Bruin's Midnight Reader

BRUIN ASYLUM

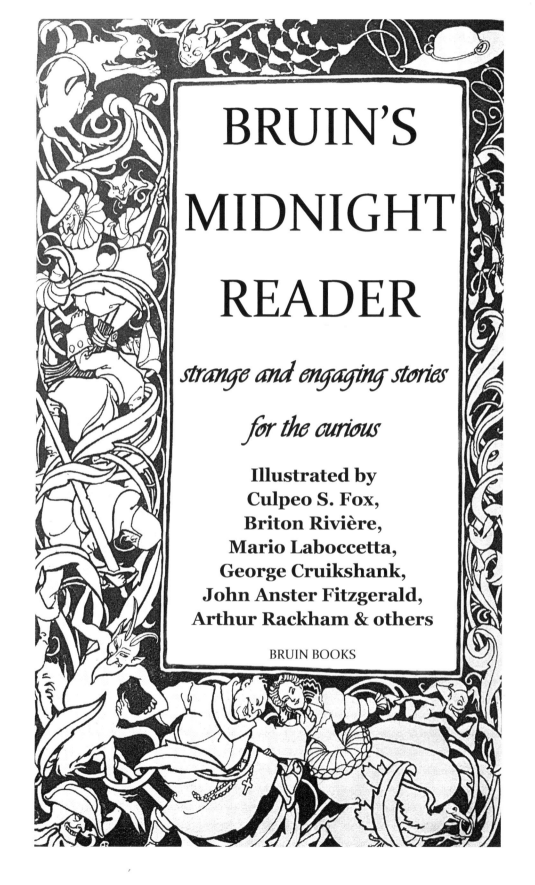

BRUIN'S MIDNIGHT READER

strange and engaging stories

for the curious

**Illustrated by
Culpeo S. Fox,
Briton Rivière,
Mario Laboccetta,
George Cruikshank,
John Anster Fitzgerald,
Arthur Rackham & others**

BRUIN BOOKS

"The Speciality of the House" ©1948 Stanley Ellen, originally appeared in *Ellery Queen's Mystery Magazine;* Reproduced with permission of Curtis Brown Ltd, London, on behalf of the Estate of Stanley Ellen.

"White Lies" from *World's End and Other Stories* by Paul Theroux. Copyright © 1980 Paul Theroux, used by permission of The Wylie Agency LLC.

"Typhoid Mary" by Hans Heinz Ewers, new translation ©2021 Joe Bandel; published by permission of the translator.

"Clairvoyance" ©1932 D. K. Broster; originally appeared in *A Fire of Driftwood* (1932); used by permission of St Hilda's College, Oxford.

"The Little Red Owl" ©1951 Margaret St. Clair, originally appeared in 1951 *Weird Tales,* Vol. 43 No. 5; Reprinted with permission of McIntosh & Otis, Inc. NY, NY.

"IT" ©1940 Theodore Sturgeon, originally appeared in *Unknown* in 1940; published by permission of The Theodore Sturgeon Literary Trust c/o The Lotts Agency, Ltd.

"The Saliva Tree" ©1965 Brian Aldiss, originally appeared in *The Magazine of Fantasy and Science Fiction*; reproduced with permission of Curtis Brown Ltd, London, on behalf of the Estate of Brian Aldiss.

"The Seed of the Sepulcher" ©1933 Clark Ashton Smith, originally appeared in *Weird Tales* 1933; published by permission of CASiana Literary Enterprises, the Literary Estate of Clark Ashton Smith.

"Hand to Mouth" ©2011 Reggie Oliver, originally appeared in *Haunts: Reliquaries of the Dead* (2011 Ulysses Press) and was later collected in *Flowers of the Sea* (2013 Tartarus Press); published by permission of the author.

"The House" ©1960 Fredric Brown; first appeared in *Fantastic*, August 1960, published by permission of the Fredric Brown Literary Estate, represented by Barry N. Malzberg.

"In the Penal Colony" by Franz Kafka; new translation ©2021 Culpeo S. Fox; published by permission of the translator.

"Feathers" ©2022 by Jonathan Eeds; used by permission of the author.

All other stories and poems are in the public domain; see back of book for more info.

Illustrations ©2021 by Culpeo S. Fox

Story selection and notes: Jonathan Eeds
Contributing Editor: David Richards
Cover Design: Michelle Policicchio

This book was crafted in the USA but is printed globally.
Printed in the USA
ISBN 978-1-7372106-1-0
Published March 2022
Bruin Books, LLC
Eugene, Oregon, USA

BRUIN'S MIDNIGHT READER

Table of Contents

a guide for the lost

PART I: THE INHUMAN CONDITION
assorted cruelties and callous indulgences

PART II: A PRAYER FOR THE INNOCENTS
a profound jealousy of the young

PART III: THE OUTER DARK

natural & unnatural horrors

PART IV: WE ARE THE HAUNTED HOUSES

whatever walked there, walked alone

PART V: CANDLE SMOKE
gothic romances and delightfully malevolent folklore

PART VI: A MIDNIGHT NOVEL
something old that's something new

Part I

THE INHUMAN CONDITION

assorted cruelties and callous indulgences

THE HUMAN SPECIES has a genius for beauty and brutality. Our ancestors built gorgeous marble temples and then coldly sacrificed virgins beneath those same sun-bathed pillars. How can we explain this shocking contrast within our kind? One thing is true: when the beautiful and brutal are combined we cannot look away. Our dark fascination possesses us. We surrender to the guilty thrill of witnessing the suffering of others. One theory is that there is something cathartic about it—a dislocated exorcism of our own darker tendencies. Another theory is that we simply all love a scary story. If the latter theory sounds more reasonable, then you have come to the right place.

Welcome to "Bruin's Midnight Reader", a sweeping survey of strange and engaging stories. Harnessing a full three centuries of fine (albeit macabre) fiction and poetry, you will find something weird and wonderful in the pages that follow.

The inhuman condition is our first area of exploration. The conte cruel (the cruel tale) emerged from European literature in the 19th century. H. P. Lovecraft (perhaps you've heard of him) described the conte cruel as ". . . less a part of the weird tradition than a class peculiar to itself—the so-called conte cruel, in which the wrenching of the emotions is accomplished through dramatic tantalizations, frustrations, and gruesome physical horrors." (Well said, sir, but perhaps it would be simpler to say that they are stories with a mean-streak.) . . . And so, here in Part I we offer a connoisseur's selection of man's inhumanity to man. You will find appetizers, first courses, second courses, main dishes, and supremely sweet desserts—all guaranteed to give you bad dreams if you fail to imbibe an alcoholic digestif before bed.

Stanley Ellin's much-revered "The Specialty of the House" kicks things off quite nicely. This perfectly crafted story caused quite a sensation when it was first published. It originated as an entry for an Ellery Queen Mystery Magazine story contest. Those judges had good taste, for Mr. Ellin would go on to win three Edgar awards over his distinguished career.

Next comes "White Lies" by best-selling author Paul Theroux, who is best known for his novels (his 29th was published April 2021) and travelogues (twenty at last count). His shorter works are overlooked treasures. "White Lies" draws on Mr. Theroux's extensive experiences in Africa, where he was a Peace Corps volunteer in Malawi and an instructor in Uganda. In this story we encounter a smug outsider who discovers that there are more perils in Africa than political upheaval.

Our third entry is Joe Bandel's translation of Hans Heinz Ewers little known story, "Typhoid Mary". Can impulsive destructive behavior be spread like a virus by someone who is immune to its pitfalls? This new translation appears here for the first time and is a wonderfully wicked example of decadent fiction.

The reader can enjoy a romping reprieve from the cerebral with the story that follows: Richard Connell's "The Most Dangerous Game." This essential adventure story never fails to enthrall.

Culpeo Fox's new translation of Franz Kafka's "In the Penal Colony" firmly directs us back to the European weird tale tradition. While writing this bizarre story of crime and punishment, Kafka may have been thinking of the penal colony that operated on Devil's Island in French Guiana, and more specifically was recalling the Dreyfus affair—a fascinating case of injustice too complicated to explore here. In Kafka's penal colony all human rights are abandoned and justice is meted out with exquisite irony and torture. (If interested, one can visit the Museum of Medieval Torture Instruments in Kafka's Prague—just in case a traveler grows bored of Prague's many other enchantments.)

Leaving the penal colony we immediately encounter D. K. Broster's "Clairvoyance". Broster is a greatly underrated writer and this may be her best tale. Setting the stage with a benign and humorous opening, the story's shock ending is a sock to solar plexus —metaphorically speaking of course.

We complete our exhibit of assorted cruelties with a story appearing for the first time anywhere: "Feathers" by Jonathan Eeds. Our editors are keenly sensitive to the possibility that the story may not live up to the standards of the beloved time-tested stories that surround it. Therefore, Bruin Books is offering any dissatisfied customers a refund of 29¢ for this one story only. The refund amount accounts for the approximate space the story occupies in this volume. The aforementioned "dissatisfied customer" may apply for the refund by sending in their original receipt of purchase and including a sum of 50¢ to cover refund return postage. Complete satisfaction is our goal!

So without further ado let's begin our journey through the inhuman condition. Please leave your humanity at the door . . .

The Speciality of the House

by Stanley Ellin

"AND THIS," said Laffler, "is Sbirro's." Costain saw a square brownstone facade identical with the others that extended from either side into the clammy darkness of the deserted street. From the barred windows of the basement at his feet, a glimmer of light showed behind heavy curtains.

"Lord," he observed, "it's a dismal hole, isn't it?"

"I beg you to understand," said Laffler stiffly, "that Sbirro's is the restaurant without pretensions. Besieged by these ghastly, neurotic times, it has refused to compromise. It is perhaps the last important establishment in this city lit by gas jets. Here you will find the same honest furnishings, the same magnificent Sheffield service, and possibly, in a far corner, the very same spider webs that were remarked by the patrons of a half century ago!"

"A doubtful recommendation," said Costain, "and hardly sanitary."

"When you enter," Laffler continued, "you leave the insanity of this year, this day, and this hour, and you find yourself for a brief span restored in spirit, not by opulence, but by dignity, which is the lost quality of our time."

Costain laughed uncomfortably. "You make it sound more like a cathedral than a restaurant," he said.

In the pale reflection of the street lamp overhead, Laffler peered at his companion's face. "I wonder," he said abruptly, "whether I have not made a mistake in extending this invitation to you."

Costain was hurt. Despite an impressive title and large salary, he was no more than a clerk to this pompous little man, but he was impelled to make some display of his feelings. "If you wish," he said coldly, "I can make other plans for my evening with no trouble."

With his large, cow-like eyes turned up to Costain, the mist drifting into the ruddy, full moon of his face, Laffler seemed strangely ill at ease. Then "No, no," he said at last, "absolutely not. It's important that you

1

dine at Sbirro's with me." He grasped Costain's arm firmly and led the way to the wrought-iron gate of the basement. "You see, you're the sole person in my office who seems to know anything at all about good food. And on my part, knowing about Sbirro's but not having some appreciative friend to share it is like having a unique piece of art locked in a room where no one else can enjoy it."

Costain was considerably mollified by this. "I understand there are a great many people who relish that situation."

"I'm not one of that kind!" Laffler said sharply. "And having the secret of Sbirro's locked in myself for years has finally become unendurable." He fumbled at the side of the gate and from within could be heard the small, discordant jangle of an ancient pull-bell. An interior door opened with a groan, and Costain found himself peering into a dark face whose only discernible feature was a row of gleaming teeth.

"Sair?" said the face.

"Mr. Laffler and a guest."

"Sair," the face said again, this time in what was clearly an invitation. It moved aside and Costain stumbled down a single step behind his host. The door and gate creaked behind him, and he stood blinking in a small foyer. It took him a moment to realize that the figure he now stared at was his own reflection in a gigantic pier glass that extended from floor to ceiling. "Atmosphere," he said under his breath and chuckled as he followed his guide to a seat.

He faced Laffler across a small table for two and peered curiously around the dining room. It was no size at all, but the half-dozen guttering gas jets which provided the only illumination threw such a deceptive light that the walls flickered and faded into uncertain distance.

There were no more than eight or ten tables about, arranged to insure the maximum privacy. All were occupied, and the few waiters serving them moved with quiet efficiency. In the air were a soft clash and scrape of cutlery and a soothing murmur of talk. Costain nodded appreciatively.

Laffler breathed an audible sigh of gratification. "I knew you would share my enthusiasm," he said. "Have you noticed, by the way, that there are no women present?"

Costain raised inquiring eyebrows.

"Sbirro," said Laffler, "does not encourage members of the fair sex to enter the premises. And, I can tell you, his method is decidedly effective. I had the experience of seeing a woman get a taste of it not long ago. She sat at a table for not less than an hour waiting for service which was never forthcoming."

"Didn't she make a scene?"

"She did." Laffler smiled at the recollection. "She succeeded in annoying the customers, embarrassing her partner, and nothing more."

"And what about Mr. Sbirro?"

"He did not make an appearance. Whether he directed affairs from behind the scenes, or was not even present during the episode, I don't know. Whichever it was, he won a complete victory. The woman never reappeared nor, for that matter, did the witless gentleman who by bringing her was really the cause of the entire contretemps."

"A fair warning to all present," laughed Costain.

A waiter now appeared at the table. The chocolate dark skin, the thin, beautifully molded nose and lips, the large liquid eyes, heavily lashed, and the silver white hair so heavy and silken that it lay on the skull like a cap, all marked him definitely as an East Indian of some sort, Costain decided. The man arranged the stiff table linen, filled two tumblers from a huge, cut-glass pitcher, and set them in their proper places.

"Tell me," Laffler said eagerly, "is the special being served this evening?"

The waiter smiled regretfully and showed teeth as spectacular as those of the majordomo. "I am so sorry, sair. There is no special this evening."

Laffler's face fell into lines of heavy disappointment. "After waiting so long. It's been a month already, and I hoped to show my friend here..."

"You understand the difficulties, sair."

"Of course, of course." Laffler looked at Costain sadly and shrugged. "You see, I had in mind to introduce you to the greatest treat that Sbirro's offers, but unfortunately it isn't on the menu this evening."

The waiter said, "Do you wish to be served now, sair?" and Laffler nodded. To Costain's surprise the waiter made his way off without waiting for any instructions.

"Have you ordered in advance?" he asked.

"Ah," said Laffler, "I really should have explained. Sbirro's offers no choice whatsoever. You will eat the same meal as everyone else in this room. Tomorrow evening you would eat an entirely different meal, but again without designating a single preference."

"Very unusual," said Costain, "and certainly unsatisfactory at times. What if one doesn't have a taste for the particular dish set before him?"

"On that score," said Laffler solemnly, "you need have no fears. I give you my word that no matter how exacting your tastes, you will relish every mouthful you eat in Sbirro's."

Costain looked doubtful, and Laffler smiled. "And consider the subtle advantages of the system," he said. "When you pick up the menu of a popular restaurant, you find yourself confronted with innumerable choices. You are forced to weigh, to evaluate, to make uneasy decisions which you may instantly regret. The effect of all this is a tension which, however slight, must make for discomfort.

"And consider the mechanics of the process. Instead of a hurly-burly of sweating cooks rushing about a kitchen in a frenzy to prepare a hundred varying items, we have a chef who stands serenely alone, bringing all his talents to bear on one task, with all assurance of a complete triumph!"

"Then you have seen the kitchen?"

"Unfortunately, no," said Laffler sadly. "The picture I offer is hypothetical, made of conversational fragments I have pieced together over the years. I must admit, though, that my desire to see the functioning of the kitchen here comes very close to being my sole obsession nowadays."

"But have you mentioned this to Sbirro?"

"A dozen times. He shrugs the suggestion away."

"Isn't that a rather curious foible on his part?"

"No, no," Laffler said hastily, "a master artist is never under the compulsion of petty courtesies. Still," he sighed, "I have never given up hope."

The waiter now reappeared bearing two soup bowls which he set in place with mathematical exactitude, and a small tureen from which he slowly ladled a measure of clear, thin broth. Costain dipped his spoon into the broth and tasted it with some curiosity. It was delicately flavored, bland to the verge of tastelessness. Costain frowned, tentatively reached for the salt and pepper cellars, and discovered there were none on the table. He looked up, saw Laffler's eyes on him, and although unwilling to compromise with his own tastes, he hesitated to act as a damper on Laffler's enthusiasm. Therefore he smiled and indicated the broth.

"Excellent," he said.

Laffler returned his smile. "You do not find it excellent at all," he said coolly. "You find it flat and badly in need of condiments. I know this," he continued as Costain's eyebrows shot upward, "because it was my own reaction many years ago, and because like yourself I found myself reaching for salt and pepper after the first mouthful. I also learned with surprise that condiments are not available in Sbirro's."

Costain was shocked. "Not even salt!" he exclaimed.

"Not even salt. The very fact that you require it for your soup stands as evidence that your taste is unduly jaded. I am confident that you will now make the same discovery that I did: by the time you have nearly finished your soup, your desire for salt will be nonexistent."

Laffler was right; before Costain had reached the bottom of his plate, he was relishing the nuances of the broth with steadily increasing delight. Laffler thrust aside his own empty bowl and rested his elbows on the table. "Do you agree with me now?"

"To my surprise," said Costain, "I do."

As the waiter busied himself clearing the table, Laffler lowered his voice significantly. "You will find," he said, "that the absence of condiments is but one of several noteworthy characteristics which mark Sbirro's. I may as well prepare you for these. For example, no alcoholic beverages of any sort are served here, nor for that matter any beverage except clear, cold water, the first and only drink necessary for a human being."

"Outside of mother's milk," suggested Costain dryly.

"I can answer that in like vein by pointing out that the average patron of Sbirro's has passed that primal stage of his development."

Costain laughed. "Granted," he said.

"Very well. There is also a ban on the use of tobacco in any form."

"But, good heavens," said Costain, "doesn't that make Sbirro's more a teetotaler's retreat than a gourmet's sanctuary?"

"I fear," said Laffler solemnly, "that you confuse the words, *gourmet* and *gourmand*. The gourmand, through glutting himself, requires a wider and wider latitude of experience to stir his surfeited senses, but the very nature of the gourmet is simplicity. The ancient Greek in his coarse chiton savoring the ripe olive; the Japanese in his bare room contemplating the curves of a single flower stem—these are the true gourmets."

"But an occasional drop of brandy or pipeful of tobacco," said Costain dubiously, "are hardly overindulgence."

"By alternating stimulant and narcotic," said Laffler, "you seesaw the delicate balance of your taste so violently that it loses its most precious quality: the appreciation of fine food. During my years as a patron of Sbirro's, I have proved this to my satisfaction."

"May I ask," said Costain, "why you regard the ban on these things as having such deep esthetic motives? What about such mundane reasons as the high cost of a liquor license, or the possibility that patrons would object to the smell of tobacco in such confined quarters?"

Laffler shook his head violently. "If and when you meet Sbirro," he said, "you will understand at once that he is not the man to make decisions on a mundane basis. As a matter of fact, it was Sbirro himself who first made me cognizant of what you call 'esthetic' motives."

"An amazing man," said Costain as the waiter prepared to serve the entree.

Laffler's next words were not spoken until he had savored and swallowed a large portion of meat. "I hesitate to use superlatives," he said, "but to my way of thinking, Sbirro represents man at the apex of his civilization!"

Costain cocked an eyebrow and applied himself to his roast which rested in a pool of stiff gravy ungarnished by green or vegetable. The thin steam rising from it carried to his nostrils a subtle, tantalizing odor which made his mouth water. He chewed a piece as slowly and thoughtfully as if he were analyzing the intricacies of a Mozart symphony. The range of taste he discovered was really extraordinary, from the pungent nip of the crisp outer edge to the peculiarly flat, yet soul-satisfying ooze of blood which the pressure of his jaws forced from the half-raw interior.

Upon swallowing he found himself ferociously hungry for another piece, and then another, and it was only with an effort that he prevented himself from wolfing down all his share of the meat and gravy without waiting to get the full voluptuous satisfaction from each mouthful. When he had scraped his platter clean, he realized that both he and Laffler had completed the entire course without exchanging a single word. He commented on this, and Laffler said, "Can you see any need for words in the presence of such food?"

Costain looked around at the shabby, dimly-lit room, the quiet diners, with a new perception. "No," he said humbly, "I cannot. For any doubts I had I apologize unreservedly. In all your praise of Sbirro's there was not a single word of exaggeration."

"Ah," said Laffler delightedly. "And that is only part of the story. You heard me mention the special which unfortunately was not on the menu tonight. What you have just eaten is as nothing when compared to the absolute delights of that special!"

"Good Lord!" cried Costain. "What is it? Nightingale's tongues? Filet of unicorn?"

"Neither," said Laffler. "It is lamb."

"Lamb?"

Laffler remained lost in thought for a minute. "If," he said at last, "I were to give you in my own unstinted words my opinion of this dish, you would judge me completely insane. That is how deeply the mere thought of it affects me. It is neither the fatty chop, nor the too solid leg; it is, instead, a select portion of the rarest sheep in existence and is named after the species—lamb Amirstan."

Costain knit his brow. "Amirstan?"

"A fragment of desolation almost lost on the border which separates Afghanistan and Russia. From chance remarks dropped by Sbirro, I gather it is no more than a plateau which grazes the pitiful remnants of a flock of superb sheep. Sbirro, through some means or other, obtained rights to the traffic in this flock and is, therefore, the sole restaurateur ever to have lamb Amirstan on his bill of fare. I can tell you that the appearance of this dish is a rare occurrence indeed, and luck is the only guide in determining for the clientele the exact date when it will be served."

"But surely," said Costain, "Sbirro could provide some advance knowledge of this event."

"The objection to that is simply stated," said Laffler. "There exists in this city a huge number of professional gluttons. Should advance information slip out, it is quite likely that they will, out of curiosity, become familiar with the dish and thenceforth supplant the regular patrons at these tables."

"But you don't mean to say," objected Costain, "that these few people present are the only ones in the entire city, or for that matter, in the whole wide world, who know of the existence of Sbirro's!"

"Very nearly. There may be one or two regular patrons who, for some reason, are not present at the moment."

"That's incredible."

"It is done," said Laffler, the slightest shade of menace in his voice, "by every patron making it his solemn obligation to keep the secret. By accepting my invitation this evening you automatically assume that obligation. I hope you can be trusted with it."

Costain flushed. "My position in your employ should vouch for me. I only question the wisdom of a policy which keeps such magnificent food away from so many who would enjoy it."

"Do you know the inevitable result of the policy *you* favor?" asked Laffler bitterly. "An influx of idiots who would nightly complain that they are never served roast duck with chocolate sauce. Is that picture tolerable to you?"

"No," admitted Costain, "I am forced to agree with you."

Laffler leaned back in his chair wearily and passed his hand over his eyes in an uncertain gesture. "I am a solitary man," he said quietly, "and not by choice alone. It may sound strange to you, it may border on eccentricity, but I feel to my depths that this restaurant, this warm haven in a coldly insane world, is both family and friend to me."

And Costain, who to this moment had never viewed his companion as other than tyrannical employer or officious host, now felt an overwhelming pity twist inside his comfortably expanded stomach.

~§~

By the end of two weeks the invitations to join Laffler at Sbirro's had become something of a ritual. Every day, at a few minutes after five, Costain would step out into the office corridor and lock his cubicle behind him; he would drape his overcoat neatly over his left arm, and peer into the glass of the door to make sure his Homburg was set at the proper angle. At one time he would have followed this by lighting a cigarette, but under Laffer's prodding he had decided to give abstinence a fair trial. Then he would start down the corridor, and Laffler would fall in step at his elbow, clearing his throat. "Ah, Costain. No plans for this evening, I hope."

"No," Costain would say, "I'm footloose and fancy-free," or "At your service," or something equally inane. He wondered at times whether it would not be more tactful to vary the ritual with an occasional refusal, but the glow with which Laffler received his answer, and the rough friendliness of Laffler's grip on his arm, forestalled him.

Among the treacherous crags of the business world, reflected Costain, what better way to secure your footing than friendship with one's employer. Already, a secretary close to the workings of the inner office had commented publicly on Laffler's highly favorable opinion of Costain. That was all to the good.

And the food! The incomparable food at Sbirro's! For the first time in his life, Costain, ordinarily a lean and bony man, noted with gratification that he was certainly gaining weight; within two weeks his bones had disappeared under a layer of sleek, firm flesh, and here and there were even signs of incipient plumpness. It struck Costain one night, while surveying himself in his bath, that the rotund Laffler, himself, might have been a spare and bony man before discovering Sbirro's.

So there was obviously everything to be gained and nothing to be lost by accepting Laffler's invitations. Perhaps after testing the heralded wonders of lamb Amirstan and meeting Sbirro, who thus far had not made an appearance, a refusal or two might be in order. But certainly not until then.

That evening, two weeks to a day after his first visit to Sbirro's, Costain had both desires fulfilled: he dined on lamb Amirstan, and he met Sbirro. Both exceeded all his expectations.

When the waiter leaned over their table immediately after seating them and gravely announced: "Tonight is special, sair," Costain was shocked to find his heart pounding with expectation. On the table before him he saw Laffler's hands trembling violently. But it isn't natural, he thought suddenly. Two full grown men, presumably intelligent and in the full possession of their senses, as jumpy as a pair of cats waiting to have their meat flung at them!

"This is it!" Laffler's voice startled him so that he almost leaped from his seat. "The culinary triumph of all times! And faced by it you are embarrassed by the very emotions it distills."

"How did you know that?" Costain asked faintly.

"How? Because a decade ago I underwent your embarrassment. Add to that your air of revulsion and it's easy to see how affronted you are by the knowledge that man has not yet forgotten how to slaver over his meat."

"And these others," whispered Costain, "do they all feel the same thing?"

"Judge for yourself."

Costain looked furtively around at the nearby tables. "You are right," he finally said. "At any rate, there's comfort in numbers."

Laffler inclined his head slightly to the side. "One of the numbers," he remarked, "appears to be in for a disappointment."

Costain followed the gesture. At the table indicated a gray-haired man sat conspicuously alone, and Costain frowned at the empty chair opposite him.

"Why, yes," he recalled, "that very stout, bald man, isn't it? I believe it's the first dinner he's missed here in two weeks."

"The entire decade more likely," said Laffler sympathetically. "Rain or shine, crisis or calamity, I don't think he's missed an evening at Sbirro's since the first time I dined here. Imagine his expression when he's told that, on his very first defection, lamb Amirstan was the *plat de jour.*"

Costain looked at the empty chair again with a dim discomfort. "His very first?" he murmured.

"Mr. Laffler! And friend! I am so pleased. So very, very pleased. No, do not stand; I will have a place made." Miraculously a seat appeared under the figure standing there at the table. The lamb Amirstan will be an unqualified success, hurr? I myself have been stewing in the miserable kitchen all the day, prodding the foolish chef to do everything just so. The 'just so' is the important part, hurr? But I see your friend does not know me. An introduction, perhaps?"

The words ran in a smooth, fluid eddy. They rippled, they purred, they hypnotized Costain so that he could do no more than stare. The mouth that uncoiled this sinuous monologue was alarmingly wide, with thin mobile lips that curled and twisted with every syllable. There was a flat nose with a straggling line of hair under it; wide-set eyes, almost oriental in appearance, that glittered in the unsteady flare of gaslight; and the long, sleek hair that swept back from high on the unwrinkled forehead—hair so pale that it might have been bleached of all color. An amazing face surely, and the sight of it tortured Costain with the conviction that it was somehow familiar. His brain twitched and prodded but could not stir up any solid recollection.

Laffler's voice jerked Costain out of his study. "Mr. Sbirro. Mr. Costain, a good friend and associate." Costain rose and shook the proffered hand. It was warm and dry, flint-hard against his palm.

"I am so very pleased, Mr. Costain. So very, very pleased," purred the voice. "You like my little establishment, hurr? You have a great treat in store, I assure you."

Laffler chuckled. "Oh, Costain's been dining here regularly for two weeks," he said. "He's by way of becoming a great admirer of yours, Sbirro."

The eyes were turned on Costain. "A very great compliment. You compliment me with your presence and I return same with my food, hurr? But the lamb Amirstan is far superior to anything of your past experience, I assure you. All the trouble of obtaining it, all the difficulty of preparation, is truly merited."

Costain strove to put aside the exasperating problem of that face. "I have wondered," he said, "why with all these difficulties you mention, you even bother to present lamb Amirstan to the public. Surely your other dishes are excellent enough to uphold your reputation."

Sbirro smiled so broadly that his face became perfectly round. "Perhaps it is a matter of the psychology, hurr? Someone discovers a wonder and must share it with others. He must fill his cup to the brim, perhaps, by observing the so evident pleasure of those who explore it with him. Or," he shrugged, "perhaps it is just a matter of good business."

"Then in the light of all this," Costain persisted, "and considering all the conventions you have imposed on your customers, why do you open the restaurant to the public instead of operating it as a private club?"

The eyes abruptly glinted into Costain's, then turned away. "So perspicacious, hurr? Then I will tell you. Because there is more privacy in a public eating place than in the most exclusive club in existence! Here no one inquires of your affairs; no one desires to know the intimacies of your life. Here the business is eating. We are not curious about names and addresses or the reasons for the coming and going of our guests. We welcome you when you are here; we have no regrets when you are here no longer. That is the answer, hurr?"

Costain was startled by this vehemence. "I had no intention of prying," he stammered.

Sbirro ran the tip of his tongue over his thin lips. "No, no," he reassured, "you are not prying. Do not let me give you that impression. On the contrary, I invite your questions."

"Oh, come, Costain," said Laffler. "Don't let Sbirro intimidate you. I've known him for years and I guarantee that his bark is worse than his bite. Before you know it, he'll be showing you all the privileges of the house—outside of inviting you to visit his precious kitchen, of course."

"Ah," smiled Sbirro, "for that, Mr. Costain may have to wait a little while. For everything else I am at his beck and call."

Laffler slapped his hand jovially on the table. "What did I tell you!" he said. "Now let's have the truth, Sbirro. Has anyone, outside of your staff, ever stepped into the sanctum sanctorum?"

Sbirro looked up. "You see on the wall above you," he said earnestly, "the portrait of one to whom I did the honor. A very dear friend and a patron of most long standing, he is evidence that my kitchen is not inviolate."

Costain studied the picture and started with recognition. "Why," he said excitedly, "that's the famous writer—you know the one, Laffler—he used to do such wonderful short stories and cynical bits and then suddenly took himself off and disappeared in Mexico!"

"Of course!" cried Laffler, "and to think I've been sitting under his portrait for years without even realizing it!" He turned to Sbirro. "A dear friend, you say? His disappearance must have been a blow to you."

Sbirro's face lengthened. "It was, it was, I assure you. But think of it this way, gentlemen: he was probably greater in his death than in his life, hurr? A most tragic man, he often told me that his only happy hours were spent here at this very table. Pathetic, is it not? And to think the only favor I could ever show him was to let him witness the mysteries of my kitchen, which is, when all is said and done, no more than a plain, ordinary kitchen."

"You seem very certain of his death," commented Costain. "After all, no evidence has ever turned up to substantiate it."

Sbirro contemplated the picture. "None at all," he said softly. "Remarkable, hurr?"

With the arrival of the entree Sbirro leaped to his feet and set about serving them himself. With his eyes alight he lifted the casserole from the tray and sniffed at the fragrance from within with sensual relish. Then, taking great care not to lose a single drop of gravy, he filled two platters with chunks of dripping meat. As if exhausted by this task, he sat back in his chair, breathing heavily. "Gentlemen," he said, "to your good appetite."

Costain chewed his first mouthful with great deliberation and swallowed it. Then he looked at the empty tines of his fork with glazed eyes.

"Good God!" he breathed.

"It is good, hurr? Better than you imagined?"

Costain shook his head dazedly. "It is as impossible," he said slowly, "for the uninitiated to conceive the delights of lamb Amirstan as for mortal man to look into his own soul."

"Perhaps—" Sbirro thrust his head so close that Costain could feel the warm, fetid breath tickle his nostrils— "perhaps you have just had a glimpse into your soul, hurr?"

Costain tried to draw back slightly without giving offence. "Perhaps." He laughed. "And a gratifying picture it made: all fang and claw. But without intending any disrespect, I should hardly like to build my church on *lamb en casserole.*"

Sbirro rose and laid a hand gently on his shoulder. "So perspicacious," he said. "Sometimes when you have nothing to do, nothing, perhaps, but sit for a very little while in a dark room and think of this world—what it is and what it is going to be—then you must turn your thoughts a little to the significance of the Lamb in religion. It will be so interesting. And now—" he bowed deeply to both men— "I have held you long enough from your dinner. I was most happy," he said, nodding to Costain, "and I am sure we will meet again." The teeth gleamed, the eyes glittered, and Sbirro was gone down the aisle of tables.

Costain twisted around to stare after the retreating figure. "Have I offended him in some way?" he asked.

Laffler looked up from his plate. "Offended him? He loves that kind of talk. Lamb Amirstan is a ritual with him; get him started and he'll be back at you a dozen times worse than a priest making a conversion."

Costain turned to his meal with the face still hovering before him. "Interesting man," he reflected. "Very."

It took him a month to discover the tantalizing familiarity of that face and when he did, he laughed aloud in his bed. Why, of course! Sbirro might have sat as the model for the Cheshire cat in *Alice!*

~§~

He passed this thought on to Laffler the very next evening as they pushed their way down the street to the restaurant against a chill, blustering wind. Laffler only looked blank.

"You may be right," he said, "but I'm not a fit judge. It's a far cry back to the days when I read the book. A far cry, indeed."

As if taking up his words, a piercing howl came ringing down the street and stopped both men short in their tracks. "Someone's in trouble there," said Laffler. "Look!"

Not far from the entrance to Sbirro's two figures could be seen struggling in the near darkness. They swayed back and forth and suddenly tumbled into a writhing heap on the sidewalk. The piteous howl went up again, and Laffler, despite his girth, ran toward it at a fair speed with Costain tagging cautiously behind.

Stretched out full-length on the pavement was a slender figure with the dusky complexion and white hair of one of Sbirro's servitors. His fingers were futilely plucking at the huge hands which encircled his throat, and his knees pushed weakly up at the gigantic bulk of a man who brutally bore down with his full weight.

Laffler came up panting. "Stop this!" he shouted. "What's going on here?"

The pleading eyes almost bulging from their sockets turned toward Laffler. "Help, sair. This man—drunk—"

"Drunk am I, ya dirty—" Costain saw now that the man was a sailor in a badly soiled uniform. The air around him reeked with the stench of liquor. "Pick me pocket and then call me drunk, will ya!" He dug his fingers in harder, and his victim groaned.

Laffler seized the sailor's shoulder. "Let go of him, do you hear! Let go of him at once!" he cried, and the next instant was sent careening into Costain, who staggered back under the force of the blow.

The attack on his own person sent Laffler into immediate and berserk action. Without a sound he leaped at the sailor, striking and kicking furiously at the unprotected face and flanks. Stunned at first, the man came to his feet with a rush and turned on Laffler. For a moment they stood locked together, and then as Costain joined the attack, all three went sprawling to the ground. Slowly Laffler and Costain got to their feet and looked down at the body before them.

"He's either out cold from liquor," said Costain, "or he struck his head going down. In any case, it's a job for the police."

"No, no, sair!" The waiter crawled weakly to his feet, and stood swaying. "No police, sair. Mr. Sbirro do not want such. You understand, sair." He caught hold of Costain with a pleading hand, and Costain looked at Laffler.

"Of course not," said Laffler. "We won't have to bother with the police. They'll pick him up soon enough, the murderous sot. But what in the world started all this?"

"That man, sair. He make most erratic way while walking, and with no meaning I push against him. Then he attack me, accusing me to rob him."

"As I thought." Laffler pushed the waiter gently along. "Now go in and get yourself attended to."

The man seemed ready to burst into tears. "To you, sair, I owe my life. If there is anything I can do—"

Laffler turned into the areaway that led to Sbirro's door. "No, no, it was nothing. You go along, and if Sbirro has any questions send him to me. I'll straighten it out."

"My life, sair," were the last words they heard as the inner door closed behind them.

"There you are, Costain," said Laffler, as a few minutes later he drew his chair under the table, "civilized man in all his glory. Reeking with alcohol, strangling to death some miserable innocent who came too close."

Costain made an effort to gloss over the nerve-shattering memory of the episode. "It's the neurotic cat that takes to alcohol," he said. "Surely there's a reason for that sailor's condition."

"Reason? Of course there is. Plain atavistic savagery!" Laffler swept his arm in an all-embracing gesture. "Why do we all sit here at our meat? Not only to appease physical demands, but because our atavistic selves cry for release. Think back, Costain. Do you remember that I once described Sbirro as the epitome of civilization? Can you now see why? A brilliant man, he fully understands the nature of human beings. But unlike lesser men he bends all his efforts to the satisfaction of our innate nature without resultant harm to some innocent bystander."

"When I think back on the wonders of lamb Amirstan," said Costain, "I quite understand what you're driving at. And, by the way, isn't it nearly due to appear on the bill of fare? It must have been over a month ago that it was last served."

The waiter, filling the tumblers, hesitated. "I am so sorry, sair. No special this evening."

"There's your answer," Laffler grunted, "and probably just my luck to miss out on it altogether the next time."

Costain stared at him. "Oh, come, that's impossible."

"No, blast it." Laffler drank off half his water at a gulp and the waiter immediately refilled the glass. "I'm off to South America for a surprise tour of inspection. One month, two months, Lord knows how long."

"Are things that bad down there?"

"They could be better." Laffler suddenly grinned. "Mustn't forget it takes very mundane dollars and cents to pay the tariff at Sbirro's."

"I haven't heard a word of this around the office."

"Wouldn't be a surprise tour if you had. Nobody knows about this except myself—and now you. I want to walk in on them completely un-expected. Find out what flim-flammery they're up to down there. As far as the office is concerned, I'm off on a jaunt somewhere. Maybe recuperating in some sanatorium from my hard work. Anyhow, the business will be in good hands. Yours, among them."

"Mine?" said Costain, surprised.

"When you go in tomorrow you'll find yourself in receipt of a promotion, even if I'm not there to hand it to you personally. Mind you, it has nothing to do with our friendship either; you've done fine work, and I'm immensely grateful for it."

Costain reddened under the praise. "You don't expect to be in tomorrow. Then you're leaving tonight?"

Laffler nodded. "I've been trying to wangle some reservations. If they come through, well, this will be in the nature of a farewell celebration."

"You know," said Costain slowly, "I devoutly hope that your reservetions don't come through. I believe our dinners here have come to mean more to me than I ever dared imagine."

The waiter's voice broke in. "Do you wish to be served now, sair?" and they both started.

"Of course, of course," said Laffler sharply, "I didn't realize you were waiting."

"What bothers me," he told Costain as the waiter turned away, "is the thought of the lamb Amirstan I'm bound to miss. To tell you the truth, I've already put off my departure a week, hoping to hit a lucky night, and now I simply can't delay any more. I do hope that when you're sitting over your share of lamb Amirstan, you'll think of me with suitable regrets."

Costain laughed. "I will indeed," he said as he turned to his dinner.

Hardly had he cleared the plate when a waiter silently reached for it. It was not their usual waiter, he observed; it was none other than the victim of the assault.

"Well," Costain said, "how do you feel now? Still under the weather?"

The waiter paid no attention to him. Instead, with the air of a man under great strain, he turned to Laffler. "Sair," he whispered. "My life. I owe it to you. I can repay you!"

Laffler looked up in amazement, then shook his head firmly. "No," he said. "I want nothing from you, understand? You have repaid me sufficiently with your thanks. Now get on with your work and let's hear no more about it."

The waiter did not stir an inch, but his voice rose slightly. "By the body and blood of your God, sair, I will help you even if you do not want! *Do not go into the kitchen, sair.* I trade you my life for yours, sair, when I speak this. Tonight or any night of your life, do not go into the kitchen at Sbirro's!"

Laffler sat back, completely dumbfounded. "Not go into the kitchen? Why shouldn't I go into the kitchen if Mr. Sbirro ever took it into his head to invite me there? What's all this about?"

A hard hand was laid on Costain's back, and another gripped the waiter's arm. The waiter remained frozen to the spot, his lips compressed, his eyes downcast.

"What is all *what* about, gentlemen?" purred the voice. "So opportune an arrival. In time as ever, I see, to answer all the questions, hurr?"

Laffler breathed a sigh of relief. "Ah, Sbirro, thank heaven you're here. This man is saying something about my not going into your kitchen. Do you know what he means?"

The teeth showed in a broad grin. "But of course. This good man was giving you advice in all amiability. It so happens that my too emotional chef heard some rumor that I might have a guest into his precious kitchen, and he flew into a fearful rage. Such a rage, gentlemen! He even threatened to give notice on the spot, and you can understand what that would mean to Sbirro's, hurr? Fortunately, I succeeded in showing him what a signal honor it is to have an esteemed patron and true connoisseur observe him at his work firsthand, and now he is quite amenable. Quite, hurr?"

He released the waiter's arm. "You are at the wrong table," he said softly. "See that it does not happen again."

The waiter slipped off without daring to raise his eyes and Sbirro drew a chair to the table. He seated himself and brushed his hand lightly over his hair. "Now I am afraid that the cat is out of the bag, hurr? This invitation to you, Mr. Laffler, was to be a surprise; but the surprise is gone, and all that is left is the invitation."

Laffler mopped beads of perspiration from his forehead. "Are you serious?" he said huskily. "Do you mean that we are really to witness the preparation of your food tonight?"

Sbirro drew a sharp fingernail along the tablecloth, leaving a thin, straight line printed in the linen. "Ah," he said, "I am faced with a dilemma of great proportions." He studied the line soberly. "You, Mr. Laffler, have been my guest for ten long years. But our friend here—"

Costain raised his hand in protest. "I understand perfectly. This invitation is solely to Mr. Laffler, and naturally my presence is embarrassing. As it happens, I have an early engagement for this evening and must be on my way anyhow. So you see there's no dilemma at all, really."

"No," said Laffler, "absolutely not. That wouldn't be fair at all. We've been sharing this until now, Costain, and I won't enjoy the experience half as much if you're not along. Surely Sbirro can make his conditions flexible, this one occasion."

They both looked at Sbirro who shrugged his shoulders regretfully.

Costain rose abruptly. "I'm not going to sit here, Laffler, and spoil your great adventure. And then, too," he bantered, "think of that ferocious chef waiting to get his cleaver on you. I prefer not to be at the scene. I'll just say goodbye," he went on, to cover Laffler's guilty silence, "and leave you to Sbirro. I'm sure he'll take pains to give you a good show." He held out his hand and Laffler squeezed it painfully hard.

"You're being very decent, Costain," he said. "I hope you'll continue to dine here until we meet again. It shouldn't be too long."

Sbirro made way for Costain to pass. "I will expect you," he said. *"Au 'voir."*

Costain stopped briefly in the dim foyer to adjust his scarf and fix his Homburg at the proper angle. When he turned away from the mirror, satisfied at last, he saw with a final glance that Laffler and Sbirro were already at the kitchen door, Sbirro holding the door invitingly wide with one hand, while the other rested, almost tenderly, on Laffler's meaty shoulders.

White Lies

by Paul Theroux

NORMALLY, in describing the life cycle of ectoparasites for my notebook, I went into great detail, since I hoped to publish an article about the strangest ones when I returned home from Africa. The one exception was *Dermatobia bendidense*. I could not give it my name; I was not its victim. And the description? One word: *Jerry*. I needed nothing more to remind me of the discovery, and though I fully intend to test my findings in the pages of an entomological journal, the memory is still too horrifying for me to reduce it to science.

Jerry Benda and I shared a house on the compound of a bush school. Every Friday and Saturday night he met an African girl named Ameena at the Rainbow Bar and brought her home in a taxi. There was no scandal: no one knew. In the morning, after breakfast, Ameena did Jerry's ironing (I did my own) and the black cook carried her back to town on the crossbar of his old bike. That was a hilarious sight. Returning from my own particular passion, which was collecting insects in the fields near our house, I often met them on the road: Jika in his cook's khakis and skullcap pedaling the long-legged Ameena—I must say she reminded me of a highly desirable insect. They yelped as they clattered down the road, the deep ruts making the bicycle bell hiccup like an alarm clock. A stranger would have assumed these Africans were man and wife, making an early morning foray to the market. The local people paid no attention.

Only I knew that these were the cook and mistress of a young American who was regarded at the school as very charming in his manner and serious in his work. The cook's laughter was a nervous giggle—he was afraid of Ameena. But he was devoted to Jerry and far too loyal to refuse to do what Jerry asked of him.

Jerry was deceitful, but at the time I did not think he was imaginative enough to do any damage. And yet his was not the conventional double life that most white people led in Africa. Jerry had certain ambitions: ambition makes more liars than egotism does. But Jerry was so careful, his lies such modest calculations, he was always believed. He said he was from Boston. "Belmont actually," he told me, when I said I was from Medford. His passport—*Bearer's address*—said Watertown. He felt he had to conceal it. That explained a lot: the insecurity of living on the lower slopes of the long hill, between the smoldering steeples of Boston and the clean, high-priced air of Belmont. We are probably no more class conscious than the British, but when we make class an issue it seems more than snobbery. It becomes a bizarre spectacle, a kind of attention seeking, and I cannot hear an American speaking of his social position without thinking of a human fly, one of those tiny men in grubby capes whom one sometimes sees clinging to the brickwork of a tall building.

What had begun as fantasy had, after six months of his repeating it in our insignificant place, made it seem like fact. Jerry didn't know Africa: his one girl friend stood for the whole continent. And of course he lied to her. I had the impression that it was one of the reasons Jerry wanted to stay in Africa. If you tell enough lies about yourself, they take hold. It becomes impossible ever to go back, since that means facing the truth. In Africa, no one could dispute what Jerry said he was: a wealthy Bostonian, from a family of some distinction, adventuring in Third World philanthropy before inheriting his father's business.

Rereading the above, I think I may be misrepresenting him. Although he was undeniably a fraud in some ways, his fraudulence was the last thing you noticed about him. What you saw first was a tall good-natured person in his early twenties, confidently casual, with easy charm and a gift for ingenious flattery. When I told him I had majored in entomology he called me "Doctor." This later became "Doc." He showed exaggerated respect to the gardeners and washerwomen at the school, using the politest phrases when he spoke to them. He always said "sir" to the students ("You, sir, are a lazy little creep"), which baffled them and won them over. The cook adored him, and even the cook's cook—who was lame and fourteen and ragged—liked Jerry to the point where the poor boy would go through the compound stealing flowers from the Inkpens' garden to decorate our table. While I was merely tolerated as an unattractive and near-sighted bug collector, Jerry was courted by the British wives in the compound. The wife of the new headmaster, Lady Alice (Sir Godfrey Inkpen had been knighted for his work in the Civil Service) usually stopped in to see Jerry when her husband was away. Jerry was gracious with her and anxious to make a good impression.

Privately, he said, "She's all tits and teeth."

"Why is it," he said to me one day, "that the white women have all the money and the black ones have all the looks?"

"I didn't realize you were interested in money."

"Not for itself, Doc," he said. "I'm interested in what it can buy."

~§~

No matter how hard I tried, I could not get used to hearing Ameena's squawks of pleasure from the next room, or Jerry's elbows banging against the wall. At any moment, I expected their humpings and slappings to bring down the boxes of mounted butterflies I had hung there. At breakfast, Jerry was his urbane self, sitting at the head of the table while Ameena cackled.

He held a teapot in each hand. "What will it be, my dear? Chinese or Indian tea? Marmalade or jam? Poached or scrambled? And may I suggest a kipper?"

"*Wopusa!*" Ameena would say. "Idiot!"

She was lean, angular, and wore a scarf in a handsome turban on her head. "I'd marry that girl tomorrow," Jerry said, "if she had fifty grand." Her breasts were full and her skin was like velvet; she looked majestic, even doing the ironing. And when I saw her ironing, it struck me how Jerry inspired devotion in people.

But not any from me. I think I resented him most because he was new. I had been in Africa for two years and had replaced any ideas of sexual conquest with the possibility of a great entomological discovery. But he was not interested in my experience. There was a great deal I could have told him. In the meantime, I watched Jika taking Ameena into town on his bicycle, and I added specimens to my collection.

~§~

Then, one day, the Inkpens' daughter arrived from Rhodesia to spend her school holidays with her parents.

We had seen her the day after she arrived, admiring the roses in her mother's garden, which adjoined ours. She was about seventeen, and breathless and damp; and so small I at once imagined this pink butterfly struggling in my net. Her name was Petra (her parents called her "Pet"), and her pretty bloom was recklessness and innocence. Jerry said, "I'm going to marry her."

"I've been thinking about it," he said the next day. "If I just invite her I'll look like a wolf. If I invite the three of them it'll seem as if I'm stage-managing it. So I'll invite the parents—for some inconvenient time—and they'll have no choice but to ask me if they can bring the daughter along, too. *They'll* ask *me* if they can bring her. Good thinking? It'll have to be after dark—they'll be afraid of someone raping her. Sunday's always family day, so how about Sunday at seven? High tea. They will deliver her into my hands."

The invitation was accepted. And Sir Godfrey said, "I hope you don't mind if we bring our daughter—"

More than anything, I wished to see whether Jerry would bring Ameena home that Saturday night. He did—I suppose he did not want to arouse Ameena's suspicions—and on Sunday morning it was break-fast as usual and "What will it be my dear?"

But everything was not as usual. In the kitchen, Jika was making a cake and scones. The powerful fragrance of baking, so early on a Sunday morning, made Ameena curious. She sniffed and smiled and picked up her cup. Then she asked: What was the cook making?

"Cakes," said Jerry. He smiled back at her.

Jika entered timidly with some toast.

"You're a better cook than I am," Ameena said in Chinyanja. "I don't know how to make cakes."

Jika looked terribly worried. He glanced at Jerry.

"Have a cake," said Jerry to Ameena.

Ameena tipped the cup to her lips and said slyly, "Africans don't eat cakes for breakfast."

"*We* do," said Jerry, with guilty rapidity. "It's an old American custom."

Ameena was staring at Jika. When she stood up he winced. Ameena said, "I have to make water." It was one of the few English sentences she knew.

Jerry said, "I think she suspects something."

As I started to leave with my net and my chloroform bottle I heard a great fuss in the kitchen, Jerry telling Ameena not to do the ironing, Ameena protesting, Jika groaning. But Jerry was angry, and soon the bicycle was bumping away from the house: Jika pedaling, Ameena on the crossbar.

"She just wanted to hang around," said Jerry. "Guess what the bitch was doing? She was ironing a drip-dry shirt!"

~§~

It was early evening when the Inkpens arrived, but night fell before tea was poured. Petra sat between her proud parents, saying what a super house we had, what a super school it was, how super it was to have a holiday here. Her monotonous ignorance made her even more desirable.

Perhaps for our benefit—to show her off—Sir Godfrey asked her leading questions. "Mother tells me you've taken up knitting" and "Mother says you've become quite a whiz at math." Now he said, "I hear you've been doing some riding."

"Heaps, actually," said Petra. Her face was shining. "There are some stables near the school."

Dances, exams, picnics, house parties: Petra gushed about her Rhodesian school. And in doing so she made it seem a distant place—not an African country at all, but a special preserve of superior English recreations.

"That's funny," I said. "Aren't there Africans there?"

Jerry looked sharply at me.

"Not at the school," said Petra. "There are some in town. The girls call them nig-nogs." She smiled. "But they're quite sweet actually."

"The Africans, dear?" asked Lady Alice.

"The girls," said Petra.

Her father frowned.

Jerry said, "What do you think of this place?"

"Honestly, I think it's super."

"Too bad it's so dark at the moment," said Jerry. "I'd like to show you my frangipani."

"Jerry's famous for that frangipani," said Lady Alice.

Jerry had gone to the French windows to indicate the general direction of the bush. He gestured toward the darkness and said, "It's somewhere over there."

"I see it," said Petra.

The white flowers and the twisted limbs of the frangipani were clearly visible in the headlights of an approaching car.

Sir Godfrey said, "I think you have a visitor."

The Inkpens were staring at the taxi. I watched Jerry. He had turned pale, but kept his composure. "Ah, yes," he said, "it's the sister of one of our pupils." He stepped outside to intercept her, but Ameena was too quick for him. She hurried past him, into the parlor where the Inkpens sat dumbfounded. Then Sir Godfrey, who had been surprised into silence, stood up and offered Ameena his chair.

Ameena gave a nervous grunt and faced Jerry. She wore the black satin cloak and sandals of a village Muslim. I had never seen her in anything but a tight dress and high heels; in that long cloak she looked like a very dangerous fly which had buzzed into the room on stiff wings.

"How nice to see you," said Jerry. Every word was right, but his voice had become shrill. "I'd like you to meet—"

Ameena flapped the wings of her cloak in embarrassment and said, "I cannot stay. And I am sorry for this visit." She spoke in her own language. Her voice was calm and even apologetic.

"Perhaps she'd like to sit down," said Sir Godfrey, who was still standing.

"I think she's fine," said Jerry, backing away slightly.

Now I saw the look of horror on Petra's face. She glanced up and down, from the dark shawled head to the cracked feet, then gaped in bewilderment and fear.

At the kitchen door, Jika stood with his hands over his ears.

"Let's go outside," said Jerry in Chinyanja.

"It is not necessary," said Ameena. "I have something for you. I can give it to you here."

Jika ducked into the kitchen and shut the door.

"Here," said Ameena. She fumbled with her cloak.

Jerry said quickly, "No," and turned as if to avert the thrust of a dagger.

But Ameena had taken a soft gift-wrapped parcel from the folds of her cloak. She handed it to Jerry and, without turning to us, flapped out of the room. She became invisible as soon as she stepped into the darkness. Before anyone could speak, the taxi was speeding away from the house.

Lady Alice said, "How very odd."

"Just a courtesy call," said Jerry, and amazed me with a succession of plausible lies. "Her brother's in Form Four—a very bright boy, as a matter of fact. She was rather pleased by how well he'd done in his exams. She stopped in to say thanks."

"That's *very* African," said Sir Godfrey.

"It's lovely when people drop in," said Petra. "It's really quite a compliment."

Jerry was smiling weakly and eyeing the window, as if he expected Ameena to thunder in once again and split his head open. Or perhaps not. Perhaps he was congratulating himself that it had all gone so smoothly.

Lady Alice said, "Well, aren't you going to open it?"

"Open what?" said Jerry, and then he realized that he was holding the parcel. "You mean this?"

"I wonder what it could be," said Petra.

I prayed that it was nothing frightening. I had heard stories of jilted lovers sending aborted fetuses to the men who had wronged them.

"I adore opening parcels," said Petra.

Jerry tore off the wrapping paper, but satisfied himself that it was nothing incriminating before he showed it to the Inkpens.

"Is it a shirt?" said Lady Alice.

"It's a beauty," said Sir Godfrey.

It was red and yellow and green, with embroidery at the collar and cuffs; an African design. Jerry said, "I should give it back. It's a sort of bribe, isn't it?"

"Absolutely not," said Sir Godfrey. "I insist you keep it."

"Put it on!" said Petra.

Jerry shook his head. Lady Alice said, "Oh, do!"

"Some other time," said Jerry. He tossed the shirt aside and told a long humorous story of his sister's wedding reception on the family yacht. And before the Inkpens left he asked Sir Godfrey with old-fashioned formality if he might be allowed to take Petra on a day trip to the local tea estate.

"You're welcome to use my car if you like," said Sir Godfrey.

~§~

It was only after the Inkpens had gone that Jerry began to tremble. He tottered to a chair, lit a cigarette, and said, "That was the worst hour of my life. Did you see her? Jesus! I thought that was the end. But what did I tell you? She suspected something!"

"Not necessarily," I said.

He kicked the shirt—I noticed he was hesitant to touch it—and said, "What's this all about then?"

"As you told Inky—it's a present."

"She's a witch," said Jerry. "She's up to something."

"You're crazy," I said. "What's more, you're unfair. You kicked her out of the house. She came back to ingratiate herself by giving you a present—a new shirt for all the ones she didn't have a chance to iron. But she saw our neighbors. I don't think she'll be back."

"What amazes me," said Jerry, "is your presumption. I've been sleeping with Ameena for six months, while you've been playing with yourself. And here you are trying to tell me about her! You're incredible."

Jerry had the worst weakness of the liar: he never believed anything you told him.

I said, "What are you going to do with the shirt?"

Clearly this had been worrying him. But he said nothing.

Late that night, working with my specimens I smelled acrid smoke. I went to the window. The incinerator was alight; Jika was coughing and stirring the flames with a stick.

~§~

The next Saturday, Jerry took Petra to the tea estate in Sir Godfrey's gray Humber. I spent the day with my net, rather resenting the thought that Jerry had all the luck. First Ameena, now Petra. And he had ditched Ameena. There seemed no end to his arrogance or—what was more annoying—his luck. He came back to the house alone. I vowed that I would not give him a chance to do any sexual boasting. I stayed in my room, but less than ten minutes after he arrived home he was knocking on my door.

"I'm busy," I yelled.

"Doc, this is serious."

He entered rather breathless, fever-white and apologetic. This was not someone who had just made a sexual conquest—I knew as soon as I saw him that it had all gone wrong. So I said, "How does she bump?"

He shook his head. He looked very pale. He said, "I couldn't."

"So she turned you down." I could not hide my satisfaction.

"She was screaming for it," he said, rather primly. "She's seventeen, Doc. She's locked in a girls' school half the year. She even found a convenient haystack. But I had to say no. In fact, I couldn't get away from her fast enough."

"Something *is* wrong," I said. "Do you feel all right?"

He ignored the question. "Doc," he said, "remember when Ameena barged in. Just think hard. Did she touch me? Listen, this is important."

I told him I could not honestly remember whether she had touched him. The incident was so pathetic and embarrassing I had tried to blot it out.

"I knew something like this was going to happen. But I don't understand it." He was talking quickly and unbuttoning his shirt. Then he took it off. "Look at this. Have you ever seen anything like it?"

At first I thought his body was covered by welts. But what I had taken to be welts were a mass of tiny reddened patches, like fly bites, some already swollen into bumps. Most of them—and by far the worst— were on his back and shoulders. They were as ugly as acne and had given his skin that same shine of infection.

"It's interesting," I said.

"Interesting!" he screamed. "It looks like syphilis and all you can say is it's interesting. Thanks a lot."

"Does it hurt?"

"Not too much," he said. "I noticed it this morning before I went out. But I think they've gotten worse. That's why nothing happened with Petra. I was too scared to take my shirt off."

"I'm sure she wouldn't have minded if you'd kept it on."

"I couldn't risk it," he said. "What if it's contagious?"

He put calamine lotion on it and covered it carefully with gauze, and the next day it was worse. Each small bite had swelled to a pimple, and some of them seemed on the point of erupting: a mass of small warty boils. That was on Sunday. On Monday I told Sir Godfrey that Jerry had a bad cold and could not teach. When I got back to the house that afternoon, Jerry said that it was so painful he couldn't lie down. He had spent the afternoon sitting bolt upright in a chair.

"It was that shirt," he said. "Ameena's shirt. She did something to it."

I said, "You're lying. Jika burned that shirt—remember?"

"She touched me," he said. "Doc, maybe it's not a curse—I'm not superstitious anyway. Maybe she gave me syph."

"Let's hope so."

"What do you mean by that!"

"I mean, there's a cure for syphilis."

"Suppose it's not that?"

"We're in Africa," I said,

This terrified him, as I knew it would.

He said, "Look at my back and tell me if it looks as bad as it feels."

He crouched under the lamp. His back was grotesquely inflamed, The eruptions had become like nipples, much bigger and with a bruised discoloration. I pressed one, He cried out. Watery liquid leaked from a pustule.

"That hurt!" he said.

"Wait." I saw more infection inside the burst boil—a white clotted mass, I told him to grit his teeth. "I'm going to squeeze this one."

I pressed it between my thumbs and as I did a small white knob protruded. It was not pus—not liquid. I kept on pressing and Jerry yelled with shrill ferocity until I was done. Then I showed him what I had squeezed from his back; it was on the tip of my tweezers—a live maggot.

"It's a worm!"

"A larva,"

"You know about these things. You've seen this before, haven't you?"

I told him the truth. I had never seen one like it before in my life. It was not in any textbook I had ever seen. And I told him more: there were, I said, perhaps two hundred of them, just like the one wriggling on my tweezers, in those boils on his body.

Jerry began to cry.

~§~

That night I heard him writhing in his bed, and groaning, and if I had not known better I would have thought Ameena was with him. He turned and jerked and thumped like a lover maddened by desire; and he whimpered, too, seeming to savor the kind of pain that is indistinguishable from sexual pleasure. But it was no more passion than the movement of those maggots in his flesh. In the morning, gray with sleeplessness, he said he felt like a corpse. Truly, he looked as if he was being eaten alive.

An illness you read about is never as bad as the real thing. Boy Scouts are told to suck the poison out of snakebites. But a snakebite—swollen and black and running like a leper's sore—is so horrible I can't imagine anyone capable of staring at it, much less putting his mouth on it. It was that way with Jerry's boils. All the textbooks on earth could not have prepared me for their ugliness, and what made them even more repellent was the fact that his face and hands were free of them. He was infected from his neck to his waist, and down his arms; his face was haggard, and in marked contrast to his sores.

I said, "We'll have to get you to a doctor."

"A witch doctor."

"You're serious!"

He gasped and said, "I'm dying, Doc. You have to help me."

"We can borrow Sir Godfrey's car. We could be in Blantyre by midnight."

Jerry said, "I can't last until midnight."

"Take it easy," I said. "I have to go over to the school. I'll say you're still sick. I don't have any classes this afternoon when I get back I'll see if I can do anything for you."

"There are witch doctors around here," he said. "You can find one—they know what to do. It's a curse."

I watched his expression change as I said, "Maybe it's the curse of the white worm." He deserved to suffer, after what he had done, but his face was so twisted in fear, I added, "There's only one thing to do. Get those maggots out. It might work."

"Why did I come to this fucking place!"

But he shut his eyes and was silent: he knew why he had left home.

When I returned from the school ("And how is our ailing friend?" Sir Godfrey had asked at morning assembly), the house seemed empty. I had a moment of panic, thinking that Jerry—unable to stand the pain—had taken an overdose. I ran into the bedroom. He lay asleep on his side, but woke when I shook him.

"Where's Jika?" I said.

"I gave him the week off," said Jerry. "I didn't want him to see me. What are you doing?"

I had set out a spirit lamp and my surgical tools: tweezers, a scalpel, cotton, alcohol, bandages. He grew afraid when I shut the door and shone the lamp on him.

"I don't want you to do it," he said. "You don't know anything about this. You said you'd never seen this thing before."

I said, "Do you want to die?"

He sobbed and lay flat on the bed. I bent over him to begin. The maggots had grown larger, some had broken the skin, and their ugly heads stuck out like beads. I lanced the worst boil, between his shoulder blades. Jerry cried out and arched his back, but I kept digging and prodding, and I found that heat made it simpler. If I held my cigarette lighter near the wound the maggot wriggled, and by degrees, I eased it out. The danger lay in their breaking: if I pulled too hard some would be left in the boil to decay, and that I said would kill him.

By the end of the afternoon I had removed only twenty or so, and Jerry had fainted from the pain. He woke at nightfall. He looked at the saucer beside the bed and saw the maggots jerking in it—they had worked themselves into a white knot—and he screamed. I had to hold him until he calmed down. And then I continued.

I kept at it until very late. And I must admit that it gave me a certain pleasure. It was not only that Jerry deserved to suffer for his deceit—and his suffering was that of a condemned man; but also what I told him had been true: this was a startling discovery for me, as an entomologist. I had never seen such creatures before.

It was after midnight when I stopped. My hand ached, my eyes hurt from the glare, and I was sick to my stomach. Jerry had gone to sleep. I switched off the light and left him to his nightmares.

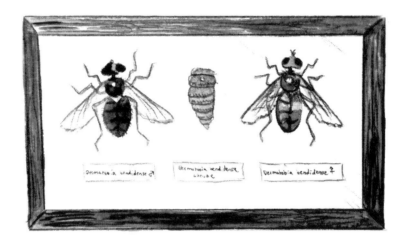

~§~

He was slightly better by morning. He was still pale, and the opened boils were crusted with blood, but he had more life in him than I had seen for days. And yet he was brutally scarred. I think he knew this: he looked as if he had been whipped.

"You saved my life," he said.

"Give it a few days," I said.

He smiled. I knew what he was thinking. Like all liars—those people who behave like human flies on our towering credulity—he was preparing his explanation. But this would be a final reply: he was preparing his escape.

"I'm leaving," he said. "I've got some money—and there's a night bus—" He stopped speaking and looked at my desk. "What's that?"

It was the dish of maggots, now as full as a rice pudding.

"Get rid of them!"

"I want to study them," I said. "I think I've earned the right to do that. But I'm off to morning assembly—what shall I tell Inky?"

"Tell him I might have this cold for a long time."

He was gone when I got back to the house; his room had been emptied, and he'd left me his books and his tennis racket with a note. I made what explanations I could. I told the truth: I had no idea where he had gone. A week later, Petra went back to Rhodesia, but she told me she would be back. As we chatted over the fence I heard Jerry's voice: *She's screaming for it.* I said, "We'll go horseback riding."

"Super!"

The curse of the white worm: Jerry had believed me. But it was the curse of impatience—he had been impatient to get rid of Ameena, impatient for Petra, impatient to put on a shirt that had not been ironed. What a pity it was that he was not around when the maggots hatched, to see them become flies I had never seen. He might have admired the way I expertly pickled some and sealed others in plastic and mounted twenty of them on a tray.

And what flies they were! It was a species that was not in any book, and yet the surprising thing was that in spite of their differently shaped wings (like a Muslim woman's cloak) and the shape of their bodies (a slight pinch above the thorax, giving them rather attractive waists), their life cycle was the same as many others of their kind: they laid their eggs on laundry and these larvae hatched at body heat and burrowed into the skin to mature. Of course, laundry was always ironed—even drip-dry shirts—to kill them. Everyone who knew Africa knew that.

Typhoid Mary

by Hans Heinz Ewers

a new translation by Joe Bandel

THE LITTLE HOLE was only dimly lit. The windows were covered, the tables pushed together and covered with a green cloth, so that it looked like one large table. Behind it sat six people: Erwin Ehrhardt, Siegfried Lowenstein, Count Thassilo Thun, Walter von Ayx, Hans dell'Greco and Randolph Ulbing. A seventh chair was empty.

In front of the green table, almost in the middle of the room, stood a large leather chair, and next to it a small end table. There was an ashtray on it, a box of matches, and a pack of cigarettes. There was not much else in the room.

The six men waited. They scarcely spoke. Fragments of jazz came from hotel Carmen across the bay.

Siegfried Lowenstein was an attorney in his 40s. A Jew—but even more, a Rhinelander. A war veteran of four years who had been awarded the blue Max—him!

Sir Hans dell'Greco was from Trieste. He was a ship's lieutenant of the former Austrian Navy. And now that Rome was paying his pension, he was trying to rebuild his Gorze era property which had been destroyed by the Italians.

Thassilo Thun was a Bohemian Baron of some obscure lineage. He was in his fifties. His watery blue eyes fluttered, and his lips trembled.

Dr. Erwin Erhardt was an industrial engineer from the Rhine. Engineer and inventor. Very rich, very elegant, and distinguished, dark haired and slender.

Randolph Ulbing was short and round. White, blonde hair—his hands looked like those of a butcher with manicured nails. He was CEO of the Ulbing branches in Hamburg and New York. An American citizen— so his millions were secure.

Baron Walter von Ayx was a painter and lived in Munich. His hair was gray, even though he was not yet thirty years old.

All six waited, smoked and drank, but didn't speak.

Then the door opened, and Colonel Lionel Thursby stepped inside. He wore small scars from his Göttinger student days on his left cheek—and a large red one across his forehead: which came from Flanders. His black eyes glowed.

"She's here!" He said.

A lady entered. Tall and slender. The colonel locked the door behind her and removed the key. Without speaking he motioned to the big chair in the middle of the room. Then he went to the table, placed the key in front of the attorney, who sat in the middle, and sat down in the empty chair by the window.

The tall woman didn't sit down.

"Why did you lock the door?" She cried. "Am I to be held here by force?"

Dr. Lowenstein nodded, "It appears that way."

The woman took a step forward.

"This looks like a tribunal. Are you perhaps wanting to sit in judgement over me?"

Again, the attorney nodded, "It appears that way."

She laughed out loud.

"Please," she said, "I am completely at your disposal."

She sat down in the easy chair, crossed her legs, and lit a cigarette.

"Go ahead gentlemen, I am curious."

The attorney stared across at her. He hadn't seen the woman in eight years—and she was exactly the same as she had been before. She hadn't aged a bit. She wiggled her narrow feet, which were stuck into pointed gray shoes. Her silk stockings were gray like her charmeuse dress. She wore an old Spanish shawl over her shoulders, whose colored flowers were so faded they were almost lost in the deep violet. She carried long deerskin gloves in one hand and in the other a small purse adorned with pearls. Her skin was tanned, quite healthy. A pearl necklace wound through her rich dark hair, and another, even larger one lay around her throat. But her rings bore black pearls. Perhaps she was not beautiful—but she looked as if she could have a very beautiful sister. Only her eyes were striking, yellow gold with brown, green, and white, like those of a large forest toad.

"How old is she anyway?" The attorney asked himself. He had seen her that morning by the pool in a black swimming suit—none of the other ladies had a figure like hers. She is certainly older than forty, he considered, probably closer to fifty or even older. And no one that encountered her thinks she is older that twenty-five. It is amazing he thought.

Marie Stuyvesant flicked the ash into the ash tray.

"Seriously, gentlemen," she said calmly, "would one of you like to explain what this is all about, because I don't see the humor in it. Especially today I'm not in the mood for jokes because I have just received some news that has troubled me."

The attorney picked up a telegram from the table.

"Perhaps it is the same one that we received. Young Dr. Terhune has shot himself in Zürich!—But you will soon see dear lady, that we are not here to play jokes."

Marie Stuyvesant interrupted him:

"Why the 'dear lady'—Friedel?" She smiled at him. "You have aged a bit since the last time I saw you! And where is that bushy hair?—but please, will you just tell me what this seriousness is all about? Look, I am not entirely unprepared. You want something of me—I've known that for a long time. Last winter I met Count Thun at the opera in Vienna—in casual conversation I mentioned that I didn't yet know where I wanted to spend the spring. Two months later he wrote to me and recommended Isle Brioni—I would like it—it had everything that I could desire. Quiet—and yet the best of company. Solitude, if I wanted it, and dance and music if I wanted something else. And—and—well, in short: everything. Then four weeks later he wrote me again, asking whether I had received his letter—and if I had decided to travel to Isle Brioni? Really—I only decided to go because this courtesy was so unlike him that I had come to suspect that he had some other intentions. But he was right to give me that bit of advice and I am very grateful to him for it.

"The first person I encountered on the pier—was Colonel Thursby; he told me that he was now working for the embassy in Rome and had come here to recuperate. But he did not tell me that he knew I would be coming here. Then five days later dell'Greco came and today, exactly two weeks after my arrival, you are all here! Because of me, right Friedel?"

The attorney nodded, "Most certainly."

"Thank you," said the beautiful woman, "that is certainly very flattering. But it now appears to me that there is no one here whom I have not had some kind of dispute with. It does seem rather strange that you would entice me here—because that is what really happened—and then follow me. It must certainly be good for the hotel—seven guests at the same time!"

"There could have easily been seventy and even more!" Said Dr. Lowenstein. "Ladies and gentlemen, and in a way, we represent all the others."

"So, a type of advisory board," said Marie, "and you gentlemen represent the absent shareholders! It certainly appears that I have in some way injured your corporation, and that is why you have compelled me—and permit me to say, in a very original way, to appear before your Tribunal! So, present your case, Mr. Chairman."

"In these years, Ms. Marie Stuyvesant, there is much that happens in this world that smacks of force rather than justice. Once we determined to hold you, we didn't care all that much if things went right and proper. You can understand that. The main thing is now that we have you here, we can share with you what we have to say. And as for there being seven of us, I am of the opinion that we represent all of humanity, at least as far as they, directly or indirectly have come in contact with you or ever will. I bid you very much, Lady Marie, to calmly listen to us—we believe, that we can share things about yourself that you don't even know—or at least never from our perspective. You will have plenty of opportunity to answer and then—to act."

He opened the leather briefcase in front of him and took out a thick stack of papers.

"This letter," he continued, "gave the impetus to our action. Colonel Thursby sent it to Dr. Erhardt over a year ago—who then shared it with me."

"You must hate me very much Colonel," the woman turned to the Englander.

"Most certainly," said the Englander. "You have driven two of my brothers and my sister to their graves. You have turned my life into a hell—oh most certainly I hate you!"

Marie Stuyvesant shrugged her shoulders. "Continue Friedel!"

"We discussed what could be done. I will not hide from you that for a long time we debated on whether it would be possible, to turn you over to the authorities, or turn to judges and psychiatrists in an attempt to rid society of you. We only dropped this idea, because—even though the poison of Marie Stuyvesant enjoys an almost international acclaim—we could see that there was scarcely any valid evidence that could be used against you. So, we decided to deal with it ourselves. We sat down with everyone we knew or heard of that had ever been in contact with you; in a small number of cases, we found solid proof in which, through the influence of your personality, through your drawings and your books, these people met their downfall. We spent this past year collecting material for this case, Marie Stuyvesant, from out of hundreds of hidden crevasses in all parts of Europe and the Americas and if I might be permitted to say, from around the entire world. Naturally, it is not in the slightest complete, but there is more than enough material, to give you— Ms. Stuyvesant, a clear picture of what your life means for the rest of human society."

He took a notebook out of the briefcase and handed it to the painter who was sitting on his right.

"This is," he declared, "a monograph by your friend, the young Dr. Ramon de Ayala about—"

Ms. Marie interrupted him. "The gentleman was never my friend. He visited me during the war years at my studio in Seville—twice—three times at the most. At the time I had a craving for cocaine, and he provided it for me."

"That is certainly correct," confirmed Dr. Lowenstein, "the young Spaniard provided you with what you wanted. Unfortunately, he then took cocaine himself."

"I didn't encourage him to do that," declared the lady.

"That is also true," answered the attorney. "Don Ramon wrote that himself. Yet, he saw you take cocaine and then took it himself. He became addicted to it. Today he is in an institution and—incurable. From him we received this very interesting monograph over the case of Jorge Quintero —which if you compare them with your own case does form a striking analogy. Many such cases of germ carriers have often been observed, but this presentation is especially clear and simple. A brief summary of the facts will be enough for us, I have provided a short excerpt—would you be so kind as to read it to us, Baron!"

Walter von Ayx read:

"Jorge Quintero was born 1882 in Ronda, Andalusia, a son of farmers. During his military service he served with his regiment for a time in Morocco. It was later determined that during this time several soldiers had been infected with typhoid. After the regiment returned to Malaga a genuine epidemic broke out. After his discharge from the military Quintero worked on various farms as a laborer in the Vega area of Grenada—and on every single farm he infected the household with typhus. At the time the simple peasants were so alarmed at these events, that Jorge, who had always been loved for being a pleasant, hardworking, and handsome man—was openly considered as the bearer of misfortune. Then he found a job as a nurse in a hospital in Granada, because in the army he had trained to work in the infirmary. Scarcely two weeks later a typhus epidemic broke out in the hospital that took the lives of no less than fifty-four people. The hospital had to be provisionally shut down and the personnel were dismissed. Jorge then found employment in various places in Granada, Jaen and later in Seville—and in all those places he infected people with typhoid. Finally, he once more found work as a nurse in Seville, and none of the doctors in the hospital knew anything about his past history. Several months later the worst outbreak of typhus that Seville had ever seen occurred at that hospital—the death toll was nearly fourteen hundred. Through a coincidence suspicion fell on Jorge—a farmer's wife recognized him as the fellow, who, she thought, had brought death into her house. Her husband and two of her children had been killed by typhus. This woman raised such an outcry, both in the hospital and on the streets, that she was finally taken into custody. When questioned she made convincing statements—they investigated and solidly determined, that what she was saying was true. In no time at all the entire past history of the unfortunate man was determined— He willingly provided all the places where he had worked, and it only needed to be confirmed. Quintero was then arrested and placed in solitary confinement, but soon released after the court hearing, because there was not the slightest bit of evidence. But he voluntarily agreed to be locked up in a room in the hospital for observation. This voluntary confinement, during which the most prominent bacteriologists in Spain were kept occupied, lasted eight months. After this time, they had to release him— because of the constant pressure of public opinion and from the local press, which made things increasingly difficult for the hospital management. Despite the most stringent precautions new cases of typhus continued to appear—seven inpatients as well as one young doctor had died. If Spain would have had a little island for a leper colony, they would most certainly have sent him there—rightly or wrongly! But now they had to once more let him loose among humanity. It was the old Jesuit Father Don José Hoyos, known as the most passionate Jaimist in all of Spain, who found a solution. He traveled to Seville, searched up the unfortunate Jorge Quintero and—"

At this point Dr. Lowenstein interrupted the discourse.

"Thank you, Baron. We will read the conclusion later."

"That's a shame," said Ms. Marie Stuyvesant. "I am very interested in the ending. The story itself is not new to me—at the time all of Seville was talking about it. Naturally I understand quite well what you are trying to say, dear Sir. Your Jorge was, or still is, a carrier of typhus.

Whoever is not immune will get infected by him. And so, you think that I am a carrier for some typhus of the soul—and it is much, much more dangerous than that carried by the Andalusian farmer's son. Is that it?"

"Yes," nodded the attorney. "And now we have a Jesuit that is successful in bringing a solution to Quinero's case. First, he began with trying to make the poor fellow understand the nature of his predicament—which all the doctors working on his case had still not made clear to him. The same thing that we would like to try with you, Ms. Marie Stuyvesant. We have a tremendous amount of evidence here, and I am convinced, that in every single case you will openly, perhaps laughingly, admit to us that everything is true down to the smallest detail. It appears that there are a considerable number of people who are immune to typhus, even without being inoculated. Unfortunately, there has not yet been a vaccine of the soul for the disease you carry—and even if a large number of individuals were immune to this or any other toxin that you are the carrier of, the full implication of your—please excuse the ugly word—manyfold vices or evil influences are so great, that scarcely one out of a thousand would not be infected. You see, Quintero can only be held accountable for the typhoid contagion—while you are able to infect people with hundreds of vices, of which every single one is even more dangerous."

He paused, coughed, reached for the carafe, and poured himself a glass of water.

Ms. Marie Stuyvesant laughed:

"Since when do you drink water, Friedel?"

The attorney raised the glass to his lips—but then set it back down again.

"Since my successful attempt to cut myself loose from you, Marie! It took eight detoxifications in three sanatoriums before I finally learned to stop drinking. Because I—thanks to you! Was nearly unsavable. Since then!"

"You are forgetting something, Friedel," the lady in gray said. "Even before I made your acquaintance you could drink a good glass—isn't that true?"

"Yes, yes," cried the attorney. "Certainly, I drank, like any good student! But through you—through you alone, I became a drunkard!"

Mary Stuyvesant put down her cigarette.

"Well—and now you are all healed—so much for the better! Yet I don't see any reason why I shouldn't have a glass of wine to drink—I think the gentlemen are not being very gallant."

She looked across the green table.

"Mr. dell'Greco—you have a Chablis there in front of you—won't you bring me a glass?"

The Italian sprang up immediately, placed a glass on her table and filled it. Then he set the bottle down next to her.

"My pleasure—" he murmured, and then went back to his seat.

The tall woman raised her glass. Slowly she said:

"To your health, Dr. Siegfried Lowenstein! It is much more fitting that I now address you so! Because the Friedel that I once knew, would never have toasted me with a glass of water!"

For the second time the attorney took up the glass of water, put it to his lips, moistening them. He took a swallow—then fiercely slammed the glass back down on the table. He stared at the woman, bit his lips.

"The devil take me," he whispered, "the devil take me—"

Then with a quick movement he grabbed the bottle of red wine that was sitting in front of his neighbor, the Baron, filled his water glass to the top, and emptied it in one gulp.

"Oh," smiled Marie Stuyvesant, "oh—"

Silently Dr. Lowenstein shoved the portfolio to the right; Ulbing, the financier, took it up.

"Our investigations have not been one sided, good Lady," he began. "If we on one side present all the evil that you have brought into the world, we also want to present the other side, and as much as possible have collected, that which speaks in your favor. That is what I have been entrusted with—the gentlemen have especially selected me, because it is my nature to be very skeptical and critical and not to take things at face value. Even though I have every reason not to think favorably of you. You have, as you will remember, good lady, once persuaded me to make a certain investment, that—shall we say—did not meet the customary requirements of the old Ulbing bank."

She interrupted him.

"You bore me! You know very well that I know nothing of business matters. You bore me, exactly like you did once before, those many years ago in Hamburg, with those dreary proposals of all kinds of combinations and possibilities, forcing me, very much against my will, to listen to them. At the time I told you that your views on business ethics seemed exceptionally childish to me. That every filthy rich man, as far as I was concerned, got their gold from stealing and robbing, that each one of them was a swindler, a cheat, or a thief. One or the other. And that is most certainly right; because that's the only way a man can make the money of others flow into his own pockets. Only, I think, such a man should at least be honest with themselves and not do as you did, always attempting to justify your actions, and with each newly swindled million go complaining through the world as remorse incarnate. All of that was very theoretical, I had no idea what kind of business you were involved in, and I have certainly never earned a penny through your business dealings."

Randolf Ulbing nodded.

"It was exactly as you say, good lady! But I thought about what you said to me, and after a long time, came to the conclusion that you were correct. Today I am even more than ever of this opinion, especially after the experiences of the past year. I have acted like every other profit maker and today am several million richer than I was at the time."

"You should be grateful to me," said Ms. Stuyvesant.

"I am not grateful to you," he retorted. "The reputation of the ancient House of Ulbing, as founded by my great-grandfather, was spotless in the financial world like no other House. It remained that way until right up to the day—when you explained it all to me! Inquire about our reputation today. I have increased the capital of the House tenfold—I have not done anything different than the other Houses—but have done very much, many things that my ancestors would never have even considered doing before, or myself either. I can easily justify any of these machinations before the court—even to myself, when I am sitting in my office. Yet I cannot help but be seized with disgust when I open a newspaper and from out of every line the troubles of the world stare out at me, troubles that I so cleverly take advantage of for myself. I followed your advice—and it has made my life miserable."

"I have no desire," said the woman, "to listen to your bull shit! What I told you was no special wisdom of mine—it has been printed and repeated a thousand times. You never paid any attention to it before! And now, that you should suddenly hear it from my own mouth and be so strongly influenced, that is your own fault!"

"I am not lying to you," replied the banker. "Because it was your influence alone. That which my watered-down stock honesty instinctively recoiled at—sounded like a universal truth when it came from your lips. And so good lady, it is your fault as well as mine!"

Ms. Marie threw her cigarette far out into the room. Her voice rang sharp and clear.

"Mr. Ulbing," she said, "you are not a good-looking man, you already know that! It is no pleasure to look at you!—Do you shave yourself? In any case, I don't understand how you can look at yourself in the mirror every day and not cut your own throat! It would certainly be an end to all your remorse!"

Dr. Erhardt repressed a quick smile.

"Let's not get too personal!" He said. "Mr. Randolph is more of a gentleman than you think, Ms. Stuyvesant. What he has to say, is flattering enough for you!"

The banker picked up a sheaf of papers.

"I have determined, good lady—and you can believe me, that I have resisted this conclusion with both hands and feet—that you are one of the most kindhearted, decent, upstanding persons, that has ever lived. Ms. Marie Stuyvesant is completely incapable of any base or mean activity. Her boundless love for all animals is known by everyone, that ever comes in contact with her. It is even more certain that she has loaned or given away more than three quarters of her not inconsiderable income, without demanding any interest. Year in and year out Ms. Stuyvesant has supported young artists and students—and has done it in such a manner, that none of them ever felt she was giving alms. During and after the war years she acted in such an unselfish manner—"

The lady in gray slapped her gloves against her knee.

"That's enough, Mr. Ulbing!" She cried. "While I don't like it that you all see me as a criminal, it is certainly even more unpleasant—yes, even unbearable, that you want to list my little virtues. I urgently ask the gentlemen to desist."

Banker Ulbing hesitated, turned with a glance to the other gentlemen.

"Lowenstein," said Dr. Erhardt," you have agreed to be the chairman?"

The attorney startled. He again took the bottle from the Baron, filled his glass, and emptied it in short swallows.

"Give me the files," he murmured. Mr. von Ayx handed them back to him.

"I think," he continued, "that the gentlemen are in agreement, to adhere to the wishes of the lady. It is only to justify our own actions that we have gathered this potentially rich material, I would like you to know. We know very well, that the good is quickly forgotten, while the evil swells up and grows. We are all completely convinced, that we have only discovered a small portion of the good, that you have done in your life. We have determined that in at least three cases you have put your life at risk to save another—in one instance it was only for a dog. —More than once you have personally demonstrated your courage, which even the best shock troops would accord the highest honors—and have demonstrated dozens of times exactly the same proud courage, the same high regard for everything, that opposes you. Never have you caused anyone any grief. And I am well-permitted to say: we know of no other woman of greater magnanimity—"

"Friedel!" said the woman. And it rang like a reproach.

"Just a moment!" he continued. "I must say this, because it clarifies a good portion of the immense possibilities of your influence. You may rightly be considered, Ms. Marie Stuyvesant, as the most elegant woman of our century. You have more taste—in every respect—than the best artists of our age. Your extraordinary talent with a pen and a brush have long been counted among those of modern art and literature. It is not easy for someone to withstand your natural charm and grace. Oh please, don't interrupt me—I am almost finished, even if I could sing your praises in this manner for hours. Only one more thing I must bring up, because it is something, which came as a complete surprise to most of us. It is the fact that you—Ms. Marie Stuyvesant—even though you have been wading knee deep through pools of sin and hells of temptation, still have the purest soul of any human today."

"Amen," said the woman. "And with that I hope this chapter is closed!"

"According to your wish!" Continued the attorney. "But before we open the next, you have to admit that we have thoroughly studied the facts and given you full credit for what you have done. Also, everything that we have just presented, makes it scarcely necessary for you to even speak—it also serves a final purpose in exposing the immense phenomenon of your influence. Mr. dell'Greco, will you please read a few excerpts from out of our files—it would take much too long if we completely read all of them."

The Naval Lieutenant who was sitting at the furthest left end of the green table began to read:

"In the year 1910 an unusual epidemic broke out among the students of the Munich Art Academy—the young people were drinking ether by the dozens. An entire group of them perished miserably—"

"Excuse me," Erwin Erhardt interrupted the Italian. "I would like to ask a few questions of Ms. Stuyvesant—am I permitted to hope that she will answer me?"

"Certainly," the lady nodded.

"What started this epidemic—naturally you know about it. They say that you started it?"

Ms. Marie shrugged her shoulders.

"I occasionally drank ether, like I—occasionally—take any other narcotic. It is highly likely that some of the young students were there. It is quite possible, that they themselves then took ether and even encouraged others."

"We have," the engineer continued, "in our files a number of such cases—and they are, as you say, regarding almost all of them, narcotics. You, Ms. Stuyvesant, were never addicted to alcohol, morphine, or cocaine; never a habitual user of muscarine, mescal, opium, or heroin—or anything else. But very many people who saw you take these narcotics, heard you talk of them or read about them in some of your books, took them, and many of these people became occasional users. Several of them perished, died in institutions, or committed suicide. What for you was an occasional thrill, perhaps a pleasant hour, was for many others a slow death. Through whom were you introduced to opium, Count Thun?"

"Through one of the good lady's books," the Count said calmly. I don't regret it. I know that I have become scarcely much of a man, in the conventional sense. I know that I will perish through opium—and know what a bitter end that is. Yet, I don't regret it—what happened to me personally, is not because of her."

The lady in gray looked at him and her voice almost rang with gratitude.

"Count, what are you smoking?"

"It is pathetic—I can only get mixtures out of India—and at exorbitant prices."

"I thought as much," said Ms. Marie. "That's why I asked. I have some of the best Chinese Opium—and will have some sent to your room, Count!" She interrupted herself laughing. "Or is that perhaps an attempt to influence a judge?"

"We are not your judges," said Dr. Lowenstein. "There is only one person that is permitted to sit in judgement of you—and you will soon enough hear his name! Please continue to read."

Sir dell'Greco took up another sheet of paper.

"Here are clippings out of magazines and newspapers, brochures and books—they are all about Ms. Marie Stuyvesant's art dealings. They vary in theme, in all kinds of tones, shimmer in all kinds of colors, but in one way they are all the same, namely how she has had a tremendous influence on promoting this type of art. And also, that this influence is the most pernicious that an artist has ever produced. 'For generations to come', says this one, people will not be able to resist this poison. The striking feature of this art is that there are those in the world, those, as Schiller would say, 'the gods graciously cover with night and grayness,' those who step with light feet and don't describe anything horrible at all. Everything is natural, nothing is unnatural—this is the dogma—and because of that it is not abnormal, perverse, or unnatural. It can all appear very beautiful—and indeed, far more often, appears as normal, common. But then if it is beautiful—that makes it good. It is not a lie to say that in all the drawings of Stuyvesant, like in her papers everything is in fact, of a higher beauty—this beauty is so tangible that the hands can grasp it, and that makes it harder to pull away from. So that the public in all countries, and most especially the youth, drink in this art—drink it in greedily, turn away from normal everyday things in disgust and seek the labyrinth of the night life. Unfortunately, the perverse is not as beautiful to them, instead they merely become wrapped in the magical cloak of this art; and there stands not only a gifted artist to instruct, but even more of the masses that have been seduced. They run after the will-o-the-wisp, and run rejoicing, into the swamp; believing, they will find beauty, only to finally end up in the mud and filth. Every principal, every University lecturer, every judge can bear witness to the soul shattering effects, that this type of art invokes—if they themselves are not already infected by it."

"Ms. Stuyvesant," Dr. Erhardt continued, "do you believe that this critic is correct?"

She answered:

"I don't read my books and I don't critique them. I write them—that is all. Like I draw my illustrations. Should I then draw and write differently? Do you demand that a hedgehog give birth to a rhinoceros, that an ostrich lay caviar!"

Erwin Erhardt thought: "This woman is amazing—"

"Proceed," the attorney turned to Mr. dell'Greco. The naval lieutenant took up his file again.

"We have various detailed reports about the so-called Stuyvesant Balls. They were already here before the outbreak of the war, but have become quite fashionable all over Europe during these past years. Two of our reports appear especially interesting, one from out of Zurich, the other from Stockholm. All the participants appeared in the bizarre costumes of your black and white illustrations, in which these so called 'sexy outfits' were developed to the highest levels of refinement—"

"Would you tell me," Engineer Ernhardt asked, "how this all came about? Ever new variations and styles with the same theme, Ms. Stuyvesant, in your illustrations. A person dressed in such a way that he exudes an irresistible sexual attraction. I possess all of your illustrations and have seen very many outfits that are based upon them. Doubtless, the highest recognition of this art is that the bizarre thrill, which it evokes is so strong that it would make even a plaster statue sigh with passion!"

Ms. Marie lit another cigarette.

"Then, dear Sir, I must have fewer feelings than a plaster statue! But that is perhaps the reason, because I know what works—and why it works. You see, the entire clothing industry is completely full of 'sexy outfits', as the learned call them, or at least it attempts to. But all these outfits down through the centuries were designed by amateurs, by tailors, cleaning women—dilettantes, who didn't have a clue. At least kings, dukes and generals understood when they insulted their handsome Lieutenants by turning them into sexy dolls. It is amazing gentlemen, how all the sages of this world run around, their heads stuffed full of deep knowledge—and they still don't know the simplest things. Clothing, my revered gentlemen, whether made of feathers or furs, or consisting of trousers or skirts, is created by us to serve as a protection against the elements. But beautiful clothing has only one purpose: to attract the eye of the opposite sex. That's why the peacock has his radiant plumage, the lion his proud mane. Whoever cannot see what nature herself teaches us—is born blind. That my outfits are sexually attractive is certainly true—in exactly the same way the birds of paradise or the lemon moths are. And I would like to say, Count Thun, that you made a much better impression on the young ladies when you were stuck in a Hussar's uniform!"

There was no reply so the Italian continued.

"Everywhere these Balls degenerated into the most shameful orgies. The notorious 'Quat'z Arts' Balls in Paris were nothing in comparison to those of Ms. Stuyvesant. All they did with their shamelessness was to bring the two sexes together, while these are celebrations of every kind of perverse lust. It is most certain, that no other time showed such a boundless neglect of morals as ours, and this is because—"

Ms. Marie Stuyvesant burst out laughing.

"—I carry the blame for that! —Oh, you moralist! Our time is more open, that is all! Immoral? Oh, dear God, it is just as moral and immoral as any other time has been. Is there anything immoral about sexuality? Perhaps because it is simply natural? Well, does that make all of nature— unnatural! Because the sex lives of the entire animal world are full of thousands of wild combinations, which any decent man would find exceptionally abnormal and perverse. But even the animal world must seem moderate compared to the exceptionally variegated love life of the plant world! Just take a closer look into nature—anyone who maintains that it is in any way normal and natural, according to your terms of what is natural, is either a liar or a complete idiot! But in the end—we humans —also belong to nature!"

"You misunderstand us," declared Erwin Erhardt. "None of us suffer from moralistic tendencies, and none of us are thinking of trying to blame you for that. If you would have listened to all that Mr. dell'Greco had to say, you would have easily noticed what our intentions really are. These Balls—which occupy thousands of conversations and to which thousands go to in all cities—are not in themselves any more significant, than any other fad that you will always find in the cities. What is important is the masses of people that attend them. What is important is that the young people turn away from their work in droves, and have only one thing in their heads, to live in their senses. What is important is that the norms, which have shaped our societies through many centuries—whether rightly or wrongly, is not of our concern—have been broken and laughingly ridiculed. These morays have certainly held our instincts in strong bonds— You, Ms. Stuyvesant, have torn these chains asunder. We cannot spend the entire day pointing out every instance—we can only provide you a couple of examples—but these examples are typical, and you could find a thousand others just like them! Please, Colonel Thursby, will you enlighten the Lady on the parts of her story which for the most part is still unknown to her."

Colonel Lionel Thursby stood up; his fingers gripped the bottle of whiskey that was sitting in front of him and held it tightly.

"You will recall, Madam Stuyvesant, that you gave a speech in London in 1913. At the time I was very enamored with you and had followed you all around the world for many years. At the invitation of the Lotus Club, you spoke of several of your causes. At the same time there was a display of your drawings and paintings in another room of the club. That evening I brought my sister and brothers along, who had known about my infatuation with you for a long time and were curious to meet you in person. That evening you read a story about two brothers who were in love with each other—you remember which story I'm talking about. Well, that which you spoke of was the case with my brothers. You certainly didn't put this unholy inclination into them, but you were the one, that inspired them to turn their harmless brotherly affections for each other into something less innocent—and encouraged it to blossom. You taught my brothers that everything that has roots, has its own right to exist, to blossom and to bear fruit. It was through you that they first learned what kind of love they shared! Then came, what had to come—the two surrendered to their strong passions. Six weeks later I found out about it—after six months the servants learned of it—after a year all of London knew. When my brothers—both army officers—were stationed with their regiments at the outbreak of the war, they received very chilly receptions from the men. They cursed them—and finally outright rejected them. And the two shot themselves—together that same night!"

"That is very unfortunate," said Ms. Stuyvesant. "I have never met the two gentlemen, Colonel; you forgot to introduce them to me."

"But you met my sister, Madam, right?" Screamed the Colonel. "She came to you after the performance. Then to your hotel on the next day and traveled with you as you left London the day after that."

The lady in gray nodded. "Yes, she did. She followed me, just like you did, Colonel. Burdened me with her feelings, exactly like you did with your feelings, feelings which I, even with the best of will, could not return—for you or for her. I am sorry Colonel, but I am a loner, don't forget that! How can you demand that I give myself to anyone, male or female, who desires me?"

"My sister came back to London," said the Colonel, "two weeks after the deaths of my brothers. She followed them—they found her poisoned, with your photo in her hand."

"But you, Dear Colonel, you are still alive!" said Marie Stuyvesant. "Alive, and wanting to make me responsible for something, that you wouldn't care anything at all about, if it had happened to anyone else."

The Colonel screamed: "I live—because death doesn't want me! I have loved you since the very first day I saw you. I am bound to you by three deaths—in this past year I have had no thoughts at all except for one: Marie Stuyvesant! I hate you—hate you, Madam—and know very well—that it is love, like it always was! And that it will never end—until—until—"

He stammered; then suddenly sat down wiping the beads of sweat from his forehead with a silk handkerchief.

Dr. Ernhardt said quickly: "May I ask you, Ms. Stuyvesant, how many people have lost their lives in a similar manner, like Ms. Thursby? Or how many such cases you are aware of? We, ourselves, have been able to determine—"

Ms. Marie interrupted him: "Put a couple more zeroes on it if it makes you happy! I don't see what difference it makes."

Dr. Lowenstein gulped down one glass after another.

"But we do, Marie Stuyvesant," he cried, "we do! One case means nothing—but when you take all of them together, that is something else. And that is what we are speaking of—these gentlemen, that are sitting here across from you—and we know that it is easier to grasp something that we know from personal experience. That is why we are sharing these things with you from our own personal lives. We have promised not to spare ourselves in this—you have seen how openly the gentlemen speak. Even Sir dell'Greco believes that you are the cause of his life being in ruin. You know that his wife is an extraordinarily beautiful woman, who is loved everywhere. Today this woman is a great international whore, who travels from one health spa to another and belongs to anyone who can afford her. A single, small remark you once made is to blame for her behavior."

"Am I permitted to ask which remark that was?" Said the lady in gray.

"The dell'Grecos made your acquaintance in Porto rose two years ago; both were great admirers of your art and naturally very happy to be allowed to get to know you better. Isabelle dell'Greco was very attached to you—every word that you spoke, she treated like gospel. You sketched both Mr. dell'Greco as well as his wife Isabelle—and it was during one of these sittings that you laid your sketchbook down on your knee and said: 'I must do something different this time!' When Mrs. Isabelle asked, you answered, 'My God, he has a magnificent figure! A genuine model! But there is something terribly boring as well—tell me, Mrs. Isabelle, isn't he sometimes frightfully boring?'"

"Yes, good heavens, gentlemen," cried Ms. Marie, "wasn't I right? Just look at the good Hans—despite his good looks he is boring enough to make me want to puke!"

Sir dell'Greco coughed: "Your Grace—your Grace—! Perhaps it is so—it is certainly so if you say it is! But my wife saw it then for the first time—and from that day on I was boring to her—as you say: boring enough to make you want to puke! She left me—found someone else—and perhaps he became boring as well after a short time. And because of that—"

"Is that also typical?" asked Ms. Marie.

The attorney nodded. "It is typical in that there is something that you said, in all innocence—that in another person's brain is capable of taking on a totally different meaning. Look, Ms. Marie, at the white hairs of my neighbor, the young Baron von Ayx. They turned white in a few months—not through romance, not through some fearful experience. But as always—through you, even though he has just now seen you for the first time in his life. Several years ago, Ms. Marie, one evening you were gambling in a casino in San Sebastian; and had just lost some twenty thousand Pesetas. Then you went with several other well-known ladies and gentlemen who had also been unlucky that evening to a coffeehouse. While the others were in genuine bad moods, you, for the most part, were in an extraordinarily good mood. You paid for your coffee with a hundred franc note that you unexpectedly found in your purse and gave the rest to the waiter as a tip. You made fun of the gloomy faces of the others and philosophized, that the true charm of a high stakes game is that the money doesn't really have any value anymore. That you only collect yellow, red, blue, and white chips or give them away and after a short time completely lose any sense of the value of money. And that you sense this sovereign sensation even more deeply after you have just lost every-thing, and not after you win. It happened that there was a gentleman nearby totally unknown to you, who overheard what you said and was very taken with it. This same gentleman, who never gambled himself, years later told his friend, the Baron von Ayx about it. The young painter—who had until this time never even considered touching a card or trying his luck at any other form of gambling, was deeply impressed with this seemingly innocent remark. He felt a strange lust to gamble—resisted it for a week, and then at the next opportunity sat down at the baccarat table in a club. After that he was stuck to that table—losing his fortune in six months as well as that of his mother. The sensation that gambling brought you, unfortunately, didn't ever come to him—but his gray hair will remind him of you for the rest of his life."

Marie Stuyvesant observed the young painter carefully. "I find that he dresses exceptionally well," she noted.

Attorney Lowenstein paged through the file.

"Another page!" He began once more. "You have, from time to time, Ms. Marie, felt the desire to appear on stage. In some cases, even plays that you directed yourself. Each one was a small sensation and most certainly a success. Not on account of theatrical talent, but because of the influence of your strong personality, which even made technical glitches seem charming and not failures."

"Is that a crime?" asked Marie Stuyvesant.

"No more than any of the other things that we have been discussing," declared the attorney. "Only there is one thing, that your example drove a crowd of young people to the stage who would never have thought of doing it before. And all of them believed that they could be successful despite a lack of talent and education simply through strength of personality—believing, they could simply go straight from the street onto the stage and be successful at it. The theater directors scarcely knew who to save from all the children, suffering from Stuyvesant mania, as it was called among the performers of the stage. A strong personality is naturally very hard to find—and the end of the story is that the vast army of prostitutes was made that much richer."

The attorney picked up another page and continued without even pausing:

"Here are a number of cases grouped together which even though very different have one thing in common, they involve cases of absurd bets. In one of your stories, Marie, there was a man who believed that he could do anything and because of that he made all kinds of improbable wagers. In this man you have described a good portion of yourself, because you also gladly make such bets—and most of the time easily win them. I, myself, was there the time you bet that you would raise a little flag on the top of the tower of the Cologne cathedral. You prepared yourself ahead of time, seeking out the best roofer in the city as a teacher, taking on a series of easier objects—and then finally winning the bet. Once in Rome you made the bet that you would go around in men's clothing for three months living your life as before. You did it, visited clubs, theaters, concerts, and churches—winning your bet. The hero of your story bet—but I don't need to tell you that. Very well—these people whose names are listed here, wanted to do the same as you, seeking honor and fame in doing crazy things. It could be that several succeeded—but not these! I have here a list of fourteen names—four of them paid for their foolishness with their lives. One young lady ended up in a lunatic asylum for several years, two are crippled for life. The rest are well and healthy today—but have paid for their lust to make such bets by suffering with long illnesses."

The attorney paused, emptied his glass, and took up another sheet of paper.

"Here, Ms. Marie, we have the cases—"

But the lady in gray interrupted him.

"It is enough," she said calmly. "I will not lie—everything, that you have determined, happened exactly as you say. If I think about it, gentlemen, I can come up with several other instances that you don't know about. Just yesterday I received a letter from a doctor in Amsterdam, that showers me with the heaviest reproach. You see, somewhere I once supported the ancient belief that it was a crime to keep incurable mental illness, completely crippled or idiotic children and the like alive in those conditions for many years. Society not only has the right, but the duty to terminate them. You all know that this position has been raised for years by scientific authorities in all countries all over the world—and naturally the doctor in Amsterdam knows this just as well as you do. Well—this doctor had an idiotic little daughter that made his life and that of his wife into a living hell. Finally, he decided, in agreement with his wife, to put an end to this daily torment: he poisoned the child. Yet his wife took this death—which should have been her salvation—so to heart, that she, presumably in a complete nervous breakdown, threw herself out of the window. But the doctor, broken down at the fate of his wife, went and turned himself in to the authorities. He was immediately arrested and sent me this letter from prison: I and I alone, he wrote, carry the blame for all his misfortune! Because it was my plea alone for the known demand that had fallen into his hands through coincidence and in the end, it was the final deciding factor that caused him to do it. Without me his wife and child would still be alive—without me he would not be accused of murder and sitting in prison."

She opened her purse, took out the letter and laid it in front of him on the table.

"Here, gentlemen, is the letter. I will not be responding to it—add it to your files if you want. It is, as far as I know, the last instance of that which you want to consider and certainly a fine example of your hypothesis. I have prepared more if you would like to see, but I think that we have more than enough and can now bring this to a close. Will you now please tell me what it is that you want from me?"

Attorney Dr. Lowenstein was not to be hurried. He gathered the papers that had been strewn right and left all over the table, arranged them carefully and put them back in his briefcase. Since no one spoke, he finally asked, "Do any of the gentlemen have anything else to say?"

The others declined.

Then he said: "Then I believe that we can bring this to a close. Since neither side has raised any objection to the factual basis of the case; we can consider them as completely proven. We have agreed ahead of time upon the division of the following roles. While I should lead the proceedings, and the individual gentlemen would act as witnesses as needed. Dr. Erhardt is to play the part of public prosecutor, to indict you as betrayer of society—of humanity. We have chosen him on purpose, because he is the only one of the seven of us that has no special reason to hate you, Ms. Marie. Dr. Erhardt has never had the honor of meeting you and has never been in any type of relationship with you—he is most certainly not biased. Please begin, Doctor!"

Dr. Erwin Erhardt began immediately:

"I received the afore mentioned letter from Colonel Thursby a year ago, the same hour, that the book dealer sent your newest portfolio; in fact, I had been asked to have a look at your drawings. Colonel Thursby is an old friend of mine from my student days—I was aware that this man would have never written such a letter if he knew of any other way to avoid it. He related everything that you have heard out of my own mouth this evening—and added a description of his state of mind, which made a heart wrenching impression. From him came the stimulus, that something must be done, to stop and control the person through whom so much misery came into this world. In that moment I felt sympathy for the Colonel—and became even more resolved in these feelings after a look at your drawings, Ms. Stuyvesant. I immediately called up attorney Lowenstein, who came immediately, and we consulted through the night. The following day we set to work—the result you already know. I am, Ms. Stuyvesant, a sincere admirer of your incredible art. I know that its suggestiveness is perhaps unique—and bow to this suggestiveness as well as to the artwork itself. But even this restless admiration cannot cloud my clear gaze, in which I—and which has grown sharper and more discerning during this past year—have been able to recognize, that your influence, Ms. Stuyvesant, is one of the most unholy that the world has ever known. Through your books and your drawings, you have turned masses of simple, decent individuals into just as many that are no longer fit for society—and in many cases your creations have caused even much, much more damage. But even if you had never written or drawn anything—the infectious, suggestive influence of your personality is strong enough, almost always, to poison everyone it encounters with its sweet poison. This poison, Ms. Stuyvesant, you carry inside of you, and when it is expressed, it doesn't harm you at all. Of Jorge Quintero, the typhoid carrier from Andalusia, it was reported to us that he was very good-natured, friendly, hard-working, and well-liked by everyone. Multiply that many hundred-fold and you will get an idea of your own image. Your great magnanimity is recognized everywhere—and it would be very hard to find anyone as hard working as you, Ms. Marie Stuyvesant. You have, as do so many important people, an instinctive avoidance of praise of any kind—and therefore I will not continue this any further. But I would like to note that this avoidance is grounded upon nothing other than, a very refined sense of shame, which in you, Ms. Stuyvesant, is much more strongly developed than in so many other people.

"Jorge Quintero certainly had only the best intentions for his fellowman—and against his will brought them torment, disease, and death. And that is exactly what you do, Ms. Stuyvesant! You, like him, turn the Mephistophelian principle into its opposite—you are of the power that always wants to do good and always does evil! Always—always and forever on your life's path; it is your unavoidable destiny!

"Now, Ms. Stuyvesant, let me tell you the end of the unfinished story of your companion in fate, Jorge. The old priest, Don José Hoyos, searched him out, lived together with him for a week, fearlessly risking his own life, in order to save those of so many others. During this time, he had long conversations about what he, Quintero represented to the rest of humanity. Up to that time the simple man had no conception of what it meant. At first, he, a completely healthy person, could not understand how he could infect other people—and had treated this suspicion as a vile slander rejecting it completely. After the doctors had explained things to him this gradually turned into feeling sorry for himself—a feeling that was very much in character for Andalusians—but also a feeling of importance because he was of such interest to all the doctors, the newspapers, and the entire public. Father Hoyos didn't take any of this away from him, but he gradually convinced him that he was a danger to society, making him understand that his own life meant the certain death of others—of whom many others were certainly much more important than he himself was. He told him that there was no authority and no power in the world that could do anything against him, that there was no law that had been broken. Others, who murdered people, could be arrested, and punished—but not him, because he had not intended to murder anyone, indeed, he had not known that being close to others brought death. But now he knew—and even though no policeman could arrest him, he would be no better than a murderer if he kept on killing people. No judge would stop him, so he must be his own judge.

"Slowly Jorge Quintero began to understand the old priest. But he was a devout Christian and knew very well what the priest was asking— suicide. But it was a terrible sin to take one's own life—

"Don José showed him the way. Had he ever heard of St. Apollonia?

"Yes, Jorge knew of her. She was the one with the plier that pulled the huge tooth, the one that you prayed to when you had a toothache. The priest told him the story of this saint. She was condemned to be burned to death. As soon as the pyre was lit, the devout woman was seized with such a longing for a martyr's death, that she couldn't wait for the executioner to seize her. She herself jumped into the blaze.

"That was suicide—yet the Catholic Church didn't consider it as such.

"And what of the devout woman's soul?

"And the devout nuns of Seeben. In the Benedictine cloister in Brixen they trembled in fear when the French invaded the land. Andreas Hofer, Speckbacher, Father Haspinger and their people had to withdraw deep into the mountains. The Jacobite troops were already in the valley, and the nuns knew what awaited them. Rape, robbing them of their innocence. So, they jumped out of the windows into the deep gorge, dashing their poor bodies on the boulders. And even though the loss of bodily innocence in this case would not have stained the moral purity of their souls, and even though the nuns must have known this—the Church proclaimed them free from guilt.

"But he, Jorge Quintero, certainly had even greater reasons than these women. If he gave up his own life—oh, it would be a free willing martyr's death given for the lives of his countrymen.

"Then—in the last moment he would feel the remorse, which the Church demanded. And if he couldn't feel this remorse for himself, then God in his mercy would grant him forgiveness.

"This, he a priest of God, would guarantee—and he was so convinced of this, that he promised him a Christian burial in consecrated ground.

"And Don José said:

"'If it is God's will—I will not get infected. If he wills differently—then let me be the last sacrifice, dear brother.'"

"The two of them spent three days in confession and passionate prayer. Then Jorge Quintero stabbed himself with his folding knife.

"The Jesuit Father kept his word. Despite all the protests of the clergy within the city he ensured that his friend was buried in the cemetery—he himself accompanied him to his final resting place.

"Two days later he came down with typhus; in three days he was dead.

"He was the unlucky last sacrifice.

"Ms. Marie Stuyvesant, we have decided to imitate the method of the old priest. Like he did with Quintero, we have attempted to convince you, what a terrible influence your life and works mean for humanity. We are not allowed to offer you the consolation that the priest could give for his confessional—because it is grounded in a faith that you don't share. As Jorge Quintero himself said, a higher Judge stands over him, and because of the mercy of this Judge the old priest could absolve him of his sin. Over you, Ms. Stuyvesant, stands no one. You are the last and final judge.

"We have nothing more to add—our work is complete. We turn it over to the many-sided criminal, the poisoner and murderess, Marie Stuyvesant. And to your own Judge: Marie Stuyvesant. In the interests of humanity, we pray for a just judgement."

Erwin Erhardt remained standing upright for a while and then sat back down.

No one spoke, not a sound in the entire hall. You could hear the harsh cries of a seagull coming from the sea.

Minutes passed by. Once the lady gave a laugh—then it was quiet again.

Finally, she spoke.

"I don't understand much of legal process, but I do know that after the prosecutor the defense is allowed to speak. You, gentlemen, have given out roles—but it appears that you have neglected this one. You don't want me to speak in my own defense—otherwise you would not have immediately wanted me to pass judgement. In accordance with your wishes, gentlemen, I renounce all defense. It is most certainly extremely rare to let the accused sit in judgement of themselves. I think that he would have every right to refuse to sit as Judge. That would certainly be the most comfortable thing for me to do. You see, gentlemen, the analogy between my case and that of your Andalusian disease carrier has a large hole in it—I am amazed that you didn't see it yourselves. Because in reality, the poor devil was not at all—his own judge. The priest judged and condemned him when he convinced him that divine justice required him to give up his life, and that his death alone would free humanity from the danger of becoming infected by him. Jorge Quintero's role was only that of the announcer—the executioner. He carried out the sentence that had been pronounced upon him. You are requesting the same from me. You, gentlemen, have long since passed judgement, and only desire that I, myself, carry it out. But you are not as honorable as the Jesuit father— Despite the intensive work of an entire year, you are far from convincing me, like the priest convinced his confessional. Don Jose assumed responsibility before the entire world and before the Divine Judgement, on which he deeply believed, for what he did—and he paid for it with his own life. You, gentlemen, have not taken on any responsibility at all—and are not in the slightest danger, because you are all—forgiven! Apart from Doctor Erhardt—you have long, long ago been infected by me, if indeed such an infection is possible. Now you wash your hands in innocence— and leave the judgement to me—and after that to carry it out.

"Very well, gentlemen, I will not refuse to sit as judge. And this is my judgement: I declare myself free!

"You have, gentlemen, presented the case of Jorge Quintero based on a Christian world view. But God created this man—created him just as he was. With a severe defect on one side—the disease of typhus of which he was a carrier. But on the other side, with an even greater portion: he carried a strong antibody, that made him immune to the poison of typhus. What he did, he had to do. So, he carried his guilt to the Divine Judge- ment. But a human pronounced that judgement over him—and because he was himself a human, he believed in this judgement and in his guilt. Now the case of such an innocent enemy of mankind like this happens very rarely—but is in no way that rare among other creatures. Isn't every viper a danger to humans? Isn't the rat a carrier of Cholera? The mosquito of malaria? But who would try to get these mosquitos, rats, and vipers to kill themselves? Society maintains that it has this right—I personally am of the opinion that it does not! But that is beside the point— The basic right of society is to protect itself and to destroy what- ever is a danger to it. That is why we exterminate rats, snakes, murderers and so many others. When society in certain cases doesn't dare eradicate that which poisons—like Quintero—that is certainly only the fault of society—which doesn't consider it that serious! If I choose to consider the poisonous cobra as sacred, then I must accept the consequences, as those in India do. It is still unharmed no matter how many people it poisons to death. Jorge Quintero was a disease carrier—well then, it was up to society to stop him, to destroy him! If they cannot, if they won't—how can they then demand, that the poor poisonous viper act like a human and do what society itself doesn't have the courage to do?

"You say, gentlemen, that I am a much worse plague on humanity than that of the Andalusian peasant. Through my drawings and my books, still even more through my personality I have—you say—infected humanity with all kinds of poisons. I am immune myself—yet every hour, on all sides I exhale a deadly pestilence. But whom, gentlemen, could Quintero infect with typhus? Not the few that were as immune as he was. The disease carriers—really, he would hardly encounter them. And not the others, the ones that were naturally immune, and finally not the people that had been inoculated against typhus. I think it is exactly the same with me. No one can be infected by me who is immune, by nature or because of strong antibodies—whatever kind of antibodies that might be. Because my poison is a poison of the soul, and I can think of many divine antidotes—whether it be religion, philosophy, or some other strong faith. To all these people I present no danger at all. The bacillus can only harm those whose bodies are receptive to it. It is not the disease alone; it must find a suitable host. And so it is, I think, also with me. The spark, that might radiate from me, can only burst into flame, when it encounters suitable tinder.

"I am convinced, gentlemen, that no powerful sorcerer can somehow draw out of a person, that which is not in him to begin with. This applies to the good as well as to the bad. No one will become a poet, that is not born to be a poet—and no one will become a murderer, who has not had the possibility of becoming a murderer slumbering within him from birth! But perhaps, perhaps, some unknown magic word will throw that tightly locked door of the soul wide open!

"And that is all that I do, gentlemen! Only that! You say—I infect many souls? I believe that is not true at all. I believe furthermore that I only encourage the external development of something that is already growing in the soul, the seed of which was there from the beginning. You think that doesn't make any difference? I believe it does!

"You call me, Doctor Erhardt, a part of the power, that always wants to do good and always does evil! As flattering as that sounds; I must disagree. I have never wanted to do neither good nor bad. Really, I have done some good—and as you know, a lot of evil—but a result for one side or the other has never been my intention. If I have any intention at all, I can express it—to paraphrase Goethe—I believe that everything that exists—before it dies—has the right to live in its own way. In doing that it can die as it pleases.

"Gentlemen, we stand in two camps, between which there can be no agreement. You represent the great humanitarian belief, that the welfare of collective society is the only criterion against which all things should be measured. Contrary to that, I am completely indifferent to the welfare and misery of humanity. I know a millionaire in New York, who for over twenty years, has established many little milk stations across the city; and daily at his own expense thousands of poor children are nourished with the milk. There is no question at all, that this beautiful gesture has made many children healthy, perhaps even saved the lives of many of them. This man is considered a great benefactor of humanity—but in my own eyes he has only done, in his own way, something which makes him happy, found a way to spend his money. If only out of the hundred thousands of children, who drank his milk over the years, a single Rembrandt would appear, then I could be grateful to him—unfortunately I have not heard of any. A Dante or a Beethoven, a Napoleon or a Goethe should have all the privileges of a divine being—but the man of the masses of humanity has only one privilege, which is to die. And it is no concern of mine at which speed it happens.

"I have, as you say, gentlemen, breathed many poisons into many souls, or, as I prefer to say, provided many starving poisonous plants with the fertilizer they needed to blossom and flourish. So, Baron Ayx became a gambler, Isabel dell'Greco became a prostitute. Count Thun became an Opium addict, Financier Ulbing a swindler and attorney Lowenstein an alcoholic. But you forget: none of you became something that you were not before. And if your beautiful wife, Mr. dell'Greco, had remained true to you—she still would have the soul of a prostitute. She proved that when she left you and ran to another. And you, Friedel, would have remained an alcoholic if you had taken twenty cures, lived in the most abstaining country in the world and never touched another drop of wine!

"You, gentlemen, you sit above me to judge me—for yourself and at the same time representing many others, who are exactly like you! Every one of you has a vice—and every one of you knows that I am free of it! I have tasted every single one of all the temptations, tried every sin that I knew of; have experienced the sensation that every temptation brings, thoroughly experienced it. But only for one purpose; to become acquainted with it. You, gentlemen, you, and those like you; you are the slaves of some little temptation. But I, I am Mistress over all of them. And because I am free, because I stand above them—that is why you persecute me!

"Your desire—deeply convinced of your own insignificance—my own annihilation! Then you closet yourselves together and believe in your pathetic collective belief, that a nothing and still another nothing and many thousand nothings are in the end a mighty force!

"You confuse yourself, gentlemen! You don't even have enough power to destroy the hated creature that now stands before you! You place the verdict in my own hands; well then, I proclaim myself free."

Marie Stuyvesant didn't raise her voice. She spoke very calmly, very quietly and with conviction. She didn't wait for a reaction from the seven gentlemen; she said:

"I thank you gentlemen, now you can go."

No one answered, they sat and didn't move.

Then Count Thun stood up, took the key from the table, walked with uncertain steps to the door. Sir dell'Greco close behind him—they went out, leaving the door wide open. Financier Ulbing stood up, then the young painter and attorney Lowenstein. Slowly they came out from behind the table.

Colonel Thursby came back—remained standing in front of the lady. His black eyes flickered and then sank, his lips twitched. Despite that—he couldn't find the words. He bit his lips—then went out like the others.

She watched him go, smiled. Put her cigarette down, then stood up. Sighed softly. Then she went to the window, drew the curtains back, looked out at the bay, over which the moon lay.

There was still one person in the hall. He came back, stepped up to her. Spoke:

"I am Erwin Erhardt. Engineer, manufacturer, inventor. Rich enough —if you reckon in dollars."

She turned around:

"You? —Didn't you say that I have never done anything to you? —What do you want?"

He said quietly:

"Will you marry me?"

"Must it be like that, doctor? —The air is sticky in here—don't you agree? Come along, we will do a little sailing in the moonlight."

The Most Dangerous Game

by Richard Connell

"OFF THERE to the right—somewhere—is a large island," said Whitney. "It's rather a mystery—"

"What island is it?" Rainsford asked.

"The old charts call it 'Ship-Trap Island,'" Whitney replied. "A suggestive name, isn't it? Sailors have a curious dread of the place. I don't know why. Some superstition—"

"Can't see it," remarked Rainsford, trying to peer through the dank tropical night that was palpable as it pressed its thick warm blackness in upon the yacht.

"You've good eyes," said Whitney, with a laugh, "and I've seen you pick off a moose moving in the brown fall bush at four hundred yards, but even you can't see four miles or so through a moonless Caribbean night."

"Nor four yards," admitted Rainsford. "Ugh! It's like moist black velvet."

"It will be light enough in Rio," promised Whitney. "We should make it in a few days. I hope the jaguar guns have come from Purdey's. We should have some good hunting up the Amazon. Great sport, hunting."

"The best sport in the world," agreed Rainsford.

"For the hunter," amended Whitney. "Not for the jaguar."

"Don't talk rot, Whitney," said Rainsford. "You're a big-game hunter, not a philosopher. Who cares how a jaguar feels?"

"Perhaps the jaguar does," observed Whitney.

"Bah! They've no understanding."

"Even so, I rather think they understand one thing—fear. The fear of pain and the fear of death."

"Nonsense," laughed Rainsford. "This hot weather is making you soft, Whitney. Be a realist. The world is made up of two classes—the hunters and the hunted. Luckily, you and I are hunters. Do you think we've passed that island yet?"

"I can't tell in the dark. I hope so."

"Why?" asked Rainsford.

"The place has a reputation—a bad one."

"Cannibals?" suggested Rainsford.

"Hardly. Even cannibals wouldn't live in such a God-forsaken place. But it's gotten into sailor lore, somehow. Didn't you notice that the crew's nerves seemed a bit jumpy today?"

"They were a bit strange, now you mention it. Even Captain Nielsen—"

"Yes, even that tough-minded old Swede, who'd go up to the devil himself and ask him for a light. Those fishy blue eyes held a look I never saw there before. All I could get out of him was 'This place has an evil name among seafaring men, sir.' Then he said to me, very gravely, 'Don't you feel anything?'—as if the air about us was actually poisonous. Now, you mustn't laugh when I tell you this—I did feel something like a sudden chill.

"There was no breeze. The sea was as flat as a plate-glass window. We were drawing near the island then. What I felt was a—a mental chill; a sort of sudden dread."

"Pure imagination," said Rainsford.

"One superstitious sailor can taint the whole ship's company with his fear."

"Maybe. But sometimes I think sailors have an extra sense that tells them when they are in danger. Sometimes I think evil is a tangible thing—with wave lengths, just as sound and light have. An evil place can, so to speak, broadcast vibrations of evil. Anyhow, I'm glad we're getting out of this zone. Well, I think I'll turn in now, Rainsford."

"I'm not sleepy," said Rainsford. "I'm going to smoke another pipe up on the afterdeck."

"Good night, then, Rainsford. See you at breakfast."

"Right. Good night, Whitney."

There was no sound in the night as Rainsford sat there but the muffled throb of the engine that drove the yacht swiftly through the darkness, and the swish and ripple of the wash of the propeller.

Rainsford, reclining in a steamer chair, indolently puffed on his favorite brier. The sensuous drowsiness of the night was on him. *It's so dark,* he thought, *that I could sleep without closing my eyes; the night would be my eyelids—*

An abrupt sound startled him. Off to the right he heard it, and his ears, expert in such matters, could not be mistaken. Again he heard the sound, and again. Somewhere, off in the blackness, someone had fired a gun three times.

Rainsford sprang up and moved quickly to the rail, mystified. He strained his eyes in the direction from which the reports had come, but it was like trying to see through a blanket. He leaped upon the rail and balanced himself there, to get greater elevation; his pipe, striking a rope, was knocked from his mouth. He lunged for it; a short, hoarse cry came from his lips as he realized he had reached too far and had lost his balance. The cry was pinched off short as the blood-warm waters of the Caribbean Sea closed over his head.

He struggled up to the surface and tried to cry out, but the wash from the speeding yacht slapped him in the face and the salt water in his open mouth made him gag and strangle. Desperately he struck out with strong strokes after the receding lights of the yacht, but he stopped before he had swum fifty feet. A certain cool-headedness had come to him; it was not the first time he had been in a tight place. There was a chance that his cries could be heard by someone aboard the yacht, but that chance was slender and grew more slender as the yacht raced on. He wrestled himself out of his clothes and shouted with all his power. The lights of the yacht became faint and ever-vanishing fireflies; then they were blotted out entirely by the night.

Rainsford remembered the shots. They had come from the right, and doggedly he swam in that direction, swimming with slow, deliberate strokes, conserving his strength. For a seemingly endless time he fought the sea. He began to count his strokes; he could do possibly a hundred more and then—Rainsford heard a sound. It came out of the darkness, a high screaming sound, the sound of an animal in an extremity of anguish and terror. He did not recognize the animal that made the sound; he did not try to; with fresh vitality he swam toward the sound. He heard it again; then it was cut short by another noise, crisp, staccato. "Pistol shot," muttered Rainsford, swimming on.

Ten minutes of determined effort brought another sound to his ears—the most welcome he had ever heard—the muttering and growling of the sea breaking on a rocky shore. He was almost on the rocks before he saw them; on a night less calm he would have been shattered against them. With his remaining strength he dragged himself from the swirling waters. Jagged crags appeared to jut up into the opaqueness; he forced himself upward, hand over hand. Gasping, his hands raw, he reached a flat place at the top. Dense jungle came down to the very edge of the cliffs. What perils that tangle of trees and underbrush might hold for him did not concern Rainsford just then. All he knew was that he was safe from his enemy, the sea, and that utter weariness was on him. He flung himself down at the jungle edge and tumbled headlong into the deepest sleep of his life.

When he opened his eyes he knew from the position of the sun that it was late in the afternoon. Sleep had given him new vigor; a sharp hunger was picking at him. He looked about him, almost cheerfully.

"Where there are pistol shots, there are men. Where there are men, there is food," he thought. But what kind of men, he wondered, in so forbidding a place? An unbroken front of snarled and ragged jungle fringed the shore.

He saw no sign of a trail through the closely knit web of weeds and trees; it was easier to go along the shore, and Rainsford floundered along by the water. Not far from where he landed, he stopped.

Some wounded thing—by the evidence, a large animal—had thrashed about in the underbrush; the jungle weeds were crushed down and the moss was lacerated; one patch of weeds was stained crimson. A small, glittering object not far away caught Rainsford's eye and he picked it up. It was an empty cartridge.

"A twenty-two," he remarked. "That's odd. It must have been a fairly large animal too. The hunter had his nerve with him to tackle it with a light gun. It's clear that the brute put up a fight. I suppose the first three shots I heard was when the hunter flushed his quarry and wounded it. The last shot was when he trailed it here and finished it."

He examined the ground closely and found what he had hoped to find—the print of hunting boots. They pointed along the cliff in the direction he had been going. Eagerly he hurried along, now slipping on a rotten log or a loose stone, but making headway; night was beginning to settle down on the island.

Bleak darkness was blacking out the sea and jungle when Rainsford sighted the lights. He came upon them as he turned a crook in the coast line; and his first thought was that he had come upon a village, for there were many lights. But as he forged along he saw to his great astonishment that all the lights were in one enormous building—a lofty structure with pointed towers plunging upward into the gloom. His eyes made out the shadowy outlines of a palatial chateau; it was set on a high bluff, and on three sides of it cliffs dived down to where the sea licked greedy lips in the shadows.

"Mirage," thought Rainsford. But it was no mirage, he found, when he opened the tall-spiked iron gate. The stone steps were real enough; the massive door with a leering gargoyle for a knocker was real enough; yet above it all hung an air of unreality.

He lifted the knocker, and it creaked up stiffly, as if it had never before been used. He let it fall, and it startled him with its booming loudness. He thought he heard steps within; the door remained closed. Again Rainsford lifted the heavy knocker, and let it fall. The door opened then—opened as suddenly as if it were on a spring—and Rainsford stood blinking in the river of glaring gold light that poured out. The first thing Rainsford's eyes discerned was the largest man Rainsford had ever seen— a gigantic creature, solidly made and black bearded to the waist. In his hand the man held a long-barreled revolver, and he was pointing it straight at Rainsford's heart.

Out of the snarl of beard two small eyes regarded Rainsford.

"Don't be alarmed," said Rainsford, with a smile which he hoped was disarming. "I'm no robber. I fell off a yacht. My name is Sanger Rainsford of New York City."

The menacing look in the eyes did not change. The revolver pointing as rigidly as if the giant were a statue. He gave no sign that he understood Rainsford's words, or that he had even heard them. He was dressed in uniform—a black uniform trimmed with gray astrakhan.

"I'm Sanger Rainsford of New York," Rainsford began again. "I fell off a yacht. I am hungry."

The man's only answer was to raise with his thumb the hammer of his revolver. Then Rainsford saw the man's free hand go to his forehead in a military salute, and he saw him click his heels together and stand at attention. Another man was coming down the broad marble steps, an erect, slender man in evening clothes. He advanced to Rainsford and held out his hand.

In a cultivated voice marked by a slight accent that gave it added precision and deliberateness, he said, "It is a very great pleasure and honor to welcome Mr. Sanger Rainsford, the celebrated hunter, to my home."

Automatically Rainsford shook the man's hand.

"I've read your book about hunting snow leopards in Tibet, you see," explained the man. "I am General Zaroff."

Rainsford's first impression was that the man was singularly handsome; his second was that there was an original, almost bizarre quality about the general's face. He was a tall man past middle age, for his hair was a vivid white; but his thick eyebrows and pointed military mustache were as black as the night from which Rainsford had come. His eyes, too, were black and very bright. He had high cheekbones, a sharp-cut nose, a spare, dark face—the face of a man used to giving orders, the face of an aristocrat. Turning to the giant in uniform, the general made a sign. The giant put away his pistol, saluted, withdrew.

"Ivan is an incredibly strong fellow," remarked the general, "but he has the misfortune to be deaf and dumb. A simple fellow, but, I'm afraid, like all his race, a bit of a savage."

"Is he Russian?"

"He is a Cossack," said the general, and his smile showed red lips and pointed teeth. "So am I.

"Come," he said, "we shouldn't be chatting here. We can talk later. Now you want clothes, food, rest. You shall have them. This is a most restful spot."

Ivan had reappeared, and the general spoke to him with lips that moved but gave forth no sound.

"Follow Ivan, if you please, Mr. Rainsford," said the general. "I was about to have my dinner when you came. I'll wait for you. You'll find that my clothes will fit you, I think."

It was to a huge, beam-ceilinged bedroom with a canopied bed big enough for six men that Rainsford followed the silent giant. Ivan laid out an evening suit, and Rainsford, as he put it on, noticed that it came from a London tailor who ordinarily cut and sewed for none below the rank of duke.

The dining room to which Ivan conducted him was in many ways remarkable. There was a medieval magnificence about it; it suggested a baronial hall of feudal times with its oaken panels, its high ceiling, its vast refectory tables where twoscore men could sit down to eat. About the hall were mounted heads of many animals—lions, tigers, elephants, moose, bears; larger or more perfect specimens Rainsford had never seen. At the great table the general was sitting, alone.

"You'll have a cocktail, Mr. Rainsford," he suggested. The cocktail was surpassingly good; and, Rainsford noted, the table appointments were of the finest—the linen, the crystal, the silver, the china.

They were eating *borsch*, the rich, red soup with whipped cream so dear to Russian palates. Half apologetically General Zaroff said, "We do our best to preserve the amenities of civilization here. Please forgive any lapses. We are well off the beaten track, you know. Do you think the champagne has suffered from its long ocean trip?"

"Not in the least," declared Rainsford. He was finding the general a most thoughtful and affable host, a true cosmopolite. But there was one small trait of the general's that made Rainsford uncomfortable. Whenever he looked up from his plate he found the general studying him, appraising him narrowly.

"Perhaps," said General Zaroff, "you were surprised that I recognized your name. You see, I read all books on hunting published in English, French, and Russian. I have but one passion in my life, Mr. Rainsford, and it is the hunt."

"You have some wonderful heads here," said Rainsford as he ate a particularly well-cooked *filet mignon*. "That Cape buffalo is the largest I ever saw."

"Oh, that fellow. Yes, he was a monster."

"Did he charge you?"

"Hurled me against a tree," said the general. "Fractured my skull. But I got the brute."

"I've always thought," said Rainsford, "that the Cape buffalo is the most dangerous of all big game."

For a moment the general did not reply; he was smiling his curious, red-lipped smile. Then he said slowly, "No. You are wrong, sir. The Cape buffalo is not the most dangerous big game." He sipped his wine. "Here in my preserve on this island," he said in the same slow tone, "I hunt more dangerous game."

Rainsford expressed his surprise. "Is there big game on this island?"

The general nodded. "The biggest."

"Really?"

"Oh, it isn't here naturally, of course. I have to stock the island."

"What have you imported, general?" Rainsford asked. "Tigers?"

The general smiled. "No," he said. "Hunting tigers ceased to interest me some years ago. I exhausted their possibilities, you see. No thrill left in tigers, no real danger. I live for danger, Mr. Rainsford."

The general took from his pocket a gold cigarette case and offered his guest a long black cigarette with a silver tip; it was perfumed and gave off a smell like incense.

"We will have some capital hunting, you and I," said the general. "I shall be most glad to have your society."

"But what game—" began Rainsford.

"I'll tell you," said the general. "You will be amused, I know. I think I may say, in all modesty, that I have done a rare thing. I have invented a new sensation. May I pour you another glass of port?"

"Thank you, general."

The general filled both glasses, and said, "God makes some men poets. Some He makes kings, some beggars. Me He made a hunter. My hand was made for the trigger, my father said. He was a very rich man with a quarter of a million acres in the Crimea, and he was an ardent sportsman. When I was only five years old he gave me a little gun, specially made in Moscow for me, to shoot sparrows with. When I shot some of his prize turkeys with it, he did not punish me; he complimented me on my marksmanship. I killed my first bear in the Caucasus when I was ten. My whole life has been one prolonged hunt. I went into the army—it was expected of noblemen's sons—and for a time commanded a division of Cossack cavalry, but my real interest was always the hunt. I have hunted every kind of game in every land. It would be impossible for me to tell you how many animals I have killed."

The general puffed at his cigarette.

"After the debacle in Russia I left the country, for it was imprudent for an officer of the Czar to stay there. Many noble Russians lost everything. I, luckily, had invested heavily in American securities, so I shall never have to open a tearoom in Monte Carlo or drive a taxi in Paris. Naturally, I continued to hunt—grizzlies in your Rockies, crocodiles in the Ganges, rhinoceroses in East Africa. It was in Africa that the Cape buffalo hit me and laid me up for six months. As soon as I recovered I started for the Amazon to hunt jaguars, for I had heard they were unusually cunning. They weren't." The Cossack sighed. "They were no match at all for a hunter with his wits about him, and a high-powered rifle. I was bitterly disappointed. I was lying in my tent with a splitting headache one night when a terrible thought pushed its way into my mind. Hunting was beginning to bore me! And hunting, remember, had been my life. I have heard that in America businessmen often go to pieces when they give up the business that has been their life."

"Yes, that's so," said Rainsford.

The general smiled. "I had no wish to go to pieces," he said. "I must do something. Now, mine is an analytical mind, Mr. Rainsford. Doubtless that is why I enjoy the problems of the chase."

"No doubt, General Zaroff."

"So," continued the general, "I asked myself why the hunt no longer fascinated me. You are much younger than I am, Mr. Rainsford, and have not hunted as much, but you perhaps can guess the answer."

"What was it?"

"Simply this: hunting had ceased to be what you call a 'sporting proposition.' It had become too easy. I always got my quarry. Always. There is no greater bore than perfection."

The general lit a fresh cigarette.

"No animal had a chance with me anymore. That is no boast; it is a mathematical certainty. The animal had nothing but his legs and his instinct. Instinct is no match for reason. When I thought of this it was a tragic moment for me, I can tell you."

Rainsford leaned across the table, absorbed in what his host was saying.

"It came to me as an inspiration what I must do," the general went on.

"And that was?"

The general smiled the quiet smile of one who has faced an obstacle and surmounted it with success. "I had to invent a new animal to hunt," he said.

"A new animal? You're joking."

"Not at all," said the general. "I never joke about hunting. I needed a new animal. I found one. So I bought this island, built this house, and here I do my hunting. The island is perfect for my purposes—there are jungles with a maze of trails in them, hills, swamps—"

"But the animal, General Zaroff?"

"Oh," said the general, "it supplies me with the most exciting hunting in the world. No other hunting compares with it for an instant. Every day I hunt, and I never grow bored now, for I have a quarry with which I can match my wits."

Rainsford's bewilderment showed in his face.

"I wanted the ideal animal to hunt," explained the general. "So I said, 'What are the attributes of an ideal quarry?' And the answer was, of course, 'It must have courage, cunning, and above all, it must be able to reason.'"

"But no animal can reason," objected Rainsford.

"My dear fellow," said the general, "there is one that can."

"But you can't mean—" gasped Rainsford.

"And why not?"

"I can't believe you are serious, General Zaroff. This is a grisly joke."

"Why should I not be serious? I am speaking of hunting."

"Hunting? Great Guns, General Zaroff, what you speak of is murder."

The general laughed with entire good nature. He regarded Rainsford quizzically. "I refuse to believe that so modern and civilized a young man as you seem to be harbors romantic ideas about the value of human life. Surely your experiences in the war—"

"Did not make me condone cold-blooded murder," finished Rainsford stiffly.

Laughter shook the general. "How extraordinarily droll you are!" he said. "One does not expect nowadays to find a young man of the educated class, even in America, with such a naive, and, if I may say so, mid-Victorian point of view. It's like finding a snuffbox in a limousine. Ah, well, doubtless you had Puritan ancestors. So many Americans appear to have had. I'll wager you'll forget your notions when you go hunting with me. You've a genuine new thrill in store for you, Mr. Rainsford."

"Thank you, I'm a hunter, not a murderer."

"Dear me," said the general, quite unruffled, "again that unpleasant word. But I think I can show you that your scruples are quite ill-founded."

"Yes?"

"Life is for the strong, to be lived by the strong, and, if needs be, taken by the strong. The weak of the world were put here to give the strong pleasure. I am strong. Why should I not use my gift? If I wish to hunt, why should I not? I hunt the scum of the earth: sailors from tramp ships—lascars, blacks, Chinese, whites, mongrels—a thoroughbred horse or hound is worth more than a score of them."

"But they are men," said Rainsford hotly.

"Precisely," said the general. "That is why I use them. It gives me pleasure. They can reason, after a fashion. So they are dangerous."

"But where do you get them?"

The general's left eyelid fluttered down in a wink. "This island is called 'Ship Trap,'" he answered. "Sometimes an angry god of the high seas sends them to me. Sometimes, when Providence is not so kind, I help Providence a bit. Come to the window with me."

Rainsford went to the window and looked out toward the sea.

"Watch! Out there!" exclaimed the general, pointing into the night. Rainsford's eyes saw only blackness, and then, as the general pressed a button, far out to sea Rainsford saw the flash of lights.

The general chuckled. "They indicate a channel," he said, "where there's none; giant rocks with razor edges crouch like a sea monster with wide-open jaws. They can crush a ship as easily as I crush this nut." He dropped a walnut on the hardwood floor and brought his heel grinding down on it. "Oh, yes," he said, casually, as if in answer to a question, "I have electricity. We try to be civilized here."

"Civilized? And you shoot down men?"

A trace of anger was in the general's black eyes, but it was there for but a second; and he said, in his most pleasant manner, "Dear me, what a righteous young man you are! I assure you I do not do the thing you suggest. That would be barbarous. I treat these visitors with every consideration. They get plenty of good food and exercise. They get into splendid physical condition. You shall see for yourself tomorrow."

"What do you mean?"

"We'll visit my training school," smiled the general. "It's in the cellar. I have about a dozen pupils down there now. They're from the Spanish bark *San Lucar* that had the bad luck to go on the rocks out there. A very inferior lot, I regret to say. Poor specimens and more accustomed to the deck than to the jungle." He raised his hand, and Ivan, who served as waiter, brought thick Turkish coffee. Rainsford, with an effort, held his tongue in check.

"It's a game, you see," pursued the general blandly. "I suggest to one of them that we go hunting. I give him a supply of food and an excellent hunting knife. I give him three hours' start. I am to follow, armed only with a pistol of the smallest caliber and range. If my quarry eludes me for three whole days, he wins the game. If I find him" —the general smiled— "he loses."

"Suppose he refuses to be hunted?"

"Oh," said the general, "I give him his option, of course. He need not play that game if he doesn't wish to. If he does not wish to hunt, I turn him over to Ivan. Ivan once had the honor of serving as official knouter to the Great White Czar, and he has his own ideas of sport. Invariably, Mr. Rainsford, invariably they choose the hunt."

"And if they win?"

The smile on the general's face widened. "To date I have not lost," he said. Then he added, hastily: "I don't wish you to think me a braggart, Mr. Rainsford. Many of them afford only the most elementary sort of problem. Occasionally I strike a tartar. One almost did win. I eventually had to use the dogs."

"The dogs?"

"This way, please. I'll show you."

The general steered Rainsford to a window. The lights from the windows sent a flickering illumination that made grotesque patterns on the courtyard below, and Rainsford could see moving about there a dozen or so huge black shapes; as they turned toward him, their eyes glittered greenly.

"A rather good lot, I think," observed the general. "They are let out at seven every night. If anyone should try to get into my house—or out of it—something extremely regrettable would occur to him." He hummed a snatch of song from the *Folies Bergère*.

"And now," said the general, "I want to show you my new collection of heads. Will you come with me to the library?"

"I hope," said Rainsford, "that you will excuse me tonight, General Zaroff. I'm really not feeling well."

"Ah, indeed?" the general inquired solicitously. "Well, I suppose that's only natural, after your long swim. You need a good, restful night's sleep. Tomorrow you'll feel like a new man, I'll wager. Then we'll hunt, eh? I've one rather promising prospect—"

Rainsford was hurrying from the room.

"Sorry you can't go with me tonight," called the general. "I expect rather fair sport—a big, strong, black. He looks resourceful—Well, good night, Mr. Rainsford; I hope you have a good night's rest."

The bed was good, and the pajamas of the softest silk, and he was tired in every fiber of his being, but nevertheless Rainsford could not quiet his brain with the opiate of sleep. He lay, eyes wide open. Once he thought he heard stealthy steps in the corridor outside his room. He sought to throw open the door; it would not open. He went to the window and looked out. His room was high up in one of the towers. The lights of the chateau were out now, and it was dark and silent; but there was a fragment of sallow moon, and by its wan light he could see, dimly, the courtyard. There, weaving in and out in the pattern of shadow, were black, noiseless forms; the hounds heard him at the window and looked up, expectantly, with their green eyes. Rainsford went back to the bed and lay down. By many methods he tried to put himself to sleep. He had achieved a doze when, just as morning began to come, he heard, far off in the jungle, the faint report of a pistol.

General Zaroff did not appear until luncheon. He was dressed faultlessly in the tweeds of a country squire. He was solicitous about the state of Rainsford's health.

"As for me," sighed the general, "I do not feel so well. I am worried, Mr. Rainsford. Last night I detected traces of my old complaint."

To Rainsford's questioning glance the general said, "Ennui. Boredom."

Then, taking a second helping of *crêpes Suzette*, the general explained: "The hunting was not good last night. The fellow lost his head. He made a straight trail that offered no problems at all. That's the trouble with these sailors; they have dull brains to begin with, and they do not know how to get about in the woods. They do excessively stupid and obvious things. It's most annoying. Will you have another glass of Chablis, Mr. Rainsford?"

"General," said Rainsford firmly, "I wish to leave this island at once."

The general raised his thickets of eyebrows; he seemed hurt. "But, my dear fellow," the general protested, "you've only just come. You've had no hunting—"

"I wish to go today," said Rainsford. He saw the dead black eyes of the general on him, studying him. General Zaroff's face suddenly brightened.

He filled Rainsford's glass with venerable Chablis from a dusty bottle.

"Tonight," said the general, "we will hunt—you and I."

Rainsford shook his head. "No, general," he said. "I will not hunt."

The general shrugged his shoulders and delicately ate a hothouse grape. "As you wish, my friend," he said. "The choice rests entirely with you. But may I not venture to suggest that you will find my idea of sport more diverting than Ivan's?"

He nodded toward the corner to where the giant stood, scowling, his thick arms crossed on his hogshead of chest.

"You don't mean—" cried Rainsford.

"My dear fellow," said the general, "have I not told you I always mean what I say about hunting? This is really an inspiration. I drink to a foeman worthy of my steel—at last." The general raised his glass, but Rainsford sat staring at him.

"You'll find this game worth playing," the general said enthusiastically. "Your brain against mine. Your woodcraft against mine. Your strength and stamina against mine. Outdoor chess! And the stake is not without value, eh?"

"And if I win—" began Rainsford huskily.

"I'll cheerfully acknowledge myself defeat if I do not find you by midnight of the third day," said General Zaroff. "My sloop will place you on the mainland near a town."

The general read what Rainsford was thinking.

"Oh, you can trust me," said the Cossack. "I will give you my word as a gentleman and a sportsman. Of course you, in turn, must agree to say nothing of your visit here."

"I'll agree to nothing of the kind," said Rainsford.

"Oh," said the general, "in that case—But why discuss that now? Three days hence we can discuss it over a bottle of *Veuve Clicquot*, unless—"

The general sipped his wine.

Then a businesslike air animated him. "Ivan," he said to Rainsford, "will supply you with hunting clothes, food, a knife. I suggest you wear moccasins; they leave a poorer trail. I suggest, too, that you avoid the big swamp in the southeast corner of the island. We call it Death Swamp. There's quicksand there. One foolish fellow tried it. The deplorable part of it was that Lazarus followed him. You can imagine my feelings, Mr. Rainsford. I loved Lazarus; he was the finest hound in my pack. Well, I must beg you to excuse me now. I always take a siesta after lunch. You'll hardly have time for a nap, I fear. You'll want to start, no doubt. I shall not follow till dusk. Hunting at night is so much more exciting than by day, don't you think? Au revoir, Mr. Rainsford, au revoir." General Zaroff, with a deep, courtly bow, strolled from the room.

From another door came Ivan. Under one arm he carried khaki hunting clothes, a haversack of food, a leather sheath containing a long-bladed hunting knife; his right hand rested on a cocked revolver thrust in the crimson sash about his waist.

~§~

Rainsford had fought his way through the bush for two hours. "I must keep my nerve. I must keep my nerve," he said through tight teeth.

He had not been entirely clearheaded when the chateau gates snapped shut behind him. His whole idea at first was to put distance between himself and General Zaroff; and to this end, he had plunged along, spurred on by the sharp rowers of something very like panic. Now he had got a grip on himself, had stopped, and was taking stock of himself and the situation. He saw that straight flight was futile; inevitably it would bring him face to face with the sea. He was in a picture with a frame of water, and his operations, clearly, must take place within that frame.

"I'll give him a trail to follow," muttered Rainsford, and he struck off from the rude path he had been following into the trackless wilderness. He executed a series of intricate loops; he doubled on his trail again and again, recalling all the lore of the fox hunt, and all the dodges of the fox. Night found him leg-weary, with hands and face lashed by the branches, on a thickly wooded ridge. He knew it would be insane to blunder on through the dark, even if he had the strength. His need for rest was imperative and he thought, "I have played the fox, now I must play the cat of the fable." A big tree with a thick trunk and outspread branches was nearby, and taking care to leave not the slightest mark, he climbed up into the crotch, and stretching out on one of the broad limbs, after a fashion, rested. Rest brought him new confidence and almost a feeling of security. Even so zealous a hunter as General Zaroff could not trace him there, he told himself; only the devil himself could follow that complicated trail through the jungle after dark. But perhaps the general was a devil—

An apprehensive night crawled slowly by like a wounded snake and sleep did not visit Rainsford, although the silence of a dead world was on the jungle. Toward morning when a dingy gray was varnishing the sky, the cry of some startled bird focused Rainsford's attention in that direction. Something was coming through the bush, coming slowly, carefully, coming by the same winding way Rainsford had come. He flattened himself down on the limb, and through a screen of leaves almost as thick as tapestry, he watched. . . . That which was approaching was a man.

It was General Zaroff. He made his way along with his eyes fixed in utmost concentration on the ground before him. He paused, almost beneath the tree, dropped to his knees and studied the ground. Rainsford's impulse was to hurl himself down like a panther, but he saw that the general's right hand held something metallic—a small automatic pistol.

The hunter shook his head several times, as if he were puzzled. Then he straightened up and took from his case one of his black cigarettes; its pungent incenselike smoke floated up to Rainsford's nostrils.

Rainsford held his breath. The general's eyes had left the ground and were traveling inch by inch up the tree. Rainsford froze there, every muscle tensed for a spring. But the sharp eyes of the hunter stopped before they reached the limb where Rainsford lay; a smile spread over his brown face. Very deliberately he blew a smoke ring into the air; then he turned his back on the tree and walked carelessly away, back along the trail he had come. The swish of the underbrush against his hunting boots grew fainter and fainter.

The pent-up air burst hotly from Rainsford's lungs. His first thought made him feel sick and numb. The general could follow a trail through the woods at night; he could follow an extremely difficult trail; he must have uncanny powers; only by the merest chance had the Cossack failed to see his quarry.

Rainsford's second thought was even more terrible. It sent a shudder of cold horror through his whole being. Why had the general smiled? Why had he turned back?

Rainsford did not want to believe what his reason told him was true, but the truth was as evident as the sun that had by now pushed through the morning mists. The general was playing with him! The general was saving him for another day's sport! The Cossack was the cat; he was the mouse. Then it was that Rainsford knew the full meaning of terror.

"I will not lose my nerve. I will not."

He slid down from the tree, and struck off again into the woods. His face was set and he forced the machinery of his mind to function. Three hundred yards from his hiding place he stopped where a huge dead tree leaned precariously on a smaller, living one. Throwing off his sack of food, Rainsford took his knife from its sheath and began to work with all his energy.

The job was finished at last, and he threw himself down behind a fallen log a hundred feet away. He did not have to wait long. The cat was coming again to play with the mouse.

Following the trail with the sureness of a bloodhound came General Zaroff. Nothing escaped those searching black eyes, no crushed blade of grass, no bent twig, no mark, no matter how faint, in the moss. So intent was the Cossack on his stalking that he was upon the thing Rainsford had made before he saw it. His foot touched the protruding bough that was the trigger. Even as he touched it, the general sensed his danger and leaped back with the agility of an ape. But he was not quite quick enough; the dead tree, delicately adjusted to rest on the cut living one, crashed down and struck the general a glancing blow on the shoulder as it fell; but for his alertness, he must have been smashed beneath it. He staggered, but he did not fall; nor did he drop his revolver. He stood there, rubbing his injured shoulder, and Rainsford, with fear again gripping his heart, heard the general's mocking laugh ring through the jungle.

"Rainsford," called the general, "if you are within sound of my voice, as I suppose you are, let me congratulate you. Not many men know how to make a Malay man-catcher. Luckily for me I, too, have hunted in Malacca. You are proving interesting, Mr. Rainsford. I am going now to have my wound dressed; it's only a slight one. But I shall be back. I shall be back."

When the general, nursing his bruised shoulder, had gone, Rainsford took up his flight again. It was flight now, a desperate, hopeless flight, that carried him on for some hours. Dusk came, then darkness, and still he pressed on. The ground grew softer under his moccasins; the vegetation grew ranker, denser; insects bit him savagely.

Then, as he stepped forward, his foot sank into the ooze. He tried to wrench it back, but the muck sucked viciously at his foot as if it were a giant leech. With a violent effort, he tore his feet loose. He knew where he was now. Death Swamp and its quicksand.

His hands were tight closed as if his nerve were something tangible that someone in the darkness was trying to tear from his grip. The softness of the earth had given him an idea. He stepped back from the quicksand a dozen feet or so and, like some huge prehistoric beaver, he began to dig.

Rainsford had dug himself in in France when a second's delay meant death. That had been a placid pastime compared to his digging now. The pit grew deeper; when it was above his shoulders, he climbed out and from some hard saplings cut stakes and sharpened them to a fine point. These stakes he planted in the bottom of the pit with the points sticking up. With flying fingers he wove a rough carpet of weeds and branches and with it he covered the mouth of the pit. Then, wet with sweat and aching with tiredness, he crouched behind the stump of a lightning-charred tree.

He knew his pursuer was coming; he heard the padding sound of feet on the soft earth, and the night breeze brought him the perfume of the general's cigarette. It seemed to Rainsford that the general was coming with unusual swiftness; he was not feeling his way along, foot by foot. Rainsford, crouching there, could not see the general, nor could he see the pit. He lived a year in a minute. Then he felt an impulse to cry aloud with joy, for he heard the sharp crackle of the breaking branches as the cover of the pit gave way; he heard the sharp scream of pain as the pointed stakes found their mark. He leaped up from his place of concealment. Then he cowered back. Three feet from the pit a man was standing, with an electric torch in his hand.

"You've done well, Rainsford," the voice of the general called. "Your Burmese tiger pit has claimed one of my best dogs. Again you score. I think, Mr. Rainsford, I'll see what you can do against my whole pack. I'm going home for a rest now. Thank you for a most amusing evening."

At daybreak Rainsford, lying near the swamp, was awakened by a sound that made him know that he had new things to learn about fear. It was a distant sound, faint and wavering, but he knew it. It was the baying of a pack of hounds.

Rainsford knew he could do one of two things. He could stay where he was and wait. That was suicide. He could flee. That was postponing the inevitable. For a moment he stood there, thinking. An idea that held a wild chance came to him, and, tightening his belt, he headed away from the swamp.

The baying of the hounds drew nearer, then still nearer, nearer, ever nearer. On a ridge Rainsford climbed a tree. Down a watercourse, not a quarter of a mile away, he could see the bush moving. Straining his eyes, he saw the lean figure of General Zaroff; just ahead of him Rainsford made out another figure whose wide shoulders surged through the tall jungle weeds; it was the giant Ivan, and he seemed pulled forward by some unseen force; Rainsford knew that Ivan must be holding the pack in leash.

They would be on him any minute now. His mind worked frantically. He thought of a native trick he had learned in Uganda. He slid down the tree. He caught hold of a springy young sapling and to it he fastened his hunting knife, with the blade pointing down the trail; with a bit of wild grapevine he tied back the sapling. Then he ran for his life. The hounds raised their voices as they hit the fresh scent. Rainsford knew now how an animal at bay feels.

He had to stop to get his breath. The baying of the hounds stopped abruptly, and Rainsford's heart stopped too. They must have reached the knife.

He shinned excitedly up a tree and looked back. His pursuers had stopped. But the hope that was in Rainsford's brain when he climbed died, for he saw in the shallow valley that General Zaroff was still on his feet. But Ivan was not. The knife, driven by the recoil of the springing tree, had not wholly failed.

Rainsford had hardly tumbled to the ground when the pack took up the cry again.

"Nerve, nerve, nerve!" he panted, as he dashed along. A blue gap showed between the trees dead ahead. Ever nearer drew the hounds. Rainsford forced himself on toward that gap. He reached it. It was the shore of the sea. Across a cove he could see the gloomy gray stone of the chateau. Twenty feet below him the sea rumbled and hissed. Rainsford hesitated. He heard the hounds. Then he leaped far out into the sea . . .

When the general and his pack reached the place by the sea, the Cossack stopped. For some minutes he stood regarding the blue-green expanse of water. He shrugged his shoulders. Then he sat down, took a drink of brandy from a silver flask, lit a cigarette, and hummed a bit from *Madame Butterfly*.

~§~

General Zaroff had an exceedingly good dinner in his great paneled dining hall that evening. With it he had a bottle of *Pol Roger* and half a bottle of *Chambertin*. Two slight annoyances kept him from perfect enjoyment. One was the thought that it would be difficult to replace Ivan; the other was that his quarry had escaped him; of course, the American hadn't played the game—so thought the general as he tasted his after-dinner liqueur. In his library he read, to soothe himself, from the works of Marcus Aurelius. At ten he went up to his bedroom. He was deliciously tired, he said to himself, as he locked himself in. There was a little moonlight, so, before turning on his light, he went to the window and looked down at the courtyard. He could see the great hounds, and he called, "Better luck another time," to them. Then he switched on the light.

A man, who had been hiding in the curtains of the bed, was standing there.

"Rainsford!" screamed the general. "How in God's name did you get here?"

"Swam," said Rainsford. "I found it quicker than walking through the jungle."

The general sucked in his breath and smiled. "I congratulate you," he said. "You have won the game."

Rainsford did not smile. "I am still a beast at bay," he said, in a low, hoarse voice. "Get ready, General Zaroff."

The general made one of his deepest bows. "I see," he said. "Splendid! One of us is to furnish a repast for the hounds. The other will sleep in this very excellent bed. On guard, Rainsford."

. . . He had never slept in a better bed, Rainsford decided.

In the Penal Colony

by Franz Kafka

a new translation by Culpeo S. Fox

"IT is an extraordinary apparatus," the officer said to the traveler and gave the machine that was so well known to him an admiring gaze. The traveler followed the commandant's invitation out of mere politeness when he had asked him to attend the execution of a soldier who was condemned for disobedience and insulting a superior. The general interest in this execution was not very high. Here in this deep, sandy valley that was surrounded by bleak slopes from all sides, beside the traveler and the officer the only people present were the convict—a dull, broad-mouthed fellow with unkempt hair and face—and a soldier who held the heavy chain which connected the smaller chains to which the convict was bound at his feet and wrist bones, as well as by his neck, and which all were also connected to each other by linked chains.

The traveler had little appreciation for the machine and walked up and down behind the convict with vague disinterest; meanwhile, the officer was preparing some last arrangements—soon he was seen crawling beneath the apparatus, which was set deep in the ground, and then again he would climb up a ladder to investigate the upper parts. Those were jobs which were usually left for a machinist to do, but the officer did them with great zeal; perhaps this was because he was such an admirer of the apparatus and believed no one else could be trusted with these tasks.

"Now, everything's done!" he finally cried and climbed down the ladder. He was immensely tired, breathing with his mouth wide open and dabbing his neck with the two delicate lady's handkerchiefs he kept tucked in the collar of his uniform.

Instead of asking about the machine, which is what the officer had expected, the traveler said: "These uniforms are way too heavy for the tropics."

"Why, yes", the officer replied, washing the oil and grease off his hands in a bucket full of water nearby. "They represent home, though; and we don't want to forsake our homeland. —But now, look at the apparatus," he added immediately, drying his hands with a towel and pointing at the machine simultaneously. "Up to this point, everything had to be done manually, but now the apparatus is working all by itself." The traveler nodded and followed him. The officer, who was intent on avoiding any possible incidents, said: "Of course, there can be malfunctions. I hope none will occur today, but you must always be prepared. After all, the apparatus is supposed to run twelve hours without any interruption. However, if there are any malfunctions, they are really small and immediately taken care of."

"Don't you want to take a seat?" he asked eventually, pulling one chair from a pile of wicker chairs, and offering it to the traveler, who could not refuse. He now sat on the edge of a pit, into which he flung a quick glance. It wasn't all that deep. At one side of the pit all the earth was piled up to a wall. At the other, there was the machine.

"I don't know," the officer said, "whether the commandant has already explained the apparatus to you." The traveler made an uncertain gesture. For the officer, this was the best possible outcome as he now was in the position to explain the machine himself. "This apparatus," he said, grasping a connecting rod to which he leaned himself against, "is an invention of our previous commandant. I assisted during its earliest tests and was also involved in all stages of its development. However, all the credit for this invention belongs to him alone. Have you heard of our previous commandant? You have not? Well, I'm not claiming too much when I tell you that the entire creation of this penal colony is his work. We, his friends, knew at his deathbed that the facility of this penal colony is designed in such a way that his successor would not be able to change anything of the old ways for many years to come, no matter how many plans he may have in his head. And our prediction came true; the new commandant should have known it. Pity that you weren't able to meet the previous commandant! But–" the officer interrupted himself here– "I'm chatting and his apparatus is standing here before us. As you can see, it is made from three components. Over time, each respective part has earned a nickname. The one beneath is named the Bed, the upper part we call the Inscriber and the middle one here, the floating one, is called the Harrow."

"The Harrow?" the traveler asked. He wasn't paying close attention because the sun was intensely shining within this shadeless valley and it was getting hard to collect one's thoughts. The officer thus appeared even more admirable to him, standing there with his tight, parade-like surcoat, all complete with epaulettes and braids, explaining his matter with such enthusiasm—all the while pointing things out here and there with his screwdriver. The soldier seemed to be in a similar mood as the traveler. He had coiled the convict's chains around both his wrists and was now leaning with one hand against his rifle, his head tilted as if oblivious to everything. The traveler wasn't at all surprised by that, since the officer was speaking in French and it was quite certain that neither the soldier nor the convict understood the language. It seemed all the more peculiar, however, that the convict did his best to follow the officer's explanations. With a certain kind of sleepy persistence, he would glance at wherever the officer was pointing, and when the latter was interrupted by the traveler with a question he'd also—just like the officer—rest his gaze upon the traveler.

"Yes, the Harrow," the officer said, "the name fits. These needles are arranged like those of a harrow and they also function just like a harrow, even though only at one place and—much more artistic. You'll understand it in a minute. Here, the condemned man is laid out in the Bed. —You see, I want to describe the apparatus first and then continue with the procedure afterwards. This way you'll be able to follow it better. Also, one cogwheel within the Inscriber is quite worn; it's screeching during the procedure, so much that it's almost impossible to understand each other. Unfortunately, getting replacement parts is also anything but easy. —So, here's the Bed, just as I said. It is completely covered with a layer of cotton wool; you'll understand its purpose soon enough. On top of this wool the condemned man is laid out on his stomach, naked of course. Here are straps for his hands and feet, and here for his neck—to tie him up. Here, at the head of the Bed where the man, as I've said, lies face down is this little lump fold of felt; you can easily adjust it in a way that it can be inserted into the man's mouth. Its purpose is to prevent him from screaming and biting his tongue in two. Of course the man must take this felt, otherwise these straps will break his neck."

"This is cotton wool?" the traveler asked and leaned forward.

"Yes, of course," the officer said, smiling, "touch it yourself." He took the traveler's hand and led it to the Bed. "It is specially prepared cotton wool, which is why it looks so unusual; I'll get back to its purpose later."

The traveler was almost won over by the machine. Keeping his hand over his eyes to protect them from the sun, he studied the apparatus. It was a very massive thing. The Bed and the Inscriber were about the same size and seemed like two dark chests. The Inscriber was built approximately two meters above the Bed; both were connected through four brass rods which were gleaming in the sun. In between these chests, there was the Harrow hanging on a band of steel.

The officer had hardly noticed the traveler's earlier indifference, yet he now detected an awakening interest, which was growing for the first time. Therefore, he stopped with his explanations to not disturb the traveler's close inspections. The convict imitated the traveler; but since he was unable to keep his hand over his eyes, he would just gaze upwards with his eyes uncovered.

"So, now the man is lying down . . ." the traveler said, leaning over in the seat and crossing his legs.

"Yes," the officer said, pushing his cap back a bit and running his hand over the hot face, "but now, listen up! The Bed as well as the Inscriber do have their own electric batteries; the Bed needs it for itself, the Inscriber needs it for the Harrow. As soon as the man is tied up, the Bed is set in motion. It's moving with tiny, very rapid quivers, sideways as well as up and down. You may have seen similar machines in lunatic asylums—the difference with our apparatus, however, is that everything is exactly calculated to the smallest movement—because you have to be extremely precise and coordinated with the movements of the Harrow. The Harrow itself is doing the main job in performing the execution."

"What is the sentence anyway?" the traveler asked.

"You don't know about that either?" the officer said greatly surprised and bit his lip. "Excuse me if my explanations are disorganized. I greatly beg your pardon. You see, prior to this the commandant was the one to explain everything; the new one, however, doesn't follow this honorable duty—not even with such an esteemed visitor." The traveler tried to dismiss this honor with a gesture, but the officer insisted on expressing himself: "The fact that he didn't provide any insight regarding our sentencing practices to our esteemed guest is one more change from how things were done—" There was a curse on lips, but he contained himself and said only: "I wasn't informed, it is not my fault. With that said, though, I may add that I'm the best equipped to explain our ways of sentencing, for here I carry—" he patted his breast pocket "—the respective constructions drawn by our previous commandant."

"Constructions drawn by the commandant himself?" the traveler asked. "Why, was he a jack of all trades? Was he soldier, judge, engineer, chemist and technical artist?"

„Es ist ein eigentümlicher
Apparat", sagte der Offizier
zu dem Forschungsreisenden (...)

"He was indeed," the officer said, nodding, and with a lingering, pondering look in his eyes. Then he glanced at his hands; to touch these drawings, they didn't seem clean enough to him. Therefore, he went to the bucket of water, washing them once more. Then he pulled out a small leather folder and said: "Our sentence doesn't seem severe. The law, which the condemned man has violated, will be inscribed on his body with the Harrow. This convict for example—" the officer pointed to the man "—will receive the following on his body: 'Honor your superior!'"

The traveler briefly glanced at the man; when the officer had pointed at him, he had lowered his head, seemingly focusing all the power of his hearing to find out what has been said. But the movements of his rubbery lips pressed together apparently showed that he could not understand anything at all. The traveler had many different questions in mind, but after looking at the convict he merely asked: "Does he know his sentence?"

"No," the officer said and was about to continue with his explanations but the traveler interrupted him:

"He doesn't know his own sentence?"

"No," the officer said once more; he paused for a moment as if seeking another rational behind the traveler's question, then said: "Telling him would be of no use. He will get to know it on his own body after all." The traveler was about to fall silent at this point when he felt the convict's eyes on him; he seemed to ask whether he could approve the procedure which the officer had explained.

Thus the traveler, who already had leaned back, bent forward again and asked: "But he is aware that he has been condemned, isn't he?"

"He isn't aware of that either," the officer said and smiled at the traveler as if he was awaiting some more odd revelations.

"No," the traveler said and wiped his forehead. "So the convict also doesn't know how his defense was received?"

"There has been no opportunity for him to be defended," the officer said and looked to the side, as if he was talking to himself, not wanting to embarrass the traveler with things so self-explanatory.

"But there must have been an opportunity to defend himself," the traveler said and got up from his chair.

The officer realized that his explanations of the apparatus were in danger of being delayed a long while; so he went to the traveler, took him by the arm, pointed at the convict (who was now aware that he had become center of attention and so stood stiffly erect, and even gave his chains a yank), and said: "So, it is like this. In this penal colony, I've been appointed judge. Despite my young age. Because I also was at the old commandant's side regarding all matters of punishment and it is also me who knows the apparatus best. The tenet which I follow is: 'Guilt is always beyond doubt'. Other courts cannot follow this principle, for they are made of many people, having even higher courts above them. This is not the case here, or at least, it wasn't when the old commandant was still around. The new one, however, has already shown himself inclined to interfere in my court, although I could successfully fend him off so far—and I will continue in being successful. . . . You wanted to have this case explained to you; well, it is as simple as any other. This morning, a captain has brought charge that this man, who was assigned to him as servant and sleeps at his door, had been caught sleeping on duty. It is his job to get up at every striking of the hour to salute in front of the captain's door. Not a hard job by any means, but it is one of significance since he is expected to be fresh and awake during both his guard assignment and servant's duties. The captain wanted to check on the servant last night to ensure he was fulfilling his task. And on the stroke of two, he had opened the door and found the man curled up and sleeping. So he took out his riding crop and hit him across the face. But instead of getting up and begging for forgiveness, the man grabbed the captain by his legs, crying: 'Get that whip away, or else I'll eat you.' . . . So, those are the facts. The captain came to me an hour ago, I noted his statements and determined the sentence right afterwards. Then, I ordered to have this man chained up. It was all very easy. If I had questioned the man first, he would have lied to me, resulting in confusion only. He would have lied, and if I had succeeded to refute his lies, he would have replaced them with new lies, and so on. But now, I do have him here and I won't let him go again. . . . So, has everything been explained well enough? Anyway, time is flying and the execution should be starting, and I'm not even done with prepar-ing the apparatus itself yet." He urged the traveler to sit down once more, before approaching the machine again and said: "As you can see, the Harrow matches the human shape; this is the harrow for the upper body, here are the harrows for the legs. As for the head, well, these small cutters are designated for that. Do you understand?" He leaned forward to the traveler with a friendly expression, eager to provide the most elaborate of explanations.

The traveler looked at the Harrow with a frown. The explanation about the trial had left him unsatisfied. However, he had to tell himself this was a penal colony after all; this was a place where special rules were necessary and where one had to operate in a military manner. Beyond that, though, he secretly had some hopes in the new commandant who seemed to have plans for introducing a new form of trial (even though a bit slowly,) which the rather narrow-minded officer was unable to grasp. Following these exact thoughts the traveler asked: "Will the commandant be present at the execution?"

"It is not for certain," the officer replied; he seemed quite embarrassed by this sudden question and his friendly expression distorted a bit. "This is exactly why we have to hurry. I'll even have to shorten my explanation, as much as it hurts me to do so. But, tomorrow, as soon as the apparatus is cleaned up again, I could—getting so dirty in the process is its only flaw—catch up with more detailed explanations. So as for now, let's proceed with the indispensable things only. . . . As soon as the man is lying on the Bed which itself starts quivering, the Harrow sinks onto the body. It positions itself automatically, so that the needles touch the body only lightly. When that is done, this steel cable stiffens up immediately, turning into a rod. And now, the game is on. An uninitiated person would notice no external difference among the punishments. The Harrow seems to be working uniformly. Quivering and shivering, it seems to punctuate the body—itself quivering because of the Bed—with its needles. Now, to make it possible for everyone to observe the sentence procedure, the Harrow is made of glass. That design created some technical difficulties with fixing the needles inside but success came after many attempts. We spared no effort whatsoever. And now, everyone can see through the glass how the inscription takes form onto the body. Don't you want to come closer and examine these needles?"

The traveler stood up very slowly, went to the machine and leaned toward the Harrow. "You see," the officer said, "two kinds of needles arranged in various rows. Each long needle having a shorter one positioned right next to it. The long one does the writing, you understand, and the short one is squirting out water to wash off the blood and keep the inscription always clean. The bloody water is then channeled through some grooves right here where it finally flows through this main gutter, leading right to the pit." The officer traced the exact path that the bloody water had to go with his finger. Taking the demonstration even further, he captured a bot of the water at the outlet pipe with both hands; at that point, the traveler raised his head, stepped backwards, and searched for his chair with his hand. Much to his horror, he saw that the convict also had followed the officer's invitation to observe the Harrow up close. His chains tightened and he pulled the drowsy soldier a little further, so that he was now bending over the glass. One could see that he was timidly searching for whatever the two gentlemen had observed before, but was failing to comprehend because he hadn't listened to any of the explanation. He looked here and there. He shuffled this way and that way, his eyes fixed over the glass. The traveler felt the urge to pull him back, for what he was doing there was probably punishable. But he was held back by the officer with one hand; with the other, the officer picked a piece of dirt from the wall and then threw it at the soldier. The soldier opened his eyes with a start. Realizing what the convict had dared to do, he dropped the rifle, braced his feet firmly to the ground, and pulled the convict back in such a harsh way that the man fell. He looked down at him, watching him wriggling and rattling with his chains. "Get him up!" the officer yelled, for he realized that the traveler was being distracted by the convict a bit too much. The traveler, leaning over the Harrow without much thought about it, was only interested in what was happening to the convict. "Get control of him!" the officer yelled once more; he ran around the machine, grabbed the convict under his armpits and helped the soldier to get him (now slipping several times) back onto his feet.

"Why, now I know everything," the traveler said as the officer returned to him.

"Except for the most important thing," the officer replied, then took the traveler by the arm and pointed up high: "There within the Inscriber is the wheelwork responsible for the Harrow's movements and this exact wheelwork mimics the Inscription and its sentence. I'm still using the drawings made by the former commandant. Here they are–" He pulled some sheets out the leather portfolio. "–unfortunately I cannot hand them over to you, as they are the most precious things that I possess. Sit down, I'll show them to you from a short distance so that you can see them well." He showed the first sheet. The traveler would have loved to say something intelligent, but all he could see were some lines running into each other and overlapping like a maze; they covered the sheet so densely that one could only hardly see some white spaces in between.

"Read it," the officer said.

"I can't," the traveler replied.

"Why, it's all clear," the officer said.

"Well, it is quite artistic," the traveler said evasively, "but I can't decipher it."

"Yes," the officer said, started laughing and put the diagram away again, "it's no calligraphy for schoolchildren. One needs to study it for a while. But I'm sure that you would understand it eventually. It must not be an easy inscribing, of course; after all, it should not kill a man instantly. That usually happens within twelve hours. The sixth hour is set to be the turning point. Thus, there must be many, many embellishments that accompany the script; the actual script moves around the body in a narrow belt only—the rest of the body is reserved for decorative applications. Can you now appreciate the work of the Harrow and the apparatus as a whole? —Look!" He jumped up the ladder, turned a wheel and cried: "Watch out, step aside!" and it all started moving. If the wheel had not screeched, it would have been marvelous. Noticeably irritated by the annoying wheel, the officer threatened it with a clenched fist; he then opened his arms at the traveler in an apologizing manner and quickly climbed down again to view the moving machine from below. Still, something wasn't right, and he realized that now; he climbed up once more, reached inside of the Inscriber with both hands, then slid down at a pole instead of using the ladder to get down faster. He yelled into the traveler's ear to make himself understandable, straining his voice with the utmost tension: "Do you understand the process now? The Harrow has started writing; as soon as it has finished the first draft onto the man's back, the cotton wool starts rolling, slowly turning the body to the side so the Harrow has new space to fill. Meanwhile, the body parts wounded by the inscription are now lying on the cotton wool, stopping the bleeding immediately, thanks to its special preparation, and preparing everything for the second engraving of the script. Here, these prongs at the edge of the Harrow rip the cotton wool off the wounds while the body is still rotating, throwing them into the pit and the Harrow can engage once more. This way, it writes deeper and deeper, twelve hours of it. During the first six hours the condemned man is as alive as before, except that he is just in pain. Two hours into the process, the felt is removed, because now, the man has no energy left to scream anymore. Here, in this electrically heated bowl at the head of the Bed, there is warm rice pudding which he can take with his tongue—if he wants to. I can tell you, no one ever misses out on this opportunity. I know of absolutely no one, and I can draw from a lot of experience. It is not before the sixth hour passes until he finally loses his will to eat. I'd usually kneel right here then to observe this phenomenon. Only rarely does the man swallow his last bite; instead, he'd just turns it within his mouth and spits it into the pit. I need to duck at this point; otherwise I'd get it all in my face. But oh, how silent the man falls once the sixth hour has passed! Even the most stupid of them suddenly understand. It starts around the eyes. Spreading from there. A wondrous view, almost tempting one to join the process and lay below the Harrow. Nothing else is happening anyway, the man only starts to decipher the script, pursing his lips as if he was listening. As yourself have seen, it is not easy to decipher the script with one's mere eyes. But our man, he deciphers it through his wounds. It is a lot of work, I might add, requiring six hours to complete. But then, the Harrow impales him eventually and spits him out right into the pit, where he splashes all over the bloody water and cotton wool. Then, the sentence is over. And we—the soldier and I, simply bury him just like that."

With his hands in his pockets, the traveler leaned his ear toward the officer and watched the machine doing its work. The convict watched as well, although without any understanding. He bent down a little and followed the moving needles when the soldier, instructed by the officer, cut his shirt and trousers from behind, prompting them to fall off. He was about to grab them and cover his bareness; but the soldier held him up high, shaking the last rags from him. The officer turned the machine off and the convict was laid out beneath the Harrow amid the sudden silence. The chains were exchanged with straps, and in the first moments it almost seemed like a relief for the convict. And now, the Harrow was positioned a bit deeper, because the convict was quite a sickly man. He shuddered as the tips of the needles touched his skin; while the soldier was still busy with his right hand, the convict stretched out his left hand, not sure what to do with it. It was, however, pointed in the direction of where the traveler was standing. The officer steadily observed him from the side, as if he was eager to read from his expression whether the execution, which he had explained superficially at least, left any impression.

The strap ripped off. The soldier most likely had pulled on it a bit too strong. The officer moved to help and the soldier showed him the damaged piece of strap. The officer went to him and said, his face turned towards the traveler: "The apparatus is a complex piece, so of course pieces break or rip here and there; but that should not lessen one's overall opinion. By the way, there is an immediate replacement for the strap ready; I'll just use one of the chains. However, it may affect the mobility of the right arm." And while applying the chain, he said: "You see, the resources to maintain the apparatus are now quite limited. We had a free fund for this exact purpose when the old commandant was still around. There used to be a storeroom where we could draw from all kinds of replacement parts. I will admit, I was rather wasteful when it comes to the use of it; I mean, back then! Not nowadays, with the new commandant and his claims that all is done under the pretext of fighting the old establishment. Now, the fund is all under his own control—and when I ask for a new strap, he demands the ripped one as proof—but the problem is that not only would it take up to ten days for a new strap to arrive, the new one would also be of much poorer quality—there is almost no use for it. But how am I supposed to operate the apparatus without a functioning strap? No one cares about that."

The traveler thought about it. It is always a very questionable thing to interfere in unfamiliar matters. He was neither a citizen of the penal colony, nor was he a citizen of the state to which it belonged. When he was about to condemn the ways of this execution or even hinder it, one could say: *Well, you are still a stranger, aren't you? You better shut your mouth.* There was nothing he could have said against this; he could have only added that he didn't understand himself in this peculiar case; after all, the only purpose of his travels was to observe, not to interfere with the ways trials are conducted. However, the urge was indeed very tempting. There was no doubt about the execution's inhumanity and injustice. Not a single soul could ascribe any kind of selfishness to the traveler since the convict was neither a friend nor a fellow countryman, and he surely also did not evoke any kind of sympathy. The traveler himself had come with letters of high authority, and he had been welcomed with some great courtesy. The mere fact that he had been invited to this execution in the first place implied that his opinion about this trial was sought. This seemed even more evident, as the commandant —as he had now clearly learned—was no supporter of how the process was handled, opposing the officer in an almost antagonistic manner.

Suddenly the traveler heard a shout of rage coming from the officer. He had just painstakingly tried to put the felted stub into the convict's mouth when the man closed his eyes in a sudden attack of nausea, causing him to throw up. The officer hurried to yank him up onto the stump, turning his head towards the pit; but it was too late. The vomit flew all over the machine. "That's all the commandant's fault!" the officer cried, angrily jolting the brass rods at the front, "—the apparatus being drowned in filth like a pigsty!" With quivering hands, he showed the traveler what just had happened. "Haven't I made this clear enough to the commandant, for hours and hours, that a condemned man must not be served any food one day prior to his execution? But alas, the new, mild administration begs to differ. Before the condemned man is taken away, the commandant's ladies are stuffing him up with sweets. All his life he has known nothing else but the taste of stinking fish and now, he must eat sweets! I mean, it would be possible, I would not mind, but why on earth does no one care about getting a new felted stub, as I have requested three months ago? How could anyone take this felt in one's mouth without disgust? After all, it has been sucked at and bitten into by more than a hundred men while they were dying!"

The convict had his head laid down with a serene expression, while the soldier was busy cleaning up the machine with the prisoner's shirt. The officer went to the traveler, who, in some intuitive notion, stepped back, but the officer took him by the hand and pulled him aside. "I want to tell you something just between you and me," he said. "I am allowed to do so, am I?"

"Of course," the traveler replied and listened with lowered eyes.

"At this point—within this colony, the trial and its execution which you are about to witness has no open supporters anymore. I am the only defender left. At the same time, I am the only defender of the old commandant's legacy. I can't think of expanding the process anymore; I need all my powers to keep what is already there. When the old commandant was still alive, the colony was full of supporters. While I do partly have the same persuasiveness that he did, I'm lacking his powers completely. Therefore, his supporters hide themselves—there are still many, but no one who would openly admit it. So, if you were about to visit a teahouse during an execution day and keep your ears open, you might catch ambiguous remarks only. Those are all supporters; but considering the current commandant and his equally current views, they're of no use. Thus, I am asking you now: Should this apparatus, a life's work, go to waste—" he pointed to the machine— "just because of this commandant and his women are influencing him? Is anyone allowed to let this happen? Even if you're just a stranger, visiting our isle for some days? Still, we got no time to lose, someone is planning against my judicial authority. There are already discussions within the commandant's headquarters where I am not brought in; even your very visit seems more than indicative of this whole affair. People are cowards, so they send you, a stranger. . . . Oh, how different executions used to be in earlier days! The whole valley was literally flooded with people the day before the process; they all came only to see. Early in the morning, the commandant would appear together with his ladies; fanfares would wake the whole encampment; I brought the news that everything was set up and ready. All of society—no high-ranked official was allowed to miss out—gathered around the apparatus. You see that pile of wicker armchairs over there? Nothing but a sad remnant of that time. The apparatus was cleaned and polished, and for almost every execution I would prepare some new replacement parts. In front of hundreds of eyes—every spectator was standing on tiptoes up to that hill over there. The condemned man was laid below the Harrow by the commandant himself. What now a common soldier is appointed to do used to be my job, the job of Chief Justice—an honorable task. And now, the execution began! No jarring note would disturb the apparatus' work. Some of the spectators would not even watch anymore, but instead lay in the sand with their eyes closed; they all knew: *Now justice was happening.* All one could hear in this silence were the sighs of the condemned man, muffled by the felted stub. Nowadays, the apparatus fails to get a louder sigh out of the condemned man, a noise that even the felt cannot lessen; but back in the days, the needles would squeeze out a corrosive liquid which is not allowed anymore. Well, and then the sixth hour came! It was near impossible to allow everyone to have a better look from up close. The commandant, in his wisdom, ordered that the children would especially be taken care of. I, however, thanks to my position, was always allowed to be close by. Very often, I would just squat down, having two little children in my arms on each side. Oh, how we all adored the expression of glorification from the tortured face, how we all held our cheeks in the glow of this beautiful justice which was finally achieved and already fading again! Those were the days, my friend!" Apparently, the officer had forgotten who was standing there before him. He had hugged the traveler and laid his head on his shoulder. The traveler found himself greatly embarrassed by this; impatiently, he looked over the officer's head. Meanwhile, the soldier was done with his cleaning task and now filled some rice pudding into the bowl. As soon as the convict, who had fully recovered again, took notice of this and tried to snatch up some of the pudding with his tongue. The soldier pushed him away several times, as this bowl seemed to be meant for a later time; but it was just as improper to see the soldier grabbing into the bowl himself with his dirty hands and eating some of the pudding right in front of the hungry convict.

The officer quickly collected himself. "I didn't want to affect you in any way," he said. "I know, it's nearly impossible to make someone understand how things used to be. With that said, the apparatus is still working, functioning on its own. It is still operating even when it is standing in this valley all alone. And the dead body will still gently fall into the pit at the end, even though there are no people anymore to gather over the pit like flies—thousands of them. Back then, we had to arrange some strong railing around the pit; it was torn away a long time ago."

The traveler wanted to turn his face away from the officer, so he started looking around aimlessly. The officer believed that he was observing the desolation of the valley; thus, he took him by his hands, turned him around to look into his eyes and asked: "Do you feel the shame?"

But the traveler kept silent. The officer let go of him after a while. With legs apart and hands resting on his hips, the officer stood still and looked at the ground. But then, he smiled at the traveler with an encouraging expression and said: "Yesterday, when the commandant invited you, I was nearby. I overheard the invitation. I know the commandant. I understood at once what he had intended with that invitation. Even though he has enough power to operate against me, he wouldn't dare yet; however, he exposes me to the opinion of a much-respected stranger. That's what he does—a careful calculation. You've been on the island for two days now, and you neither know the old commandant, nor his way of thinking; you're caught up in your own European ways. Perhaps you're opposed to the general idea of the death penalty from the get-go, and thus you are especially opposed to mechanical executions. On top of that, you witness the process in such a sad way, with a slightly damaged machine, without any public participation. Considering all of this (this is how the commandant thinks about it,) wouldn't it be possible that you have no appreciation for my kind of procedure? And in case you do indeed have no appreciation for it (and I'm still thinking on the commandant's behalf,) you will tell me so, because you surely trust your well-tested beliefs. You may have indeed seen the ways of many different folks and cultures and learned to respect them, and therefore you probably would not speak against our procedure with all your power—as you would otherwise do so in your own country. But the commandant does not even need that. A hasty and casual word, carelessly spoken, is enough. It doesn't even have to reflect your own beliefs if only it does meet his own ideas. Oh, I'm sure that he will interrogate you with all his cunning. And his women will sit in circles, perking up their ears. You may say: 'In our homeland, trial is different', or 'among us, a convict is questioned before the verdict', or 'at home, torture was a thing of the medieval ages'. All those remarks are legitimate, in that they seem appropriate to you—innocent remarks that don't affect my procedure at all. But how will the commandant take them? Oh, I can see him, our good commandant, how he pushes the chair away immediately. I see him hurrying to the balcony. I see his ladies following him. I hear his voice—the women call it the voice of thunder—and then, well, he then says: 'An excellent explorer from the West who was appointed to inspect judicial procedures in all countries has just decided that our ways of execution, modeled after old customs, is inhumane. A verdict like this, coming from such an honored person, would make it impossible to conduct an execution of this kind anymore. Thus, from this day on, I will order . . . and so on'. You want to interfere, what he proclaims up there is not what you have said. You didn't call my procedure inhumane—the opposite is the case. Drawing on your deep understanding, you believe it to be one of the most humane and dignified of all, you marvel at the apparatus just as much—but, it's too late. You can't reach the balcony which is full of women already; you try to make yourself seen; you want to scream; but suddenly, there is the hand of a lady, covering your mouth—and I? The old commandant's life work, and now mine—we both go for nothing."

The traveler had to suppress a smile. So, the job he had thought to be extremely difficult was, in fact, that easy. He evasively said: "You are overestimating my influence; the commandant has read my credentials, he knows that I'm no expert in the field of judicial procedures. If I was about to express an opinion, it would be the opinion of an everyman—not any more significant than the opinion of someone else; certainly much less important than the opinion of the commandant who, as far as I believe, has the final word in these matters. If his opinion is as negative as you assume, then I fear that the procedure has indeed come to an end—without any of my own humble assistance."

Did the officer understand already? No, he did not. He vividly shook his head, and then briefly looked at the convict and the soldier who both stopped eating the rice with a flinch. He came very close to the traveler, but avoided meeting his eyes. Instead, he gazed at a random point on his jacket and then said, quieter than before: "You don't know the commandant. To him and us all, you are—and please forgive my expression—in a way rather innocent. And your influence, believe you me, can't be held high enough. I was happy beyond reason when I heard that you alone would attend the execution. I know, the commandant's order was supposed to wound me, but now I'll turn it to my advantage. Not at all distracted by false insinuations and spiteful looks—which could not have been avoided if the execution had been attended by more people—you have now listened to my explanations. You have seen the apparatus and you are about to witness the execution itself. Your verdict is settled already, I'm sure. But in case there are still little uncertainties remaining, be sure that witnessing the execution will terminate them all. And now, I'm asking you: Please help me with the commandant!"

The traveler didn't allow him to talk any further. "How could I do that," he cried out, "this is absolutely impossible. I can neither help nor hinder you."

"You could do it," the officer said. The traveler watched with growing concern that the officer was clenching his fists. "You could do it," he repeated, this time with even more urgency in his voice. "I've got a plan that has to work. You think your influence would make no difference. I know that it would. But, in case you're right, wouldn't it be still necessary to try everything we can to keep this procedure? Thus, listen to my plan! To make it happen we have to make sure that you keep silent about the procedure. As long as no one is directly asking you, you must not say a single word. Your remarks need to be brief and vague; one should notice that it's hard for you to talk about it, that you are indeed bitter, that you— in case you have to openly express yourself—are about to break into curses. I'm not asking you to lie, not at all. All you need to do is reply with very short answers, like: 'Yes, I've seen the execution', or 'Yes, I've listened to all explanations'. Just that and nothing else. There is enough reason for the bitterness that people should be able to clearly see it in your face, even if it doesn't impress the commandant. He, of course, will completely misunderstand it—interpret it in his own way. That is the basis of my plan. Tomorrow at headquarters, and under authority of the commandant, there will be a great discussion among all higher-ranked officials. The commandant, of course, knows very well how to make a spectacle out of this. A gallery is already built which is always full of spectators. I'm forced to attend these discussions, but ah, I'm shaken by reluctance. Now, you will be invited to this meeting for sure; if everything goes according to my plan, this invitation will soon turn into an urgent request. But, in case you won't be invited for whatever reason, you must demand an invitation. If you do so, you will receive it without a doubt. So tomorrow then, you'll be sitting together with the ladies in the comman- dant's box. From time to time he'll check for you to be up there with brief looks. After some various and trivial agenda items which exist only for the spectators—usually it's about harbor constructions, always harbor constructions! . . . the discussion will then shift to the judicial process. If it is not initiated by the commandant, I'll take care of making it happen. I'll get up and proclaim the news of today's execution. Just very briefly, just this one announcement. An announcement like that may be not typical there, but I'll do it anyway. The commandant will thank me, as always, with a friendly smile and then, because he can't hold it back, will take advantage of the situation. 'There has been,' he will exclaim just like that, or in a similar manner, 'an announcement of the execution. I only wanted to add that this execution was witnessed by the same great explorer who has visited our colony and of whom you all already know.

Today's discussion is graced by his presence, which makes this a gathering of great significance. Don't we want to raise the question to this great explorer, how he judges the procedure of both the trial and the execution which has been carried out and is modeled after the old ways?' Of course, now there is applause everywhere, an universal agreement—with me being the loudest of them all. The commandant bows before you and says: 'So then, on behalf of everyone, I ask for your impressions of our judicial system.' And it is here that you to step up to the railing. Place your hands on the railing so everyone can see them, or otherwise the ladies will grab your fingers and play with them. . . . And then, finally, it is your turn to speak. I don't know how I am going to bear the tension of those hours until then. In your speech, you don't have to mince matters. Boldly speak the truth, lean over the railing, roar even—why yes, share your opinion with the commandant through shouts, an opinion full of determination! But perhaps, you don't want to do that, as it opposes your very character. Perhaps people of your kind behave way differently in such a situation, but that is also completely legitimate and fine. You don't have to get up—just make a few remarks. Say them in a whisper so that the officials beneath can just hear you, that's enough—you don't even have to talk about the lack of public attendance during the execution, about the screeching wheel, the ripped strap, the disgusting felt . . . no, leave everything else to me and believe me, if my speech doesn't chase him out of the room, it will force him to his knees for sure, in such a way that he has no choice but to acknowledge the truth: Old commandant, I bow down before you . . . —that, that is my plan. Do you want to help me to carry it out? Why, of course you do! And even more than that, you absolutely have to." And the officer grabbed the traveler by both his arms, looking him straight in the eyes with a heavy sigh. The last few sentences he had been screaming in such a way that even the soldier and the convict were paying attention. Even though they still could not understand a thing. And yet, they had stopped eating and, still chewing, gazed at the traveler.

The traveler had known from the very beginning that there was only one answer he could give. He had experienced way too much in his life for him to be deterred. Deep down, he was just being honest and unafraid. Still, he now hesitated for a moment as he looked at the soldier and the convict. But eventually, he said what he had to say: "No." The officer's eyes blinked several times, but he did not take his gaze off the traveler. "Do you want an explanation?" the traveler asked. The officer kept silent and nodded. "I opposed this procedure," the traveler now said, "even before I was witness to it. I won't abuse your trust in any way, of course. To be honest, I was actually wondering whether I am entitled to intervene against this procedure and whether this intervention of mine would be successful. And I knew to whom I had to turn for this: the commandant of course. You made this fact even clearer to me—but without reinforcing my decision. The opposite is the case; your strong conviction does affect me, although it won't change my mind."

The officer still didn't say a word; he turned to the machine, grabbed one of the brass rods and then, leaning back a little, gazed up at the Inscriber, as if he was checking that everything was all right. The soldier and the convict apparently had become friends meanwhile; the convict— even though difficult to do because of his position and being all tied up— signaled the soldier, who was leaning toward him. The convict whispered something into his ear, and the soldier nodded.

The traveler went after the officer and said: "You don't know yet what I am going to do. Even though I will share my opinion about this procedure with the commandant, I won't do it during a public discussion —but in private; I also won't stay long enough that I could be invited to any public meeting anyway. I'm going to leave tomorrow morning. At least, I will board my ship."

The officer didn't seem to have listened. "So . . . the procedure has not convinced you," he said, more to himself, and smiled. He smiled like an elder would smile over the naïvety of a child, keeping his real thoughts hidden behind that smile.

"Well . . . it's time then," he eventually said, suddenly looking at the traveler with bright eyes, seemingly communicating a certain kind of de- mand, or even appeal for participation.

"It's time for what?" the traveler asked uneasily. But he didn't re- ceive any reply.

"You are free," the officer told the convict in his own language. The latter didn't believe him at first. "Well, you are a free," the officer insisted. And for the first time, there was a real glimmer of life in the convict's face. Could it be true? Was it just a sudden mood of the officer, able to change at any moment? Was it the traveler, who had brought him this reprieve? What was it? These things his face seemed to ask. But not for long. Whatever it was, he wanted to be truly free, if he was allowed to be and he started to struggle and shake, as much as the Harrow would permit him to.

"You're going to tear the straps," the officer yelled, "be still! We'll undo them already." And giving the soldier a sign, he set to work on him.

During the process, the convict didn't say anything, but he laughed softly. Soon, he was able to look left to the officer, and then right to where the soldier was standing—and he also did not forget the traveler.

"Pull him out," the officer ordered the soldier. One had to be careful here because of the Harrow; the convict already had some small wounds on his back, thanks to his own impatience.

From now on, though, the officer was no longer concerned with the convict. He went instead to the traveler and pulled out the leather booklet again, flipping through it until he found the page he wanted, and showed it to the traveler.

"Read it," he said.

"I can't," the traveler replied. "I already told you that I can't decipher these pages."

"Why, look closely at this page," the officer said and stepped right next to the traveler, so they could read it together. But when this also did not help, he raised his little finger high over the paper, as if the page must not be touched under any circumstances, trying to make it easier for the traveler to read. The traveler did try, mainly to satisfy the officer—but it was to no avail. Now, the officer even began to spell the inscription, and then continued to read it in context. "'Be just!'—it states," he said, "now, you can read it, yeah?" The traveler bowed so low over the paper that the officer pulled it away a bit, afraid that it could be touched. The traveler said no more, but it was clear that he still could not read a thing. "'Be just!'—it states," the officer repeated.

"That may be so," the traveler said. "I do believe that's written there."

"Well then," the officer said, half-way satisfied at least, and climbed the ladder, taking the page with him. With the utmost care, he positioned the paper onto the Inscriber and apparently rearranged the wheelwork completely. It was a very demanding task; the wheels probably were very small. He was examining everything so precisely that sometimes, the officer's head would disappear inside the Inscriber.

The traveler patiently watched this work from below; his neck grew stiff and his eyes stung from the sunlight. The soldier and the convict were keeping each other busy meanwhile. The convict's shirt and trousers, which had both fallen into the pit, were pulled out by the soldier using the tip of his bayonet. The shirt was incredibly dirty and the convict washed it in the bucket of water. While he was putting his clothes on, both the soldier and the convict had to burst into loud laughter, for his shirt and trousers were split up the back. Perhaps, the convict felt responsible to entertain the soldier; with his ripped clothing, he turned and circled before the soldier who was squatting on the ground and laughing so hard that he had to slap his knee. However, they hastened to restrain themselves, remembering the presence of the two gentlemen.

When the officer had finally finished his work, he observed everything with a smile; then, he suddenly closed the cover of the Inscriber which had been open the whole time, came down, looked into the pit and then at the convict, noticing with satisfaction that he had retrieved his clothing. Then he went to the bucket of water to wash his hands; too late he realized the disgusting dirt and grew upset that he could not clean his hands now. Eventually, he pushed them into the sand—an option that did not satisfy him, yet was something that he had to accept—and started to unbutton his uniform. When he did that, the two lady's handkerchiefs, which had been tucked behind his collar, fell into his hands. "Here, take your handkerchiefs," he said and threw them over to the convict. And to the traveler he explained: "Gifts from the ladies."

Despite the apparent rush with which he pulled off his uniform, eventually disrobing completely, he took great care in handling each piece of clothing; he would even brush the silver braids on his tunic with his fingers, shaking a tassel into place. But, what didn't quite fit the picture was the fact that he reluctantly threw each piece away and into the pit as soon as he was finished handling it. The last item that he had left to him was his short sword, as well as its harness. He pulled the sword out of its scabbard and broke it into pieces; then, he took all the pieces—the broken sword, the harness, and the scabbard—and threw them away in such a fierce manner that it made a loud racket in the pit.

And now, he stood there, naked. The traveler bit his lip and said nothing. Although he knew what was about to happen, he didn't feel entitled to hinder the officer in any way. If this judicial process, to which the officer was so devoted, was truly about to get terminated—probably because of the traveler's intervention, which he felt obliged to do—then the officer was acting completely rational. The traveler felt that he would have done the same.

The soldier and the convict didn't understand at first; they didn't even watch. The convict was quite happy to have received the handkerchiefs back, although he wasn't allowed to enjoy them for very long, because the soldier unexpectantly snatched them away. He tucked them behind his belt and the convict tried to retrieve them, but the soldier was too wary for him. It all resulted in a fight, although not-too-serious and half-joking. Only when the officer was standing there completely naked did they stop and paid attention. The convict seemed especially struck by the ironic turn of events. What had happened to him was now happening to the officer. Perhaps matters were being carried to extreme this time. It probably was the foreign traveler who had ordered this turnabout. So, this was vengeance. Without having suffered all that long, he was still avenged in the end. A broad, silent laugh appeared on his face and lingered there.

But the officer had now turned to the machine. If it hadn't been clear earlier how in tune with this machine he was, one would be shocked by how well he handled it now—how eagerly it obeyed his touch. He only had to approach the Harrow with his hand and immediately it rose and sank several times until it had reached the right position to welcome him. He only needed to touch the Bed by the edges to make it quiver. The felt stub moved up to his mouth all by itself. One could see that the officer was hesitating, not quite ready to accept, but this hesitation lasted for only a moment before he finally submitted and took it between his teeth. Everything was set up and ready. Only the straps were hanging from the sides. But they were obviously unnecessary; the officer did not need to be strapped. At that point, the convict noticed the lose straps as well and he quickly concluded that the execution wasn't complete unless they were fastened. He eagerly waved at the soldier and they both ran to the machine to strap the officer up. The officer already had one leg stretched out to kick the crank that activated the Inscriber. Then he saw the two men approaching; thus, he pulled his leg back and allowed himself to be strapped up. Now, however, he was unable to stroke the crank anymore. Neither the soldier nor the convict knew how to work it and the traveler was determined not to lift a finger. But that wasn't necessary. As soon as the straps were attached the machine began its work. The bed was quivering, the needles started dancing on the officer's skin, the Harrow swung up and down. The traveler had already been staring for quite some time when he suddenly remembered that one wheel within the Inscriber should have screeched. But all was quiet, one could not hear the slightest buzz.

Because of its hushed efficiency, the machine seemed to disappear. The traveler looked over at the soldier and the convict. The convict was the livelier one; everything about the machine seemed to interest him. He bent down at times, stretching out his forefinger and pointing at something to show the soldier. The traveler felt greatly embarrassed by that. He was determined to stay until the end, yet he questioned whether he was able to bear the sight of these two men any longer. "Go home," he said. The soldier may have followed this order, but to the convict it felt like an outright punishment. With his hands folded he pleaded and begged to stay, and when the traveler shook his head, unwilling to give in, he even knelt down. Seeing that his orders were ineffective he went over to them to chase the two away. Then he heard a sound coming from the Inscriber. He looked up. Was one of the wheels damaged after all? But it was something else. Slowly, the cover of the Inscriber lifted, only to fall open completely. The teeth of a cog wheel was bared. Soon afterwards they lifted and the whole wheel was exposed. It was as if an unknown force was pressing the Inscriber so that no space for the wheel remained; it turned to the edge of the Inscriber where it fell, still rolling upright in the sand until it finally came to a halt. But there was already another wheel rising in its place and many others followed: big ones, small ones—a confusion of gears, and the same sequence happened to all of them. Surely the Inscriber had to be empty now, but the process kept repeating, with a new large cluster emerging, then falling and rolling in the sand until it finally lay still. Witnessing all of this, the convict had completely forgotten the traveler's order—the gearwork utterly fascinated him. He was tempted to grab one of the wheels and urge the soldier to help him, but at every attempt he pulled his hand away, startled by the next falling wheel that would scare him as it started to roll.

The traveler, however, felt very disturbed. The machine was apparently breaking; its seemingly gentle operation had been a ruse and he felt that it was solely up to him to look after the officer, now that the fellow wasn't able to take care of himself anymore. But since the falling gear had grabbed all his attention, he had failed to look after the rest of the machine. Now, after the last wheel had fallen out of the Inscriber, he bent over the Harrow and a new, even more unpleasant surprise awaited him. The Harrow did not write. It would only stab. And the Bed wasn't turning the body, but hoisted it into the needles instead, shaking and quivering. The traveler wanted to interfere, bringing it all to a halt—that wasn't the torture that the officer had planned to attain. This was outright murder. He stretched out his hands, but at this exact moment the Harrow shot up, turning the impaled body on its side—the normal sequence, but only in the twelfth hour. The blood was flooding in hundreds of streams, but not mixed with water, for the water tubes had failed as well. And now, the last thing also failed: the body did not come loose from the long needles. The officer's blood streamed out, but his body hung over the pit without falling. The Harrow was about to return to its default position, but stayed over the pit where it was, as if it had realized that it could not free itself from its load. "Please help!" the traveler cried out to the soldier and the convict as he grabbed the officer's feet. He wanted to position himself against the feet so the other two could grab the officer's head from the other side and thusly ease him slowly from the needles. Yet, the two could not make up their minds whether to come and help—the convict actually turned around and looked away. The traveler had to come over to them, forcing them to get the officer by the head. At this point, he unwillingly looked right at the corpse's face. It was as it had been throughout his life; there was no trace of the promised salvation. What everyone else had found in that machine, the officer had not. His lips were sealed and pressed together. His eyes were wide open and seemed alive, his gaze calm and determined, and through his forehead had gone the tip of the large iron needle.

~§~

As the traveler reached the first houses in the colony, with the soldier and the convict following behind him, the soldier pointed out one and said: "Here, that's the teahouse."

On the ground floor there was a deep room, almost reminiscent of a cave, with smoke-covered walls and ceiling. It was all wide open on the street side. Although the teahouse did not differ greatly from the other houses of the colony which were all rather dilapidated (except for the commandant's palatial buildings,) it still left an impression on the traveler, reminding him of a distant memory and the powerful feeling of long forgotten times. He came closer, followed by his companions, and stepped through the unoccupied tables which were standing in front of the teahouse and in the street. He took a deep breath and inhaled the cool, stifling air that came from inside. "The old one is buried here," the soldier said. "The chaplain didn't allow him a place in the cemetery. People were uncertain for a while what to do with him, but eventually he was buried right here. I'm sure the officer didn't tell you about that, for he would have been much ashamed. He even tried to dig him up a few times at night, but he was always chased away."

"Where is the grave?" asked the traveler, who found it hard to believe the soldier.

Both the soldier and the convict immediately ran in front of him and pointed with outstretched hands to where the grave was. They led the traveler to the back wall where some guests were occupying a few tables. They probably were dock workers—strong men with short and shiny, black beards. None wore a coat and their shirts were torn—poor, humili- ated folk. As the traveler approached, some of them got up, pressing themselves against the wall. They looked at him. "He's a stranger," came the whispering all around the traveler. "He wants to see the grave." They pushed one of the tables aside and beneath it, there really was a gravestone. It was just a simple stone, low enough to be hidden under a table, and there was an inscription in tiny letters. The traveler had to kneel to properly read it. It said:

> "Here lies the old commandant. His followers who are not allowed to have names anymore, buried him in this grave and made this stone. There is a prophecy that the commandant will rise once more after a certain number of years and lead his followers out of this house and into a new conquest of the colony. Be faithful and wait!"

As the traveler had read this and got up again, he saw the men standing all around him and smiling—as if they had also read the inscription, found it ridiculous, and were now asking him to agree. The traveler acted oblivious to their unspoken insinuation, but shared some coins among them. He waited as the table was pushed back over the grave again, then left the teahouse and headed to the harbor.

The soldier and the convict had found some acquaintances in the teahouse who held them back. Still, they must have broken free from them because the traveler was still in the middle of a long staircase leading to the boats when they ran after him. They probably wanted to force the traveler to take them with him in the last minute. When the traveler argued at the bottom of the stairs with a sailor about his up- coming passage to the steamer, the two of them came rushing down the steps in silence; they didn't dare to make a scene. But as soon as they reached the bottom, the traveler was already on board and the sailor cast the boat off the shore. They still could have jumped into the boat, but the traveler had picked up a heavily knotted rope from the boat deck and threatened them. It was enough to hold them back.

Clairvoyance

by D. K. Broster

"YES, it's certainly a lovely place," said Mr. Alfred Pickering, the Australian wool-grower come 'home,' as he looked out through the open French window of the library of Strode Manor onto the great lawn with the lake in the distance. "Of all the houses I've seen in the last couple of months, this is the only one which in the least bears out the description sent me. I think you house agents have mistaken your job, you know; you ought to go in for writing fiction."

Mr. Simpkins (of Pottinger, Simpkins and Marrow) sniggered. "Oh, come, sir! We have to do our best for our clients."

"Well, you don't seem to have succeeded here," retorted Mr. Pickering, "attractive as the place is. I can't understand its having stood empty all this time. How long did you say it was since Mr. Strode went abroad—five years?"

"Fancy his leaving all the beautiful furniture in the house, too!" commented his wife.

"But it has all been well cared for, as you can see," replied Mr. Simpkins, looking complacently round. "As you say, madam, there's beautiful things in the house—antiques, too. Mr. Strode was a noted collector. But his best china—pots they call Bing, or Ming, or some such comic name—is lent to the Victoria and Albert Museum."

"Those, too, are the sort of things you see in museums," remarked Mr. Pickering, with his eyes upon the fan-shaped arrangement on the only wall where bookcases did not rise too high for such a display, and where the elaborate inlay of an early seventeenth-century German arque-bus shouldered the tapering length and complicated hilt of a Spanish rapier or the unfamiliar mechanism of a wheel-lock pistol.

"This is the study, I suppose," said comfortable-looking Mrs. Pickering. "But I am sure that if I tried to read in here, I should always be looking out at that beautiful view."

"Yes, madam," agreed Mr. Simpkins, towering over her in his long, light overcoat; "yes, especially when the famous rhododendrons by the lake are in bloom. And, of course, if the house was occupied the grounds would look more as they used to do—not but what the lawn is mown regularly now. But a property always appears to much better advantage when there is someone in it."

"What I can't understand," reiterated the Australian, "is why in five years there hasn't been someone in it, or why it hasn't been bought, since you say Mr. Strode would prefer to sell."

"Well, sir," responded Mr. Simpkins, with a slight tinge of constraint, "it's not everyone who requires a large place like this, all furnished. Gentlemen who would take a lease of a property of this size usually have their own furniture; still more so those who might wish to purchase it."

"Yes, I suppose that's true. But when a man comes back from the underside of the globe like me, he's glad to find a home all ready to step into. And I should have thought there might have been other chaps in the same position. Have you had nobody after it in five years?"

"Oh, several people, Mr. Pickering, several," the house agent assured him in haste. "But for some of them the Manor was too big, for others too small. There's always a something, as the saying is." He broke off suddenly. "Would you kindly excuse me for a moment, sir? There's the gardener out there wanting to speak to me, I see, before he goes home to his dinner."

"I call it charming," repeated Mr. Pickering, as the agent hurried out into the verandah and vanished. "Don't you think so, too, Polly?"

But plump little Mrs. Pickering did not seem to share his enthusiasm. "If you ask me," she said slowly, "I believe there *is* a 'something' about this place which frightens everyone away, for all it seems so bright and has been so well kept up. Just now, when I was looking out at the lake there . . ." She stopped.

"But it was you, little woman, who said you'd always be looking at it if you lived here!"

"I'm not so sure, now, that I should," responded his wife, drawing her breath in sharply. "And, Alfred, didn't you notice, when we stopped the car at that little farm outside the village and asked the way, just before we met Mr Simpkins, the girl looked almost scared? I wonder if the Manor is supposed to be haunted?"

Her husband chuckled. "The only objection to haunted houses that I've ever heard of is that you can't get servants to stay in 'em. Otherwise I should be no end pleased to have an ancestor clanking round in chains, even if it wasn't my own ancestor. If there's a Johnny of that sort here, so much the better!

"Alfred, are you really thinking of buying the place?"

"I'm inclined to, if you're agreeable, old lady. I like it fine. The house may not be as old as these fellows make out, but it's none the worse for that, and the grounds only want a little attention—almost a park, they are, too. I should like to buy it lock, stock, and barrel, furniture, books, and curios—including those queer old guns (if they are guns) and swords and things there." He surveyed the trophy of weapons for a moment. "I could put my two bushmen's spears in with them . . . Hullo, why has this sheath got no sword in it? Japanese work, by the look of it, like that figure in armour over there near you."

Mrs. Pickering was now by the door, looking down at something. "I don't think this cheap rug is worth buying!" she observed critically. "An absolutely shoddy thing—on a valuable carpet like this, too!" She stooped, turned back the rug in question, and became quite silent.

At that moment the lank form of Mr. Simpkins reappeared at the French window, and him Mr. Pickering, still examining the display of weapons, addressed over his shoulder. "I say, isn't there a sword or something missing from here?"

But the house agent did not answer because at the same instant Mrs. Pickering also said, in a voice so queer that her husband immediately turned round: "I see now why this rug was put here. But . . . what made that stain?"

Mr. Pickering came over to view the place. The representative of Pottinger, Simpkins and Marrow followed, more slowly. Colour had sprung into his cadaverous cheeks. "Well, madam, it's hard for me to answer that question, isn't it?" he asked, in a manner attempting the semi-jovial. "Not having lived in the house, you see . . . Oh, something spilt, I should say, by one of the caretakers we've had here; and, after trying to get the mark out, the woman's gone and bought that cheap rug and put it down to cover the damage. But the carpet could easily be turned round, in which case that side of it would be—"

"Yes, of course it could!" broke in Mr. Pickering cheerfully. His Polly really looked quite strange and upset. "What's come to you, my girl? Accidents will happen!"

"I want to know what the accident was!" repeated his wife, with an odd, pale persistence most unlike her.

"My dear, how can Mr. Simpkins possibly tell us? It's unfortunate there should be a stain, but I can't see that it's of any importance how it came there."

"Allow me, madam," quoth Mr Simpkins, stooping and replacing the rug. "I will instruct the present caretaker to have a try to get the mark out. I suggest that you come out into the garden now, sir, and have a look at this side of the house . . . Madam, I am afraid you are feeling indisposed; shall I fetch you some water?"

"My dear Polly, what's got you?" exclaimed her husband in alarm, putting his arm round her plump contours. "Here, I believe I have my flask with me; yes." And with one hand he pulled it out. "Sit down there, dear, on the sofa, and have a drop of this, perhaps with a little water, if Mr. Simpkins will kindly fetch some."

"No!" said Mrs. Pickering, shuddering violently. "No, I won't sit down in this room. Take me out of it quickly—no, no, no, Alfred, not through that window—that's worse, much worse! And for God's sake don't have anything to do with the house! Something dreadful has happened in this room."

And as her husband, thoroughly frightened (for she was not by nature an hysterical or fanciful woman), hurried her through the door, she burst into tears.

"Most unfortunate," said Mr. Simpkins about an hour and a half later to his partner in their office in the little county town. "Blanked unfortunate! He was all for taking it, perhaps even for buying it, the Colonial."

"I hope you didn't call him that, Simmie," replied Mr. Marrow, who in shape resembled his name-sake of the vegetable kingdom. "Dominions they are nowadays, Australians."

Mr. Simpkins took no notice. "Yes, I believe he would have bought it if that blessed wife of his hadn't gone off into hysterics in the library. Perhaps I oughtn't to have taken them in there; but if I had made any difficulty about it that would have seemed odd, too."

"What made her go into hysterics?"

"She had moved the rug. It's true that it is an unusual place for a rug to be. But God alone knows what put the suspicion into her head, because the mark don't look like that now—not to my thinking. Funny thing was that at the same moment—the very same moment, mind you—the chap himself saw that the sword was missing; said something about it, too, but I took no notice. (The sheath ought not to be on the wall at all.) And then in a minute or two he had to take her out of the room, fairly howling. Queer creatures, women, damned queer!"

Mr. Marrow, about to light a cigarette, paused. "I think, considering what you and me know about the library of the Manor, we may say that they are. And now it almost looks as if it was a case with this Mrs. Pickering, too, of—what do they call it?—the thing that caused all the trouble five years ago."

"You surely don't mean that she is what they said at the inquest that poor girl was?"

"No, no; I mean the business that started it—clair . . . what the devil is it called?—clairvoyance."

"Oh, that! But if this Mrs. Pickering had had clairvoyance she would have seen—"

"What it's a good thing for her that she didn't see," finished Mr. Marrow, achieving the lighting of his cigarette. "But, damn it all, we've lost yet another possible tenant. I suppose they must have heard something, in spite of all the trouble we took that they shouldn't speak to anyone in the village and get wind of it like the last people did."

"I don't think it was that. And yet when he had soothed her down and got her into the car—for she said she must go straight back to London—he asked me right out, there in the drive: 'Has there been a murder or a suicide taken place in that room? Now tell me the truth, as man to man.'"

"And what did you say, as man to man?"

"I told him the truth, of course. I said: 'No, no murder or suicide took place in that room, I give you my word.' So he asks: 'What did take place there, then?' looking a bit as if he had caught the horrors from his wife, though he didn't seem at all that sort. (No more did she, to do her justice.) I says: 'My dear sir, the house being Queen Anne, lots of things that we know nothing about must have happened in that library.' 'Queen Anne!' says he. 'Queen Victoria, more like! But something very unpleasant took place there, and at a guess five years ago. I shall not take the house. Send in your bill for any expenses you may have been put to over this visit.' Then he got into his car and slammed the door; and that was the last I saw of them. All the woman's fault, like the . . . the affair in the library."

"That's a bit hard," observed Mr. Marrow judicially. "It wasn't really the poor girl's fault; if anybody's, it was Strode's—at least, he was responsible. You may remember that if the medical evidence hadn't been so positive that it was impossible to hypnotise a person into doing a thing like that, he might have been sent for trial. Did these Pickerings find out that he left the very day after the inquest; just walked out of the house and has never been near it since, in all these years?"

"Not from me, you bet . . . Well, there's nothing to be done but to go on with that advertisement, 'To Americans and others', because it seems pretty hopeless to get anybody else—unless the place could be given another name. No one in England is likely to have forgotten the 'Strode Manor tragedy'."

"We might head the ad with this, which I saw used the other day, and by a London firm, I fancy: *'Situate amid inconceivable rurality'*. Not true of the Manor, exactly, but that's no matter. It's a taking expression, that's the main thing."

Mr. Simpkins did not reply. His eyes had a rapt, glassy look; an idea was being born.

"I believe," he said at last, "that if we could hook an American we should do better *not* to keep the story quiet, but to boost it to him for all it was worth. Wouldn't a hundred per cent Yank be likely to find it full of 'pep'?"

"Simmie," exclaimed Mr. Marrow, "you've hit it! We might even get more for the place . . . when we find the right oil-king!"

2

THE CLOSE-SHAVEN LAWNS were brilliantly green, the great rhododendrons in their full rosy magnificence, when the horror happened, five years before. The villagers said that the bushes had never bloomed so luxuriantly since; but then they never went into the grounds to see. They were afraid of meeting her, the delicate pale girl with *those* hands, or perhaps the little boy . . .

It was not exactly a party; Edward Strode did not like them. But Persis, his seventeen-year-old daughter, had her friend Cynthia Storrington staying with her, even as Mr. and Mrs. Strode had the elegant Mrs. Fleming stopping with them; and three girls and a couple of youths of Persis' acquaintance had come to tea and tennis. Moreover, Catherine, the youngest child—the two boys in-between were away at school—was celebrating her birthday and playing with half a dozen small companions of both sexes, under due supervision from nurses, down by the lake and its red and pink bastions of blossom. But though Mrs. Strode had earlier presided over the tea-table in the drawing-room on the other side of the house, she was now sitting with some embroidery on the sofa in the library, where were also Mrs. Fleming, in a Paris frock of extreme simplicity and expensiveness, smoking a cigarette in a long amber holder, and Edward Strode himself, with his little pointed Elizabethan beard, carefully mending a torn page in a recently acquired manuscript.

"Where ever did you get that charming design, Marian?' suddenly asked the guest, coming to the sofa and stooping over Mrs. Strode with a lazy, boneless grace. "Not from any shop, I am sure."

"No. I adapted it from a *tsuba* of Edward's."

"Mercy on us, what's a *tsuba*?"

"The guard of a Japanese sword," replied Mrs. Strode, stitching away. "He has quite a quantity of them, some with very agreeable designs indeed. I have used the best already. This one is actually from the guard of his precious Sadamune katana on the wall there, and, not being detached like the others, was a little more difficult to copy, since I would not let him take it off for me." She held up her work. "Any design on a *tsuba* must fit into its more or less circular shape, you see. These little drooping stems are rice."

"But it is exquisite!' exclaimed Mrs. Fleming. "A miracle of design—and of ingenuity. I should like to see the original. A trifle out of place on a sword-hilt, though, somehow—rice."

Edward Strode looked up. "Some hilts have plum blossoms, bamboos blown by the wind, peonies, or twisted water-weeds. I will get the sword down for you with pleasure, Erica; it is one of my proudest treasures. I have not had it long, however. The *tsuba*, as it happens, has been rather a sore point ever since Jenkinson was here a fortnight ago, for he had the impudence to say that he was not sure if it was genuine." He made a wry face.

"But the sword—"

"Oh, the sword is genuine enough, and rare, and very old; a poem in steel—a signed poem, too. It's infernal nonsense about the guard, course; still, I shall not be quite at ease until a better authority than Jenkinson has seen it."

"But, Edward," protested Mrs. Fleming, "surely you are an authority on . . . what do you call the things?"

Edward Strode smiled his infrequent smile. "There are seven hundred different specimens of these guards in the South Kensington Museum alone, for there exist about seventy different schools and sub-schools in the art of *tsuba*-making." He was bringing down the sword, scabbard and all from the wall—a long-sword, a katana, slightly curved, with the usual long pommel wrapped round and round in an open pattern with dark silk braid, which allowed the pearly incrustations of the ray-skin mount to show through its interstices. The sheath, of magnolia wood ornamented with strips of cane, was old and shabby; but had it been lavishly decorated one would not have looked at it again when the blade was out—as its owner, almost reverently, drew it out now; so mirror-bright was the steel, so perfect in line, so smooth and flawless its marvelous surface. Indeed, Mrs. Fleming, forgetting her desire to examine the guard, said, with something like a gasp: "You say this is very old—it can't be!"

"It was forged about six hundred years ago; it is dated. Sadamune, the famous swordsmith who made it, worked in the early part of the fourteenth century."

"In the thirteen hundreds! Edward, it's impossible! It might have been made yesterday! Why, the blade of that slim, pointed sword on the wall there—I happened to be examining it yesterday—which I suppose is not so old, looks far older, for it is all flecked and pitted."

"And yet that rapier is three hundred years the junior of this sword. It is a reputed Toledo blade, too. But, my dear Erica, compared with the work of the great Japanese swordsmiths, even the swords of Damascus and Toledo are, as a French authority puts it, but the efforts of children. Japanese swords are incomparably the most beautiful that the world has ever produced. Do you know that no European sword has ever possessed an edge like this, because if it had, the whole sword would be as brittle as glass (since European swords are of the same hardness all over). But here the body of the blade—the very bright part —is of softer temper to avoid the risk of breakage. I have cut through a floating scarf with this beautiful thing, and I daresay it would go with the same ease through a man's leg, bone and all—I have not tried."

"What is that kind of wavy mistiness along the edge?" asked Mrs. Fleming, bending over the weapon.

"That is the *yakiba*, the tempering, patterned so on purpose. There are thirty-two main designs of *yakiba*."

"Good heavens!"

"Now I will show you an interesting thing," said her host, well mounted on his subject. "You see where the *yakiba* comes round to the point of the blade—the *boshi*—and takes a different pattern?"

"Yes, if you can call anything so ghostly and indeterminate a pattern. I suppose you will tell me that there are several different classes of that?"

"As a matter of fact, there are. Well, this particular one is characteristic only of the smith who made this sword, Sadamune, the great Masamune's favorite pupil; and the shape represents the upper part of the head of Jizo, the god who looks after children, and who is generally represented as a young and handsome man with a beautiful smile."

"Mrs. Fleming laughed. "Alas, I can't make out anything remotely suggesting the head of any man, handsome or ugly. But I do see that the sword is a thing of beauty, cold and deadly perhaps, but exquisite. Now I must look at the guard."

"You do see the sword's beauty?" said Edward Strode eagerly. "I am glad of that. As to its coldness, there is a Japanese poem which says that a drawn sword brings a cool breeze into a house even at midsummer. Swords, you know, were formerly in Japan objects of veneration, almost of worship; the swordsmiths lived a semi-religious life, and the forging of a sword was practically a religious ceremony, requiring a ceremonial costume."

"The forging then," commented the visitor, "was hardly of a piece with that in the *Ring*—I mean when Siegfried, clad in his customary hearth-rug, bangs away at 'Nothung' on Covent Garden stage! So these are your bending rice-stalks, Marian. What workmanship! What metal is the guard made of, Edward?"

"Iron—pierced iron."

"And what are these tiny gold dragons on the hilt, under the binding?"

"Those are the *menuki*, to give a better grip," explained Mr. Strode. 'The hilt, of course, is more recent than the blade, the *tsuba* too, even if it is really of the school of Miochin, as it purports to be . . . Hallo, Persis, have your visitors gone?"

"Yes, Daddy, but only just," replied his elder daughter, appearing at the French window, and sniffing at the big creamy rose which she had plucked from the verandah. "They said they were too hot for any more tennis, lazy pigs, so we went back to the drawing-room and played the 'willing' game—you know. Oh, and Daddy," she stepped into the room, "such an interesting thing happened. You know how you blindfold a person and put your hands on their shoulders, two of you, and 'will' them to do something or other. "Yes," as her father frowned impatiently, "I know you think it silly, but listen! Cynthia said she was ready to be "willed"; so we blind-folded her and told her to make her mind a blank, and we settled that she should go to the little table with the snuff-boxes and vinaigrettes, and pick out the china snuff-box which has that darling little landscape, and take it over and put it in a particular place on the mantelpiece. Well, after we had willed a bit she started off, slowly, and went to the table with us—it was Joan and I—and picked out the box from the others all right—"

"I detest this playing with the fringes of a serious subject like hypnotism," growled Mr. Strode.

"Yes, I know, darling, but listen! Directly Cynthia got the snuff-box into her hands she began to feel it all over in a curious way; then, instead of taking it to the mantelpiece, she suddenly sat down and held the snuff-box right, and began to talk very fast; we could not make out much of what she was saying, and, in fact, it hardly sounded like her voice. Presently the tears began to run down her face, and she seemed so unhappy that we took the snuff-box away from her, and unbandaged her eyes; and after a bit she woke up and was just the same as usual . . . Daddy, I shan't stay to be looked at like that. Smell this, and you'll feel better!" She thrust the great rose into her father's face, laughed, and sped out again by the way she had come.

"That's rather a curious thing, Edward," remarked Mrs. Strode after a moment, laying down her embroidery. "Cynthia could not have known the story of the last owner of the porcelain snuff-box."

"The girl is apparently a sensitive," replied her husband, sliding the Japanese sword carefully back into its sheath . . . "She's what is commonly called clairvoyant—though to my thinking clairvoyance can nearly always be explained by thought transference from the mind of some other person present."

"But not in this case," said Mrs. Strode quietly. "Persis knows nod about that little box."

"Cynthia's tears were justified, then?" inquired Mrs. Fleming.

"The last owner of the porcelain snuff-box was certainly unhappy," replied Mrs Strode. "But only Edward and I know that."

"Then the girl is undoubtedly a sensitive!" exclaimed Mrs. Fleming. "It seems to me a gift that should be cultivated; it would be invaluable to a collector, for instance . . . Why, of course, Edward, here is a splendid chance of getting some light on the problem of your *tsuba*! Have Cynthia in and see what she says!"

"I am afraid I should not attach much weight to it. I am skeptical about clairvoyance, for the reason I have mentioned."

"Yet you admit that the girl must be a sensitive. Test her!"

"Another time," said Mr. Strode, "Have you finished looking at the *tsuba*, Erica?"

"But Cynthia is leaving tomorrow, Edward," his wife reminded him, as she selected a fresh thread of silk. "By the morning train, in fact, directly after breakfast."

"So you see that there is no time like the present," urged Mrs. Fleming with a laugh. "You could try her on something else first. Robert" (she was referring to her husband) "would be so pleased, poor jealous darling, to hear that your Mino da Fiesole Virgin and Child, for instance, was only 'of the school'."

"I don't imagine," said Edward Strode dryly, "that, however jealous Fleming is, he would be satisfied with such an ascription on the authority of an ignorant girl of seventeen. But the manifestation is interesting, none the less."

"Then for heaven's sake let us go and see it!" cried Mrs. Fleming. "Perhaps Cynthia is even now describing the past occupants of those William and Mary chairs in the drawing-room!"

"You forget, there is only Persis with her now," remarked Mrs. Strode. "The game is over."

"And in any case, I should not have joined in that childishness, observed her husband. "If I made such an experiment at all it would be quietly in here. But of course it is arrant nonsense to imagine that the child could tell one anything of value on a disputed point—anything about the maker of this *tsuba*, for instance."

"One Japanese looking much like another Japanese, even to a clairvoyant," suggested Mrs. Fleming. "On the other hand, suppose the *tsuba* was turned out in Birmingham—don't look so outraged, Edward, I'm sure it wasn't. But do have Cynthia in and see what happens! Marian, do make him!"

Mrs. Strode put down her work. "I will go and ask her to come in here if you are so set on it, Erica. Shall I, Edward?"

Half reluctantly, her husband nodded, and she left the room.

"This should be most interesting," said Mrs. Fleming, laying aside her cigarette-holder. Taking up a strip of old brocade from the back of the sofa, she spread its faded silver gilt and roses over the whole length of the sheathed *katana*, still upon the table, leaving only the guard exposed. "You know how to start her off, Edward—since it seems that is the method to start her? I have played at it, too . . . But I was forgetting," she added on a different note, "I was quite forgetting that you know something of hypnotism, as of most things; so she ought to respond very readily if you 'will' her to see a Japanese of the proper period working at those charming ears of rice!"

The door opened.

"Here's Cynthia, ready to oblige," announced Persis. "What can she do for you, Daddy?"

Her father fingered his little pointed beard. "My dear," said Mrs. Fleming, coming forward, "it is really I who want you to—oh no, I must not tell you exactly what. But we hear that you were so clever about . . . something in the drawing-room."

"Was I?" asked Cynthia Storrington, opening wider her innocent, dreamy-looking eyes. She was a girl for whom the word 'ethereal' might have been especially minted, a tall slip of a girl with ash-blonde hair and very delicate features, wearing a green dress the color of an early beech-leaf.

Mrs. Strode reappeared. "There is something on the table here, Cynthia, that my husband wants to make an experiment about, if you will help him."

"But how can I," asked the girl. She glanced shyly at Mr. Strode. "Oh no, I'd rather not, I think. It was only a game, you know, just now in the drawing-room."

"And I don't consider it any more than a game, Cynthia," said her host quickly. "And if you would really rather not—"

"Oh, Cynthia, do!" pleaded Mrs. Fleming.

"Cynthia, don't be a goat!" admonished Persis more bluntly and perhaps more efficaciously. And she added in an audible whisper, as she went nearer to her friend: "You can make up what you jolly well please!"

"But I don't make up!" protested Cynthia, wrinkling her white forehead. "I don't know what I say!"

"Or do, either? Didn't you know you were crying?"

Cynthia turned crimson. "Don't torment her, Persis!" said that damsel's mother. "My dear Cynthia, take no notice of her, or of anybody else; go back to the drawing-room!"

But Edward Strode had his eyes fixed upon the girl. Perhaps it was the first time that he had ever been quite aware of her particular quality, though it was not her first visit to the Manor. And Cynthia, supersensitive as she evidently was, seemed to be conscious of something unusual in his gaze. She looked at him, then away. "I will try if you like, Mr. Strode."

"Thank you," said he briefly; and Mrs. Fleming added: "That is very sporting of you, Cynthia." Then Persis produced a silk handkerchief of her elder brother's which had evidently served the same purpose previously, and tied it over the dreamy eyes.

"Who is going to do it?" she asked, knotting the ends. "You and I, Daddy?'

"No, not you, because you do not know what the problem is. Mrs. Fleming, who does, will assist in this . . . game of Blind Man's Buff." It was plain that he was ill at ease, ashamed, almost, at taking part, to please his old friend, in what he considered a childish performance.

The two laid their hands lightly on the girl's slim shoulders, and for a few minutes there was complete silence in the room itself. But from without floated in the cries and laughter of the children chasing each other about the rhododendrons, away by the lake, and the sleepy, liquid notes of distant wood-pigeons. Cynthia in her leaf-green frock had stood at first like an image; then, all at once, but still with an automaton-like stiffness, she, and the couple with her, began to move towards the library table. Mrs. Strode and Persis watched them. A little pressure easily directs a blindfolded and susceptible young thing, thought Mrs. Strode skeptically; she had resumed her seat on the sofa and her embroidery.

As she made this reflection there came a knock at the door—for Mr. Strode's sanctuary was never entered without permission. Persis darted out.

She returned. "Bother!" she said in a low voice to her mother. "It's Major Whittingham, come about a license or something. He wants to see Daddy most particularly, Morton says, and can't wait. He wouldn't keep him more than a couple of minutes. He's in the drawing-room."

Edward Strode heard. "Then I am afraid I must go to him. We had, however, hardly begun." He removed his hands. "My dear Cynthia, a thousand apologies! If you can spare the time to stay here we can resume when I return; I shall not be long."

"Shall I take off the handkerchief?" asked the disappointed Mrs. Fleming as their host left the room; and without waiting for an answer she untied it. "There, sit down, Cynthia; I don't expect Mr. Strode will be more than a few minutes."

Still as if she were in one piece Cynthia obeyed, seating herself in the chair drawn up to the table; and almost immediately one long, slender hand began to search over the table's surface. The other she had put up to her eyes. It occurred to Mrs. Fleming that the girl was further "gone" than she had thought, and that perhaps it was not altogether good to have called her back so abruptly.

"I know," said Cynthia suddenly, in a slightly unusual voice, "what you want me to touch. It is here somewhere." She brought down her other hand, and that, too, began to pass over the nearer portion of the table, sweeping about like a blind person's. Together they reached, one the shrouded and sheathed blade, the other the shrouded pommel of the Japanese sword.

"Cynthia, what are you keeping your eyes shut for?" asked Mrs.

Strode sharply, leaning forward from the sofa. "Open them, child!"

But Cynthia's eyes were still shut when her left hand clutched the sword through the strip of brocade; still shut when with a couple of imperious gestures she first flung off the strip and then, somewhat to the consternation of the two ladies, drew off the sheath of the katana and threw that, too, upon the floor. The long, keen blade gleamed naked on the library table.

"You'll cut yourself," remonstrated Mrs. Fleming almost nervously. "And it isn't the blade that we want to know about . . . Whatever is the girl playing at?"

For while the fingers of Cynthia's right hand were clutching the braided ray-skin of the pommel, the fingers of the left felt along the blade, leaving little patches on the unsullied steel.

"You'll catch it for doing that!" muttered Persis, who knew that no ungloved hand must ever touch that sacred surface.

"Sadamune made it," said Cynthia in a hoarse whisper. "He never made a better blade. My great-great-grandfather carried it in a sheath of inlaid iron; my grandfather had a scabbard of gold lacquer made for it, and I—"

She broke off and opened her eyes. They had changed color and character alike; bright and fierce, they were staring out of the window in front of her, and her mouth, the young, fresh mouth of seventeen, was set in a thin, cruel line.

Mrs. Strode was already off the sofa. "Cynthia," she said in a tone of authority, "put down that sword at once!"

Cynthia had not in truth taken it up; it still lay on the table, though the pommel was in her grip. But instead of obeying she laughed, and broke into a run of meaningless syllables, in which the word *wakizasbi* kept recurring. Mrs. Strode, if no one else, recognized the Japanese name for the lesser sword which always accompanied the *katana* in a *dabnio's* sash.

"Persis," said Mrs. Fleming breathlessly, "go for your father quickly! She—this must be stopped!"

"Oh, Cynthia, don't be a goat!" adjured Persis, for the second and last time; and with the words laid a rather timid hand on her friend's shoulder from behind.

And at that Cynthia jumped up, brandishing the *katana* as though it were of straw, her eyes, which were not her eyes anymore, blazing with an unholy rapture, and the strange language still hissing from her altered mouth.

"Daddy, Daddy!" screamed Persis, hurling herself through the doorway, "Daddy, come at once . . . *Daddy!*"

"She's gone crazy," said Mrs. Strode quickly. "We must get the sword away from her! Catch her arm, Erica!"

"*I* shall make a sheath for it of my enemies!" sang Cynthia, reverting all at once to English. She had backed to the edge of the open French window, dragging with her Mrs. Fleming, who, unable to get hold of her right arm, had seized the left. On the threshold Cynthia flung her off, and as she stumbled brought down that flashing miracle of sharpness. It did not need a man's arm behind it. Catching Mrs. Fleming between neck and shoulder, going with joy through the soft blue Doucet gown and the chalcedony necklace which matched it, the incomparable edge sliced through the artery and half the neck. Mrs. Fleming fell outside in the verandah, screaming; and there, in a very short time, died.

For one instant Mrs. Strode had retreated towards the sofa. She might, if she had been very quick, have got unharmed from the room—for she had forgotten the children at the far end of the lawn—but she was by nature a brave woman. Catching up in a bunch the heavy bear-skin rug at her feet she came on again, intending to throw it over that terrible young figure by the window, now whirling the long *katana* about in all directions and chanting unintelligibilities at the top of its voice. "Edward will be here in a moment," Marian Strode was telling herself, "Edward and no doubt Major Whittingham, too. If I can just get this over her head . . . or over the sword even . . . O God, if only Erica were not screaming like that! . . ."

But bear-skins were nothing to the Sadamune blade. It flashed once; hair, pelt, and mounting parted like butter, and the head of Jizo bit deep into the top of Mrs. Strode's left arm. She dropped the rug, and this time made a rush for the door. The sword instantly pursued her. But she was saved by the figure in Japanese armor standing in the corner, for even as she sank down, almost against the door-panels, she heard Cynthia striking madly at the grinning mask under the helmet, and the steel clattering on the lacquered body-plates. That, too, ceased, as she went into darkness . . . Two minutes more, and her husband, bursting in, had caught her up in his arms, while out under the pale roses of the verandah Major Whittingham, as pale as they, was just realizing that it was of no avail to linger over what lay there. And where was the girl?

Cynthia was gone—to worse. The children by the rhododendrons, thinking it a game, had run to meet her. But Jizo, the protector of children, killed only one outright, and he a rather uninteresting little boy.

The rhododendrons saved the rest, even the maimed. She could not easily get in among those flowering fastnesses, or did not trouble to attempt it, slashing at their heads of bloom instead. So the Sadamune blade was stained with green as well before consciousness of what she had done came to the girl . . . if it ever came. She may have jumped from the diving-board still in the full frenzy of whatever centuries-old blood-lust the touch of the sword had communicated to her, or she may have awakened. One of the children's nurses, herself injured, was the only witness of the end. The young Death gave a cry which might have been either a laugh or a shriek, then, holding the wet *katana* high above her head, jumped straight off the spring-board into the lake. The nurse, before she herself fainted among the rhododendron stems, saw that she went down like a stone.

When the slayer was found she might have been Ophelia. There were no stains on the green dress and her hands were empty and clean. The poem in steel lies quiet at the bottom of the lake, with its lovely luster tarnished and water-weeds growing through the tracery of the disputed *tsuba*. Perhaps when the right oil-king is found to take Strode Manor he will have it retrieved, for it is very valuable.

Feathers

by Jonathan Eeds

THE returning students ruined a perfectly lovely daydream about spearfishing. The bus driver stiffened his spine with resolve and dutifully squared his official unified-district cap. The children streamed in like remnants of his dream: a school of baby barracuda, darting, shoving, feisty, playful. A husky boy with a sloppy manner teased the driver with his souvenir bird-toy, then swung into his seat with a resounding *womp*. The driver managed a half-smile, pretending to find the children charming, then leaned over the steering wheel and gazed straight down the gravel drive that led to the open road. He waited for the teacher to wrap things up in the parking lot. Once Ms. Branwen got onboard she would take control of the riot-in-progress and count heads. Calm would be restored.

Standing beside the bus' folding doors, Davis proudly looked on as the last child boarded. His smile was wide and easy. He shook Ms. Branwen's chalk-dry hand and accepted a neat bundle of papers wrapped in the thickest rubber band he had ever seen. These were the children's artistic impressions of their visit to the *Anadarko Raptor Center*. He was pleasantly surprised with himself for entirely enjoying the past hour with the kids. He shared his beaming expression with Ella, but she was having none of it. She frowned and looked at her boots.

The bus rumbled away, dipping into the shady canopy of Doug-firs and big-leaf maples. The maple leaves, big as catcher's mitts, held a ghostly sheen of gravel dust.

Ella was still scowling as they climbed the gentle slope to the gift shop. Davis had grown a little weary of Ella's "poetic" moods and so decided to egg her on just for fun.

"Boy that was great," he said. "Don't you think? The kids were so enthusiastic. You can sign me up for the next field trip."

"Count on it," she said. "I don't have time for tours."

"Ah, the kids are so sweet. How else can we gen-up new funding?"

"From school kids?" she said incredulously.

"From their *parents*. Some of them are sure to bring their parents back this weekend. Better have the giftshop stocked up."

Ella conceded this with a grunt, then said, "What are those?"

"I had the kids draw their favorite bird. Should I hang them up?"

"Sure. Let's have a look first."

Davis handed over the stack. Ella undid the rubber band and slipped into over her forearm. Most of the drawings were of the Northern Pygmy Owl (*Glaucidium gnoma*). Everyone one loved the pygmy owl. It was as small as a mouse but had eyes the size of tea saucers. One drawing showed Davis' pudgy form lecturing a row of one-dimensional stick-kids. A leering vulture perched on his padded arm.

"I think that's supposed to be a red-tailed hawk," Davis said as he stood next to her. The top of Davis' nut-brown dome barely topped Ella's rounded shoulder. "Pretty good likeness of me, though. Handsome devil."

Ella extracted a drawing that looked as if it had been tortured by little grubby hands. "Wow," she said. It was more of an exhalation than a comment. Without saying another word she stuffed the remaining stack back into Davis' hands and marched past the owl-pens. Hopping every other step she entered her office next to the gift shop. Her shoulder clipped the rack of "The Little Red Owl" books and sent it spinning. A flock of Little Red Owls flew in frantic circles under the eaves. Davis followed Ella inside and found her flattening the drawing on her desktop. She nudged her cell phone and coffee cup aside, then moved them back in to kitty-corner the curling paper.

She sat down, propped her elbows on the blotter and gazed over the drawing as if she was studying an ancient and mysterious parchment. She looked at the hovering Davis, her deep scowl eased by curiosity.

"Look at this. What do you see?"

He leaned in: "A crow. We don't have any crows in recovery. Maybe they saw one picking through the dumpster."

"Notice anything particularly interesting about this crow?"

"Well . . . it's mangy . . . it looks really sad . . . and . . . it's speaking." Davis pointed at the squiggly speech coming out of the bird's beak.

"'Me hate all,'" Ella read aloud. "What do you think it means?"

"Maybe the kid's got emotional problems," Davis shrugged. "Are you concerned about little, umm, Mickey's welfare?"

"You know me better than that," Ella chided. "Take a closer look. See there? The bird's tongue? It's forked."

"A devil's tongue," Davis observed. "The kid definitely has issues."

"I think this bird's real, but Mickey didn't see it here."

Ella jerked her jean-jacket off the back of her desk chair and threw it on. She made sure her car keys were in the right-hand pocket, then snatched her cell phone and buried into the other pocket.

"Ella . . . what's going on—?"

Ella silently stared at him for a moment, as if struggling whether to share her thoughts. "Not only is that bird real," she said at last, "it's my bird. My bird, Davis! And I want it back."

~§~

Ella drove to the Mt. Crane Elementary School in an excited state. She had never been there before and so had to punch its location into the nav-aid app on her cell phone. As soon as she locked the location she felt foolish using it for a three-mile trip.

She swung into the school parking lot and felt a flutter of despair when she saw that the lot was nearly empty. She exited her Mini, unfolding like a origami stork onto the clean asphalt, and stood tall and lanky in front of the visitors sign. Her jet black hair ruffled in the mellow spring breeze. The mournful tinkling of tetherball chains drifted in from the playground.

Ella was about to enter the front office when she spotted Ms. Branwen coming down the breezeway. She pulled a trolley full of folders, colorful binders, and disheveled stacks of loose papers. A glossy red purse sat on top of the plastic crate and served as a paperweight.

"Ms. Branwen," Ella called.

Ms. Branwen was startled by Ella's sudden appearance, but as soon as she recognized her she smiled. "Did we leave something behind?"

"Yeah—a kid," Ella said straight-faced, but when she heard the gasp of horror she quickly course corrected: "Sorry, sorry. Bad joke."

Ms. Branwen smiled in relief. "You know that happened to me once."

Ella continued in a more conciliatory tone. "Sorry I touched a nerve. I hope your class had a nice visit. Thanks for all the beautiful drawings."

"The children had a great time," she said. "I had no idea all that was up there, hidden in the woods. It's like a miniature game reserve."

"Not enough people know about us. That's the problem. We're always scraping for funds."

Ms. Branwen thought it odd that Ella had made a special trip just to hit her up for a donation. "I put five dollars in the box," she said flatly.

"Oh, thanks for that, but that's not why I'm here. It's about Mickey."

"Mickey? . . . *What'd* he do?"

"Nothing. Don't worry. It's about his drawing. It's very unusual. I was hoping to speak to him about it?"

"I see some pretty strange drawings," she said. "What'd it show?"

"Just a crow, but there's a weird caption: 'Me hate all.'"

"Ah, *that* crow," Ms. Branwen said. "He's always drawing that bird. A talking bird, yeah?—but that's the first time I heard that one. I can see why you were alarmed by it."

"You're not concerned about the boy?" Ella said, trying to coax more information out of her. "Maybe something going on at home?"

"No way. Mickey comes from a home straight out of a fifties sitcom. Like I said, kids draw some *pretty weird* things. Mickey's talking bird is nothing compared to what I've seen—popping heads, gun-spray, bloody knives . . . All the violent stuff gets reported to Child Services Division."

"Good to know," Ella said. "I just had to ask. Honestly, I'm more interested in the drawing for *scientific* reasons."

"Oh?"

"Is it possible to talk to Mickey about his drawing?"

"You're kidding."

"I'm serious. Just a couple of questions."

"Well, you can come back on Monday at 2PM. It chaos then because the buses are all loading, but I can hold Mickey back long enough for you to talk to him."

"I meant now. Can I talk to him now?"

"Now you're really pulling my leg."

"I'm completely serious. Can you call his mom, or something?"

"What's the big hurry?" Ms. Branwen scoffed, and then added in a playful tone: "It's the *weekend—yay.*"

Ella quickly racked her brain for all the possible scenarios that would compel this skeptical teacher to help her.

"Did you look at the drawing?" Ella said.

"I might have glanced at it. Why?"

No way she looked at it, Ella concluded. She immediately felt more at ease with the lie she was about to tell.

"Then you may not have noticed how mangy the bird is. It's infected with a parasite. Mickey accurately drew a *Petronius bacillus*–a rare louse that carries a nasty germ. You said Mickey draws the bird all the time?"

"Yes—well, for the last month anyway. Before that he drew Pikachu."

"Does he actually have this bird, you think? Has he ever mentioned that he has a bird?"

"Not that I recall."

"I don't think we can wait on this. The boy may be in danger."

"Oh dear."

"Can you call the mom, ask if I can come to the house? . . . I'll do anything for the school if you help me. Donate some books, give some of my time. This is really important."

"Anything?" Ms. Branwen chimed.

Ella nodded.

"Well then, can you bring a bald eagle to our next school assembly?" she proposed. "It's our school mascot."

~§~

Ms. Branwen arranged for the visit over the phone. She said it was best if she tagged along. Ella was happy to have her serve as a social shield. As a life-long loner, Ella knew how to manipulate people but not how to connect with them well enough to resolve delicate issues. She got through life by way of her aggressive but charmless intellect.

Mickey's mom, Mrs. Mullins, conducted a two-minute screening of Ella's intentions before letting the two ladies into the living room. Ella, not a time-waster by any means, held Mickey's drawing rather close to Mrs. Mullins face and said: "Is this bird real?"

"Mickey rescued a crow with a broken wing. He likes drawing it."

"Where'd he find it?"

"In the park. It was hurt and the other crows were pecking at it. They would have pecked it to death if Mickey hadn't chased them away with his baseball bat."

"The bird may be diseased," Ms. Branwen broke in. "It could be infectious."

"There's nothing wrong with that bird," Mrs. Mullins countered. "Mickey nursed it back to health. He loves that bird."

"You should be proud of Mickey," Ella said. "The raptor center receives all kinds of wounded birds, but nobody ever cares enough about the crows to bring them in. People think they're vermin."

Ella attempted to adorn her comment with a sympathetic look, but her cold obsidian eyes betrayed the effort. Mrs. Mullins flinched and took a half-step back.

"I *am* proud of him," she affirmed. "It's the first time he's shown any real responsibility. It's just a dumb bird, though. I don't much like it."

"They're smarter than dogs, you know. They use tools, recognize faces . . . How old is Mickey?"

"Seven and a half."

"Um, great age. Some scientists believe that a crow's intelligence is equal to that of a seven-year old child. It's a generally held belief that a crow can be taught to talk. Not mimic, converse intelligently. Does Mickey talk to his crow?"

"Talk? Er—"

Ella nodded at a puffy gray cat that was imperiously perched on a tasseled chair cushion.

"Lovely cat. Do you talk to it?"

"Of course . . . *don't I, Dollie?*" The feline sphinx narrowed its eyes and drew back its ears so that they looked like velvet horns. "—I swear she can read my mind."

"A proper grimalkin, then?" Ella said. "Your familiar."

"A wha—?" Mrs. Mullins looked to Ms. Branwen for help.

"Ella just wants to make sure Mickey's bird is healthy," Ms. Branwen said. "Can we see Mickey, *please*?"

"I have to get dinner started."

"Me too. We won't take long—will we, Ella?"

Ella nodded.

"He's in his room playing a game."

Mickey's room was cluttered but clean. His bed was tightly made, almost in military fashion. He had a few books strewn about, and he was carelessly sitting crossed-leg on a few of them as he played his computer game. His club-wielding avatar was collecting coins along a rainbow bridge and lopping off any troll-heads popping out of the pavers.

Ella's attention was drawn to the walls, where several of Mickey's crow drawings were hung. *Crow on a branch. Crow on the roof. Crow swimming in an enormous birdbath.* In each the crow was saying something. None of the bird-talk made sense to Ella.

Mickey had barely looked up from his game when his door swung open and didn't pay any attention as the adults jabbered overhead.

"Mickey, pause the game," Mrs. Mullins shouted into his ear. "Big surprise! Ms. Branwen is here to see you, and she brought a friend from the raptor center."

"Hi, Ms. Branwen," Mickey beamed at them with a gap-tooth smile.

"Did you have fun at the raptor center?" Ms. Branwen said.

"Yeah! Mom, can we go back there?"

Mrs. Mullins squeezed out a smile and said, "Sure, a family trip."

"I don't want Dora to come," Mickey said, pouting a little. "Just you, me and Dad. Ok, Mom?"

"I like your drawing," Ella said and held it up, then motioned toward the walls. "You have a lot of nice bird pictures."

"That's La-la, my bird."

"La-la? How funny. My name's Ella. Our names rhyme."

Mickey was unimpressed by this.

"You saved La-la didn't you? You saved her from the other mean crows."

"They were going to murder her."

"Wow! What a hero! Do you want to hear something else funny? When crows get together—all together, like they did in the park that day, they call it 'a murder of crows.' Isn't that funny?"

Mickey gave Ella a dull, quizzical look. His fingers twitched on the controls. He badly wanted to return to his game.

"Can you show me La-la?"

Ella was crouching down now, her bended knee barely grazing Mickey's. She did her best to lock on his flittering eyes. Her closeness made him squirm.

"That won't be possible right now," Mrs. Mullins asserted.

Ella's head whipped back in time to see Mrs. Mullins calm her quivering lower lip. "Not possible? Why not? The bird may be diseased."

"I need to consult with my husband," she said, her voice warbly yet protective. "It's a father and son project."

"Consult? You're not buying a car. I just want to see the bird."

"Are you always this rude?" Mrs. Mullins said, visibly shaken but standing her ground.

Ella let out a deep sigh and rose to her feet. "Forgive me. Long day."

"We should be going," Ms. Branwen said, tugging on Ella's sleeve.

Ella agreed but then turned to Mickey. "I really do you like your drawings. Can I have some of them?"

"Sure."

"I'll hang them up at the raptor center. You can see them when you come for a visit. You and your family can visit for free."

That put a big smile on Mickey's face. All was well now so Ms. Branwen and Mrs. Mullins filed out of the room. Ella was at the tail-end of the exodus and used her strategic positioning to abruptly close the door without leaving the room. She turned and pressed her back against the door. Mickey thought this was strange but started playing his game anyway.

"Mickey, do you talk to La-la?"

Mickey nodded without stopping his game. The magic coins rang like little bells.

" . . . and does La-la talk back to you? 'Me hate all.' Did she say that?"

Mickey looked up and slowly nodded in the affirmative.

"Thank you for saving her, Mickey, but La-la belongs to me and I want her back."

"She loves me. She told me so."

"I have some good things to trade." She looked around Mickey's room. "You have quite a collection of stuffed animals. Did you see all the stuffies in the raptor center gift shop? Owls, eagles, even penguins. You can have anything you like from the gift shop. Wouldn't that be a fair trade?"

"But she loves me."

"You fixed her wing. Such a kind, grown-up act, but she really can't love you—not really. Birds have different feelings than us. They're cold, calculating. What about this: what was your favorite bird at the raptor center?"

"The midget owl," he said with a thumbs-up and a cockeyed smile.

"Of course it was. Everyone loves the pygmy owl. Maybe we can work something out."

"Yeah!" Mickey pumped his fist in the air but Ella couldn't tell if it was a reaction to her offer or to some triumph in his game.

"We got a deal, Mickey?"

"Sure, Ms. Ella, but you got it backwards."

"What'd I get backwards, dear?"

"What she said. La-la didn't say, "Me hate all.'

"No?"

"She said, 'All hate me.' You got it backwards."

~§~

The two ladies were well into living room before realizing that Ella was not trailing behind them. Mrs. Mullins hooked round Ms. Branwen and furiously started back down the hallway, but Ella emerged from Mickey's room and quietly closed his door.

"Sorry about that," she said. "I stumbled over one of mickey's toys on the way out and jammed the door closed. I had trouble with the child-proof guard on the doorknob. Can you believe it?"

"Thanks for your time, Mrs. Mullins," Ms. Branwen said, feeling the urgent need to defuse tempers. "Ella, can you drive me back to my car now?"

"Yeah, let's go. Sorry for my manners, Mrs. Mullins. I can be abrupt. Tough upbringing . . . There is one thing, though."

"What now?" she said impatiently.

"Are you aware that crows are considered to be migratory birds?"

"So."

"Migratory birds are protected by the federal statutes. It's against the law to kill or capture a migratory bird. They play a critical role in our ecosphere. It's a federal crime, in fact. There's a hefty fine. You're in violation of federal law by keeping that bird."

"Oh, dear."

"As a sworn officer of the state I can't ignore the circumstances for very long, so be sure to *consult* with your husband tonight."

Mrs. Mullins nodded, her will defeated at last.

~§~

Ms. Branwen slammed the door to Ella's car with a curt goodbye. Her sensible heels clicked on the pavement as she strode across the school parking lot. The grounds were empty, the light dwindling. When she spied the dull blue silhouette of her Toyota Corolla she mumbled a prayer never to see Ella again, eagle or no eagle.

As Ella drove away and headed for home she smirked to herself in the rearview mirror. She was starting to feel better about how things were turning out, but the shrill chirp of her cell phone disrupted her good humor. She liked to use her phone for everything *except* talking.

"What do you want, Davis?" she said.

"Hello to you too," Davis said. "Where are you?"

"On my way home. Why?"

"You need to turn your bumper round and come back to the center."

"Why?"

"I got a guy here you're going to want to talk to."

"Jesus, Davis—Why?"

"Just come back, Ella. Come back."

~§~

The horizon was a brooding smear of violet and vermilion. A penetrating chill settled into the earth as darkness clawed over the eastern ridge . Wind-tossed grass and grain lay still after a restless day.

Ella sped into the parking lot, her headlights sweeping across the fir-boughs, her snarling tires slinging loose gravel against Davis's Bronco. The lights were on inside her office and she could see two broad-shouldered shadows huddled around the computer. Two hulking males bullshitting over cups of coffee.

As soon as she slammed her car door the chicken farmer's dogs began barking and leaping onto the chain-link fence. The dogs were kenneled at the back of the farmhouse that squatted on the hilltop. As far as Ella knew, the house had been there forever, and it was a major nuisance to everything she was trying to accomplish at the raptor center. The dogs snarled and snapped at her scent, almost choking on their hatred. It was the same reaction whenever they caught a whiff of Ella. Inexplicably, they hated her, and her only, for they were mildly indifferent to all others who crossed the raptor center grounds. Ella didn't even know the old farmer's name but she had had many terse conversations with him about his dogs. They had the birds on edge, she'd complain, and whenever they bark or howl the birds in the uppermost pens go into a frenzy. I'll try to quiet them, he'd say in a terse, gravelly voice, and then step back into a veil of smoky shadows and shut the door.

Ella stormed up the hill and lobbed a handful of heavy stones over the farmer's fence. "Shut your damned dogs up!" She shouted as her volley sailed into their pen and battered the junk scattered there. One clanked against an abandoned wash machine and another cracked the window of a collapsing tool shed. She could see the drunken silhouette of the old man stagger out of his easy chair and then weakly plop down again, defeated by gravity. Ella threw one more stone that sent the chickens into a raucous whirlwind of panic. Worried the guy might come out with his shotgun, Ella clomped back through damp clumps of grass and unfurling bracken, plunging at last into the halo of the compound lights with jarring strides.

She stormed into the office, her shoulders tense and her eyes locked on her own fury.

"Dogs again?" David said, looking up from the computer screen.

"They'll tear that old bastard to pieces one day," Ella said as she ripped off her jacket. "It'll be sweet justice."

"You and those dogs," Davis said and chuckled hoarsely. "Pull up a chair Ella. We've got a guest. This is Bill Rollins. Bill, Ella."

They shook hands. Bill's tortoise-shell callouses gave his hand the feel of a muscular claw, but his smile was frank, his eyes honest.

"What's up guys?" Ella said and crossed her arms.

"I wasn't sure where else to go," Bill said. "The county's not helping. My hands are tied by the state . . . and the feds—*Jeez*!"

"And . . . ?"

"I'm a cattle rancher. My cows graze on a hundred acres south of here. A lot of it's rough terrain—steep hills ending in a box canyon. Oak trees, scrub. The point is that I can't just look out my window and see how things are doing. By the time I made the rounds I already had two cows mutilated, and a half-dozen sheep. Something's killing them. It's as if their precious parts—their eyes, tongue, kidneys—had been removed by a surgeon. No coyote or cougar does that."

"Cattle mutilation?" Ella said, locking her folded arms even tighter. "So, based upon your suspenseful insinuations I am guessing that you are about to tell me that a *UFO did this*?"

"Why would I come to the raptor center about a *U*—"

"As a matter of fact," Davis broke in, "these are *identified* flying objects: *Coragyps atratus*."

Davis turned his computer screen so that Ella could see a winged demon perched on a bloodied lamb.

"A Black vulture," Ella said. "That's impossible. We're way out of their range—two thousand miles out, and two mountain ranges. You're looking at a stock photo taken in Arkansas."

"I saw a buzzard just like this one in my pasture," Bill insisted.

"It must have been a Turkey vulture. The Black vulture is migratory but rarely leaves its range in the southeast. In recent years they have been spotted at Cartel massacres along the border, but not in California and certainly not Oregon."

"Evil drawn to evil," Davis said.

"These aren't evil birds. They're following their instincts."

"Evil instincts," Davis said. "We've been reading about them."

"Look Ella," Bill said, his voice quietly desperate. "I know what a turkey vulture looks like. My guy's got a black head, not red. This picture is exactly what I saw."

"Ok, ok, sorry . . . assuming that you are correct . . . we have some American black vultures that have strayed *way* off track . . . what kind of assistance can we provide?"

"I'd like you to kill them, but I know you can't do that. I can't even do it because they're protected by law, although I can't understand why. I want you to help me collect enough evidence of the damage so that I can go to the state with it. An outsider's expert opinion. The Lieutenant Governor's office said they'd try to help if I can give them something more to act on."

"Honestly, Bill," Ella shrugged, "nobody's going to care much if you kill a couple of buzzards. Why get big government involved?"

"How long have you lived in Anadarko, Ella? The Governor wants to outlaw my diesel tractor. The County Commissioner wants to regulate and tax water rights that have been in my family for generations. And the Mayor? Well, she's very concerned about my cow farts . . ."

"Ella, we can go to Bill's ranch and take photos. Maybe we can tranq one of them, verify that they are Black vultures. Do the laws protect migratory birds that have strayed outside their normal range?"

"Who knows?"

"Can you help?" Bill said, his crumpled cap in hand.

"It would be interesting to capture one and put a tracker on it. Can you meet me and Davis here in the morning and take us out to your place?"

"You got it. What time?"

"At the crack of dawn . . . say, 9 am?"

~§~

Davis was waiting in his chugging Ford Bronco when Ella wound her Mini up the raptor center drive. The only other car in the lot belonged to the Maisey twins. Other than Davis, they were Ella's most reliable volunteers, although they preferred to run the gift shop to caring for the birds. Ella thought they were an odd pair but Davis did whatever they asked. All the repairs, feeding, and cleaning fell to Davis.

Ella climbed aboard the Bronco and said, "No Bill?"

"Something came up. He gave me directions to his ranch, though. Here's a sketch of his property with the best observation points marked."

"Can we stop for coffee?"

"Totally out of the way." Davis chopped his hand in a direction away from town.

"Swing her around, Big D. I'm not doing this without coffee."

"As you wish, buttercup," Davis said, swinging his Bronco left instead of right.

Ella unzipped the canvass case that held the unassembled pieces of her tranquilizer. She held up a vial filled with amber-colored animal tranq, her eyes lingering on it as if studying the individual molecules held within. She tilted the casing a couple of times before laying it back in the case's plastic chamber. The dart consisted of four parts: the liquid chamber that had to be filled with the sleep-inducing serum, a screw-on needle, a pressure chamber behind the serum chamber, and a screw-on rubber feather with a silicon sleeve that covered a hole in the side of the barrel. The needle was solely for penetration; the knock-out shot spewed out of the side port when the sleeve was pushed back upon impact.

Davis gave her a side glance and said, "Ever use one of those things?"

"Nope, but I watched a YouTube video. I'm good."

"It doesn't look like any gun I've seen."

"It's not a gun," she said as she zipped the case shut. "It's a blow-dart."

"Come on, Ella. We're not playing around here—a blow-dart?"

"Whose playing? A gun, like your rifle, could scare the birds off. They're very wary of farmers with guns. The blow-dart looks like a walking stick. There's nothing scary about it."

"Trying to blend in are you?" Davis teased. "I couldn't help noticing your shocking pink sweatshirt and dayglow yellow socks."

"How am I supposed to dress?"

Davis smugly ran his hand from his olive-drab cap to his camo cargo pants.

"Good work, Treebeard. The village elders will be proud." Then she pointed into the strip-mall parking lot. "Don't forget my coffee."

~§~

Twenty minutes later they were rumbling over a dirt road that sharply weaved round boulders and gnarled tree roots twisting out of the bank. Ella was still trying to drink her coffee but the rough road made that a challenge. Davis seemed to be steering for the roughest patches. Ella glanced at the cattle rancher's hand-drawn map and instructed Davis to pull behind three closely huddled ash trees. A quarter mile away thirty or so cows clustered in the open pasture. A couple vultures were lazily circling above the bovines. A small group yearlings broke from the main herd and were placidly roaming across the field, nosing the grass for fresh tufts. The others were content to graze where they were in the overly-cropped grass. A calf tussled around its mother, groping for a teat on her milk-swollen udder. At the edge of the herd a very pregnant cow was lowing mournfully, obviously suffering from contractions. None of the other cows paid the slightest attention, but the two buzzards over-head were drawn to the sounds of distress. They tightened their circles over the birthing cow.

Davis lowered his binoculars.

"Those could be our vultures. They've got ugly black heads instead of ugly red heads."

"I think you're right, but we won't know for sure until I tranq one. Can I see those?"

Davis handed her the binoculars.

"You don't think they'd attack a full-grown cow, do you?" he said while Ella quietly studied the birds' stealthy descent. "I think they may try to separate that calf from its mother."

"Hmmm," Ella said, adjusting the focus on the binoculars. "The mother wouldn't have it. Do you see any bulls around?"

"No."

"Me either. That's why those two birds are getting bolder. You're right, though. Those are black vultures. I'm certain of it."

"Great! We'll have this wrapped up in time for lunch . . . Hey, the birds look like they're coming down. They're getting lower and lower."

Ella handed back the field glasses. "Let's get closer. We can circle around behind those trees."

"Better grab our gear first."

Davis returned from the Bronco and handed Ella her case. He had his rifle strapped on his shoulder. He patted the canvas strap pressing into his broad, beefy chest. "Just in case."

Ella opened her kit and assembled the blow-dart gun with surprising dexterity for someone who Davis thought of as being "all thumbs." She inserted a dart and adjusted the chamber pressure so that it was ready to shoot. Then she opened what looked like a cigarette case and scanned the extra four darts before closing the case and slipping it into her sweat-shirt side-pocket.

"A-hunting we will go," Davis mumbled as they trudged past a hedge of impenetrable blackberry vines. Davis was a step behind Ella as she weaved through the shady grove. When she paused abruptly he immediately halted and checked her expression in anticipation of their next move. Her face flushed with excitement as she observed the unfolding drama in the field.

"I think they're interested in that cow giving birth," she said, her breathing quick, her voice hushed.

"They want the placenta?" Davis said, incredulous.

"Sure they do. Think of all those nutrients. But they want the calf, too. Easy pickens—tender, helpless. Imagine eating something just as its taking its first real breath."

Davis felt a surge of repulsion, then anger. His hand tightened on his gun strap. "Let's go!"

Ella raised a hand: "Hold up."

At that moment, one of the vultures settled gently onto the birthing cow's rear haunches. The heifer gave a start but was in too much pain to much notice her passenger. Her eyes rolled as she let out a string of suffering bellows. Through the glasses it looked like the vulture was being as gentle as possible, conciliatory even, as it contrived to calm the mother's anxiety. "Son of a bitch," Davis seethed as he watched the deceitful posturing of the scavenger.

Ella pointed across the pasture. "We can get close enough if we reposition behind that oak over there. Nice and easy, okay?"

They used the tree trunks and bramble for cover. A covey of quail shot out of the tall thistles and gave them a start. When they reached the oak tree the cow bellowed in pain. Her puttering bassoon notes ratcheted into choking screams. She was breaching.

Ella rested the blow-gun in the crook of a broken branch, then she reached into her hoodie and removed her cell phone. She started filming the cow giving birth, zooming in on the vulture's reactions to the cow's dilation. The vulture leaned over the cow's upraised tail like a sinister mid-wife, bobbing and cocking its head in anticipation.

"What the—" Davis blurted when he saw that she was filming.

"*Shhh!* I'm recording . . ."

The cow dropped to her knees and rolled on her side. Wild-eyed, she looked back at the emerging calf, which was still wiggling inside the birthing sack. The vulture lowered its head, as if encouraging the mother to breathe, to push. Then it hopped onto the turf and watched as the calf slid from the grossly enlarged vulva. The second vulture, still circling overhead, screamed a vicious, jealous cry. The grounded vulture cocked its head skyward for a moment, then began tugging at the fetal membrane—delicately at first, but soon resorting to increasing savagery to tear it open. The gangly, saturated legs of the newborn struggled to break free.

And Ella was getting it all filmed. She was the hardened scientist now, passionate for knowledge, impervious to sentiments. Her heart pounded with excitement. She was an ice-cold chronicler of nature's savage power. Here was a rare carrion bird, having drifted far from its harsh and humid environs, wreaking absolute havoc on a bucolic pasture nestled in gentle hills. The raw savagery was mesmerizing.

But then an explosive gunshot rang out inches from her ear, jarring her nervous system like an sledge-hammer. Her hands spasmed and she dropped her cell phone (still recording) into a fresh cow pie. She bent over, jamming her palm over her left ear, as if that was going to block the explosion that had already happened. "What the fuck, Davis!" she screamed and looked at him, her nose creased in anger, her lips snarling.

Davis saw none of that. Fascination seized his face as he gazed at the crazy scene in the pasture. The buzzard's head was no longer there—only a flopping neck remained, and yet the bird's nervous system had the frenetic energy to launch into a final frenzied tail-spin, its legs sprinting and stumbling ahead, spooking the cows into a lazy stampede across the dry creek-bed.

Ella glared at Davis, but he responded with a wry half-turned smile.

"I like cows," he said and slipped the smoking rifle onto his shoulder.

~§~

They waited in furtive silence for over an hour. Davis had never seen Ella this angry before, but he knew her well enough to leave her be. The strained emotions and hay-scented air tired him and he dosed off to the sweet song of a meadowlark. The second vulture eventually landed and scarfed up all that was left of the placenta. Mother and new-born had moved on to a plusher pasture beyond the creek-bed. Ella got her shot off while Davis was still napping against a tree trunk. The vulture staggered, hopped, then toppled over in a heap. After placing the tracking device on the bird's leg, she trotted back to the observation tree and waited there with Davis, who was wiping the sleep from of his eyes. Forty-five minutes later, the bird groggily arose from the grass, hopped a few times, then took flight in an oblique angle over the hillside. Ella turned on her receiver and they could hear the bird's transmitter bleeping away.

"Well, we both got our bird," Davis said cheerfully, but Ella's cool gaze cast a dark chill in his bones.

He drove Ella back to the raptor center, then served his afternoon of banishment by cleaning the pens and delousing the birds while listening to talk radio on his headset.

~§~

Davis was already in the raptor center office when Ella entered, her keys still jingling because she was expecting the door to be locked.

"You're early," she said, hardly glancing at Davis as she dumped her gear into her office chair.

"I wanted to smooth things over," Davis said. "Make some points, you know, by looking *dedicated*."

"I don't pay you anything, so . . ."

"Yeah, that occurred to me after I'd already been sitting here a half-hour. But it wasn't a total waste of time. It gave me a chance to ponder the mysteries of Mickey."

"Oh yeah . . .?"

"Actually, I should say the mysteries of Mickey's bird. I was looking through those other drawings you brought from his house."

"You rifled my desk?"

"You told me to hang them up, and *as* I was hanging them up I couldn't help but notice that 'La-la' was scribbled on one of them. Crows don't sing *tra-la-la* like wrens or vespers. They croak like toads. Sounds like a beer belch to me. So, why make the crow sing like that?"

"It isn't singing. It's saying its name. Mickey named the bird La-la."

"La-la," Davis repeated thoughtfully. "Cute. Almost sounds like your name. La-la. *El-la*. Quite a coincidence, yeah?"

"Not a coincidence, Davis. I told you it was my bird."

"That's right, you did. Mickey's crow was once your crow, and he somehow knew to name it after you? This is all pretty confusing."

"This is how you get on my good side? By pestering me?"

Ella's expression assumed an absent-minded searching look, then she strode to a metal file cabinet, dropped into a crouch and yanked the lowest of the drawers open. She pulled out a half-inch thick manuscript that was bound by old-fashioned brass rivets. A red thumb-drive also came out. She turned and faced Davis with both items raised, one in each hand.

"My doctoral thesis," she said. "My *rejected* doctoral thesis, I should say. And this video recording was an attachment to the thesis, but it was never considered by the board. Remember me talking about my thesis?"

"Sure, Ella," Davis responded cautiously. He could see that Ella's anxiety level was rising by the moment. "It came up in your job interview. You were still pursuing your doctorate. It gave you an edge over the other candidates."

"That's right. You were on the hiring committee and so you know all about it. The truth is that I gave up on ever getting my doctorate, but admitting it wouldn't have got me hired, and I needed this job. When my thesis was rejected the review board used it to shame me, ridicule me. I was told that my methods were pseudo-science. They were hair-brained. I was a fraud!"

"Better to put all that behind you," Davis said, knowing now he had pushed Ella too far. He attempted to reel her back in. "You're here among friends now. We know your value. You *saved* the center, for God's sake." But her anxiety mounted as she paced back and forth in front of his desk.

"One of them—this fat fuck with hanging jowls and a Colonel Sanders goatee—called me Dr. *Moreau*. Dr. Moreau, yeah, just because I split their tongues with a scalpel? Because I altered their libidos with sonic pulses? Experimented with psychedelic molds and rare earth magnets? My methods weren't cruel. My ideas weren't bizarre—they were edgy, novel!" She paused to massage the back of her neck. Her puffed-up posture suddenly deflated and she seemed to shrink before his eyes.

". . . I'm done with all of it," she murmured, her voice losing its emotion. "After my thesis was rejected I got drunk and set the birds free. They're all gone. And the golden irony of it all: I now run a broken-down bird-farm."

Davis nodded knowingly, then said: "I can see why you didn't reveal any of this during the interview. That blistering bitterness I have come to love so dearly may have been misunderstood by the other members of the hiring committee."

Ella smirked.

"I always liked you, Davis," she said and slid the thumb drive into the USB port of her laptop. She clicked on a media file and fast-forwarded through several scenes that showed Ella working in front of a bird-pen full of crows. She paused the frame when she came across a single bird on a perch. She reversed the feed, then hit play and turned the volume up. "I was on the verge of a major breakthrough in avian communications," she said over her shoulder.

The Ella on the tape was younger, slimmer, confident. Her profile showed a creamy complexion, her eyes were bright and lively. She wore radiant red lipstick—Davis had never seen her wear lipstick, never thought of her as particularly feminine. She was in fact beautiful, exuberant, beguiling. *Who was this person?*

The recording showed Ella training a single crow that strode back forth on a wooden pole, bobbing its head and ruffling its feathers. It was attentive to Ella's every move, bowing and bobbing like a diminutive courtier.

"Say 'I love you, Ella.' Come on, kiss-kiss, 'I love you, Ella.'

"Love you La-la."

"Goood. Have a treat. Taste good? Now say, 'Ella is the sun and

moon to me.' Come on . . ."

"La-la sun and moon to me!"

Davis stepped closer to the monitor and said, "Ella, that's fantastic, but what's the difference between this bird and a parrot? Why all the controversy?"

"Watch . . ."

"What are you going to do today?"

"Talk to La-la."

"Hmmm. Nice. What else?"

"Teach other birrrds."

"Teach them what?"

"Teach to love La-la."

"Oh, I like that. What else?

"Teach talk. Teach count. Loud book talk."

Ella shut-off the video stream.

"She didn't tell Mickey her name was La-la. She was calling for me, calling for Ella." She snapped her laptop shut and leveled a weary gaze at Davis. "I told you she was my bird."

~§~

Later that day, Ella drove back to the Mullins house. She had called ahead and obtained permission to visit Mickey again. It took quite a bit of negotiations to wear Mickey's mom down. She finally won the battle by assuring her that the Feds were not going to show up at her doorstep with a warrant for the bird. Knowing that she was still on terribly shaky ground she stopped at the chocolate shop and bought a box of huckleberry truffles as peace offering. When she got out of her car in front of the Mullins' residence, though, Ella carried two boxes. The truffle box sat on a much bigger carton with holes punched in it. There was a temperature and handling warning label on all four sides, plus a statement in bold green letters: LIVE ANIMALS!

Mickey bounded out before Ella has a chance to press the bell. He hopped around the porch with the uninhibited joy that only children anticipating gifts can exhibit. Mrs. Mullins accepted the truffle box after wiping her hands on a sauce-stained apron. The door closed behind them and Ella came out again in under five minutes. Mickey hugged Ella's legs before dashing back into the house. Mrs. Mullins closed the door as Ella stepped off the porch, but she watched from a slit in the curtains to make sure Ella drove away. Ella still had the animal box cradled in her arms. As she walked back to her car it was clear that something was rustling and bumping inside the carton.

~§~

Before locking up for the day Ella cleaned out one of the portable cages. As she was wiping the wire gate with an alcohol pad, the Maisey twins walked into her office in single file then stood shoulder to shoulder in front of Ella's workbench.

"The gift shop's all locked up," said one.

"Only one customer today," said the other. "A Little Red Owl bookmark."

Ella nodded thoughtfully then refocused on her cleaning. She expected the twins' muffled footsteps to leave her office but they had not budged.

"Something bothering you ladies?" Ella said, looking from one face to the other.

The left-hand twin said, "The pygmy owl cage is empty."

"The bird is gone," said the right-hand twin.

"Oh!" Ella said. "I'm sure it's nothing. Were there any classroom visits scheduled for today?"

"No," they said together, their voices synchronized in a clipped, insinuating tone.

"Did you check the quarantine pens?"

"Yes."

"No bird."

"It's probably just hiding in its cage," Ella said, then smiled. "It's good at hiding."

"I doubt it."

"The pygmy owl is A-W-O-L."

Ella slowly rose to her feet and reemphasized rather menacingly: "It's hiding."

The twins' faces blushed in succession and they took a step back, then one of them noticed the live-animal carton on the floor next to Ella. The box rocked a little and something inside made an unearthly clicking sound.

Ella looked down at the box then glared at the twins.

"I'll lock up."

They hesitated because they had something else to say: "We're going to take a vacation."

"We might not come back," the more forceful twin added, her voice twisting like a screw.

Ella only nodded and sat down. The Maisey twins left without further ado, making little squeaky sighs of displeasure as they passed through the door. The hurt they intended to inflict with their departure went unfelt. Ella was used to driving people away. It was to be expected.

That night it rained and rained and rained. When the clouds finally broke the moon shimmered in every gutter. The next morning the town of Anadarko was as clean and shiny as a baptized baby.

~§~

Mrs. Mullins was trying to do too much at one time. She had dinner simmering (perhaps burning) on the stove. She corralled Mickey in his room and was forcing him to read from his chapter book. She still had to call the garbage company and ask why the trash hadn't been picked up but the recycling had. The cat was weaving in and out of her busy legs, begging to be fed because it was way past feeding time. And she was also trying to vacuum the entire house because it was a shambles. Mickey's room was especially bad and so she started there. "Keep reading," she warned as she moved in with her rattling canister and twisting hose. "Get up on your bed so that I can get under it." Mickey hopped on the bed and started playing with the toys he had left there. Mrs. Mullins worked the vacuum hose around the skirt of the bedspread, then cautiously slipped it in a few inches under the bed. A marble was sucked up and began spinning like mad in the see-through cylinder. Then she nudged something that felt like a roll-up sock that went thumping up the tube. When it hit the canister there was a cyclone of feathers and tiny bones. Mrs. Mullins couldn't stop the machine. She couldn't work the power button. The feathery detritus spun and spun with insane, wailing velocity.

And poor Mickey—well, he looked on in complete terror.

~§~

The tracking receiver had gone silent for three days. Ella was mysteriously distracted by something else and had become derelict in her tracking duties. When Davis made some noise about it she plopped the receiver on her desk and attempted to tune the bird in but got only static. Either it was dead, had shed the tracker, or had moved out of range.

Ella asked Davis to fixed an old TV antenna to highest point in the compound and run a cable from it into the office. "Now where am I going to find an old TV antenna?" Davis asked. "Go where they smash-up the old RV's for scrap metal," she suggested. And that's exactly what he did. Davis triumphantly returned in the afternoon with a TV antenna, a satellite dish (just in case) and a pristine folding lawn chair he had found still strapped beneath a Winnebago. To save time he clapped the antenna onto the utility shed with bailing wire. It wasn't the highest point but it looked like the safest spot for it. There was only so much risk Davis was willing to take for Ella. As he put away the ladder Ella attached the cable to the auxiliary port on her receiver.

Waves of static greeted Davis as he came through the door. Ella was hunched over the receiver, fidgeting with the frequency dial. "I haven't used this since college. Sometimes the old technology's the best."

"You don't have to tell me that," Davis said as he unfolded his lounge chair and sat next to Ella. "Look, my new office chair has a beer holder."

"If we can pick up a signal we can lock it in with the direction finder," she said hopefully. "Then we can go mobile. We'll probably lose the signal as soon as we disconnect from the antenna, but we'll pick it up again when we get closer. Chances are the bird is either circling above a field or is on the ground, eating."

"How will we know how far to go?"

"I thought of that. We'll measure the wavelength of the signal, then make a calculation based on the curvature of the earth—accounting for the declination of the sun, of course . . . *Or* we could just use our eyeballs."

"Oh," Davis said, then took an imaginary sip from his imaginary beer.

~§~

A half-hour later they were driving north in Davis' Bronco. The faint beeping of the receiver grew stronger, then started to fade as the road rounded a pillared boulder that had licorice ferns sprouting from every crevice. The dusty windshield was blinking with sun-splashes and tree-shadows.

"At last!" Ella cried as they broke out of the woods and were zipping along the open terrain of the valley floor. "Signal's strong now. Start looking for our bird."

"That could be it," Davis said pointing out of his lowered window, "circling above those firs. Oh! There's more."

"A lot more. We've got to get closer. Looks like they're flocking. Weird. Vultures don't flock."

As the veil of fir trees slid below the knoll one bird became two, then a dozen, then thirty or more. The flock broke from its inverted cone-shaped pattern and shot directly over the Bronco. Davis slowed the car and opened all the windows. Unlike geese that honked continuously when flying in formation, the vultures formed no aerodynamic V's and made no audible chatter, yet when they were directly overhead their flapping wings pulsated like a hellish whirlwind.

"Looks like a gathering storm," Davis said as he cranked the car around.

"More like a *summoned* storm," Ella said. "Hit the gas, Davis. They're heading back towards the raptor center."

"Maybe the Maisey twins are sun-bathing and caught their eye," Davis said as he twisted the steering wheel. "Now there's a tasty snack."

"They quit, you pervert," she snarked. "Faster, Davis. They're swarming the raptor center. The birds will go nuts and injure themselves."

The Bronco skidded to a gravel-spewing stop and they hopped out. Ella ran up the hill, then spun around. "Where are they? I can hear them, but they're not here."

"Up the hill! They're all over that guy's roof—the guy with the dogs. There must be a hundred of them."

Davis reached into his Bronco, retrieved his gun, then flung the unzipped canvass case aside and checked the breech.

"Davis!" Ella shouted. "We're inside city limits. You can't shoot that gun!"

"But he's not. That guy's in county."

Davis stalked up the hill and steadied his stance on a natural ledge just above the southern-most pens. The vultures watched him from the roofline. He flicked the safety off and eased his left hand down the stock, then gripped it firmly. A throaty chorus of clicks and trills swept along the roofbeam.

Davis found an open patch of sky and fired his rifle a half-dozen times. The carrion birds clamored and scratched and clawed aloft with colliding wings. Chaotic shadows darkened the sky as they scattered over the eastern ridgeline. Dust and chicken feathers roiled up from the bare earth and billowed through the cyclone fence. Davis stood fast, amazed by the fury he had unleashed. Ella muttered something as she pass him and struggled up the hill. It wasn't an easy climbed because it was a steep bluff. The chicken farmer's compound had a commanding view of the bird sanctuary below. Davis slung the rifle on his shoulder and joined Ella at the farmer's fence-line. "What a mess!" she gasped.

Davis touched her shoulder and said, "We can get in through that gate." Ella nodded and they walked along the wire fence, which was posted right up to the sharp drop of the ridgeline. They had to hang onto the fence at narrow points. As they circled the pens they saw dozens of dead chickens, some of them torn to pieces, some of them just lying limp. Feathers floated through the slanting shadows.

"Oh my God," Ella said as she unlatched the gate. "The farmer's hurt."

Davis hurried pass Ella and crouched down next to the farmer, who was stretched out face down on the sunbaked clay. His heavily calloused elbows stuck out like wings. His wrists and hands were hidden beneath his broad belly. The barrel of a shotgun jutted out from under his slumped shoulder. David checked his pulse. There was none. He squinted up at Ella. "He's dead."

"Did the vultures get him?" Ella said as she rested her palms on her bent knees. She was quietly panting and drops of her sweat pinged an empty grain tray.

"Doesn't look like it," Davis said as he struggled to his feet.

"Did he shoot himself by accident?"

"He never fired the gun. Looks like he wanted to, though. I think he just collapsed—heart attack, stroke, who knows."

"Couldn't take the loss of his chickens . . . " Ella said ironically.

"Where are the dogs?" Davis said. "Ah, Man! There's one. *Sweet Jesus*—on the fence, other side of the coop."

Ella walked toward the dog, bewildered and disgusted by what she saw: a hundred pound mongrel impaled on a row of wrought iron fence stakes. Over the years the farmer had pieced his fence together with a menagerie of materials. The dog hung from a fancy section that more belonged at the entryway of a gated estate. Davis joined her. His breathing was labored. He didn't understand what he was looking at. Why didn't the dog leap over the section of upended pallets? Davis finally decided it was a panicky move made by a mindless brute.

"I hated that dog, but I never—"

"It's OK, Ella. The farmer wasn't exactly Mr. Popularity either. I wouldn't call this a crime scene, but we should be careful not to touch anything more. Let's call the police. He lived alone, right?"

"Yeah, but there were two dogs: this one and a bitch."

"It's gone," David said. "Must have slipped though that tear in the fence. Looks fresh. Fur's stuck to the wire."

"Let's go, Davis."

"Yeah, let's go. I'll make the call outside the fence."

~§~

After all the excitement, the following week felt pleasantly mundane. The nasty business at the chicken farm only rated a two-paragraph story in the weekly paper. The coroner ruled the farmer's death as heart failure. Not much to gossip about there, so the *Anadarko Ledger* gave more space to the Tri-City swim meet and the gem show at the fairgrounds. The Black vultures were never seen in the valley again. Very few residents were even aware the rare carrion birds had passed through. Ella and Davis continued with their daily duties and spoke little of it, although Davis still puzzled over the incident a great deal. He felt a lingering sadness for the dead dog and the brutality of its demise.

One morning Davis and Ella were hanging out in the main office before the raptor center opened for the day. Davis was drinking a cup of coffee and polishing a brass hinge he wanted use on the gift shop's screen door. Ella was coddling her crow.

"I love you. I love you," she cooed.

"Ella Pretty," the crow cooed back and accepted a hand-fed tidbit. It toddled back and forth on the smooth redwood perch Davis had carved and sanded.

"You know something, Ella?" he said as he nonchalantly wiped the henge.

"What, Davis?"

"I sure miss the Maisey twins."

"Un-huh," she said without giving Davis so much as a glance.

"I think they miss me, too. They called me the other day. There was two of them and one of me, so that makes it a conference call. You know what they said?"

Ella shrugged, disinterested.

"They said that you stole the Pygmy Owl and traded it for your crow."

"Didn't happen," Ella said, unfazed. She smiled and stroked her crow's glossy bobbing head.

"Well, the pygmy owl's gone, in case you haven't noticed. Its cage is empty, cold, unlit. Feed bin's bare. Explain that."

Ella smirked at Davis and raised a small cage that had been hidden behind her desk. The missing pygmy owl innocently blinked at Davis.

"Our little friend needed some TLC so I took it home," she explained and lowered the cage. "Is that okay with you?"

"Ah! I never doubted you," Davis assured her while his face flushed crimson. "I told the twins they must be wrong. Ridiculous, but . . . what *did* you give Mickey for that fabulous crow of yours?"

"Oh, a pygmy owl," she sighed.

Davis gave Ella his best baffled expression.

Without looking away from her preening crow, Ella pointed at the mini-museum nestled in the gift shop alcove. There stood a taxidermist display of regional raptors—a kestrel, a barn owl, a merlin, and what used to be a pygmy owl. The shopworn owl was now replaced by a sequined parrot from the gift shop bins. The information placard that succinctly explained the range, behavior, and diet of the *Glaucidium gnoma* remained in place.

"By God, she does have a sense of humor!" Davis declared and laughed until he was consumed by a coughing fit. He turned away, embarrassed by his lack of control.

Once his pulse calmed and things were quiet for a while he said, "We really haven't talked about what happened up there on the hill. I can't get that poor dog out of my mind. It was a nasty brute, but I love dogs, all dogs. It's heartbreaking. Why did it commit suicide by jumping on the pickets?"

"You can't know that," Ella said. "It panicked. That's all."

"You're probably right," Davis said and set the hinge aside. "Still . . . why?"

"You'll get over it, Davis. Haven't you enjoyed the peace and quiet?"

"Sure," he said. He thought about working on the screen door but then had another thought and tossed the henge into his top drawer.

"Didn't you say you added a security camera along the south fence?"

"It's mounted in the Lodgepole pine closest to the chicken farm. I wanted to keep an eye on the place in case I needed to take him to court over the dogs. Won't need to now . . . The camera's perfectly legal," she added, heading off any self-righteous outcry from Davis.

"Does the camera record?"

"I think so. I haven't played with it since it was put up."

"I want to find the footage from that day the vultures swarmed the chicken farm. I don't know why we didn't think of looking at it before."

"Knock yourself out. The camera hard drive is in the utility room. Just pull what you need and watch it on your laptop."

"Aren't you curious?"

"Nope."

~§~

It only took a few minutes for Davis to route the external hard drive through his laptop. The video files were date stamped and so it was easy to search for the day and time he needed. The camera angle, due to the height and position of the pine tree, was elevated slightly above the hilltop and so was able to catch a decent view of the chicken coop, the fenced-off yard, and a section of the farmhouse behind it.

He watched everything is reverse as he searched for the bird-swarm. The first bit of evidence was all the commotion of the police, fire, and ambulance crews. Then there was suddenly no activity, only an empty yard. Skipping ahead he saw Ella and himself poking around the yard, then nothing again. During the quiet stretch the sparse foliage oddly quivered in the backward breeze, then came an implosion of buzzards in response to Davis' rifle. The chicken farmer was laying on the ground, just as they had found him, then he stumbled backwards up to his feet, his face stretched with a terrible grimace of pain, which was then replaced by anger as he walked backward round the coop and toward his house. There was an odd movement off to the side—a vulture that was particularly animated, its jerky movements almost comical. The man slipped out of view: the frame slid down his hips, knees, boots—until he was gone altogether. The big male dog ran passed in reverse, its tail between its legs then its hackles raised in fury, its lips curled, teeth snapping, barking—but there was no sound on the tape of course. Thankfully, the camera hadn't captured the dog's terrible impalement. Another pair of dog ears and tail scurried backwards—a smaller dog, and so this must have been the bitch. Then there was a commotion round a wooden box with a blanket hanging over the edge. One of the buzzards was tottering in the gravel patch next to the box. It looked sick as if upchucking something. It was difficult to tell what was happening. Before he could make sense of it, the buzzards began to thin out by leaping backwards up into the air. It looked as if they had been blown away by a powerful wind, one by one. Finally all was quiet, motionless.

Davis felt jittery. Something had just happened that he couldn't quite comprehend, something corkscrewing in his subconscious. He gave a sideways glance at Ella, who was still preening her bird. He had never seen her so happy and contented.

"Does this thing zoom in?" He said weakly, his face pale, his lips oddly parched.

"Use the mouse," she said without looking up.

"Easy for you to say," Davis mumbled but he got the hang of it after a few tries. He paused the image then restarted it so that he could watch in real-time as the birds swarmed the yard. He zoomed in on the wooden box at full power. Some furry things weakly squirmed in the folds of the blanket. He slowed the video and saw tiny tails and floppy ears, little eye slits, some open, some closed. The buzzard landed awkwardly beside the box and dramatically arched its wings in a show of dominance and exaltation. It snatched the first puppy, tossed its head back, and swallowed it whole. The lump in its throat dropped as it choked the puppy down. The other newborns, oblivious to what was happening, crawled into the newly open space, groping for what was missing. The buzzard picked them up one by one, until there were no more. A shadow fell across the brazen bird, the shadow of a man with a hoisted rifle. The bird looked up at the man and made a hacking motion with its fleshy head. With its beak open and its black tongue twitching like a finger, the bird appeared to be laughing at the man. The shadow collapsed without a shot fired.

Davis slapped his laptop closed and emptied his stomach into a garbage can.

"Davis!" Ella finally looked up. "What the—"

"It was the worst thing I've ever seen," he said wiping his mouth on his sleeve. "You have to see it for yourself. No! Don't watch it. Don't ever watch it. Erase it."

"If you say so, Davis," Ella said kindly and handed him a tissue.

Davis hovered over the trash can. He breathed in his own vile fumes. His bowed head and arching spine gave him a humped-back appearance. The desk lamp highlighted the frosty hairs on his rosy ear-points. He was bent, submissive, and when he gazed at Ella he realized how truly special she was. The crow had given her that crucial missing piece, and she had given the crow a love it would not otherwise have. Ella's pale aquiline nose and delicate moon-turned chin gave her a storybook charm. She was enchanting. Yet she still had the innocence of someone unaware of the powers within. She summoned the birds. Ella had. With only an unspoken desire. And Davis was a part of it all, part of her sphere, and he was happy to be of use at last.

He would do anything for pretty Ella.

Part II

A PRAYER FOR THE INNOCENTS

a profound jealousy of the young

IT'S TIME to consider the softer side of horror: tormenting helpless children. This section focuses on children in peril, and we are not referring to the ones subjected to the Starbucks-fueled enthusiasm of soccer moms and dads. Although there is a long tradition of threatened, mutated, and maligned children in fairy tales, there is little of this frivolity found today outside of Young Adult literature . . . and of course your average schoolyard. We've rounded up some of the tastiest Gobshockers available, beginning with the "Doll's Ghost" by F. Marion Crawford. This story has a wonderful old world feel to it and features a possessed doll that has the heart of an angel. The fear and suspense of a lost child give Crawford's neat little tale a razor-sharp edge, but it's an edge that is ultimately sweetened by some calming sentimentality. You'll love it!

"The Boy Who Sought the Shudders" is a new adaption of the original Grimm's Fairy Tale. It's a delightful bit of weirdness that granny probably never read to you.

"The Little Red Owl" by Margaret St. Clair is one of our favorite weird tales of all time. Read it and find out why.

Our next gem, M. R. James' "Lost Hearts", is one of the Cambridge provost's famous Christmas Ghost Stories. It's not one you normally find anthologized. This is a mystery, for it is quite malicious and grip-ping—not nearly as subtle as most of his stories. After reading it you'll wish that he had written more stories involving innocent children, especially stories as nasty as *this one.*

Following James' heartfelt entry comes Theodore Sturgeon's classic monster tale, "IT". Arguably an inspiration for "Swamp Thing" and the glut of zombie stories and films that would come decades later, the story—a genuine tour de force—stands as a hallmark of the genre. It's one of those stories that can be reread every year, with new layers and nuances discovered each time. In my mind there is more than one innocent in the story, for I begrudgingly feel some sympathy for that dripping abomination that crawls out of the woods.

Our exploration of youthful horrors concludes with one of the most underappreciated stories in weird fiction; "Seaton's Aunt" by Walter de la Mare is about the life-long nightmare suffered by a pampered English schoolboy. Our Edwardian Richie Rich seems spoiled but he is on a slow-burn of terror with his dear old auntie. De la Mare's writing style is beautiful, so refined, that one is tempted to linger on every finely wrought sentence—but don't do that because there are a lot of other stories to read.

And now, shall we continue with our assessment of Evil—this time from a child's point of view. . . ? Our special children's section is rated PG for Potentially Gruesome. It is recommended that you only share these stories with those darling nieces and nephews who like to kick you in the shin.

The Doll's Ghost

by F. Marion Crawford

IT WAS A TERRIBLE ACCIDENT, and for one moment the splendid machinery of Cranston House got out of gear and stood still. The butler emerged from the retirement in which he spent his elegant leisure, two grooms of the chambers appeared simultaneously from opposite directions, there were actually housemaids on the grand staircase, and those who remember the facts most exactly assert that Mrs. Pringle herself positively stood upon the landing. Mrs. Pringle was the housekeeper. As for the head nurse, the under nurse, and the nursery maid, their feelings cannot be described. The head nurse laid one hand upon the polished marble balustrade and stared stupidly before her, the under nurse stood rigid and pale, leaning against the polished marble wall, and the nursery-maid collapsed and sat down upon the polished marble step, just beyond the limits of the velvet carpet, and frankly burst into tears.

The Lady Gwendolen Lancaster-Douglas-Scroop, youngest daughter of the ninth Duke of Cranston, and aged six years and three months, picked herself up quite alone, and sat down on the third step from the foot of the grand staircase in Cranston House.

"Oh!" exclaimed the butler, and he disappeared again.

"Ah!" responded the grooms of the chambers, as they also went away.

"It's only that doll," Mrs. Pringle was distinctly heard to say, in a tone of contempt.

The under nurse heard her say it. Then the three nurses gathered round Lady Gwendolen and patted her, and gave her unhealthy things out of their pockets, and hurried her out of Cranston House as fast as they could, lest it should be found out upstairs that they had allowed the Lady Gwendolen Lancaster-Douglas-Scroop to tumble down the grand staircase with her doll in her arms. And as the doll was badly broken, the nursery-maid carried it, with the pieces, wrapped up in Lady Gwendolen's little cloak. It was not far to Hyde Park, and when they had reached a quiet place they took means to find out that Lady Gwendolen had no bruises. For the carpet was very thick and soft, and there was thick stuff under it to make it softer.

Lady Gwendolen Douglas-Scroop sometimes yelled, but she never cried. It was because she had yelled that the nurse had allowed her to go downstairs alone with Nina, the doll, under one arm, while she steadied herself with her other hand on the balustrade, and trod upon the polished marble steps beyond the edge of the carpet. So she had fallen, and Nina had come to grief.

When the nurses were quite sure that she was not hurt, they unwrapped the doll and looked at her in her turn. She had been a very beautiful doll, very large, and fair, and healthy, with real yellow hair, and eyelids that would open and shut over very grown-up dark eyes. Moreover, when you moved her right arm up and down she said "Pa-pa," and when you moved the left she said "Ma-ma," very distinctly.

"I heard her say 'Pa' when she fell," said the under nurse, who heard everything. "But she ought to have said 'Pa-pa.'"

"That's because her arm went up when she hit the step," said the head nurse. "She'll say the other 'Pa' when I put it down again."

"Pa," said Nina, as her right arm was pushed down, and speaking through her broken face. It was cracked right across, from the upper corner of the forehead, with a hideous gash, through the nose and down to the little frilled collar of the pale green silk Mother Hubbard frock, and two little three-cornered pieces of porcelain had fallen out.

"I'm sure it's a wonder she can speak at all, being all smashed," said the under nurse.

"You'll have to take her to Mr. Puckler," said her superior. "It's not far, and you'd better go at once."

Lady Gwendolen was occupied in digging a hole in the ground with a little spade, and paid no attention to the nurses.

"What are you doing?" enquired the nursery-maid, looking on.

"Nina's dead, and I'm diggin' her a grave," replied her ladyship thoughtfully.

"Oh, she'll come to life again all right," said the nursery-maid.

The under nurse wrapped Nina up again and departed. Fortunately a kind soldier, with very long legs and a very small cap, happened to be there; and as he had nothing to do, he offered to see the under nurse safely to Mr. Puckler's and back.

Mr. Bernard Puckler and his little daughter lived in a little house in a little alley, which led out off a quiet little street not very far from Belgrave Square. He was the great doll doctor, and his extensive practice lay in the most aristocratic quarter. He mended dolls of all sizes and ages, boy dolls and girl dolls, baby dolls in long clothes, and grown-up dolls in fashionable gowns, talking dolls and dumb dolls, those that shut their eyes when they lay down, and those whose eyes had to be shut for them by means of a mysterious wire. His daughter Else was only just over twelve years old, but she was already very clever at mending dolls' clothes, and at doing their hair, which is harder than you might think, though the dolls sit quite still while it is being done.

Mr. Puckler had originally been a German, but he had dissolved his nationality in the ocean of London many years ago, like a great many foreigners. He still had one or two German friends, however, who came on Saturday evenings, and smoked with him and played picquet or "skat" with him for farthing points, and called him "Herr Doctor," which seemed to please Mr. Puckler very much.

He looked older than he was, for his beard was rather long and ragged, his hair was grizzled and thin, and he wore horn-rimmed spectacles. As for Else, she was a thin, pale child, very quiet and neat, with dark eyes and brown hair that was plaited down her back and tied with a bit of black ribbon. She mended the dolls' clothes and took the dolls back to their homes when they were quite strong again.

The house was a little one, but too big for the two people who lived in it. There was a small sitting-room on the street, and the workshop was at the back, and there were three rooms upstairs. But the father and daughter lived most of their time in the workshop, because they were generally at work, even in the evenings.

Mr. Puckler laid Nina on the table and looked at her a long time, till the tears began to fill his eyes behind the horn-rimmed spectacles. He was a very susceptible man, and he often fell in love with the dolls he mended, and found it hard to part with them when they had smiled at him for a few days. They were real little people to him, with characters and thoughts and feelings of their own, and he was very tender with them all. But some attracted him especially from the first, and when they were brought to him maimed and injured, their state seemed so pitiful to him that the tears came easily. You must remember that he had lived among dolls during a great part of his life, and understood them.

"How do you know that they feel nothing?" he went on to say to Else. "You must be gentle with them. It costs nothing to be kind to the little beings, and perhaps it makes a difference to them."

And Else understood him, because she was a child, and she knew that she was more to him than all the dolls.

He fell in love with Nina at first sight, perhaps because her beautiful brown glass eyes were something like Else's own, and he loved Else first and best, with all his heart. And, besides, it was a very sorrowful case. Nina had evidently not been long in the world, for her complexion was perfect, her hair was smooth where it should be smooth, and curly where it should be curly, and her silk clothes were perfectly new. But across her face was that frightful gash, like a sabre-cut, deep and shadowy within, but clean and sharp at the edges. When he tenderly pressed her head to close the gaping wound, the edges made a fine grating sound, that was painful to hear, and the lids of the dark eyes quivered and trembled as though Nina were suffering dreadfully.

"Poor Nina!" he exclaimed sorrowfully. "But I shall not hurt you much, though you will take a long time to get strong."

He always asked the names of the broken dolls when they were brought to him, and sometimes the people knew what the children called them, and told him. He liked "Nina" for a name. Altogether and in every way she pleased him more than any doll he had seen for many years, and he felt drawn to her, and made up his mind to make her perfectly strong and sound, no matter how much labour it might cost him.

Mr. Puckler worked patiently a little at a time, and Else watched him. She could do nothing for poor Nina, whose clothes needed no mending. The longer the doll doctor worked, the more fond he became of the yellow hair and the beautiful brown glass eyes. He sometimes forgot all the other dolls that were waiting to be mended, lying side by side on a shelf, and sat for an hour gazing at Nina's face, while he racked his ingenuity for some new invention by which to hide even the smallest trace of the terrible accident.

She was wonderfully mended. Even he was obliged to admit that; but the scar was still visible to his keen eyes, a very fine line right across the face, downwards from right to left. Yet all the conditions had been most favourable for a cure, since the cement had set quite hard at the first attempt and the weather had been fine and dry, which makes a great difference in a dolls' hospital.

At last he knew that he could do no more, and the under nurse had already come twice to see whether the job was finished, as she coarsely expressed it.

"Nina is not quite strong yet," Mr. Puckler had answered each time, for he could not make up his mind to face the parting.

And now he sat before the square deal table at which he worked, and Nina lay before him for the last time with a big brown paper box beside her. It stood there like her coffin, waiting for her, he thought. He must put her into it, and lay tissue paper over her dear face, and then put on the lid, and at the thought of tying the string his sight was dim with tears again. He was never to look into the glassy depths of the beautiful brown eyes any more, nor to hear the little wooden voice say "Pa-pa" and "Ma-ma." It was a very painful moment.

In the vain hope of gaining time before the separation, he took up the little sticky bottles of cement and glue and gum and colour, looking at each one in turn, and then at Nina's face. And all his small tools lay there, neatly arranged in a row, but he knew that he could not use them again for Nina. She was quite strong at last, and in a country where there should be no cruel children to hurt her she might live a hundred years, with only that almost imperceptible line across her face to tell of the fearful thing that had befallen her on the marble steps of Cranston House.

Suddenly Mr. Puckler's heart was quite full, and he rose abruptly from his seat and turned away.

"Else," he said unsteadily, "you must do it for me. I cannot bear to see her go into the box."

So he went and stood at the window with his back turned, while Else did what he had not the heart to do.

"Is it done?" he asked, not turning round. "Then take her away, my dear. Put on your hat, and take her to Cranston House quickly, and when you are gone I will turn round."

Else was used to her father's queer ways with the dolls, and though she had never seen him so much moved by a parting, she was not much surprised.

"Come back quickly," he said, when he heard her hand on the latch. "It is growing late, and I should not send you at this hour. But I cannot bear to look forward to it anymore."

When Else was gone, he left the window and sat down in his place before the table again, to wait for the child to come back. He touched the place where Nina had lain, very gently, and he recalled the softly tinted pink face, and the glass eyes, and the ringlets of yellow hair, till he could almost see them.

The evenings were long, for it was late in the spring. But it began to grow dark soon, and Mr. Puckler wondered why Else did not come back.

She had been gone an hour and a half, and that was much longer than he had expected, for it was barely half a mile from Belgrave Square to Cranston House. He reflected that the child might have been kept waiting, but as the twilight deepened he grew anxious, and walked up and down in the dim workshop, no longer thinking of Nina, but of Else, his own living child, whom he loved.

An undefinable, disquieting sensation came upon him by fine degrees, a chilliness and a faint stirring of his thin hair, joined with a wish to be in any company rather than to be alone much longer. It was the beginning of fear.

He told himself in strong German-English that he was a foolish old man, and he began to feel about for the matches in the dusk. He knew just where they should be, for he always kept them in the same place, close to the little tin box that held bits of sealing-wax of various colours, for some kinds of mending. But somehow he could not find the matches in the gloom.

Something had happened to Else, he was sure, and as his fear increased, he felt as though it might be allayed if he could get a light and see what time it was. Then he called himself a foolish old man again, and the sound of his own voice startled him in the dark. He could not find the matches.

The window was grey still; he might see what time it was if he went close to it, and he could go and get matches out of the cupboard afterwards. He stood back from the table, to get out of the way of the chair, and began to cross the board floor.

Something was following him in the dark. There was a small pattering, as of tiny feet upon the boards. He stopped and listened, and the roots of his hair tingled. It was nothing, and he was a foolish old man. He made two steps more, and he was sure that he heard the little pattering again. He turned his back to the window, leaning against the sash so that the panes began to crack, and he faced the dark. Everything was quite still, and it smelt of paste and cement and wood-filings as usual.

"Is that you, Else?" he asked, and he was surprised by the fear in his voice.

There was no answer in the room, and he held up his watch and tried to make out what time it was by the grey dusk that was just not darkness. So far as he could see, it was within two or three minutes of ten o'clock. He had been a long time alone. He was shocked, and frightened for Else, out in London so late, and he almost ran across the room to the door. As he fumbled for the latch, he distinctly heard the running of the little feet after him.

"Mice!" he exclaimed feebly, just as he got the door open.

He shut it quickly behind him, and felt as though some cold thing had settled on his back and were writhing upon him. The passage was quite dark, but he found his hat and was out in the alley in a moment, breathing more freely, and surprised to find how much light there still was in the open air. He could see the pavement clearly under his feet, and far off in the street to which the alley led he could hear the laughter and calls of children, playing some game out of doors. He wondered how he could have been so nervous, and for an instant he thought of going back into the house to wait quietly for Else. But instantly he felt that nervous fright of something stealing over him again. In any case it was better to walk up to Cranston House and ask the servants about the child. One of the women had perhaps taken a fancy to her, and was even now giving her tea and cake.

He walked quickly to Belgrave Square, and then up the broad streets, listening as he went, whenever there was no other sound, for the tiny footsteps. But he heard nothing, and was laughing at himself when he rang the servants' bell at the big house. Of course, the child must be there.

The person who opened the door was quite an inferior person, for it was a back door, but affected the manners of the front, and stared at Mr. Puckler superciliously under the strong light.

No little girl had been seen, and he knew "nothing about no dolls."

"She is my little girl," said Mr. Puckler tremulously, for all his anxiety was returning tenfold, "and I am afraid something has happened."

The inferior person said rudely that "nothing could have happened to her in that house, because she had not been there, which was a jolly good reason why;" and Mr. Puckler was obliged to admit that the man ought to know, as it was his business to keep the door and let people in. He wished to be allowed to speak to the under nurse, who knew him; but the man was ruder than ever, and finally shut the door in his face.

When the doll doctor was alone in the street, he steadied himself by the railing, for he felt as though he were breaking in two, just as some dolls break, in the middle of the backbone.

Presently he knew that he must be doing something to find Else, and that gave him strength. He began to walk as quickly as he could through the streets, following every highway and byway which his little girl might have taken on her errand. He also asked several policemen in vain if they had seen her, and most of them answered him kindly, for they saw that he was a sober man and in his right senses, and some of them had little girls of their own.

It was one o'clock in the morning when he went up to his own door again, worn out and hopeless and broken-hearted. As he turned the key in the lock, his heart stood still, for he knew that he was awake and not dreaming, and that he really heard those tiny footsteps pattering to meet him inside the house along the passage.

But he was too unhappy to be much frightened any more, and his heart went on again with a dull regular pain, that found its way all through him with every pulse. So he went in, and hung up his hat in the dark, and found the matches in the cupboard and the candlestick in its place in the corner.

Mr. Puckler was so much overcome and so completely worn out that he sat down in his chair before the work-table and almost fainted, as his face dropped forward upon his folded hands. Beside him the solitary candle burned steadily with a low flame in the still warm air.

"Else! Else!" he moaned against his yellow knuckles. And that was all he could say, and it was no relief to him. On the contrary, the very sound of the name was a new and sharp pain that pierced his ears and his head and his very soul. For every time he repeated the name it meant that little Else was dead, somewhere out in the streets of London in the dark.

He was so terribly hurt that he did not even feel something pulling gently at the skirt of his old coat, so gently that it was like the nibbling of a tiny mouse. He might have thought that it was really a mouse if he had noticed it.

"Else! Else!" he groaned right against his hands.

Then a cool breath stirred his thin hair, and the low flame of the one candle dropped down almost to a mere spark, not flickering as though a draught were going to blow it out, but just dropping down as if it were tired out. Mr. Puckler felt his hands stiffening with fright under his face; and there was a faint rustling sound, like some small silk thing blown in a gentle breeze. He sat up straight, stark and scared, and a small wooden voice spoke in the stillness.

"Pa-pa," it said, with a break between the syllables.

Mr. Puckler stood up in a single jump, and his chair fell over backwards with a smashing noise upon the wooden floor. The candle had almost gone out.

It was Nina's doll voice that had spoken, and he should have known it among the voices of a hundred other dolls. And yet there was something more in it, a little human ring, with a pitiful cry and a call for help, and the wail of a hurt child. Mr. Puckler stood up, stark and stiff, and tried to look round, but at first he could not, for he seemed to be frozen from head to foot.

Then he made a great effort, and he raised one hand to each of his temples, and pressed his own head round as he would have turned a doll's. The candle was burning so low that it might as well have been out altogether, for any light it gave, and the room seemed quite dark at first. Then he saw something. He would not have believed that he could be more frightened than he had been just before that. But he was, and his knees shook, for he saw the doll standing in the middle of the floor, shining with a faint and ghostly radiance, her beautiful glassy brown eyes fixed on his. And across her face the very thin line of the break he had mended shone as though it were drawn in light with a fine point of white flame.

Yet there was something more in the eyes, too; there was something human, like Else's own, but as if only the doll saw him through them, and not Else. And there was enough of Else to bring back all his pain and to make him forget his fear.

"Else! My little Else!" he cried aloud.

The small ghost moved, and its doll-arm slowly rose and fell with a stiff, mechanical motion.

"Pa-pa," it said.

It seemed this time that there was even more of Else's tone echoing somewhere between the wooden notes that reached his ears so distinctly, and yet so far away. Else was calling him, he was sure.

His face was perfectly white in the gloom, but his knees did not shake any more, and he felt that he was less frightened.

"Yes, child! But where? Where?" he asked. "Where are you, Else?"

"Pa-pa!"

The syllables died away in the quiet room. There was a low rustling of silk, the glassy brown eyes turned slowly away, and Mr. Puckler heard the pitter-patter of the small feet in the bronze kid slippers as the figure ran straight to the door. Then the candle burned high again, the room was full of light, and he was alone.

Mr. Puckler passed his hand over his eyes and looked about him. He could see everything quite clearly, and he felt that he must have been dreaming, though he was standing instead of sitting down, as he should have been if he had just waked up. The candle burned brightly now. There were the dolls to be mended, lying in a row with their toes up. The third one had lost her right shoe, and Else was making one. He knew that, and he was certainly not dreaming now. He had not been dreaming when he had come in from his fruitless search and had heard the doll's footsteps running to the door. He had not fallen asleep in his chair. How could he possibly have fallen asleep when his heart was breaking? He had been awake all the time.

He steadied himself, set the fallen chair upon its legs, and said to himself again very emphatically that he was a foolish old man. He ought to be out in the streets looking for his child, asking questions, and enquiring at the police stations, where all accidents were reported as soon as they were known, or at the hospitals.

"Pa-pa!"

The longing, wailing, pitiful little wooden cry rang from the passage, outside the door, and Mr. Puckler stood for an instant with white face, transfixed and rooted to the spot. A moment later his hand was on the latch. Then he was in the passage, with the light streaming from the open door behind him.

Quite at the other end he saw the little phantom shining clearly in the shadow, and the right hand seemed to beckon to him as the arm rose and fell once more. He knew all at once that it had not come to frighten him but to lead him, and when it disappeared, and he walked boldly towards the door, he knew that it was in the street outside, waiting for him. He forgot that he was tired and had eaten no supper, and had walked many miles, for a sudden hope ran through and through him, like a golden stream of life.

And sure enough, at the corner of the alley, and at the corner of the street, and out in Belgrave Square, he saw the small ghost flitting before him. Sometimes it was only a shadow, where there was other light, but then the glare of the lamps made a pale green sheen on its little Mother Hubbard frock of silk; and sometimes, where the streets were dark and silent, the whole figure shone out brightly, with its yellow curls and rosy neck. It seemed to trot along like a tiny child, and Mr. Puckler could almost hear the pattering of the bronze kid slippers on the pavement as it ran. But it went very fast, and he could only just keep up with it, tearing along with his hat on the back of his head and his thin hair blown by the night breeze, and his horn-rimmed spectacles firmly set upon his broad nose.

On and on he went, and he had no idea where he was. He did not even care, for he knew certainly that he was going the right way.

Then at last, in a wide, quiet street, he was standing before a big, sober-looking door that had two lamps on each side of it, and a polished brass bell-handle, which he pulled.

And just inside, when the door was opened, in the bright light, there was the little shadow, and the pale green sheen of the little silk dress, and once more the small cry came to his ears, less pitiful, more longing.

"Pa-pa!"

The shadow turned suddenly bright, and out of the brightness the beautiful brown glass eyes were turned up happily to his, while the rosy mouth smiled so divinely that the phantom doll looked almost like a little angel just then.

"A little girl was brought in soon after ten o'clock," said the quiet voice of the hospital doorkeeper. "I think they thought she was only stunned. She was holding a big brown-paper box against her, and they could not get it out of her arms. She had a long plait of brown hair that hung down as they carried her."

"She is my little girl," said Mr. Puckler, but he hardly heard his own voice.

He leaned over Else's face in the gentle light of the children's ward, and when he had stood there a minute the beautiful brown eyes opened and looked up to his.

"Pa-pa!" cried Else, softly, "I knew you would come!"

Then Mr. Puckler did not know what he did or said for a moment, and what he felt was worth all the fear and terror and despair that had almost killed him that night. But by and by Else was telling her story, and the nurse let her speak, for there were only two other children in the room, who were getting well and were sound asleep.

"They were big boys with bad faces," said Else, "and they tried to get Nina away from me, but I held on and fought as well as I could till one of them hit me with something, and I don't remember any more, for I tumbled down, and I suppose the boys ran away, and somebody found me there. But I'm afraid Nina is all smashed."

"Here is the box," said the nurse. "We could not take it out of her arms till she came to herself. Should you like to see if the doll is broken?"

And she undid the string cleverly, but Nina was all smashed to pieces. Only the gentle light of the children's ward made a pale green sheen in the folds of the little Mother Hubbard frock.

The Boy Who Sought the Shudders

by Wilhelm and Jacob Grimm

specially adapted for this edition by Jonathan Eeds

THERE was once a father who had two sons. One boy was clever and sensible. He knew how to get the job done. The younger one was the complete opposite. He was dull-witted, a bit lazy, and possessed neither imagination nor insight.

When people saw him, they said: "Oh boy, his father will have plenty of trouble with him. He'll be sponging off the old man his entire life."

Whenever there was anything to be done, the eldest son always had to do it. That was a given. But if his Father sent the older boy to fetch anything late in the evening and the way led through the churchyard, or any other dreary place, he would balk: "Oh no, Father, not there; it makes me shudder!" Handy as he was, the older boy was afraid of dark places. Everyone has their limitations.

In the evening, when stories were being told round the fire that made one's flesh creep, the listeners would moan: "Oh, you make me shudder!" The youngest son, sitting in the corner and listening intently, could not imagine what they meant. "They always say 'It makes me shudder! It makes me shudder!' Well, it doesn't make me shudder a bit. Not a tingle! It must be something I can't understand." His mind never took him to uncomfortable places. He often dozed during the scariest of stories. Still, over time, he developed an obsession for the shudders.

Now it happened one day that his father said to him: "My lad, though you have an aversion to work you *are* growing big and strong. You must learn something by which you can make a living. You have to contribute! See what pains your brother takes—so diligent and hard-working, but you sit around waiting for life to happen."

"Well, Father," he answered, "I am quite ready to learn something.

Most of all, I would very much like to learn how to shudder, for I know nothing about that."

The elder son laughed when he heard him, and thought: "Good heavens! What a fool my brother is; he will never do any good as long as he lives."

But his father sighed, and answered: "It's easy enough to learn how to shudder, but you won't make your bread by it."

Soon after, the sexton (who looked after the churchyard in all manner of things: sweeping, bell-ringing and grave-digging) came to the house on a visit, and the father confided his troubles with his youngest son to him. He told him how stupid he was, and how he never could learn anything. "Would you believe that when I asked him how he was going to make his living, he said he would like to learn how to shudder?"

"If that's all," assured the sexton, "he may learn something of that from me. Just let me have him, and I'll soon put the polish on him. He'll be willing to pull a plough himself once I'm done with him."

The father was pleased, for he thought: "The lad will gain something from a hard lesson in life."

So the sexton took him home with him and told the lad that it was his job to ring the church bells.

A few days later, the sexton woke the boy at midnight and told him to get up into the tower to ring the bells. "You shall soon be taught how to shudder!" the sexton thought, as he crept stealthily up the stairs beforehand.

When the lad got up into the tower, and turned round to catch hold of the bell rope, he saw a white figure standing on the steps opposite the belfry window.

"Who's there?" he cried; but the ghostly figure neither moved nor answered.

"Answer," cried the lad, "or get out of the way. You have no business here in the night."

Wanting to make sure the lad would think he was a ghost, the sexton did not stir. He would scare him yet!

The lad cried for the second time: "What do you want here? Speak if you are an honest fellow, or I'll throw you down the stairs."

The sexton did not think he would go to such lengths, so he made no sound, and stood as still as if he were made of stone.

Then the lad called to him the third time, and, as he had no answer, he took a run and threw the ghost down the stairs. He fell down ten steps, and remained lying in a corner in a crumpled heap.

Then he rang the bells as if nothing had occurred. Afterwards he trudged to his corner pallet in the sexton's house, and, without saying a word to anybody, went to bed and was soon fast asleep.

The sexton's wife waited a long time for her husband to come home, but, as he never came back, she got frightened, and woke up the lad from his peaceful slumber.

"Don't you know what has become of my husband?" she asked. "He went up into the church tower before you."

"No," answered the Lad. "There was somebody standing on the stairs opposite the belfry window, and, as he would neither answer me nor go away, I took him to be a rogue and threw him downstairs. Go and see if it was your husband; I should be sorry if it were."

The woman hurried away and found her husband lying in the corner, moaning and clutching a broken leg. She helped him down, and then hastened with loud cries to the lad's father.

"Your son has brought about a great misfortune; he has thrown my husband downstairs and broken his leg. Take the good-for-nothing fellow away, out of our house!"

The father was horrified, and, going back with her, gave the lad a good scolding.

"What is the meaning of this inhuman prank? The evil one must have put it into your head."

"Father," answered the lad, "just listen to me. I am quite innocent. He stood there in the dark, like a man with some wicked design. I did not know who it was, and I warned him three times to speak, or to go away!"

"My God!" said his father. "You bring nothing but disaster. Leave my sight. I will have nothing more to do with you."

"Gladly, Father. But please allow me to wait until daylight; then I will go away, and learn to shudder. Then, at least, I shall have one skill to make my living by."

"Learn what you like," said his Father. "It's all the same to me. Here are fifty thalers for you. I am not heartless. Go out into the world, and don't tell a creature where you come from, or who your father is, for you will only bring shame to this house."

"As you please, Father. If that is all you want, I can easily fulfill your wishes."

At daybreak, the lad put his fifty thalers into his pocket, and went out along the high road, repeating over and over to himself as he went: "If only I could shudder, if only I could shudder."

A man came by and overheard the words the lad was saying to himself, and when they had gone a little further, and came within sight of the gallows, he said: "See, there is the tree where those seven men have been wedded to the ropemaker's daughter, and are now learning to fly. Sit down below them, and when night comes you will soon learn to shudder."

"That sounds easy enough," said the lad. "And if I learn to shudder tonight you shall have my fifty thalers. Come back and check on me early tomorrow morning."

Then the lad went up to the gallows, and sat down under them to wait till night came. The seven bodies swayed with the slightest breeze. The creaky ropes made an eerie music.

Since he was cold he lighted a fire, but at midnight the wind grew so cold that not even the flames would keep him warm.

The wind blew the men on the gallows backwards and forwards, so that they swung against each other, bumping arms and shoulders as if they wrestled one another. This unearthly site made him think: "Here am I freezing by the fire, but how much colder they must be up there. How sad and awkward."

And as he was very compassionate, he mounted the ladder, undid them, and brought all seven down one by one.

Then he stoked the fire and placed them round it to warm themselves. They sat there and never moved, even when the fire caught their clothing and started little flames that burned up their pant legs.

"Behave!—or I will hang you all up again."

The dead men, of course, could not hear, and remained silent while their paltry rags burned.

Then he grew angry, and said: "If you won't take care of yourselves, I can't help you. And I won't be burnt with you!"

So he hung them all up again in a row. He thought it was no use being nice to people. He sat down by the fire and went to sleep again.

Next morning, the man, wanting to get his fifty thalers, came to him and said: "Now do you know what shuddering means?"

"No," he said; "how should I have learnt it? Those fellows up there never opened their mouths, and they were so stupid that they let the few poor rags they had about them burn."

The man saw that no thalers would be his that day, and so he went away, saying: "Never in my life have I seen such a fellow as this."

The lad also went on his way, and again began saying to himself: "Oh, if only I could learn to shudder, if only I could learn to shudder."

A carter, walking behind him and leading a wagon of wares, heard this, and asked: "Who are you?"

"I don't know," answered the youth.

"Who is your father?"

"That I must not say."

"What are you always mumbling in your beard?"

"Ah," answered the youth, "I want to learn to shudder, but no one can teach me."

"Stop your silly chatter," said the carter. "Just you come with me, and I'll see that you find what you want."

The youth climbed aboard the carter's overfilled wagon and went down the road with him. In the evening they reached an inn, where they meant to pass the night. As they entered, the lad loudly moaned, "Oh, if only I could learn to shudder, if only I could learn to shudder."

The landlord, who heard him, laughed, and said: "If that's what you want, there should be plenty of opportunity for you here."

"I will not be a party to this," said the landlady. "So many a prying fellow has already paid the penalty with his life. It would be a sin and a shame if those bright eyes should not see the light of day again."

The landlord gave his wife a shuttering gaze.

Not noticing the brewing tension, the youth said: "I will learn the shudders somehow, however hard it may be. I have been banished from my family's house for not knowing it."

He gave the innkeepers no peace until the landlord finally told him that there was an enchanted castle a little way off, where anyone could be made to shudder, if he could spend three nights in it. No one had survived its terrors, so he would be taking a huge risk even to enter the gates.

"As a matter of fact," the landlord said and gave the lad a knowing wink, "the King has promised his daughter to anyone who dared do it."

"The King's daughter?" the lad said. His face looked dreamy and slack-jawed.

". . . the prettiest maiden the sun has ever shone on," the Landlord added. He went on to say that there were also great treasures hidden in the castle, watched over by evil spirits, enough to make any poor man rich who could break the spell. Already many had gone in, but none had ever come out. That was the problem. All had failed.

Next morning the youth went to the King, and said: "By your leave, I should like to pass three nights in the enchanted castle."

The King looked at him, and since he took a fancy to him (due to his pampered life the King had become something of a dullard himself,) he said: "You may ask for three things to take into the castle with you, but they must be lifeless things."

The boy thought for a minute before answering: "I ask for a fire, a turning-lathe, and a cooper's bench with the knife."

The King had all three carried into the castle for him.

When night fell, the youth went up to the castle and made a bright fire in one of the rooms. He put the cooper's bench with the knife near the fire, and seated himself on the turning-lathe.

"Oh, if only I could shudder," he said; "but I shan't learn it here either. This place seems rather homey—much better accommodations than I am accustomed to."

Towards midnight he wanted to stoke up the fire, and, as he was enlivening the flames with a bellows, something in one corner began to shriek: "*Mkgnao, Mkgnao,* how coooo*o*ld we are now!"

"You fools!" the boy cried. "What do you shriek for? If you are cold, come and warm yourselves by the fire."

As he spoke, two big black cats bounded up and sat down, one on each side of him, and stared at him with wild, fiery eyes.

After a time, when they had warmed themselves, they said: "Young fellow, shall we have a game of cards?"

"Why not?" he answered; "but show me your paws first."

The cats willingly complied by stretching out their claws. They were quite proud of them.

"Oh," said he, "what long nails you have! Wait, I must first trim them for you." Thereupon he seized them by the throats, put them on the cutting-board and fastened their feet to the workbench. "I have looked at your fingers," said he, "and my desire for card-playing has gone." He struck them dead and threw them into the moat. Something terrible rose from the depths and engulphed them, then sank again with a burp. No sooner had he got rid of these two cats, and was about to sit down by his fire again, than crowds of black cats and dogs swarmed out of every corner, more and more of them piling out of everywhere.

They howled horribly, recklessly trampled on his fire, and nearly put it out.

For a time the boy looked quietly on, but the increasing riot of fur and howls got to be too much, so he seized his cooper's knife and cried: "Away with you, you rascally pack," and swung his knife like a whirling dervish. Some of the devilish creatures sprang away, the others he killed and threw into the water: *flip, flop, plop!*

When he came back he scraped the embers of his fire together again, and warmed himself. *Peace at last,* he thought. He could hardly keep his eyes open and felt the greatest desire to go to sleep. He looked round, and in one corner he saw a big bed.

"That's the very thing," he said, and lay down in it. As soon as he closed his eyes, the bed began to move, and soon it was tearing round and round the castle. "Very good!" he said. "The faster the better!" The bed rolled on as if it were dragged by six horses; over thresholds and stairs, up and down. It was a good way to see all the sights.

Suddenly it went *hop, hop, hop,* and turned topsy-turvy, so that it lay upon him like a musty mountain. Feeling no pain, his heart pounding only a little, he pitched the pillows and blankets into the air, slipped out from under the bed, and said: "Now anyone may ride who likes."

Then he lay down by his fire and slept till daylight. He was so tired that the cold stone felt like clover.

In the morning the King came to check on the boy, and when he saw him lying on the floor, he thought the ghosts had killed him. So he said: "It's a sad pity, for such a handsome fellow. I had such high hopes."

But the Youth heard him, sat up, stretched and said: "It has not come to that yet."

The King was surprised and delighted, and asked him how he had got on.

"Pretty well!" he answered. "One night is gone, I suppose I shall get through the others too."

When the landlord saw him he said: "I never thought I should see you alive again. Have you learnt how to shudder now?"

"No," he answered; "it's all in vain. If only someone would tell me how. How can I shudder?"

The second night came, and up he went again and sat down by the fire, and began his old song: "Oh, if only I could learn to shudder." He was becoming something of a one-note chanticleer.

In the middle of the night a great noise and uproar began, first softly, nearly inaudible, but slowly growing until it was thunderously loud . . . then for a short time an abrupt and utter silence fell on the room. Only the *plish, plish* of a leaky trough could be heard.

At last, with a loud scream, half the body of a man tumbled down the chimney in front of him.

"Hullo!" the half-man said. "You haven't seen a pair of legs, have you?"

The noise began again, and, amidst shrieks and howls, the other half fell down.

"Give me a moment," the youth said; "I'll stoke the fire to warm your toes."

When this was done, and he looked round, the two halves had come together and a hideous man sat in the boy's place.

"Ho now! We didn't agree to that," said the youth. "The bench is mine. Get up!"

The man wanted to push him out of the way, but the lad would not have it, flung him aside, and reclaimed his seat.

Then more men fell down the chimney, one after the other, and they fetched nine human shin bones and two skulls, and began to play skittles.

The youth felt inclined to join them, and cried: "I say, can I play too?"

"Yes, if you've got any money."

"Money enough," he answered, "but your skittle-balls aren't quite round."

Then he took the skulls and turned them on the lathe till they were quite round. "Now they will roll better," he said. "Here goes! The more, the merrier!"

So he played with them and lost some money, but when it struck twelve everything disappeared in a pitiful poof. He lay down, and was soon fast asleep.

Next morning the King came again to look after him, and said: "Well, how did you get on this time?"

"I played skittles," he answered, "and lost a few coins. Since I am staying here rent-free I guess that doesn't matter."

"Did you learn to shudder?"

"Not a bit. I only made merry. Oh, if I could but find out how to shudder. Why can't I feel the shudders . . .?" The King was already on his way out the door as soon as he heard the boy commence his monotonous appeals.

On the third night he again sat down on his bench, and said quite savagely: "If only I could shudder!"

When it grew late, six tall men came in carrying a coffin on planks. The youth recognized the cadaver and said: "Hullo there! That must be my cousin who died a few days ago." And he cheerily beckoned the corpse: "Come, dear cousin, come along."

The men put the coffin on the floor, and he went up and took the lid off so that the dead man was fully exposed. He felt the face, and it was as cold as ice. "Wait," he said; "I will warm him."

Then he went to the fire and warmed his palm. He pressed it on

the ashen face, but the dead man remained cold. A bit of funereal rouge came off on the boy's hand when he pulled it away. Undeterred, the boy took the cadaver out of the coffin, laid it across his shoulder and carried it to the fire. There he sat the corpse up properly. Kneeling before his cousin, he vigorously rubbed its limp arms to make the blood circulate.

But it was all no good. Dead is dead, after all. Next, it came into his head that if two people were in bed together, they warmed each other. So he put the dead man in the bed, covered him up, and lay down beside him. To fill the awkward silence, he told the reticent corpse about his adventures up till this point.

After a time the dead man grew warm, and began to move. The boy's thrilling story seemed to stimulate him.

Then the youth said: "There, you see, cousin of mine, have I not warmed you?"

But the dead man rose up and cried: "*Yesssss*. Now, I will strangle you! If only to shut you up!"

"What!" said he, "is that all the thanks I get? Back you go into your coffin then." So saying, he lifted him up, threw him into the box and fastened down the lid. Then the six men came back and carried the coffin away.

"Nice work, fellas," he muttered as they left. "But look at me, will ya? Not a shudder in my bones. I shall never learn it here."

Just then a huge man appeared. He was frightful to look at—old and gnarled like a swamp oak, with a long mossy beard that ended in a curling fork. Clickity-crawly things dropped off his nightshirt as he staggered forward. Everything about him was crooked.

"Oh, you miserable wastrel!" he cried. "You shall soon learn what shuddering is, for you shall die!"

"Not so fast," said the Youth. He was munching on an apple and so had to finish his chewing. Tossing the core aside he continued, "That makes no sense whatsoever. Explain it to me. If I am to learn shuddering, how can I do that while dead and numb on a slab? Your plan is absurd."

"Is it now?" hissed the old monster. "I will make short work of you,"

"Oh, listen to you! Don't you boast. I am as strong as you, and very likely much stronger."

"We shall see about that," said the Old Man. "If you are the stronger, I will let you go. Come; we will settle this."

Then he led him through numberless dark passages to a smithy, took an axe, and with one blow struck one of the anvils into the earth.

"I can better that," said the youth, and went to the other anvil. The

Old Man moved closer so that he could see—close enough that his white beard momentarily hung over the anvil.

Seeing his chance the youth quickly swung the axe and split the anvil with one blow, catching hold of the Old Man's beard at the same time.

"Now, I have you ensnared," said the youth, "and you will be the one to die."

Then he seized an iron rod and tormented the old man with it in various imaginative ways, till the codger shrieked for mercy and promised him great riches if he would *only-please-stop*.

Nodding in agreement the youth pulled out the axe and released him. Keeping his promise, the old man led him back into the castle but grumbled the whole way: "It's a waste of good anvils . . . Do you have any idea how long it took me to grow this beard?. . . I suppose you'll complain about all this once you're back in the village. . . there's no tolerance anymore . . ." Once in the cellar, he showed the lad three chests of gold.

"Here are my conditions . . ." he said, raising a knobby finger for emphasis. "One chest is for the poor, one for the King, and one for you. Er . . . I could use a little recompense if you've enjoyed your stay here at the enchanted castle."

"That sounds satisfactory," the youth said.

The clock struck twelve, and the ghost disappeared, leaving the youth alone in the dark.

"I must manage to get out somehow," he said, and groped about till he found his way back to his room, where he lay down by the fire and went to sleep.

Next morning the King came and said: "Certainly by now you must have learnt how to shudder."

"Alas, no," said he. "What can it be? My cousin rose from the dead to no avail, and an old man with a beard came and showed me a lot of gold. But what shuddering is . . . oh! . . . that is something no man can tell me."

Then said the King: "I regret that you did not find what you sought, but you *have* broken the spell on the castle, and so you shall marry my daughter."

"That is all very well," he said; "but still I don't know what shuddering is."

The gold was carried from the castle, and the royal wedding was scheduled, but, happy as the young prince was, and much as he loved his princess, he was always saying: "Oh, if only I could learn to shudder, if only I could feel the shudders."

At last his bride-to-be was vexed by his obsession, and her maid-in-waiting said: "Take heart, my dear. I know the ways of men. I can help you; he shall be taught the meaning of shuddering."

The maid hurried out to the brook which ran through the garden and got a pail full of cold water teeming with hundreds of little fishes.

And so on the night of their nuptials, when the young prince was asleep, his wife turned back the covers and poured the cold water over him, and all the little silver fishes wiggled up and down his body with icy animation.

The prince awoke and cried: "I am shuddering, dear wife. I have the shudders! Now I know what shuddering is!"

And so the boy who sought the shudders found them at last. It *was* his wedding night, after all.

The Little Red Owl

by Margaret St. Clair

"BY NOW the fire was getting close to Billy and Gwendolyn," Charles said unctuously. "They could feel the heat against their faces, and it frightened them. All around them the leaves and branches were bursting into flame. They pulled as hard as they could against the ropes the Vulture Man had tied them with, but they could not get loose. Billy began to scream."

He paused in his narrative and looked archly at the children. They were listening intently. He observed with pleasure that they were both pale with excitement and what was pretty certainly distress. "What do you think happened to Billy and Gwendolyn?" he urged them. "Go on, tell me what you think happened to them."

"I know!" Peter said, almost shouting, "I know! The Little Red Owl came and got them out!"

"I'm afraid not," Charles answered smoothly. "Don't you remember, I told you at the beginning of the story tonight that the Little Red Owl has been hurt? He's not strong the way he used to be. The Vulture Man caught him and broke the bones in both his wings. Now he can't fly. All he can do is lie on the ground. And the broken wings hurt him very much."

Charles transferred his attention to Carlotta, who was chewing anxiously on the end of one of her short blonde braids. "What do you think happened, Lottie?" he asked.

She pulled the wisp of hair out of her mouth. "He's not really hurt, is he, Uncle Charles?" she asked anxiously. "Not the Little Red Owl? He's all right. He'll save them. You're just making it up."

Charles sighed. "Both the Little Red Owl's wings are broken," he said patiently. "He can't help Billy and Gwendolyn. He needs help himself, Carlotta. Do you know what is going to happen to Billy and Gwendolyn?"

She put her arm around Peter and hugged him up to her. "What,

174

Uncle Charles?" she asked, as if the contact with her brother strengthened her.

"Why, they're going to be badly burned. Perhaps they will even die before the fire goes out. Do you remember how much your arm hurt when you burned it last week, Lottie?" He pointed to the band aid on Carlotta's forearm. "Well, then."

Lottie's face puckered up. Her small chest heaved. For a moment Charles thought she was going to scream or slap at him. Then she began pulling her brother toward the door. "Come on, Peter," she said, almost in a whisper. "It's time for bed."

From the hallway she spoke to her uncle in a clear if somewhat wobbling voice. "I don't care what you say. I don't believe it. The Little Red Owl . . . the Little Red Owl isn't hurt. He's all right!"

Charles heard her and her brother stumbling down the hall toward their bedroom. For a moment his eyebrows went up. Then he relaxed. He chuckled. This defiance, of course, meant that Lottie was frightened. Not ill-pleased with himself, he rose from his chair.

~§~

Mrs. Morris, his housekeeper, was in the back sitting room. Under the placid light of a floor lamp she was knitting steadily away on a blue pullover for Peter. After a moment she put her work down and looked at him.

"Are the children all right, sir?" she asked in her pleasant voice. "I thought their voices sounded a little worked-up."

"I was telling them rather an exciting story," Charles said easily. "You know how children are."

"Yes, sir." Mrs. Morris hesitated. "Why do you tell them stories like that, sir? Just before they go to bed?"

Why, indeed? Charles thought. He felt his throat contract in an inaudible chuckle. For he loved them, he loved children, he loved Billy and Gwendolyn—no, their names were Carlotta and Peter—tenderly. "They enjoy the excitement," he said lightly. "Didn't you like ghost stories yourself when you were young?"

"Oh, ghost stories." Mrs. Morris' face relaxed. She stuck the needle in her knitting, put it in the knitting bag. "I'll tuck them in, sir," she said. "I wouldn't want them to have bad dreams."

She went out. Charles, left alone in the room, stood on the hearth rug jingling the change in his pockets restlessly. Should he have a drink?

No, he wasn't thirsty. He picked up a newspaper and put it down again. At last he pulled an armchair up to the fire. He sat down, picked up the poker, began to tap with it against the burning logs. A cloud of sparks darted up.

Charles watched, smiling. Whenever the swarm of sparks started to die away, he tapped on the logs again. At last he laid the poker aside and sank back in his chair. He began to plan the story he would tell the children on the next day.

~§~

The morning was rainy, in the afternoon there were scattered showers. It was not until later afternoon that Mrs. Morris thought it advisable to let the children out of the house. Charles watched from his study window.

Shouting and laughing, the children ran straight for the wall. Since the wall was less than five feet high it wasn't—Charles thought—exactly dangerous, but it had for the children the special attraction of the disapproved. Lottie clambered up first and then, from her eminence, gave Peter a helping hand. Soon, arms outstretched, they were balancing dramatically as they tightrope walked.

It began to grow dark. Charles came up to them, walking quietly in the dusk. "Lottie," he said, "it's time for you two to go in. I have a new story to tell you tonight."

From under her upraised arm Lottie peered at him. "I don't want to go in," she said sullenly. "Peter and I, we don't like your old stories. We don't want to listen to them."

"Carlotta, do you know what happens to little girls who are rude?"

"N-no," she answered uneasily. He could see that she was getting scared.

"They fall down and break their bones" he said impressively. "It hurts them very much. Carlotta, you're going to fall and break your arms and legs, like the Little Red Owl. That's because you were rude to me."

Lottie's mouth opened. She stared at him. Then she turned to run. Her foot caught. Over she went.

She began to scream hysterically. What a fuss about nothing, Charles thought, going up to her. Because of course she hadn't broken anything; bones at her age were soft, not brittle. Even though she should have. He tried to pick her up, and she crawled away from him, shrieking. And then of course Mrs. Morris had to come out.

Carlotta's knees were bathed and bandaged, she and Peter were given supper on a tray in their bedroom. Mrs. Morris spent a long time with them before she closed the door behind her and came out.

There would, Charles expected, be some kind of interview. He was standing on the hearth rug waiting when she came in.

"I want to speak to you about the children, sir," she said, plunging.

The courage of the timid! Charles thought. "Yes?" he said. He was careful to get the inflection of the word exactly right.

She moistened her lips. "Lottie says—Lottie tells me that you threatened her, sir. She says you told her she would fall and break her bones. As a punishment."

"She was exceedingly rude to me," Charles responded indifferently. Not that it would do him any good to be indifferent—it was an article of faith with Mrs. Morris that children were always right.

"Maybe so, sir. But you mustn't talk to her like that. She might really have hurt herself." She hesitated. "I'll have to tell her mother, sir, when Mrs. Gibbs gets back."

"Tell away," Charles answered, though he could feel himself trembling. It was the unfairness that bothered him. "Carlotta was unbearably rude."

Mrs. Morris bowed her head. It might have been in agreement. After an instant's silence, she continued. "And, sir, you must not tell them any more of those stories. I won't have that."

"Won't?" Charles mocked her.

"Yes, sir. Won't." She looked at him. Her face softened. "I think you ought to see a doctor, sir," she said. "You're not well."

"I never felt better in my life!" It was true. The energy, the force that filled him—it was like a fountain of life bubbling up. He was in love with them. Until now he had not really lived.

"I don't mean that kind of a doctor, sir. I mean—somebody who knows about the nerves. I beg your pardon, Mr. Gibbs. But I can see that as far as your nerves go, you're not well."

There were heavy candlesticks over the mantel. Charles clenched his hands in his pockets. No, he wouldn't. "Perhaps you're right, Mrs. Morris," he said disarmingly. "I haven't been quite myself lately. When Mrs. Gibbs comes back, I'll certainly go see someone."

"Thank you, sir. I'm sure it would do you good."

~§~

Her righteous back receded in the hall. But now what was he to do? If he told Mrs. Morris to go, pack her things, get out, *get out*, her first action would be to communicate with Sally Gibbs. And that would mean having his sister-in-law to deal with. Charles grimaced.

After a moment he sat down in the armchair and began prodding absorbedly at the fire.

The days passed slowly, emptily. He kept away from the children and they kept out of his way. Mrs. Morris was always near them, watchful, well-mannered, alert. He had not known time could pass so slowly. He had nothing to live for now.

At the end of the week he went to the city to see a dealer in rare books. "Oh, yes, Mr. Gibbs," the man said pleasantly: "I've a new book, only came in yesterday, in which I think you might be interested. "Here," he handed a copy of *The Secret Museum of Naples* to him.

Charles pushed it away distastefully. "No, not that," he said, trying to keep the scorn out of his voice. "I'll tell you the sort of thing I want." He went into details.

The bookseller listened intently, smiling at first, and then beginning to frown. "Let me see," he said when Charles paused. "Would this be it?" He got a large floppy folio from under the counter and opened it a page.

Charles couldn't help smiling at the picture, but he had to refuse the book. Once more he explained his wants.

"I'm afraid I can't help you," the dealer said at last. "You can see yourself that such a book would be rather, h'um, rather special. I doubt that it exists. A child's coloring book, you say, with a particular picture. Let me think."

He wrinkled up his forehead. Then he scribbled an address on a sheet from a note pad and handed it to Charles. "That's the artist who did the picture you were just admiring," he said. "You might find it worthwhile to talk to him."

The artist's studio was on the third floor, a big, empty room whose walls were decorated with innocuous flower pastels. The artist himself was a small man with a tight face and watchful eyes. After Charles had talked to him for a while, however, he became more friendly. He got out a portfolio of his drawings; they were very amusing, very amusing indeed. Not at all like the pastels on the wall. Charles congratulated him on his talent. And the artist showed a gratifying readiness at understanding what it was Charles wanted him to do.

He drew a sketch; it was even better than the ideas Charles had had. He knew a printer who could, he thought, reproduce the picture as

Charles wanted it. The sum the artist wanted for making the drawing and overseeing its insertion in the books—Charles thought it would be better to have two of them prepared—was certainly large. It was so large that Charles hesitated briefly. But after all, why not? What is money given us for, if not to enjoy ourselves?

~§~

On the eleventh day the artist telephoned from the city to say that the books were ready. Would Mr. Gibbs come after them? Certainly, Charles said, certainly. His fingers trembled with excitement as he dressed.

"It's page six," the artist said, giving him the picture books. "Of course, until it has been gone over, it doesn't look like much.

Charles examined the inserted page, and nodded. Page six could not be distinguished, superficially, from any of the other pages. It, like they, bore on its surface numerous tiny colored dots, widely spaced, and an occasional solid line.

"I had the printer run off some extra copies of the page," the artist said, picking up a brush. "I'll show you how it comes out. Watch." He dipped the blush in water and began to paint the water carefully over a loose sheet which bore the numeral 6. "There! What do you think of it?"

Charles could only nod with satisfaction. A beautiful job! Of course, the children would probably smear it. It was unlikely that they would paint as carefully as the artist had done. But enough would come through —there was plenty on the page—to have an effect. Oh, yes.

He paid the painter, and left. He carried the books, an innocuous brown paper parcel, under his arm. All the way home, in the taxi, in the station, on the train, he kept caressing it. The feel of the paper against his fingertips delighted him.

It was such a pleasant afternoon that he decided to walk from the station to his house. It would give him more time to plan and anticipate. But when he was about a block away from home he remembered, with a stab of dismay, something he'd forgotten to plan for: Mrs. Morris. Oh, dear.

How could he get her out of the house? A faked telephone message? No, his voice couldn't possibly pass for that of Mrs. Morris' daughter Jean. A telegram? But telegrams always have the name of the receiving office at the top, and Jean lived in Connecticut. If Mrs. Morris noticed *that* little discrepancy, the fat would be in the fire.

Was his whole Argosy of enjoyment going to be wrecked on the rock of Mrs. Morris? After all the trouble he had gone to? It was abominable. His lips shook. But, after all, perhaps he was distressing himself for nothing. It would be difficult to get Mrs. Morris out of the house; but was getting her out of the house absolutely necessary? Wouldn't there, indeed, be an especially subtle pleasure in going ahead with what he was going to do while she was present? He'd have to be careful, but he could manage it. Satisfied, Charles began to hum lightly as he walked along.

~§~

When he got home he gave Mrs. Morris the parcel. "I bought these for the children in the city," he said. "Happened to see them in the window of a novelty shop. Do you think Lottie and her brother will care for them?"

Mrs. Morris undid the string. The dubiety left her face as she looked at the lettering on the covers of the big gay paper books. "The Paint-With-Water Color Book," she read aloud. "All you need is water and a brush."

"You understand how it works?" Charles said carefully. "You just take a paintbrush and water, and paint over the pages inside. And the water makes the colors and the pictures come out."

Mrs. Morris nodded. "Yes, I know. Jeanie used to have a coloring book like that."

She began to flip over the pages. Page one. Page three. Page five. Page seven. She hadn't noticed anything. Charles felt weak with pleasure. He licked his lips.

"Yes, they'll like them," Mrs. Morris said. "Thank you, Mr. Gibbs, for thinking of the children. I'm glad you're feeling better. They've been wanting something to do. I'll go give the paint books to them now." She went out.

Charles sighed at the exquisiteness of the moment. She was cooperating delightfully. And he'd been right, it was much better fun to do it this way.

He took off his shoes. In stockinged feet, he slid into the hall. He listened. He heard a babble of excited voices, then the rush of water in the bathroom. Lottie was saying something to Peter, something about spilling. (So typical of Lottie, the pretense of neatness. He wasn't fooled by it.) The children, it was clear, were getting water and starting at once on their painting books. How long would it take them to get to page six?

After supper he listened again. Mrs. Morris was ironing in the kitchen. The bouse was quiet except for the occasional murmur of the children's voices. Charles was keyed-up and tense, but he found he didn't mind waiting at all. There was something quite delightful in the thought of the children painting steadily ahead, while their industry brought them nearer and nearer to page six.

His hearing seemed exceptionally acute. He could hear the pages rustle as the children turned them, the weak scratch of their brushes on the paper, even the gurgle of the water as the brushes were dipped.

The moment came as he had imagined it, at the end of a long silence. Lottie gave a faint cry. A chair was pushed back. Still remembering caution, Charles ran down the hall on tiptoe to their room.

The paint book was open on the table. Both Lottie and Peter were looking at it. It must be Lottie's book, for the painting had been done with considerable care.

~§~

The picture was even better than Charles had remembered. The Little Red Owl hung upside down, crucified through his shattered wings. The flames, the blood, the beautiful blood dripping from his eyes. And, in the background, Billy and Gwendolyn.

Charles grasped Lottie by the shoulder. Now that the time had come, he forgot what he had meant to say. He shook her. He said, "That's what happened to the Little Red Owl."

Carlotta pulled out of his grip. She faced him. She was pale. But her eyes shone. "The picture's a big lie," she said.

Charles drew in his breath. Defiance? It was impossible; he'd had the picture made so she'd be convinced.

"I'll tell you how it really was," Carlotta said. Her voice rose.

"The Little Red Owl's not hurt! When the bad Vulture Man tried to catch him, the Little Red Owl flew in his face. The Vulture Man fell down. And the fire roared up over him. Then the Little Red Owl went and saved Billy and Gwendolyn. They got away. They're safe." She hesitated. Her breath was coming in gasps. Then she tore the picture out of the book. It left a jagged edge. Using both hands, she crumpled it up.

Oh, she thought she was a heroine! Charles caught her once more and began to shake her. She felt small and soft under his hands. Would her bones be brittle, like plant stems, or would they bend before they could break?

"You little . . . little . . . to tear a thing like that!" He hit her savagely, forgetting caution, and then again. Peter began to scream; Charles couldn't attend to both of them at once. It was almost a relief when Mrs. Morris came running in.

He was helped by dignity, pride, self-respect. He managed to listen to her tirade with his head proudly erect, and when she halted for breath he said coldly, "Are you quite through?"

But there is a price set on such severe self-control, and later he had to pay it. After Mrs. Morris had herded the children upstairs to her room for safekeeping, he sat huddled over the fire in the sitting room, shivering without being able to stop himself. His hands were shaking too much for him to be able to pick up the poker.

Why hadn't he silenced her? Charles asked himself. He could have hit her repeatedly on the mouth. He was stronger than she was. But the moment had passed. He couldn't possibly nerve himself to it now. Too late. Now Mrs. Morris was in the kitchen telephoning, calling number after number as she tried to locate Sally Gibbs.

What would happen? Well, he rather thought Sally would tell Mrs. Gibbs to take the children to some hotel and stay with them tonight. But that wasn't quite what he meant. What would happen to him?

His attention wandered. He tried to concentrate on what Mrs. Morris was saying, but gave it up after a second. His fate would be decided after all, he rather thought, not by what Mrs. Morris was saying, but by the sentences of a quite different voice, the voice he had begun to hear within his head.

He listened. The outer world sank away through gauzy layers into a profound silence. The . . . the children. Yes. He started to get up. Then he sat down in his chair again. He took a newspaper from the table beside him. He folded it carefully into a long, many layered lath-shape. He thrust the end of the newspaper into the flames in the grate.

~§~

"Were you scared, Lottie?" Peter asked. After their experience their mother had taken them to a psychologist who specialized in children. He had advised that they be allowed to talk if they wished, but not pressed to it. This was the first time that either one of them had referred to what had happened, even to the other one.

They had been playing earlier in the day with plasticine. Lottie pressed a blob of it out from under her fingernail before answering.

"Yes," she said honestly, "when he broke the door down. Why, Peter? Weren't you?"

"Not then," her brother answered with a hint of superiority. "I thought Mrs. Morris would come for us."

"But when you saw how the hall was all on fire, Peter? He'd set it on fire behind him, so nobody could get in to us."

"Yes, I was scared then, Lottie. But you know what scared me most? It was when I saw how his face was all wet and shiny and the light from the fire shined on his face."

"*Shone*," his sister corrected automatically. "What I minded most was when he came in the room. All the smoke and fire."

"When did you stop being scared, Lottie?"

"When I heard him whistle."

"Who whistle?" Peter asked uncertainly. "Uncle Charles?"

"Oh, Peter, don't be silly. You're older than that. You'll know. *Him*."

"Oh. His whistle's pretty, isn't it?"

"Um-hum. Low and sweet and soft. Not like an owl, really. More like a dove."

"Lottie—did it really happen?"

Carlotta stared at him. "Did *what* really happen?" she demanded. "You mean, did the Little Red Owl really lead us through the smoke over to the window? And show us how to climb down the drainpipe to the rose bed? Of course he did."

"No, not that. Just because you're bigger, Lottie, you don't need to think you're the only one that knows things. I mean, did he really fly in Uncle Charles's face?"

Carlotta did not answer immediately. She went over to the window and looked out. The children's nursery was on the second floor. She could see a streetlamp and a portion of the quiet street. "I didn't see him do it," she said, without turning. "But I heard the noise. And I saw Uncle Charles fall."

Mrs. Gibbs came in. "Bedtime, darlings," she said brightly. "Come along."

They were taken to the bathroom, washed, tooth-brushed, toileted. Mrs. Gibbs saw them into bed with hugs and kisses. She turned out the light. There was a silence. Then Lottie said, "If you want to, Peter, you can sleep in my bed tonight."

"All right." He crossed the room to her, skirting the play table and a couple of chairs. They snuggled together in the bed.

"Do you think we'll ever see him again?" Peter asked when they were settled. "The Little Red Owl?"

"Maybe," Lottie said thoughtfully, "maybe we would if we were scared or in trouble. Maybe he'd come for us then and help. I'll tell you, Peter. Let's try real hard to dream about him tonight. Maybe if we try real hard we can see him." Her voice was rich with longing. "Our own dear Little Red Owl."

There was a silence. Then Lottie said, "Have you still got the feather he gave you, Peter? Are you taking good care of it?"

In the darkness Peter nodded. "Don't you worry, Lottie," he said sleepily. "I've got it in a good safe place. Yes."

Lost Hearts

by M. R. James

IT WAS, as far as I can ascertain, in September of the year 1811 that a post-chaise drew up before the door of Aswarby Hall, in the heart of Lincolnshire. The little boy who was the only passenger in the chaise, and who jumped out as soon as it had stopped, looked about him with the keenest curiosity during the short interval that elapsed between the ringing of the bell and the opening of the hall door. He saw a tall, square, red-brick house, built in the reign of Anne; a stone-pillared porch had been added in the purer classical style of 1790; the windows of the house were many, tall and narrow, with small panes and thick white woodwork. A pediment, pierced with a round window, crowned the front. There were wings to right and left, connected by curious glazed galleries, supported by colonnades, with the central block. These wings plainly contained the stables and offices of the house. Each was surmounted by an ornamental cupola with a gilded vane.

An evening light shone on the building, making the window-panes glow like so many fires. Away from the Hall in front stretched a flat park studded with oaks and fringed with firs, which stood out against the sky. The clock in the church-tower, buried in trees on the edge of the park, only its golden weather-cock catching the light, was striking six, and the sound came gently beating down the wind. It was altogether a pleasant impression, though tinged with the sort of melancholy appropriate to an evening in early autumn, that was conveyed to the mind of the boy who was standing in the porch waiting for the door to open to him.

The post-chaise had brought him from Warwickshire, where, some six months before, he had been left an orphan. Now, owing to the gener-ous offer of his elderly cousin, Mr Abney, he had come to live at Aswarby. The offer was unexpected, because all who knew anything of Mr Abney looked upon him as a somewhat austere recluse, into whose steady-going household the advent of a small boy would import a new and, it seemed, incongruous element. The truth is that very little was known of Mr Abney's pursuits or temper. The Professor of Greek at Cambridge had been heard to say that no one knew more of the religious beliefs of the later pagans than did the owner of Aswarby. Certainly his library contained all the then available books bearing on the Mysteries, the Orphic poems, the worship of Mithras, and the Neo-Platonists. In the marble-paved hall stood a fine group of Mithras slaying a bull, which had been imported from the Levant at great expense by the owner. He had contributed a description of it to the Gentleman's Magazine, and he had written a remarkable series of articles in the Critical Museum on the superstitions of the Romans of the Lower Empire. He was looked upon, in fine, as a man wrapped up in his books, and it was a matter of great surprise among his neighbours that he should ever have heard of his orphan cousin, Stephen Elliott, much more that he should have volunteered to make him an inmate of Aswarby Hall.

Whatever may have been expected by his neighbours, it is certain that Mr Abney—the tall, the thin, the austere—seemed inclined to give his young cousin a kindly reception. The moment the front-door was opened he darted out of his study, rubbing his hands with delight.

"How are you, my boy?—how are you? How old are you?" said he— "that is, you are not too much tired, I hope, by your journey to eat your supper?"

"No, thank you, sir," said Master Elliott; "I am pretty well."

"That's a good lad," said Mr Abney. "And how old are you, my boy?"

It seemed a little odd that he should have asked the question twice in the first two minutes of their acquaintance.

"I'm twelve years old next birthday, sir," said Stephen.

"And when is your birthday, my dear boy? Eleventh of September, eh? That's well—that's very well. Nearly a year hence, isn't it? I like—ha, ha!—I like to get these things down in my book. Sure it's twelve? Certain?"

"Yes, quite sure, sir."

"Well, well! Take him to Mrs Bunch's room, Parkes, and let him have his tea—supper—whatever it is."

"Yes, sir," answered the staid Mr Parkes; and conducted Stephen to the lower regions.

Mrs Bunch was the most comfortable and human person whom Stephen had as yet met in Aswarby. She made him completely at home; they were great friends in a quarter of an hour: and great friends they remained. Mrs Bunch had been born in the neighbourhood some fifty-five years before the date of Stephen's arrival, and her residence at the

Hall was of twenty years' standing. Consequently, if anyone knew the ins and outs of the house and the district, Mrs Bunch knew them; and she was by no means disinclined to communicate her information.

Certainly there were plenty of things about the Hall and the Hall gardens which Stephen, who was of an adventurous and inquiring turn, was anxious to have explained to him. "Who built the temple at the end of the laurel walk? Who was the old man whose picture hung on the staircase, sitting at a table, with a skull under his hand?" These and many similar points were cleared up by the resources of Mrs Bunch's powerful intellect. There were others, however, of which the explanations furnished were less satisfactory.

One November evening Stephen was sitting by the fire in the house-keeper's room reflecting on his surroundings.

"Is Mr Abney a good man, and will he go to heaven?" he suddenly asked, with the peculiar confidence which children possess in the ability of their elders to settle these questions, the decision of which is believed to be reserved for other tribunals.

"Good?—bless the child!" said Mrs Bunch. "Master's as kind a soul as ever I see! Didn't I never tell you of the little boy as he took in out of the street, as you may say, this seven years back? And the little girl, two years after I first come here?"

"No. Do tell me all about them, Mrs Bunch—now, this minute!"

"Well," said Mrs Bunch, "the little girl I don't seem to recollect so much about. I know master brought her back with him from his walk one day, and give orders to Mrs Ellis, as was housekeeper then, as she should be took every care with. And the pore child hadn't no one belonging to her—she telled me so her own self—and here she lived with us a matter of three weeks it might be; and then, whether she were some think of a gipsy in her blood or what not, but one morning she out of her bed afore any of us had opened a eye, and neither track nor yet trace of her have I set eyes on since. Master was wonderful put about, and had all the ponds dragged; but it's my belief she was had away by them gipsies, for there was singing round the house for as much as an hour the night she went, and Parkes, he declare as he heard them a-calling in the woods all that afternoon. Dear, dear! A hodd child she was, so silent in her ways and all, but I was wonderful taken up with her, so domesticated she was— surprising."

"And what about the little boy?" said Stephen.

"Ah, that pore boy!" sighed Mrs Bunch. "He were a foreigner— Jevanny he called hisself—and he come a-tweaking his 'urdy-gurdy' round and about the drive one winter day, and master 'ad him in that minute, and ast all about where he came from, and how old he was, and how he made his way, and where was his relatives, and all as kind as heart could wish. But it went the same way with him. They're a hunruly lot, them foreign nations, I do suppose, and he was off one fine morning just the same as the girl. Why he went and what he done was our question for as much as a year after; for he never took his 'urdy-gurdy, and there it lays on the shelf."

The remainder of the evening was spent by Stephen in miscellaneous cross-examination of Mrs Bunch and in efforts to extract a tune from the hurdy-gurdy.

That night he had a curious dream. At the end of the passage at the top of the house, in which his bedroom was situated, there was an old disused bathroom. It was kept locked, but the upper half of the door was glazed, and, since the muslin curtains which used to hang there had long been gone, you could look in and see the lead-lined bath affixed to the wall on the right hand, with its head towards the window.

On the night of which I am speaking, Stephen Elliott found himself, as he thought, looking through the glazed door. The moon was shining through the window, and he was gazing at a figure which lay in the bath.

His description of what he saw reminds me of what I once beheld myself in the famous vaults of St Michan's Church in Dublin, which possess the horrid property of preserving corpses from decay for centuries. A figure inexpressibly thin and pathetic, of a dusty leaden colour, enveloped in a shroud-like garment, the thin lips crooked into a faint and dreadful smile, the hands pressed tightly over the region of the heart.

As he looked upon it, a distant, almost inaudible moan seemed to issue from its lips, and the arms began to stir. The terror of the sight forced Stephen backwards, and he awoke to the fact that he was indeed standing on the cold boarded floor of the passage in the full light of the moon. With a courage which I do not think can be common among boys of his age, he went to the door of the bathroom to ascertain if the figure of his dream were really there. It was not, and he went back to bed.

Mrs Bunch was much impressed next morning by his story, and went so far as to replace the muslin curtain over the glazed door of the bathroom. Mr Abney, moreover, to whom he confided his experiences at breakfast, was greatly interested, and made notes of the matter in what he called "his book".

The spring equinox was approaching, as Mr Abney frequently reminded his cousin, adding that this had been always considered by the ancients to be a critical time for the young: that Stephen would do well to take care of himself, and to shut his bedroom window at night; and that Censorinus had some valuable remarks on the subject. Two incidents that occurred about this time made an impression upon Stephen's mind.

The first was after an unusually uneasy and oppressed night that he had passed—though he could not recall any particular dream that he had had.

The following evening Mrs Bunch was occupying herself in mending his nightgown.

"Gracious me, Master Stephen!" she broke forth rather irritably, "how do you manage to tear your nightdress all to flinders this way? Look here, sir, what trouble you do give to poor servants that have to darn and mend after you!"

There was indeed a most destructive and apparently wanton series of slits or scorings in the garment, which would undoubtedly require a skilful needle to make good. They were confined to the left side of the chest—long, parallel slits, about six inches in length, some of them not quite piercing the texture of the linen. Stephen could only express his entire ignorance of their origin: he was sure they were not there the night before.

"But," he said, "Mrs Bunch, they are just the same as the scratches on the outside of my bedroom door; and I'm sure I never had anything to do with making them."

Mrs Bunch gazed at him open-mouthed, then snatched up a candle, departed hastily from the room, and was heard making her way upstairs. In a few minutes she came down.

"Well," she said, "Master Stephen, it's a funny thing to me how them marks and scratches can 'a' come there—too high up for any cat or dog to 'ave made 'em, much less a rat: for all the world like a Chinaman's finger-nails, as my uncle in the tea-trade used to tell us of when we was girls together. I wouldn't say nothing to master, not if I was you, Master Stephen, my dear; and just turn the key of the door when you go to your bed."

"I always do, Mrs Bunch, as soon as I've said my prayers."

"Ah, that's a good child: always say your prayers, and then no one can't hurt you."

Herewith Mrs Bunch addressed herself to mending the injured nightgown, with intervals of meditation, until bed-time. This was on a Friday night in March, 1812.

On the following evening the usual duet of Stephen and Mrs Bunch was augmented by the sudden arrival of Mr Parkes, the butler, who as a rule kept himself rather to himself in his own pantry. He did not see that Stephen was there: he was, moreover, flustered and less slow of speech than was his wont.

"Master may get up his own wine, if he likes, of an evening," was his first remark. "Either I do it in the daytime or not at all, Mrs Bunch. I don't know what it may be: very like it's the rats, or the wind got into the cellars; but I'm not so young as I was, and I can't go through with it as I have done."

"Well, Mr Parkes, you know it is a surprising place for the rats, is the Hall."

"I'm not denying that, Mrs Bunch; and, to be sure, many a time I've heard the tale from the men in the shipyards about the rat that could speak. I never laid no confidence in that before; but tonight, if I'd de-meaned myself to lay my ear to the door of the further bin, I could pretty much have heard what they was saying."

"Oh, there, Mr Parkes, I've no patience with your fancies! Rats talking in the wine-cellar indeed!"

"Well, Mrs Bunch, I've no wish to argue with you: all I say is, if you choose to go to the far bin, and lay your ear to the door, you may prove my words this minute."

"What nonsense you do talk, Mr Parkes—not fit for children to listen to! Why, you'll be frightening Master Stephen there out of his wits."

"What! Master Stephen?" said Parkes, awaking to the consciousness of the boy's presence. "Master Stephen knows well enough when I'm a-playing a joke with you, Mrs Bunch."

In fact, Master Stephen knew much too well to suppose that Mr Parkes had in the first instance intended a joke. He was interested, not altogether pleasantly, in the situation; but all his questions were unsuc-cessful in inducing the butler to give any more detailed account of his experiences in the wine-cellar.

We have now arrived at March 24, 1812. It was a day of curious experiences for Stephen: a windy, noisy day, which filled the house and the gardens with a restless impression. As Stephen stood by the fence of the grounds, and looked out into the park, he felt as if an endless pro-cession of unseen people were sweeping past him on the wind, borne on resistlessly and aimlessly, vainly striving to stop themselves, to catch at something that might arrest their flight and bring them once again into contact with the living world of which they had formed a part. After luncheon that day Mr Abney said:

"Stephen, my boy, do you think you could manage to come to me tonight as late as eleven o'clock in my study? I shall be busy until that time, and I wish to show you something connected with your future life which it is most important that you should know. You are not to mention this matter to Mrs Bunch nor to anyone else in the house; and you had better go to your room at the usual time."

Here was a new excitement added to life: Stephen eagerly grasped at the opportunity of sitting up till eleven o'clock. He looked in at the library door on his way upstairs that evening, and saw a brazier, which he had often noticed in the corner of the room, moved out before the fire; an old silver-gilt cup stood on the table, filled with red wine, and some written sheets of paper lay near it. Mr Abney was sprinkling some incense on the brazier from a round silver box as Stephen passed, but did not seem to notice his step.

The wind had fallen, and there was a still night and a full moon. At about ten o'clock Stephen was standing at the open window of his bedroom, looking out over the country. Still as the night was, the mysterious population of the distant moon-lit woods was not yet lulled to rest. From time to time strange cries as of lost and despairing wanderers sounded from across the mere. They might be the notes of owls or waterbirds, yet they did not quite resemble either sound. Were not they coming nearer? Now they sounded from the nearer side of the water, and in a few moments they seemed to be floating about among the shrubberies. Then they ceased; but just as Stephen was thinking of shutting the window and resuming his reading of *Robinson Crusoe*, he caught sight of two figures standing on the gravelled terrace that ran along the garden side of the Hall—the figures of a boy and girl, as it seemed; they stood side by side, looking up at the windows. Something in the form of the girl recalled irresistibly his dream of the figure in the bath. The boy inspired him with more acute fear.

Whilst the girl stood still, half smiling, with her hands clasped over her heart, the boy, a thin shape, with black hair and ragged clothing, raised his arms in the air with an appearance of menace and of unappeasable hunger and longing. The moon shone upon his almost transparent hands, and Stephen saw that the nails were fearfully long and that the light shone through them. As he stood with his arms thus raised, he disclosed a terrifying spectacle. On the left side of his chest there opened a black and gaping rent; and there fell upon Stephen's brain, rather than upon his ear, the impression of one of those hungry and desolate cries that he had heard resounding over the woods of Aswarby all that evening.

In another moment this dreadful pair had moved swiftly and noiselessly over the dry gravel, and he saw them no more.

Inexpressibly frightened as he was, he determined to take his candle and go down to Mr Abney's study, for the hour appointed for their meeting was near at hand. The study or library opened out of the front-hall on one side, and Stephen, urged on by his terrors, did not take long in getting there. To effect an entrance was not so easy. It was not locked, he felt sure, for the key was on the outside of the door as usual. His repeated knocks produced no answer. Mr Abney was engaged: he was speaking. What! why did he try to cry out? And why was the cry choked in his throat? Had he, too, seen the mysterious children? But now everything was quiet, and the door yielded to Stephen's terrified and frantic pushing.

On the table in Mr Abney's study certain papers were found which explained the situation to Stephen Elliott when he was of an age to understand them. The most important sentences were as follows:

"It was a belief very strongly and generally held by the ancients—of whose wisdom in these matters I have had such experience as induces me to place confidence in their assertions—that by enacting certain processes, which to us moderns have something of a barbaric complexion, a very remarkable enlightenment of the spiritual faculties in man may be attained: that, for example, by absorbing the personalities of a certain number of his fellow-creatures, an individual may gain a complete ascendancy over those orders of spiritual beings which control the elemental forces of our universe.

"It is recorded of Simon Magus that he was able to fly in the air, to become invisible, or to assume any form he pleased, by the agency of the soul of a boy whom, to use the libellous phrase employed by the author of the Clementine Recognitions, he had 'murdered'. I find it set down, moreover, with considerable detail in the writings of Hermes Trismegistus, that similar happy results may be produced by the absorption of the hearts of not less than three human beings below the age of twenty-one years. To the testing of the truth of this receipt I have devoted the greater part of the last twenty years, selecting as the *corpora vilia* of my experiment such persons as could conveniently be removed without occasioning a sensible gap in society. The first step I effected by the removal of one Phoebe Stanley, a girl of gipsy extraction, on March 24, 1792. The second, by the removal of a wandering Italian lad, named Giovanni Paoli, on the night of March 23, 1805. The final 'victim'—to employ a word repugnant in the highest degree to my feelings—must be my cousin, Stephen Elliott. His day must be this March 24, 1812.

"The best means of effecting the required absorption is to remove the heart from the living subject, to reduce it to ashes, and to mingle them with about a pint of some red wine, preferably port. The remains of the first two subjects, at least, it will be well to conceal: a disused bathroom or wine-cellar will be found convenient for such a purpose. Some annoyance may be experienced from the psychic portion of the subjects, which popular language dignifies with the name of ghosts. But the man of philosophic temperament—to whom alone the experiment is appropriate—will be little prone to attach importance to the feeble efforts of these beings to wreak their vengeance on him. I contemplate with the liveliest satisfaction the enlarged and emancipated existence which the experiment, if successful, will confer on me; not only placing me beyond the reach of human justice (so-called), but eliminating to a great extent the prospect of death itself."

Mr Abney was found in his chair, his head thrown back, his face stamped with an expression of rage, fright, and mortal pain. In his left side was a terrible lacerated wound, exposing the heart. There was no blood on his hands, and a long knife that lay on the table was perfectly clean. A savage wild-cat might have inflicted the injuries. The window of the study was open, and it was the opinion of the coroner that Mr Abney had met his death by the agency of some wild creature. But Stephen Elliott's study of the papers I have quoted led him to a very different conclusion.

IT

by Theodore Sturgeon

IT WALKED IN THE WOODS.

It was never born. It existed. Under the pine needles the fires burn, deep and smokeless in the mold. In heat and in darkness and decay there is growth. There is life and there is growth. It grew, but it was not alive. It walked unbreathing through the woods, and thought and saw and was hideous and strong, and it was not born and it did not live. It grew and moved about without living.

It crawled out of the darkness and hot damp mold into the cool of a morning. It was huge. It was lumped and crusted with its own hateful substances, and pieces of it dropped off as it went its way, dropped off and lay writhing, and stilled, and sank putrescent into the forest loam.

It had no mercy, no laughter, no beauty. It had strength and great intelligence. And—perhaps it could not be destroyed. It crawled out of its mound in the wood and lay pulsing in the sunlight for a long moment. Patches of it shone wetly in the golden glow, parts of it were nubbled and flaked. And whose dead bones had given it the form of a man?

It scrabbled painfully with its half-formed hands, beating the ground and the bole of a tree. It rolled and lifted itself up on its crumbling elbows, and it tore up a great handful of herbs and shredded them against its chest, and it paused and gazed at the gray-green juices with intelligent calm. It wavered to its feet, and seized a young sapling and destroyed it, folding the slender trunk back on itself again and again, watching attentively the useless, fibered splinters. And it snatched up a fear-frozen field-creature, crushing it slowly, letting blood and pulpy flesh and fur ooze from between its fingers, run down and rot on the forearms.

It began searching.

~§~

Kimbo drifted through the tall grasses like a puff of dust, his bushy tail curled tightly over his back and his long jaws agape. He ran with an easy lope, loving his freedom and the power of his flanks and furry shoulders. His tongue lolled listlessly over his lips. His lips were black and serrated, and each tiny pointed liplet swayed with his doggy gallop. Kimbo was all dog, all healthy animal.

He leaped high over a boulder and landed with a startled yelp as a long-eared cony shot from its hiding place under the rock. Kimbo hurtled after it, grunting with each great thrust of his legs. The rabbit bounced just ahead of him, keeping its distance, its ears flattened on its curving back and its little legs nibbling away at distance hungrily. It stopped, and Kimbo pounced, and the rabbit shot away at a tangent and popped into a hollow log. Kimbo yelped again and rushed snuffling at the log, and knowing his failure, curvetted but once around the stump and ran on into the forest. The thing that watched from the wood raised its crusted arms and waited for Kimbo.

Kimbo sensed it there, standing dead-still by the path. To him it was a bulk which smelled of carrion not fit to roll in, and he snuffled distaste-fully and ran to pass it.

The thing let him come abreast and dropped a heavy twisted fist on him. Kimbo saw it coming and curled up tight as he ran, and the hand clipped stunningly on his rump, sending him rolling and yipping down the slope. Kimbo straddled to his feet, shook his head, shook his body with a deep growl, came back to the silent thing with green murder in his eyes. He walked stiffly, straight-legged, his tail as low as his lowered head and a ruff of fury round his neck. The thing raised its arm again, waited.

Kimbo slowed, then flipped himself through the air at the monster's throat. His jaws closed on it; his teeth clicked together through a mass of filth, and he fell choking and snarling at its feet. The thing leaned down and struck twice, and after the dog's back was broken, it sat beside him and began to tear him apart.

~§~

"Be back in an hour or so," said Alton Drew, picking up his rifle from the corner behind the wood box. His brother laughed.

"Old Kimbo 'bout runs your life, Alton," he said.

"Ah, I know the ol' devil," said Alton. "When I whistle for him for half an hour and he don't show up, he's in a jam or he's treed something wuth shootin' at. The ol' son of a gun calls me by not answerin'."

Cory Drew shoved a full glass of milk over to his nine-year-old daughter and smiled. "You think as much o' that houn' dog o' yours as I do of Babe here."

Babe slid off her chair and ran to her uncle. "Gonna catch me the bad fella, Uncle Alton?" she shrilled. The "bad fella" was Cory's invention —the one who lurked in corners ready to pounce on little girls who chased the chickens and played around mowing machines and hurled green apples with powerful young arms at the sides of the hogs, to hear the synchronized thud and grunt; little girls who swore with an Austrian accent like an ex-hired man they had had; who dug caves in haystacks till they tipped over, and kept pet crawfish in tomorrow's milk cans, and rode work horses to a lather in the night pasture.

"Get back here and keep away from Uncle Alton's gun!" said Cory. "If you see the bad fella, Alton, chase him back here. He has a date with Babe here for that stunt of hers last night." The preceding evening, Babe had kind-heartedly poured pepper on the cows' salt block.

"Don't worry, kiddo," grinned her uncle, "I'll bring you the bad fella's hide if he don't get me first."

~§~

Alton Drew walked up the path toward the wood, thinking about Babe. She was a phenomenon—a pampered farm child. Ah well—she had to be. They'd both loved Clissa Drew, and she'd married Cory, and they had to love Clissa's child. Funny thing, love. Alton was a man's man, and thought things out that way; and his reaction to love was a strong and frightened one. He knew what love was because he felt it still for his brother's wife and would feel it as long as he lived for Babe. It led him through his life, and yet he embarrassed himself by thinking of it. Loving a dog was an easy thing, because you and the old devil could love one another completely without talking about it. The smell of gun smoke and wet fur in the rain were perfume enough for Alton Drew, a grunt of satisfaction and the scream of something hunted and hit were poetry enough. They weren't like love for a human, that choked his throat so he could not say words he could not have thought of anyway. So Alton loved his dog Kimbo and his Winchester for all to see, and let his love for his brother's women, Clissa and Babe, eat at him quietly and unmentioned.

His quick eyes saw the fresh indentations in the soft earth behind the boulder, which showed where Kimbo had turned and leaped with a single surge, chasing the rabbit. Ignoring the tracks, he looked for the nearest place where a rabbit might hide, and strolled over to the stump. Kimbo had been there, he saw, and had been there too late. "You're an ol' fool," muttered Alton. "Y' can't catch a cony by chasin' it. You want to cross him up some way." He gave a peculiar trilling whistle, sure that Kimbo was digging frantically under some nearby stump for a rabbit that was three counties away by now. No answer. A little puzzled, Alton went back to the path. "He never done this before," he said softly.

He cocked his .32-40 and cradled it. At the county fair someone had once said of Alton Drew that he could shoot at a handful of corn and peas thrown in the air and hit only the corn. Once he split a bullet on the blade of a knife and put two candles out. He had no need to fear anything that could be shot at. That's what he believed.

~§~

The thing in the woods looked curiously down at what it had done to Kimbo, and tried to moan the way Kimbo had before he died. It stood a minute storing away facts in its foul, unemotional mind. Blood was warm. The sunlight was warm. Things that moved and bore fur had a muscle to force the thick liquid through tiny tubes in their bodies. The liquid coagulated after a time. The liquid on rooted green things was thinner and the loss of a limb did not mean loss of life. It was very interesting, but the thing, the mold with a mind, was not pleased. Neither was it displeased. Its accidental urge was a thirst for knowledge, and it was only—interested.

It was growing late, and the sun reddened and rested awhile on the hilly horizon, teaching the clouds to be inverted flames. The thing threw up its head suddenly, noticing the dusk. Night was ever a strange thing, even for those of us who have known it in life. It would have been frightening for the monster had it been capable of fright, but it could only be curious; it could only reason from what it had observed.

What was happening? It was getting harder to see. Why? It threw its shapeless head from side to side. It was true—things were dim, and growing dimmer. Things were changing shape, taking on a new and darker color. What did the creatures it had crushed and torn apart see? How did they see? The larger one, the one that had attacked, had used two organs in its head. That must have been it, because after the thing had torn off two of the dog's legs it had struck at the hairy muzzle; and the dog, seeing the blow coming, had dropped folds of skin over the organs—closed its eyes. Ergo, the dog saw with its eyes. But then after the dog was dead, and its body still, repeated blows had had no effect on the eyes. They remained open and staring. The logical conclusion was, then, that a being that had ceased to live and breathe and move about lost the use of its eyes. It must be that to lose sight was, conversely, to die. Dead things did not walk about. They lay down and did not move. Therefore the thing in the wood concluded that it must be dead, and so it lay down by the path, not far away from Kimbo's scattered body, lay down and believed itself dead.

~§~

Alton Drew came up through the dusk to the wood. He was frankly worried. He whistled again, and then called, and there was still no response, and he said again, "The ol' flea-bus never done this before," and shook his heavy head. It was past milking time, and Cory would need him. "Kimbo!" he roared. The cry echoed through the shadows, and Alton flipped on the safety catch of his rifle and put the butt on the ground beside the path. Leaning on it, he took off his cap and scratched the back of his head, wondering. The rifle butt sank into what he thought was soft earth; he staggered and stepped into the chest of the thing that lay beside the path. His foot went up to the ankle in its yielding rottenness, and he swore and jumped back.

"*Whew!* Somp'n sure dead as hell there! Ugh!" He swabbed at his boot with a handful of leaves while the monster lay in the growing blackness with the edges of the deep footprint in its chest sliding into it, filling it up. It lay there regarding him dimly out of its muddy eyes, thinking it was dead because of the darkness, watching the articulation of Alton Drew's joints, wondering at this new uncautious creature.

Alton cleaned the butt of his gun with more leaves and went on up the path, whistling anxiously for Kimbo.

~§~

Clissa Drew stood in the door of the milk shed, very lovely in red-checked gingham and a blue apron. Her hair was clean yellow, parted in the middle and stretched tautly back to a heavy braided knot. "Cory! Alton!" she called a little sharply.

"Well?" Cory responded gruffly from the barn, where he was stripping off the Ayrshire. The dwindling streams of milk plopped pleasantly into the froth of a full pail.

"I've called and called," said Clissa. "Supper's cold, and Babe won't eat until you come. Why—where's Alton?"

Cory grunted, heaved the stool out of the way, threw over the stanchion lock and slapped the Ayrshire on the rump. The cow backed and filled like a towboat, clattered down the line and out into the barn-yard. "Ain't back yet."

"Not back?" Clissa came in and stood beside him as he sat by the next cow, put his forehead against the warm flank. "But, Cory, he said he'd—"

"Yeh, yeh, I know. He said he'd be back fer the milkin'. I heard him. Well, he ain't."

"And you have to—Oh, Cory, I'll help you finish up. Alton would be back if he could. Maybe he's—"

"Maybe he's treed a blue jay," snapped her husband. "Him an' that damn dog." He gestured hugely with one hand while the other went on milking. "I got twenty-six head o' cows to milk. I got pigs to feed an' chickens to put to bed. I got to toss hay for the mare and turn the team out. I got harness to mend and a wire down in the night pasture. I got wood to split an' carry." He milked for a moment in silence, chewing on his lip. Clissa stood twisting her hands together, trying to think of something to stem the tide. It wasn't the first time Alton's hunting had interfered with the chores. "So I got to go ahead with it. I can't interfere with Alton's spoorin'. Every damn time that hound o' his smells out a squirrel I go without my supper. I'm getting' sick and—"

"Oh, I'll help you!" said Clissa. She was thinking of the spring, when Kimbo had held four hundred pounds of raging black bear at bay until Alton could put a bullet in its brain, the time Babe had found a bear cub and started to carry it home, and had fallen into a freshet, cutting her head. You can't hate a dog that has saved your child for you, she thought.

"You'll do nothin' of the kind!" Cory growled. "Get back to the house. You'll find work enough there. I'll be along when I can. Dammit, Clissa, don't cry! I didn't mean to—Oh, shucks!" He got up and put his arms around her. "I'm wrought up," he said. "Go on now. I'd no call to speak that way to you. I'm sorry. Go back to Babe. I'll put a stop to this for good tonight. I've had enough. There's work here for four farmers an' all we've got is me an' that . . . that huntsman.

"Go on now, Clissa."

"All right," she said into his shoulder. "But, Cory, hear him out first when he comes back. He might be unable to come back. He might be unable to come back this time. Maybe he . . . he—"

"Ain't nothin' kin hurt my brother that a bullet will hit. He can take care of himself. He's got no excuse good enough this time. Go on, now. Make the kid eat."

Clissa went back to the house, her young face furrowed. If Cory quarreled with Alton now and drove him away, what with the drought and the creamery about to close and all, they just couldn't manage. Hiring a man was out of the question. Cory'd have to work himself to death, and he just wouldn't be able to make it. No one man could. She sighed and went into the house. It was seven o'clock, and the milking not done yet. Oh, why did Alton have to—

Babe was in bed at nine when Clissa heard Cory in the shed, slinging the wire cutters into a corner. "Alton back yet?" they both said at once as Cory stepped into the kitchen; and as she shook her head he clumped over to the stove, and lifting a lid, spat into the coals. "Come to bed," he said.

She laid down her stitching and looked at his broad back. He was twenty-eight, and he walked and acted like a man ten years older, and looked like a man five years younger. "I'll be up in a while," Clissa said.

Cory glanced at the corner behind the wood box where Alton's rifle usually stood, then made an unspellable, disgusted sound and sat down to take off his heavy muddy shoes.

"It's after nine," Clissa volunteered timidly. Cory said nothing, reaching for house slippers.

"Cory, you're not going to—"

"Not going to what?"

"Oh, nothing. I just thought that maybe Alton—"

"Alton," Cory flared. "The dog goes hunting field mice. Alton goes hunting the dog. Now you want me to go hunting Alton. That's what you want?"

"I just— He was never this late before."

"I won't do it! Go out lookin' for him at nine o'clock in the night? I'll be damned! He has no call to use us so, Clissa."

Clissa said nothing. She went to the stove, peered into the wash boiler set aside at the back of the range. When she turned around, Cory had his shoes and coat on again.

"I knew you'd go," she said. Her voice smiled though she did not.

"I'll be back durned soon," said Cory. "I don't reckon he's strayed far. It is late. I ain't feared for him, but—" He broke his 12-gauge shotgun, looked through the barrels, slipped two shells in the breech and a box of them into his pocket. "Don't wait up," he said over his shoulder as he went out.

"I won't," Clissa replied to the closed door, and went back to her stitching by the lamp.

The path up the slope to the wood was very dark when Cory went up it, peering and calling. The air was chill and quiet, and a fetid odor of mold hung in it. Cory blew the taste of it out through impatient nostrils, drew it in again with the next breath, and swore. "Nonsense," he muttered. "Houn' dawg. Huntin', at ten in th' night, too. Alton!" he bellowed. "Alton Drew!" Echoes answered him, and he entered the wood. The huddled thing he passed in the dark heard him and felt the vibrations of his footsteps and did not move because it thought it was dead.

Cory strode on, looking around and ahead and not down since his feet knew the path.

"Alton!"

"That you, Cory?"

Cory Drew froze. That corner of the wood was thickly set and as dark as a burial vault. The voice he heard was choked, quiet, penetrating.

"Alton?"

"I found Kimbo, Cory."

"Where the hell have you been?" shouted Cory furiously. He disliked this pitch-darkness; he was afraid at the tense hopelessness of Alton's voice, and he mistrusted his ability to stay angry at his brother.

"I called him, Cory. I whistled at him, an' the ol' devil didn't answer."

"I can say the same for you, you . . . you louse. Why weren't you to milkin'? Where are you? You caught in a trap?"

"The houn' never missed answerin' me before, you know," said the tight, monotonous voice from the darkness.

"Alton! What the devil's the matter with you? What do I care if your mutt didn't answer? Where—"

"I guess because he ain't never died before," said Alton, refusing to be interrupted.

"You *what?*" Cory clicked his lips together twice and then said, "Alton, you turned crazy? What's that you say?"

"Kimbo's dead."

"Kim . . . oh! Oh!" Cory was seeing that picture again in his mind— Babe sprawled unconscious in the freshet, and Kimbo raging and snapping against a monster bear, holding her back until Alton could get there. "What happened, Alton?" he asked more quietly.

"I aim to find out. Someone tore him up."

"Tore him up?"

"There ain't a bit of him left tacked together, Cory. Every damn joint in his body tore apart. Guts out of him."

"Good God! Bear, you reckon?"

"No bear, nor nothin' on four legs. He's all here. None of him's been et. Whoever done it just killed him an'—tore him up."

"Good God!" Cory said again. "Who could've—" There was a long silence, then. "Come 'long home," he said almost gently.

"There's no call for you to set up by him all night."

"I'll set. I aim to be here at sunup, an' I'm going to start trackin', an' I'm goin' to keep trackin' till I find the one done this job on Kimbo."

"You're drunk or crazy, Alton."

"I ain't drunk. You can think what you like about the rest of it. I'm stickin' here."

"We got a farm back yonder. Remember? I ain't going to milk twenty-six head o' cows again in the mornin' like I did jest now, Alton."

"Somebody's got to. I can't be there. I guess you'll just have to, Cory."

"You dirty scum!" Cory screamed. "You'll come back with me now or I'll know why!"

Alton's voice was still tight, half-sleepy. "Don't you come no nearer, bud."

Cory kept moving toward Alton's voice.

"I said"—the voice was very quiet now—*"Stop where you are."* Cory kept coming. A sharp click told of the release of the .32-40's safety. Cory stopped.

"You got your gun on me, Alton?" Cory whispered.

"Thass right, bud. You ain't a-trompin' up these tracks for me. I need 'em at sunup."

A full minute passed, and the only sound in the blackness was that of Cory's pained breathing. Finally:

"I got my gun, too, Alton. Come home."

"You can't see to shoot me."

"We're even on that."

"We ain't. I know just where you stand, Cory. I been here four hours."

"My gun scatters."

"My gun kills."

Without another word Cory Drew turned on his heel and stamped back to the farm.

~§~

Black and liquidescent it lay in the blackness, not alive, not under-standing death, believing itself dead. Things that were alive saw and moved about. Things that were not alive could do neither. It rested its muddy gaze on the line of trees at the crest of the rise, and deep within it thoughts trickled wetly. It lay huddled, dividing its new-found facts, dissecting them as it had dissected live things when there was light; comparing, concluding, pigeonholing.

The trees at the top of the slope could just be seen, as their trunks were a fraction of a shade lighter than the dark sky behind them. At length they, too, disappeared, and for a moment sky and trees were a monotone. The thing knew it was dead now, and like many a being before it, it wondered how long it must stay like this. And then the sky beyond the trees grew a little lighter. That was a manifestly impossible occur-rence, thought the thing, but it could see it and it must be so. Did dead things live again? That was curious. What about dismembered dead things? It would wait and see.

The sun came hand over hand up a beam of light. A bird somewhere made a high yawning peep, and as an owl killed a shrew, a skunk pounced on another, so that the night-shift deaths and those of the day could go on without cessation. Two flowers nodded archly to each other, compar-ing their pretty clothes. A dragonfly nymph decided it was tired of looking serious and cracked its back open, to crawl out and dry gauzily. The first golden ray sheared down between the trees, through the grasses, passed over the mass in the shadowed bushes. "I am alive again," thought the thing that could not possibly live. "I am alive, for I see clearly." It stood up on its thick legs, up into the golden glow. In a little while the wet flakes that had grown during the night dried in the sun, and when it took its first steps, they cracked off and a small shower of them fell away. It walked up the slope to find Kimbo, to see if he, too, were alive again.

~§~

Babe let the sun come into her room by opening her eyes. Uncle Alton was gone—that was the first thing that ran through her head. Dad had come home last night and had shouted at mother for an hour. Alton was plumb crazy. He'd turned a gun on his own brother. If Alton ever came ten feet into Cory's land, Cory would fill him so full of holes, he'd look like a tumbleweed. Alton was lazy, shiftless, selfish, and one or two other things of questionable taste but undoubted vividness. Babe knew her father. Uncle Alton would never be safe in this county.

She bounced out of bed in the enviable way of the very young, and ran to the window. Cory was trudging down to the night pasture with two bridles over his arm, to get the team. There were kitchen noises from downstairs.

Babe ducked her head in the washbowl and shook off the water like a terrier before she toweled. Trailing clean shirt and dungarees, she went to the head of the stairs, slid into the shirt, and began her morning ritual with the trousers. One step down was a step through the right leg. One more, and she was into the left. Then, bouncing step by step on both feet, buttoning one button per step, she reached the bottom fully dressed and ran into the kitchen. "Didn't Uncle Alton come back a-tall, Mum?"

"Morning, Babe. No, dear." Clissa was too quiet, smiling too much, Babe thought shrewdly. Wasn't happy.

"Where'd he go, Mum?"

"We don't know, Babe. Sit down and eat your breakfast."

"What's a misbegotten, Mum?" the Babe asked suddenly. Her mother nearly dropped the dish she was drying. "Babe! You must never say that again!"

"Oh. Well, why is Uncle Alton, then?"

"Why is he what?"

Babe's mouth muscled around an outsize spoonful of oatmeal. "A misbe—"

"Babe!"

"All right, Mum," said Babe with her mouth full. "Well, why?"

"I told Cory not to shout last night," Clissa said half to herself.

"Well, whatever it means, he isn't," said Babe with finality. "Did he go hunting again?"

"He went to look for Kimbo, darling."

"Kimbo? Oh Mummy, is Kimbo gone, too? Didn't he come back either?"

"No dear. Oh, please, Babe, stop asking questions!"

"All right. Where do you think they went?"

"Into the north woods. Be quiet."

Babe gulped away at her breakfast. An idea struck her; and as she thought of it she ate slower and slower, and cast more and more glances at her mother from under the lashes of her tilted eyes. It would be awful if daddy did anything to Uncle Alton. Someone ought to warn him.

Babe was halfway to the woods when Alton's .32-40 sent echoes giggling up and down the valley.

~§~

Cory was in the south thirty, riding a cultivator and cussing at the team of grays when he heard the gun. "Hoa," he called to the horses, and sat a moment to listen to the sound. "One-two-three. Four," he counted. "Saw someone, blasted away at him. Had a chance to take aim and give him another, careful. My God!" He threw up the cultivator points and steered the team into the shade of three oaks. He hobbled the gelding with swift tosses of a spare strap, and headed for the woods. "Alton a killer," he murmured, and doubled back to the house for his gun. Clissa was standing just outside the door.

"Get shells!" he snapped and flung into the house. Clissa followed him. He was strapping his hunting knife on before she could get a box off the shelf. "Cory—"

"Hear that gun, did you? Alton's off his nut. He don't waste lead. He shot at someone just then, and he wasn't fixin' to shoot pa'tridges when I saw him last. He was out to get a man. Gimme my gun."

"Cory, Babe—"

"You keep her here. Oh, God, this is a helluva mess. I can't stand much more." Cory ran out the door.

Clissa caught his arm: "Cory I'm trying to tell you. Babe isn't here. I've called, and she isn't here."

Cory's heavy, young-old face tautened. "Babe—Where did you last see her?"

"Breakfast." Clissa was crying now.

"She say where she was going?"

"No. She asked a lot of questions about Alton and where he'd gone."

"Did you say?"

Clissa's eyes widened, and she nodded, biting the back of her hand.

"You shouldn't ha' done that, Clissa," he gritted, and ran toward the woods, Clissa looking after him, and in that moment she could have killed herself.

Cory ran with his head up, straining with his legs and lungs and eyes at the long path. He puffed up the slope to the woods, agonized for breath after the forty-five minutes' heavy going. He couldn't even notice the damp smell of mold in the air.

He caught a movement in a thicket to his right, and dropped. Struggling to keep his breath, he crept forward until he could see clearly. There was something in there, all right. Something black, keeping still. Cory relaxed his legs and torso completely to make it easier for his heart to pump some strength back into them, and slowly raised the 12-gauge until it bore on the thing hidden in the thicket.

"Come out!" Cory said when he could speak.

Nothing happened.

"Come out or by God I'll shoot!" rasped Cory.

There was a long moment of silence, and his finger tightened on the trigger.

"You asked for it," he said, and as he fired, the thing leaped sideways into the open, screaming.

It was a thin little man dressed in sepulchral black, and bearing the rosiest baby-face Cory had ever seen. The face was twisted with fright and pain. The man scrambled to his feet and hopped up and down saying over and over, "Oh, my hand. Don't shoot again! Oh, my hand. Don't shoot again!" He stopped after a bit, when Cory had climbed to his feet, and he regarded the farmer out of sad china-blue eyes. "You shot me," he said reproachfully, holding up a little bloody hand. "Oh, my goodness."

Cory said, "Now, who the hell are you?"

The man immediately became hysterical, mouthing such a flood of broken sentences that Cory stepped back a pace and half-raised his gun in self-defense. It seemed to consist mostly of "I lost my papers," and "I didn't do it," and "It was horrible. Horrible. Horrible," and "The dead man," and "Oh, don't shoot again."

Cory tried twice to ask him a question, and then he stepped over and knocked the man down. He lay on the ground writhing and moaning and blubbering and putting his bloody hand to his mouth where Cory had hit him.

"Now what's going on around here?"

The man rolled over and sat up. "I didn't do it!" he sobbed. "I didn't. I was walking along and I heard the gun and I heard some swearing and an awful scream and I went over there and peeped and I saw the dead man and I ran away and you came and I hid and you shot me and—"

"Shut up!" The man did, as if a switch had been thrown. "Now," said Cory, pointing along the path, "you say there's a dead man up there?"

The man nodded and began crying in earnest. Cory helped him up. "Follow this path back to my farmhouse," he said. "Tell my wife to fix up your hand. Don't tell her anything else. And wait there until I come.

Hear?"

"Yes. Thank you. Oh, thank you. *Snff.*"

"Go on now." Cory gave him a gentle shove in the right direction and went alone, in cold fear, up the path to the spot where he had found Alton the night before. He found him here now, too, and Kimbo. Kimbo and Alton had spent several years together in the deepest friendship; they had hunted and fought and slept together, and the lives they owed each other were finished now. They were dead together.

It was terrible that they died the same way. Cory Drew was a strong man, but he gasped and fainted dead away when he saw what the thing of the mold had done to his brother and his brother's dog.

~§~

The little man in black hurried down the path, whimpering and holding his injured hand as if he rather wished he could limp with it. After a while the whimper faded away, and the hurried stride changed to a walk as the gibbering terror of the last hour receded. He drew two deep breaths, said: "My goodness!" and felt almost normal. He bound a linen handkerchief around his wrist, but the hand kept bleeding. He tried the elbow, and that made it hurt. So he stuffed the handkerchief back in his pocket and simply waved the hand stupidly in the air until the blood clotted. He did not see the great moist horror that clumped along behind him, although his nostrils crinkled with its foulness.

The monster had three holes close together on its chest, and one hole in the middle of its slimy forehead. It had three close-set pits in its back and one on the back of its head. These marks were where Alton Drew's bullets had struck and passed through. Half of the monster's shapeless face was sloughed away, and there was a deep indentation on its shoulder. This was what Alton Drew's gun butt had done after he clubbed it and struck at the thing that would not lie down after he put his four bullets through it. When these things happened the monster was not hurt or angry. It only wondered why Alton Drew acted that way. Now it followed the little man without hurrying at all, matching his stride step by step and dropping little particles of muck behind it.

The little man went on out of the wood and stood with his back against a big tree at the forest's edge, and he thought. Enough had happened to him here. What good would it do to stay and face a horrible murder inquest, just to continue this silly, vague search? There was supposed to be the ruin of an old, old hunting lodge deep in this wood somewhere, and perhaps it would hold the evidence he wanted. But it was a vague report—vague enough to be forgotten without regret. It would be the height of foolishness to stay for all the hick-town red tape that would follow that ghastly affair back in the wood. Ergo, it would be ridiculous to follow that farmer's advice, to go to his house and wait for him. He would go back to town.

The monster was leaning against the other side of the big tree.

The little man snuffled disgustedly at a sudden overpowering odor of rot. He reached for his handkerchief, fumbled and dropped it. As he bent to pick it up, the monster's arm *whuffed* heavily in the air where his head had been—a blow that would certainly have removed that baby-face protuberance. The man stood up and would have put the handkerchief to his nose had it not been so bloody. The creature behind the tree lifted its arm again just as the little man tossed the handkerchief away and stepped out into the field, heading across country to the distant highway that would take him back to town. The monster pounced on the handkerchief, picked it up, studied it, tore it across several times and inspected the tattered edges. Then it gazed vacantly at the disappearing figure of the little man, and finding him no longer interesting, turned back into the woods.

~§~

Babe broke into a trot at the sound of the shots. It was important to warn Uncle Alton about what her father had said, but it was more interesting to find out what he had bagged. Oh, he'd bagged it, all right. Uncle Alton never fired without killing. This was about the first time she had ever heard him blast away like that. Must be a bear, she thought excitedly, tripping over a root, sprawling, rolling to her feet again, without noticing the tumble. She'd love to have another bearskin in her room. Where would she put it? Maybe they could line it and she could have it for a blanket. Uncle Alton could sit on it and read to her in the evening—Oh, no. No. Not with this trouble between him and dad. Oh, if she could only do something! She tried to run faster, worried and anticipating, but she was out of breath and went more slowly instead.

At the top of the rise by the edge of the woods she stopped and looked back. Far down in the valley lay the south thirty. She scanned it carefully, looking for her father. The new furrows and the old were sharply defined, and her keen eyes saw immediately that Cory had left the line with the cultivator and had angled the team over to the shade trees without finishing his row. That wasn't like him. She could see the team now, and Cory's pale-blue denim was nowhere in sight. She giggled lightly to herself as she thought of the way she would fool her father. And the little sound of laughter drowned out, for her, the sound of Alton's hoarse dying scream.

She reached and crossed the path and slid through the brush beside it. The shots came from up around here somewhere. She stopped and listened several times, and then suddenly heard something coming toward her, fast. She ducked under cover, terrified, and a little baby-faced man in black, his blue eyes wide with horror, crashed blindly past her, the leather case he carried catching on the branches. It spun a moment and then fell right in front of her. The man never missed it.

Babe lay there for a long moment and then picked up the case and faded into the woods. Things were happening too fast for her. She wanted Uncle Alton, but she dared not call. She stopped again and strained her ears. Back toward the edge of the wood she heard her father's voice, and another's—probably the man who had dropped the briefcase. She dared not go over there. Filled with enjoyable terror, she thought hard, then snapped her fingers in triumph. She and Alton had played Injun many times up here; they had a whole repertoire of secret signals. She had practiced birdcalls until she knew them better than the birds themselves. What would it be? Ah—bluejay. She threw back her head and by some youthful alchemy produced a nerve-shattering screech that would have done justice to any jay that ever flew. She repeated it, and then twice more.

The response was immediate—the call of a bluejay, four times, spaced two and two. Babe nodded to herself happily. That was the signal that they were to meet immediately at The Place. The Place was a hideout that he had discovered and shared with her, and not another soul knew of it; an angle of rock beside a stream not far away. It wasn't exactly a cave, but almost. Enough so to be entrancing. Babe trotted happily away toward the brook. She had just known that Uncle Alton would remember the call of the bluejay, and what it meant.

In the tree that arched over Alton's scattered body perched a large jay bird, preening itself and shining in the sun. Quite unconscious of the presence of death, hardly noticing the Babe's realistic cry, it screamed again four times, two and two.

~§~

It took Cory more than a moment to recover himself from what he had seen. He turned away from it and leaned weakly against a pine, panting. Alton. That was Alton lying there, in—parts. "God! God, God, God—"

Gradually his strength returned, and he forced himself to turn again. Stepping carefully, he bent and picked up the .32-40. Its barrel was bright and clean, but the butt and stock were smeared with some kind of stinking rottenness. Where had he seen the stuff before? Somewhere—no matter. He cleaned it off absently, throwing the befouled bandanna away afterward. Through his mind ran Alton's words—was that only last night?—*"I'm gain' to start trackin'. An' I'm gain' to keep trackin' till I find the one done this job on Kimbo."*

Cory searched shrinkingly until he found Alton's box of shells. The box was wet and sticky. That made it—better, somehow. A bullet wet with Alton's blood was the right thing to use. He went away a short distance, circled around till he found heavy footprints, then came back.

"I'm a-trackin' for you, bud," he whispered thickly, and began. Through the brush he followed its wavering spoor, amazed at the amount of filthy mold about, gradually associating it with the thing that had killed his brother. There was nothing in the world for him anymore but hate and doggedness. Cursing himself for not getting Alton home last night, he followed the tracks to the edge of the woods. They led him to a big tree there, and there he saw something else—the footprints of the little city man. Nearby lay some tattered scraps of linen, and—what was that?

Another set of prints—small ones. Small, stub-toed ones.

"Babe!"

No answer. The wind sighed. Somewhere a bluejay called. Babe stopped and turned when she heard her father's voice, faint with distance, piercing.

"Listen at him holler," she crooned delightedly. "Gee, he sounds mad." She sent a jay bird's call disrespectfully back to him and hurried to The Place.

It consisted of a mammoth boulder beside the brook. Some upheaval in the glacial age had cleft it, cutting out a huge V-shaped chunk. The widest part of the cleft was at the water's edge, and the narrowest was hidden by bushes. It made a little ceilingless room, rough and uneven and full of pot-holes and cavelets inside, and yet with quite a level floor. The open end was at the water's edge.

Babe parted the bushes and peered down the cleft.

"Uncle Alton!" she called softly. There was no answer. Oh, well, he'd be along. She scrambled in and slid down to the floor.

She loved it here. It was shaded and cool, and the chattering stream filled it with shifting golden lights and laughing gurgles. She called again, on principle, and then perched on an outcropping to wait. It was only then she realized that she still carried the little man's briefcase.

She turned it over a couple of times and then opened it. It was divided in the middle by a leather wall. On one side were a few papers in a large yellow envelope, and on the other some sandwiches, a candy bar, and an apple. With a youngster's complacent acceptance of manna from heaven, Babe fell to. She saved one sandwich for Alton, mainly because she didn't like its highly spiced bologna. The rest made quite a feast.

She was a little worried when Alton hadn't arrived, even after she had consumed the apple core. She got up and tried to skim some flat pebbles across the roiling brook, and she stood on her hands, and she tried to think of a story to tell herself, and she tried just waiting. Finally, in desperation, she turned again to the briefcase, took out the papers, curled up by the rocky wall and began to read them. It was something to do, anyway.

There was an old newspaper clipping that told about strange wills that people had left. An old lady had once left a lot of money to whoever would make the trip from the Earth to the Moon and back. Another had financed a home for cats whose masters and mistresses had died. A man left thousands of dollars to the first person who could solve a certain mathematical problem and prove his solution. But one item was blue-penciled. It was:

> One of the strangest of wills still in force is that of Thaddeus M. Kirk, who died in 1920. It appears that he built an elaborate mausoleum with burial vaults for all the remains of his family. He collected and removed caskets from all over the country to fill the designated niches. Kirk was the last of his line; there were no relatives when he died. His will stated that the mausoleum was to be kept in repair permanently, and that a certain sum was to be set aside as a reward for whoever could produce the body of his grandfather, Roger Kirk, whose niche is still empty. Anyone finding this body is eligible to receive a substantial fortune.

Babe yawned vaguely over this, but kept on reading because there was nothing else to do. Next was a thick sheet of business correspond-dence, bearing the letterhead of a firm of lawyers. The body of it ran:

> In regard to your query regarding the will of Thaddeus Kirk, we are authorized to state that his grandfather was a man about five feet, five inches, whose left arm had been broken and who had a triangular silver plate set into his skull. There is no information as to the whereabouts of his death. He disappeared and was declared legally dead after the lapse of fourteen years.
>
> The amount of the reward as stated in the will, plus accrued interest, now amounts to a fraction over sixty-two thousand dollars. This will be paid to anyone who produces the remains, providing that said remains answer descriptions kept in our private files.

There was more, but Babe was bored. She went on to the little black notebook. There was nothing in it but penciled and highly abbreviated records of visits to libraries; quotations from books with titles like "History of Angelina and Tyler Counties" and "Kirk Family History." Babe threw that aside, too. Where could Uncle Alton be?

She began to sing tunelessly, "Tumalumalum tum, ta ta ta," pretending to dance a minuet with flowing skirts like a girl she had seen in the movies. A rustle of the bushes at the entrance to The Place stopped her. She peeped upward, saw them being thrust aside. Quickly she ran to a tiny cul-de-sac in the rock wall, just big enough for her to hide in. She giggled at the thought of how surprised Uncle Alton would be when she jumped out at him.

She heard the newcomer come shuffling down the steep slope of the crevice and land heavily on the floor. There was something about the sound—What was it? It occurred to her that though it was a hard job for a big man like Uncle Alton to get through the little opening in the bushes, she could hear no heavy breathing. She heard no breathing at all!

Babe peeped out into the main cave and squealed in utmost horror. Standing there was, not Uncle Alton, but a massive caricature of a man: a huge thing like an irregular mud doll, clumsily made. It quivered and parts of it glistened and parts of it were dried and crumbly. Half of the lower left part of its face was gone, giving it a lopsided look. It had no perceptible mouth or nose, and its eyes were crooked, one higher than the other, both a dingy brown with no whites at all. It stood quite still looking at her, its only movement a steady unalive quivering.

It wondered about the queer little noise Babe had made. Babe crept far back against a little pocket of stone, her brain running round and round in tiny circles of agony. She opened her mouth to cry out, and could not. Her eyes bulged and her face flamed with the strangling effort, and the two golden ropes of her braided hair twitched and twitched as she hunted hopelessly for a way out. If only she were out in the open—or in the wedge-shaped half-cave where the thing was—or home in bed!

The thing clumped toward her, expressionless, moving with a slow inevitability that was the sheer crux of horror. Babe lay wide-eyed and frozen, mounting pressure of terror stilling her lungs, making her heart shake the whole world. The monster came to the mouth of the little pocket, tried to walk to her and was stopped by the sides. It was such a narrow little fissure, and it was all Babe could do to get in. The thing from the wood stood straining against the rock at its shoulders, pressing harder and harder to get to Babe. She sat up slowly, so near to the thing that its odor was almost thick enough to see, and a wild hope burst through her voiceless fear. It couldn't get in! It couldn't get in because it was too big!

The substance of its feet spread slowly under the tremendous strain and at its shoulder appeared a slight crack. It widened as the monster unfeelingly crushed itself against the rock, and suddenly a large piece of the shoulder came away and the being twisted slushily three feet farther in. It lay quietly with its muddy eyes fixed on her, and then brought one thick arm up over its head and reached.

Babe scrambled in the inch farther she had believed impossible, and the filthy clubbed hand stroked down her back, leaving a trail of muck on the blue denim of the shirt she wore. The monster surged suddenly and, lying full length now, gained that last precious inch. A black hand seized one of her braids, and for Babe the lights went out.

When she came to, she was dangling by her hair from that same crusted paw. The thing held her high, so that her face and its featureless head were not more than a foot apart. It gazed at her with a mild curiosity in its eyes, and it swung her slowly back and forth. The agony of her pulled hair did what fear could not do—gave her a voice. She screamed. She opened her mouth and puffed up her powerful young lungs, and she sounded off. She held her throat in the position of the first scream, and her chest labored and pumped more air through the frozen throat. Shrill and monotonous and infinitely piercing, her screams.

The thing did not mind. It held her as she was, and watched. When it had learned all it could from this phenomenon, it dropped her jarringly, and looked around the half-cave, ignoring the stunned and huddled Babe. It reached over and picked up the leather briefcase and tore it twice across as if it were tissue. It saw the sandwich Babe had left, picked it up, crushed it, dropped it.

Babe opened her eyes, saw that she was free, and just as the thing turned back to her she dove between its legs and out into the shallow pool in front of the rock, paddled across and hit the other bank screaming. A vicious little light of fury burned in her; she picked up a grapefruit-sized stone and hurled it with all her frenzied might. It flew low and fast, and struck squashily on the monster's ankle. The thing was just taking a step toward the water; the stone caught it off balance, and its unpracticed equilibrium could not save it. It tottered for a long, silent moment at the edge and then splashed into the stream. Without a second look Babe ran shrieking away.

Cory Drew was following the little gobs of mold that somehow indicated the path of the murderer, and he was nearby when he first heard her scream. He broke into a run, dropping his shotgun and holding the .32-40 ready to fire. He ran with such deadly panic in his heart that he ran right past the huge cleft rock and was a hundred yards past it before she burst out through the pool and ran up the bank. He had to run hard and fast to catch her, because anything behind her was that faceless horror in the cave, and she was living for the one idea of getting away from there. He caught her in his arms and swung her to him, and she screamed on and on and on.

Babe didn't see Cory at all, even when he held her and quieted her.

~§~

The monster lay in the water. It neither liked nor disliked this new element. It rested on the bottom, its massive head a foot beneath the surface, and it curiously considered the facts that it had garnered. There was the little humming noise of Babe's voice that sent the monster questing into the cave. There was the black material of the brief case that resisted so much more than green things when he tore it. There was the little two-legged one who sang and brought him near, and who screamed when he came. There was this new cold moving thing he had fallen into. It was washing his body away. That had never happened before. That was interesting. The monster decided to stay and observe this new thing. It felt no urge to save itself; it could only be curious.

The brook came laughing down out of its spring, ran down from its source beckoning to the sunbeams and embracing freshets and helpful brooklets. It shouted and played with streaming little roots, and nudged the minnows and pollywogs about in its tiny backwaters. It was a happy brook. When it came to the pool by the cloven rock it found the monster there, and plucked at it. It soaked the foul substances and smoothed and melted the molds, and the waters below the thing eddied darkly with its diluted matter. It was a thorough brook. It washed all it touched, persistently. Where it found filth, it removed filth; and if there were layer on layer of foulness, then layer by foul layer it was removed. It was a good brook. It did not mind the poison of the monster, but took it up and thinned it and spread it in little rings round rocks downstream, and let it drift to the rootlets of water plants, that they might grow greener and lovelier. And the monster melted.

"I am smaller," the thing thought. "That is interesting. I could not move now. And now this part of me which thinks is going, too. It will stop in just a moment, and drift away with the rest of the body. It will stop thinking and I will stop being, and that, too, is a very interesting thing."

So the monster melted and dirtied the water, and the water was clean again, washing and washing the skeleton that the monster had left. It was not very big, and there was a badly-healed knot on the left arm. The sunlight flickered on the triangular silver plate set into the pale skull, and the skeleton was very clean now. The brook laughed about it for an age.

They found the skeleton, six grimlipped men who came to find a killer. No one had believed Babe, when she told her story days later. It had to be days later because Babe had screamed for seven hours without stopping, and had lain like a dead child for a day. No one believed her at all, because her story was all about the bad fella, and they knew that the bad fella was simply a thing that her father had made up to frighten her with. But it was through her that the skeleton was found, and so the men at the bank sent a check to the Drews for more money than they had ever dreamed about. It was old Roger Kirk, sure enough, that skeleton, though it was found five miles from where he had died and sank into the forest floor where the hot molds builded around his skeleton and emerged—a monster.

So the Drews had a new barn and fine new livestock and they hired four men. But they didn't have Alton. And they didn't have Kimbo. And Babe screams at night and has grown very thin.

Seaton's Aunt

by Walter de la Mare

I HAD HEARD rumours of Seaton's Aunt long before I actually encountered her. Seaton, in the hush of confidence, or at any little show of toleration on our part, would remark, "My aunt," or "My old aunt, you know," as if his relative might be a kind of cement to an *entente cordiale*.

He had an unusual quantity of pocket-money; or, at any rate, it was bestowed on him in unusually large amounts; and he spent it freely, though none of us would have described him as an "awfully generous chap." "Hullo, Seaton," we would say, "the old Begum?"

At the beginning of term, too, he used to bring back surprising and exotic dainties in a box with a trick padlock that accompanied him from his first appearance at Gummidge's in a billy-cock hat to the rather abrupt conclusion of his schooldays.

From a boy's point of view he looked distastefully foreign, with his yellow skin, and slow chocolate-coloured eyes, and lean weak figure. Merely for his looks he was treated by most of us true-blue Englishmen with condescension, hostility, or contempt. We used to call him "Pongo," but without any much better excuse for the nickname than his skin. He was, that is, in one sense of the term what he assuredly was not in the other sense—a sport.

Seaton and I, as I may say, were never in any sense intimate at school; our orbits only intersected in class. I kept deliberately aloof from him. I felt vaguely he was a sneak, and remained quite unmollified by advances on his side, which, in a boy's barbarous fashion, unless it suited me to be magnanimous, I haughtily ignored.

We were both of us quick-footed, and at Prisoner's Base used occasionally to hide together. And so I best remember Seaton—his narrow watchful face in the dusk of a summer evening; his peculiar crouch, and his inarticulate whisperings and mumblings. Otherwise he played all games slackly and limply; used to stand and feed at his locker with a crony or two until his "tuck" gave out; or waste his money on some out-landish fancy or other. He bought, for instance, a silver bangle, which he wore above his left elbow, until some of the fellows showed their masterly contempt of the practice by dropping it nearly red-hot down his neck.

It needed, therefore, a rather peculiar taste, a rather rare kind of schoolboy courage and indifference to criticism, to be much associated with him. And I had neither the taste nor, perhaps, the courage. None the less, he did make advances, and on one memorable occasion went to the length of bestowing on me a whole pot of some outlandish mulberry-coloured jelly that had been duplicated in his term's supplies. In the exuberance of my gratitude I promised to spend the next half-term holi-day with him at his aunt's house.

I had clean forgotten my promise when, two or three days before the holiday, he came up and triumphantly reminded me of it.

"Well, to tell you the honest truth, Seaton, old chap—" I began graciously; but he cut me short.

"My aunt expects you," he said; "she is very glad you are coming. She's sure to be quite decent to you, Withers."

I looked at him in sheer astonishment; the emphasis was so uncalled for. It seemed to suggest an aunt not hitherto hinted at, and a friendly feeling on Seaton's side that was far more disconcerting than welcome.

~§~

We reached his home partly by train, partly by a lift in an empty farm-cart, and partly by walking. It was a whole-day holiday, and we were to sleep the night; he lent me extraordinary nightgear, I remember. The village street was unusually wide, and was fed from a green by two converging roads, with an inn, and a high green sign at the corner. About a hundred yards down the street was a chemist's shop—a Mr. Tanner's. We descended the two steps into his dusky and odorous interior to buy, I remember, some rat poison. A little beyond the chemist's was the forge. You then walked along a very narrow path, under a fairly high wall, nod-ding here and there with weeds and tufts of grass, and so came to the iron garden-gates, and saw the high, flat house behind its huge sycamore. A coach-house stood on the left of the house, and on the right a gate led into a kind of rambling orchard. The lawn lay away over to the left again, and at the bottom (for the whole garden sloped gently to a sluggish and rushy pond-like stream) was a meadow.

We arrived at noon, and entered the gates out of the hot dust beneath the glitter of the dark-curtained windows. Seaton led me at once through the little garden-gate to show me his tadpole pond, swarming with what (being myself not in the least interested in low life) I considered the most horrible creatures—of all shapes, consistencies and sizes, but with whom Seaton seemed to be on the most intimate of terms. I can see his absorbed face now as he sat on his heels and fished the slimy things out in his sallow palms. Wearying at last of these pets, we loitered about awhile in an aimless fashion. Seaton seemed to be listening, or at any rate waiting, for something to happen or for someone to come. But nothing did happen and no one came.

That was just like Seaton. Anyhow, the first view I got of his aunt was when, at the summons of a distant gong, we turned from the garden, very hungry and thirsty, to go in to luncheon. We were approaching the house when Seaton suddenly came to a standstill. Indeed, I have always had the impression that he plucked at my sleeve. Something, at least, seemed to catch me back, as it were, as he cried, "Look out, there she is!"

She was standing at an upper window which opened wide on a hinge, and at first sight she looked an excessively tall and overwhelming figure. This, however, was mainly because the window reached all but to the floor of the bedroom. She was in reality rather an under-sized woman, in spite of her long face and big head. She must have stood, I think, unusually still, with eyes fixed on us, though this impression may be due to Seaton's sudden warning and to my consciousness of the cautious and subdued air that had fallen on him at sight of her. I know that, without the least reason in the world, I felt a kind of guiltiness, as if I had been "caught." There was a silvery star pattern sprinkled on her black silk dress, and even from the ground I could see the immense coils of her hair and the rings on her left hand which was held fingering the small jet buttons of her bodice. She watched our united advance without stirring, until, imperceptibly, her eyes raised and lost themselves in the distance, so that it was out of an assumed reverie that she appeared suddenly to awaken to our presence beneath her when we drew close to the house.

"So this is your friend, Mr. Smithers, I suppose?" she said, bobbing to me.

"Withers, aunt," said Seaton. "It's much the same," she said, with eyes fixed on me. "Come in, Mr. Withers, and bring him along with you."

She continued to gaze at me—at least, I think she did so. I know that the fixity of her scrutiny and her ironical "Mr." made me feel peculiarly uncomfortable. None the less she was extremely kind and attentive to me, though, no doubt, her kindness and attention showed up more vividly against her complete neglect of Seaton. Only one remark that I have any recollection of she made to him: "When I look on my nephew, Mr. Smithers, I realise that dust we are, and dust shall become. You are hot, dirty, and incorrigible, Arthur."

She sat at the head of the table, Seaton at the foot, and I, before a wide waste of damask tablecloth, between them. It was an old and rather close dining-room, with windows thrown wide to the green garden and a wonderful cascade of fading roses. Miss Seaton's great chair faced this window, so that its rose-reflected light shone full on her yellowish face, and on just such chocolate eyes as my schoolfellow's, except that hers were more than half-covered by unusually long and heavy lids.

There she sat, steadily eating, with those sluggish eyes fixed for the most part on my face; above them stood the deep-lined fork between her eyebrows; and above that the wide expanse of a remarkable brow beneath its strange steep bank of hair. The lunch was copious, and consisted, I remember, of all such dishes as are generally considered too rich and too good for the schoolboy digestion—lobster mayonnaise, cold game sausages, an immense veal and ham pie farced with eggs, truffles, and numberless delicious flavours; besides kickshaws, creams and sweetmeats. We even had wine, a half-glass of old darkish sherry each.

Miss Seaton enjoyed and indulged an enormous appetite. Her example and a natural schoolboy voracity soon overcame my nervousness of her, even to the extent of allowing me to enjoy to the best of my bent so rare a spread. Seaton was singularly modest; the greater part of his meal consisted of almonds and raisins, which he nibbled surreptitiously and as if he found difficulty in swallowing them.

I don't mean that Miss Seaton "conversed" with me. She merely scattered trenchant remarks and now and then twinkled a baited question over my head. But her face was like a dense and involved accompaniment to her talk. She presently dropped the "Mr.," to my intense relief, and called me now Withers, or Wither, now Smithers, and even once towards the close of the meal distinctly Johnson, though how on earth my name suggested it, or whose face mine had reanimated in memory, I cannot conceive.

"And is Arthur a good boy at school, Mr. Wither?" was one of her many questions. "Does he please his masters? Is he first in his class? What does the reverend Dr. Gummidge think of him, eh?"

I knew she was jeering at him, but her face was adamant against the least flicker of sarcasm or facetiousness. I gazed fixedly at a blushing crescent of lobster.

"I think you're eighth, aren't you, Seaton?"

Seaton moved his small pupils towards his aunt. But she continued to gaze with a kind of concentrated detachment at me.

"Arthur will never make a brilliant scholar, I fear," she said, lifting a dexterously-burdened fork to her wide mouth.

After luncheon she proceeded me up to my bedroom. It was a jolly little bedroom, with a brass fender and rugs and a polished floor, on which it was possible, I afterwards found, to play "snow-shoes." Over the washstand was a little black-framed water-colour drawing, depicting a large eye with an extremely fishlike intensity in the spark of light on the dark pupil; and in "illuminated" lettering beneath was printed very minutely, "Thou God, Seest *me*," followed by a long looped monogram, "S.S.," in the corner. The other pictures were all of the sea: brigs on blue water; a schooner overtopping chalk cliffs; a rocky island of prodigious steepness, with two tiny sailors dragging a monstrous boat up a shelf of beach.

"This is the room, Withers, my brother William died in when a boy. Admire the view!"

I looked out of the window across the tree-tops. It was a day hot with sunshine over the green fields, and the cattle were standing swishing their tails in the shallow water. But the view at the moment was only exaggeratedly vivid because I was horribly dreading that she would presently enquire after my luggage, and I had not brought even a toothbrush. I need have had no fear. Hers was not that highly-civilised type of mind that is stuffed with sharp, material details. Nor could her ample presence be described as in the least motherly.

"I would never consent to question a schoolfellow behind my nephew's back," she said, standing in the middle of the room, "but tell me, Smithers, why is Arthur so unpopular? You, I understand, are his only close friend." She stood in a dazzle of sun, and out of it her eyes regarded me with such leaden penetration beneath their thick lids that I doubt if my face concealed the least thought from her. "But there, there," she added very suavely, stooping her head a little, "don't trouble to answer me. I never extort an answer. Boys are queer fish. Brains might perhaps have suggested his washing his hands before luncheon; but—not my choice, Smithers. God forbid! And now, perhaps, you would like to go into the garden again. I cannot actually see from here, but I should not be surprised if Arthur is now skulking behind that hedge."

He was. I saw his head come out and take a rapid glance at the windows.

"Join him, Mr. Smithers; we shall meet again, I hope, at the tea-table. The afternoon I spend in retirement."

Whether or not, Seaton and I had not been long engaged with the aid of two green switches in riding round and round a lumbering old grey horse we found in the meadow, before a rather bunched-up figure appeared, walking along the field-path on the other side of the water, with a magenta parasol studiously lowered in our direction throughout our slow progress, as if that were the magnetic needle and we the fixed Pole.

Seaton at once lost all nerve in his riding. At the next lurch of the old mare's heels he toppled over in the grass, and I slid off the sleek broad back to join him where he stood, rubbing his shoulder and sourly watching the rather pompous figure till it was out of sight.

"Was that your aunt, Seaton?" I enquired; but not till then. He nodded.

"Why didn't she take any notice of us, then?"

"She never does."

"Why not?"

"Oh, she knows all right, without; that's the dam awful part of it." Seaton was about the only fellow at Gummidge's who ever had the ostentation to use bad language. He had suffered for it too. But it wasn't, I think, bravado. I believe he really felt certain things more intensely than most of the other fellows, and they were generally things that fortunate and average people do not feel at all—the peculiar quality, for instance, of the British schoolboy's imagination.

"I tell you, Withers," he went on moodily, slinking across the meadow with his hands covered up in his pockets, "she sees everything. And what she doesn't see she knows without."

"But how?" I said, not because I was much interested, but because the afternoon was so hot and tiresome and purposeless, and it seemed more of a bore to remain silent. Seaton turned gloomily and spoke in a very low voice.

"Don't appear to be talking of her, if you wouldn't mind. It's—because she's in league with the devil." He nodded his head and stooped to pick up a round flat pebble. "I tell you," he said, still stooping, "you fellows don't realise what it is. I know I'm a bit close and all that. But so would you be if you had that old hag listening to every thought you think."

I looked at him, then turned and surveyed one by one the windows of the house.

"Where's your pater?" I said awkwardly.

"Dead, ages and ages ago, and my mother too. She's not my aunt by right."

"What is she, then?"

"I mean she's not my mother's sister, because my grandmother married twice; and she's one of the first lot. I don't know what you call her, anyhow she's not my real aunt."

"She gives you plenty of pocket-money."

Seaton looked steadfastly at me out of his flat eyes. "She can't give me what's mine. When I come of age half the whole lot will be mine; and what's more"—he turned his back on the house—"I'll make her hand over every blessed shilling of it."

I put my hands in my pockets and stared at Seaton; "Is it much?"

He nodded.

"Who told you?"

He got suddenly very angry; a darkish red came into his cheeks, his eyes glistened, but he made no answer, and we loitered listlessly about the garden until it was time for tea . . .

Seaton's aunt was wearing an extraordinary kind of lace jacket when we sidled sheepishly into the drawing-room together. She greeted me with a heavy and protracted smile, and bade me bring a chair close to the little table.

"I hope Arthur has made you feel at home," she said, as she handed me my cup in her crooked hand. "He don't talk much to me; but then I'm an old woman. You must come again, Wither, and draw him out of his shell. You old snail!" She wagged her head at Seaton, who sat munching cake and watching her intently.

"And we must correspond, perhaps." She nearly shut her eyes at me. "You must write and tell me everything behind the creature's back."

I confess I found her rather disquieting company. The evening drew on. Lamps were brought in by a man with a nondescript face and very quiet footsteps. Seaton was told to bring out the chess-men. And we played a game, she and I, with her big chin thrust over the board at every move as she gloated over the pieces and occasionally croaked "Check!"— after which she would sit back inscrutably staring at me. But the game was never finished. She simply hemmed me defencelessly in with a cloud of men that held me impotent, and yet one and all refused to administer to my poor flustered old king a merciful coup de grâce.

"There," she said as the clock struck ten— "a drawn game, Withers.

We are very evenly matched. A very creditable defence, Withers. You know your room. There's supper on a tray in the dining-room. Don't let the creature over-eat himself. The gong will sound three-quarters of an hour before a punctual breakfast." She held out her cheek to Seaton, and he kissed it with obvious perfunctoriness. With me she shook hands.

"An excellent game," she said cordially, "but my memory is poor, and"—she swept the pieces helter-skelter into the box— "the result will never be known." She raised her great head far back. "Eh?"

It was a kind of challenge, and I could only murmur: "Oh, I was absolutely in a hole, you know!" when she burst out laughing and waved us both out of the room.

Seaton and I stood and ate our supper, with one candlestick to light us, in a corner of the dining-room. "Well, and how would you like it?" he said very softly, after cautiously poking his head round the doorway.

"Like what?"

"Being spied on—every blessed thing you do and think?"

"I shouldn't like it at all," I said, "if she does."

"And yet you let her smash you up at chess!"

"I didn't let her!" I said, indignantly.

"Well, you funked it, then."

"And I didn't funk it either," I said; "she's so jolly clever with her knights."

Seaton stared fixedly at the candle. "You wait, that's all," he said slowly. And we went upstairs to bed.

I had not been long in bed, I think, when I was cautiously awakened by a touch on my shoulder. And there was Seaton's face in the candle-light—and his eyes looking into mine.

"What's up?" I said, rising quickly to my elbow.

"Don't scurry," he whispered, "or she'll hear. I'm sorry for waking you, but I didn't think you'd be asleep so soon."

"Why, what's the time, then?" Seaton wore, what was then rather unusual, a night-suit, and he hauled his big silver watch out of the pocket in his jacket.

"It's a quarter to twelve. I never get to sleep before twelve—not here."

"What do you do, then?"

"Oh, I read and listen."

"Listen?"

Seaton stared into his candle-flame as if he were listening even then. "You can't guess what it is. All you read in ghost stories, that's all rot. You can't see much, Withers, but you know all the same."

"Know what?"

"Why, that they're there."

"Who's there?" I asked fretfully, glancing at the door.

"Why, in the house. It swarms with 'em. Just you stand still and listen outside my bedroom door in the middle of the night. I have, dozens of times; they're all over the place."

"Look here, Seaton," I said, "you asked me to come here, and I didn't mind chucking up a leave just to oblige you, and because I'd promised; but don't get talking a lot of rot, that's all, or you'll know the difference when we get back."

"Don't fret," he said coldly, turning away. "I shan't be at school long. And what's more, you're here now, and there isn't anybody else to talk to. I'll chance the other."

"Look here, Seaton," I said, "you may think you're going to scare me with a lot of stuff about voices and all that. But I'll just thank you to clear out; and you may please yourself about pottering about all night."

He made no answer; he was standing by the dressing-table looking across his candle into the looking-glass; he turned and stared slowly round the walls.

"Even this room's nothing more than a coffin. I suppose she told you—'It's exactly the same as when my brother William died'—trust her for that! And good luck to him, say I. Look at that." He raised his candle close to the little water-colour I have mentioned. "There's hundreds of eyes like that in this house; and even if God does see you, He takes precious good care you don't see Him. And it's just the same with them. I tell you what, Withers, I'm getting sick of all this. I shan't stand it much longer."

The house was silent within and without, and even in the yellowish radiance of the candle a faint silver showed through the open window on my blind. I slipped off the bedclothes, wide awake, and sat irresolute on the bedside.

"I know you're only guying me," I said angrily, "but why is the house full of—what you say? Why do you hear—what you do hear? Tell me that, you silly fool!"

Seaton sat down on a chair and rested his candlestick on his knee. He blinked at me calmly.

"She brings them," he said, with lifted eyebrows.

"Who? Your aunt?"

He nodded.

"How?"

"I told you," he answered pettishly. "She's in league. You don't know. She as good as killed my mother; I know that. But it's not only her by a long chalk. She just sucks you dry. I know. And that's what she'll do for me; because I'm like her—like my mother, I mean. She simply hates to see me alive. I wouldn't be like that old she-wolf for a million pounds. And so"—he broke off, with a comprehensive wave of his candlestick— "they're always here. Ah, my boy, wait till she's dead! She'll hear something then, I can tell you. It's all very well now, but wait till then! I wouldn't be in her shoes when she has to clear out—for something. Don't you go and believe I care for ghosts, or whatever you like to call them. We're all in the same box. We're all under her thumb."

He was looking almost nonchalantly at the ceiling at the moment, when I saw his face change, saw his eyes suddenly drop like shot birds and fix themselves on the cranny of the door he had just left ajar. Even from where I sat I could see his colour change; he went greenish. He crouched without stirring, simply fixed. And I, scarcely daring to breathe, sat with creeping skin, simply watching him. His hands relaxed, and he gave a kind of sigh.

"Was that one?" I whispered, with a timid show of jauntiness. He looked round, opened his mouth, and nodded. "What?" I said. He jerked his thumb with meaningful eyes, and I knew that he meant that his aunt had been there listening at our door cranny.

"Look here, Seaton," I said once more, wriggling to my feet. "You may think I'm a jolly noodle; just as you please. But your aunt has been civil to me and all that, and I don't believe a word you say about her, that's all, and never did. Every fellow's a bit off his pluck at night, and you may think it a fine sport to try your rubbish on me. I heard your aunt come upstairs before I fell asleep. And I'll bet you a level tanner she's in bed now. What's more, you can keep your blessed ghosts to yourself. It's a guilty conscience, I should think."

Seaton looked at me curiously, without answering for a moment. "I'm not a liar, Withers; but I'm not going to quarrel either. You're the only chap I care a button for; or, at any rate, you're the only chap that's ever come here; and it's something to tell a fellow what you feel. I don't care a fig for fifty thousand ghosts, although I swear on my solemn oath that I know they're here. But she"—he turned deliberately—"you laid a tanner she's in bed, Withers; well, I know different. She's never in bed much of the night, and I'll prove it, too, just to show you I'm not such a nolly as you think I am. Come on!"

"Come on where?"

"Why, to see."

I hesitated. He opened a large cupboard and took out a small dark dressing-gown and a kind of shawl-jacket. He threw the jacket on the bed and put on the gown. His dusky face was colourless, and I could see by the way he fumbled at the sleeves he was shivering. But it was no good showing the white feather now. So I threw the tasselled shawl over my shoulders and, leaving our candle brightly burning on the chair, we went out together and stood in the corridor.

"Now then, listen!" Seaton whispered.

We stood leaning over the staircase. It was like leaning over a well, so still and chill the air was all around us. But presently, as I suppose happens in most old houses, began to echo and answer in my ears a medley of infinite small stirrings and whisperings. Now out of the distance an old timber would relax its fibres, or a scurry die away behind the perishing wainscoat. But amid and behind such sounds as these I seemed to begin to be conscious, as it were, of the lightest of footfalls, sounds as faint as the vanishing remembrance of voices in a dream. Seaton was all in obscurity except his face; out of that his eyes gleamed darkly, watching me.

"You'd hear, too, in time, my fine soldier," he muttered. "Come on!"

He descended the stairs, slipping his lean fingers lightly along the balusters. He turned to the right at the loop, and I followed him barefooted along a thickly-carpeted corridor. At the end stood a door ajar. And from here we very stealthily and in complete blackness ascended five narrow stairs. Seaton, with immense caution, slowly pushed open a door, and we stood together looking into a great pool of duskiness, out of which, lit by the feeble clearness of a night-light, rose a vast bed. A heap of clothes lay on the floor; beside them two slippers dozed, with noses each to each, two yards apart. Somewhere a little clock ticked huskily. There was a rather close smell of lavender and *eau de cologne*, mingled with the fragrance of ancient sachets, soap, and drugs. Yet it was a scent even more peculiarly commingled than that.

And the bed! I stared warily in; it was mounded gigantically, and it was empty.

Seaton turned a vague pale face, all shadows: "What did I say?" he muttered. "Who's—who's the fool now, I say? How are we going to get back without meeting her, I say? Answer me that! Oh, I wish to goodness you hadn't come here, Withers."

He stood visibly shivering in his skimpy gown, and could hardly speak for his teeth chattering. And very distinctly, in the hush that followed his whisper, I heard approaching a faint unhurried voluminous rustle. Seaton clutched my arm, dragged me to the right across the room to a large cupboard, and drew the door close to on us. And presently, as with bursting lungs I peeped out into the long, low, curtained bedroom, waddled in that wonderful great head and body. I can see her now, all patched and lined with shadow, her tied-up hair (she must have had enormous quantities of it for so old a woman), her heavy lids above those flat, slow, vigilant eyes. She just passed across my ken in the vague dusk; but the bed was out of sight.

We waited on and on, listening to the clock's muffled ticking. Not the ghost of a sound rose up from the great bed. Either she lay archly listening or slept a sleep serener than an infant's. And when, it seemed, we had been hours in hiding and were cramped, chilled, and half suffocated, we crept out on all fours, with terror knocking at our ribs, and so down the five narrow stairs and back to the little candle-lit blue-and-gold bedroom.

Once there, Seaton gave in. He sat livid on a chair with closed eyes.

"Here," I said shaking his arm, "I'm going to bed; I've had enough of this foolery; I'm going to bed." His lips quivered, but he made no answer. I poured out some water into my basin and, with that cold pictured azure eye fixed on us, bespattered Seaton's sallow face and forehead and dabbled his hair. He presently sighed and opened fish-like eyes.

"Come on!" I said. "Don't get shamming, there's a good chap. Get on my back if you like, and I'll carry you into your bedroom."

He waved me away and stood up. So, with my candle in one hand, I took him under the arm and walked him along according to his direction down the corridor. His was a much dingier room than mine, and littered with boxes, paper, cages, and clothes. I huddled him into bed and turned to go. And suddenly—I can hardly explain it now—a kind of cold and deadly terror swept over me. I almost ran out of the room, with eyes fixed rigidly in front of me, blew out my candle, and buried my head under the bedclothes.

When I awoke, roused not by a gong, but by a long-continued tapping at my door, sunlight was raying in on cornice and bedpost, and birds were singing in the garden. I got up, ashamed of the night's folly, dressed quickly, and went downstairs. The breakfast-room was sweet with flowers and fruit and honey. Seaton's aunt was standing in the garden beside the open French windows, feeding a great flutter of birds. I watched her for a moment, unseen. Her face was set in a deep reverie beneath the shadow of a big loose sun-hat. It was deeply lined, crooked, and, in a way I can't describe, fixedly vacant and strange. I coughed, and she turned at once with a prodigious smile to enquire how I had slept. And in that mysterious way by which we learn each other's secret thoughts without a sentence spoken I knew that she had followed every word and movement of the night before, and was triumphing over my affected innocence and ridiculing my friendly and too easy advances.

We returned to school, Seaton and I, lavishly laden, and by rail all the way. I made no reference to the obscure talk we had had, and resolutely refused to meet his eyes or to take up the hints he let fall. I was relieved—and yet I was sorry—to be going back, and strode on as fast as I could from the station, with Seaton almost trotting at my heels. But he insisted on buying more fruit and sweets—my share of which I accepted with a very bad grace. It was uncomfortably like a bribe; and, after all, I had no quarrel with his rum old aunt, and hadn't really believed half the stuff he had told me.

I saw as little of him as I could after that. He never referred to our visit or resumed his confidences, though in class I would sometimes catch his eyes fixed on mine, full of a mute understanding, which I easily affected not to understand. He left Gummidge's, as I have said, rather abruptly, though I never heard of anything to his discredit. And I did not see him or have any news of him again till by chance we met one summer afternoon in the Strand.

~§~

He was dressed rather oddly in a coat too large for him and a bright silky tie. But we instantly recognised one another under the awning of a cheap jeweller's shop. He immediately attached himself to me and dragged me off, not too cheerfully, to lunch with him at an Italian restaurant nearby. He chattered about our old school, which he remembered only with dislike and disgust; told me cold-bloodedly of the disastrous fate of one or two of the old fellows who had been among his chief tormentors; insisted on an expensive wine and the whole gamut of the foreign menu; and finally informed me, with a good deal of niggling, that he had come up to town to buy an engagement-ring.

And of course: "How is your aunt?" I enquired at last.

He seemed to have been awaiting the question. It fell like a stone into a deep pool, so many expressions flitted across his long un-English face.

"She's aged a good deal," he said softly, and broke off.

"She's been very decent," he continued presently after, and paused again. "In a way." He eyed me fleetingly. "I dare say you heard that—she—that is, that we—had lost a good deal of money."

"No," I said.

"Oh, yes!" said Seaton, and paused again. And somehow, poor fellow, I knew in the clink and clatter of glass and voices that he had lied to me; that he did not possess, and never had possessed, a penny beyond what his aunt had squandered on his too ample allowance of pocket-money.

"And the ghosts?" I enquired quizzically. He grew instantly solemn, and, though it may have been my fancy, slightly yellowed. But "You are making game of me, Withers," was all he said.

He asked for my address, and I rather reluctantly gave him my card.

"Look here, Withers," he said, as we stood together in the sunlight on the kerb, saying good-bye, "here I am, and—and it's all very well. I'm not perhaps as fanciful as I was. But you are practically the only friend I have on earth—except Alice. . . . And there—to make a clean breast of it, I'm not sure that my aunt cares much about my getting married. She doesn't say so, of course. You know her well enough for that." He looked sidelong at the rattling gaudy traffic.

"What I was going to say is this: would you mind coming down? You needn't stay the night unless you please, though, of course, you know you would be awfully welcome. But I should like you to meet my—to meet Alice; and then, perhaps, you might tell me your honest opinion of—of the other too."

I vaguely demurred. He pressed me. And we parted with a half promise that I would come. He waved his ball-topped cane at me and ran off in his long jacket after a bus.

A letter arrived soon after, in his small weak handwriting, giving me full particulars regarding route and trains. And without the least curiosity, even, perhaps, with some little annoyance that chance should have thrown us together again, I accepted his invitation and arrived one hazy midday at his out-of-the-way station to find him sitting on a low seat under a clump of double hollyhocks, awaiting me.

His face looked absent and singularly listless; but he seemed, none the less, pleased to see me.

We walked up the village street, past the little dingy apothecary's and the empty forge, and, as on my first visit, skirted the house together, and, instead of entering by the front door, made our way down the green path into the garden at the back. A pale haze of cloud muffled the sun; the garden lay in a grey shimmer—its old trees, its snap-dragoned faintly glittering walls. But now there was an air of slovenliness where before all had been neat and methodical. In a patch of shallowly-dug soil stood a worn-down spade leaning against a tree. There was an old broken wheelbarrow. The roses had run to leaf and briar; the fruit-trees were unpruned. The goddess of neglect brooded in secret.

"You ain't much of a gardener, Seaton," I said, with a sigh of ease.

"I think, do you know, I like it best like this," said Seaton. "We haven't any man now, of course. Can't afford it." He stood staring at his little dark square of freshly-turned earth. "And it always seems to me," he went on ruminatingly, "that, after all we are nothing better than inter-lopers on the earth, disfiguring and staining wherever we go. I know it's shocking blasphemy to say so, but then it's different here, you see. We are further away."

"To tell you the truth, Seaton, I don't quite see," I said; "but it isn't a new philosophy, is it? Anyhow, it's a precious beastly one."

"It's only what I think," he replied, with all his odd old stubborn meekness. We wandered on together, talking little, and still with that expression of uneasy vigilance on Seaton's face. He pulled out his watch as we stood gazing idly over the green meadows and the dark motionless bulrushes.

"I think, perhaps, it's nearly time for lunch," he said. "Would you like to come in?"

We turned and walked slowly towards the house, across whose windows I confess my own eyes, too, went restlessly wandering in search of its rather disconcerting inmate. There was a pathetic look of draggled-ness, of want of means and care, rust and overgrowth and faded paint. Seaton's aunt, a little to my relief, did not share our meal. Seaton carved the cold meat, and dispatched a heaped-up plate by an elderly servant for his aunt's private consumption. We talked little and in half-suppressed tones, and sipped a bottle of Madeira which Seaton had rather heedfully fetched out of the great mahogany sideboard.

I played him a dull and effortless game of chess, yawning between the moves he himself made almost at haphazard, and with attention elsewhere engaged. About five o'clock came the sound of a distant ring, and Seaton jumped up, overturning the board, and so ending a game that else might have fatuously continued to this day. He effusively excused himself, and after some little while returned with a slim, dark, rather sallow girl of about nineteen, in a white gown and hat, to whom I was presented with some little nervousness as his "dear old friend and schoolfellow."

We talked on in the pale afternoon light, still, as it seemed to me, and even in spite of a real effort to be clear and gay, in a half-suppressed, lack-lustre fashion. We all seemed, if it were not my fancy, to me expectant, to be rather anxiously awaiting an arrival, the appearance of someone who all but filled our collective consciousness. Seaton talked least of all, and in a restless interjectory way, as he continually fidgeted from chair to chair. At last he proposed a stroll in the garden before the sun should have quite gone down.

Alice walked between us. Her hair and eyes were conspicuously dark against the whiteness of her gown. She carried herself not ungracefully, and yet without the least movement of her arms and body, and answered us both without turning her head. There was a curious provocative reserve in that impassive and rather long face, a half-unconscious strength of character.

And yet somehow I knew—I believe we all knew—that this walk, this discussion of their future plans was a futility. I had nothing to base such a cynicism on, except only a vague sense of oppression, the foreboding remembrance of the inert invincible power in the background, to whom optimistic plans and lovemaking and youth are as chaff and thistle-down. We came back silent, in the last light. Seaton's aunt was there—under an old brass lamp. Her hair was as barbarously massed and curled as ever. Her eyelids, I think, hung even a little heavier in age over their slow-moving inscrutable pupils. We filed in softly out of the evening, and I made my bow.

"In this short interval, Mr. Withers," she remarked amiably, "you have put off youth, put on the man. Dear me, how sad it is to see the young days vanishing! Sit down. My nephew tells me you met by chance —or act of Providence, shall we call it?—and in my beloved Strand! You, I understand, are to be best man—yes, best man, or am I divulging secrets?" She surveyed Arthur and Alice with overwhelming graciousness. They sat apart on two low chairs and smiled in return.

"And Arthur—how do you think Arthur is looking?"

"I think he looks very much in need of a change," I said deliberately.

"A change! Indeed?" She all but shut her eyes at me and with an exaggerated sentimentality shook her head. "My dear Mr. Withers! Are we not all in need of a change in this fleeting, fleeting world?" She mused over the remark like a connoisseur. "And you," she continued, turning abruptly to Alice, "I hope you pointed out to Mr. Withers all my pretty bits?"

"We walked round the garden," said Alice, looking out of the window. "It's a very beautiful evening."

"Is it?" said the old lady, starting up violently. "Then on this very beautiful evening we will go in to supper. Mr. Withers, your arm; Arthur, bring your bride."

I can scarcely describe with what curious ruminations I led the way into the faded, heavy-aired dining-room, with this indefinable old creature leaning weightily on my arm—the large flat bracelet on the yellow-laced wrist. She fumed a little, breathed rather heavily, as if with an effort of mind rather than of body; for she had grown much stouter and yet little more proportionate.

And to talk into that great white face, so close to mine, was a queer experience in the dim light of the corridor, and even in the twinkling crystal of the candles. She was naïve —appallingly naïve; she was sudden and superficial; she was even arch; and all these in the brief, rather puffy passage from one room to the other, with these two tongue-tied children bringing up the rear. The meal was tremendous. I have never seen such a monstrous salad. But the dishes were greasy and over-spiced, and were indifferently cooked. One thing only was quite unchanged—my hostess's appetite was as Gargantuan as ever. The old solid candelabra that lighted us stood before her high-back chair. Seaton sat a little removed, with his plate almost in darkness.

And throughout this prodigious meal his aunt talked, mainly to me, mainly at Seaton, with an occasional satirical courtesy to Alice and muttered explosions of directions to the servant. She had aged, and yet, if it be not nonsense to say so, seemed no older. I suppose to the Pyramids a decade is but as the rustling down of a handful of dust. And she reminded me of some such unshakable prehistoric. She certainly was an amazing talker—racy, extravagant, with a delivery that was perfectly overwhelming. As for Seaton—her flashes of silence were for him. On her enormous volubility would suddenly fall a hush: acid sarcasm would be left implied; and she would sit softly moving her great head, with eyes fixed full in a dreamy smile; but with her whole attention, one could see, slowly, joyously absorbing his mute discomfiture.

She confided in us her views on a theme vaguely occupying at the moment, I suppose, all our minds. "We have barbarous institutions, and so must put up, I suppose, with a never-ending procession of fools—of fools ad infinitum. Marriage, Mr. Withers, was instituted in the privacy of a garden; sub Rosa, as it were. Civilization flaunts it in the glare of day.

The dull marry the poor; the rich the effete; and so our New Jerusalem is peopled with naturals, plain and coloured, at either end. I detest folly; I detest still more (if I must be frank, dear Arthur), mere cleverness. Mankind has simply become a tailless host of indistinctive animals. We should never have taken to Evolution, Mr. Withers. 'Natural Selection!'—little gods and fishes!—the deaf for the dumb. We should have used our brains—intellectual pride, the ecclesiastics call it. And by brains I mean—what do I mean, Alice?—I mean, my dear child"—and she laid two gross fingers on Alice's narrow sleeve—"I mean courage. Consider it, Arthur. I read that the scientific world is once more beginning to be afraid of spiritual agencies. Spiritual agencies that tap, and actually float, bless their hearts! I think just one more of those mulberries—thank you.

"They talk about 'blind Love,'" she ran inconsequently on as she helped herself, with eyes roving on the dish, "but why blind? I think, do you know, from weeping over its rickets. After all, it is we plain women that triumph, Mr. Withers, beyond the mockery of time. Alice, now! Fleeting, fleeting is youth, my child. What's that you were confiding to your plate, Arthur? Satirical boy. He laughs at his old aunt: nay, but thou didst laugh. He detests all sentiment. He whispers the most acid asides. Come, my love, we will leave these cynics; we will go and commiserate with each other on our sex. The choice of two evils, Mr. Smithers!" I opened the door, and she swept out as if borne on a torrent of unintelligible indignation; and Arthur and I were left in the clear four-flamed light alone.

For a while we sat in silence. He shook his head at my cigarette-case, and I lit a cigarette. Presently he fidgeted in his chair and poked his head forward into the light. He paused to rise and shut again the shut door.

"How long will you be?" he said, standing by the table.

I laughed.

"Oh, it's not that!" he said, in some confusion. "Of course, I like to be with her. But it's not that. The truth is, Withers, I don't care about leaving her too long with my aunt."

I hesitated. He looked at me questioningly.

"Look here, Seaton," I said, "you know well enough that I don't want to interfere in your affairs, or to offer advice where it is not wanted. But don't you think perhaps you may not treat your aunt quite in the right way? As one gets old, you know, a little give and take. I have an old godmother, or something. She talks, too . . . A little allowance: it does no harm. But hang it all, I'm no talker."

He sat down with his hands in his pockets and still with his eyes fixed almost incredulously on mine. "How?" he said.

"Well, my dear fellow, if I'm any judge—mind, I don't say that I am— but I can't help thinking she thinks you don't care for her; and perhaps takes your silence for—for bad temper. She has been very decent to you, hasn't she?"

"*Decent*? My God!" said Seaton.

I smoked on in silence; but he continued to look at me with that peculiar concentration I remembered of old.

"I don't think, perhaps, Withers," he began presently, "I don't think you quite understand. Perhaps you are not quite our kind. You always did, just like the other fellows, guy me at school. You laughed at me that night you came to stay here—about the voices and all that. But I don't mind being laughed at— because I know."

"Know what?" It was the same old system of dull question and evasive answer.

"I mean I know that what we see and hear is only the smallest fraction of what is. I know she lives quite out of this. She talks to you; but it's all make-believe. It's all a 'parlour game'. She's not really with you; only pitting her outside wits against yours and enjoying the fooling. She's living on inside, on what you're rotten without. That's what it is—a cannibal feast. She's a spider. It doesn't much matter what you call it. It means the same kind of thing. I tell you, Withers, she hates me; and you can scarcely dream what that hatred means. I used to think I had an inkling of the reason. It's oceans deeper than that. It just lies behind: herself against myself. Why, after all, how much do we really understand of anything? We don't even know our own histories, and not a tenth, not a tenth of the reasons. What has life been to me?—nothing but a trap. And when one is set free, it only begins again. I thought you might understand; but you are on a different level: that's all."

"What on earth are you talking about?" I said contemptuously, in spite of myself.

"I mean what I say," he said gutturally. "All this outside's only make-believe—but there! what's the good of talking? So far as this is concerned I'm as good as done. You wait."

Seaton blew out three of the candles, and, leaving the vacant room in semidarkness, we groped our way along the corridor to the drawing-room. There a full moon stood shining in at the long garden windows. Alice sat stooping at the door, with her hands clasped, looking out, alone.

"Where is she?" Seaton asked in a low tone.

Alice looked up; their eyes met in a kind of instantaneous understanding, and the door immediately afterwards opened behind us.

"Such a moon!" said a voice that, once heard, remained unfor-gettably on the ear. "A night for lovers, Mr. Withers, if ever there was one. Get a shawl, my dear Arthur, and take Alice for a little promenade. I dare say we old cronies will manage to keep awake. Hasten, hasten, Romeo! My poor, poor Alice, how laggard a lover!"

Seaton returned with a shawl. They drifted out into the moonlight. My companion gazed after them till they were out of hearing, turned to me gravely, and suddenly twisted her white face into such a convulsion of contemptuous amusement that I could only stare blankly in reply.

"Dear innocent children!" she said, with inimitable unctuousness. "Well, well, Mr. Withers, we poor seasoned old creatures must move with the times. Do you sing?"

I scouted the idea.

"Then you must listen to my playing. Chess"—she clasped her forehead with both cramped hands—"chess is now completely beyond my poor wits."

She sat down at the piano and ran her fingers in a flourish over the keys. "What shall it be? How shall we capture them, those passionate hearts? That first fine careless rapture? Poetry itself." She gazed softly into the garden a moment, and presently, with a shake of her body, began to play the opening bars of Beethoven's "Moonlight" Sonata. The piano was old and woolly. She played without music. The lamplight was rather dim. The moonbeams from the window lay across the keys. Her head was in shadow. And whether it was simply due to her personality or to some really occult skill in her playing I cannot say: I only know that she gravely and deliberately set herself to satirize the beautiful music. It brooded on the air, disillusioned, charged with mockery and bitterness. I stood at the window; far down the path I could see the white figure glimmering in that pool of colourless light. A few faint stars shone, and still that amazing woman behind me dragged out of the unwilling keys her wonderful grotesquerie of youth, and love, and beauty. It came to an end. I knew the player was watching me. "Please, please, go on!" I murmured, without turning. "Please go on playing, Miss Seaton."

No answer was returned to my rather fluttering sarcasm, but I knew in some indefinite way that I was being acutely scrutinized, when sud-denly there followed a procession of quiet, plaintive chords which broke at last softly into the hymn, "A Few More Years Shall Roll".

I confess it held me spellbound. There is a wistful, strained, plangent pathos in the tune; but beneath those masterly old hands it cried softly and bitterly the solitude and desperate estrangement of the world. Arthur and his lady-love vanished from my thoughts. No one could put into a rather hackneyed old hymn-tune such an appeal who had never known the meaning of the words. Their meaning, anyhow, isn't commonplace.

I turned very cautiously and glanced at the musician. She was leaning forward a little over the keys, so that at the approach of my cautious glance she had but to turn her face into the thin flood of moonlight for every feature to become distinctly visible. And so, with the tune abruptly terminated, we steadfastly regarded one another, and she broke into a chuckle of laughter.

"Not quite so seasoned as I supposed, Mr. Withers. I see you are a real lover of music. To me it is too painful. It evokes too much thought—."

I could scarcely see her little glittering eyes under their penthouse lids.

"And now," she broke off crisply, "tell me, as a man of the world, what do you think of my new niece?"

I was not a man of the world, nor was I much flattered in my stiff and dullish way of looking at things by being called one; and I could answer her without the least hesitation.

"I don't think, Miss Seaton, I'm much of a judge of character. She's very charming."

"A brunette?"

"I think I prefer dark women."

"And why? Consider, Mr. Withers; dark hair, dark eyes, dark cloud, dark night, dark vision, dark death, dark grave, dark!"

Perhaps the climax would have rather thrilled Seaton, but I was too thick-skinned. "I don't know much about all that," I answered rather pompously. "Broad daylight's difficult enough for most of us."

"Ah," she said, with a sly inward burst of satirical laughter.

"And I suppose," I went on, perhaps a little nettled, "it isn't the actual darkness one admires, it's the contrast of the skin, and the colour of the eyes, and—and their shining. Just as," I went blundering on, too late to turn back, "just as you only see the stars in the dark. It would be a long day without any evening. As for death and the grave, I don't suppose we shall much notice that." Arthur and his sweetheart were slowly returning along the dewy path. "I believe in making the best of things."

"How very interesting!" came the smooth answer. "I see you are a philosopher, Mr. Withers. H'm! 'As for death and the grave, I don't suppose we shall much notice that.' Very interesting . . . And I'm sure," she added in a particularly suave voice, "I profoundly hope so." She rose slowly from her stool. "You will take pity on me again, I hope. You and I would get on famously—kindred spirits—elective affinities. And, of course, now that my nephew's going to leave us, now that his affections are centered on another, I shall be a very lonely old woman . . . Shall I not, Arthur?"

Seaton blinked stupidly. "I didn't hear what you said, aunt."

"I was telling our old friend, Arthur, that when you are gone I shall be a very lonely old woman."

"Oh, I don't think so," he said in a strange voice.

"He means, Mr. Withers, he means, my dear child," she said, sweeping her eyes over Alice, "he means that I shall have memory for company—heavenly memory—the ghosts of other days. Sentimental boy! And did you enjoy our music, Alice? Did I really stir that youthful heart? . . . O, O, O," continued the horrible old creature, "you billers and cooers, I have been listening to such flatteries, such confessions! Beware, beware, Arthur, there's many a slip." She rolled her little eyes at me, she shrugged her shoulders at Alice, and gazed an instant stonily into her nephew's face.

I held out my hand. "Good night, good night!" she cried. "He that fights and runs away. Ah, good night, Mr. Withers; come again soon!" She thrust out her cheek at Alice, and we all three filed slowly out of the room.

Black shadow darkened the porch and half the spreading sycamore. We walked without speaking up the dusty village street. Here and there a crimson window glowed. At the fork of the highroad I said good-bye. But I had taken hardly more than a dozen paces when a sudden impulse seized me.

"Seaton!" I called.

He turned in the moonlight.

"You have my address; if by any chance, you know, you should care to spend a week or two in town between this and the—the Day, we should be delighted to see you."

"Thank you, Withers, thank you," he said in a low voice.

"I dare say"—I waved my stick gallantly to Alice—"I dare say you will be doing some shopping; we could all meet," I added laughing.

"Thank you, thank you, Withers—immensely," he repeated.

And so we parted.

But they were out of the jog-trot of my prosaic life. And being of a stolid and incurious nature, I left Seaton and his marriage, and even his aunt, to themselves in my memory, and scarcely gave a thought to them until one day I was walking up the Strand again, and passed the flashing gloaming of the covered-in jeweller's shop where I had accidentally encountered my old schoolfellow in the summer. It was one of those still close autumnal days after a rainy night. I cannot say why, but a vivid recollection returned to my mind of our meeting and of how suppressed Seaton had seemed, and of how vainly he had endeavoured to appear assured and eager. He must be married by now, and had doubtless returned from his honeymoon. And I had clean forgotten my manners, had sent not a word of congratulation, nor—as I might very well have done, and as I knew he would have been immensely pleased at my doing—the ghost of a wedding-present.

On the other hand, I pleaded with myself, I had had no invitation. I paused at the corner of Trafalgar Square, and at the bidding of one of those caprices that seize occasionally on even an unimaginative mind, I suddenly ran after a green bus that was passing, and found myself bound on a visit I had not in the least foreseen.

The colours of autumn were over the village when I arrived. A beautiful late afternoon sunlight bathed thatch and meadow. But it was close and hot. A child, two dogs, a very old woman with a heavy basket I encountered. One or two incurious tradesmen looked idly up as I passed by. It was all so rural and so still, my whimsical impulse had so much flagged, that for a while I hesitated to venture under the shadow of the sycamore-tree to enquire after the happy pair. I deliberately passed by the faint-blue gates and continued my walk under the high green and tufted wall. Hollyhocks had attained their topmost bud and seeded in the little cottage gardens beyond; the Michaelmas daisies were in flower; a sweet warm aromatic smell of fading leaves was in the air. Beyond the cottages lay a field where cattle were grazing, and beyond that I came to a little churchyard. Then the road wound on, pathless and houseless, among gorse and bracken. I turned impatiently and walked quickly back to the house and rang the bell.

The rather colourless elderly woman who answered my enquiry informed me that Miss Seaton was at home, as if only taciturnity forbade her adding, "But she doesn't want to see you."

"Might I, do you think, have Mr. Arthur's address?" I said.

She looked at me with quiet astonishment, as if waiting for an explanation.

Not the faintest of smiles came into her thin face.

"I will tell Miss Seaton," she said after a pause. "Please walk in."

She showed me into the dingy undusted drawing-room, filled with evening sunshine and with the green-dyed light that penetrated the leaves overhanging the long French windows. I sat down and waited on and on, occasionally aware of a creaking footfall overhead. At last the door opened a little, and the great face I had once known peered round at me. For it was enormously changed; mainly, I think, because the old eyes had rather suddenly failed, and so a kind of stillness and darkness lay over its calm and wrinkled pallor.

"Who is it?" she asked.

I explained myself and told her the occasion of my visit.

She came in and shut the door carefully after her and, though the fumbling was scarcely perceptible, groped her way to a chair. She had on an old dressing-gown, like a cassock, of a patterned cinnamon colour.

"What is it you want?" she said, seating herself and lifting her blank face to mine.

"Might I just have Arthur's address?" I said deferentially. "I am so sorry to have disturbed you.

"H'm. You have come to see my nephew?"

"Not necessarily to see him, only to hear how he is, and, of course, Mrs. Seaton, too. I am afraid my silence must have appeared to . . ."

"He hasn't noticed your silence," croaked the old voice out of the great mask; "besides, there isn't any Mrs. Seaton."

"Ah, then," I answered, after a momentary pause, "I have not seemed so black as I painted myself! And how is Miss Outram?"

"She's gone into Yorkshire," answered Seaton's aunt.

"And Arthur too?"

She did not reply, but simply sat blinking at me with lifted chin, as if listening, but certainly not for what I might have to say. I began to feel rather at a loss.

"You were no close friend of my nephew's, Mr. Smithers?" she said presently.

"No," I answered, welcoming the cue, "and yet, do you know, Miss Seaton, he is one of the very few of my old schoolfellows I have come across in the last few years, and I suppose as one gets older one begins to value old associations . . ." My voice seemed to trail off into a vacuum. "I thought Miss Outram," I hastily began again, "a particularly charming girl. I hope they are both quite well."

Still the old face solemnly blinked at me in silence.

"You must find it very lonely, Miss Seaton, with Arthur away?"

"I was never lonely in my life," she said sourly. "I don't look to flesh and blood for my company. When you've got to be my age, Mr. Smithers (which God forbid), you'll find life a very different affair from what you seem to think it is now. You won't seek company then, I'll be bound. It's thrust on you." Her face edged round into the clear green light, and her eyes groped, as it were, over my vacant, disconcerted face. "I dare say, now," she said, composing her mouth, "I dare say my nephew told you a good many tarradiddles in his time. Oh, yes, a good many, eh? He was always a liar. What, now, did he say of me? Tell me, now." She leant forward as far as she could, trembling, with an ingratiating smile.

"I think he is rather superstitious," I said coldly, "but, honestly, I have a very poor memory, Miss Seaton."

"Why?" she said. "I haven't."

"The engagement hasn't been broken off, I hope."

"Well, between you and me," she said, shrinking up and with an immensely confidential grimace, "it has."

"I'm sure I'm very sorry to hear it. And where is Arthur?"

"Eh?"

"Where is Arthur?"

We faced each other mutely among the dead old bygone furniture.

Past all my scrutiny was that large, flat, grey, cryptic countenance. And then, suddenly, our eyes for the first time really met. In some indescribable way out of that thick-lidded obscurity a far small something stooped and looked out at me for a mere instant of time that seemed of almost intolerable protraction.

Involuntarily I blinked and shook my head. She muttered something with great rapidity, but quite inarticulately; rose and hobbled to the door. I thought I heard, mingled in broken mutterings, something about tea.

"Please, please, don't trouble," I began, but could say no more, for the door was already shut between us. I stood and looked out on the long-neglected garden. I could just see the bright greenness of Seaton's old tadpole pond. I wandered about the room. Dusk began to gather, the last birds in that dense shadowiness of trees had ceased to sing. And not a sound was to be heard in the house. I waited on and on, vainly speculating. I even attempted to ring the bell; but the wire was broken, and only jangled loosely at my efforts.

I hesitated, unwilling to call or to venture out, and yet more unwilling to linger on, waiting for a tea that promised to be an exceedingly comfortless supper. And as darkness drew down, a feeling of the utmost unease and disquietude came over me. All my talks with Seaton returned on me with a suddenly enriched meaning. I recalled again his face as we had stood hanging over the staircase, listening in the small hours to the inexplicable stirrings of the night. There were no candles in the room; every minute the autumnal darkness deepened. I cautiously opened the door and listened, and with some little dismay withdrew, for I was uncertain of my way out. I even tried the garden, but was confronted under a veritable thicket of foliage by a padlocked gate. It would be a little too ignominious to be caught scaling a friend's garden fence!

Cautiously returning into the still and musty drawing-room, I took out my watch, and gave the incredible old woman ten minutes in which to reappear. And when that tedious ten minutes had ticked by I could scarcely distinguish its hands. I determined to wait no longer, drew open the door, and, trusting to my sense of direction, groped my way through the corridor that I vaguely remembered led to the front of the house.

I mounted three or four stairs, and, lifting a heavy curtain, found myself facing the starry fanlight of the porch. From here I glanced into the gloom of the dining-room. My fingers were on the latch of the outer door when I heard a faint stirring in the darkness above the hall. I looked up and became conscious of, rather than saw, the huddled old figure looking down on me.

There was an immense hushed pause. Then, "Arthur, Arthur," whispered an inexpressibly peevish, rasping voice, "is that you? Is that you, Arthur?" I can scarcely say why, but the question horribly startled me. No conceivable answer occurred to me. With head craned back, hand clenched on my umbrella, I continued to stare up into the gloom, in this fatuous confrontation.

"Oh, oh," the voice croaked. "It is you, is it? That disgusting man! . . . Go away out. Go away out."

Hesitating no longer, I caught open the door and, slamming it behind me, ran out into the garden, under the gigantic old sycamore, and so out at the open gate.

I found myself half up the village street before I stopped running. The local butcher was sitting in his shop reading a piece of newspaper by the light of a small oil-lamp. I crossed the road and enquired the way to the station. And after he had with minute and needless care directed me, I asked casually if Mr. Arthur Seaton still lived with his aunt at the big house just beyond the village. He poked his head in at the little parlour door.

"Here's a gentleman enquiring after young Mr. Seaton, Millie," he said. "He's dead, ain't he?"

"Why, yes, bless you," replied a cheerful voice from within. "Dead and buried these three months or more—young Mr. Seaton. And just before he was to be married, don't you remember, Bob?"

I saw a fair young woman's face peer over the muslin of the little door at me.

"Thank you," I replied, "then I go straight on?"

"That's it, sir; past the pond, bear up the hill a bit to the left, and then there's the station lights before your eyes."

We looked intelligently into each other's faces in the beam of the smoky lamp. But not one of the many questions in my mind could I put into words.

And again I paused irresolutely a few paces further on. It was not fancy, merely a foolish apprehension of what the raw-boned butcher might "think" that prevented my going back to see if I could find Seaton's grave in the benighted churchyard. There was precious little use in pottering about in the muddy dark, merely to discover where he was buried. And yet I felt a little uneasy. My rather horrible thought was that, so far as I was concerned—one of his extremely few friends—he had never been much better than "buried" in my mind.

Part III

THE OUTER DARK

natural and unnatural horrors

WHAT CAN ONE SAY about interstellar multi-dimensional horror that hasn't already been said? Obviously I have no idea. It is a confusing topic, and to quote that astronaut who disappeared some years ago beyond the moons of Jupiter: "My God, it's full of stars."

The stories presented here for your amusement are a combination of cosmic and ecological horror. Cosmic horror involves forces that pose an existential threat—an encroachment from beyond our sphere, usually spawning in a bit of space dust or clawing out of an alternate dimension. These stories may include elder gods not found in any known religion. Ecological horror—or as I prefer to call her: Mother Unnature—concerns our physical world gone wild.

"The Dead Valley" by Ralph Adams Cram is not so much a story of cosmic horror as it is an expression of the Super Natural, or Super Nature. The narrative is set up under the guise of a pass-along tale—"I heard it from a friend . . ." In our story two young boys cross the mountains to buy a puppy and stumble upon a toxic valley that is both frightening and deadly. It is hinted that the lads have found a supernatural breech of our world—a hellish impingement beyond our understanding, yet this cosmic horror tale is more grounded than we know. It seems Mother Nature has some real nasty inclinations. I present Exhibit A— the Mazuku, which is Swahili for "evil wind." Unstable volcanic pockets sometimes vent highly noxious clouds of CO_2—a killer cloud that hugs the ground, just like something from a John Carpenter movie. Whether based on fact or the work of a fevered imagination, "The Dead Valley" is a milestone of American weird fiction.

Algernon Blackwood's "The Willows" will forever cement its author's reputation and well deserves its vaunted place in the pantheon of supernatural fiction. It is one of the first, if not the first, story of cosmic horror. Like "The

Dead Valley" the plot is set in motion by two traveling companions. This time, while canoeing down the stretch of the Danube that meanders through the remote plains of Hungary, the explorers encounter a force of nature that is totally out of sync with human experience. Stranded on a sandy island midstream, waiting for better conditions before shoving off, they slowly realize that a creeping, consuming force is revealing itself. The story's effect is absolutely chilling, and made more powerful by our inability to fully understand it. The very best supernatural stories show us that there is a thin veil between our reality and the nether world. This plays through Blackwood's body of work and is one of the many reasons he is considered a grandmaster of the genre.

"The Seed From the Sepulcher" is the work of one of the most fertile minds of horror fiction, Clark Ashton Smith. Smith was a writer, poet and artist who lived most of his life in Auburn, California—an old gold-mining town in the Sierra Mountain foothills. He corresponded with H. P. Lovecraft and Robert E. Howard, and this trio of distant friends would define 20th century weird fiction. "The Seed From the Sepulcher" is a powerhouse tale about the darker forces of nature. Again we find two men on a canoe trip (this section could have been called "Two Men in a Boat")—a low-budget, rundown expedition to collect rare orchids along the banks of Venezuela's Orinoco River. Daring to enter a vine-choked tomb in the search of forbidden relics they discover something even more rare in the ruins. Once you've read the story you won't be able to get it out of your head.

"That Damned Thing" by Ambrose Bierce is further proof that cosmic horror existed before you-know-who came along. This is a very short story but carries big ideas that have been expanded by later writers. Told in Bierce's fiercely sardonic style, the plot intriguingly slides from a court inquiry regarding a mysterious death to the dead man's diary that was never fully allowed into evidence. We—the reader—see the evidence but never fully learn the truth.

Our final entry is the Nebula award-winning novella "The Saliva Tree" by the science fiction grand-master and three-time Hugo winning author, Brian Aldiss. Written as a homage to H. G. Wells on the centenary of Well's birth, it is a playful tribute to Wellsian ideas and ideals. Why this story has never been filmed is a complete mystery. It has a pastoral Victorian setting, a great mix of country-folk and lay-about university types, lots of charming farm animals, plus a god-awful monster—all of it very photogenic. In any case it will play well in the theater-of-the-mind.

The Dead Valley

by Ralph Adams Cram

I HAVE A FRIEND, Olof Ehrensvärd, a Swede by birth, who yet, by reason of a strange and melancholy mischance of his early boyhood, has thrown his lot with that of the New World. It is a curious story of a headstrong boy and a proud and relentless family: the details do not matter here, but they are sufficient to weave a web of romance around the tall yellow-bearded man with the sad eyes and the voice that gives itself perfectly to plaintive little Swedish songs remembered out of childhood. In the winter evenings we play chess together, he and I, and after some close, fierce battle has been fought to a finish—usually with my own defeat—we fill our pipes again, and Ehrensvärd tells me stories of the far, half-remembered days in the fatherland, before he went to sea: stories that grow very strange and incredible as the night deepens and the fire falls together, but stories that, nevertheless, I fully believe.

One of them made a strong impression on me, so I set it down here, only regretting that I cannot reproduce the curiously perfect English and the delicate accent which to me increased the fascination of the tale. Yet, as best I can remember it, here it is.

~§~

"I never told you how Nils and I went over the hills to Hallsberg, and how we found the Dead Valley, did I? Well, this is the way it happened. I must have been about twelve years old, and Nils Sjöberg, whose father's estate joined ours, was a few months younger. We were inseparable just at that time, and whatever we did, we did together.

"Once a week it was market day in Engelholm, and Nils and I went always there to see the strange sights that the market gathered from all the surrounding country. One day we quite lost our hearts, for an old man

245

from across the Elfborg had brought a little dog to sell, that seemed to us the most beautiful dog in all the world. He was a round, woolly puppy, so funny that Nils and I sat down on the ground and laughed at him, until he came and played with us in so jolly a way that we felt that there was only one really desirable thing in life, and that was the little dog of the old man from across the hills. But alas! we had not half money enough wherewith to buy him, so we were forced to beg the old man not to sell him before the next market day, promising that we would bring the money for him then. He gave us his word, and we ran home very fast and implored our mothers to give us money for the little dog.

"We got the money, but we could not wait for the next market day. Suppose the puppy should be sold! The thought frightened us so that we begged and implored that we might be allowed to go over the hills to Hallsberg where the old man lived, and get the little dog ourselves, and at last they told us we might go. By starting early in the morning we should reach Hallsberg by three o'clock, and it was arranged that we should stay there that night with Nils's aunt, and, leaving by noon the next day, be home again by sunset.

"Soon after sunrise we were on our way, after having received minute instructions as to just what we should do in all possible and impossible circumstances, and finally a repeated injunction that we should start for home at the same hour the next day, so that we might get safely back before nightfall.

"For us, it was magnificent sport, and we started off with our rifles, full of the sense of our very great importance: yet the journey was simple enough, along a good road, across the big hills we knew so well, for Nils and I had shot over half the territory this side of the dividing ridge of the Elfborg. Back of Engelholm lay a long valley, from which rose the low mountains, and we had to cross this, and then follow the road along the side of the hills for three or four miles, before a narrow path branched off to the left, leading up through the pass.

"Nothing occurred of interest on the way over, and we reached Hallsberg in due season, found to our inexpressible joy that the little dog was not sold, secured him, and so went to the house of Nils's aunt to spend the night.

"Why we did not leave early on the following day, I can't quite remember; at all events, I know we stopped at a shooting range just outside of the town, where most attractive pasteboard pigs were sliding slowly through painted foliage, serving so as beautiful marks. The result was that we did not get fairly started for home until afternoon, and as we found ourselves at last pushing up the side of the mountain with the sun dangerously near their summits, I think we were a little scared at the prospect of the examination and possible punishment that awaited us when we got home at midnight.

"Therefore we hurried as fast as possible up the mountain side, while the blue dusk closed in about us, and the light died in the purple sky. At first we had talked hilariously, and the little dog had leaped ahead of us with the utmost joy. Latterly, however, a curious oppression came on us; we did not speak or even whistle, while the dog fell behind, following us with hesitation in every muscle.

"We had passed through the foothills and the low spurs of the mountains, and were almost at the top of the main range, when life seemed to go out of everything, leaving the world dead, so suddenly silent the forest became, so stagnant the air. Instinctively we halted to listen.

"Perfect silence—the crushing silence of deep forests at night; and more, for always, even in the most impenetrable fastnesses of the wooded mountains, is the multitudinous murmur of little lives, awakened by the darkness, exaggerated and intensified by the stillness of the air and the great dark: but here and now the silence seemed unbroken even by the turn of a leaf, the movement of a twig, the note of night bird or insect. I could hear the blood beat through my veins; and the crushing of the grass under our feet as we advanced with hesitating steps sounded like the falling of trees.

"And the air was stagnant—dead. The atmosphere seemed to lie upon the body like the weight of sea on a diver who has ventured too far into its awful depths. What we usually call silence seems so only in relation to the din of ordinary experience. This was silence in the absolute, and it crushed the mind while it intensified the senses, bringing down the awful weight of inextinguishable fear.

"I know that Nils and I stared towards each other in abject terror, listening to our quick, heavy breathing, that sounded to our acute senses like the fitful rush of waters. And the poor little dog we were leading justified our terror. The black oppression seemed to crush him even as it did us. He lay close on the ground, moaning feebly, and dragging himself painfully and slowly closer to Nils's feet. I think this exhibition of utter animal fear was the last touch, and must inevitably have blasted our reason—mine anyway; but just then, as we stood quaking on the bounds of madness, came a sound, so awful, so ghastly, so horrible, that it seemed to rouse us from the dead spell that was on us.

"In the depth of the silence came a cry, beginning as a low, sorrowful moan, rising to a tremulous shriek, culminating in a yell that seemed to tear the night in sunder and rend the world as by a cataclysm. So fearful was it that I could not believe it had actual existence: it passed previous experience, the powers of belief, and for a moment I thought it the result of my own animal terror, an hallucination born of tottering reason.

"A glance at Nils dispelled this thought in a flash. In the pale light of the high stars he was the embodiment of all possible human fear, quaking with an ague, his jaw fallen, his tongue out, his eyes protruding like those of a hanged man. Without a word we fled, the panic of fear giving us strength, and together, the little dog caught close in Nils's arms, we sped down the side of the cursed mountains—anywhere, goal was of no account: we had but one impulse—to get away from that place.

"So under the black trees and the far white stars that flashed through the still leaves overhead, we leaped down the mountainside, regardless of path or landmark, straight through the tangled underbrush, across mountain streams, through fens and copses, anywhere, so only that our course was downward.

"How long we ran thus, I have no idea, but by and by the forest fell behind, and we found ourselves among the foothills, and fell exhausted on the dry short grass, panting like tired dogs.

"It was lighter here in the open, and presently we looked around to see where we were, and how we were to strike out in order to find the path that would lead us home. We looked in vain for a familiar sign. Behind us rose the great wall of black forest on the flank of the mountain: before us lay the undulating mounds of low foothills, unbroken by trees or rocks, and beyond, only the fall of black sky bright with multitudinous stars that turned its velvet depth to a luminous gray.

"As I remember, we did not speak to each other once: the terror was too heavy on us for that, but by and by we rose simultaneously and started out across the hills.

"Still the same silence, the same dead, motionless air—air that was at once sultry and chilling: a heavy heat struck through with an icy chill that felt almost like the burning of frozen steel. Still carrying the helpless dog, Nils pressed on through the hills, and I followed close behind. At last, in front of us, rose a slope of moor touching the white stars. We climbed it wearily, reached the top, and found ourselves gazing down into a great, smooth valley, filled halfway to the brim with—what?

"As far as the eye could see stretched a level plain of ashy white, faintly phosphorescent, a sea of velvet fog that lay like motionless water, or rather like a floor of alabaster, so dense did it appear, so seemingly capable of sustaining weight. If it were possible, I think that sea of dead white mist struck even greater terror into my soul than the heavy silence or the deadly cry—so ominous was it, so utterly unreal, so phantasmal, so impossible, as it lay there like a dead ocean under the steady stars. Yet through that mist *we must go*! there seemed no other way home, and, shattered with abject fear, mad with the one desire to get back, we started down the slope to where the sea of milky mist ceased, sharp and distinct around the stems of the rough grass.

"I put one foot into the ghostly fog. A chill as of death struck through me, stopping my heart, and I threw myself backward on the slope. At that instant came again the shriek, close, close, right in our ears, in ourselves, and far out across that damnable sea I saw the cold fog lift like a water-spout and toss itself high in writhing convolutions towards the sky. The stars began to grow dim as thick vapor swept across them, and in the growing dark I saw a great, watery moon lift itself slowly above the palpitating sea, vast and vague in the gathering mist.

"This was enough: we turned and fled along the margin of the white sea that throbbed now with fitful motion below us, rising, rising, slowly and steadily, driving us higher and higher up the side of the foothills.

"It was a race for life; that we knew. How we kept it up I cannot understand, but we did, and at last we saw the white sea fall behind us as we staggered up the end of the valley, and then down into a region that we knew, and so into the old path. The last thing I remember was hearing a strange voice, that of Nils, but horribly changed, stammer brokenly, 'The dog is dead!' and then the whole world turned around twice, slowly and resistlessly, and consciousness went out with a crash.

"It was some three weeks later, as I remember, that I awoke in my own room, and found my mother sitting beside the bed. I could not think very well at first, but as I slowly grew strong again, vague flashes of recollection began to come to me, and little by little the whole sequence of events of that awful night in the Dead Valley came back. All that I could gain from what was told me was that three weeks before I had been found in my own bed, raging sick, and that my illness grew fast into brain fever. I tried to speak of the dread things that had happened to me, but I saw at once that no one looked on them save as the hauntings of a dying frenzy, and so I closed my mouth and kept my own counsel.

"I must see Nils, however, and so I asked for him. My mother told me that he also had been ill with a strange fever, but that he was now quite well again. Presently they brought him in, and when we were alone I began to speak to him of the night on the mountain. I shall never forget

the shock that struck me down on my pillow when the boy denied everything: denied having gone with me, ever having heard the cry, having
seen the valley, or feeling the deadly chill of the ghostly fog. Nothing
would shake his determined ignorance, and in spite of myself I was
forced to admit that his denials came from no policy of concealment, but
from blank oblivion.

"My weakened brain was in a turmoil. Was it all but the floating
phantasm of delirium? Or had the horror of the real thing blotted Nils's
mind into blankness so far as the events of the night in the Dead Valley
were concerned? The latter explanation seemed the only one, else how
explain the sudden illness which in a night had struck us both down? I
said nothing more, either to Nils or to my own people, but waited, with a
growing determination that, once well again, I would find that valley if it
really existed.

"It was some weeks before I was really well enough to go, but finally,
late in September, I chose a bright, warm, still day, the last smile of the
dying summer, and started early in the morning along the path that led to
Hallsberg. I was sure I knew where the trail struck off to the right, down
which we had come from the valley of dead water, for a great tree grew by
the Hallsberg path at the point where, with a sense of salvation, we had
found the home road. Presently I saw it to the right, a little distance
ahead.

"I think the bright sunlight and the clear air had worked as a tonic to
me, for by the time I came to the foot of the great pine, I had quite lost
faith in the verity of the vision that haunted me, believing at last that it
was indeed but the nightmare of madness. Nevertheless, I turned sharply
to the right, at the base of the tree, into a narrow path that led through a
dense thicket. As I did so I tripped over something. A swarm of flies sung
into the air around me, and looking down I saw the matted fleece, with
the poor little bones thrusting through, of the dog we had bought in
Hallsberg.

"Then my courage went out with a puff, and I knew that it all was
true, and that now I was frightened. Pride and the desire for adventure
urged me on, however, and I pressed into the close thicket that barred my
way. The path was hardly visible: merely the worn road of some small
beasts, for, though it showed in the crisp grass, the bushes above grew
thick and hardly penetrable. The land rose slowly, and rising grew
clearer, until at last I came out on a great slope of hill, unbroken by trees
or shrubs, very like my memory of that rise of land we had topped in
order that we might find the dead valley and the icy fog. I looked at the

sun; it was bright and clear, and all around insects were humming in the autumn air, and birds were darting to and fro. Surely there was no danger, not until nightfall at least; so I began to whistle, and with a rush mounted the last crest of brown hill.

"There lay the Dead Valley! A great oval basin, almost as smooth and regular as though made by man. On all sides the grass crept over the brink of the encircling hills, dusty green on the crests, then fading into ashy brown, and so to a deadly white, this last color forming a thin ring, running in a long line around the slope. And then? Nothing. Bare, brown, hard earth, glittering with grains of alkali, but otherwise dead and barren. Not a tuft of grass, not a stick of brushwood, not even a stone, but only the vast expanse of beaten clay.

"In the midst of the basin, perhaps a mile and a half away, the level expanse was broken by a great dead tree, rising leafless and gaunt into the air. Without a moment's hesitation I started down into the valley and made for this goal. Every particle of fear seemed to have left me, and even the valley itself did not look so very terrifying. At all events, I was driven by an overwhelming curiosity, and there seemed to be but one thing in the world to do—to get to that tree! As I trudged along over the hard earth, I noticed that the multitudinous voices of birds and insects had died away. No bee or butterfly hovered through the air, no insects leaped or crept over the dull earth. The very air itself was stagnant.

"As I drew near the skeleton tree, I noticed the glint of sunlight on a kind of white mound around its roots, and I wondered curiously. It was not until I had come close that I saw its nature.

"All around the roots and barkless trunk was heaped a wilderness of little bones. Tiny skulls of rodents and of birds, thousands of them, rising about the dead tree and streaming off for several yards in all directions, until the dreadful pile ended in isolated skulls and scattered skeletons. Here and there a larger bone appeared—the thigh of a sheep, the hoofs of a horse, and to one side, grinning slowly, a human skull.

"I stood quite still, staring with all my eyes, when suddenly the dense silence was broken by a faint, forlorn cry high over my head. I looked up and saw a great falcon turning and sailing downward just over the tree. In a moment more she fell motionless on the bleaching bones.

"Horror struck me, and I rushed for home, my brain whirling, a strange numbness growing in me. I ran steadily, on and on. At last I glanced up. Where was the rise of hill? I looked around wildly. Close before me was the dead tree with its pile of bones. I had circled it round and round, and the valley wall was still a mile and a half away.

"I stood dazed and frozen. The sun was sinking, red and dull, towards the line of hills. In the east the dark was growing fast. Was there still time? *Time!* It was not *that* I wanted, it was *will*! My feet seemed clogged as in a nightmare. I could hardly drag them over the barren earth. And then I felt the slow chill creeping through me. I looked down. Out of the earth a thin mist was rising, collecting in little pools that grew ever larger until they joined here and there, their currents swirling slowly like thin blue smoke. The western hills halved the copper sun. When it was dark I should hear that shriek again, and then I should die. I knew that, and with every remaining atom of will I staggered towards the red west through the writhing mist that crept clammily around my ankles, retarding my steps.

"And as I fought my way off from the tree, the horror grew, until at last I thought I was going to die. The silence pursued me like dumb ghosts, the still air held my breath, the hellish fog caught at my feet like cold hands.

"But I won! though not a moment too soon. As I crawled on my hands and knees up the brown slope, I heard, far away and high in the air, the cry that already had almost bereft me of reason. It was faint and vague, but unmistakable in its horrible intensity. I glanced behind. The fog was dense and pallid, heaving undulously up the brown slope. The sky was gold under the setting sun, but below was the ashy gray of death. I stood for a moment on the brink of this sea of hell, and then leaped down the slope. The sunset opened before me, the night closed behind, and as I crawled home weak and tired, darkness shut down on the Dead Valley."

The Willows

by Algernon Blackwood

I.

AFTER leaving Vienna, and long before you come to Budapest, the Danube enters a region of singular loneliness and desolation, where its waters spread away on all sides regardless of a main channel, and the country becomes a swamp for miles upon miles, covered by a vast sea of low willow-bushes. On the big maps this deserted area is painted in a fluffy blue, growing fainter in color as it leaves the banks, and across it may be seen in large straggling letters the word *Sümpfe*, meaning marshes.

In high flood this great acreage of sand, shingle-beds, and willow-grown islands is almost topped by the water, but in normal seasons the bushes bend and rustle in the free winds, showing their silver leaves to the sunshine in an ever-moving plain of bewildering beauty. These willows never attain to the dignity of trees; they have no rigid trunks; they remain humble bushes, with rounded tops and soft outline, swaying on slender stems that answer to the least pressure of the wind; supple as grasses, and so continually shifting that they somehow give the impression that the entire plain is moving and alive. For the wind sends waves rising and falling over the whole surface, waves of leaves instead of waves of water, green swells like the sea, too, until the branches turn and lift, and then silvery white as their underside turns to the sun.

Happy to slip beyond the control of the stern banks, the Danube here wanders about at will among the intricate network of channels intersecting the islands everywhere with broad avenues down which the waters pour with a shouting sound; making whirlpools, eddies, and foaming rapids; tearing at the sandy banks; carrying away masses of shore and willow-clumps; and forming new islands innumerably which shift daily in size and shape and possess at best an impermanent life, since the flood-time obliterates their very existence.

Properly speaking, this fascinating part of the river's life begins soon after leaving Pressburg, and we, in our Canadian canoe, with gipsy tent and frying-pan on board, reached it on the crest of a rising flood about mid-July. That very same morning, when the sky was reddening before sunrise, we had slipped swiftly through still-sleeping Vienna, leaving it a couple of hours later a mere patch of smoke against the blue hills of the Wienerwald on the horizon; we had breakfasted below Fischeramend under a grove of birch trees roaring in the wind; and had then swept on the tearing current past Orth, Hainburg, Petronell (the old Roman Carnuntum of Marcus Aurelius), and so under the frowning heights of Thelsen on a spur of the Carpathians, where the March steals in quietly from the left and the frontier is crossed between Austria and Hungary.

Racing along at twelve kilometers an hour soon took us well into Hungary, and the muddy waters—sure sign of flood—sent us aground on many a shingle-bed, and twisted us like a cork in many a sudden belching whirlpool before the towers of Pressburg (Hungarian, Poszóny) showed against the sky; and then the canoe, leaping like a spirited horse, flew at top speed under the grey walls, negotiated safely the sunken chain of the Fliegende Brucke ferry, turned the corner sharply to the left, and plunged on yellow foam into the wilderness of islands, sandbanks, and swamp-land beyond—the land of the willows.

The change came suddenly, as when a series of bioscope pictures snaps down on the streets of a town and shifts without warning into the scenery of lake and forest. We entered the land of desolation on wings, and in less than half an hour there was neither boat nor fishing-hut nor red roof, nor any single sign of human habitation and civilization within sight. The sense of remoteness from the world of humankind, the utter isolation, the fascination of this singular world of willows, winds, and waters, instantly laid its spell upon us both, so that we allowed laughingly to one another that we ought by rights to have held some special kind of passport to admit us, and that we had, somewhat audaciously, come without asking leave into a separate little kingdom of wonder and magic —a kingdom that was reserved for the use of others who had a right to it, with everywhere unwritten warnings to trespassers for those who had the imagination to discover them.

Though still early in the afternoon, the ceaseless buffetings of a most tempestuous wind made us feel weary, and we at once began casting about for a suitable camping-ground for the night. But the bewildering character of the islands made landing difficult; the swirling flood carried us in shore and then swept us out again; the willow branches tore our hands as we seized them to stop the canoe, and we pulled many a yard of sandy bank into the water before at length we shot with a great sideways blow from the wind into a backwater and managed to beach the bows in a cloud of spray. Then we lay panting and laughing after our exertions on the hot yellow sand, sheltered from the wind, and in the full blaze of a scorching sun, a cloudless blue sky above, and an immense army of dancing, shouting willow bushes, closing in from all sides, shining with spray and clapping their thousand little hands as though to applaud the success of our efforts.

"What a river!" I said to my companion, thinking of all the way we had traveled from the source in the Black Forest, and how he had often been obliged to wade and push in the upper shallows at the beginning of June.

"Won't stand much nonsense now, will it?" he said, pulling the canoe a little farther into safety up the sand, and then composing himself for a nap.

I lay by his side, happy and peaceful in the bath of the elements—water, wind, sand, and the great fire of the sun—thinking of the long journey that lay behind us, and of the great stretch before us to the Black Sea, and how lucky I was to have such a delightful and charming traveling companion as my friend, the Swede.

We had made many similar journeys together, but the Danube, more than any other river I knew, impressed us from the very beginning with its *aliveness*. From its tiny bubbling entry into the world among the pinewood gardens of Donaueschingen, until this moment when it began to play the great river-game of losing itself among the deserted swamps, unobserved, unrestrained, it had seemed to us like following the growth of some living creature. Sleepy at first, but later developing violent desires as it became conscious of its deep soul, it rolled, like some huge fluid being, through all the countries we had passed, holding our little craft on its mighty shoulders, playing roughly with us sometimes, yet always friendly and well-meaning, till at length we had come inevitably to regard it as a Great Personage.

How, indeed, could it be otherwise, since it told us so much of its secret life? At night we heard it singing to the moon as we lay in our tent, uttering that odd sibilant note peculiar to itself and said to be caused by the rapid tearing of the pebbles along its bed, so great is its hurrying speed. We knew, too, the voice of its gurgling whirlpools, suddenly bubbling up on a surface previously quite calm; the roar of its shallows and swift rapids; its constant steady thundering below all mere surface sounds; and that ceaseless tearing of its icy waters at the banks. How it stood up and shouted when the rains fell flat upon its face! And how its laughter roared out when the wind blew up-stream and tried to stop its growing speed! We knew all its sounds and voices, its tumblings and foamings, its unnecessary splashing against the bridges; that self-conscious chatter when there were hills to look on; the affected dignity of its speech when it passed through the little towns, far too important to laugh; and all these faint, sweet whisperings when the sun caught it fairly in some slow curve and poured down upon it till the steam rose.

It was full of tricks, too, in its early life before the great world knew it. There were places in the upper reaches among the Swabian forests, when yet the first whispers of its destiny had not reached it, where it elected to disappear through holes in the ground, to appear again on the other side of the porous limestone hills and start a new river with another name; leaving, too, so little water in its own bed that we had to climb out and wade and push the canoe through miles of shallows.

And a chief pleasure, in those early days of its irresponsible youth, was to lie low, like Brer Fox, just before the little turbulent tributaries came to join it from the Alps, and to refuse to acknowledge them when in, but to run for miles side by side, the dividing line well marked, the very levels different, the Danube utterly declining to recognize the newcomer. Below Passau, however, it gave up this particular trick, for there the Inn comes in with a thundering power impossible to ignore, and so pushes and incommodes the parent river that there is hardly room for them in the long twisting gorge that follows, and the Danube is shoved this way and that against the cliffs, and forced to hurry itself with great waves and much dashing to and fro in order to get through in time. And during the fight our canoe slipped down from its shoulder to its breast, and had the time of its life among the struggling waves. But the Inn taught the old river a lesson, and after Passau it no longer pretended to ignore new arrivals.

This was many days back, of course, and since then we had come to know other aspects of the great creature, and across the Bavarian wheat plain of Straubing she wandered so slowly under the blazing June sun that we could well imagine only the surface inches were water, while below there moved, concealed as by a silken mantle, a whole army of Undines, passing silently and unseen down to the sea, and very leisurely too, lest they be discovered.

Much, too, we forgave her because of her friendliness to the birds and animals that haunted the shores. Cormorants lined the banks in lonely places in rows like short black palings; grey crows crowded the shingle-beds; storks stood fishing in the vistas of shallower water that opened up between the islands, and hawks, swans, and marsh birds of all sorts filled the air with glinting wings and singing, petulant cries. It was impossible to feel annoyed with the river's vagaries after seeing a deer leap with a splash into the water at sunrise and swim past the bows of the canoe; and often we saw fawns peering at us from the underbrush, or looked straight into the brown eyes of a stag as we charged full tilt round a corner and entered another reach of the river. Foxes, too, everywhere haunted the banks, tripping daintily among the driftwood and disappearing so suddenly that it was impossible to see how they managed it.

But now, after leaving Pressburg, everything changed a little, and the Danube became more serious. It ceased trifling. It was half-way to the Black Sea, within seeming distance almost of other, stranger countries where no tricks would be permitted or understood. It became suddenly grown-up, and claimed our respect and even our awe. It broke out into three arms, for one thing, that only met again a hundred kilometers farther down, and for a canoe there were no indications which one was intended to be followed.

"If you take a side channel," said the Hungarian officer we met in the Pressburg shop while buying provisions, "you may find yourselves, when the flood subsides, forty miles from anywhere, high and dry, and you may easily starve. There are no people, no farms, no fishermen. I warn you not to continue. The river, too, is still rising, and this wind will increase."

The rising river did not alarm us in the least, but the matter of being left high and dry by a sudden subsidence of the waters might be serious, and we had consequently laid in an extra stock of provisions. For the rest, the officer's prophecy held true, and the wind, blowing down a perfectly clear sky, increased steadily till it reached the dignity of a westerly gale.

It was earlier than usual when we camped, for the sun was a good hour or two from the horizon, and leaving my friend still asleep on the hot sand, I wandered about in desultory examination of our hotel. The island, I found, was less than an acre in extent, a mere sandy bank standing some two or three feet above the level of the river. The far end, pointing into the sunset, was covered with flying spray which the tremendous wind drove off the crests of the broken waves. It was triangular in shape, with the apex up stream.

I stood there for several minutes, watching the impetuous crimson flood bearing down with a shouting roar, dashing in waves against the bank as though to sweep it bodily away, and then swirling by in two foaming streams on either side. The ground seemed to shake with the shock and rush, while the furious movement of the willow bushes as the wind poured over them increased the curious illusion that the island itself actually moved. Above, for a mile or two, I could see the great river descending upon me; it was like looking up the slope of a sliding hill, white with foam, and leaping up everywhere to show itself to the sun.

The rest of the island was too thickly grown with willows to make walking pleasant, but I made the tour, nevertheless. From the lower end the light, of course, changed, and the river looked dark and angry. Only the backs of the flying waves were visible, streaked with foam, and pushed forcibly by the great puffs of wind that fell upon them from behind. For a short mile it was visible, pouring in and out among the islands, and then disappearing with a huge sweep into the willows, which closed about it like a herd of monstrous antediluvian creatures crowding down to drink. They made me think of gigantic sponge-like growths that sucked the river up into themselves. They caused it to vanish from sight. They herded there together in such overpowering numbers.

Altogether it was an impressive scene, with its utter loneliness, its bizarre suggestion; and as I gazed, long and curiously, a singular emotion began to stir somewhere in the depths of me. Midway in my delight of the wild beauty, there crept, unbidden and unexplained, a curious feeling of disquietude, almost of alarm.

A rising river, perhaps, always suggests something of the ominous; many of the little islands I saw before me would probably have been swept away by the morning; this resistless, thundering flood of water touched the sense of awe. Yet I was aware that my uneasiness lay deeper far than the emotions of awe and wonder. It was not that I felt. Nor had it directly to do with the power of the driving wind—this shouting hurricane that might almost carry up a few acres of willows into the air and scatter them like so much chaff over the landscape. The wind was simply enjoying itself, for nothing rose out of the flat landscape to stop it, and I was conscious of sharing its great game with a kind of pleasurable excitement. Yet this novel emotion had nothing to do with the wind. Indeed, so vague was the sense of distress I experienced, that it was impossible to trace it to its source and deal with it accordingly, though I was aware somehow that it had to do with my realization of our utter insignificance before this unrestrained power of the elements about me. The huge-grown river had something to do with it too—a vague, unpleasant idea that we had somehow trifled with these great elemental forces in whose power we lay helpless every hour of the day and night. For here, indeed, they were gigantically at play together, and the sight appealed to the imagination.

But my emotion, so far as I could understand it, seemed to attach itself more particularly to the willow bushes, to these acres and acres of willows, crowding, so thickly growing there, swarming everywhere the eye could reach, pressing upon the river as though to suffocate it, standing in dense array mile after mile beneath the sky, watching, waiting, listening. And, apart quite from the elements, the willows connected themselves subtly with my malaise, attacking the mind insidiously somehow by reason of their vast numbers, and contriving in some way or other to represent to the imagination a new and mighty power, a power, moreover, not altogether friendly to us.

Great revelations of nature, of course, never fail to impress in one way or another, and I was no stranger to moods of the kind. Mountains overawe and oceans terrify, while the mystery of great forests exercises a spell peculiarly its own. But all these, at one point or another, somewhere link on intimately with human life and human experience. They stir comprehensible, even if alarming, emotions. They tend on the whole to exalt.

With this multitude of willows, however, it was something far different, I felt. Some essence emanated from them that besieged the heart. A sense of awe awakened, true, but of awe touched somewhere by a vague terror. Their serried ranks, growing everywhere darker about me as the shadows deepened, moving furiously yet softly in the wind, woke in me the curious and unwelcome suggestion that we had trespassed here upon the borders of an alien world, a world where we were intruders, a world where we were not wanted or invited to remain—where we ran grave risks perhaps!

The feeling, however, though it refused to yield its meaning entirely to analysis, did not at the time trouble me by passing into menace. Yet it never left me quite, even during the very practical business of putting up the tent in a hurricane of wind and building a fire for the stew-pot. It remained, just enough to bother and perplex, and to rob a most delightful camping-ground of a good portion of its charm. To my companion, however, I said nothing, for he was a man I considered devoid of imagination. In the first place, I could never have explained to him what I meant, and in the second, he would have laughed stupidly at me if I had.

There was a slight depression in the center of the island, and here we pitched the tent. The surrounding willows broke the wind a bit.

"A poor camp," observed the imperturbable Swede when at last the tent stood upright, "no stones and precious little firewood. I'm for moving on early tomorrow—eh? This sand won't hold anything."

But the experience of a collapsing tent at midnight had taught us many devices, and we made the cozy gipsy house as safe as possible, and then set about collecting a store of wood to last till bed-time. Willow bushes drop no branches, and driftwood was our only source of supply. We hunted the shores pretty thoroughly. Everywhere the banks were crumbling as the rising flood tore at them and carried away great portions with a splash and a gurgle.

"The island's much smaller than when we landed," said the accurate Swede. "It won't last long at this rate. We'd better drag the canoe close to the tent, and be ready to start at a moment's notice. I shall sleep in my clothes."

He was a little distance off, climbing along the bank, and I heard his rather jolly laugh as he spoke.

"By Jove!" I heard him call, a moment later, and turned to see what had caused his exclamation. But for the moment he was hidden by the willows, and I could not find him.

"What in the world's this?" I heard him cry again, and this time his voice had become serious.

I ran up quickly and joined him on the bank. He was looking over the river, pointing at something in the water.

"Good heavens, it's a man's body!" he cried excitedly. "Look!"

A black thing, turning over and over in the foaming waves, swept rapidly past. It kept disappearing and coming up to the surface again. It was about twenty feet from the shore, and just as it was opposite to where we stood it lurched round and looked straight at us. We saw its eyes reflecting the sunset, and gleaming an odd yellow as the body turned over. Then it gave a swift, gulping plunge, and dived out of sight in a flash.

"An otter, by gad!" we exclaimed in the same breath, laughing.

It was an otter, alive, and out on the hunt; yet it had looked exactly like the body of a drowned man turning helplessly in the current. Far below it came to the surface once again, and we saw its black skin, wet and shining in the sunlight.

Then, too, just as we turned back, our arms full of driftwood, another thing happened to recall us to the riverbank. This time it really was a man, and what was more, a man in a boat. Now a small boat on the

Danube was an unusual sight at any time, but here in this deserted region, and at flood time, it was so unexpected as to constitute a real event. We stood and stared.

Whether it was due to the slanting sunlight, or the refraction from the wonderfully illumined water, I cannot say, but, whatever the cause, I found it difficult to focus my sight properly upon the flying apparition. It seemed, however, to be a man standing upright in a sort of flat-bottomed boat, steering with a long oar, and being carried down the opposite shore at a tremendous pace. He apparently was looking across in our direction, but the distance was too great and the light too uncertain for us to make out very plainly what he was about. It seemed to me that he was gesticulating and making signs at us. His voice came across the water to us shouting something furiously, but the wind drowned it so that no single word was audible. There was something curious about the whole appearance—man, boat, signs, voice—that made an impression on me out of all proportion to its cause.

"He's crossing himself!" I cried. "Look, he's making the sign of the Cross!"

"I believe you're right," the Swede said, shading his eyes with his hand and watching the man out of sight. He seemed to be gone in a moment, melting away down there into the sea of willows where the sun caught them in the bend of the river and turned them into a great crimson wall of beauty. Mist, too, had begun to ruse, so that the air was hazy.

"But what in the world is he doing at nightfall on this flooded river?" I said, half to myself. "Where is he going at such a time, and what did he mean by his signs and shouting? D'you think he wished to warn us about something?"

"He saw our smoke, and thought we were spirits probably," laughed my companion. "These Hungarians believe in all sorts of rubbish; you remember the shopwoman at Pressburg warning us that no one ever landed here because it belonged to some sort of beings outside man's world! I suppose they believe in fairies and elementals, possibly demons, too. That peasant in the boat saw people on the islands for the first time in his life," he added, after a slight pause, "and it scared him, that's all."

The Swede's tone of voice was not convincing, and his manner lacked something that was usually there. I noted the change instantly while he talked, though without being able to label it precisely.

"If they had enough imagination," I laughed loudly—I remember trying to make as much *noise* as I could—"they might well people a place like this with the old gods of antiquity. The Romans must have haunted all this region more or less with their shrines and sacred groves and elemental deities."

The subject dropped and we returned to our stew-pot, for my friend was not given to imaginative conversation as a rule. Moreover, just then I remember feeling distinctly glad that he was not imaginative; his stolid, practical nature suddenly seemed to me welcome and comforting. It was an admirable temperament, I felt; he could steer down rapids like a red Indian, shoot dangerous bridges and whirlpools better than any white man I ever saw in a canoe. He was a grand fellow for an adventurous trip, a tower of strength when untoward things happened. I looked at his strong face and light curly hair as he staggered along under his pile of driftwood (twice the size of mine!), and I experienced a feeling of relief. Yes, I was distinctly glad just then that the Swede was—what he was, and that he never made remarks that suggested more than they said.

"The river's still rising, though," he added, as if following out some thoughts of his own, and dropping his load with a gasp. "This island will be under water in two days if it goes on."

"I wish the *wind* would go down," I said. "I don't care a fig for the river."

The flood, indeed, had no terrors for us; we could get off at ten minutes' notice, and the more water the better—we liked it. It meant an increasing current and the obliteration of the treacherous shingle-beds that so often threatened to tear the bottom out of our canoe.

Contrary to our expectations, the wind did not go down with the sun. It seemed to increase with the darkness, howling overhead and shaking the willows round us like straws. Curious sounds accompanied it sometimes, like the explosion of heavy guns, and it fell upon the water and the island in great flat blows of immense power. It made me think of the sounds a planet must make, could we only hear it, driving along through space.

But the sky kept wholly clear of clouds, and soon after supper the full moon rose up in the east and covered the river and the plain of shouting willows with a light like the day.

We lay on the sandy patch beside the fire, smoking, listening to the noises of the night round us, and talking happily of the journey we had already made, and of our plans ahead. The map lay spread in the door of the tent, but the high wind made it hard to study, and presently we lowered the curtain and extinguished the lantern. The firelight was enough to smoke and see each other's faces by, and the sparks flew about overhead like fireworks. A few yards beyond, the river gurgled and hissed, and from time to time a heavy splash announced the falling away of further portions of the bank.

Our talk, I noticed, had to do with the faraway scenes and incidents of our first camps in the Black Forest, or of other subjects altogether remote from the present setting, for neither of us spoke of the actual moment more than was necessary—almost as though we had agreed tacitly to avoid discussion of the camp and its incidents. Neither the otter nor the boatman, for instance, received the honor of a single mention, though ordinarily these would have furnished discussion for the greater part of the evening. They were, of course, distinct events in such a place.

The scarcity of wood made it a business to keep the fire going, for the wind, that drove the smoke in our faces wherever we sat, helped at the same time to make a forced draught. We took it in turn to make some foraging expeditions into the darkness, and the quantity the Swede brought back always made me feel that he took an absurdly long time finding it; for the fact was I did not care much about being left alone, and yet it always seemed to be my turn to grub about among the bushes or scramble along the slippery banks in the moonlight. The long day's battle with wind and water—such wind and such water!—had tired us both, and an early bed was the obvious program. Yet neither of us made the move for the tent. We lay there, tending the fire, talking in desultory fashion, peering about us into the dense willow bushes, and listening to the thunder of wind and river. The loneliness of the place had entered our very bones, and silence seemed natural, for after a bit the sound of our voices became a trifle unreal and forced; whispering would have been the fitting mode of communication, I felt, and the human voice, always rather absurd amid the roar of the elements, now carried with it something almost illegitimate. It was like talking out loud in church, or in some place where it was not lawful, perhaps not quite *safe*, to be overheard.

The eeriness of this lonely island, set among a million willows, swept by a hurricane, and surrounded by hurrying deep waters, touched us both, I fancy. Untrodden by man, almost unknown to man, it lay there beneath the moon, remote from human influence, on the frontier of another world, an alien world, a world tenanted by willows only and the souls of willows. And we, in our rashness, had dared to invade it, even to make use of it! Something more than the power of its mystery stirred in me as I lay on the sand, feet to fire, and peered up through the leaves at the stars. For the last time I rose to get firewood.

"When this has burnt up," I said firmly, "I shall turn in," and my companion watched me lazily as I moved off into the surrounding shadows.

For an unimaginative man I thought he seemed unusually receptive that night, unusually open to suggestion of things other than sensory. He too was touched by the beauty and loneliness of the place. I was not altogether pleased, I remember, to recognize this slight change in him, and instead of immediately collecting sticks, I made my way to the far point of the island where the moonlight on plain and river could be seen to better advantage. The desire to be alone had come suddenly upon me; my former dread returned in force; there was a vague feeling in me I wished to face and probe to the bottom.

When I reached the point of sand jutting out among the waves, the spell of the place descended upon me with a positive shock. No mere "scenery" could have produced such an effect. There was something more here, something to alarm.

I gazed across the waste of wild waters; I watched the whispering willows; I heard the ceaseless beating of the tireless wind; and, one and all, each in its own way, stirred in me this sensation of a strange distress. But the *willows* especially; forever they went on chattering and talking among themselves, laughing a little, shrilly crying out, sometimes sighing—but what it was they made so much to-do about belonged to the secret life of the great plain they inhabited. And it was utterly alien to the world I knew, or to that of the wild yet kindly elements. They made me think of a host of beings from another plane of life, another evolution altogether, perhaps, all discussing a mystery known only to themselves. I watched them moving busily together, oddly shaking their big bushy heads, twirling their myriad leaves even when there was no wind. They moved of their own will as though alive, and they touched, by some incalculable method, my own keen sense of the *horrible*.

There they stood in the moonlight, like a vast army surrounding our camp, shaking their innumerable silver spears defiantly, formed all ready for an attack.

The psychology of places, for some imaginations at least, is very vivid; for the wanderer, especially, camps have their "note" either of welcome or rejection. At first it may not always be apparent, because the busy preparations of tent and cooking prevent, but with the first pause— after supper usually—it comes and announces itself. And the note of this willow-camp now became unmistakably plain to me; we were interlopers, trespassers; we were not welcomed. The sense of unfamiliarity grew upon me as I stood there watching. We touched the frontier of a region where our presence was resented. For a night's lodging we might perhaps be tolerated; but for a prolonged and inquisitive stay—No! by all the gods of the trees and wilderness, no! We were the first human influences upon this island, and we were not wanted. *The willows were against us.*

Strange thoughts like these, bizarre fancies, borne I know not whence, found lodgment in my mind as I stood listening. What, I thought, if, after all, these crouching willows proved to be alive; if suddenly they should rise up, like a swarm of living creatures, marshaled by the gods whose territory we had invaded, sweep towards us off the vast swamps, booming overhead in the night—and then *settle down!* As I looked it was so easy to imagine they actually moved, crept nearer, retreated a little, huddled together in masses, hostile, waiting for the great wind that should finally start them a-running. I could have sworn their aspect changed a little, and their ranks deepened and pressed more closely together.

The melancholy shrill cry of a night-bird sounded overhead, and suddenly I nearly lost my balance as the piece of bank I stood upon fell with a great splash into the river, undermined by the flood. I stepped back just in time, and went on hunting for firewood again, half laughing at the odd fancies that crowded so thickly into my mind and cast their spell upon me. I recalled the Swede's remark about moving on next day, and I was just thinking that I fully agreed with him, when I turned with a start and saw the subject of my thoughts standing immediately in front of me. He was quite close. The roar of the elements had covered his approach.

"You've been gone so long," he shouted above the wind, "I thought something must have happened to you."

But there was that in his tone, and a certain look in his face as well, that conveyed to me more than his usual words, and in a flash I understood the real reason for his coming. It was because the spell of the place had entered his soul too, and he did not like being alone.

"River still rising," he cried, pointing to the flood in the moonlight, "and the wind's simply awful."

He always said the same things, but it was the cry for companionship that gave the real importance to his words.

"Lucky," I cried back, "our tent's in the hollow. I think it'll hold all right." I added something about the difficulty of finding wood, in order to explain my absence, but the wind caught my words and flung them across the river, so that he did not hear, but just looked at me through the branches, nodding his head.

"Lucky if we get away without disaster!" he shouted, or words to that effect; and I remember feeling half angry with him for putting the thought into words, for it was exactly what I felt myself. There was disaster impending somewhere, and the sense of presentiment lay unpleasantly upon me.

We went back to the fire and made a final blaze, poking it up with our feet. We took a last look round. But for the wind the heat would have been unpleasant. I put this thought into words, and I remember my friend's reply struck me oddly: that he would rather have the heat, the ordinary July weather, than this "diabolical wind."

Everything was snug for the night; the canoe lying turned over beside the tent, with both yellow paddles beneath her; the provision sack hanging from a willow-stem, and the washed-up dishes removed to a safe distance from the fire, all ready for the morning meal.

We smothered the embers of the fire with sand, and then turned in. The flap of the tent door was up, and I saw the branches and the stars and the white moonlight. The shaking willows and the heavy buffetings of the wind against our taut little house were the last things I remembered as sleep came down and covered all with its soft and delicious forgetfulness.

II.

SUDDENLY I found myself lying awake, peering from my sandy mattress through the door of the tent. I looked at my watch pinned against the canvas, and saw by the bright moonlight that it was past twelve o'clock—the threshold of a new day—and I had therefore slept a couple of hours. The Swede was asleep still beside me; the wind howled as before; something plucked at my heart and made me feel afraid. There was a sense of disturbance in my immediate neighborhood.

I sat up quickly and looked out. The trees were swaying violently to and fro as the gusts smote them, but our little bit of green canvas lay snugly safe in the hollow, for the wind passed over it without meeting enough resistance to make it vicious. The feeling of disquietude did not pass, however, and I crawled quietly out of the tent to see if our belongings were safe. I moved carefully so as not to waken my companion. A curious excitement was on me.

I was halfway out, kneeling on all fours, when my eye first took in that the tops of the bushes opposite, with their moving tracery of leaves, made shapes against the sky. I sat back on my haunches and stared. It was incredible, surely, but there, opposite and slightly above me, were shapes of some indeterminate sort among the willows, and as the branches swayed in the wind they seemed to group themselves about these shapes, forming a series of monstrous outlines that shifted rapidly beneath the moon. Close, about fifty feet in front of me, I saw these things.

My first instinct was to waken my companion, that he too might see them, but something made me hesitate—the sudden realization, probably, that I should not welcome corroboration; and meanwhile I crouched there staring in amazement with smarting eyes. I was wide awake. I remember saying to myself that I was *not* dreaming.

They first became properly visible, these huge figures, just within the tops of the bushes—immense, bronze-colored, moving, and wholly independent of the swaying of the branches. I saw them plainly and noted, now I came to examine them more calmly, that they were very much larger than human, and indeed that something in their appearance proclaimed them to be *not human* at all. Certainly they were not merely the moving tracery of the branches against the moonlight. They shifted independently. They rose upwards in a continuous stream from earth to sky, vanishing utterly as soon as they reached the dark of the sky. They were interlaced one with another, making a great column, and I saw their limbs and huge bodies melting in and out of each other, forming this serpentine line that bent and swayed and twisted spirally with the contortions of the wind-tossed trees. They were nude, fluid shapes, passing up the bushes, *within* the leaves almost—rising up in a living column into the heavens. Their faces I never could see. Unceasingly they poured upwards, swaying in great bending curves, with a hue of dull bronze upon their skins.

I stared, trying to force every atom of vision from my eyes. For a long time I thought they *must* every moment disappear and resolve themselves into the movements of the branches and prove to be an optical illusion. I searched everywhere for a proof of reality, when all the while I understood quite well that the standard of reality had changed. For the longer I looked the more certain I became that these figures were real and living, though perhaps not according to the standards that the camera and the biologist would insist upon.

Far from feeling fear, I was possessed with a sense of awe and wonder such as I have never known. I seemed to be gazing at the personified elemental forces of this haunted and primeval region. Our intrusion had stirred the powers of the place into activity. It was we who were the cause of the disturbance, and my brain filled to bursting with stories and legends of the spirits and deities of places that have been acknowledged and worshipped by men in all ages of the world's history. But, before I could arrive at any possible explanation, something impelled me to go farther out, and I crept forward on the sand and stood upright. I felt the ground still warm under my bare feet; the wind tore at my hair and face; and the sound of the river burst upon my ears with a sudden roar. These things, I knew, were real, and proved that my senses were acting normally. Yet the figures still rose from earth to heaven, silent, majestically, in a great spiral of grace and strength that over-whelmed me at length with a genuine deep emotion of worship. I felt that I must fall down and worship—absolutely worship.

Perhaps in another minute I might have done so, when a gust of wind swept against me with such force that it blew me sideways, and I nearly stumbled and fell. It seemed to shake the dream violently out of me. At least it gave me another point of view somehow. The figures still remained, still ascended into heaven from the heart of the night, but my reason at last began to assert itself. It must be a subjective experience, I argued—none the less real for that, but still subjective. The moonlight and the branches combined to work out these pictures upon the mirror of my imagination, and for some reason I projected them outwards and made them appear objective. I knew this must be the case, of course. I took courage, and began to move forward across the open patches of sand. By Jove, though, was it all hallucination? Was it merely subjective? Did not my reason argue in the old futile way from the little standard of the known?

I only know that great column of figures ascended darkly into the sky for what seemed a very long period of time, and with a very complete measure of reality as most men are accustomed to gauge reality. Then suddenly they were gone!

And, once they were gone and the immediate wonder of their great presence had passed, fear came down upon me with a cold rush. The esoteric meaning of this lonely and haunted region suddenly flamed up within me, and I began to tremble dreadfully. I took a quick look round— a look of horror that came near to panic—calculating vainly ways of escape; and then, realizing how helpless I was to achieve anything really effective, I crept back silently into the tent and lay down again upon my sandy mattress, first lowering the door-curtain to shut out the sight of the willows in the moonlight, and then burying my head as deeply as possible beneath the blankets to deaden the sound of the terrifying wind.

III.

AS though further to convince me that I had not been dreaming, I remember that it was a long time before I fell again into a troubled and restless sleep; and even then only the upper crust of me slept, and underneath there was something that never quite lost consciousness, but lay alert and on the watch.

But this second time I jumped up with a genuine start of terror. It was neither the wind nor the river that woke me, but the slow approach of something that caused the sleeping portion of me to grow smaller and smaller till at last it vanished altogether, and I found myself sitting bolt upright—listening.

Outside there was a sound of multitudinous little patterings. They had been coming, I was aware, for a long time, and in my sleep they had first become audible. I sat there nervously wide awake as though I had not slept at all. It seemed to me that my breathing came with difficulty, and that there was a great weight upon the surface of my body. In spite of the hot night, I felt clammy with cold and shivered. Something surely was pressing steadily against the sides of the tent and weighing down upon it from above. Was it the body of the wind? Was this the pattering rain, the dripping of the leaves? The spray blown from the river by the wind and gathering in big drops? I thought quickly of a dozen things.

Then suddenly the explanation leaped into my mind: a bough from the poplar, the only large tree on the island, had fallen with the wind. Still half caught by the other branches, it would fall with the next gust and crush us, and meanwhile its leaves brushed and tapped upon the tight canvas surface of the tent. I raised a loose flap and rushed out, calling to the Swede to follow.

But when I got out and stood upright I saw that the tent was free. There was no hanging bough; there was no rain or spray; nothing approached.

A cold, grey light filtered down through the bushes and lay on the faintly gleaming sand. Stars still crowded the sky directly overhead, and the wind howled magnificently, but the fire no longer gave out any glow, and I saw the east reddening in streaks through the trees. Several hours must have passed since I stood there before watching the ascending figures, and the memory of it now came back to me horribly, like an evil dream. Oh, how tired it made me feel, that ceaseless raging wind! Yet, though the deep lassitude of a sleepless night was on me, my nerves were tingling with the activity of an equally tireless apprehension, and all idea of repose was out of the question. The river I saw had risen further. Its thunder filled the air, and a fine spray made itself felt through my thin sleeping shirt.

Yet nowhere did I discover the slightest evidence of anything to cause alarm. This deep, prolonged disturbance in my heart remained wholly unaccounted for.

My companion had not stirred when I called him, and there was no need to waken him now. I looked about me carefully, noting everything; the turned-over canoe; the yellow paddles—two of them, I'm certain; the provision sack and the extra lantern hanging together from the tree; and, crowding everywhere about me, enveloping all, the willows, those endless, shaking willows. A bird uttered its morning cry, and a string of duck passed with whirring flight overhead in the twilight. The sand whirled, dry and stinging, about my bare feet in the wind.

I walked round the tent and then went out a little way into the bush, so that I could see across the river to the farther landscape, and the same profound yet indefinable emotion of distress seized upon me again as I saw the interminable sea of bushes stretching to the horizon, looking ghostly and unreal in the wan light of dawn. I walked softly here and there, still puzzling over that odd sound of infinite pattering, and of that pressure upon the tent that had wakened me. It *must* have been the wind, I reflected—the wind bearing upon the loose, hot sand, driving the dry particles smartly against the taut canvas—the wind dropping heavily upon our fragile roof.

Yet all the time my nervousness and malaise increased appreciably.

I crossed over to the farther shore and noted how the coast-line had altered in the night, and what masses of sand the river had torn away. I dipped my hands and feet into the cool current, and bathed my forehead. Already there was a glow of sunrise in the sky and the exquisite freshness of coming day. On my way back I passed purposely beneath the very bushes where I had seen the column of figures rising into the air, and midway among the clumps I suddenly found myself overtaken by a sense of vast terror. From the shadows a large figure went swiftly by. Someone passed me, as sure as ever man did . . .

It was a great staggering blow from the wind that helped me forward again, and once out in the more open space, the sense of terror diminished strangely. The winds were about and walking, I remember saying to myself, for the winds often move like great presences under the trees. And altogether the fear that hovered about me was such an unknown and immense kind of fear, so unlike anything I had ever felt before, that it woke a sense of awe and wonder in me that did much to counteract its worst effects; and when I reached a high point in the middle of the island from which I could see the wide stretch of river, crimson in the sunrise, the whole magical beauty of it all was so overpowering that a sort of wild yearning woke in me and almost brought a cry up into the throat.

But this cry found no expression, for as my eyes wandered from the plain beyond to the island round me and noted our little tent half hidden among the willows, a dreadful discovery leaped out at me, compared to which my terror of the walking winds seemed as nothing at all.

For a change, I thought, had somehow come about in the arrangement of the landscape. It was not that my point of vantage gave me a different view, but that an alteration had apparently been effected in the relation of the tent to the willows, and of the willows to the tent. Surely the bushes now crowded much closer—unnecessarily, unpleasantly close. *They had moved nearer.*

Creeping with silent feet over the shifting sands, drawing imperceptibly nearer by soft, unhurried movements, the willows had come closer during the night. But had the wind moved them, or had they moved of themselves? I recalled the sound of infinite small patterings and the pressure upon the tent and upon my own heart that caused me to wake in terror. I swayed for a moment in the wind like a tree, finding it hard to keep my upright position on the sandy hillock. There was a suggestion here of personal agency, of deliberate intention, of aggressive hostility, and it terrified me into a sort of rigidity.

Then the reaction followed quickly. The idea was so bizarre, so absurd, that I felt inclined to laugh. But the laughter came no more readily than the cry, for the knowledge that my mind was so receptive to such dangerous imaginings brought the additional terror that it was through our minds and not through our physical bodies that the attack would come, and was coming.

The wind buffeted me about, and, very quickly it seemed, the sun came up over the horizon, for it was after four o'clock, and I must have stood on that little pinnacle of sand longer than I knew, afraid to come down to close quarters with the willows. I returned quietly, creepily, to the tent, first taking another exhaustive look round and—yes, I confess it—making a few measurements. I paced out on the warm sand the distances between the willows and the tent, making a note of the shortest distance particularly.

I crawled stealthily into my blankets. My companion, to all appearances, still slept soundly, and I was glad that this was so. Provided my experiences were not corroborated, I could find strength somehow to deny them, perhaps. With the daylight I could persuade myself that it was all a subjective hallucination, a fantasy of the night, a projection of the excited imagination.

Nothing further came in to disturb me, and I fell asleep almost at once, utterly exhausted, yet still in dread of hearing again that weird sound of multitudinous pattering, or of feeling the pressure upon my heart that had made it difficult to breathe.

IV.

THE SUN was high in the heavens when my companion woke me from a heavy sleep and announced that the porridge was cooked and there was just time to bathe. The grateful smell of frizzling bacon entered the tent door.

"River still rising," he said, "and several islands out in mid-stream have disappeared altogether. Our own island's much smaller."

"Any wood left?" I asked sleepily.

"The wood and the island will finish tomorrow in a dead heat," he laughed, "but there's enough to last us till then."

I plunged in from the point of the island, which had indeed altered a lot in size and shape during the night, and was swept down in a moment to the landing-place opposite the tent. The water was icy, and the banks flew by like the country from an express train. Bathing under such conditions was an exhilarating operation, and the terror of the night seemed cleansed out of me by a process of evaporation in the brain. The sun was blazing hot; not a cloud showed itself anywhere; the wind, however, had not abated one little jot.

Quite suddenly then the implied meaning of the Swede's words flashed across me, showing that he no longer wished to leave post-haste, and had changed his mind. "Enough to last till tomorrow"—he assumed we should stay on the island another night. It struck me as odd. The night before he was so positive the other way. How had the change come about?

Great crumblings of the banks occurred at breakfast, with heavy splashings and clouds of spray which the wind brought into our frying-pan, and my fellow-traveler talked incessantly about the difficulty the Vienna-Pesth steamers must have to find the channel in flood. But the state of his mind interested and impressed me far more than the state of the river or the difficulties of the steamers. He had changed somehow since the evening before. His manner was different—a trifle excited, a trifle shy, with a sort of suspicion about his voice and gestures. I hardly know how to describe it now in cold blood, but at the time I remember being quite certain of one thing—that he had become frightened?

He ate very little breakfast, and for once omitted to smoke his pipe. He had the map spread open beside him, and kept studying its markings.

"We'd better get off sharp in an hour," I said presently, feeling for an opening that must bring him indirectly to a partial confession at any rate. And his answer puzzled me uncomfortably: "Rather! If they'll let us."

"Who'll let us? The elements?" I asked quickly, with affected indifference.

"The powers of this awful place, whoever they are," he replied, keeping his eyes on the map. "The gods are here, if they are anywhere at all in the world."

"The elements are always the true immortals," I replied, laughing as naturally as I could manage, yet knowing quite well that my face reflected my true feelings when he looked up gravely at me and spoke across the smoke:

"We shall be fortunate if we get away without further disaster."

This was exactly what I had dreaded, and I screwed myself up to the point of the direct question. It was like agreeing to allow the dentist to extract the tooth; it *had* to come anyhow in the long run, and the rest was all pretence.

"Further disaster! Why, what's happened?"

"For one thing—the steering paddle's gone," he said quietly.

"The steering paddle gone!" I repeated, greatly excited, for this was our rudder, and the Danube in flood without a rudder was suicide. "But what—"

"And there's a tear in the bottom of the canoe," he added, with a genuine little tremor in his voice.

I continued staring at him, able only to repeat the words in his face somewhat foolishly. There, in the heat of the sun, and on this burning sand, I was aware of a freezing atmosphere descending round us. I got up to follow him, for he merely nodded his head gravely and led the way towards the tent a few yards on the other side of the fireplace. The canoe still lay there as I had last seen her in the night, ribs uppermost, the paddles, or rather, *the* paddle, on the sand beside her.

"There's only one," he said, stooping to pick it up. "And here's the rent in the base-board."

It was on the tip of my tongue to tell him that I had clearly noticed *two* paddles a few hours before, but a second impulse made me think better of it, and I said nothing. I approached to see.

There was a long, finely made tear in the bottom of the canoe where a little slither of wood had been neatly taken clean out; it looked as if the tooth of a sharp rock or snag had eaten down her length, and investigation showed that the hole went through. Had we launched out in her without observing it we must inevitably have foundered. At first the water would have made the wood swell so as to close the hole, but once out in mid-stream the water must have poured in, and the canoe, never more than two inches above the surface, would have filled and sunk very rapidly.

"There, you see an attempt to prepare a victim for the sacrifice," I heard him saying, more to himself than to me, "two victims rather," he added as he bent over and ran his fingers along the slit.

I began to whistle—a thing I always do unconsciously when utterly nonplussed—and purposely paid no attention to his words. I was determined to consider them foolish.

"It wasn't there last night," he said presently, straightening up from his examination and looking anywhere but at me.

"We must have scratched her in landing, of course," I stopped whistling to say. "The stones are very sharp."

I stopped abruptly, for at that moment he turned round and met my eye squarely. I knew just as well as he did how impossible my explanation was. There were no stones, to begin with.

"And then there's this to explain too," he added quietly, handing me the paddle and pointing to the blade.

A new and curious emotion spread freezingly over me as I took and examined it. The blade was scraped down all over, beautifully scraped, as though someone had sand-papered it with care, making it so thin that the first vigorous stroke must have snapped it off at the elbow.

"One of us walked in his sleep and did this thing," I said feebly, "or—or it has been filed by the constant stream of sand particles blown against it by the wind, perhaps."

"Ah," said the Swede, turning away, laughing a little, "you can explain everything."

"The same wind that caught the steering paddle and flung it so near the bank that it fell in with the next lump that crumbled," I called out after him, absolutely determined to find an explanation for everything he showed me.

"I see," he shouted back, turning his head to look at me before disappearing among the willow bushes.

Once alone with these perplexing evidences of personal agency, I think my first thoughts took the form of "One of us must have done this thing, and it certainly was not I." But my second thought decided how impossible it was to suppose, under all the circumstances, that either of us had done it. That my companion, the trusted friend of a dozen similar expeditions, could have knowingly had a hand in it, was a suggestion not to be entertained for a moment. Equally absurd seemed the explanation that this imperturbable and densely practical nature had suddenly become insane and was busied with insane purposes.

Yet the fact remained that what disturbed me most, and kept my fear actively alive even in this blaze of sunshine and wild beauty, was the clear certainty that some curious alteration had come about in his *mind*—that he was nervous, timid, suspicious, aware of goings on he did not speak about, watching a series of secret and hitherto unmentionable events—waiting, in a word, for a climax that he expected, and, I thought, expected very soon. This grew up in my mind intuitively—I hardly knew how.

I made a hurried examination of the tent and its surroundings, but the measurements of the night remained the same. There were deep hollows formed in the sand I now noticed for the first time, basin-shaped and of various depths and sizes, varying from that of a tea-cup to a large bowl. The wind, no doubt, was responsible for these miniature craters, just as it was for lifting the paddle and tossing it towards the water. The rent in the canoe was the only thing that seemed quite inexplicable; and, after all, it *was* conceivable that a sharp point had caught it when we landed. The examination I made of the shore did not assist this theory, but all the same I clung to it with that diminishing portion of my intelligence which I called my "reason." An explanation of some kind was an absolute necessity, just as some working explanation of the universe is necessary—however absurd—to the happiness of every individual who seeks to do his duty in the world and face the problems of life. The simile seemed to me at the time an exact parallel.

I at once set the pitch melting, and presently the Swede joined me at the work, though under the best conditions in the world the canoe could not be safe for traveling till the following day. I drew his attention casually to the hollows in the sand.

"Yes," he said, "I know. They're all over the island. But *you* can explain them, no doubt!"

"Wind, of course," I answered without hesitation. "Have you never watched those little whirlwinds in the street that twist and twirl everything into a circle? This sand's loose enough to yield, that's all."

He made no reply, and we worked on in silence for a bit. I watched him surreptitiously all the time, and I had an idea he was watching me. He seemed, too, to be always listening attentively to something I could not hear, or perhaps for something that he expected to hear, for he kept turning about and staring into the bushes, and up into the sky, and out across the water where it was visible through the openings among the willows. Sometimes he even put his hand to his ear and held it there for several minutes. He said nothing to me, however, about it, and I asked no questions. And meanwhile, as he mended that torn canoe with the skill and address of a red Indian, I was glad to notice his absorption in the work, for there was a vague dread in my heart that he would speak of the changed aspect of the willows. And, if he had noticed *that*, my imagination could no longer be held a sufficient explanation of it.

At length, after a long pause, he began to talk.

"Queer thing," he added in a hurried sort of voice, as though he wanted to say something and get it over. "Queer thing. I mean, about that otter last night."

I had expected something so totally different that he caught me with surprise, and I looked up sharply.

"Shows how lonely this place is. Otters are awfully shy things—"

"I don't mean that, of course," he interrupted. "I mean—do you think—did you think it really was an otter?"

"What else, in the name of Heaven, what else?"

"You know, I saw it before you did, and at first it seemed—so *much* bigger than an otter."

"The sunset as you looked upstream magnified it, or something," I replied.

He looked at me absently a moment, as though his mind were busy with other thoughts.

"It had such extraordinary yellow eyes," he went on half to himself.

"That was the sun too," I laughed, a trifle boisterously. "I suppose you'll wonder next if that fellow in the boat—"

I suddenly decided not to finish the sentence. He was in the act again of listening, turning his head to the wind, and something in the expression of his face made me halt. The subject dropped, and we went on with our caulking. Apparently he had not noticed my unfinished sentence. Five minutes later, however, he looked at me across the canoe, the smoking pitch in his hand, his face exceedingly grave.

"I *did* rather wonder, if you want to know," he said slowly, "what that thing in the boat was. I remember thinking at the time it was not a man. The whole business seemed to rise quite suddenly out of the water."

I laughed again boisterously in his face, but this time there was impatience, and a strain of anger too, in my feeling.

"Look here now," I cried, "this place is quite queer enough without going out of our way to imagine things! That boat was an ordinary boat, and the man in it was an ordinary man, and they were both going downstream as fast as they could lick. And that otter *was* an otter, so don't let's play the fool about it!"

He looked steadily at me with the same grave expression. He was not in the least annoyed. I took courage from his silence.

"And, for Heaven's sake," I went on, "don't keep pretending you hear things, because it only gives me the jumps, and there's nothing to hear but the river and this cursed old thundering wind."

"You *fool!*" he answered in a low, shocked voice, "you utter fool. That's just the way all victims talk. As if you didn't understand just as well as I do!" he sneered with scorn in his voice, and a sort of resignation. "The best thing you can do is to keep quiet and try to hold your mind as firm as possible. This feeble attempt at self-deception only makes the truth harder when you're forced to meet it."

My little effort was over, and I found nothing more to say, for I knew quite well his words were true, and that *I* was the fool, not *he*. Up to a certain stage in the adventure he kept ahead of me easily, and I think I felt annoyed to be out of it, to be thus proved less psychic, less sensitive than himself to these extraordinary happenings, and half ignorant all the time of what was going on under my very nose. *He knew* from the very beginning, apparently. But at the moment I wholly missed the point of his words about the necessity of there being a victim, and that we ourselves were destined to satisfy the want. I dropped all pretense thenceforward, but thenceforward likewise my fear increased steadily to the climax.

"But you're quite right about one thing," he added, before the subject passed, "and that is that we're wiser not to talk about it, or even to think about it, because what one *thinks* finds expression in words, and what one *says*, happens."

That afternoon, while the canoe dried and hardened, we spent trying to fish, testing the leak, collecting wood, and watching the enormous flood of rising water. Masses of driftwood swept near our shores sometimes, and we fished for them with long willow branches. The island grew perceptibly smaller as the banks were torn away with great gulps and splashes. The weather kept brilliantly fine till about four o'clock, and then for the first time for three days the wind showed signs of abating. Clouds began to gather in the south-west, spreading thence slowly over the sky.

This lessening of the wind came as a great relief, for the incessant roaring, banging, and thundering had irritated our nerves. Yet the silence that came about five o'clock with its sudden cessation was in a manner quite as oppressive. The booming of the river had everything in its own way then; it filled the air with deep murmurs, more musical than the wind noises, but infinitely more monotonous. The wind held many notes, rising, falling always beating out some sort of great elemental tune; whereas the river's song lay between three notes at most—dull pedal notes, that held a lugubrious quality foreign to the wind, and somehow seemed to me, in my then nervous state, to sound wonderfully well the music of doom.

It was extraordinary, too, how the withdrawal suddenly of bright sunlight took everything out of the landscape that made for cheerfulness; and since this particular landscape had already managed to convey the suggestion of something sinister, the change of course was all the more unwelcome and noticeable. For me, I know, the darkening outlook became distinctly more alarming, and I found myself more than once calculating how soon after sunset the full moon would get up in the east, and whether the gathering clouds would greatly interfere with her lighting of the little island.

With this general hush of the wind—though it still indulged in occasional brief gusts—the river seemed to me to grow blacker, the willows to stand more densely together. The latter, too, kept up a sort of independent movement of their own, rustling among themselves when no wind stirred, and shaking oddly from the roots upwards. When common objects in this way become charged with the suggestion of horror, they stimulate the imagination far more than things of unusual appearance; and these bushes, crowding huddled about us, assumed for me in the darkness a bizarre *grotesquerie* of appearance that lent to them somehow the aspect of purposeful and living creatures. Their very ordinariness, I felt, masked what was malignant and hostile to us. The forces of the region drew nearer with the coming of night. They were focusing upon our island, and more particularly upon ourselves. For thus, somehow, in the terms of the imagination, did my really indescribable sensations in this extraordinary place present themselves.

I had slept a good deal in the early afternoon, and had thus recovered somewhat from the exhaustion of a disturbed night, but this only served apparently to render me more susceptible than before to the obsessing spell of the haunting. I fought against it, laughing at my feelings as absurd and childish, with very obvious physiological explanations, yet, in spite of every effort, they gained in strength upon me so that I dreaded the night as a child lost in a forest must dread the approach of darkness.

The canoe we had carefully covered with a waterproof sheet during the day, and the one remaining paddle had been securely tied by the Swede to the base of a tree, lest the wind should rob us of that too. From five o'clock onwards I busied myself with the stew-pot and preparations for dinner, it being my turn to cook that night. We had potatoes, onions, bits of bacon fat to add flavor, and a general thick residue from former stews at the bottom of the pot; with black bread broken up into it the result was most excellent, and it was followed by a stew of plums with sugar and a brew of strong tea with dried milk. A good pile of wood lay close at hand, and the absence of wind made my duties easy. My companion sat lazily watching me, dividing his attentions between cleaning his pipe and giving useless advice—an admitted privilege of the off-duty man. He had been very quiet all the afternoon, engaged in re-caulking the canoe, strengthening the tent ropes, and fishing for driftwood while I slept. No more talk about undesirable things had passed between us, and I think his only remarks had to do with the gradual destruction of the island, which he declared was not fully a third smaller than when we first landed.

The pot had just begun to bubble when I heard his voice calling to me from the bank, where he had wandered away without my noticing. I ran up.

"Come and listen," he said, "and see what you make of it." He held his hand cupwise to his ear, as so often before.

"*Now* do you hear anything?" he asked, watching me curiously.

We stood there, listening attentively together. At first I heard only the deep note of the water and the hissings rising from its turbulent surface. The willows, for once, were motionless and silent. Then a sound began to reach my ears faintly, a peculiar sound—something like the humming of a distant gong. It seemed to come across to us in the darkness from the waste of swamps and willows opposite. It was repeated at regular intervals, but it was certainly neither the sound of a bell nor the hooting of a distant steamer. I can liken it to nothing so much as to the sound of an immense gong, suspended far up in the sky, repeating incessantly its muffled metallic note, soft and musical, as it was repeatedly struck. My heart quickened as I listened.

"I've heard it all day," said my companion. "While you slept this afternoon it came all round the island. I hunted it down, but could never get near enough to see—to localize it correctly. Sometimes it was overhead, and sometimes it seemed under the water. Once or twice, too, I could have sworn it was not outside at all, but *within myself*—you know—the way a sound in the fourth dimension is supposed to come."

I was too much puzzled to pay much attention to his words. I listened carefully, striving to associate it with any known familiar sound I could think of, but without success. It changed in the direction, too, coming nearer, and then sinking utterly away into remote distance. I cannot say that it was ominous in quality, because to me it seemed distinctly musical, yet I must admit it set going a distressing feeling that made me wish I had never heard it.

"The wind blowing in those sand-funnels," I said determined to find an explanation, "or the bushes rubbing together after the storm perhaps."

"It comes off the whole swamp," my friend answered. "It comes from everywhere at once." He ignored my explanations. "It comes from the willow bushes somehow—"

"But now the wind has dropped," I objected. "The willows can hardly make a noise by themselves, can they?"

His answer frightened me, first because I had dreaded it, and secondly, because I knew intuitively it was true.

"It is *because* the wind has dropped we now hear it. It was drowned before. It is the cry, I believe, of the—"

I dashed back to my fire, warned by the sound of bubbling that the stew was in danger, but determined at the same time to escape further conversation. I was resolute, if possible, to avoid the exchanging of views. I dreaded, too, that he would begin about the gods, or the elemental forces, or something else disquieting, and I wanted to keep myself well in hand for what might happen later. There was another night to be faced before we escaped from this distressing place, and there was no knowing yet what it might bring forth.

"Come and cut up bread for the pot," I called to him, vigorously stirring the appetizing mixture. That stew-pot held sanity for us both, and the thought made me laugh.

He came over slowly and took the provision sack from the tree, fumbling in its mysterious depths, and then emptying the entire contents upon the ground-sheet at his feet.

"Hurry up!" I cried; "it's boiling."

The Swede burst out into a roar of laughter that startled me. It was forced laughter, not artificial exactly, but mirthless.

"There's nothing here!" he shouted, holding his sides.

"Bread, I mean."

"It's gone. There is no bread. They've taken it!"

I dropped the long spoon and ran up. Everything the sack had contained lay upon the ground-sheet, but there was no loaf.

The whole dead weight of my growing fear fell upon me and shook me. Then I burst out laughing too. It was the only thing to do: and the sound of my laughter also made me understand his. The stain of psychical pressure caused it—this explosion of unnatural laughter in both of us; it was an effort of repressed forces to seek relief; it was a temporary safety-valve. And with both of us it ceased quite suddenly.

"How criminally stupid of me!" I cried, still determined to be consistent and find an explanation. "I clean forgot to buy a loaf at Pressburg. That chattering woman put everything out of my head, and I must have left it lying on the counter or—"

"The oatmeal, too, is much less than it was this morning," the Swede interrupted.

Why in the world need he draw attention to it? I thought angrily.

"There's enough for tomorrow," I said, stirring vigorously, "and we can get lots more at Komorn or Gran. In twenty-four hours we shall be miles from here."

"I hope so—to God," he muttered, putting the things back into the sack, "unless we're claimed first as victims for the sacrifice," he added with a foolish laugh. He dragged the sack into the tent, for safety's sake, I suppose, and I heard him mumbling to himself, but so indistinctly that it seemed quite natural for me to ignore his words.

Our meal was beyond question a gloomy one, and we ate it almost in silence, avoiding one another's eyes, and keeping the fire bright. Then we washed up and prepared for the night, and, once smoking, our minds unoccupied with any definite duties, the apprehension I had felt all day long became more and more acute. It was not then active fear, I think, but the very vagueness of its origin distressed me far more that if I had been able to ticket and face it squarely. The curious sound I have likened to the note of a gong became now almost incessant, and filled the stillness of the night with a faint, continuous ringing rather than a series of distinct notes. At one time it was behind and at another time in front of us. Sometimes I fancied it came from the bushes on our left, and then again from the clumps on our right. More often it hovered directly overhead like the whirring of wings. It was really everywhere at once, behind, in front, at our sides and over our heads, completely surrounding us. The sound really defies description. But nothing within my knowledge is like that ceaseless muffled humming rising off the deserted world of swamps and willows.

We sat smoking in comparative silence, the strain growing every minute greater. The worst feature of the situation seemed to me that we did not know what to expect, and could therefore make no sort of preparation by way of defense. We could anticipate nothing. My explanations made in the sunshine, moreover, now came to haunt me with their foolish and wholly unsatisfactory nature, and it was more and more clear to us that some kind of plain talk with my companion was inevitable, whether I liked it or not. After all, we had to spend the night together, and to sleep in the same tent side by side. I saw that I could not get along much longer without the support of his mind, and for that, of course, plain talk was imperative. As long as possible, however, I postponed this little climax, and tried to ignore or laugh at the occasional sentences he flung into the emptiness.

Some of these sentences, moreover, were confoundedly disquieting to me, coming as they did to corroborate much that I felt myself; corroboration, too—which made it so much more convincing—from a totally different point of view. He composed such curious sentences, and hurled them at me in such an inconsequential sort of way, as though his main line of thought was secret to himself, and these fragments were mere bits he found it impossible to digest. He got rid of them by uttering them. Speech relieved him. It was like being sick.

"There are things about us, I'm sure, that make for disorder, disintegration, destruction, our destruction," he said once, while the fire blazed between us. "We've strayed out of a safe line somewhere."

And, another time, when the gong sounds had come nearer, ringing much louder than before, and directly over our heads, he said as though talking to himself:

"I don't think a gramophone would show any record of that. The sound doesn't come to me by the ears at all. The vibrations reach me in another manner altogether, and seem to be within me, which is precisely how a fourth dimensional sound might be supposed to make itself heard."

I purposely made no reply to this, but I sat up a little closer to the fire and peered about me into the darkness. The clouds were massed all over the sky, and no trace of moonlight came through. Very still, too, everything was, so that the river and the frogs had things all their own way.

"It has that about it," he went on, "which is utterly out of common experience. It is *unknown*. Only one thing describes it really; it is a non-human sound; I mean a sound outside humanity."

Having rid himself of this indigestible morsel, he lay quiet for a time, but he had so admirably expressed my own feeling that it was a relief to have the thought out, and to have confined it by the limitation of words from dangerous wandering to and fro in the mind.

The solitude of that Danube camping-place, can I ever forget it? The feeling of being utterly alone on an empty planet! My thoughts ran incessantly upon cities and the haunts of men. I would have given my soul, as the saying is, for the "feel" of those Bavarian villages we had passed through by the score; for the normal, human commonplaces; peasants drinking beer, tables beneath the trees, hot sunshine, and a ruined castle on the rocks behind the red-roofed church. Even the tourists would have been welcome.

Yet what I felt of dread was no ordinary ghostly fear. It was infinitely greater, stranger, and seemed to arise from some dim ancestral sense of terror more profoundly disturbing than anything I had known or dreamed of. We had "strayed," as the Swede put it, into some region or some set of conditions where the risks were great, yet unintelligible to us; where the frontiers of some unknown world lay close about us. It was a spot held by the dwellers in some outer space, a sort of peep-hole whence they could spy upon the earth, themselves unseen, a point where the veil between had worn a little thin. As the final result of too long a sojourn here, we should be carried over the border and deprived of what we called "our lives," yet by mental, not physical, processes. In that sense, as he said, we should be the victims of our adventure—a sacrifice.

It took us in different fashion, each according to the measure of his sensitiveness and powers of resistance. I translated it vaguely into a personification of the mightily disturbed elements, investing them with the horror of a deliberate and malefic purpose, resentful of our audacious intrusion into their breeding-place; whereas my friend threw it into the unoriginal form at first of a trespass on some ancient shrine, some place where the old gods still held sway, where the emotional forces of former worshippers still clung, and the ancestral portion of him yielded to the old pagan spell.

At any rate, here was a place unpolluted by men, kept clean by the winds from coarsening human influences, a place where spiritual agencies were within reach and aggressive. Never, before or since, have I been so attacked by indescribable suggestions of a "beyond region," of another scheme of life, another revolution not parallel to the human. And in the end our minds would succumb under the weight of the awful spell, and we should be drawn across the frontier into *their* world.

Small things testified to the amazing influence of the place, and now in the silence round the fire they allowed themselves to be noted by the mind. The very atmosphere had proved itself a magnifying medium to distort every indication: the otter rolling in the current, the hurrying boatman making signs, the shifting willows, one and all had been robbed of its natural character, and revealed in something of its other aspect—as it existed across the border to that other region. And this changed aspect I felt was now not merely to me, but to the race. The whole experience whose verge we touched was unknown to humanity at all. It was a new order of experience, and in the true sense of the word *unearthly.*

"It's the deliberate, calculating purpose that reduces one's courage to zero," the Swede said suddenly, as if he had been actually following my thoughts. "Otherwise imagination might count for much. But the paddle, the canoe, the lessening food—"

"Haven't I explained all that once?" I interrupted viciously.

"You have," he answered dryly; "you have indeed."

He made other remarks too, as usual, about what he called the "plain determination to provide a victim"; but, having now arranged my thoughts better, I recognized that this was simply the cry of his frightened soul against the knowledge that he was being attacked in a vital part, and that he would be somehow taken or destroyed. The situation called for a courage and calmness of reasoning that neither of us could compass, and I have never before been so clearly conscious of two persons in me—the one that explained everything, and the other that laughed at such foolish explanations, yet was horribly afraid.

Meanwhile, in the pitchy night the fire died down and the wood pile grew small. Neither of us moved to replenish the stock, and the darkness consequently came up very close to our faces. A few feet beyond the circle of firelight it was inky black. Occasionally a stray puff of wind set the willows shivering about us, but apart from this not very welcome sound a deep and depressing silence reigned, broken only by the gurgling of the river and the humming in the air overhead.

We both missed, I think, the shouting company of the winds.

At length, at a moment when a stray puff prolonged itself as though the wind were about to rise again, I reached the point for me of saturation, the point where it was absolutely necessary to find relief in plain speech, or else to betray myself by some hysterical extravagance that must have been far worse in its effect upon both of us. I kicked the fire into a blaze, and turned to my companion abruptly. He looked up with a start.

"I can't disguise it any longer," I said; "I don't like this place, and the darkness, and the noises, and the awful feelings I get. There's something here that beats me utterly. I'm in a blue funk, and that's the plain truth. If the other shore was—different, I swear I'd be inclined to swim for it!"

The Swede's face turned very white beneath the deep tan of sun and wind. He stared straight at me and answered quietly, but his voice betrayed his huge excitement by its unnatural calmness. For the moment, at any rate, he was the strong man of the two. He was more phlegmatic, for one thing.

"It's not a physical condition we can escape from by running away," he replied, in the tone of a doctor diagnosing some grave disease; "we must sit tight and wait. There are forces close here that could kill a herd of elephants in a second as easily as you or I could squash a fly. Our only chance is to keep perfectly still. Our insignificance perhaps may save us."

I put a dozen questions into my expression of face, but found no words. It was precisely like listening to an accurate description of a disease whose symptoms had puzzled me.

"I mean that so far, although aware of our disturbing presence, they have not *found* us—not 'located' us, as the Americans say," he went on. "They're blundering about like men hunting for a leak of gas. The paddle and canoe and provisions prove that. I think they *feel* us, but cannot actually see us. We must keep our minds quiet—it's our minds they feel. We must control our thoughts, or it's all up with us."

"Death, you mean?" I stammered, icy with the horror of his suggestion.

"Worse—by far," he said. "Death, according to one's belief, means either annihilation or release from the limitations of the senses, but it involves no change of character. *You* don't suddenly alter just because the body's gone. But this means a radical alteration, a complete change, a horrible loss of oneself by substitution—far worse than death, and not even annihilation. We happen to have camped in a spot where their region touches ours, where the veil between has worn thin"—horrors! he was using my very own phrase, my actual words—"so that they are aware of our being in their neighborhood."

"But *who* are aware?" I asked.

I forgot the shaking of the willows in the windless calm, the humming overhead, everything except that I was waiting for an answer that I dreaded more than I can possibly explain.

He lowered his voice at once to reply, leaning forward a little over the fire, an indefinable change in his face that made me avoid his eyes and look down upon the ground.

"All my life," he said, "I have been strangely, vividly conscious of another region—not far removed from our own world in one sense, yet wholly different in kind—where great things go on unceasingly, where immense and terrible personalities hurry by, intent on vast purposes compared to which earthly affairs, the rise and fall of nations, the destinies of empires, the fate of armies and continents, are all as dust in the balance; vast purposes, I mean, that deal directly with the soul, and not indirectly with mere expressions of the soul—"

"I suggest just now—" I began, seeking to stop him, feeling as though I was face to face with a madman. But he instantly overbore me with his torrent that *had* to come.

"You think," he said, "it is the spirit of the elements, and I thought perhaps it was the old gods. But I tell you now it is—*neither*. These would be comprehensible entities, for they have relations with men, depending upon them for worship or sacrifice, whereas these beings who are now about us have absolutely nothing to do with mankind, and it is mere chance that their space happens just at this spot to touch our own."

The mere conception, which his words somehow made so convincing, as I listened to them there in the dark stillness of that lonely island, set me shaking a little all over. I found it impossible to control my movements.

"And what do you propose?" I began again.

"A sacrifice, a victim, might save us by distracting them until we could get away," he went on, "just as the wolves stop to devour the dogs and give the sleigh another start. But—I see no chance of any other victim now."

I stared blankly at him. The gleam in his eye was dreadful. Presently he continued.

"It's the willows, of course. The willows *mask* the others, but the others are feeling about for us. If we let our minds betray our fear, we're lost, lost utterly." He looked at me with an expression so calm, so determined, so sincere, that I no longer had any doubts as to his sanity. He was as sane as any man ever was. "If we can hold out through the night," he added, "we may get off in the daylight unnoticed, or rather, *undiscovered.*"

"But you really think a sacrifice would—"

That gong-like humming came down very close over our heads as I spoke, but it was my friend's scared face that really stopped my mouth.

"Hush!" he whispered, holding up his hand. "Do not mention them more than you can help. Do not refer to them *by name*. To name is to reveal; it is the inevitable clue, and our only hope lies in ignoring them, in order that they may ignore us."

"Even in thought?" He was extraordinarily agitated.

"Especially in thought. Our thoughts make spirals in their world. We must keep them *out of our minds* at all costs if possible."

I raked the fire together to prevent the darkness having everything its own way. I never longed for the sun as I longed for it then in the awful blackness of that summer night.

"Were you awake all last night?" he went on suddenly.

"I slept badly a little after dawn," I replied evasively, trying to follow his instructions, which I knew instinctively were true, "but the wind, of course—"

"I know. But the wind won't account for all the noises."

"Then you heard it too?"

"The multiplying countless little footsteps I heard," he said, adding, after a moment's hesitation, "and that other sound—"

"You mean above the tent, and the pressing down upon us of something tremendous, gigantic?"

He nodded significantly.

"It was like the beginning of a sort of inner suffocation?" I said.

"Partly, yes. It seemed to me that the weight of the atmosphere had been altered—had increased enormously, so that we should have been crushed."

"And that," I went on, determined to have it all out, pointing upwards where the gong-like note hummed ceaselessly, rising and falling like wind. "What do you make of that?"

"It's *their* sound," he whispered gravely. "It's the sound of their world, the humming in their region. The division here is so thin that it leaks through somehow. But, if you listen carefully, you'll find it's not above so much as around us. It's in the willows. It's the willows themselves humming, because here the willows have been made symbols of the forces that are against us."

I could not follow exactly what he meant by this, yet the thought and idea in my mind were beyond question the thought and idea in his. I realized what he realized, only with less power of analysis than his. It was on the tip of my tongue to tell him at last about my hallucination of the ascending figures and the moving bushes, when he suddenly thrust his face again close into mine across the firelight and began to speak in a very earnest whisper. He amazed me by his calmness and pluck, his apparent control of the situation. This man I had for years deemed unimaginative, stolid!

"Now listen," he said. "The only thing for us to do is to go on as though nothing had happened, follow our usual habits, go to bed, and so forth; pretend we feel nothing and notice nothing. It is a question wholly of the mind, and the less we think about them the better our chance of escape. Above all, don't *think*, for what you think happens!"

"All right," I managed to reply, simply breathless with his words and the strangeness of it all; "all right, I'll try, but tell me one more thing first. Tell me what you make of those hollows in the ground all about us, those sand-funnels?"

"No!" he cried, forgetting to whisper in his excitement. "I dare not, simply dare not, put the thought into words. If you have not guessed I am glad. Don't try to. *They* have put it into my mind; try your hardest to prevent their putting it into yours."

He sank his voice again to a whisper before he finished, and I did not press him to explain. There was already just about as much horror in me as I could hold. The conversation came to an end, and we smoked our pipes busily in silence.

Then something happened, something unimportant apparently, as the way is when the nerves are in a very great state of tension, and this small thing for a brief space gave me an entirely different point of view. I chanced to look down at my sand-shoe—the sort we used for the canoe—and something to do with the hole at the toe suddenly recalled to me the London shop where I had bought them, the difficulty the man had in fitting me, and other details of the uninteresting but practical operation. At once, in its train, followed a wholesome view of the modern skeptical world I was accustomed to move in at home. I thought of roast beef, and ale, motor-cars, policemen, brass bands, and a dozen other things that proclaimed the soul of ordinariness or utility. The effect was immediate and astonishing even to myself. Psychologically, I suppose, it was simply a sudden and violent reaction after the strain of living in an atmosphere of things that to the normal consciousness must seem impossible and incredible. But, whatever the cause, it momentarily lifted the spell from my heart, and left me for the short space of a minute feeling free and utterly unafraid. I looked up at my friend opposite.

"You damned old pagan!" I cried, laughing aloud in his face. "You imaginative idiot! You superstitious idolater! You—"

I stopped in the middle, seized anew by the old horror. I tried to smother the sound of my voice as something sacrilegious. The Swede, of course, heard it too—the strange cry overhead in the darkness—and that sudden drop in the air as though something had come nearer.

He had turned ashen white under the tan. He stood bolt upright in front of the fire, stiff as a rod, staring at me.

"After that," he said in a sort of helpless, frantic way, "we must go! We can't stay now; we must strike camp this very instant and go on— down the river."

He was talking, I saw, quite wildly, his words dictated by abject terror—the terror he had resisted so long, but which had caught him at last.

"In the dark?" I exclaimed, shaking with fear after my hysterical outburst, but still realizing our position better than he did. "Sheer madness! The river's in flood, and we've only got a single paddle. Besides, we only go deeper into their country! There's nothing ahead for fifty miles but willows, willows, willows!"

He sat down again in a state of semi-collapse. The positions, by one of those kaleidoscopic changes nature loves, were suddenly reversed, and the control of our forces passed over into my hands. His mind at last had reached the point where it was beginning to weaken.

"What on earth possessed you to do such a thing?" he whispered with the awe of genuine terror in his voice and face.

I crossed round to his side of the fire. I took both his hands in mine, kneeling down beside him and looking straight into his frightened eyes.

"We'll make one more blaze," I said firmly, "and then turn in for the night. At sunrise we'll be off full speed for Komorn. Now, pull yourself together a bit, and remember your own advice about *not thinking fear!*"

He said no more, and I saw that he would agree and obey. In some measure, too, it was a sort of relief to get up and make an excursion into the darkness for more wood. We kept close together, almost touching, groping among the bushes and along the bank. The humming overhead never ceased, but seemed to me to grow louder as we increased our distance from the fire. It was shivery work!

We were grubbing away in the middle of a thickish clump of willows where some driftwood from a former flood had caught high among the branches, when my body was seized in a grip that made me half drop upon the sand. It was the Swede. He had fallen against me, and was clutching me for support. I heard his breath coming and going in short gasps.

"Look! By my soul!" he whispered, and for the first time in my experience I knew what it was to hear tears of terror in a human voice. He was pointing to the fire, some fifty feet away. I followed the direction of his finger, and I swear my heart missed a beat.

There, in front of the dim glow, *something was moving*.

I saw it through a veil that hung before my eyes like the gauze drop-curtain used at the back of a theater—hazily a little. It was neither a human figure nor an animal. To me it gave the strange impression of being as large as several animals grouped together, like horses, two or three, moving slowly. The Swede, too, got a similar result, though expressing it differently, for he thought it was shaped and sized like a clump of willow bushes, rounded at the top, and moving all over upon its surface—"coiling upon itself like smoke," he said afterwards.

"I watched it settle downwards through the bushes," he sobbed at me. "Look, by God! It's coming this way! Oh, oh!"—he gave a kind of whistling cry. "*They've found us.*"

I gave one terrified glance, which just enabled me to see that the shadowy form was swinging towards us through the bushes, and then I collapsed backwards with a crash into the branches. These failed, of course, to support my weight, so that with the Swede on top of me we fell in a struggling heap upon the sand. I really hardly knew what was happening. I was conscious only of a sort of enveloping sensation of icy fear that plucked the nerves out of their fleshly covering, twisted them this way and that, and replaced them quivering. My eyes were tightly shut; something in my throat choked me; a feeling that my consciousness was expanding, extending out into space, swiftly gave way to another feeling that I was losing it altogether, and about to die.

An acute spasm of pain passed through me, and I was aware that the Swede had hold of me in such a way that he hurt me abominably. It was the way he caught at me in falling.

But it was the pain, he declared afterwards, that saved me; it caused me to *forget them* and think of something else at the very instant when they were about to find me. It concealed my mind from them at the moment of discovery, yet just in time to evade their terrible seizing of me. He himself, he says, actually swooned at the same moment, and that was what saved him.

I only know that at a later date, how long or short is impossible to say, I found myself scrambling up out of the slippery network of willow branches, and saw my companion standing in front of me holding out a hand to assist me. I stared at him in a dazed way, rubbing the arm he had twisted for me. Nothing came to me to say, somehow.

"I lost consciousness for a moment or two," I heard him say. "That's what saved me. It made me stop thinking about them."

"You nearly broke my arm in two," I said, uttering my only connected thought at the moment. A numbness came over me.

"That's what saved *you!*" he replied. "Between us, we've managed to set them off on a false tack somewhere. The humming has ceased. It's gone—for the moment at any rate!"

A wave of hysterical laughter seized me again, and this time spread to my friend too—great healing gusts of shaking laughter that brought a tremendous sense of relief in their train. We made our way back to the fire and put the wood on so that it blazed at once. Then we saw that the tent had fallen over and lay in a tangled heap upon the ground.

We picked it up, and during the process tripped more than once and caught our feet in sand.

"It's those sand-funnels," exclaimed the Swede, when the tent was up again and the firelight lit up the ground for several yards about us. "And look at the size of them!"

All round the tent and about the fireplace where we had seen the moving shadows there were deep funnel-shaped hollows in the sand, exactly similar to the ones we had already found over the island, only far bigger and deeper, beautifully formed, and wide enough in some instances to admit the whole of my foot and leg.

Neither of us said a word. We both knew that sleep was the safest thing we could do, and to bed we went accordingly without further delay, having first thrown sand on the fire and taken the provision sack and the paddle inside the tent with us. The canoe, too, we propped in such a way at the end of the tent that our feet touched it, and the least motion would disturb and wake us.

In case of emergency, too, we again went to bed in our clothes, ready for a sudden start.

V.

IT was my firm intention to lie awake all night and watch, but the exhaustion of nerves and body decreed otherwise, and sleep after a while came over me with a welcome blanket of oblivion. The fact that my companion also slept quickened its approach. At first he fidgeted and constantly sat up, asking me if I "heard this" or "heard that." He tossed about on his cork mattress, and said the tent was moving and the river had risen over the point of the island, but each time I went out to look I returned with the report that all was well, and finally he grew calmer and lay still. Then at length his breathing became regular and I heard unmistakable sounds of snoring—the first and only time in my life when snoring has been a welcome and calming influence.

This, I remember, was the last thought in my mind before dozing off.

A difficulty in breathing woke me, and I found the blanket over my face. But something else besides the blanket was pressing upon me, and my first thought was that my companion had rolled off his mattress on to my own in his sleep. I called to him and sat up, and at the same moment it came to me that the tent was *surrounded*. That sound of multitudinous soft pattering was again audible outside, filling the night with horror.

I called again to him, louder than before. He did not answer, but I missed the sound of his snoring, and also noticed that the flap of the tent was down. This was the unpardonable sin. I crawled out in the darkness to hook it back securely, and it was then for the first time I realized positively that the Swede was not here. He had gone.

I dashed out in a mad run, seized by a dreadful agitation, and the moment I was out I plunged into a sort of torrent of humming that surrounded me completely and came out of every quarter of the heavens at once. It was that same familiar humming—gone mad! A swarm of great invisible bees might have been about me in the air. The sound seemed to thicken the very atmosphere, and I felt that my lungs worked with difficulty.

But my friend was in danger, and I could not hesitate.

The dawn was just about to break, and a faint whitish light spread upwards over the clouds from a thin strip of clear horizon. No wind stirred. I could just make out the bushes and river beyond, and the pale sandy patches. In my excitement I ran frantically to and fro about the island, calling him by name, shouting at the top of my voice the first words that came into my head. But the willows smothered my voice, and the humming muffled it, so that the sound only traveled a few feet round me. I plunged among the bushes, tripping headlong, tumbling over roots, and scraping my face as I tore this way and that among the preventing branches.

Then, quite unexpectedly, I came out upon the island's point and saw a dark figure outlined between the water and the sky. It was the Swede. And already he had one foot in the river! A moment more and he would have taken the plunge.

I threw myself upon him, flinging my arms about his waist and dragging him shorewards with all my strength. Of course he struggled furiously, making a noise all the time just like that cursed humming, and using the most outlandish phrases in his anger about "going *inside* to Them," and "taking the way of the water and the wind," and God only knows what more besides, that I tried in vain to recall afterwards, but which turned me sick with horror and amazement as I listened. But in the end I managed to get him into the comparative safety of the tent, and flung him breathless and cursing upon the mattress where I held him until the fit had passed.

I think the suddenness with which it all went and he grew calm, coinciding as it did with the equally abrupt cessation of the humming and pattering outside—I think this was almost the strangest part of the whole business perhaps. For he had just opened his eyes and turned his tired face up to me so that the dawn threw a pale light upon it through the doorway, and said, for all the world just like a frightened child:

"My life, old man—it's my life I owe you. But it's all over now anyhow. They've found a victim in our place!"

Then he dropped back upon his blankets and went to sleep literally under my eyes. He simply collapsed, and began to snore again as healthily as though nothing had happened and he had never tried to offer his own life as a sacrifice by drowning. And when the sunlight woke him three hours later—hours of ceaseless vigil for me—it became so clear to me that he remembered absolutely nothing of what he had attempted to do, that I deemed it wise to hold my peace and ask no dangerous questions.

He woke naturally and easily, as I have said, when the sun was already high in a windless hot sky, and he at once got up and set about the preparation of the fire for breakfast. I followed him anxiously at bathing, but he did not attempt to plunge in, merely dipping his head and making some remark about the extra coldness of the water.

"River's falling at last," he said, "and I'm glad of it."

"The humming has stopped too," I said.

He looked up at me quietly with his normal expression. Evidently he remembered everything except his own attempt at suicide.

"Everything has stopped," he said, "because—"

He hesitated. But I knew some reference to that remark he had made just before he fainted was in his mind, and I was determined to know it.

"Because 'They've found another victim'?" I said, forcing a little laugh.

"Exactly," he answered, "exactly! I feel as positive of it as though—as though—I feel quite safe again, I mean," he finished.

He began to look curiously about him. The sunlight lay in hot patches on the sand. There was no wind. The willows were motionless. He slowly rose to feet.

"Come," he said; "I think if we look, we shall find it."

He started off on a run, and I followed him. He kept to the banks, poking with a stick among the sandy bays and caves and little back-waters, myself always close on his heels.

"Ah!" he exclaimed presently, "ah!"

The tone of his voice somehow brought back to me a vivid sense of the horror of the last twenty-four hours, and I hurried up to join him. He was pointing with his stick at a large black object that lay half in the water and half on the sand. It appeared to be caught by some twisted willow roots so that the river could not sweep it away. A few hours before the spot must have been under water.

"See," he said quietly, "the victim that made our escape possible!"

And when I peered across his shoulder I saw that his stick rested on the body of a man. He turned it over. It was the corpse of a peasant, and the face was hidden in the sand. Clearly the man had been drowned, but a few hours before, and his body must have been swept down upon our island somewhere about the hour of the dawn—*at the very time the fit had passed*.

"We must give it a decent burial, you know."

"I suppose so," I replied. I shuddered a little in spite of myself, for there was something about the appearance of that poor drowned man that turned me cold.

The Swede glanced up sharply at me, an undecipherable expression on his face, and began clambering down the bank. I followed him more leisurely. The current, I noticed, had torn away much of the clothing from the body, so that the neck and part of the chest lay bare.

Halfway down the bank my companion suddenly stopped and held up his hand in warning; but either my foot slipped, or I had gained too much momentum to bring myself quickly to a halt, for I bumped into him and sent him forward with a sort of leap to save himself. We tumbled together on to the hard sand so that our feet splashed into the water. And, before anything could be done, we had collided a little heavily against the corpse.

The Swede uttered a sharp cry. And I sprang back as if I had been shot.

At the moment we touched the body there rose from its surface the loud sound of humming—the sound of several hummings—which passed with a vast commotion as of winged things in the air about us and disappeared upwards into the sky, growing fainter and fainter till they finally ceased in the distance. It was exactly as though we had disturbed some living yet invisible creatures at work.

My companion clutched me, and I think I clutched him, but before either of us had time properly to recover from the unexpected shock, we saw that a movement of the current was turning the corpse round so that it became released from the grip of the willow roots. A moment later it had turned completely over, the dead face uppermost, staring at the sky. It lay on the edge of the main stream. In another moment it would be swept away.

The Swede started to save it, shouting again something I did not catch about a "proper burial"—and then abruptly dropped upon his knees on the sand and covered his eyes with his hands. I was beside him in an instant.

I saw what he had seen.

For just as the body swung round to the current the face and the exposed chest turned full towards us, and showed plainly how the skin and flesh were indented with small hollows, beautifully formed, and exactly similar in shape and kind to the sand-funnels that we had found all over the island.

"Their mark!" I heard my companion mutter under his breath. "Their awful mark!"

And when I turned my eyes again from his ghastly face to the river, the current had done its work, and the body had been swept away into mid-stream and was already beyond our reach and almost out of sight, turning over and over on the waves like an otter.

The Seed from the Sepulcher

by Clark Ashton Smith

"YES, I found the place," said Falmer. "It's a queer sort of place, pretty much as the legends describe it." He spat quickly into the fire, as if the act of speech had been physically distasteful to him, and, half averting his face from the scrutiny of Thone, stared with morose and somber eyes into the jungle-matted Venezuelan darkness. Thone, still weak and dizzy from the fever that had incapacitated him for continuing their journey to its end, was curiously puzzled. Falmer, it seemed to him, had undergone an inexplicable change during the three days of his absence—a change so elusive and shadowy in some of its phases that Thone was unable to delimit it fully in his thoughts. Other phases, however, were all too obvious. Falmer, even during extreme hardship or jungle illness, had been heretofore unquenchably loquacious and cheerful. Now he seemed sullen, uncommunicative, as if his mind were preoccupied with far-off things of disagreeable import. His bluff face had grown hollow—even pointed—and his eyes had narrowed to secretive slits. Thone was troubled by these changes, though he tried to dismiss his impressions as mere distempered fancies due to the influence of the ebbing fever.

"But can't you tell me what the place was like?" he persisted.

"There isn't much to tell," said Falmer, in a queer grumbling tone. "Just a few crumbling walls overgrown and half-displaced by the forest trees, and a few falling pillars netted with lianas."

"But didn't you find the burial-pit of the Indian legend, where the gold was supposed to be?"

"Oh, yes, I found it. The place has started to cave in from above, so there wasn't much difficulty about that—but there was no treasure." Falmer's voice had taken on a forbidding surliness; and Thone decided to refrain from further questioning.

"I guess," he commented lightly, "that we had better stick to orchid-hunting. Treasure trove doesn't seem to be in our line. By the way, did you find any unusual flowers or plants during the trip?"

"Hell, no," Falmer snapped. His face had gone suddenly ashen in the firelight, and his eyes had assumed a set glare that might have meant either fear or anger. "Shut up, can't you? I don't want to talk. I've had a headache all day—some damned Venezuelan fever coming on, I suppose. We'd better head for the Orinoco tomorrow, even if we are both sick. I've had all I want of this trip."

James Falmer and Roderick Thone, professional orchid-hunters, with two Indian guides, had been following an obscure tributary of the upper Orinoco. The country was rich in rare flowers; and, beyond its floral wealth, they had been drawn by vague but persistent rumors among the local tribes concerning the existence of a ruined city somewhere on this tributary: a city that contained a burial-pit in which vast treasures of gold, silver and jewels had been interred together with the dead of some nameless people. These rumors were never first-hand, but the two men had thought it worthwhile to investigate them. Thone had fallen sick while they were still a full day's journey from the supposed site of the ruins, and Falmer had gone on in a canoe with one of the Indians, leaving the other to attend to Thone. He had returned at nightfall of the third day following his departure.

Thone decided after a while, as he lay staring at his companion, that the latter's taciturnity and moroseness were perhaps due to disappointment over his failure to find the treasure. It must have been that—together with some tropical infection working in his blood. However, he admitted doubtfully to himself, it was not like Falmer to be disappointed or downcast under such circumstances. Greediness for mere wealth, as far as he had occasion to observe, was not in the man's nature.

Falmer did not speak again, but sat glaring before him as if he saw something invisible to others beyond the labyrinth of fire-touched boughs and lianas in which the whispering, stealthy darkness crouched. Somehow, there was a shadowy fear in his aspect. Thone continued to watch him, and saw that the Indians, impassive and cryptic, were also watching him, as if with some obscure expectancy. The riddle was too much for Thone, and he gave it up after a while, lapsing into restless, fever-turbulent slumber, from which he awakened at intervals to see the set face of Falmer, dimmer and more distorted each time with the slowly dying fire. At last it became a half-human thing, devoured by inhuman shadows and twisted by the ever-changing horror of those febrile dreams.

Thone felt stronger in the morning: his brain was clear, his pulse tranquil once more; and he saw with mounting concern the mysterious indisposition of Falmer, who seemed to rouse and exert himself with great difficulty, speaking hardly a word and moving with singular stiffness and sluggishness. He appeared to have forgotten his announced project of returning toward the Orinoco, and Thone took entire charge of the preparations for departure. His companion's condition puzzled him more and more: the signs were not born of any malady with which he was familiar. There was no fever and the symptoms were wholly obscure and ambiguous. However, on general principles, he administered a stiff dose of quinine to Falmer before they started.

The paling saffron of a sultry dawn sifted upon them through the jungle-tops as they loaded their belongings into the dugouts and pushed off down the slow current. Thone sat near the bow of one of the boats, with Falmer in the rear, and a large bundle of orchid roots and part of their equipment filling the middle. The two Indians, taciturn and stolid, occupied the other boat, together with the rest of the supplies.

It was a monotonous journey. The river wound like a sluggish olive snake between dark, interminable walls of forest, from which, at intervals, the goblin faces of orchids leaned and leered. There were no sounds other than the splash of paddles, the furious chattering of monkeys and petulant cries of strange, fiery-colored birds. The sun rose above the jungle and poured down a waveless tide of torrid brilliance.

Thone rowed steadily, looking back over his shoulder at times to address Falmer with some casual remark or friendly question. The latter, with dazed eyes and features that were queerly pale and pinched in the sunlight, sat dully erect and made no effort to use his paddle, seeming to lack both the strength and the inclination. He offered no reply to the solicitous queries of Thone, but shook his head at intervals with a sort of shuddering motion that was plainly automatic and involuntary, rather than the expression of common negation. After a while he began to moan thickly, as if in pain or delirium.

They went on in this manner for several hours; the heat grew more oppressive between the stifling, airless walls of jungle. Thone became aware of a shriller cadence in the moans of his sick companion. Looking back, he saw that Falmer had removed his sunhelmet, seemingly oblivious of the murderous heat, and was clawing at the crown of his head with frantic fingers. Convulsions shook his entire body, and the dugout began to rock dangerously as he tossed to and fro in a long paroxysm of manifest agony. His voice mounted to a ceaseless, high, unhuman shrieking.

Thone made a quick decision. There was a break in the lining palisade of somber forest, and he headed the boat for shore immediately.

The Indians followed, whispering between themselves and eyeing the sick man with glances of apprehensive awe and terror that puzzled Thone tremendously. He felt that there was some devilish mystery about the whole affair; and he could not imagine what was wrong with Falmer. All the known manifestations of malignant tropical diseases rose before him like a rout of hideous phantasms; but among them, he could not recognize the thing that had assailed his companion.

Having gotten Falmer ashore on a semi-circle of liana-latticed beach without the aid of the reluctant guides, who seemed unwilling to touch or approach the sick man, Thone administered a heavy hypodermic injection of morphine from his medicine chest. This appeared to ease Falmer's suffering, and the convulsions ceased. Thone, taking advantage of their remission, proceeded to examine the crown of Falmer's head.

He was startled to find amid the thick disheveled hair a hard and pointed lump which resembled strangely the tip of a beginning horn, rising under the still unbroken skin. As if endowed with erectile and resistless life, it seemed to grow beneath his fingers.

At the same time, abruptly and mysteriously, Falmer opened his eyes and appeared to regain full consciousness, as if he had overcome not only the effects of the hypodermic but the stupor of the unknown malady. For a few minutes, he was more his normal self than at any time since his return from the ruins. He began to talk, as if he were anxious to relieve his mind of some oppressing burden. His voice was peculiarly thick and toneless, but Thone, listening in half-comprehending horror, was able to follow his mutterings and piece them together.

"The pit! The pit!" said Falmer. "The infernal thing that was in the pit, in the deep sepulcher! . . . I wouldn't go back there for the treasure of a dozen El Dorados . . . I didn't tell you much about those ruins, Thone. Somehow it was hard—impossibly hard—to talk.

"I guess the Indian knew there was something wrong with those ruins. He led me to the place all right . . . but he wouldn't tell me anything about it; and he waited by the riverside while I searched for the treasure.

"Great grey walls there were, older than the jungle—old as death and time—not like anything I have ever seen. They must have been quarried and reared by people from some forgotten continent or lost planet. They loomed and leaned at mad, unnatural angles, threatening to crush the trees about them. And there were columns, too: thick, swollen columns of unholy form, whose abominable carvings the jungle had not wholly screened from view.

"My God! that accursed burial-pit! There was no trouble finding it.

The pavement above had broken through quite recently, I think. A big tree had pried with its boa-like roots between the yard-deep flagstones that were buried beneath centuries of mould. One of the flags had been tilted back on the pavement, and another had fallen through into the pit. There was a large hole, whose bottom I could see dimly in the forest-strangled light. Something glimmered palely at the bottom; but I could not be sure what it was.

"I had taken along a coil of rope, as you remember. I tied one end to a main root of the tree, dropped the other through the opening, and went down like a monkey. When I got to the bottom I could see little at first in the gloom, except for the whitish glimmering all around me, at my feet. Something broke and crunched beneath me when I began to move—something that was unspeakably brittle and friable. I turned on my flash-light, and saw that the place was fairly littered with bones—human skeletons lay tumbled everywhere. They must have been very old, for they dissolved into powder at a touch.

"The place was a huge sepulchral chamber. After awhile, as I wandered about with the flashlight, I found the steps that led to the blocked-up entrance. But if any treasure had been buried with the bodies, it must have been removed long ago. I groped around amid the bones and dust, feeling pretty much like a ghoul, but couldn't find anything of value, not even a bracelet or a finger-ring on any of the skeletons.

"It wasn't until I thought of climbing out that I noticed the real horror. I didn't mind those skeletons so much: they were lying in atti-tudes of repose, even if they were a little crowded and it seemed that their owners must have died natural deaths—natural, that is, as we reckon such things.

"Then, in one of the corners—the corner nearest to the opening in the roof—I looked up and saw it in the webby shadows. Ten feet above my head it hung, and I had almost touched it, unknowingly, when I des-cended the rope.

"It looked like a sort of weird lattice-work at first. Then I saw that the lattice was partly formed of human bones—a complete skeleton, very tall and stalwart, like that of a warrior. I wouldn't have cared if it had been hanging there in any normal fashion—if it had been suspended by metal chains, for instance, or had merely been nailed to the walls. The horror lay in the thing that grew out of the skull—the white, withered thing like a set of fantastic antlers ending in myriads of long and stringy tendrils that had spread themselves on the wall, climbing upward till they reached the roof. They must have lifted the skeleton, or body, along with them as they climbed.

"I examined the thing with my flashlight, and found new horrors. It must have been a plant of some sort, and apparently it had started to grow in the cranium. Some of the branches had issued from the cloven crown, others through the eye-holes and the noseholes, to flare upward. And the roots of the blasphemous thing had gone downward, trellising themselves on every bone. The very toes and fingers were ringed with them, and they drooped in writhing coils. Worst of all, the ones that had issued from the toe-ends *were rooted in a second skull*, which dangled just below, with fragments of the broken-off root system. There was a litter of fallen bones on the floor in the corner, but I didn't care to inspect it.

"The sight made me feel a little weak, somehow—and more than a little nauseated—that abhorrent, inexplicable mingling of the human and the plant. I started to climb the rope, in a feverish hurry to get out, but the thing fascinated me, in its abominable fashion, and I couldn't help pausing to study it a little more when I had climbed half-way. I leaned toward it too fast, I guess, and the rope began to sway, bringing my face lightly against the leprous, antler-shaped boughs above the skull.

"Something broke—I don't know what—possibly a sort of pod on one of the branches. Anyway, I found my head enveloped in a cloud of pearl-grey powder, very light, fine, and scentless. The stuff settled on my hair, it got into my nose and eyes, nearly choking and blinding me. I tried to shake it off as well as I could. Then I climbed on and pulled myself through the opening . . ."

As if the effort of coherent narration had been too heavy a strain, Falmer lapsed into disconnected mumblings, some of which were inaudible. The mysterious malady, whatever it was, returned upon him, and his delirious ramblings were mixed with groans of torture. But at moments he regained a flash of coherence.

"My head! My head!" he muttered. "There must be something in my brain, something that grows and spreads; I tell you, I can feel it there. I haven't felt right at any time since I left the burial-pit . . . My mind has been queer ever since . . . It must have been the spores of the ancient devil-plant . . . The spores have taken root . . . the thing is splitting my skull, going down into my brain—a plant that springs out of a human cranium, as if from a flower-pot!"

The dreadful convulsions began once more, and Falmer writhed uncontrollably in his companion's arms, shrieking with agony. Thone, sick at heart, and horribly shocked by his sufferings, abandoned all effort at restraint and took up the hypodermic. With much difficulty, he managed to inject a triple dose into one of the wildly tossing arms, and Falmer grew quiet by degrees and lay with open glassy eyes, breathing stertorously. Thone, for the first time, perceived an odd protrusion of his eye-balls, which seemed about to start from their sockets, making it impossible for the lids to close, and lending the drawn, contorted features an expression of mad horror and extravagant ghastliness. It was as if something were pushing Falmer's eyes from his head.

Thone, trembling with sudden weakness and terror, felt that he was involved in some unnatural web of nightmare. He could not, dared not, believe the story Falmer had told him, and its implications. The thing was too monstrous, too fantastic; and, assuring himself that his companion had imagined it all, had been ill throughout with the incubation of some strange fever, he stooped over and found that the horn-shaped lump on Falmer's head had now broken through the skin.

Increasingly, with a sense of unreality, he stared at the object that his prying fingers had touched and revealed amid the matted hair. It was unmistakably a plant-bud of some sort, with involuted folds of pale green and bloody pink that seemed about to expand. The thing issued from above the central suture of the skull; and the thought occurred to the horror-sick observer that it had somehow taken root in the very bone; had gone downward, as Falmer had feared, into the brain.

A nausea swept upon Thone, and he recoiled from the lolling head and its baleful outgrowth, averting his gaze. His fever, he felt, was returning; there was a woeful debility in all his limbs; and he heard the muttering voices of incipient delirium through the quinine-induced ringing in his ears. His eyes blurred with a deathly mist, as if the miasma of some equatorial fen had arisen visibly before him.

He fought to subdue his illness and impotence. He must not give way to it wholly; he must go on with Falmer and the Indians, and reach the nearest trading station, many days away on the Orinoco, where Falmer could receive aid.

As if through sheer volition, the clinging vapor cleared from his eyes, and he felt a resurgence of strength. He looked around for the two guides, and saw, with a start of uncomprehending surprise, that they had vanished. Then, peering further, he observed that one of the boats—the dugout used by the Indians—had also disappeared. It was all too evident that he and Falmer had been deserted. Perhaps the Indians had known what was wrong with the sick man, and had been afraid. Their apprehensive glances, their covert whisperings, their patent unwillingness to approach Falmer, all seemed to confirm this. At any rate, they were gone, and they had taken much of the camp equipment and most of the provisions with them.

Thone turned once more to the supine body of Falmer, conquering his fear and repugnance with effort. Something must be done, and they must go on while Falmer still lived. One of the boats remained; and even if Thone became too ill to ply the paddle, the current would still carry them downstream.

Resolutely, he drew out his clasp-knife and, stooping over the stricken man, he excised the protruding bud, cutting as close to the scalp itself as he could with safety. The thing was unnaturally tough and rubbery; it exuded a thin, sanious fluid; and he shuddered when he saw its internal structure, full of nerve-like filaments, with a core that suggested cartilage. He flung it aside quickly on the river sand. Then, lifting Falmer in his arms, he lurched and staggered toward the remaining boat. He fell more than once, and lay half-swooning across the inert body. Alternately carrying and dragging his burden, he reached the boat at last. With the remainder of his failing strength, he contrived to prop Falmer in the stern against the pile of equipment.

His fever was mounting apace. Dimly, with a swimming brain, and legs that bent beneath him like river reeds, he went back for the medicine-kit. After much delay, with tedious, half-delirious exertions, he pushed off from the shore, and got the boat into mid-stream. He paddled with nerveless, mechanical strokes, hardly knowing what he did, till the fever mastered him wholly and the oar slipped from oblivious fingers . . .

After that, he seemed to be drifting through a hell of strange dreams illumed by an intolerable, glaring sun. He went on in this way for cycles, and then floated into a phantom-peopled darkness, and slumber haunted by innominable voices and faces, all of which became at last the voice and face of Falmer, detailing over and over again a hideous story which Thone still seemed to hear in the utmost abyss of sleep.

He awoke in the yellow glare of dawn, with his brain and his senses comparatively clear. His illness had left a great languor, but his first thought was of Falmer. He twisted about, nearly falling overboard in his debility, and sat facing his companion.

Falmer still reclined, half-sitting, half-lying, against the pile of blankets and other impedimenta. His knees were drawn up, his hands clasping them as if in tetanic rigor. His features had grown as wan and stark and ghastly as those of a dead man, and his whole aspect was one of mortal rigidity. It was this, however, that caused Thone to gasp with unbelieving horror—a horror in which he found himself hoping that

Falmer really *was* dead.

During the interim of Thone's delirium and his lapse into slumber, which must have been a whole afternoon and night, the monstrous plant-bud, merely stimulated, it would seem, by the act of excision, had grown again with preternatural and abhorrent rapidity, from Falmer's head. A loathsome pale-green stem was mounting thickly and had started to branch like antlers after attaining a height of six or seven inches.

More dreadful than this, if possible, similar growths had issued from the eyes; and their heavy stems, climbing vertically across the forehead, had entirely displaced the eye-balls. Already they were branching like the thing that mounted from the crown. The antlers were all tipped with pale vermilion. Each of them appeared to quiver with repulsive animation, nodding rhythmically in the warm, windless air . . . From the mouth another stem protruded, curling upward like a long and whitish tongue. It had not yet begun to bifurcate.

Thone closed his eyes to shut away the shocking vision. Behind his lids, in a yellow dazzle of light, he still saw the cadaverous, deathly features, the climbing stems that quivered against the dawn like ghastly hydras of tomb-etiolated green. They seemed to be waving toward him, growing and lengthening visibly as they waved. He opened his eyes again, and fancied, with a start of new terror, that the antlers were actually taller than they had been a few moments previous.

After that, he sat watching them in a sort of baleful paralysis, with horror curdled at his heart. The illusion of the plant's visible growth and freer movement—if it was illusion—increased upon him by accelerative degrees. Falmer, however, did not stir, and his white, parchment face seemed to shrivel and fall in, as if the roots of the growth were draining him of blood, were devouring his very flesh in their insatiable and ghoulish hunger.

Shuddering, Thone wrenched his eyes away and stared at the river shore. The stream had widened, and the current had grown more sluggish. He sought to recognize their location, looking in vain for some familiar landmark in the monotonous dull-green cliffs of jungle that lined the margin. All was strange to him, and he felt hopelessly lost and alienated. He seemed to be drifting on an unknown tide of nightmare and madness, companioned by something more frightful than corruption itself.

His mind began to wander with an odd inconsequence, coming back always, in a sort of closed circle, to the growth that was devouring Falmer.

With a flash of scientific curiosity, he found himself wondering to what genus it belonged. It was neither fungus nor pitcher-plant, nor anything that he had ever encountered or heard of in his explorations. It must have come, as Falmer had suggested, from an alien world; it was nothing that the earth could conceivably have nourished.

He felt, with a comforting assurance, that Falmer was dead, for the roots of the thing must have long since penetrated the brain. That at least, was a mercy. But even as he shaped the thought, he heard a low, guttural moaning, and, peering at Falmer in horrible startlement, saw that his limbs and body were twitching slightly. The twitching increased, and took on a rhythmic regularity, though at no time did it resemble the agonized and violent convulsions of the previous day. It was plainly automatic, like a sort of galvanism; and Thone saw that it was timed with the languorous and loathsome swaying of the plant. The effect on the watcher was insidiously mesmeric and somnolent; and once he caught himself beating the detestable rhythm with his foot.

He tried to pull himself together, groping desperately for something to which his sanity could cling. Ineluctably, he felt the return of his sickness: fever, nausea, and revulsion worse than the loathliness of death. But before he yielded to it utterly, he drew his loaded revolver from the holster and fired six times into Falmer's quivering body. He knew that he had not missed, but, after the final bullet, Falmer still moaned and twitched in unison with the evil swaying of the plant, and Thone, sliding into delirium, heard still the ceaseless, automatic moaning.

There was no time in the world of seething unreality and shoreless oblivion through which he drifted. When he came to himself again, he could not know if hours or weeks had elapsed. But he knew at once that the boat was no longer moving; and lifting himself dizzily, he saw that it had floated into shallow water and mud and was nosing the beach of a tiny, jungle-tufted isle in mid-river. The putrid odor of slime was about him like a stagnant pool, and he heard a strident humming of insects.

It was either late morning or early afternoon, for the sun was high in the still heavens. Lianas were drooping above him from the island trees like uncoiled serpents, and epiphytic orchids, marked with ophidian mottlings, leaned toward him grotesquely from lowering boughs. Immense butterflies went past on sumptuously spotted wings.

He sat up, feeling very giddy and light-headed, and faced again the horror that companioned him. The thing had grown incredibly, enormously: the three-antlered stems, mounting above Falmer's head, had become gigantic and had put out masses of ropy feelers that tossed uneasily in the air, as if searching for support—or new provender. In the topmost antler, issuing from the crown and towering above the others, a prodigious blossom had opened—a sort of fleshy disk, broad as a man's face and pale as leprosy.

Falmer's features had shrunken till the outlines of every bone were visible as if beneath tightened paper. He was a mere death's head in a mask of human skin, and his body seemed to have collapsed and fallen, leaving little more than a skeleton beneath his clothing. He was quite still now, except for the communicated quivering of the stems. The atrocious plant had sucked him dry, had eaten his vitals and his flesh.

Thone wanted to hurl himself forward in a mad impulse to grapple with the loathly growth. But a strange paralysis held him back. The plant was like a living and sentient thing—a thing that watched him, that dominated him with its unclean but superior will. And the huge blossom, as he stared, took on the dim, unnatural semblance of a face. It was somehow like the face of Falmer, but the lineaments were twisted all awry, and were mingled with those of something wholly devilish and non-human. Thone could not move—and he could not take his eyes from the blasphemous, unthinkable abnormality.

By some miracle, his fever had left him; and it did not return. Instead, there came an eternity of frozen fright and madness, in which he sat facing the mesmeric plant. It towered before him from the dry, dead shell that had been Falmer, its swollen, glutted stems and branches swaying in a gentle rhythm, its huge flower leering perpetually upon him with its impious travesty of a human face. He thought that he heard a low singing sound, ineffably, demoniacally sweet, but whether it emanated from the plant or was a mere hallucination of his overwrought senses, he could not know.

The sluggish hours went by, and a gruelling sun poured down upon him like molten lead from some titanic vessel of torture. His head swam with weakness and the fetor-laden heat; but he could not relax the rigor of his posture. There was no change in the nodding monstrosity, which seemed to have attained its full growth above the head of its victim. But after a long interim, Thone's eyes were drawn to the rigid, shrunken hands of Falmer, which still clasped the drawn-up knees in a spasmodic clutch. From the back of each hand, from the ends of the skeleton fingers, tiny white rootlets had broken and were writhing slowly in the air, groping, it seemed, for a new source of nourishment. Then, from the neck and chin, other tips were breaking, and over the whole body the clothing stirred in a curious manner, as if with the crawling and lifting of hidden lizards.

At the same time the singing grew louder, sweeter, more imperious in Thone's ears, and the swaying of the great plant assumed an indescribably seductive tempo. It was like the allurement of voluptuous sirens, the deadly languor of dancing cobras. Thone felt an irresistible compulsion: a summons was being laid upon him, and his drugged mind and body must obey it. The very fingers of Falmer, twisting viperishly, seemed beckoning to him. Then, suddenly he was on his hands and knees in the bottom of the boat.

Inch by inch, with baleful terror and equally baleful fascination contending in his brain, he crept forward, dragging himself over the disregarded bundle of orchid-plants—inch by inch, foot by foot, till his head was against the withered hands of Falmer, from which hung and floated the questing roots.

Some cataleptic spell had made him helpless. He felt the rootlets as they moved like delving fingers through his hair and over his face and neck, and started to strike in with agonizing, needle-sharp tips. He could not stir, he could not even close his lids. In a frozen stare, he saw the gold and carmine flash of a hovering butterfly as the roots began to pierce his pupils.

Deeper and deeper went the greedy roots, while new filaments grew out to enmesh him like a witch's net . . . For a while, it seemed that the dead and the living writhed together in leashed convulsions . . . At last Thone hung supine amid the lethal, ever-growing web; bloated and colossal, the plant lived on; and in its upper branches, through the still, stifling afternoon, a second flower began to unfold.

That Damned Thing

by Ambrose Bierce

I.

BY THE LIGHT of a tallow candle, which had been placed on one end of a rough table, a man was reading something written in a book. It was an old account book, greatly worn; and the writing was not, apparently, very legible, for the man sometimes held the page close to the flame of the candle to get a stronger light upon it. The shadow of the book would then throw into obscurity a half of the room, darkening a number of faces and figures; for besides the reader, eight other men were present. Seven of them sat against the rough log walls, silent and motionless, and, the room being small, not very far from the table. By extending an arm any one of them could have touched the eighth man, who lay on the table, face upward, partly covered by a sheet, his arms at his sides. He was dead.

The man with the book was not reading aloud, and no one spoke; all seemed to be waiting for something to occur; the dead man only was without expectation. From the blank darkness outside came in, through the aperture that served for a window, all the ever unfamiliar noises of night in the wilderness—the long, nameless note of a distant coyote; the stilly pulsing thrill of tireless insects in trees; strange cries of night birds, so different from those of the birds of day; the drone of great blundering beetles, and all that mysterious chorus of small sounds that seem always to have been but half heard when they have suddenly ceased, as if conscious of an indiscretion. But nothing of all this was noted in that company; its members were not overmuch addicted to idle interest in matters of no practical importance; that was obvious in every line of their rugged faces—obvious even in the dim light of the single candle. They were evidently men of the vicinity—farmers and woodmen.

The person reading was a trifle different; one would have said of him that he was of the world, worldly, albeit there was that in his attire which attested a certain fellowship with the organisms of his environment. His coat would hardly have passed muster in San Francisco: his footgear was not of urban origin, and the hat that lay by him on the floor (he was the only one uncovered) was such that if one had considered it as an article of mere personal adornment he would have missed its meaning. In countenance the man was rather prepossessing, with just a hint of sternness; though that he may have assumed or cultivated, as appropriate to one in authority. For he was a coroner. It was by virtue of his office that he had possession of the book in which he was reading; it had been found among the dead man's effects—in his cabin, where the inquest was now taking place.

When the coroner had finished reading he put the book into his breast pocket. At that moment the door was pushed open and a young man entered. He, clearly, was not of mountain birth and breeding: he was clad as those who dwell in cities. His clothing was dusty, however, as from travel. He had, in fact, been riding hard to attend the inquest.

The coroner nodded; no one else greeted him.

"We have waited for you," said the coroner. "It is necessary to have done with this business tonight."

The young man smiled. "I am sorry to have kept you," he said. "I went away, not to evade your summons, but to post to my newspaper an account of what I suppose I am called back to relate."

The coroner smiled.

"The account that you posted to your newspaper," he said, "differs probably from that which you will give here under oath."

"That," replied the other, rather hotly and with a visible flush, "is as you choose. I used manifold paper and have a copy of what I sent. It was not written as news, for it is incredible, but as fiction. It may go as a part of my testimony under oath."

"But you say it is incredible."

"That is nothing to you, sir, if I also swear that it is true."

The coroner was apparently not greatly affected by the young man's manifest resentment. He was silent for some moments, his eyes upon the floor. The men about the sides of the cabin talked in whispers, but seldom withdrew their gaze from the face of the corpse. Presently the coroner lifted his eyes and said: "We will resume the inquest."

The men removed their hats. The witness was sworn.

"What is your name?" the coroner asked.

"William Harker."

"Age?"

"Twenty-seven."

"You knew the deceased, Hugh Morgan?"

"Yes."

"You were with him when he died?"

"Near him."

"How did that happen—your presence, I mean?"

"I was visiting him at this place to shoot and fish. A part of my purpose, however, was to study him, and his odd, solitary way of life. He seemed a good model for a character in fiction. I sometimes write stories."

"I sometimes read them."

"Thank you."

"Stories in general—not yours."

Some of the jurors laughed. Against a sombre background humor shows high lights. Soldiers in the intervals of battle laugh easily, and a jest in the death chamber conquers by surprise.

"Relate the circumstances of this man's death," said the coroner. "You may use any notes or memoranda that you please."

The witness understood. Pulling a manuscript from his breast pocket he held it near the candle, and turning the leaves until he found the passage that he wanted, began to read.

II.

"...The sun had hardly risen when we left the house. We were looking for quail, each with a shotgun, but we had only one dog. Morgan said that our best ground was beyond a certain ridge that he pointed out, and we crossed it by a trail through the chaparral. On the other side was comparatively level ground, thickly covered with wild oats. As we emerged from the chaparral, Morgan was but a few yards in advance. Suddenly, we heard, at a little distance to our right, and partly in front, a noise as of some animal thrashing about in the bushes, which we could see were violently agitated.

"'We've startled a deer,' he said. 'I wish we had brought a rifle.'

"Morgan, who had stopped and was intently watching the agitated chaparral, said nothing, but had cocked both barrels of his gun, and was holding it in readiness to aim. I thought him a trifle excited, which surprised me, for he had a reputation for exceptional coolness, even in moments of sudden and imminent peril.

"'O, come!' I said. 'You are not going to fill up a deer with quail-shot, are you?'

"Still he did not reply; but, catching a sight of his face as he turned it slightly toward me, I was struck by the pallor of it. Then I understood that we had serious business on hand, and my first conjecture was that we had 'jumped' a grizzly. I advanced to Morgan's side, cocking my piece as I moved.

"The bushes were now quiet, and the sounds had ceased, but Morgan was as attentive to the place as before.

"'What is it? What the devil is it?' I asked.

"'That Damned Thing!' he replied, without turning his head. His voice was husky and unnatural. He trembled visibly.

"I was about to speak further, when I observed the wild oats near the place of the disturbance moving in the most inexplicable way. I can hardly describe it. It seemed as if stirred by a streak of wind, which not only bent it, but pressed it down—crushed it so that it did not rise, and this movement was slowly prolonging itself directly toward us.

"Nothing that I had ever seen had affected me so strangely as this unfamiliar and unaccountable phenomenon, yet I am unable to recall any sense of fear. I remember—and tell it here because, singularly enough, I recollected it then—that once, in looking carelessly out of an open window, I momentarily mistook a small tree close at hand for one of a group of larger trees at a little distance away. It looked the same size as the others, but, being more distinctly and sharply defined in mass and detail, seemed out of harmony with them. It was a mere falsification of the law of aerial perspective, but it startled, almost terrified me. We so rely upon the orderly operation of familiar natural laws that any seeming suspension of them is noted as a menace to our safety, a warning of unthinkable calamity. So now the apparently causeless movement of the herbage, and the slow, undeviating approach of the line of disturbance were distinctly disquieting. My companion appeared actually frightened, and I could hardly credit my senses when I saw him suddenly throw his gun to his shoulders and fire both barrels at the agitated grass! Before the smoke of the discharge had cleared away I heard a loud savage cry—a scream like that of a wild animal—and, flinging his gun upon the ground, Morgan sprang away and ran swiftly from the spot. At the same instant I was thrown violently to the ground by the impact of something unseen in the smoke—some soft, heavy substance that seemed thrown against me with great force.

"Before I could get upon my feet and recover my gun, which seemed to have been struck from my hands, I heard Morgan crying out as if in mortal agony, and mingling with his cries were such hoarse savage sounds as one hears from fighting dogs. Inexpressibly terrified, I struggled to my feet and looked in the direction of Morgan's retreat; and may heaven in mercy spare me from another sight like that! At a distance of less than thirty yards was my friend, down upon one knee, his head thrown back at a frightful angle, hatless, his long hair in disorder and his whole body in violent movement from side to side, backward and forward. His right arm was lifted and seemed to lack the hand—at least, I could see none. The other arm was invisible. At times, as my memory now reports this extraordinary scene, I could discern but a part of his body; it was as if he had been partly blotted out—I cannot otherwise express it—then a shifting of his position would bring it all into view again.

"All this must have occurred within a few seconds, yet in that time Morgan assumed all the postures of a determined wrestler vanquished by superior weight and strength. I saw nothing but him, and him not always distinctly. During the entire incident his shouts and curses were heard, as if through an enveloping uproar of such sounds of rage and fury as I had never heard from the throat of man or brute!

"For a moment only I stood irresolute, then, throwing down my gun, I ran forward to my friend's assistance. I had a vague belief that he was suffering from a fit or some form of convulsion. Before I could reach his side he was down and quiet. All sounds had ceased, but, with a feeling of such terror as even these awful events had not inspired, I now saw the same mysterious movement of the wild oats prolonging itself from the trampled area about the prostrate man toward the edge of a wood. It was only when it had reached the wood that I was able to withdraw my eyes and look at my companion. He was dead."

III.

THE CORONER rose from his seat and stood beside the dead man. Lifting an edge of the sheet he pulled it away, exposing the entire body, altogether naked and showing in the candle light a clay-like yellow. It had, however, broad maculations of bluish-black, obviously caused by extravasated blood from contusions. The chest and sides looked as if they had been beaten with a bludgeon. There were dreadful lacerations; the skin was torn in strips and shreds.

The coroner moved round to the end of the table and undid a silk handkerchief, which had been passed under the chin and knotted on the top of the head. When the handkerchief was drawn away it exposed what had been the throat. Some of the jurors who had risen to get a better view repented their curiosity, and turned away their faces. Witness Harker went to the open window and leaned out across the sill, faint and sick. Dropping the handkerchief upon the dead man's neck, the coroner stepped to an angle of the room, and from a pile of clothing produced one garment after another, each of which he held up a moment for inspection. All were torn, and stiff with blood. The jurors did not make a closer inspection. They seemed rather uninterested. They had, in truth, seen all this before; the only thing that was new to them being Harker's testimony.

"Gentlemen," the coroner said, "we have no more evidence, I think. Your duty has been already explained to you; if there is nothing you wish to ask you may go outside and consider your verdict."

The foreman rose—a tall, bearded man of sixty, coarsely clad.

"I should like to ask one question, Mr. Coroner," he said. "What asylum did this yer last witness escape from?"

"Mr. Harker," said the coroner, gravely and tranquilly, "from what asylum did you last escape?"

Harker flushed crimson again, but said nothing, and the seven jurors rose and solemnly filed out of the cabin.

"If you have done insulting me, sir," said Harker, as soon as he and the officer were left alone with the dead man, "I suppose I am at liberty to go?"

"Yes."

Harker started to leave, but paused, with his hand on the door latch. The habit of his profession was strong in him—stronger than his sense of personal dignity. He turned about and said:

"The book that you have there—I recognize it as Morgan's diary. You seemed greatly interested in it; you read in it while I was testifying. May I see it? The public would like—"

"The book will cut no figure in this matter," replied the official, slipping it into his coat pocket; "all the entries in it were made before the writer's death."

As Harker passed out of the house the jury reentered and stood about the table on which the now covered corpse showed under the sheet with sharp definition. The foreman seated himself near the candle, produced from his breast pocket a pencil and scrap of paper, and wrote rather laboriously the following verdict, which with various degrees of effort all signed:

"We, the jury, do find that the remains come to their death at the hands of a mountain lion, but some of us thinks, all the same, they had fits."

IV.

IN THE DIARY of the late Hugh Morgan are certain interesting entries having, possibly, a scientific value as suggestions. At the inquest upon his body the book was not put in evidence; possibly the coroner thought it not worthwhile to confuse the jury. The date of the first of the entries mentioned cannot be ascertained; the upper part of the leaf is torn away; the part of the entry remaining is as follows:

". . . would run in a half circle, keeping his head turned always toward the centre and again he would stand still, barking furiously. At last he ran away into the brush as fast as he could go. I thought at first that he had gone mad, but on returning to the house found no other alteration in his manner than what was obviously due to fear of punishment.

"Can a dog see with his nose? Do odors impress some olfactory centre with images of the thing emitting them? . . .

"Sept 2.—Looking at the stars last night as they rose above the crest of the ridge east of the house, I observed them successively disappear—from left to right. Each was eclipsed but an instant, and only a few at the same time, but along the entire length of the ridge all that were within a degree or two of the crest were blotted out. It was as if something had passed along between me and them; but I could not see it, and the stars were not thick enough to define its outline. Ugh! I don't like this . . ."

Several weeks' entries are missing, three leaves being torn from the book.

"Sept. 27.—It has been about here again—I find evidences of its presence every day. I watched again all of last night in the same cover, gun in hand, double-charged with buckshot. In the morning the fresh footprints were there, as before. Yet I would have sworn that I did not sleep—indeed, I hardly sleep at all. It is terrible, insupportable! If these amazing experiences are real I shall go mad; if they are fanciful I am mad already.

"Oct. 3.—I shall not go—it shall not drive me away. No, this is *my* house, my land. God hates a coward . . .

"Oct. 5.—I can stand it no longer; I have invited Harker to pass a few weeks with me—he has a level head. I can judge from his manner if he thinks me mad.

"Oct. 7.—I have the solution of the problem; it came to me last night—suddenly, as by revelation. How simple—how terribly simple!

"There are sounds that we cannot hear. At either end of the scale are notes that stir no chord of that imperfect instrument, the human ear. They are too high or too grave. I have observed a flock of blackbirds occupying an entire treetop—the tops of several trees—and all in full song. Suddenly—in a moment—at absolutely the same instant—all spring into the air and fly away. How? They could not all see one another—whole treetops intervened. At no point could a leader have been visible to all. There must have been a signal of warning or command, high and shrill above the din, but by me unheard. I have observed, too, the same simultaneous flight when all were silent, among not only blackbirds, but other birds—quail, for example, widely separated by bushes—even on opposite sides of a hill.

"It is known to seamen that a school of whales basking or sporting on the surface of the ocean, miles apart, with the convexity of the earth between them, will sometimes dive at the same instant—all gone out of sight in a moment. The signal has been sounded—too grave for the ear of the sailor at the masthead and his comrades on the deck—who nevertheless feel its vibrations in the ship as the stones of a cathedral are stirred by the bass of the organ.

"As with sounds, so with colors. At each end of the solar spectrum the chemist can detect the presence of what are known as 'actinic' rays. They represent colors—integral colors in the composition of light—which we are unable to discern. The human eye is an imperfect instrument; its range is but a few octaves of the real 'chromatic scale' I am not mad; there are colors that we can not see.

"And, God help me! the Damned Thing is of such a color!"

The Saliva Tree

by Brian Aldiss

*There is neither speech nor language: but their voices
are heard among them.*

PSALM XIX

"YOU know, I'm really much exercised about the Fourth Dimension,"
said the fair-haired young man, with a suitable earnestness in his voice.

"Um," said his companion, staring up at the night sky.

"It seems very much in evidence these days. Do you not think you
catch a glimpse of it in the drawings of Aubrey Beardsley?"

"Um," said his companion.

They stood together on a low rise to the east of the sleepy East
Anglian town of Cottersall, watching the stars, shivering a little in the
chill February air. They are both young men in their early twenties. The
one who is occupied with the Fourth Dimension is called Bruce Fox; he is
tall and fair, and works as junior clerk in the Norwich firm of lawyers,
Prendergast and Tout. The other, who has so far vouchsafed us only an
um or two, although he is to figure largely as the hero of our account, is
by name Gregory Rolles. He is tall and dark, with grey eyes set in his
handsome and intelligent face. He and Fox have sworn to Think Large,
thus distinguishing themselves, at least in their own minds, from all the
rest of the occupants of Cottersall in these last years of the nineteenth
century.

"There's another!" exclaimed Gregory, breaking at last from the
realm of monosyllables. He pointed a gloved finger up at the constellation
of Auriga the Charioteer. A meteor streaked across the sky like a runaway
flake of the Milky Way, and died in midair.

"Beautiful!" they said together.

"It's funny," Fox said, prefacing his words with an oft-used phrase,
"the stars and men's minds are so linked together and always have been,

316

even in the centuries of ignorance before Charles Darwin. They always seem to play an ill-defined role in man's affairs. They help me think large too, don't they you, Greg?"

"You know what I think—I think that some of those stars may be occupied. By people, I mean." He breathed heavily, overcome by what he was saying. "People who—perhaps they are better than us, live in a just society, wonderful people . . ."

"I know, Socialists to a man!" Fox exclaimed. This was one point on which he did not share his friend's advanced thinking. He had listened to Mr. Tout talking in the office, and thought he knew better than his rich friend how these socialists, of which one heard so much these days, were undermining society. "Stars full of socialists!"

"Better than stars full of Christians! Why, if the stars were full of Christians, no doubt they would already have sent missionaries down here to preach their Gospel."

"I wonder if there ever will be planetary journeys as predicted by Nunsowe Greene and Monsieur Jules Verne—" Fox said, when the appearance of a fresh meteor stopped him in midsentence.

Like the last, this meteor seemed to come from the general direction of Auriga. It travelled slowly, and it glowed red, and it sailed grandly towards them. They both exclaimed at once, and gripped each other by the arm. The magnificent spark burned in the sky, larger now, so that its red aura appeared to encase a brighter orange glow. It passed overhead (afterwards, they argued whether it had not made a slight noise as it passed), and disappeared below a clump of willow. They knew it had been near. For an instant, the land had shone with its light.

Gregory was the first to break the silence.

"Bruce, Bruce, did you see that? That was no ordinary fireball!"

"It was so big! What was it?"

"Perhaps our heavenly visitor has come at last!"

"Hey, Greg, it must have landed by your friends' farm—the Grendon place—mustn't it?"

"You're right! I must pay old Mr. Grendon a visit tomorrow and see if he or his family saw anything of this."

They talked excitedly, stamping their feet as they exercised their lungs. Their conversation was the conversation of optimistic young men, and included much speculative matter that began "Wouldn't it be wonderful if—", or "Just supposing—". Then they stopped and laughed at their own absurd beliefs.

"It must be nearly nine o'clock," Fox said at last. "I didn't mean to be so late tonight. It's funny how fast time passes. We'd best be getting back, Greg."

They had brought no lantern, since the night was both clear and dry. It was but two miles by the track back to the outlying houses of Cottersall. They stepped it out lustily, arm linked in arm in case one of them tripped in cart ruts, for Fox had to be up at five in the morning if he was to bicycle to his work punctually. The little village lay silent, or almost so. In the baker's house where Gregory lodged, a gaslight burned and a piano could be heard. As they halted smartly at the side door, Fox said slyly, "So you'll be seeing all the Grendon family tomorrow?"

"It seems probable, unless that red hot planetary ship has already borne them off to a better world."

"Tell us true, Greg—you really go to see that pretty Nancy Grendon, don't you?"

Gregory struck his friend playfully on the shoulder.

"No need for your jealousy, Bruce! I go to see the father, not the daughter. Though the one is female, the other is progressive, and that must interest me more just yet. Nancy has beauty, true, but her father— ah, her father has electricity!"

Laughing, they cheerfully shook hands and parted for the night.

On Grendon's farm, things were a deal less tranquil, as Gregory was to discover.

~§~

Gregory Rolles rose before seven next morning as was his custom. It was while he was lighting his gas mantle, and wishing the baker would install electricity, that a swift train of thought led him to reflect again on the phenomenal thing in the previous night's sky. Mrs. Fenn, the baker's wife, who had already lit his fire, brought him up hot water for washing and scalding water for shaving and, later, a mighty tray full of breakfast. Throughout this activity, and indeed while he ate his porridge and chops, Gregory remained abstracted, letting his mind wander luxuriously over all the possibilities that the "meteor" illuminated. He decided that he would ride out to see Mr. Grendon within the hour.

He was lucky in being able, at this stage in his life, to please himself largely as to how his days were spent, for his father was a person of some substance. Edward Rolles had had the fortune, at the time of the Crimean War, to meet Escoffier, and with some help from the great chef had brought onto the market a baking powder, "Eugenol", that, being slightly

more palatable and less deleterious to the human system than its rivals, had achieved great commercial success. As a result, Gregory had attended one of the Cambridge colleges.

Now, having gained a degree, he was poised on the verge of a career. But which career? He had acquired—more as result of his intercourse with other students than with those officially deputed to instruct him— some understanding of the sciences; his essays had been praised and some of his poetry published, so that he inclined towards literature; and an un-easy sense that life for everyone outside the privileged classes contained too large a proportion of misery led him to think seriously of a political career. In Divinity, too, he was well-grounded; but at least the idea of Holy Orders did not tempt him.

While he wrestled with his future, he undertook to live away from home, since his relations with his father were never smooth. By rusti- cating himself in the heart of East Anglia, he hoped to gather material for a volume tentatively entitled "Wanderings with a Socialist Naturalist", which would assuage all sides of his ambitions. Nancy Grendon, who had a pretty hand with a pencil, might even execute a little emblem for the title page . . . Perhaps he might be permitted to dedicate it to his author friend, Mr. Herbert George Wells . . .

He dressed himself warmly, for the morning was cold as well as dull, and went down to the baker's stables. When he had saddled his mare, Daisy, he swung himself up and set out along a road that the horse knew well.

The sun had been up for something over an hour, yet the sky and the landscape were drab in the extreme. Two sorts of East Anglian landscape met here, trapped by the confused wanderings of the River Oast: the unfarmable heathland and the unfarmable fen. There were few trees, and those stunted, so that the four fine elms that stood on one side of the Grendon farm made a cynosure for miles around.

The land rose slightly towards the farm, the area about the house forming something of a little island amid marshy ground and irregular stretches of water that gave back to the sky its own dun tone. The gate over the little bridge was, as always, open wide; Daisy picked her way through the mud to the stables, where Gregory left her to champ oats contentedly. Cuff and her pup, Lardie, barked loudly about Gregory's heels as usual, and he patted their heads on his way over to the house.

Nancy came hurrying out to meet him before he got to the front door.

"We had some excitement last night, Gregory," she said. He noted with pleasure she had at last brought herself to use his first name.

"Something bright and glaring!" she said. "I was retiring, when this noise come and then this light, and I rush to look out through the curtains, and there's this here great thing like an egg sinking into our pond." In her speech, and particularly when she was excited, she carried the lilting accent of Norfolk.

"The meteor!" Gregory exclaimed. "Bruce Fox and I were out last night as we were the night before, watching for the lovely Aurigids that arrive every February, when we saw an extra big one. I said then it was coming over very near here."

"Why, it almost landed on our house," Nancy said. She looked very pleasing this morning, with her lips red, her cheeks shining, and her chestnut curls all astray. As she spoke, her mother appeared in apron and cap, with a wrap hurriedly thrown over her shoulders.

"Nancy, you come in, standing freezing like that! You ent daft, girl, are you? Hello, Gregory, how be going on? I didn't reckon as we'd see you today. Come in and warm yourself."

"Good-day to you, Mrs. Grendon. I'm hearing about your wonderful meteor of last night."

"It was a falling star, according to Bert Neckland. I ent sure what it was, but it certainly stirred up the animals, that I *do* know."

"Can you see anything of it in the pond?" Gregory asked.

"Let me show you," Nancy said.

Mrs. Grendon returned indoors. She went slowly and grandly, her back very straight and an unaccustomed load before her. Nancy was her only daughter; there was a younger son, Archie, a stubborn lad who had fallen at odds with his father and now was apprenticed to a blacksmith in Norwich; and no other children living. Three infants had not survived the mixture of fogs alternating with bitter east winds that comprised the typical Cottersall winter. But no, the farmer's wife was unexpectedly gravid again, and would bear her husband another baby when the spring came in.

As Nancy led Gregory over to the pond, he saw Grendon with his two labourers working in the West Field, but they did not wave.

"Was your father not excited by the arrival last night?"

"That he was—when it happened! He went out with his shotgun, and Bert Neckland with him. But there was nothing to see but bubbles in the pond and steam over it, and this morning he couldn't discuss it, and said that work must go on whatever happen."

They stood beside the pond, a dark and extensive slab of water with rushes on the farther bank and open country beyond. As they looked at its ruffled surface, they stood with the windmill black and bulky on their left hand. It was to this that Nancy now pointed.

Mud had been splashed across the boards high up the sides of the mill; some was to be seen even on the tip of the nearest white sail. Gregory surveyed it all with interest. Nancy, however, was still pursuing her own line of thought.

"Don't you reckon Father works too hard, Gregory? When he ent outside doing jobs, he's in reading his pamphlets and his electricity manuals. He never rests but when he sleeps."

"Um. Whatever went into the pond went in with a great smack! There's no sign of anything there now, is there? Not that you can see an inch below the surface."

"You being a friend of his, Mum thought perhaps as you'd say something to him. He don't go to bed till ever so late—sometimes it's near midnight, and then he's up again at three and a half o'clock. Would you speak to him? You know Mother dassent."

"Nancy, we ought to see whatever it was that went in the pond. It can't have dissolved. How deep is the water? Is it very deep?"

"Oh, you aren't listening, Gregory Rolles! Bother the old meteor!"

"This is a matter of science, Nancy. Don't you see—"

"Oh, rotten old science, is it? Then I don't want to hear. I'm cold, standing out here. You can have a good look if you like, but I'm going in before I gets froze. It was only an old stone out of the sky, because I heard Father and Bert Neckland agree to it."

"Fat lot Bert Neckland knows about such things!" he called to her departing back. She had the prettiest ringlets on her neck, but really he didn't want to get involved with a nineteen-year old farmer's daughter. It was a pity more girls didn't believe in Free Love, as did most of his male acquaintances.

He looked down at the dark water. Whatever it *was* that had arrived last night, it was here, only a few feet from him. He longed to discover what remained of it. Vivid pictures entered his mind: his name in head-lines in *The Morning Post*, the Royal Society making him an honorary member, his father embracing him and pressing him to return home.

Thoughtfully, he walked over to the barn. Hens ran clucking out of his way as he entered and stood looking up, waiting for his eyes to adjust to the dim light. There, as he remembered it, was a little rowing boat. Perhaps in his courting days old Mr. Grendon had taken his prospective wife out for excursions on the Oast in it. Surely it had not been used in years.

He moved the long ladder over to climb and inspect it, and a cat went flying across the rafters in retreat. The inside of the boat was filthy, but two oars lay there, and it seemed intact. The craft had been hitched to its present position by two ropes thrown over a higher beam; it was a simple enough matter to lower it to the ground.

At that point, Gregory had a moment of prudence for other people's property. He went into the farm and asked Mrs. Grendon if he might embark on the pond with it. That complaisant lady said he might do as he wished, and accordingly he dragged the boat from the barn and launched it in the shallows of the pond. It floated. The boards had dried, and water leaked through a couple of seams, but not nearly enough to deter him. Climbing delicately in among the straw and filth, he pushed off.

~§~

From here, the farm, or such of it as he could see, presented a somewhat sinister aspect. The mill loomed above him, dismal and tarred black, only its sails white and creaking in the slight wind. To his other side, the blank-faced end of the barn looked immense and meaningless. Behind it he could see the backs of cowsheds with, beyond them, the raw new brick of the back of Grendon's machine house, where he made electricity. Between barn and mill, he could see the farm-house, but the upper storey only, because of the lie of the land. Its decrepit humps of thatch and the tall stack of its chimney gave it a forbidding air. He mused on the strangeness that overcame one from looking at human works from an angle from which they were never designed to be seen, and wondered if there were similar angles in nature. Presumably there were, for behind him where the pond ended were only ragged willows topping reed beds. It looked as if there should have been something else—a little land at least—but no land showed, only the willows and the watery sky.

Now he was over the approximate centre of the pond. He shipped his oars and peered over the side. There was an agitation in the water, and nothing could be seen, although he imagined much.

As he stared over the one side, the boat unexpectedly tipped to the other. Gregory swung round. The boat listed heavily to the left, so that the oars rolled over that way. He could see nothing. Yet—he heard something. It was a sound much like a hound slowly panting. And whatever made it was about to capsize the boat.

"What is it?" he said, as all the skin pricked up his back and skull.

The boat lurched, for all the world as if someone invisible were trying to get into it. Frightened, he grasped the oar, and, without thinking, swept it over that side of the rowing boat.

It struck something solid where there was only air.

Dropping the oar in surprise, he put out his hand. It touched something yielding. At the same time, his arm was violently struck.

His actions were then entirely governed by instinct. Thought did not enter the matter. He picked up the oar again and smote the thin air with it. It hit something. There was a splash, and the boat righted itself so suddenly he was almost pitched into the water. Even while it still rocked, he was rowing frantically for the shallows, dragging the boat from the water, and running for the safety of the farm-house.

Only at the door did he pause. His reason returned, his heart began gradually to stop stammering its fright. He stood looking at the seamed wood of the porch, trying to evaluate what he had seen and what had actually happened. But what had happened?

Forcing himself to go back to the pond, he stood by the boat and looked across the sullen face of the water. It lay undisturbed, except by surface ripples. He looked at the boat. A quantity of water lay in the bottom of it. He thought, all that happened was that I neatly capsized, and I let my idiot fears run away with me. Shaking his head, he pulled the boat back to the barn.

~§~

Gregory, as he often did, stayed to eat lunch at the farm, but he saw nothing of the farmer till milking time.

Joseph Grendon was in his late forties, and a few years senior to his wife. He had a gaunt solemn face and a heavy beard that made him look older than he was. For all his seriousness, he greeted Gregory civilly enough. They stood together in the gathering dusk as the cows swung behind them into their regular stalls. Together they walked into the machine house next door, and Grendon lit the oil burners that started the steam engine into motion that would turn the generator that would supply the vital spark.

"I smell the future in here," Gregory said, smiling. By now, he had forgotten the shock of the morning.

"The future will have to get on without me. I shall be dead by then." The farmer spoke as he walked, putting each word reliably before the next.

"That is what you always say. You're wrong—the future is rushing upon us."

"You ent far wrong there, Master Gregory, but I won't have no part of it, I reckon. I'm an old man now. Do you know what I was reading in one of those London papers last night? They do say as how before another half-century is out every house in the country will be supplied with electrical lighting from one big central power house in London. This here old machine won't be no good then, will it?"

"It will be the end of the gas industry, that's for sure. That will cause much unemployment."

"Well, of course, in remote districts like this here primitive place, you wouldn't get gas in a dozen centuries. But electrical lighting is easier to conduct from one place to another than gas is. Here she come!"

This last exclamation was directed at a flicker of light in the pilot bulb overhead. They stood there contemplating with satisfaction the wonderful machinery. As steam pressure rose, the great leather belt turned faster and faster, and the flicker in the pilot bulb grew stronger. Although Gregory was used to a home lit by both gas and electricity, he never felt the excitement of it as he did here, out in the wilds, where the nearest incandescent bulb was probably in Norwich, a great part of a day's journey away.

"Why did you really decide to have this plant built, Joseph?"

"Like I told you, it's safer than lanterns in the sheds and the sties and anywhere with dry straw about the place. My father had a bad fire here when I was a boy that put the wind up me proper . . . Did I ever tell you as how Bert Neckland's older brother used to work for me once, till I got this here equipment in? He was a regular Bible-thumper, he was, and do you know what he told me? He said as how this here electrical lighting was too bright and devilish to be God's work, and in consequence he refused to let it shine on him. So I told him, I said, Well, I ent having you going round with an umbrella up all hours of darkness, and I gave him his wages and I tell him to clear off out if that's the way he feels."

"And he did?"

"He ent been back here since."

"Idiot! All things are possible now. The Steam Age was wonderful in its way, or must have seemed so to the people that lived in it, but in this new Electric Age—anything's possible. Do you know what I believe, Joseph? I believe that before so very many years are up, we shall have electrical flying machines. Who knows, we may even be able to make them big enough to fly to the moon! Oh, I tell you, I just cannot wait till the New Century. By then, who knows, all men may be united in brotherhood, and then we shall see some progress."

"I don't know. I shall be united in my grave by then."

"Nonsense, you can live to be a hundred."

Now a pale flickering radiance illuminated the room. By contrast, everything outside looked black. Grendon nodded in satisfaction, made some adjustments to the burners, and they went outside.

Free from the bustle of the steam engine, they could hear the noise the cows were making. At milking time, the animals were usually quiet; something had upset them. The farmer ran quickly into the milking shed, with Gregory on his heels.

The new light, radiating from a bulb hanging above the stalls, showed the beasts of restless demeanour and rolling eye. Bert Neckland stood as far away from the door as possible, grasping his stick and letting his mouth hang open.

"What in blazes you staring at, bor?" Grendon asked.

Neckland slowly shut his mouth.

"We had a scare," he said. "Something come in here," he said.

"Did you see what it was?" Gregory asked.

"No, there weren't nothing to see. It was a ghost, that's what it was. It come right in here and touched the cows. It touched me too. It was a ghost."

The farmer snorted. "A tramp more like. You couldn't see because the light wasn't on."

His man shook his head emphatically. "Light weren't that bad. I tell you, whatever it was, it come right up to me and touched me." He stopped, and pointed to the edge of the stall. "Look there! See, I weren't telling you no lie, master. It was a ghost, and there's its wet hand-print."

They crowded round and examined the worn and chewed timber at the corner of the partition between two stalls. An indefinite patch of moisture darkened the wood. Gregory's thoughts went back to his experience on the pond, and again he felt the prickle of unease along his spine. But the farmer said stoutly "Nonsense, it's a bit of cowslime. Now you get on with the milking, Bert, and let's have no more hossing about, because I want my tea. Where's Cuff?"

Bert looked defiant.

"If you don't believe me, maybe you'll believe the bitch. She saw whatever it was and went for it. It kicked her over, but she ran it out of here."

"I'll see if I can see her," Gregory said.

He ran outside and began calling the bitch. By now it was almost entirely dark. He could see nothing in the wide space of the front yard, and so set off in the other direction, down the path towards the pig sties and the fields, calling Cuff as he went. He paused. Low and savage growls sounded ahead, under the elm trees. It was Cuff. He went slowly forward. At this moment, he cursed that electric light meant lack of lanterns, and wished too that he had a weapon.

"Who's there?" he called.

The farmer came up by his side. "Let's charge 'em!"

They ran forward. The trunks of the four great elms were clear against the western sky, with water glinting leadenly behind them. The dog became visible. As Gregory saw Cuff, she sailed into the air, whirled round, and flew at the farmer. He flung up his arms and warded off the body. At the same time, Gregory felt a rush of air as if someone unseen had run past him, and a stale muddy smell filled his nostrils. Staggering, he looked behind him. The wan light from the cowsheds spread across the path between the outhouses and the farmhouse. Beyond the light, more distantly, was the silent countryside behind the grain store. Nothing untoward could be seen.

"They killed my old Cuff," said the farmer.

Gregory knelt down beside him to look at the bitch. There was no mark of injury on her, but she was dead, her fine head lying limp.

"She knew there was something there," Gregory said. "She went to attack whatever it was and it got her first. What was it? Whatever in the world was it?"

"They killed my old Cuff," said the farmer again, unhearing. He picked the body up in his arms, turned, and carried it towards the house. Gregory stood where he was, mind and heart equally uneasy.

He jumped violently when a step sounded nearby. It was Bert Neckland. "What, did that there ghost kill the old bitch?" he asked.

"It killed the bitch certainly, but it was something more terrible than a ghost."

"That's one of them ghosts, bor. I seen plenty in my time. I ent afraid of ghosts, are you?"

"You looked fairly sick in the cowshed a minute ago."

The farmhand put his fists on his hips. He was no more than a couple of years older than Gregory, a stocky young man with a spotty complexion and a snub nose that gave him at once an air of comedy and menace. "Is that so, Master Gregory? Well, you looks pretty funky standing there now."

"I am scared. I don't mind admitting it. But only because we have something here a lot nastier than any spectre."

Neckland came a little closer.

"Then if you are so blooming windy, perhaps you'll be staying away from the farm in future."

"Certainly not." He tried to edge back into the light, but the labourer got in his way.

"If I was you, I should stay away." He emphasized his point by digging an elbow into Gregory's coat. "And just remember that Nancy was interested in me long afore you come along, bor."

"Oh, that's it, is it! I think Nancy can decide for herself in whom she is interested, don't you?"

"I'm *telling* you who she's interested in, see? And mind you don't forget, see?" He emphasized the words with another nudge. Gregory pushed his arm away angrily. Neckland shrugged his shoulders and walked off. As he went, he said. "You're going to get worse than ghosts if you keep hanging round here."

Gregory was shaken. The suppressed violence in the man's voice suggested that he had been harbouring malice for some time. Unsuspectingly, Gregory had always gone out of his way to be cordial, had regarded the sullenness as mere slow-wittedness and done his socialist best to overcome the barrier between them. He thought of following Neckland and trying to make it up with him; but that would look too feeble. Instead, he followed the way the farmer had gone with his dead bitch, and made for the house.

~§~

Gregory Rolles was too late back to Cottersall that night to meet his friend Fox. The next night, the weather became exceedingly chilly and Gabriel Woodcock, the oldest inhabitant, was prophesying snow before the winter was out (a not very venturesome prophecy to be fulfilled within forty-eight hours, thus impressing most of the inhabitants of the village, for they took pleasure in being impressed and exclaiming and saying "Well I never!" to each other). The two friends met in "The Wayfarer", where the fires were bigger, though the ale was weaker, than in the "Three Poachers" at the other end of the village.

Seeing to it that nothing dramatic was missed from his account, Gregory related the affairs of the previous day, omitting any reference to

Neckland's pugnacity. Fox listened fascinated, neglecting both his pipe and his ale.

"So you see how it is, Bruce," Gregory concluded. "In that deep pond by the mill lurks a vehicle of some sort, the very one we saw in the sky, and in it lives an invisible being of evil intent. You see how I fear for my friends there. Should I tell the police about it, do you think?"

"I'm sure it would not help the Grendons to have old Farrish bumping out there on his penny-farthing," Fox said, referring to the local representative of the law. He took a long draw first on the pipe and then on the glass. "But I'm not sure you have your conclusions quite right, Greg. Understand, I don't doubt the facts, amazing though they are. I mean, we were more or less expecting celestial visitants. The world's recent blossoming with gas and electric lighting in its cities at night must have been a signal to half the nations of space that we are now civilized down here. But have our visitants done any deliberate harm to anyone?"

"They nearly drowned me and they killed poor Cuff. I don't see what you're getting at. They haven't begun in a very friendly fashion, have they now?"

"Think what the situation must seem like to them. Suppose they come from Mars or the Moon—we know their world must be absolutely different from Earth. They may be terrified. And it can hardly be called an unfriendly act to try to get into your rowing boat. The first unfriendly act was yours, when you struck out with the oar."

Gregory bit his lip. His friend had a point. "I was scared."

"It may have been because they were scared that they killed Cuff. The dog attacked them, after all, didn't she? I feel sorry for these creatures, alone in an unfriendly world."

"You keep saying 'these'! As far as we know, there is only one of them."

"My point is this, Greg. You have completely gone back on your previous enlightened attitude. You are all for killing these poor things instead of trying to speak to them. Remember what you were saying about other worlds being full of socialists? Try thinking of these chaps as invisible socialists and see if that doesn't make them easier to deal with."

Gregory fell to stroking his chin. Inwardly, he acknowledged that Bruce Fox's words made a great impression on him. He had allowed panic to prejudice his judgement; as a result, he had behaved as immoderately as a savage in some remote corner of the Empire confronted by his first steam locomotive.

"I'd better get back to the farm and sort things out as soon as possible," he said. "If these things really do need help, I'll help them."

"That's it. But try not to think of them as 'things'. Think of them as—as—I know, as *The Aurigans*."

"Aurigans it is. But don't be so smug, Bruce. If you'd been in that boat—"

"I know, old friend. I'd have died of fright." To this monument of tact, Fox added, "Do as you say, go back and sort things out as soon as possible. I'm longing for the next instalment of this mystery. It's quite the jolliest thing since Sherlock Holmes."

~§~

Gregory Rolles went back to the farm. But the sorting out of which Bruce had spoken took longer than he expected. This was chiefly because the Aurigans seemed to have settled quietly into their new home after the initial day's troubles.

They came forth no more from the pond, as far as he could discover; at least they caused no more disturbance. The young graduate particularly regretted this since he had taken his friend's words much to heart, and wanted to prove how enlightened and benevolent he was towards this strange form of life. After some days, he came to believe the Aurigans must have left as unexpectedly as they arrived. Then a minor incident convinced him otherwise; and that same night, in his snug room over the baker's shop, he described it to his correspondent in Worcester Park, Surrey.

Dear Mr. Wells,

I must apologize for my failure to write earlier, owing to lack of news concerning the Grendon Farm affair.

Only today, the Aurigans showed themselves again!—if indeed "showed" is the right word for invisible creatures.

Nancy Grendon and I were in the orchard feeding the hens. There is still much snow lying about, and everywhere is very white. As the poultry came running to Nancy's tub, I saw a disturbance further down the orchard—merely some snow dropping from an apple bough, but the movement caught my eye, and I then saw a *procession* of falling snow proceed towards us from tree to tree. The grass is long there, and I soon noted the stalks being thrust aside by *an unknown agency!* I directed Nancy's attention to the phenomenon. The motion in the grass stopped only a few yards from us.

Nancy was startled, but I determined to acquit myself more like a

Briton than I had previously. Accordingly, I advanced and said, "Who are you? What do you want? We are your friends if you are friendly."

No answer came. I stepped forward again, and now the grass again fell back, and I could see by the way it was pressed down that the creature must have large feet. By the movement of the grasses, I could see he was running. I cried to him and ran too. He went round the side of the house, and then over the frozen mud in the farmyard I could see no further trace of him. But instinct led me forward, past the barn to the pond.

Surely enough, I then saw the cold, muddy water rise and heave, as if engulfing a body that slid quietly in. Shards of broken ice were thrust aside, and by an outward motion, I could see where the strange being went. In a flurry and a small whirlpool, he was gone, and I have no doubt dived down to the mysterious star vehicle.

These things—people—I know not what to call them—must be aquatic; perhaps they live in the canals of the Red Planet. But imagine, Sir—an invisible mankind! The idea is almost as wonderful and fantastic as something from your novel, "The Time Machine".

Pray give me your comment, and trust in my sanity and accuracy as a reporter!

Yours in friendship,

GREGORY ROLLES.

What he did not tell was the way Nancy had clung to him after, in the warmth of the parlour, and confessed her fear. And he had scorned the idea that these beings could be hostile, and had seen the admiration in her eyes, and had thought that she was, after all, a dashed pretty girl, and perhaps worth braving the wrath of those two very different people for: Edward Rolles, his father, and Ben Neckland, the farm labourer.

At that point Mrs. Grendon came in, and the two young people moved rapidly apart. Mrs. Grendon went more slowly. The new life within her was large now, and she carried herself accordingly. So as not to distress her, they told her nothing of what they had seen. Nor was there time for discussion, for the farmer and his two men came tramping into the kitchen, kicking off their boots and demanding lunch.

It was at lunch a week later, when Gregory was again at the farm, taking with him an article on electricity as a pretext for his visit, that the subject of the stinking dew was first discussed.

Grubby was the first to mention it in Gregory's hearing. Grubby, with Bert Neckland, formed the whole strength of Joseph Grendon's labour force; but whereas Neckland was considered couth enough to board in the farmhouse (he had a gaunt room in the attic), Grubby was fit only to sleep in a little flint-and-chalk hut well away from the farm building. His "house", as he dignified the miserable hut, stood below the olchard and near the sties, the occupants of which lulled Grubby to sleep with their snores.

"Reckon we ent ever had a dew like that before, Mr. Grendon," he said, his manner suggesting to Gregory that he had made this observation already this morning; Grubby never ventured to say anything original.

"Heavy as an autumn dew," said the farmer firmly, as if there had been an argument on that point.

Silence fell, broken only by a general munching and, from Grubby, a particular guzzling, as they all made their way through huge platefuls of stewed rabbit and dumplings.

"It weren't no ordinary dew, that I do know," Grubby said after a while.

"It stank of toadstools," Neckland said. "Or rotten pond water."

More munching.

"I have read of freak dews before," Gregory told the company. "And you hear of freak rains, when frogs fall out of the sky. I've even read of hailstones with live frogs and toads embedded in them."

"There's always something beyond belief as you have read of, Master Gregory," Neckland said. "But we happen to be talking about this here dew that fell right on this here farm this here morning. There weren't no frogs in it, either."

"Well it's gone now, so I can't see why you're worried about it," Nancy said.

"We ent ever had a dew like that before, Miss Nancy," Grubby said.

"I know I had to wash my washing again," Mrs. Grendon said. "I left it out all night and it stank really foul this morning."

"It may be something to do with the pond," Gregory said. "Some sort of freak of evaporation."

Neckland snorted. From his position at the top of the table, the farmer halted his shovelling operations to point a fork at Gregory.

"You may well be right there. Because I tell you what, that there dew only come down on our land and property. A yard the other side of the gate, the road was dry. Bone dry it was."

"Right you are there, master," Neckland agreed. "And while the West Field was dripping with the stuff, I saw for myself that the bracken over the hedge weren't wet at all. Ah, it's a rum go!"

"Say what you like, we ent ever had a dew like it," Grubby said. He appeared to be summing up the feeling of the company.

Leading off the parlour was a smaller room. Although it shared a massive fireplace with the parlour—for the whole house was built round and supported by this central brick stack—fires were rarely lit in the smaller room. This was the Best Room. Here Joseph Grendon occasionally retired to survey—with some severity and discomfort—his accounts. Otherwise the room was scarcely used.

After his meal, Grendon retired belching into the Best Room, and Gregory followed. This was where the farmer kept his modest store of books, his Carlyles, Ainsworths, Ruskins, and Lyttons, together with the copy of "The Time Machine" which Gregory had presented to him at Christmas, complete with a socially-inspired inscription. But the room was chiefly notable for the stuffed animals it contained, some encased in glass.

These animals had evidently been assaulted by a blunder in taxidermy, for they stood in poses that would in life have been beyond them, even supposing them to have been equipped with the extra joints and malformations indicated by their post-mortemnal shapes. They numbered among them creatures that bore chance resemblances to owls, dogs, foxes, cats, goats and calves. Only the stuffed fish carried more than a wan likeness to their living counterparts, and they had felt such an autumn after death that all their scales had been shed like leaves.

Gregory looked doubtfully at these monsters in which man's forming hand was more evident than God's. There were so many of them that some had overflowed into the parlour; in the Best Room, it was their multitude as well as their deformity that appalled. All the same, seeing how gloomily Grendon scowled over his ledger, Gregory said, thinking to cheer the older man, "You should practise some more taxidermy, Joseph."

"Ah." Without looking up.

"The hobby would be pleasant for you."

"Ah." Now he did look up. "You're young and you know only the good side of life. You're ignorant, Master Gregory, for all your university learning. You don't know how the qualities get whittled away from a man until by the time he's my age, there's only persistence left."

"That's not—"

"I shall never do another stuffing job. I ent got time! I ent really got time for nothing but this here old farm."

"But that's not true! You—"

"I say it is true, and I don't talk idle. I pass the time of day with you; I might even say I like you; but you don't *mean* nothing to me." He looked straight at Gregory as he spoke, and then slowly lowered his eyes with what might have been sadness. "Neither does Marjorie mean nothing to me now, though that was different afore we married. I got this here farm, you see, and I'm the farm and it is me."

He was stuck for words, and the beady eyes of the specimens ranged about him stared at him unhelpfully.

"Of course it's hard work," Gregory said.

"You don't understand, bor. Nobody do. This here land is no good. It's barren. Every year, it grows less and less. It ent got no more life than what these here animals have. So that means I am barren too—year by year, I got less substance."

He stood up suddenly, angry perhaps at himself.

"You better go home, Master Gregory."

"Joe, I'm terribly sorry. I wish I could help . . ."

"I know you mean kindly. You go home while the night's fine." He peered out into the blank yard. "Let's hope we don't get another stinking dewfall tonight."

~§~

The strange dew did not fall again. As a topic of conversation, it was limited, and even on the farm, where there was little new to talk about, it was forgotten in a few days. The February passed, being neither much worse nor much better than most Februaries, and ended in heavy rain-storms. March came, letting in a chilly spring over the land. The animals on the farm began to bring forth their young.

They brought them forth in amazing numbers, as if to overturn all the farmer's beliefs in the unproductiveness of his land.

"I never seen anything like it!" Grendon said to Gregory. Nor had Gregory seen the taciturn farmer so excited. He took the young man by the arm and marched him into the barn.

There lay Trix, the nannie goat. Against her flank huddled three little brown and white kids, while a fourth stood nearby, wobbling on its spindly legs.

"Four on 'em! Have you ever heard of a goat throwing off *four* kids? You better write to the papers in London about this, Gregory! But just you come down to the pigsties."

The squealing from the sties was louder than usual. As they marched down the path towards them, Gregory looked up at the great elms, their outlines dusted in green, and thought he detected something sinister in the noises, something hysterical that was perhaps matched by an element in Grendon's own bearing.

The Grendon pigs were mixed breeds, with a preponderance of Large Blacks. They usually gave litters of something like ten piglets. Now there was not a litter without fourteen in it; one enormous black sow had eighteen small pigs jostling about her. The noise was tremendous and, standing looking down on this swarming life, Gregory told himself that he was foolish to imagine anything uncanny in it; he knew so little about farm life.

" 'Course, they ent all going to live," the farmer said. "The old sows ent got enough dugs to feed that brood. But it's a record lot! I reckon you ought to write to that there 'Norwich Advertiser' about it."

Grubby lumbered up with two pails of feed, his great round face flushed as if in rapport with all the fecundity about him. "Never seen so many pigs," he said. "You ought to write to that there newspaper in Norwich about it, bor. There ent never been so many pigs."

Gregory had no chance to talk to Nancy on the subject. She and her mother had driven to town in the trap, for it was market day in Cottersall. After he had eaten with Grendon and the men—Mrs. Grendon had left them a cold lunch—Gregory went by himself to look about the farm, still with a deep and (he told himself) unreasoning sense of disturbance inside him.

A pale sunshine filled the afternoon. It could not penetrate far down into the water of the pond. But as Gregory stood by the horse trough staring at the expanse of water, he saw that it teemed with young tadpoles and frogs. He went closer. What he had regarded as a sheet of rather stagnant water was alive with small swimming things. As he looked, a great beetle surged out of the depths and seized a tadpole. The tadpoles were also providing food for two ducks that, with their young, were swimming by the reeds on the far side of the pond. And how many young did the ducks have? An armada of chicks was there, parading in and out of the rushes.

He walked round behind the barn and the cowsheds, where the ground was marshy, and across the bridge at the back of the machine house. The haystacks stood here, and behind them a wild stretch of hedge. As he went, Gregory watched for birds' nests. In the woodpile was a redstart's nest, in the marsh a meadow pipit's, in the hedge nests of Sparrows and blackbirds. All were piled high with eggs—far too many eggs.

For a minute, he stood uncertainly, then began to walk slowly back the way he had come. Nancy stood between two of the haystacks. He started in surprise at seeing her. He called her name, but she stood silent with her back to him.

Puzzled, he went forward and touched her on the shoulder. Her heads wung round. He saw her long teeth, the yellow curve of bone that had been her nose—but it was a sheep's head, falling backwards off a stick over which her old cloak had been draped. It lay on the ground by her bonnet, and he stared down at it in dismay, trying to quiet the leap of his heart. And at that moment, Neckland jumped out and caught him by the wrist.

"Ha, that gave thee a scare, my hearty, didn't it? I saw 'ee hanging round here. Why don't you get off out of here and never come back, bor? I warned you before, and I ent going to warn you again, do you hear? You leave Nancy alone, you and your books!"

Gregory wrenched his hand away.

"You did this, did you, you bloody ignorant lout? What do you think you are playing at here? How do you think Nancy or her mother would like it if they saw what you had done? Suppose I showed this to Farmer Grendon? Are you off your head, Neckland?"

"Don't you call me a ignorant lout or I'll knock off that there block of yours, that I will. I'm a-giving you a good scare, you cheeky tick, and I'm a-warning you to keep away from here."

"I don't want your warnings, and I refuse to heed them. It's up to the Grendons whether or not I come here, not you. You keep to your place and I'll keep to mine. If you try this sort of thing again, we shall come to blows."

Neckland looked less pugnacious than he had a moment ago. He said, cockily enough, "I ent afraid of you."

"Then I may give you cause to be," Gregory said. Turning on his heel, he walked swiftly away—alert at the same time for an attack from the rear. But Neckland slunk away as silently as he had come. Crossing the yard, Gregory went over to the stable and saddled Daisy. He swung himself up and rode away without bidding good-bye to anyone.

At one point, he looked over his shoulder. The farm crouched low and dark above the desolate land. Sky predominated over everything. The Earth seemed merely a strip of beach before a great tumbled ocean of air and light and space and things ill-defined; and from that ocean had come . . . he did not know, nor did he know how to find out, except by waiting and seeing if the strange vessel from the seas of space had brought evil or blessing.

Riding into Cottersall, he went straight to the market place. He saw the Grendon trap, with Nancy's little pony, Hetty, between the shafts, standing outside the grocer's shop. Mrs. Grendon and Nancy were just coming out. Jumping to the ground, Gregory led Daisy over to them and bid them good day.

"We are going to call on my friend Mrs. Edwards and her daughters," Mrs. Grendon said.

"I wondered, Mrs. Grendon, if you'd allow me to speak with Nancy privately, just for ten minutes."

Mrs. Grendon was well wrapped against the wind; she made a monumental figure as she looked at her daughter and considered.

"Seeing you talks to her at the farm, I don't see why you shouldn't talk to her here, but I don't want to cause no scandal, Master Gregory, and I'm sure I don't know where you can go to talk private. I mean, folks are more staid in their ways in Norfolk than they used to be in my young days, and I don't want any scandal. Can't it wait till you come to see us at the farm again?"

"If you would be so kind, Mrs. Grendon, I would be very obliged if I might speak privately with her now. My landlady, Mrs. Fenn, has a little downstairs parlour at the back of the shop, and I know she would let us speak there. It would be quite respectable."

"Drat respectable! Let people think what they will, I say." All the same, she stood for some time in meditation. Nancy remained by her mother with her eyes on the ground. Gregory looked at her and seemed to see her anew. Under her blue coat, fur-trimmed, she wore her orange-and-brown squared gingham dress; she had a bonnet on her head. Her complexion was pure and blemishless, her skin as firm and delicate as a plum, and her dark eyes were hidden under long lashes. Her lips were steady, pale, and clearly defined, with appealing tucks at each corner. He felt almost like a thief, stealing a sight of her beauty while she was not regarding him.

"I'm going on to Mrs. Edwards," Marjorie Grendon declared at last. "I don't care what you two do so long as you behave—but I shall, mind, if you aren't with me in a half-hour, Nancy, do you hear?"

"Yes, mother."

The baker's shop was in the next street. Gregory and Nancy walked there in silence. Gregory shut Daisy in the stable and they went together into the parlour through the back door. At this time of day, Mr. Fenn was resting upstairs and his wife looking after the shop, so the little room was empty.

Nancy sat upright in a chair and said, "Well, Gregory, what's all this about? Fancy dragging me off from my mother like that in the middle of town!"

"Nancy, don't be cross. I had to see you."

She pouted. "You come out to the old farm often enough and don't show any particular wish to see me there."

"That's nonsense. I always come to see you—lately in particular. Besides, you're more interested in Bert Neckland, aren't you?"

"Bert Neckland, indeed! Why should I be interested in him? Not that it's any of your business if I am."

"It is my business, Nancy. I love you, Nancy!"

He had not meant to blurt it out in quite that fashion, but now it was out, it was out, and he pressed home his disadvantage by crossing the room, kneeling at her feet, and taking her hands in his.

"I thought you only came out to the farm to see my father."

"It was like that at first, Nancy, but no more."

"You've got interested in farming now, haven't you? That's what you come for now, isn't it?"

"Well, I certainly am interested in the farm, but I want to talk about you. Nancy, darling Nancy, say that you like me just a little. Encourage me somewhat."

"You are a very fine gentleman, Gregory, and I feel very kind towards you, to be sure, but . . ."

"But?"

She gave him the benefit of her downcast eyes again.

"Your station in life is very different from mine, and besides—well, you don't *do* anything."

He was shocked into silence. With the natural egotism of youth, he had not seriously thought that she could have any firm objection to him; but in her words he suddenly saw the truth of his position, at least as it was revealed to her.

"Nancy—I—well, it's true I do not seem to you to be working at present. But I do a lot of reading and studying here, and I write to several important people in the world. And all the time I am coming to a great decision about what my career will be. I do assure you I am no loafer, if that's what you think."

"No, I don't think that. But Bert says you often spend a convivial evening in that there 'Wayfarer'."

"Oh, he does, does he? And what business is it of his if I do—or of yours, come to that? What a damned cheek!"

She stood up. "If you have nothing left to say but a lot of swearing, I'll be off to join my mother, if you don't mind."

"Oh, by Jove, I'm making a mess of this!" He caught her wrist. "Listen, my sweet thing. I ask you only this, that you try and look on me favourably. And also that you let me say a word about the farm. Some strange things are happening there, and I seriously don't like to think of you being there at night. All these young things being born, all these little pigs—it's uncanny!"

"I don't see what's uncanny no more than my father does. I know how hard he works, and he's done a good job rearing his animals, that's all. He's the best farmer round Cottersall by a long chalk."

"Oh, certainly. He's a wonderful man. But he didn't put seven or eight eggs into a hedge-sparrow's nest, did he? He didn't fill the pond with tadpoles and newts till it looks like a broth, did he? Something strange is happening on your farm this year, Nancy, and I want to protect you if I can."

The earnestness with which he spoke, coupled perhaps with his proximity and the ardent way he pressed her hand, went a good way toward mollifying Nancy.

"Dear Gregory, you don't know anything about farm life, I don't reckon, for all your books. But you're very sweet to be concerned."

"I shall always be concerned about you, Nancy, you beautiful creature."

"You'll make me blush!"

"Please do, for then you look even lovelier than usual!" He put an arm round her. When she looked up at him, he caught her up close to his chest and kissed her fervently.

She gasped and broke away, but not with too great haste.

"Oh, Gregory! Oh, Gregory! I must go to mother now!"

"Another kiss first! I can't let you go until I get another."

He took it, and stood by the door trembling with excitement as she left. "Come and see us again soon," she whispered.

"With dearest pleasure," he said. But the next visit held more dread than pleasure.

~§~

The big cart was standing in the yard full of squealing piglets when Gregory arrived. The farmer and Neckland were bustling about it. The farmer, shrugging into his overcoat, greeted Gregory cheerfully.

"I've a chance to make a good quick profit on these little chaps. Old sows can't feed them, but sucking pig fetches its price in Norwich, so Bert and me are going to drive over to Heigham and put them on the train."

"They're grown since I last saw them!"

"Ah, they put on over two pounds a day. Bert, we'd better get a net and spread over this lot, or they'll be diving out. They're that lively!"

The two men made their way over to the barn, clomping through the mud. Mud squelched behind Gregory. He turned.

In the muck between the stables and the cart, footprints appeared, two parallel tracks. They seemed to imprint themselves with no agency but their own. A cold flow of acute supernatural terror overcame Gregory, so that he could not move. The scene seemed to go grey and palsied as he watched the tracks come towards him.

The carthorse neighed uneasily, the prints reached the cart, the cart creaked, as if something had climbed aboard. The piglets squealed with terror. One dived clear over the wooden sides. Then a terrible silence fell.

Gregory still could not move. He heard an unaccountable sucking noise in the cart, but his eyes remained rooted on the muddy tracks. Those impressions were of something other than a man: something with dragging feet that were in outline something like a seal's flippers. Suddenly he found his voice, "Mr. Grendon!" he cried.

Only as the farmer and Bert came running from the barn with the net did Gregory dare look into the cart.

One last piglet, even as he looked, seemed to be deflating rapidly, like a rubber balloon collapsing. It went limp and lay silent among the other little empty bags of pig skin. The cart creaked. Something splashed heavily off across the farm-yard in the direction of the pond.

Grendon did not see. He had run to the cart and was staring like Gregory in dismay at the deflated corpses. Neckland stared too, and was the first to find his voice.

"Some sort of disease got 'em all, just like that! Must be one of them there new diseases from the continent of Europe!"

"It's no disease," Gregory said. He could hardly speak, for his mind had just registered the fact that there were no bones left in or amid the deflated pig bodies. "It's no disease—look, the pig that got away is still alive."

He pointed to the animal that had jumped from the cart. It had injured its leg in the process, and now lay in the ditch some feet away, panting. The farmer went over to it and lifted it out.

"It escaped the disease by jumping out," Neckland said. "Master, we better go and see how the rest of them is down in the sties."

"Ah, that we had," Grendon said. He handed the pig over to Gregory, his face set. "No good taking one alone to market. I'll get Grubby to unharness the horse. Meanwhile, perhaps you'd be good enough to take this little chap in to Marjorie. At least we can all eat a bit of roast pig for dinner tomorrow."

"Mr. Grendon, this is no disease. Have the veterinarian over from Heigham and let him examine these bodies."

"Don't you tell me how to run my farm, young man. I've got trouble enough."

Despite this rebuff, Gregory could not keep away. He had to see Nancy, and he had to see what occurred at the farm. The morning after the horrible thing happened to the pigs, he received a letter from his most admired correspondent, Mr. H. G. Wells, one paragraph of which read: "At bottom, I think I am neither optimist nor pessimist. I tend to believe both that we stand on the threshold of an epoch of magnificent progress—certainly such an epoch is within our grasp—and that we may have reached the *'fin du globe'* prophesied by our gloomier *fin de siecle* prophets. I am not at all surprised to hear that such a vast issue may be resolving itself on a remote farm near Cottersall, Norfolk—all unknown to anyone but the two of us. Do not think that I am in other than a state of terror, even when I cannot help exclaiming 'What a lark!'"

Too preoccupied to be as excited over such a letter as he would ordinarily have been, Gregory tucked it away in his jacket pocket and went to saddle up Daisy.

Before lunch, he stole a kiss from Nancy, and planted another on her over-heated left cheek as she stood by the vast range in the kitchen. Apart from that, there was little pleasure in the day. Grendon was reassured to find that none of the other piglets had fallen ill of the strange shrinking disease, but he remained alert against the possibility of it striking again. Meanwhile, another miracle had occurred. In the lower pasture, in a tumbledown shed, he had a cow that had given birth to four calves during the night. He did not expect the animal to live, but the calves were well enough, and being fed from a bottle by Nancy.

The farmer's face was dull, for he had been up all night with the labouring cow, and he sat down thankfully at the head of the table as the roast pig arrived on its platter.

It proved uneatable. In no time, they were all flinging down implements in disgust. The flesh had a bitter taste for which Neckland was the first to account.

"It's diseased!" he growled. "This here animal had the disease all the time. We didn't ought to eat this here meat or we may all be dead ourselves inside of a week."

They were forced to make a snack on cold salted beef and cheese and pickled onions, none of which Mrs. Grendon could face in her condition. She retreated upstairs in tears at the thought of the failure of her carefully prepared dish, and Nancy ran after her to comfort her.

After the dismal meal, Gregory spoke to Grendon.

"I have decided I must go to Norwich tomorrow for a few days, Mr. Grendon," he said. "You are in trouble here, I believe. Is there anything, any business, I can transact for you in the city? Can I find you a veterinary surgeon there?"

Grendon clapped his shoulder. "I know you mean well, and I thank 'ee for it, but you don't seem to realize that vetinaries cost a load of money and aren't always too helpful when they do come. Just suppose we had some young idiot here who told us all our stock is poisoned and we had to kill it? That would be a right look-out, eh?"

"Just because Gregory Rolles has plenty of money, he thinks everyone has," Neckland sneered.

The farmer turned furiously on him. "Who asked you to open your trap, bor? You keep your trap shut when there's a private conversation going on as don't concern you at all. Why aren't you out cleaning down the cowshed, since you ett all that last loaf?"

When Neckland had gone, Grendon said, "Bert's a good lad, but he don't like you at all. Now you was saying we had trouble here. But a farm is always trouble, Gregory—some years one sort of trouble, some years another. But I ent ever seen such fine growth as this year, and I tell 'ee straight I'm delighted, proper delighted. Some pigs have died, but that ent going to stop me doing my best by all the rest of 'em."

"But they will be unmarketable if they all taste like the one today."

Grendon smote his palm. "You're a real worrier. They may grow out of this bitter taste. And then again, if they don't, people have to buy them before they can taste them, don't they? I'm a poor man, Gregory, and when a bit of fortune comes my way, I can't afford to let it get away. In fact, I tell 'ee this, and even Bert don't know it yet, but tomorrow or the next day, I got Seeley the builder coming over here to put me up some more wood sheds down by Grubby's hut, to give the young animals more room."

"Good. Then let me do something for you, Joseph, in return for all your kindness to me. Let me bring a vet back from Norwich at my own expense, just to have a look round, nothing more."

"Blow me if you aren't stubborn as they come. I'm telling you, same as my dad used to say, if I finds any person on my land as I didn't ask here, I'm getting that there gun of mine down and I'm peppering him with buckshot, same as I did with them two old tramps last year. Fair enough, bor?"

"I suppose so."

"Then I must go and see to the cow. And stop worrying about what you don't understand."

After the farmer had gone, Gregory stood for a long time looking out of the window, waiting for Nancy to come down, worrying over the train of events. But the view was peaceful enough. He was the only person worrying, he reflected. Even the shrewd Mr. H. G. Wells, his correspond-dent, seemed to take his reports with a pinch of salt—he who of all men in England should sympathetically receive the news of the miraculous when it came to Earth, even if it failed to arrive in the form predicted in his recent novel, "The Wonderful Visit". Be that as it might, he was going to Norwich and the wise uncle who lived there as soon as he could—as soon, in fact, as he had kissed dear Nancy good-bye.

~§~

The wise uncle was indeed sympathetic. He was altogether a gentler man than his brother Edward, Gregory's father. He looked with sympathy at the plan of the farm that Gregory drew, he looked with sympathy at the sketch of the muddy footprint, he listened with sympathy to an account of what had happened. And at the end of it all he said, "Ghosts!"

When Gregory tried to argue with him, he said firmly, "My dear boy, I fear the modern marvels of our age have gone to your head. You know of such engineering structures as the cantilever bridge over the Firth of Forth, and you know as we all do of the colossal tower Eiffel has built in Paris—though if it stands ten years, I'll eat my hat. Now, no one will deny these things are marvellous, but they are things that rest on the ground. You're trying to tell me that engineers on this world or some other world might build a machine—a vehicle—that could fly from one heavenly body to another. Well then, *I'm* telling you that no engineer can do such a thing—and I'm not just saying that, but I'm quoting a law about it. There's a law about engineers not being able to sail in some sort of damned Eiffel Tower with engines from Mars to Earth, or the Sun to Earth, or wherever you will—a law to be read in your Bible and echoed in the pages of 'The Cornhill'. No, my boy, the modern age has gone to your head, but it's old-fashioned ghosts that have gone to your farm."

So Gregory walked into the city, and inspected the booksellers, and made several purchases, and never doubted for a moment that his uncle, though infinitely sympathetic, and adroit at slipping one a sovereign on parting, was sadly less wise than he had hitherto seemed: a discovery that seemed to reflect how Gregory had grown up and how times were changing.

But Norwich was a pleasant city and his uncle's house a comfortable house in which to stay, and he lingered there a week where he had meant to spend only three days at the most.

Consequently, conscience stirred in him when he again approached the Grendon farm along the rough road from Cottersall. He was surprised to see how the countryside had altered since he was last this way. New foliage gleamed everywhere, and even the heath looked a happier place. But as he came up to the farm, he saw how overgrown it was. Great ragged elder and towering cow parsley had shot up, so that at first they hid all the buildings. He fancied the farm had been spirited away until, spurring Daisy on, he saw the black mill emerge from behind a clump of nearby growth. The south meadows were deep in rank grass. Even the elms seemed much shaggier than before and loomed threateningly over the house.

As he clattered over the flat wooden bridge and through the open gate into the yard, Gregory noted huge hairy nettles craning out of the adjoining ditches. Birds fluttered everywhere. Yet the impression he received was one of death rather than life. A great quiet lay over the place, as if it were under a curse that eliminated noise and hope.

He realized this effect was partly because Lardie, the young bitch collie who had taken the place of Cuff, was not running up barking as she generally did with visitors. The yard was deserted. Even the customary fowls had gone. As he led Daisy into the stables, he saw a heavy piebald in the first stall and recognized it as Dr. Crouchorn's. His anxieties took more definite shape.

Since the stable was now full, he led his mare across to the stone trough by the pond and hitched her there before walking over to the house. The front door was open. Great ragged dandelions grew against the porch. The creeper, hitherto somewhat sparse, pressed into the lower windows. A movement in the rank grass caught his eye and he looked down, drawing back his riding boot. An enormous toad crouched under weed, the head of a still writhing grass snake in its mouth. The toad seemed to eye Gregory fixedly, as if trying to determine whether the man envied it its gluttony. Shuddering in disgust, he hurried into the house.

Three of Trix's kids, well grown now, strutted about the parlour, nibbling at the carpet and climbing into the massive armchairs, staring at a stuffed caricature of a goat that stood in its glass case by the window. Judging by the chaos in the room, they had been there some while, and had had a game on the table. But they possessed the room alone, and a quick glance into the kitchen revealed nobody there either.

Muffled sounds came from upstairs. The stairs curled round the massive chimneypiece, and were shut from the lower rooms by a latched door. Gregory had never been invited upstairs, but he did not hesitate. Throwing the door open, he started up the dark stairwell, and almost at once ran into a body.

Its softness told him that this was Nancy; she stood in the dark weeping. Even as he caught her and breathed her name, she broke from his grasp and ran from him up the stairs. He could hear the noises more clearly now, and the sound of crying—though at the moment he was not listening. Nancy ran to a door on the landing nearest to the top of the stairs, burst into the room beyond, and closed it. When Gregory tried the latch, he heard the bolt slide to on the other side.

"Nancy!" he called. "Don't hide from me! What is it? What's happening?"

She made no answer. As he stood there baffled against the door, the next door along the passage opened and Doctor Crouchorn emerged, clutching his little black bag. He was a tall, sombre man, with deep lines on his face that inspired such fear into his patients that a remarkable percentage of them did as he bid and recovered. Even here, he wore the top hat that, simply by remaining constantly in position, contributed to the doctor's fame in the neighbourhood.

"What's the trouble, Doctor Crouchorn?" Gregory asked, as the medical man shut the door behind him and started down the stairs. "Has the plague struck this house, or something equally terrible?"

"Plague, young man, plague? No, it is something much more unnatural than that."

He stared at Gregory unsmilingly, as if promising himself inwardly not to move a muscle again until Gregory asked the obvious.

"What did you call for, doctor?"

"The hour of Mrs. Grendon's confinement struck during the night," he said, still poised on the top step.

A wave of reliefs wept over Gregory. He had forgotten Nancy's mother! "She's had her baby? Was it a boy?"

The doctor nodded in slow motion. "She bore two boys, young man." He hesitated, and then a muscle in his face twitched and he said in a rush, "She also bore seven daughters. Nine children! And they all—they all live. It's impossible. Until I die—"

He could not finish. Tipping his hat, he hurried down the stairs, leaving Gregory to look fixedly at the wallpaper while his mind whirled as if it would convert itself into liquid. Nine children! Nine! It was as if she were no different from an animal in a sty. And the wallpaper pattern took on a diseased and livid look as if the house itself embodied sickness. The mewling cries from the bedroom seemed also the emblem of something inhuman calling its need.

He stood there in a daze, the sickly infant cries boring into him. From beyond the stone walls that oppressed him, he heard the noise of a horse ridden at hard gallop over the wooden bridge and down the track to Cottersall, dying with distance. From Nancy's room came no sound. Gregory guessed she had hidden herself from him for shame, and at last stirred himself into moving down the dark and curving stairwell. A stable cat scuttled out from under the bottom stair, a dozen baby tabbies in pursuit. The goats still held possession of the room. The fire was but scattered ashes in the hearth, and had not been tended since the crisis of the night.

"I bet you're surprised!"

Gregory swung round. From the kitchen came Grubby, clutching a wedge of bread and meat in his fist. He chewed with his mouth open, grinning at Gregory.

"Farmer Grendon be a proper ram!" he exclaimed. "Ent no other man in this county could beget himself nine kids at one go!"

"Where is the farmer?"

"I say there ent no other man in this here county—"

"Yes, I heard what you said. Where is the farmer?"

"Working, I suppose. But I tell 'ee, bor, there ent no other man—"

Leaving Grubby munching and talking, Gregory strode out into the yard. He came on Grendon round the corner of the house. The farmer had a pitchfork full of hay, which he was carrying over his shoulder into the cowsheds. Gregory stood in his way but he pushed past.

"I want to speak to you, Joseph."

"There's work to be done. Pity you can't see that."

"I want to speak about your wife."

Grendon made no reply. He worked like a demon, tossing the hay down, turning for more. In any case, it was difficult to talk. The cows and calves, closely confined, seemed to set up a perpetual uneasy noise of lowing and un-cow-like grunts. Gregory followed the farmer round to the hayrick, but the man walked like one possessed. His eyes seemed sunk into his head, his mouth was puckered until his lips were invisible. When Gregory laid a hand on his arm, he shook it off. Stabbing up another great load of hay, he swung back towards the sheds so violently that Gregory had to jump out of his way.

Gregory lost his temper. Following Grendon back into the cowshed, he swung the bottom of the two-part door shut, and bolted it on the outside. When Grendon came back, he did not budge.

"Joseph, what's got into you? Why are you suddenly so heartless? Surely your wife needs you by her?"

His eyes had a curious blind look as he turned them at Gregory. He held the pitchfork before him in both hands almost like a weapon as he said, "I been with her all night, bor, while she brought forth her increase."

"But now—"

"She got a nursing woman from Dereham Cottages with her now. I been with her all night. Now I got to see to the farm—things keep growing, you know."

"They're growing too much, Joseph. Stop and think—"

"I've no time for talking." Dropping the pitchfork, he elbowed Gregory out of the way, unbolted the door, and flung it open. Grasping Gregory firmly by the biceps of one arm, he began to propel him along to the vegetable beds down by South Meadows.

The early lettuce were gigantic here. Everything bristled out of the ground. Recklessly, Grendon ran among the lines of new green, pulling up fists full of young radish, carrots, spring onions, scattering them over his shoulder as fast as he plucked them from the ground.

"See, Gregory—all bigger than you ever seen 'em, and weeks early! The harvest is going to be a bumper. Look at the fields! Look at the orchard!" With wide gesture, he swept a hand towards the lines of trees, buried in the mounds of snow-and-pink of their blossom. "Whatever happens, we got to take advantage of it. It may not happen another year. Why—it's like a fairy story!"

He said no more. Turning, he seemed already to have forgotten Gregory. Eyes down at the ground that had suddenly achieved such abundance, he marched back towards the sheds, from whence now came the sound of Neckland washing out milk churns.

The spring sun was warm on Gregory's back. He told himself that everything looked normal. The farm was flourishing. From beyond the sties came shouts, distantly, and the sounds of men working, where the builder was preparing to erect more sheds. Perhaps, he told himself dully, he was worrying about nothing. Slowly, he walked towards the back of the house. There was nothing he could do here; it was time to return to Cottersall; but first he must see Nancy.

Nancy was in the kitchen. Neckland had brought her in a stoup of fresh milk, and she was supping it wearily from a ladle.

"Oh, Greg, I'm sorry I ran from you. I was so upset." She came to him, still holding the ladle but dangling her arms over his shoulders in a familiar way she had not used before. "Poor mother, I fear her mind is unhinged with—with bearing so many children. She's talking such strange stuff as I never heard before, and I do believe she fancies as she's a child again."

"Is it to be wondered at?" he said, smoothing her hair with his hand. "She'll be better once she's recovered from the shock."

They kissed each other, and after a minute she passed him a ladleful of milk. He drank and then spat it out in disgust.

"Ugh! What's got into the milk? Is Neckland trying to poison you or something? Have you tasted it? It's as bitter as sloes!"

She pulled a puzzled face. "I thought it tasted rather strange, but not unpleasant. Here, let me try again."

"No, it's too horrible. Some Sloan's Liniment must have got mixed in it."

Despite his warning, she put her lips to the metal spoon and sipped, then shook her head. "You're imagining things, Greg. It does taste a bit different, 'tis true, but there's nothing wrong with it."

"Sweetheart, it's horrible. I'm going to get your father to taste it, and see what he thinks."

"I wouldn't bother him just now, Greg, if I was you. You know how busy he is, and tired, and attending on mother during the night has put him back in his work. I will mention it to him at dinner—which I must now prepare. Them there goats have made such a muck in here, not to mention that Grubby! You'll stay to take a bite with us, I hope?"

"No, Nancy, I'm off now. I have a letter awaiting me that I must answer; it arrived when I was in Norwich."

She bit her lip and snapped her fingers. "There, how terrible awful you'll think me! I never asked you how you enjoyed yourself in the big city! It must be wonderful to be a man of leisure, never with no work to do nor meals to prepare."

"You still hold that against me! Listen, my lovely Nancy, this letter is from a Dr. Hudson-Ward, an old acquaintance of my father's. He is head-master of a school in Gloucester, and he wishes me to join the staff there as teacher on most favourable terms. So you see I may not be idle much longer!"

Laughing, she clung to him. "That's wonderful, my darling! What a handsome schoolmaster you will make. But Gloucester—that's over the other side of the country. I suppose we shan't be seeing you again once you get there."

"Nothing's settled yet, Nancy."

"You'll be gone in a week and we shan't never see you again. Once you get to that there old school, you will never think of your Nancy no more."

He cupped her face in his hands. "Are you my Nancy? Do you care for me?"

Her eyelashes came over her dark eyes. "Greg, things are so muddled here—I mean—yes, I do care, I dread to think I'd not see you again."

Recalling her saying that, he rode away a quarter of an hour later very content at heart—and entirely neglectful of the dangers to which he left her exposed.

~§~

Rain fell lightly as Gregory Rolles made his way that evening to the "Wayfarer" inn. His friend Bruce Fox was already there, ensconced in one of the snug seats by the ingle nook.

On this occasion, Fox was more interested in purveying details of his sister's forthcoming wedding than in listening to what Gregory had to tell, and since some of his future brother-in-law's friends soon arrived, and had to buy and be bought libation, the evening became a merry and thoughtless one. And in a short while, the ale having its good effect, Gregory also forgot what he wanted to say and began whole-heartedly to enjoy the company.

Next morning, he awoke with a heavy head and in a dismal state of mind. Mrs. Fenn, clattering round the room lighting his fire, did not improve matters; he could tell from her demeanour that he had come home late and made a noise on the stairs. But the Mrs. Fenns of this world, he reflected irritably, were born to suffer such indignities, and the more regularly the better. He told himself this thought was not in accord with his socialist principles, but they felt as sluggish as his liver this morning.

The day was too wet for him to go out and take exercise. He sat moodily in a chair by the window, delaying an answer to Dr. Hudson-Ward, the headmaster. Lethargically, he turned to a small leather-bound volume on serpents that he had acquired in Norwich a few days earlier. After a while, a passage caught his particular attention:

"Most serpents of the venomous variety, with the exception of the opisthoglyphs, release their victims from their fangs after striking. The victims die in some cases in but a few seconds while in other cases the onset of moribundity may be delayed by hours or days. The saliva of some serpents contains not only venom but a special digestive virtue. The deadly Coral Snake of Brazil, though attaining no more than a foot in length, has this virtue in abundance. Accordingly, when it bites an animal or a human being, the victim not only dies in profound agony in a matter of seconds, but his interior parts are then dissolved, so that even the bones become no more than jelly. Then may the little serpent suck all of the victim out as a kind of soup or broth from the original wound in its skin, which latter alone remains intact."

For a long while, Gregory sat where he was in the window, with the book open in his lap, thinking about the Grendon farm, and about Nancy. He reproached himself for having done so little for his friends there, and gradually resolved on a plan of action the next time he rode out; but his visit was to be delayed for some days: the wet weather had set in with more determination than the end of April and the beginning of May generally allowed.

Despite that, he heard news of Grendon on the second day of rain as he took his supper with the Fenns downstairs. That was market day, and then the baker's wife said, "That there idiot labourer on Joe Grendon's place is going to get himself locked up if he ent careful. Did you hear about him today, Master Gregory?"

"What did he do, Mrs. Fenn?"

"Why, what didn't he do? Delivered the milk round as usual, so I hear, and nobody wouldn't buy none, seeing as it has been off for the past I-don't-know-how-long. So Grubby swore terrible and vowed he had the best milk in town, and took a great sup at the churn to prove it. And then them two Betts boys started throwing stones, and of course that set Grubby off! He caught one of 'em and ducked his head in the milk, and then flung the bucket right smack through his father's nice glass window. Imagine that! So out come old man Betts and his great big missus, and they lambasts old Grubby with beansticks till he drives off cursing and vowing he'll never sell nobody good milk no more!"

The baker laughed. "That would have been a sight worth seeing of! I reckon they all gone mad out at Joe's place. Old Seeley the builder come in yesterday morning, and he reckon Joe's doing better this year than what he ever did, while everyone else round here is having a thin time. According to Seeley, Marjorie Grendon had quins, but you know old Seeley is a bit of a joker. Dr. Crouchom would have let on if she'd had quins, I reckon."

"Doctor Crouchom was weeping drunk last night, from all accounts."

"So I hear. That ent like him, be it?"

"First time it was ever known, though they do say he liked his bottle when he was a youngster."

Listening to the gossip as it shuttled back and forth between husband and wife, Gregory found little appetite for his stew. Moodily, he returned to his room and tried to concentrate on a letter to the worthy Dr. Hudson-Ward in the county of Gloucestershire. He knew he should take the job, indeed he felt inclined to do so; but first he knew he had to see Nancy safe. The indecision he felt caused him to delay answering the doctor until the next day, when he feebly wrote that he would be glad to accept the post offered at the price offered, but begged to have a week to think about it. When he took the letter down to the post woman in "The Three Poachers", the rain was still falling.

~§~

One morning, the rains were suddenly vanished, the blue and wide East Anglian skies were back, and Gregory saddled up Daisy and rode out along the miry track he had so often taken. As he arrived at the farm, Grubby and Neckland were at work in the ditch, unblocking it with shovels. He saluted them and rode in. As he was about to put the mare into the stables, he saw Grendon and Nancy standing on the patch of waste ground under the windowless east side of the house. He went slowly to join them, noting as he walked how dry the ground was here, as if no rain had fallen in a fortnight. But this observation was drowned in shock as he saw the nine little crosses Grendon was sticking into nine freshly-turned mounds of earth.

Nancy stood weeping. They both looked up as Gregory approached, but Grendon went stubbornly on with his task.

"Oh, Nancy, Joseph, I'm so sorry about this!" Gregory exclaimed. "To think that they've all—but where's the parson? Where's the parson,

Joseph? Why are *you* burying them, without a proper service or any-thing?"

"I told father, but he took no heed!" Nancy exclaimed.

Grendon had reached the last grave. He seized the last crude wooden cross, lifted it above his head and stabbed it down into the ground as if he would pierce the heart of what lay under it. Only then did he straighten and speak.

"We don't need a parson here. I've no time to waste with parsons. I have work to do if you ent."

"But these are your children, Joseph! What has got into you?"

"They are part of the farm now, as they always was." He turned, rolling his shirt sleeves further up his brawny arms, and strode off in the direction of the ditching activities.

Gregory took Nancy in his arms and looked at her tear-stained face. "What a time you must have been having these last few days!"

"I-I thought you'd gone to Gloucester, Greg! Why didn't you come? Every day I waited for you to come!"

"It was so wet and flooded."

"It's been lovely weather since you were last here. Look how everything has grown!"

"It poured with rain every single day in Cottersall."

"Well, I never! That explains why there is so much water flowing in the Oast and in the ditches. But we've had only a few light showers."

"Nancy, tell me, how did these poor little mites die?"

"I'd rather not say, if you don't mind."

"Why didn't your father get in Parson Landson? How could he be so lacking in feeling?"

"Because he didn't want anyone from the outside world to know. That's why he's sent the builders away again. You see—oh, I must tell you, my dear—it's mother. She has gone completely off her head, completely! It was the evening before last, when she took her first turn outside the back door."

"You don't mean to say she—"

"Ow, Greg, you're hurting my arms! She—she crept upstairs when we weren't noticing and she—she stifled each of the babies in turn, Greg, under the best goose-feather pillow."

He could feel the colour leaving his cheeks. Solicitously, she led him to the back of the house. They sat together on the orchard railings while he digested the words in silence.

"How is your mother now, Nancy?"

"She's silent. Father had to bar her in her room for safety. Last night she screamed a lot. But this morning she's quiet."

He looked dazedly about him. The appearance of everything was speckled, as if the return of his blood to his head had somehow infected it with a rash. The blossom had gone almost entirely from the fruit trees in the orchard and already the embryo apples showed signs of swelling. Nearby, broad beans bowed under enormous pods. Seeing his glance, Nancy dipped into her apron pocket and produced a bunch of shining crimson radishes as big as tangerines.

"Have one of these. They're crisp and wet and hot, just as they should be."

Indifferently, he accepted and bit the tempting globe. At once he had to spit the portion out. There again was that vile bitter flavour!

"Oh, but they're lovely!" Nancy protested.

"Not even 'rather strange' now-simply 'lovely'? Nancy, don't you see, something uncanny and awful is taking place here. I'm sorry, but I can't see otherwise. You and your father should leave here at once."

"*Leave* here, Greg? Just because you don't like the taste of these lovely radishes? How can we leave here? Where should we go? See this here house? My granddad died here, and his father before him. It's our *place*. We can't just up and off, not even after this bit of trouble. Try another radish."

"For heaven's sake, Nancy, they taste as if the flavour was intended for creatures with a palate completely different from ours . . . Oh . . ." He stared at her. "And perhaps they are. Nancy, I tell you—"

He broke off, sliding from the railing. Neckland had come up from one side, still plastered in mud from his work in the ditch, his collarless shirt flapping open. In his hand, he grasped an ancient and military-looking pistol.

"I'll fire this if you come nearer," he said. "It goes okey, never worry, and it's loaded, Master Gregory. Now you're a-going to listen to me!"

"Bert, put that thing away!" Nancy exclaimed. She moved forward to him, but Gregory pulled her back and stood before her.

"Don't be a bloody idiot, Neckland. Put it away!"

"I'll shoot you, bor, I'll shoot you, I swear, if you mucks about." His eyes were glaring, and the look on his dark face left no doubt that he meant what he said. "You're going to swear to me that you're going to clear off of this farm on that nag of yours and never come back again."

"I'm going straight to tell my father, Bert," Nancy warned.

The pistol twitched.

"If you move, Nancy, I warn you I'll shoot this fine chap of yours in the leg. Besides, your father don't care about Master Gregory any more—he's got better things to worry him."

"Like finding out what's happening here?" Gregory said. "Listen, Neckland, we're all in trouble. This farm is being run by a group of nasty little monsters. You can't see them because they're invisible—"

The gun exploded. As he spoke, Nancy had attempted to run off. Without hesitating, Neckland fired down at Gregory's knees. Gregory felt the shot pluck his trouser leg and knew himself unharmed. With the knowledge came rage. He flung himself at Neckland and hit him hard over the heart. Falling back, Neckland dropped the pistol and swung his fist wildly. Gregory struck him again. As he did so, the other grabbed him and they began furiously hitting each other. When Gregory broke free, Neckland grappled with him again. There was more pummelling of ribs.

"Let me go, you swine!" Gregory shouted. He hooked his foot behind Neckland's ankle, and they both rolled over onto the grass. At this point, a sort of flood bank had been raised long ago between the house and the low-lying orchard. Down this the two men rolled, fetching up sharply against the stone wall of the kitchen. Neckland got the worst of it, catching his head on the corner, and lay there stunned. Gregory found himself looking at two feet encased in ludicrous stockings. Slowly, he rose to his feet, and confronted Mrs. Grendon at less than a yard's distance. She was smiling.

He stood there, and gradually straightened his back, looking at her anxiously.

"So there you are, Jackie, my Jackalums," she said. The smile was wider now and less like a smile. "I wanted to talk to you. You are the one who knows about the things that walk on the lines, aren't you?"

"I don't understand, Mrs. Grendon."

"Don't call me that there daft old name, sonnie. You know all about the little grey things that aren't supposed to be there, don't you?"

"Oh, those . . . Suppose I said I did know?"

"The other naughty children will pretend they don't know what I mean, but you know, don't you? You know about the little grey things."

The sweat stood out on his brow. She had moved nearer. She stood close, staring into his eyes, not touching him; but he was acutely conscious that she could touch him at any moment. From the corner of his eye, he saw Neckland stir and crawl away from the house, but there were other things to occupy him.

"These little grey things," he said. "Did you save the nine babies from them?"

"They grey things wanted to kiss them, you see, but I couldn't let them. I was clever. I hid them under the goose-feather pillow and now even *I* can't find them!" She began to laugh, making a horrible low whirring sound in her throat.

"They're small and grey and wet, aren't they?" Gregory said sharply. "They've got big feet, webbed like frogs, but they're heavy and short, aren't they, and they have fangs like a snake, haven't they?"

She looked doubtful. Then her eye seemed to catch a movement. She looked fixedly to one side. "Here come one now, the female one," she said.

Gregory turned to look where she did. Nothing was visible. His mouth was dry. "How many are there, Mrs. Grendon?"

Then he saw the short grass stir, flatten, and raise near at hand, and let out a cry of alarm. Wrenching off his riding boot, he swung it in an arc, low above the ground. It struck something concealed in thin air. Almost at once, he received a terrific kick in the thigh, and fell backwards. Despite the hurt, fear made him jump up almost at once.

Mrs. Grendon was changing. Her mouth collapsed as if it would run off one corner of her face. Her head sagged to one side. Her shoulders fell. A deep crimson blush momentarily suffused her features, then drained, and as it drained she dwindled like a deflating rubber balloon. Gregory sank to his knees, whimpering, buried his face in his hands and pressed his hands to the grass. Darkness overcame him.

His senses must have left him only for a moment. When he pulled himself up again, the almost empty bag of woman's clothes was still settling slowly on the ground.

"Joseph! Joseph!" he yelled. Nancy had fled. In a distracted mixture of panic and fury, he dragged his boot on again and rushed round the house towards the cowsheds.

Neckland stood half-way between barn and mill, rubbing his skull. In his rattled state, the sight of Gregory apparently in full pursuit made him run away.

"Neckland!" Gregory shouted. He ran like mad for the other. Neckland bolted for the mill, jumped inside, tried to pull the door to, lost his nerve, and ran up the wooden stairs. Gregory bellowed after him.

The pursuit took them right up to the top of the mill. Neckland had lost too much wit even to kick over the bolt of the trapdoor. Gregory burst it up and climbed out panting. Thoroughly cowed, Neckland backed towards the opening until he was almost out on the little platform above the sails.

"You'll fall out, you idiot," Gregory warned. "Listen, Neckland, you have no reason to fear me. I want no enmity between us. There's a bigger enemy we must fight. Look!"

He came towards the low door and looked down at the dark surface of the pond. Neckland grabbed the overhead pulley for security and said nothing.

"Look down at the pond," Gregory said. "That's where the Aurigans live. My God—Bert, look, there one goes!"

The urgency in his voice made the farm hand look down where he pointed. Together, the two men watched as a depression slid over the black water; an overlapping chain of ripples swung back from it. At approximately the middle of the pond, the depression became a commotion. A small whirlpool formed and died, and the ripples began to settle.

"There's your ghost, Bert," Gregory gasped. "That must have been the one that got poor Mrs. Grendon. Now do you believe?"

"I never heard of a ghost as lived under water," Neckland gasped.

"A ghost never harmed anyone—we've already had a sample of what these terrifying things can do. Come on, Bert, shake hands, understand I bear you no hard feelings. Oh, come on, man! I know how you feel about Nancy, but she must be free to make her own choice in life."

They shook hands and grinned rather foolishly at each other.

"We better go and tell the farmer what we seen," Neckland said. "I reckon that thing done what happened to Lardie last evening."

"Lardie? What's happened to her? I thought I hadn't seen her today."

"Same as happened to the little pigs. I found her just inside the barn. Just her coat was left, that's all. No insides! Like she'd been sucked dry."

"Let's go, Bert."

~§~

It took Gregory twenty minutes to summon the council of war on which he had set his mind. The party gathered in the farmhouse, in the parlour. By this time, Nancy had somewhat recovered from the shock of her mother's death, and sat in an armchair with a shawl about her shoulders. Her father stood nearby with his arms folded, looking impatient, while Bert Neckland lounged by the door. Only Grubby was not present. He had been told to get on with the ditching.

"I'm going to have another attempt to convince you all that you are in very grave danger," Gregory said. "You won't see it for yourselves, so I—"

He paused. There was a dragging noise on the landing upstairs, a board creaked.

"Who the devil's up there?" Grendon growled. He made towards the stairwell.

"Don't go, father!" Nancy screamed, but her father flung open the door and made his way up. Gregory bit his lip. The Aurigans had never ventured into the house before.

In a moment, Grendon returned with a monstrous piglet in his arms.

"Keep the confounded animals out of the house, Nancy," he said, pushing the creature squealing out of the front door.

The interruption made Gregory realize how his nerves still jangled. He set his back to the sawdust-filled parody of a goat that watched from its case, and spoke quickly.

"The situation is that we're all animals together at present. Do you remember that strange meteor that fell out of the sky last winter, Joseph? And do you remember that ill-smelling dew early in the spring. They were not unconnected, and they are connected with all that's happening now. That meteor was a space machine of some sort, I firmly believe, and it brought in it a kind of life that—that is not so much hostile to terrestrial life as *indifferent to its quality*. The creatures from that machine—I call them Aurigans—spread the dew over the farm. It was a growth accelerator, a manure or fertilizer, that speeds growth in plants and animals."

"So much better for us!" Grendon said.

"But it's not better. The things grow wildly, yes, but the taste is altered to suit the palates of those things out there. You've seen what happened. You can't sell anything. People won't touch your eggs or milk or meat—they taste too foul."

"But that's a lot of nonsense. We'll sell in Norwich. Our produce is better than it ever was. We eat it, don't we?"

"Yes, Joseph, *you* eat it. But anyone who eats at your table is doomed. Don't you understand—you are all 'fertilized' just as surely as the pigs and chickens. Your place has been turned into a superfarm, and you are all meat to the Aurigans."

That set a silence in the room, until Nancy said in a small voice, "You

don't believe such a terrible thing."

"I suppose these unseen creatures told you all this?" Grendon said truculently.

"Judge by the evidence, as I do. Your wife—I must be brutal, Joseph—your wife was eaten, like the dog and the pigs. As everything else will be in time. The Aurigans aren't even cannibals. They aren't like us. They don't care whether we have souls or intelligences, any more than we really care whether the bullocks have."

"No one's going to eat me," Neckland said, looking decidedly white about the gills.

"How can you stop them? They're invisible, and I think they can strike like snakes. They're aquatic and I think they may be only two feet tall. How can you protect yourself?" He turned to the farmer. "Joseph, the danger is very great, and not only to us here. At first, they may have offered us no harm while they got the measure of us—otherwise I'd have died in your rowing boat. Now there's no longer doubt of their hostile intent. I beg you to let me go to Heigham and telephone to the chief of police in Norwich, or at least to the local militia, to get them to come and help us."

The farmer shook his head slowly, and pointed a finger at Gregory.

"You soon forgot them talks we had, bor, all about the coming age of socialism and how the powers of the state was going to wither away. Directly we get a bit of trouble, you want to call in the authorities. There's no harm here a few savage dogs like my old Cuff can't handle, and I don't say as I ent going to get a couple of dogs, but you'm a fule if you reckon I'm getting the authorities down here. Fine old socialist you turn out to be!"

"You have no room to talk about that!" Gregory exclaimed.

"Why didn't you let Grubby come here? If you were a socialist, you'd treat the men as you treat yourself. Instead, you leave him out in the ditch. I wanted him to hear this discussion."

The farmer leant threateningly across the table at him.

"Oh, you did, did you? Since when was this your farm? And Grubby can come and go as he likes when it's his, so put that in your pipe and smoke it, bor! Who do you just think you are?" He moved closer to Gregory, apparently happy to work off his fears as anger. "You'm trying to scare us all off this here little old bit of ground, ent you? Well, the Grendons ent a scaring sort, see! Now I'll tell you something. See that rifle there on the wall? That be loaded. And if you ent off this farm by midday, that rifle ont be on that wall no more. It'll be here, bor, right here in my two hands, and I'll be letting you have it right where you'll feel it most."

"You can't do that, father," Nancy said. "You know Gregory is a friend of ours."

"For God's sake, Joseph," Gregory said, "see where your enemy lies. Bert, tell Mr. Grendon what we saw on the pond, go on."

Neckland was far from keen to be dragged into this argument. He scratched his head, drew a red-and-white spotted kerchief from round his neck to wipe his face, and muttered, "We saw a sort of ripple on the water, but I didn't see nothing really, Master Gregory. I mean, it could have been the wind, couldn't it?"

"Now you be warned, Gregory," the farmer repeated. "You be off my land by noon by the sun, and that mare of yours, or I ont answer for it." He marched out into the pale sunshine, and Neckland followed.

Nancy and Gregory stood staring at each other. He took her hands, and they were cold.

"You believe what I was saying, Nancy?"

"Is that why the food did at one point taste bad to us, and then soon tasted well enough again?"

"It can only have been that at that time your systems were not fully adjusted to the poison. Now they are. You're being fed up, Nancy, just like the livestock—I'm sure of it! I fear for you, darling love, I fear so much. What are we to do? Come back to Cottersall with me! Mrs. Fenn has another fine little drawing-room upstairs that I'm sure she would rent."

"Now you're talking nonsense, Greg! How can I? What would people say? No, you go away for now and let the tempest of father's wrath abate, and if you could come back tomorrow, you will find he will be milder for sure, because I plan to wait on him tonight and talk to him about you. Why, he's half daft with grief and doesn't know what he says."

"All right, my darling. But stay inside as much as you can. The Aurigans have not come indoors yet, as far as we know, and it may be safer here. And lock all the doors and put the shutters over the windows before you go to bed. And get your father to take that rifle of his upstairs with him."

~§~

The evenings were lengthening with confidence towards summer now, and Bruce Fox arrived home before sunset. As he jumped from his bicycle this evening, he found his friend Gregory impatiently awaiting him.

They went indoors together, and while Fox ate a large tea, Gregory told him what had been happening at the farm that day.

"You're in trouble," Fox said. "Look, tomorrow's Sunday. I'll skip church and come out with you. You need help."

"Joseph may shoot me. He'll be certain to if I bring along a stranger. You can help me tonight by telling me where I can purchase a young dog straight away to protect Nancy."

"Nonsense, I'm coming with you. I can't bear hearing all this at second hand anyhow. We'll pick up a pup in any event—the blacksmith has a litter to be rid of. Have you got any plan of action?"

"Plan? No, not really."

"You must have a plan. Grendon doesn't scare too easily, does he?"

"I imagine he's scared well enough. Nancy says he's scared. He just isn't imaginative enough to see what he can do but carry on working as hard as possible."

"Look, I know these farmers. They won't believe anything till you rub their noses in it. What we must do is *show* him an Aurigan."

"Oh, splendid, Bruce? And how do you catch one?"

"You trap one."

"Don't forget they're invisible—hey, Bruce, yes, by Jove, you're right! I've the very idea! Look, we've nothing more to worry about if we can trap one. We can trap the lot, however many there are, and we can kill the little horrors when we have trapped them."

Fox grinned over the top of a chunk of cherry cake. "We're agreed, I suppose, that these Aurigans aren't socialist utopians any longer?"

It helped a great deal, Gregory thought, to be able to visualize roughly what the alien life form looked like. The volume on serpents had been a happy find, for not only did it give an idea of how the Aurigans must be able to digest their prey so rapidly—"a kind of soup or broth"—but presumably it gave a clue to their appearance. To live in a space machine, they would probably be fairly small, and they seemed to be semi-aquatic. It all went to make up a picture of a strange being: skin perhaps scaled like a fish, great flipper feet like a frog, barrel-like diminutive stature, and a tiny head with two great fangs in the jaw. There was no doubt but that the invisibility cloaked a really ugly-looking dwarf!

As the macabre image passed through his head, Gregory and Bruce Fox were preparing their trap. Fortunately, Grendon had offered no resistance to their entering the farm; Nancy had evidently spoken to good effect. And he had suffered another shock. Five fowls had been reduced to little but feathers and skin that morning almost before his eyes, and he was as a result sullen and indifferent to what went on. Now he was out in a distant field, working, and the two young men were allowed to carry out their plans unmolested—though not without an occasional anxious glance at the pond—while a worried Nancy looked on from the farmhouse window.

She had with her a sturdy young mongrel dog of eight months, which Gregory and Bruce had brought along, called Gyp. Grendon had obtained two ferocious hounds from a distant neighbour. These wide-mouthed brutes were secured on long running chains that enabled them to patrol from the horse trough by the pond, down the west side of the house, almost to the elms and the bridge leading over to West Field. They barked stridently most of the time and seemed to cause a general unease among the other animals, all of which gave voice restlessly this forenoon.

The dogs would be a difficulty, Nancy had said, for they refused to touch any of the food the farm could provide. It was hoped they would take it when they became hungry enough.

Grendon had planted a great board by the farm gate and on the board had painted a notice telling everyone to keep away.

Armed with pitchforks, the two young men carried flour sacks out from the mill and placed them at strategic positions across the yard as far as the gate. Gregory went to the cowsheds and led out one of the calves there on a length of binder twine under the very teeth of the barking dogs—he only hoped they would prove as hostile to the Aurigans as they seemed to be to human life.

As he was pulling the calf across the yard, Grubby appeared.

"You'd better stay away from us, Grubby. We're trying to trap one of the ghosts."

"Master, if I catch one, I shall strangle him, straight I will."

"A pitchfork is a better weapon. These ghosts are dangerous little beasts at close quarters."

"I'm strong, bor, I tell 'ee! I'd strangle un!"

To prove his point, Grubby rolled his striped and tattered sleeve even further up his arm and exposed to Gregory and Fox his enormous biceps. At the same time, he wagged his great heavy head and lolled his tongue out of his mouth, perhaps to demonstrate some of the effects of strangulation.

"It's a very fine arm," Gregory agreed. "But, look, Grubby, we have a better idea. We are going to do this ghost to death with pitchforks; if you want to join in, you'd better get a spare one from the stable."

Grubby looked at him with a sly—shy expression and stroked his throat. "I'd be better at strangling, bor. I've always wanted to strangle someone."

"Why should you want to do that, Grubby?"

The labourer lowered his voice. "I always wanted to see how difficult it would be. I'm strong, you see. I got my strength up as a lad doing some of this here strangling—but never men, you know, just cattle."

Backing away a pace, Gregory said, "This time, Grubby, it's pitchforks for us." To settle the issue, he went into the stables, got a pitchfork, and returned to thrust it into Grubby's hand.

"Let's get on with it," Fox said.

They were all ready to start. Fox and Grubby crouched down in the ditch on either side of the gate, weapons at the ready. Gregory emptied one of the bags of flour over the yard in a patch just before the gate, so that anyone leaving the farm would have to walk through it. Then he led the calf towards the pond.

The young animal set up an uneasy mooing, and most of the beasts nearby seemed to answer. The chickens and hens scattered about the yard in the pale sunshine as if demented. Gregory felt the sweat trickle down his back, although his skin was cold with the chemistries of suspense. With a slap on its rump, he forced the calf into the water of the pond. It stood there unhappily, until he led it out again and slowly back across the yard, past the mill and the grain store on his right, past Mrs. Grendon's neglected flowerbed on his left, towards the gate where his allies waited. And for all his determination not to do so, he could not stop himself looking backwards at the leaden surface of the pond to see if anything followed him. He led the calf through the gate and stopped. No tracks but his and the calf's showed in the strewn flour.

"Try it again," Fox advised. "Perhaps they are taking a nap down there."

Gregory went through the routine again, and a third and fourth time, on each occasion smoothing the flour after he had been through it. Each time, he saw Nancy watching helplessly from the house. Each time, he felt a little more sick with tension.

Yet when it happened, it took him by surprise. He had got the calf to the gate for a fifth time when Fox's shout joined the chorus of animal noises. The pond had shown no special ripple, so the Aurigan had come from some dark-purposed prowl of the farm—suddenly, its finned footsteps were marking the flour.

Yelling with excitement, Gregory dropped the rope that led the calf and ducked to one side. Seizing up an opened bag of flour by the gatepost, he flung its contents before the advancing figure.

The bomb of flour exploded all over the Aurigan. Now it was revealed in chalky outline. Despite himself, Gregory found himself screaming in sheer fright as the ghastliness was revealed in whirling white. It was especially the size that frightened: this dread thing, remote from human form, was too big for earthly nature—ten feet high, perhaps twelve! Invincible, and horribly quick, it came rushing at him with unnumbered arms striking out towards him.

~§~

Next morning, Dr. Crouchorn and his silk hat appeared at Gregory's bedside, thanked Mrs. Fenn for some hot water, and dressed Gregory's leg wound.

"You got off lightly, considering," the old man said. "But if you will take a piece of advice from me, Mr. Rolles, you will cease to visit the Grendon farm. It's an evil place and you'll come to no good there."

Gregory nodded. He had told the doctor nothing, except that Grendon had run up and shot him in the leg; which was true enough, but that it omitted most of the story.

"When will I be up again, Doctor?"

"Oh, young flesh heals soon enough, or undertakers would be rich men and doctors paupers. A few days should see you right as rain. But I'll be visiting you again tomorrow, until when you are to stay flat on your back and keep that leg motionless."

"I understand."

The doctor made a ferocious face. "You understand, but will you take heed? I'm warning you, if you take one step on that leg, it will turn purple and fall off." He nodded slowly and emphatically, and the lines on his face deepened to such a great extent that anyone familiar with the eccentriccities of his physiognomy would be inclined to estimate that he was smiling.

"I suppose I may write a letter, doctor?"

"I suppose you may, young man."

Directly Dr. Crouchorn had gone, Gregory took pen and paper and addressed some urgent lines to Nancy. They told her that he loved her very much and could not bear to think of her remaining on the farm; that he could not get to see her for a few days because of his leg wound; and that she must immediately come away on Hetty with a bag full of her things and stay at "The Wayfarer", where there was a capital room for which he would pay. That if she thought anything of him, she must put the simple plan into action this very day, and send him word round from the inn when she was established there.

With some satisfaction, Gregory read this through twice, signed it and added kisses, and summoned Mrs. Fenn with the aid of a small bell she had provided for that purpose.

He told her that the delivery of the letter was a matter of extreme urgency. He would entrust it to Tommy, the baker's boy, to deliver when his morning round was over, and would give him a shilling for his efforts. Mrs. Fenn was not enthusiastic about this, but with a little flattery was persuaded to speak to Tommy; she left the bedroom clutching both letter and shilling.

At once, Gregory began a letter, this one to Mr. H. G. Wells. It was some while since he had last addressed his correspondent, and so he had to make a somewhat lengthy report; but eventually he came to the events of the previous day.

"So horrified was I by the sight of the Aurigan (he wrote), that I stood where I was, unable to move, while the flour blew about us. And how can I now convey to you—who are perhaps the most interested person in this vital subject in all the British Isles—what the monster looked like, outlined in white? My impressions were, of course, both brief and indefinite, but the main handicap is that there is nothing on Earth to liken this weird being to!

"It appeared, I suppose, most like some horrendous goose, but the neck must be imagined as almost as thick as the body—indeed, it was almost all body, or all neck, whichever way you look at it. And on top of this neck was no head but a terrible array of various sorts of arms, a nest of writhing cilia, antennae, and whips, for all the world as if an octopus were entangled with a Portuguese Man-o'-war as big as itself, with a few shrimp and starfish legs thrown in. Does this sound ludicrous? I can only swear to you that as it bore down on me, perhaps twice my own height or more, I found it something almost too terrifying for human eyes to look on—and yet I did not see it, but merely the flour that adhered to it!

"That repulsive sight would have been the last my eyes ever dwelt on had it not been for Grubby, the simple farmhand I have had occasion to mention before.

"As I threw the flour, Grubby gave a great cry and rushed forward, dropping the pitchfork. He jumped at the creature as it turned on me. This put out our plan, which was that he and Bruce Fox should pitchfork the creature to death. Instead, he grasped it as high as he possibly might and commenced to squeeze with the full force of his mighty muscles. What a terrifying contest! What a fear-fraught combat!

"Collecting his wits, Bruce charged forward and attacked with his pitchfork. It was his battle cry that brought me back from my paralysis into action. I ran and seized Grubby's pitchfork and also charged. That thing had arms for us all! It struck out, and I have no doubt now that several arms held poisoned needle teeth, for I saw one come towards me gaping like a snake's mouth. Need I stress the danger—particularly when you recall that the effect of the flour cloud was only partial, and there were still invisible arms flailing round us I "Our saving was that the Aurigan was cowardly. I saw Bruce jab it hard, and a second later, I rammed my pitchfork right through its foot. At once it had had enough. Grubby fell to the ground as it retreated. It moved at amazing speed, back towards the pool. We were in pursuit! And all the beasts of the barnyard uttered their cries to it.

"As it launched itself into the water, we both flung our pitch-forks at its form. But it swam out strongly and then dived below the surface, leaving only ripples and a scummy trail of flour.

"We stood staring at the water for an instant, and then with common accord ran back to Grubby. He was dead. He lay face up and was no longer recognizable. The Aurigan must have struck him with its poisoned fangs as soon as he attacked. Grubby's skin was stretched tight and glistened oddly. He had turned a dull crimson. All his internal substance had been transformed to liquid by the rapid-working venoms of the Aurigan; he was like a sort of giant man-shaped rotten haggis.

"There were wound marks across his neck and throat and what had been his face, and from these wounds his substance drained, so that he slowly deflated into his trampled bed of flour and dust. Perhaps the sight of fabled Medusa's head, that turned men to stone, was no worse than this, for we stood there utterly paralyzed. It was a blast from Farmer Grendon's rifle that brought us back to life.

"He had threatened to shoot me. Now, seeing us despoiling his flour stocks and apparently about to make off with a calf, he fired at us. We had no choice but to run for it. Grendon was in no explaining mood. Good Nancy came running out to stop him, but Neckland was charging up too with the pair of savage dogs growling at the end of their chains.

"Bruce and I had ridden up on my Daisy. I had left her saddled. Bringing her out of the stable at a trot, I heaved Bruce up into the saddle and was about to climb on myself when the gun went off again and I felt a burning pain in my leg. Bruce dragged me into the saddle and we were off—I half unconscious.

"Here I lie now in bed, and should be about again in a couple of days. Fortunately, the shot did not harm any bones.

"So you see how the farm is now a place of the damned! Once, I thought it might even become a new Eden, growing the food of the gods for men like gods. Instead—alas! the first meeting between humanity and beings from another world has proved disastrous, and the Eden is become a battleground for a war of worlds. How can our anticipations for the future be anything other than gloomy?

"Before I close this over-long account, I must answer a query in your letter and pose another to you, more personal than yours to me.

"First, you question if the Aurigans are entirely invisible and say—if I may quote your letter—'Any alteration in the refractive index of the eye lenses would make vision impossible, but without such alteration the eyes would be visible as glassy globules. And for vision it is also necessary that there should be visual purple behind the retina and an opaque cornea. How then do your Aurigans manage for vision?' The answer must be that they do without eyesight as we know it, for I think they naturally maintain a complete invisibility. How they 'see' I know not, but whatever sense they use, it is effective. How they communicate I know not—our fellow made not the slightest sound when I speared his foot!—yet it is apparent they must communicate effectively. Perhaps they tried originally to communicate with us through a mysterious sense we do not possess and, on receiving no answer, assumed us to be as dumb as our dumb animals. If so, what a tragedy!

"Now to my personal enquiry. I know, sir, that you must grow more busy as you grow more famous; but I feel that what transpires here in this remote corner of East Anglia is of momentous import to the world and the future. Could you not take it upon yourself to pay us a visit here? You would be comfortable at one of our two inns, and the journey here by railway is efficient if tedious—you can easily get a regular waggon from Heigham station here, a distance of only eight miles. You could then view Grendon's farm for yourself, and perhaps one of these intersteller beings too. I feel you are as much amused as concerned by the accounts you receive from the undersigned, but I swear not one detail is exaggerated. Say you can come!

"If you need persuasion, reflect on how much delight it will give to :

"Your sincere admirer and friend,
GREGORY ROLLES."

Reading this long letter through, scratching out two superfluous adjectives, Gregory lay back in some satisfaction. He had the feeling he was still involved in the struggle although temporarily out of action.

But the late afternoon brought him disquieting news. Tommy, the baker's boy, had gone out as far as the Grendon farm. Then the ugly legends circulating in the village about the place had risen in his mind, and he had stood wondering whether he should go on. An unnatural babble of animal noise came from the farm, mixed with hammering, and when Tommy crept forward and saw the farmer himself looking as black as a puddle and building a great thing like a gibbet in the yard, he had lost his nerve and rushed back the way he came, the letter to Nancy undelivered.

Bruce Fox arrived that evening to see how his friend was, and Gregory tried to persuade him to take the letter. But Fox was able successfully to plead a prior engagement. They talked for a while, mainly running over the horrors of the previous day once more, and then Fox left.

Gregory lay on the bed worrying about Nancy until Mrs. Fenn brought up supper on a tray. At least it was clear now why the Aurigans had not entered the farm-house; they were far too large to do so. She was safe as long as she kept indoors—as far as anyone on that doomed plot was safe.

He fell asleep early that night. In the early hours of the morning, nightmare visited him. He was in a strange city where all the buildings were new and the people wore shining clothes. In one square grew a tree. The Gregory in the dream stood in a special relationship to the tree: he fed it. It was his job to push people who were passing by the tree against its surface. The tree was a saliva tree. Down its smooth bark ran quantities of saliva from red lips like leaves up in the boughs. It grew enormous on the people on which it fed. As they were thrown against it, they passed into the substance of the tree. Some of the saliva splashed onto Gregory.

But instead of dissolving him, it caused everything he touched to be dissolved. He put his arms about the girl he loved, and as his mouth went towards hers, her skin peeled away from her face.

He woke weeping desperately and fumbling blindly for the ring of the gas mantle.

~§~

Dr. Crouchom came late next morning and told Gregory he should have at least three more days complete rest for the recovery of the muscles of his leg. Gregory lay there in a state of acute dissatisfaction with himself. Recalling the vile dream, he thought how negligent he had been towards Nancy, the girl he loved. His letter to her still lay undelivered by his bedside. After Mrs. Fenn had brought up his dinner, he determined that he must see Nancy for himself. Leaving the food, he pulled himself out of bed and dressed slowly.

The leg was more painful than he had expected, but he got himself downstairs and out to the stable without too much trouble. Daisy seemed pleased to see him. He rubbed her nose and rested his head against her long cheek in sheer pleasure at being with her again.

"This may be the last time you have to undertake this particular journey, my girl," he said.

Saddling her was comparatively easy. Getting into the saddle involved much bodily anguish. But eventually he was comfortable and they turned along the familiar and desolate road to the domain of the Aurigans. His leg was worse than he had bargained for. More than once, he had to get the mare to stop while he let the throbbing subside. He saw he was losing blood plentifully.

As he approached the farm, he observed what the baker's boy had meant by saying Grendon was building a gibbet. A pole had been set up in the middle of the yard. A cable ran to the top of it, and a light was rigged there, so that the expanse of the yard could be illuminated by night.

Another change had taken place. A wooden fence had been built behind the horse trough, cutting off the pond from the farm. But at one point, ominously, a section of it had been broken down and splintered and crushed, as if some monstrous thing had walked through the barrier unheeding.

A ferocious dog was chained just inside the gate, and barking its head off, to the consternation of the poultry. Gregory dare not enter. As he stood pondering the best way to tackle this fresh problem, the door of the farmhouse opened fractionally and Nancy peeped out. He called and signalled frantically to her.

Timidly, she ran across and let him in, dragging the dog back.

Gregory hitched Daisy to the gatepost and kissed her cheek, soothed by the feel of her sturdy body in his arms.

"Where's your father?"

"My dearest, your leg, your poor leg! It's bleeding yet!"

"Never mind my leg. Where's your father?"

"He's down in South Meadow, I think."

"Good! I'm going to speak with him. Nancy, I want you to go indoors and pack some belongings. I'm taking you away with me."

"I can't leave father!"

"You must. I'm going to tell him now." As he limped across the yard, she called fearfully, "He has that there gun of his'n with him all the time— do be careful!"

The two dogs on a running chain followed him all the way down the side of the house, nearly choking in their efforts to get at him, their teeth flashing uncomfortably close to his ankles.

Near the elms, he saw that several wild birds lay in the grass. One was still fluttering feebly. He could only assume they had worn themselves out trying to feed their immense and hungry broods. Which was what would happen to the farmer in time, he reflected. He noticed Neckland below Grubby's little hut, busy sawing wood; the farmer was not with him. On impulse, Gregory turned into the sties.

It was gloomy there. In the gloom, Grendon worked. He dropped his bucket when he saw Gregory there, and came forward threateningly.

"You come back? Why don't you stay away? Can't you see the notice by the gate? I don't want you here no more, bor. I know you mean well, and I intend you no harm, but I'll kill 'ee, understand, kill 'ee if you ever come here again. I've plenty of worries without you to add to them. Now then, get you going!"

Gregory stood his ground.

"Mr. Grendon, are you as mad as your wife was before she died? Do you understand that you may meet Grubby's fate at any moment? Do you realize what you are harbouring in your pond?"

"I ent a fule. But suppose them there things do eat everything, humans included? Suppose this is now their farm? They still got to have someone tend it. So I reckon they ent going to harm me. So long as they sees me work hard, they ent going to harm me."

"You're being fattened, do you understand? For all the hard work you do, you must have put on a stone this last month. Doesn't that scare you?"

Something of the farmer's pose broke for a moment. He cast a wild look round. "I ent saying I ent scared. I'm saying I'm doing what I have to do. We don't own our lives. Now do me a favour and get out of here."

Instinctively, Gregory's glance had followed Grendon's. For the first time, he saw in the dimness the size of the pigs. Their great broad black backs were visible over the top of the sties. They were the size of young oxen.

"This is a farm of death," he said.

"Death's always the end of all of us, pig or cow or man alike."

"Right-ho, Mr. Grendon, you can think like that if you like. It's not my way of thinking, nor am I going to see your dependents suffer from your madness. Mr. Grendon, sir, I wish to ask for your daughter's hand in marriage."

~§~

For the first three days that she was away from her home, Nancy Grendon lay in her room in "The Wayfarer" near to death. It seemed as if all ordinary food poisoned her. But gradually under Doctor Crouchorn's ministration—terrified perhaps by the rage she suspected he would vent upon her should she fail to get better—she recovered her strength.

"You look so much better today," Gregory said, clasping her hand. "You'll soon be up and about again, once your system is free of all the evil nourishment of the farm."

"Greg, dearest, promise me you will not go to the farm again. You have no need to go now I'm not there."

He cast his eyes down and said, "Then you don't have to get me to promise, do you?"

"I just want to be sure we neither of us go there again. Father, I feel sure, bears a charmed life. But I-I feel now as if I'm waking from a nightmare!"

"Don't think about it! Look, I've brought you some flowers!"

He produced a clay pot overloaded with wallflowers with gigantic blooms and gave it to her.

She smiled and said. "They're so large! Greg—they're—they're from the farm, aren't they? They're unnaturally large."

"I thought you'd like a souvenir of the nicer side of your home."

With all her strength, she hurled the pot across the room. It struck the door and broke. The dark earth scattered over the boards and the flowers lay broken on the floor.

"You dare bring the curse in here! And, Greg, this means you've been back to the farm, doesn't it, since we come away together?"

He nodded his head, looking defiantly at her. "I had to see what was happening."

"Please don't go there again, Greg, please. It's as if I was now coming to my senses again—but I don't want it to be as if you was losing yours! Supposing those things followed us here to Cottersall, those Aurigans?"

"You know, Nancy, I've wondered several times why they remain on the farm as they do. You would think that once they found they could so easily defeat human beings, they would attack everyone, or send for more of their own kind and try to invade us. Yet they seem perfecdy content to remain in that one small space."

She smiled. "I may not be very clever compared with you, but I tell 'ee the answer to that one. They ent interested in going anywhere. I think there's just two of them, and they come to our little old world for a holiday in their space machine, same as we might go to Great Yarmouth for a couple of days for our honeymoon. Perhaps they're on their honeymoon."

"On honeymoon! What a ghasdy idea!"

"Well, on holiday then. That was father's idea—he says as there's just two of them, treating Earth as a quiet place to stay. People like to eat well when they're on holiday, don't they?"

He stared at Nancy aghast.

"But that's horrible! You're trying to make the Aurigans out to be *pleasant!*"

"Of course I ent, you silly ha'p'orth! But I expect they seem pleasant to each other."

"Well, I prefer to think of them as menaces."

"All the more reason for you to keep away from them!"

But to be out of sight was not to be out of mind's reach. Gregory received another letter from Dr. Hudson-Ward, a kind and encouraging one, but he made no attempt to answer it. He felt he could not bear to take up any work that would remove him from the neighbourhood, although the need to work, in view of his matrimonial plans, was now pressing; the modest allowance his father made him would not support two in any comfort. Yet he could not bring his thought to grapple with such practical problems. It was another letter he looked for, and the horrors of the farm that obsessed him. And the next night, he dreamed of the saliva tree again.

In the evening, he plucked up enough courage to tell Fox and Nancy about it. They met in the little snug at the back of "The Wayferer's" public bars, a discreet and private place with red plush on the seats. Nancy was her usual self again, and had been out for a brief walk in the afternoon sunshine.

"People wanted to give themselves to the saliva tree. And although I didn't see this for myself, I had the distinct feeling that perhaps they weren't actually killed so much as changed into something else—something less human maybe. And this time, I saw the tree was made of metal of some kind and was growing bigger and bigger by pumps—you could see through the saliva tree to big armatures and pistons, and out of the branches steam was pouring."

Fox laughed, a little unsympathetically. "Sounds to me like the shape of things to come, when even plants are grown by machinery. Events are preying on your mind, Greg! Listen, my sister is going to Norwich tomorrow, driving in her uncle's trap. Why don't the two of you go with her? She's going to buy some adornments for her bridal gown, so that should interest you, Nancy. Then you could stay with Greg's uncle for a couple of days. I assure you I will let you know immediately the Aurigans invade Cottersall, so you won't miss anything."

Nancy seized Gregory's arm. "Can we please, Gregory, can we? I ent been to Norwich for long enough and it's a fine city."

"It would be a good idea," he said doubtfully.

Both of them pressed him until he was forced to yield. He broke up the little party as soon as he decently could, kissed Nancy goodnight, and walked hurriedly back down the street to the baker's. Of one thing he was certain: if he must leave the district even for a short while, he had to have a look to see what was happening at the farm before he went.

~§~

The farm looked in the summer's dusk as it had never done before. Massive wooden screens nine feet high had been erected and hastily creosoted. They stood about in forlorn fashion, intended to keep the public gaze from the farm, but lending it unmeaning. They stood not only in the yard but at irregular intervals along the boundaries of the land, inappropriately among fruit trees, desolately amid bracken, irrelevantly in swamp. A sound of furious hammering, punctuated by the unwearying animal noises, indicated that more screens were still being built.

But what lent the place its unearthly look was the lighting. The solitary pole supporting electric light now had five companions: one by the gate, one by the pond, one behind the house, one outside the engine house, one down by the pigsties. Their hideous yellow glare reduced the scene to the sort of unlikely picture that might be found and puzzled over in the eternal midnight of an Egyptian tomb.

Gregory was too wise to try and enter by the gate. He hitched Daisy to the low branches of a thorn tree and set off over waste land, entering Grendon's property by the South Meadow. As he walked stealthily towards the distant outhouses, he could see how the farm land differed from the territory about it. The corn was already so high it seemed in the dark almost to threaten by its ceaseless whisper of movement. The fruits had ripened fast. In the strawberry beds were great strawberries like pears. The marrows lay on their dunghill like bloated bolsters, gleaming from a distant shaft of light. In the orchard, the trees creaked, weighed down by distorted footballs that passed for apples; with a heavy autumnal thud one fell over-ripe to the ground. Everywhere on the farm, there seemed to be slight movement and noise, so much so that Gregory stopped to listen.

A wind was rising. The sails of the old mill shrieked like a gull's cry as they began to turn. In the engine house, the steam engine pumped out its double unfaltering note as it generated power. The dogs still raged, the animals added their uneasy chorus. He recalled the saliva tree; here as in the dream, it was as if agriculture had become industry, and the impulses of nature swallowed by the new god of Science. In the bark of the trees rose the dark steam of novel and unknown forces.

He talked himself into pressing forward again. He moved carefully through the baffling slices of shadow and illumination created by the screens and lights, and arrived near the back door of the farmhouse. A lantern burnt In the kitchen window. As Gregory hesitated, the crunch of broken glass came from within. Cautiously, he edged himself past the window and peered in through the doorway. From the parlour, he heard the voice of Grendon. It held a curious muffled tone, as if the man spoke to himself.

"Lie there! You're no use to me. This is a trial of strength. Oh God, preserve me, to let me prove myself! Thou has made my land barren till now—now let me harvest it! I don't know what You're doing. I didn't mean to presume, but this here farm is my life. Curse 'em, curse 'em all! They're all enemies." There was more of it; the man was muttering like one drunk. With a horrid fascination, Gregory was drawn forward till he had crossed the kitchen flags and stood on the verge of the larger room. He peered round the half open door until he could see the farmer, standing obscurely in the middle of the room.

A candle stood in the neglected hearth, its flickering flame glassily reflected in the cases of maladroit animals. Evidently the house electricity had been cut to give additional power to the new lights outside.

Grendon's back was to Gregory. One gaunt and unshaven cheek was lit by candle-light. His back seemed a little bent by the weight of what he imagined his duties, yet looking at that leather-clad back now Gregory experienced a sort of reverence for the independence of the man, and for the mystery that lay under his plainness. He watched as Grendon moved out through the front door, leaving it hanging wide, and passed into the yard, still muttering to himself. He walked round the side of the house and was hidden from view as the sound of his tread was lost amid the renewed barking of dogs.

The tumult did not drown a groan from near at hand. Peering into the shadows, Gregory saw a body lying under the table. It rolled over, crunching broken glass as it did so, and exclaimed in a dazed way. Without being able to see clearly, Gregory knew it was Neckland. He climbed over to the man and propped his head up, kicking away a stuffed fish as he did so.

"Don't kill me, bor! I only want to get away from here. I only want to get away."

"Bert? It's Greg here. Bert, are you badly hurt?"

He could see some wounds. The fellow's shirt had been practically torn from his back, and the flesh on his side and back was cut from where he had rolled in the glass. More serious was a great weal over one shoulder, changing to a deeper colour as Gregory looked at it. A brawl had taken place. Under the table lay another fish, its mouth gaping as if it still died, and the pseudo-goat, one button eye of which had rolled out of its socket. The cases from which they had come lay shattered by the wall.

Wiping his face and speaking in a more rational voice, Neckland said, "Gregory? I thought as you was down Cottersall? What you doing here? He'll kill you proper if he finds you here!"

"What happened to you, Bert? Can you get up?"

The labourer was again in possession of his faculties. He grabbed Gregory's forearm and said imploringly, "Keep your voice down, for Christ's sake, or he'll hear us and come back and settle my hash for once for all! He's gone clean off his head, says as these pond things are having a holiday here. He nearly knocked my head off my shoulder with that stick of his! Lucky I got a thick head!"

"What was the quarrel about?"

"I tell you srraight, bor, I have got the wind up proper about this here farm. They things as live in the pond will eat me and suck me up like they done Grubby if I stay here any more. So I runoff when Joe Grendon weren't looking, and I come in here to gather up my traps and my bits and leave here at once. This whole place is evil, a bed of evil, and it ought to be destroyed. Hell can't be worse than this here farm!"

"So he caught you in here, did he?"

"I saw him rush in and I flung that there fish at him, and the goat. But he had me! Now I'm getting out, and I'd advise you to do the same. You must be daft, come back here like you did!"

As he spoke, he pulled himself to his feet and stood, keeping his balance with Gregory's aid. Grunting, he made his way over to the staircase.

"Bert," Gregory said, "supposing we rush Grendon and lay him out. We can then get him in the cart and all leave together."

Neckland turned to stare at him, his face hidden in shadows, nursing his shoulder with one hand.

"You try it!" he said, and then he turned and went steadily up the stairs.

Gregory stood where he was, keeping one eye on the window. He had come to the farm without any clear notion in his head, but now that the idea had been formulated, he saw that it was up to him to try and remove Grendon from his farm. He felt obliged to do it; for although he had lost his former regard for Grendon, a sort of fascination for the man held him, and he was incapable of leaving any human being, however perverse, to face alone the alien horrors of the farm. It occurred to him that he might get help from the distant houses, Dereham Cottages, if only the farmer were rendered in one way or another unable to pepper the intruders with shot.

The machine house possessed only one high window, and that was barred. It was built of brick and had a stout door which could be barred and locked from the outside. Perhaps it would be possible to lure Grendon into there; outside aid could then be obtained.

Not without apprehension, Gregory went to the open door and peered out into the confused dark. He stared anxiously at the ground for sight of a footstep more sinister than the farmer's, but there was no indication that the Aurigans were active. He stepped into the yard.

He had not gone two yards before a woman's screams rang out. The sound seemed to clamp an icy grip about Gregory's ribs, and into his mind came a picture of poor mad Mrs. Grendon. Then he recognized the voice, in its few shouted words, as Nancy's. Even before the sound cut off, he began to pelt down the dark side of the house as fast as he could run.

Only later did he realise how he seemed to be running against a great army of animal cries. Loudest was the babel of the pigs; every swine seemed to have some message deep and nervous and indecipherable to deliver to an unknown source; and it was to the sties that Gregory ran, swerving past the giant screens under the high and sickly light.

The noise in the sties was deafening. Every animal was attacking its pen with its sharp hooves. One light swung over the middle pen. With its help, Gregory saw immediately how terrible was the change that had come over the farm since his last visit. The sows had swollen enormously and their great ears clattered against their cheeks like boards. Their hirsute backs curved almost to the rafters of their prison.

Grendon was at the far entrance. In his arms he held the unconscious form of his daughter. A sack of pig feed lay scattered by his feet. He had one pen gate half open and was trying to thrust his way in against the flank of a pig whose mighty shoulder came almost level with his. He turned and stared at Gregory with a face whose blankness was more terrifying than any expression of rage.

There was another presence in the place. A pen gate near to Gregory swung open. The two sows wedged in the narrow sty gave out a terrible falsetto squealing, clearly scenting the presence of an unappeasable hunger. They kicked out blindly, and all the other animals plunged with a sympathetic fear. Struggle was useless. An Aurigan was there; the figure of Death itself, with its unwearying scythe and unaltering smile of bone, was as easily avoided as this poisoned and unseen presence. A rosy flush spread over the back of one of the sows. Almost at once, her great bulk began to collapse; in a moment, her substance had been ingested.

Gregory did not stay to watch the sickening action. He was running forward, for the farmer was again on the move. And now it was clear what he was going to do. He pushed into the end sty and dropped his daughter down into the metal food trough. At once, the sows turned with smacking jaws to deal with this new fodder. His hands free, Grendon moved to a bracket set in the wall. There lay his gun.

Now the uproar in the sties had reached its loudest. The sow whose companion had been so rapidly ingested broke free and burst into the central aisle. For a moment she stood—mercifully, for otherwise Gregory would have been trampled—as if dazed by the possibility of liberty. The place shook and the other swine fought to get to her. Brick crumbled, pen gates buckled. Gregory jumped aside as the second pig lumbered free, and next moment the place was full of grotesque fighting bodies, fighting their way to liberty.

He had reached Grendon, but the stampede caught them even as they confronted each other. A hoof stabbed down on Grendon's instep. Groaning, he bent forward, and was at once swept underfoot by his creatures. Gregory barely had time to vault into the nearest pen before they thundered by. Nancy was trying pitifully to climb out of the trough as the two beasts to which she had been offered fought to kick their way free. With a ferocious strength—without reason—almost without consciousness—Gregory hauled her up, jumped until he swung up on one of the overhead beams, wrapped a leg round the beam, hung down till he grasped Nancy, pulled her up with him.

They were safe, but the safety was not permanent. Through the din and dust, they could see that the gigantic beasts were wedged tightly in both entrances. In the middle was a sort of battlefield, where the animals fought to reach the opposite end of the building; they were gradually tearing each other to pieces—but the sties too were threatened with demolition.

"The Aurigan is here somewhere," Gregory shouted. "We aren't safe from it by any means."

"You were foolish to come here, Greg," Nancy said. "I found you had gone and I had to follow you. But Father—I don't think he even recognized me!"

At least, Gregory thought, she had not seen her father trampled underfoot. Involuntarily glancing in that direction, he saw the shotgun that Grendon had never managed to reach still lying across a bracket on the wall. By crawling along a transverse beam, he could reach it easily. Bidding Nancy sit where she was, he wriggled along the beam, only a foot or two above the heaving backs of the swine. At least the gun should afford them some protection: the Aurigan, despite all its ghastly differences from humanity, would hardly be immune to lead.

As he grasped the old-fashioned weapon and pulled it up, Gregory was suddenly filled with an intense desire to kill one of the invisible monsters. In that instant, he recalled an earlier hope he had had of them: that they might be superior beings, beings of wisdom and enlightened power, coming from a better society where higher moral codes directed the activities of its citizens. He had thought that only to such a civilization would the divine gift of travelling through interplanetary space be granted. But perhaps the opposite held true: perhaps such a great objective could be gained only by species ruthless enough to disregard more humane ends. As soon as he thought it, his mind was overpowered with a vast diseased vision of the universe, where such races as dealt in love and kindness and intellect cowered forever on their little globes, while all about them went the slayers of the universe, sailing where they would to satisfy their cruelties and their endless appetites.

He heaved his way back to Nancy above the bloody porcine fray.

She pointed mutely. At the far end, the entrance had crumbled away, and the sows were bursting forth into the night. But one sow fell and turned crimson as it fell, sogging over the floor like a shapeless bag. Another, passing the same spot, suffered the same fate.

Was the Aurigan moved by anger? Had the pigs, in their blind charging, injured it? Gregory raised the gun and aimed. As he did so, he saw a faint hallucinatory column in the air; enough dirt and mud and blood had been thrown up to spot the Aurigan and render him partly visible. Gregory fired.

The recoil nearly knocked him off his perch. He shut his eyes, dazed by the noise, and was dimly aware of Nancy clinging to him, shouting, "Oh, you marvellous man, you marvellous man! You hit that old bor right smack on target!"

He opened his eyes and peered through the smoke and dust. The shade that represented the Aurigan was tottering. It fell. It fell among the distorted shapes of the two sows it had killed, and corrupt fluids splattered over the paving. Then it rose again. They saw its progress to the broken door, and then it had gone.

For a minute they sat there, staring at each other, triumph and speculation mingling on both their faces. Apart from one badly injured beast, the building was clear of pigs now. Gregory climbed to the floor and helped Nancy down beside him. They skirted the loathsome masses as best they could and staggered into the fresh air.

Up beyond the orchard, strange lights showed in the rear windows of the farmhouse.

"It's on fire! Oh, Greg, our poor home is afire! Quick, we must gather what we can! All father's lovely cases—"

He held her fiercely, bent so that he spoke straight into her face. "Bert Neckland did this! He did it! He told me the place ought to be destroyed and that's what he did."

"Let's go, then—"

"No, no, Nancy, we must let it burn! Listen! There's a wounded

Aurigan loose here somewhere. We didn't kill him. If those things feel rage, anger, spite, they'll be set to kill us now—don't forget there's more than one of 'em! We aren't going that way if we want to live. Daisy's just across the meadow here, and she'll bear us both safe home."

"Greg, dearest, this is my home!" she cried in her despair.

The flames were leaping higher. The kitchen windows broke in a shower of glass. He was running with her in the opposite direction, shouting wildly, "I'm your home now! I'm your home now!"

Now she was running with him, no longer protesting, and they plunged together through the high rank grass.

When they gained the track and the restive mare, they paused to take breath and look back.

The house was well ablaze now. Clearly nothing could save it. Sparks had carried to the windmill, and one of the sails was ablaze. About the scene, the electric lights shone spectral and pale on the tops of their poles. An occasional running figure of a gigantic animal dived about its own purposes. Suddenly, there was a flash as of lightning and all the electric lights went out. One of the stampeding animals had knocked down a pole; crashing into the pond, it short-circuited the system.

"Let's get away," Gregory said, and he helped Nancy onto the mare. As he climbed up behind her, a roaring sound developed, grew in volume and altered in pitch. Abruptly it died again. A thick cloud of steam billowed above the pond. From it rose the space machine, rising, rising, rising, suddenly a sight to take the heart in awe. It moved up into the soft night sky, was lost for a moment, began dully to glow, was seen to be already tremendously far away.

Desperately, Gregory looked for it, but it had gone, already beyond the frail confines of the terrestrial atmosphere. An awful desolation settled on him, the more awful for being irrational, and then he thought, and cried his thought aloud, "Perhaps they were only holiday-makers here! Perhaps they enjoyed themselves here, and will tell their friends of this little globe! Perhaps Earth has a future only as a resort for millions of the Aurigan kind!"

~§~

The church clock was striking midnight as they passed the first cottages of Cottersall.

"We'll go first to the inn," Gregory said. "I can't well disturb Mrs. Fenn at this late hour, but your landlord will fetch us food and hot water and see that your cuts are bandaged."

"I'm right as rain, love, but I'd be glad of your company."

"I warn you, you shall have too much of it from now on!"

The door of the inn was locked, but a light burned inside, and in a moment the landlord himself opened to them, all eager to hear a bit of gossip he could pass on to his customer.

"So happens as there's a gentleman up in Number Three wishes to speak with you in the morning," he told Gregory. "Very nice gentleman came on the night train, only got in here an hour past, off the waggon."

Gregory made a wry face.

"My father, no doubt."

"Oh, no, sir. His name is a Mr. Wills or Wells—his signature was a mite difficult to make out."

"Wells! Mr. Wells! So he's come!" He caught Nancy's hands, shaking them in his excitement. "Nancy, one of the greatest men in England is here! There's no one more profitable for such a tale as ours! I'm going up to speak with him right away."

Kissing her lightly on the cheek, he hurried up the stairs and knocked on the door of Number Three.

PART IV

WE ARE THE HAUNTED HOUSES

whatever walked there, walked alone

IF WE CONSIDER ourselves as a soul contained within a body, then the metaphor "We are the Haunted Houses" should resonate. Our memories haunt us. Our house—our mind—has many rooms, many floors, and sometimes we enter a space that has been locked for decades. Dreams disturb us with their secret taunts. And then there is the outside world—a world filled with other people, other houses. As we stroll around in our neighborhood of souls we can't help but wonder, is it time to leave this dump?

The stories and poems assembled here explore the haunted house theme, whether it is an ancient château, a secluded cabin in the Canadian wilderness, or merely a lonely man wandering empty streets.

The poems should be familiar to most readers, but here is an opportunity to revisit them with a different perspective. Edgar Allen Poe's "The Raven" reveals a man tortured by loss and uncertainly. It's a poem that demands to be read aloud. Try it the next time you ride a crowded bus.

"The Love Song of J. Alfred Prufrock" is an early poem by T. S. Elliot, written when he was only 22, and yet it yields a presentient angst of the coming modern age. The first lines of the poem are an excerpt, in the original Italian, from Dante's "Inferno" (XXVII; 58-63), and as with the beckoning of Dante's long-dead school master, we are invited to enter Prufrock's personal underworld: "Let us go then, you and I . . ."

Some choice stories have been cherry-picked for this section. First we have Fredric Brown's short-short story "The House", which is more of a mosaic of metaphors than one of his typically well-plotted tales. Many have tried to pick it apart and find meaning in its symbology. The most likely solution is that Brown had a bad dream, woke up with an achy head, and jotted down the details he could recall. The outcome is a Lynchian excursion into Brown's psyche, and it's a wonderfully weird place.

"The Monkey's Paw" by W. W. Jacobs may be the most anthologized supernatural tale ever. It's brilliant, and we make no apologies for including it here. Even if you've read it before it's worth another knock on the door.

Algernon Blackwood is the only writer to get two notches in this collection. His "A Haunted Island" is not one of his better known stories but it still brings the big chills. Blackwood wrote quite a lot about the ancient spirits that stride the primal realms. In this story of the Canadian wilds, a law student lingers on in a rented hunting cabin after his companions have packed their guns and gone home. Hoping to cram some studying in before returning to law school, he soon discovers that he is not alone. Someone or some thing has taken a keen interest in his presence and is circling in, searching for him. The fear mounts with a beautiful intensity rarely found in tales of terror.

We complete the cycle with one of the scariest stories you are likely to read, Reggie Oliver's "Hand to Mouth". Mr. Oliver, who often illustrates his own stories and novels, covers an impressive range of creative pursuits. He is an actor, director, and playwright, in addition to being an award-winning author of three novels, eight collections of short fiction, a children's book (as writer and illustrator), and the biography of British writer Stella Gibbons, "Out of the Woodshed". "Hand to Mouth" speaks for itself, however, and a bit of a bracer may be needed at a certain point in the story, so be warned. A quick visit to the local spirits distributor beforehand is recommended.

Let us go then, you and I . . .

The Raven

by Edgar Allan Poe

Once upon a midnight dreary, while I pondered, weak and weary,
Over many a quaint and curious volume of forgotten lore—
    While I nodded, nearly napping, suddenly there came a tapping,
    As of some one gently rapping, rapping at my chamber door—
"'Tis some visitor," I muttered, "tapping at my chamber door—
      Only this and nothing more."

Ah, distinctly I remember it was in the bleak December;
And each separate dying ember wrought its ghost upon the floor.
    Eagerly I wished the morrow;—vainly I had sought to borrow
    From my books surcease of sorrow—sorrow for the lost Lenore—
For the rare and radiant maiden whom the angels name Lenore—
      Nameless *here* for evermore.

And the silken, sad, uncertain rustling of each purple curtain
Thrilled me—filled me with fantastic terrors never felt before;
    So that now, to still the beating of my heart, I stood repeating,
    "'Tis some visitor entreating entrance at my chamber door—
Some late visitor entreating entrance at my chamber door;—
      This it is and nothing more."

Presently my soul grew stronger; hesitating then no longer,
"Sir," said I, "or Madam, truly your forgiveness I implore;
    But the fact is I was napping, and so gently you came rapping,
    And so faintly you came tapping, tapping at my chamber door,
That I scarce was sure I heard you"—here I opened wide the door;—
      Darkness there and nothing more.

Deep into that darkness peering, long I stood there wondering, fearing,
Doubting, dreaming dreams no mortal ever dared to dream before;
But the silence was unbroken, and the stillness gave no token,
And the only word there spoken was the whispered word, "Lenore?"
This I whispered, and an echo murmured back the word, "Lenore!"—
    Merely this and nothing more.

Back into the chamber turning, all my soul within me burning,
Soon again I heard a tapping somewhat louder than before.
"Surely," said I, "surely that is something at my window lattice;
Let me see, then, what thereat is, and this mystery explore—
Let my heart be still a moment and this mystery explore;—
    'Tis the wind and nothing more!"

Open here I flung the shutter, when, with many a flirt and flutter,
In there stepped a stately Raven of the saintly days of yore;
Not the least obeisance made he; not a minute stopped or stayed he;
But, with mien of lord or lady, perched above my chamber door—
Perched upon a bust of Pallas just above my chamber door—
    Perched, and sat, and nothing more.

Then this ebony bird beguiling my sad fancy into smiling,
By the grave and stern decorum of the countenance it wore,
"Though thy crest be shorn and shaven, thou," I said, "art sure no craven,
Ghastly grim and ancient Raven wandering from the Nightly shore—
Tell me what thy lordly name is on the Night's Plutonian shore!"
    Quoth the Raven "Nevermore."

Much I marvelled this ungainly fowl to hear discourse so plainly,
Though its answer little meaning—little relevancy bore;
For we cannot help agreeing that no living human being
Ever yet was blest with seeing bird above his chamber door—
Bird or beast upon the sculptured bust above his chamber door,
    With such name as "Nevermore."

But the Raven, sitting lonely on the placid bust, spoke only
That one word, as if his soul in that one word he did outpour.
    Nothing further then he uttered—not a feather then he fluttered—
    Till I scarcely more than muttered "Other friends have flown before—
On the morrow *he* will leave me, as my hopes have flown before."
        Then the bird said "Nevermore."

    Startled at the stillness broken by reply so aptly spoken,
"Doubtless," said I, "what it utters is its only stock and store
    Caught from some unhappy master whom unmerciful Disaster
    Followed fast and followed faster till his songs one burden bore—
Till the dirges of his Hope that melancholy burden bore
        Of 'Never—nevermore.'"

    But the Raven still beguiling my sad fancy into smiling,
Straight I wheeled a cushioned seat in front of bird, and bust and door;
    Then, upon the velvet sinking, I betook myself to linking
    Fancy unto fancy, thinking what this ominous bird of yore—
What this grim, ungainly, ghastly, gaunt and ominous bird of yore
        Meant in croaking "Nevermore."

    This I sat engaged in guessing, but no syllable expressing
To the fowl whose fiery eyes now burned into my bosom's core;
    This and more I sat divining, with my head at ease reclining
    On the cushion's velvet lining that the lamp-light gloated o'er,
But whose velvet violet lining with the lamp-light gloating o'er,
        She shall press, ah, nevermore!

    Then, methought, the air grew denser, perfumed from an unseen censer
Swung by Seraphim whose foot-falls tinkled on the tufted floor.
    Wretch," I cried, "thy God hath lent thee–by these angels he hath sent thee
    Respite—respite and nepenthe, from thy memories of Lenore;
Quaff, oh quaff this kind nepenthe and forget this lost Lenore!"
        Quoth the Raven "Nevermore."

"Prophet!" said I, "thing of evil!—prophet still, if bird or devil!—
Whether Tempter sent, or whether tempest tossed thee here ashore,
    Desolate yet all undaunted, on this desert land enchanted—
    On this home by Horror haunted—tell me truly, I implore—
Is there—*is* there balm in Gilead?—tell me—tell me, I implore!"
        Quoth the Raven "Nevermore."

"Prophet!" said I, "thing of evil—prophet still, if bird or devil!
By that Heaven that bends above us—by that God we both adore—
    Tell this soul with sorrow laden if, within the distant Aidenn,
    It shall clasp a sainted maiden whom the angels name Lenore—
Clasp a rare and radiant maiden whom the angels name Lenore."
        Quoth the Raven "Nevermore."

"Be that word our sign in parting, bird or fiend!" I shrieked, upstarting—
"Get thee back into the tempest and the Night's Plutonian shore!
    Leave no black plume as a token of that lie thy soul hath spoken!
    Leave my loneliness unbroken!—quit the bust above my door!
Take thy beak from out my heart, and take thy form from off my door!"
        Quoth the Raven "Nevermore."

And the Raven, never flitting, still is sitting, *still* is sitting
On the pallid bust of Pallas just above my chamber door;
    And his eyes have all the seeming of a demon's that is dreaming,
    And the lamp-light o'er him streaming throws his shadow on the floor;
And my soul from out that shadow that lies floating on the floor
        Shall be lifted—nevermore!

THE HOUSE

by Fredric Brown

HE HESITATED upon the porch and looked a last long look upon the road behind him and the green trees that grew beside it and the yellow fields and the distant hill and the bright sunlight. Then he opened the door and entered and the door swung shut behind him.

He turned as it clicked and saw only blank wall. There was no knob and no keyhole, and the edges of the door, if there were edges, were so cunningly fitted into the carven paneling that he could not discern its outline.

Before him lay the cobwebbed hallway. The floor was thick with dust and through the dust wound two so slender curving trails as might have been made by two very small snakes or two very large caterpillars. They were very faint trails and he did not notice them until he was opposite the first doorway to the right, upon which was the inscription "*Semper Fidelis*" in old English lettering.

Beyond this door he found himself in a small red room, no larger than a large closet. A single chair in this room lay on its side, one leg broken and dangling by a thin splinter. On the nearest wall the only picture was a framed portrait of Benjamin Franklin. It hung askew and the glass covering it was cracked. There was no dust upon the floor and the room appeared to have been recently cleaned. In the center of the floor lay a bright curved scimitar. There were red stains upon its hilt, and upon the edge of the blade was a thick coating of green ooze. Aside from these things the room was empty. After he had stood in this room for a long time, he crossed the hallway and entered the room opposite. It was large, the size of a small auditorium, but the bare black walls made it seem smaller at first glance. There was row upon row of purple plush theater seats, but there was no stage or platform and the rows of seats started only a few inches from the blank wall they faced. There was nothing else in the room, but upon the nearest seat lay a neat pile of programs. One of these he took and found it blank save for two advertisements on the back cover, one for Prophylactic toothbrushes and the other for choice building lots in the Sub Rosa Subdivision. Upon a page near the front of the program he saw that someone had written with a lead pencil the word or name "Garfinkle." He thrust the program into his pocket and returned to the hallway, along which he walked in search of the stairs.

Behind one closed door which he passed he heard someone, obviously amateur, picking out tunes on what sounded like a Hawaiian guitar. He knocked upon this door but a scurrying of footsteps and silence was the only answer. When he opened the door and peered within he saw only a decaying corpse hanging from the chandelier, and an odor hurled itself upon him so nauseating that he closed the door hastily, and walked on to the stairway.

The stairway was narrow and winding. There was no banister, and he clung close to the wall as he ascended. He saw that the first seven steps from the bottom had been scrubbed clean but in the dust above the seventh step he saw again the two winding trails. Upon the third step from the top they converged, and vanished.

He entered the first door to his right and found himself in a spacious bedroom, lavishly furnished. He crossed immediately to the carven poster-bed and pulled aside the curtains. The bed was neatly made, and he saw a slip of paper pinned to the smoothed pillow. Upon it was written hastily in a woman's handwriting, "Denver, 1909." Upon the reverse side, neatly written in ink in another handwriting was an algebraic equation.

He left this room quietly and stopped short just outside the door to listen to a sound that came from behind a black doorway across the hall.

It was the deep voice of a man chanting in a strange and unfamiliar tongue. It rose and fell in a monotonous cadence like a Buddhist hymn, yet over and over recurred the word "Ragnarock." The word seemed vaguely familiar, and the voice sounded like his own voice, but muffled by many things. With bowed head he stood until the voice died away into a blue trembling silence and twilight crept into the hallway with the stealthiness of a practiced thief.

Then as though awakening, he walked along the now-silent hallway until he came to the third and last door and he saw that they had printed his name upon the upper panel in tiny letters of gold. Perhaps radium had been mixed with the gold for the letters glowed in the hallway's dimness.

He stood for a long moment with his hand upon the knob, and then at last he entered and closed the door behind him. He heard the click of the latch and knew that it would never open again, yet he felt no fear with this realization.

The darkness was a black, tangible thing that sprang back from him when he struck a match. He saw then that the room was a counterpart of the east bedroom of his father's house near Wilmington, the room in which he had been born. He knew, now, just where to look for candles. There were two in the drawer, and the stump of a third, and he knew that, burned one at a time, they would last for almost ten hours. He lighted the first and stood it in the brass bracket on the wall, from whence it cast dancing shadows from each chair, from the bed, and from the small waiting cradle that stood beside the bed.

Upon the table beside his mother's sewing basket lay the March, 1887, issue of *Harper's Magazine*, and he took it up and glanced idly through its pages.

At length he dropped it to the floor and thought tenderly of his wife who had died many years ago, and a faint smile trembled upon his lips as he remembered a dozen little incidents of the years of days and nights they had spent together. He thought, too, of many other things as the minutes went by.

It was not until the ninth hour when but half an inch of candle remained and darkness began to gather in the farther corners of the room and to creep closer, that he screamed, and beat and clawed at the door until his hands were a raw and bloody pulp.

The Love Song of J. Alfred Prufrock

by T. S. Eliot

S'io credesse che mia risposta fosse
A persona che mai tornasse al mondo,
Questa fiamma staria senza piu scosse.
Ma perciocche giammai di questo fondo
Non torno vivo alcun, s'i'odo il vero,
Senza tema d'infamia ti rispondo.

Let us go then, you and I,
When the evening is spread out against the sky
Like a patient etherized upon a table;
Let us go, through certain half-deserted streets,
The muttering retreats
Of restless nights in one-night cheap hotels
And sawdust restaurants with oyster-shells:
Streets that follow like a tedious argument
Of insidious intent
To lead you to an overwhelming question...
Oh, do not ask, "What is it?"
Let us go and make our visit.

In the room the women come and go
Talking of Michelangelo.

The yellow fog that rubs its back upon the window-panes,
The yellow smoke that rubs its muzzle on the window-panes
Licked its tongue into the corners of the evening,
Lingered upon the pools that stand in drains,
Let fall upon its back the soot that falls from chimneys,
Slipped by the terrace, made a sudden leap,
And seeing that it was a soft October night,
Curled once about the house, and fell asleep.

And indeed there will be time
For the yellow smoke that slides along the street,
Rubbing its back upon the window-panes;
There will be time, there will be time
To prepare a face to meet the faces that you meet;
There will be time to murder and create,
And time for all the works and days of hands
That lift and drop a question on your plate;
Time for you and time for me,
And time yet for a hundred indecisions,
And for a hundred visions and revisions,
Before the taking of a toast and tea.

In the room the women come and go
Talking of Michelangelo.

And indeed there will be time
To wonder, "Do I dare?" and, "Do I dare?"
Time to turn back and descend the stair,
With a bald spot in the middle of my hair—
(They will say: "How his hair is growing thin!")
My morning coat, my collar mounting firmly to the chin,
My necktie rich and modest, but asserted by a simple pin—
(They will say: "But how his arms and legs are thin!")
Do I dare
Disturb the universe?
In a minute there is time
For decisions and revisions which a minute will reverse.

For I have known them all already, known them all—
Have known the evenings, mornings, afternoons,
I have measured out my life with coffee spoons;
I know the voices dying with a dying fall
Beneath the music from a farther room.
   So how should I presume?

And I have known the eyes already, known them all—
The eyes that fix you in a formulated phrase,
And when I am formulated, sprawling on a pin,
When I am pinned and wriggling on the wall,
Then how should I begin
To spit out all the butt-ends of my days and ways?
   And how should I presume?

And I have known the arms already, known them all—
Arms that are braceleted and white and bare
(But in the lamplight, downed with light brown hair!)
Is it perfume from a dress
That makes me so digress?
Arms that lie along a table, or wrap about a shawl.
          And should I then presume?
          And how should I begin?

Shall I say, I have gone at dusk through narrow streets
And watched the smoke that rises from the pipes
Of lonely men in shirt-sleeves, leaning out of windows? ...

I should have been a pair of ragged claws
Scuttling across the floors of silent seas.

And the afternoon, the evening, sleeps so peacefully!
Smoothed by long fingers,
Asleep ... tired ... or it malingers,
Stretched on the floor, here beside you and me.
Should I, after tea and cakes and ices,
Have the strength to force the moment to its crisis?
But though I have wept and fasted, wept and prayed,
Though I have seen my head (grown slightly bald) brought in
    upon a platter,
I am no prophet — and here's no great matter;
I have seen the moment of my greatness flicker,
And I have seen the eternal Footman hold my coat, and snicker,
And in short, I was afraid.

And would it have been worth it, after all,
After the cups, the marmalade, the tea,
Among the porcelain, among some talk of you and me,
Would it have been worth while,
To have bitten off the matter with a smile,
To have squeezed the universe into a ball
To roll it toward some overwhelming question,
To say: "I am Lazarus, come from the dead,
Come back to tell you all, I shall tell you all"—
If one, settling a pillow by her head,
    Should say: "That is not what I meant at all.
    That is not it, at all."

And would it have been worth it, after all,
Would it have been worth while,
After the sunsets and the dooryards and the sprinkled streets,
After the novels, after the teacups, after the skirts that trail along
    the floor—
And this, and so much more?—
It is impossible to say just what I mean!
But as if a magic lantern threw the nerves in patterns on a
    screen:
Would it have been worth while
If one, settling a pillow or throwing off a shawl,
And turning toward the window, should say:
    "That is not it at all,
    That is not what I meant, at all."

No! I am not Prince Hamlet, nor was meant to be;
Am an attendant lord, one that will do
To swell a progress, start a scene or two,
Advise the prince; no doubt, an easy tool,
Deferential, glad to be of use,
Politic, cautious, and meticulous;
Full of high sentence, but a bit obtuse;
At times, indeed, almost ridiculous—
Almost, at times, the Fool.

I grow old ... I grow old ...
I shall wear the bottoms of my trousers rolled.

Shall I part my hair behind? Do I dare to eat a peach?
I shall wear white flannel trousers, and walk upon the beach.
I have heard the mermaids singing, each to each.

I do not think that they will sing to me.

I have seen them riding seaward on the waves
Combing the white hair of the waves blown back
When the wind blows the water white and black.
We have lingered in the chambers of the sea
By sea-girls wreathed with seaweed red and brown
Till human voices wake us, and we drown.

THE MONKEY'S PAW

by W. W. Jacobs

I.

WITHOUT, the night was cold and wet, but in the small parlour of Laburnam Villa the blinds were drawn and the fire burned brightly. Father and son were at chess, the former, who possessed ideas about the game involving radical changes, putting his king into such sharp and unnecessary perils that it even provoked comment from the white-haired old lady knitting placidly by the fire.

"Hark at the wind," said Mr. White, who, having seen a fatal mistake after it was too late, was amiably desirous of preventing his son from seeing it.

"I'm listening," said the latter, grimly surveying the board as he stretched out his hand. "Check."

"I should hardly think that he'd come tonight," said his father, with his hand poised over the board.

"Mate," replied the son.

"That's the worst of living so far out," bawled Mr. White, with sudden and unlooked-for violence; "of all the beastly, slushy, out-of-the-way places to live in, this is the worst. Pathway's a bog, and the road's a torrent. I don't know what people are thinking about. I suppose because only two houses in the road are let, they think it doesn't matter."

"Never mind, dear," said his wife, soothingly; "perhaps you'll win the next one."

Mr. White looked up sharply, just in time to intercept a knowing glance between mother and son. The words died away on his lips, and he hid a guilty grin in his thin grey beard.

"There he is," said Herbert White, as the gate banged to loudly and heavy footsteps came toward the door.

The old man rose with hospitable haste, and opening the door, was heard condoling with the new arrival. The new arrival also condoled with himself, so that Mrs. White said, "Tut, tut!" and coughed gently as her husband entered the room, followed by a tall, burly man, beady of eye and rubicund of visage.

"Sergeant-Major Morris," he said, introducing him.

The sergeant-major shook hands, and taking the proffered seat by the fire, watched contentedly while his host got out whiskey and tumblers and stood a small copper kettle on the fire.

At the third glass his eyes got brighter, and he began to talk, the little family circle regarding with eager interest this visitor from distant parts, as he squared his broad shoulders in the chair and spoke of wild scenes and doughty deeds; of wars and plagues and strange peoples.

"Twenty-one years of it," said Mr. White, nodding at his wife and son. "When he went away he was a slip of a youth in the warehouse. Now look at him."

"He don't look to have taken much harm," said Mrs. White, politely.

"I'd like to go to India myself," said the old man, "just to look round a bit, you know."

"Better where you are," said the sergeant-major, shaking his head. He put down the empty glass, and sighing softly, shook it again.

"I should like to see those old temples and fakirs and jugglers," said the old man. "What was that you started telling me the other day about a monkey's paw or something, Morris?"

"Nothing," said the soldier, hastily. "Leastways nothing worth hearing."

"Monkey's paw?" said Mrs. White, curiously.

"Well, it's just a bit of what you might call magic, perhaps," said the sergeant-major, offhandedly.

His three listeners leaned forward eagerly. The visitor absent-mindedly put his empty glass to his lips and then set it down again. His host filled it for him.

"To look at," said the sergeant-major, fumbling in his pocket, "it's just an ordinary little paw, dried to a mummy."

He took something out of his pocket and proffered it. Mrs. White drew back with a grimace, but her son, taking it, examined it curiously.

"And what is there special about it?" inquired Mr. White as he took it from his son, and having examined it, placed it upon the table.

"It had a spell put on it by an old fakir," said the sergeant-major, "a very holy man. He wanted to show that fate ruled people's lives, and that those who interfered with it did so to their sorrow. He put a spell on it so that three separate men could each have three wishes from it."

His manner was so impressive that his hearers were conscious that their light laughter jarred somewhat.

"Well, why don't you have three, sir?" said Herbert White, cleverly.

The soldier regarded him in the way that middle age is wont to regard presumptuous youth. "I have," he said, quietly, and his blotchy face whitened.

"And did you really have the three wishes granted?" asked Mrs. White.

"I did," said the sergeant-major, and his glass tapped against his strong teeth.

"And has anybody else wished?" persisted the old lady.

"The first man had his three wishes. Yes," was the reply; "I don't know what the first two were, but the third was for death. That's how I got the paw."

His tones were so grave that a hush fell upon the group.

"If you've had your three wishes, it's no good to you now, then, Morris," said the old man at last. "What do you keep it for?"

The soldier shook his head. "Fancy, I suppose," he said, slowly. "I did have some idea of selling it, but I don't think I will. It has caused enough mischief already. Besides, people won't buy. They think it's a fairy tale; some of them, and those who do think anything of it want to try it first and pay me afterward."

"If you could have another three wishes," said the old man, eyeing him keenly, "would you have them?"

"I don't know," said the other. "I don't know."

He took the paw, and dangling it between his forefinger and thumb, suddenly threw it upon the fire. White, with a slight cry, stooped down and snatched it off.

"Better let it burn," said the soldier, solemnly.

"If you don't want it, Morris," said the other, "give it to me."

"I won't," said his friend, doggedly. "I threw it on the fire. If you keep it, don't blame me for what happens. Pitch it on the fire again like a sensible man."

The other shook his head and examined his new possession closely. "How do you do it?" he inquired.

"Hold it up in your right hand and wish aloud," said the sergeant-major, "but I warn you of the consequences."

"Sounds like the Arabian Nights," said Mrs. White, as she rose and began to set the supper. "Don't you think you might wish for four pairs of hands for me?"

Her husband drew the talisman from pocket, and then all three burst into laughter as the sergeant-major, with a look of alarm on his face, caught him by the arm.

"If you must wish," he said, gruffly, "wish for something sensible."

Mr. White dropped it back in his pocket, and placing chairs, motioned his friend to the table. In the business of supper the talisman was partly forgotten, and afterward the three sat listening in an enthralled fashion to a second instalment of the soldier's adventures in India.

"If the tale about the monkey's paw is not more truthful than those he has been telling us," said Herbert, as the door closed behind their guest, just in time for him to catch the last train, "we shan't make much out of it."

"Did you give him anything for it, father?" inquired Mrs. White, regarding her husband closely.

"A trifle," said he, colouring slightly. "He didn't want it, but I made him take it. And he pressed me again to throw it away."

"Likely," said Herbert, with pretended horror. "Why, we're going to be rich, and famous and happy. Wish to be an emperor, father, to begin with; then you can't be henpecked."

He darted round the table, pursued by the maligned Mrs. White armed with an antimacassar.

Mr. White took the paw from his pocket and eyed it dubiously. "I don't know what to wish for, and that's a fact," he said, slowly. "It seems to me I've got all I want."

"If you only cleared the house, you'd be quite happy, wouldn't you?" said Herbert, with his hand on his shoulder. "Well, wish for two hundred pounds, then; that'll just do it."

His father, smiling shamefacedly at his own credulity, held up the talisman, as his son, with a solemn face, somewhat marred by a wink at his mother, sat down at the piano and struck a few impressive chords.

"I wish for two hundred pounds," said the old man distinctly.

A fine crash from the piano greeted the words, interrupted by a shuddering cry from the old man. His wife and son ran toward him.

"It moved," he cried, with a glance of disgust at the object as it lay on the floor.

"As I wished, it twisted in my hand like a snake."

"Well, I don't see the money," said his son as he picked it up and placed it on the table, "and I bet I never shall."

"It must have been your fancy, father," said his wife, regarding him anxiously.

He shook his head. "Never mind, though; there's no harm done, but it gave me a shock all the same."

They sat down by the fire again while the two men finished their pipes. Outside, the wind was higher than ever, and the old man started nervously at the sound of a door banging upstairs. A silence unusual and depressing settled upon all three, which lasted until the old couple rose to retire for the night.

"I expect you'll find the cash tied up in a big bag in the middle of your bed," said Herbert, as he bade them good-night, "and something horrible squatting up on top of the wardrobe watching you as you pocket your ill-gotten gains."

He sat alone in the darkness, gazing at the dying fire, and seeing faces in it. The last face was so horrible and so simian that he gazed at it in amazement. It got so vivid that, with a little uneasy laugh, he felt on the table for a glass containing a little water to throw over it. His hand grasped the monkey's paw, and with a little shiver he wiped his hand on his coat and went up to bed.

II.

In the brightness of the wintry sun next morning as it streamed over the breakfast table he laughed at his fears. There was an air of prosaic wholesomeness about the room which it had lacked on the previous night, and the dirty, shrivelled little paw was pitched on the sideboard with a carelessness which betokened no great belief in its virtues.

"I suppose all old soldiers are the same," said Mrs. White. "The idea of our listening to such nonsense! How could wishes be granted in these days? And if they could, how could two hundred pounds hurt you, father?"

"Might drop on his head from the sky," said the frivolous Herbert.

"Morris said the things happened so naturally," said his father, "that you might if you so wished attribute it to coincidence."

"Well, don't break into the money before I come back," said Herbert as he rose from the table. "I'm afraid it'll turn you into a mean, avaricious man, and we shall have to disown you."

His mother laughed, and following him to the door, watched him down the road; and returning to the breakfast table, was very happy at the expense of her husband's credulity. All of which did not prevent her from scurrying to the door at the postman's knock, nor prevent her from referring somewhat shortly to retired sergeant-majors of bibulous habits when she found that the post brought a tailor's bill.

"Herbert will have some more of his funny remarks, I expect, when he comes home," she said, as they sat at dinner.

"I dare say," said Mr. White, pouring himself out some beer; "but for all that, the thing moved in my hand; that I'll swear to."

"You thought it did," said the old lady soothingly.

"I say it did," replied the other. "There was no thought about it; I had just—What's the matter?"

His wife made no reply. She was watching the mysterious movements of a man outside, who, peering in an undecided fashion at the house, appeared to be trying to make up his mind to enter. In mental connection with the two hundred pounds, she noticed that the stranger was well dressed, and wore a silk hat of glossy newness. Three times he paused at the gate, and then walked on again. The fourth time he stood with his hand upon it, and then with sudden resolution flung it open and walked up the path. Mrs. White at the same moment placed her hands behind her, and hurriedly unfastening the strings of her apron, put that useful article of apparel beneath the cushion of her chair.

She brought the stranger, who seemed ill at ease, into the room. He gazed at her furtively, and listened in a preoccupied fashion as the old lady apologized for the appearance of the room, and her husband's coat, a garment which he usually reserved for the garden. She then waited as patiently as her sex would permit, for him to broach his business, but he was at first strangely silent.

"I—was asked to call," he said at last, and stooped and picked a piece of cotton from his trousers. "I come from 'Maw and Meggins.'"

The old lady started. "Is anything the matter?" she asked, breathlessly. "Has anything happened to Herbert? What is it? What is it?"

Her husband interposed. "There, there, mother," he said, hastily. "Sit down, and don't jump to conclusions. You've not brought bad news, I'm sure, sir;" and he eyed the other wistfully.

"I'm sorry—" began the visitor.

"Is he hurt?" demanded the mother, wildly.

The visitor bowed in assent. "Badly hurt," he said, quietly, "but he is not in any pain."

"Oh, thank God!" said the old woman, clasping her hands. "Thank God for that! Thank—"

She broke off suddenly as the sinister meaning of the assurance dawned upon her and she saw the awful confirmation of her fears in the other's averted face. She caught her breath, and turning to her slower-witted husband, laid her trembling old hand upon his. There was a long silence.

"He was caught in the machinery," said the visitor at length in a low voice.

"Caught in the machinery," repeated Mr. White, in a dazed fashion, "yes."

He sat staring blankly out at the window, and taking his wife's hand between his own, pressed it as he had been wont to do in their old courting-days nearly forty years before.

"He was the only one left to us," he said, turning gently to the visitor. "It is hard."

The other coughed, and rising, walked slowly to the window. "The firm wished me to convey their sincere sympathy with you in your great loss," he said, without looking round. "I beg that you will understand I am only their servant and merely obeying orders."

There was no reply; the old woman's face was white, her eyes staring, and her breath inaudible; on the husband's face was a look such as his friend the sergeant might have carried into his first action.

"I was to say that 'Maw and Meggins' disclaim all responsibility," continued the other. "They admit no liability at all, but in consideration of your son's services, they wish to present you with a certain sum as compensation."

Mr. White dropped his wife's hand, and rising to his feet, gazed with a look of horror at his visitor. His dry lips shaped the words, "How much?"

"Two hundred pounds," was the answer.

Unconscious of his wife's shriek, the old man smiled faintly, put out his hands like a sightless man, and dropped, a senseless heap, to the floor.

III.

In the huge new cemetery, some two miles distant, the old people buried their dead, and came back to a house steeped in shadow and silence. It was all over so quickly that at first they could hardly realize it, and remained in a state of expectation as though of something else to happen—something else which was to lighten this load, too heavy for old hearts to bear.

But the days passed, and expectation gave place to resignation—the hopeless resignation of the old, sometimes miscalled, apathy. Sometimes they hardly exchanged a word, for now they had nothing to talk about, and their days were long to weariness.

It was about a week after that the old man, waking suddenly in the night, stretched out his hand and found himself alone. The room was in darkness, and the sound of subdued weeping came from the window. He raised himself in bed and listened.

"Come back," he said, tenderly. "You will be cold."

"It is colder for my son," said the old woman, and wept afresh.

The sound of her sobs died away on his ears. The bed was warm, and his eyes heavy with sleep. He dozed fitfully, and then slept until a sudden wild cry from his wife awoke him with a start.

"The paw!" she cried wildly. "The monkey's paw!"

He started up in alarm. "Where? Where is it? What's the matter?"

She came stumbling across the room toward him. "I want it," she said, quietly. "You've not destroyed it?"

"It's in the parlour, on the bracket," he replied, marvelling. "Why?"

She cried and laughed together, and bending over, kissed his cheek.

"I only just thought of it," she said, hysterically. "Why didn't I think of it before? Why didn't you think of it?"

"Think of what?" he questioned.

"The other two wishes," she replied, rapidly. "We've only had one."

"Was not that enough?" he demanded, fiercely.

"No," she cried, triumphantly; "we'll have one more. Go down and get it quickly, and wish our boy alive again."

The man sat up in bed and flung the bedclothes from his quaking limbs. "Good God, you are mad!" he cried, aghast.

"Get it," she panted; "get it quickly, and wish—Oh, my boy, my boy!"

Her husband struck a match and lit the candle. "Get back to bed," he said, unsteadily. "You don't know what you are saying."

"We had the first wish granted," said the old woman, feverishly; "why not the second?"

"A coincidence," stammered the old man.

"Go and get it and wish," cried his wife, quivering with excitement.

The old man turned and regarded her, and his voice shook. "He has been dead ten days, and besides he—I would not tell you else, but—I could only recognize him by his clothing. If he was too terrible for you to see then, how now?"

"Bring him back," cried the old woman, and dragged him toward the door. "Do you think I fear the child I have nursed?"

He went down in the darkness, and felt his way to the parlour, and then to the mantelpiece. The talisman was in its place, and a horrible fear that the unspoken wish might bring his mutilated son before him ere he could escape from the room seized upon him, and he caught his breath as he found that he had lost the direction of the door. His brow cold with sweat, he felt his way round the table, and groped along the wall until he found himself in the small passage with the unwholesome thing in his hand.

Even his wife's face seemed changed as he entered the room. It was white and expectant, and to his fears seemed to have an unnatural look upon it. He was afraid of her.

"Wish!" she cried, in a strong voice.

"It is foolish and wicked," he faltered.

"Wish!" repeated his wife.

He raised his hand. "I wish my son alive again."

The talisman fell to the floor, and he regarded it fearfully. Then he sank trembling into a chair as the old woman, with burning eyes, walked to the window and raised the blind.

He sat until he was chilled with the cold, glancing occasionally at the figure of the old woman peering through the window. The candle-end, which had burned below the rim of the china candlestick, was throwing pulsating shadows on the ceiling and walls, until, with a flicker larger than the rest, it expired. The old man, with an unspeakable sense of relief at the failure of the talisman, crept back to his bed, and a minute or two afterward the old woman came silently and apathetically beside him.

Neither spoke, but lay silently listening to the ticking of the clock. A stair creaked, and a squeaky mouse scurried noisily through the wall. The darkness was oppressive, and after lying for some time screwing up his courage, he took the box of matches, and striking one, went downstairs for a candle.

At the foot of the stairs the match went out, and he paused to strike another; and at the same moment a knock, so quiet and stealthy as to be scarcely audible, sounded on the front door.

The matches fell from his hand and spilled in the passage. He stood motionless, his breath suspended until the knock was repeated. Then he turned and fled swiftly back to his room, and closed the door behind him. A third knock sounded through the house.

"What's that?" cried the old woman, starting up.

"A rat," said the old man in shaking tones—"a rat. It passed me on the stairs."

His wife sat up in bed listening. A loud knock resounded through the house.

"It's Herbert!" she screamed. "It's Herbert!"

She ran to the door, but her husband was before her, and catching her by the arm, held her tightly.

"What are you going to do?" he whispered hoarsely.

"It's my boy; it's Herbert!" she cried, struggling mechanically. "I forgot it was two miles away. What are you holding me for? Let go. I must open the door."

"For God's sake don't let it in," cried the old man, trembling.

"You're afraid of your own son," she cried, struggling. "Let me go. I'm coming, Herbert; I'm coming."

There was another knock, and another. The old woman with a sudden wrench broke free and ran from the room. Her husband followed to the landing, and called after her appealingly as she hurried downstairs. He heard the chain rattle back and the bottom bolt drawn slowly and stiffly from the socket. Then the old woman's voice, strained and panting.

"The bolt," she cried, loudly. "Come down. I can't reach it."

But her husband was on his hands and knees groping wildly on the floor in search of the paw. If he could only find it before the thing outside got in. A perfect fusillade of knocks reverberated through the house, and he heard the scraping of a chair as his wife put it down in the passage against the door. He heard the creaking of the bolt as it came slowly back, and at the same moment he found the monkey's paw, and frantically breathed his third and last wish.

The knocking ceased suddenly, although the echoes of it were still in the house. He heard the chair drawn back, and the door opened. A cold wind rushed up the staircase, and a long loud wail of disappointment and misery from his wife gave him courage to run down to her side, and then to the gate beyond. The streetlamp flickering opposite shone on a quiet and deserted road.

A Haunted Island

by Algernon Blackwood

THE FOLLOWING events occurred on a small island of isolated position in a large Canadian lake, to whose cool waters the inhabitants of Montreal and Toronto flee for rest and recreation in the hot months. It is only to be regretted that events of such peculiar interest to the genuine student of the psychical should be entirely uncorroborated. Such unfortunately, however, is the case.

Our own party of nearly twenty had returned to Montreal that very day, and I was left in solitary possession for a week or two longer, in order to accomplish some important "reading" for the law which I had foolishly neglected during the summer.

It was late in September, and the big trout and maskinonge were stirring themselves in the depths of the lake, and beginning slowly to move up to the surface waters as the north winds and early frosts lowered their temperature. Already the maples were crimson and gold, and the wild laughter of the loons echoed in sheltered bays that never knew their strange cry in the summer.

With a whole island to oneself, a two-storey cottage, a canoe, and only the chipmunks, and the farmer's weekly visit with eggs and bread, to disturb one, the opportunities for hard reading might be very great. It all depends!

The rest of the party had gone off with many warnings to beware of Indians, and not to stay late enough to be the victim of a frost that thinks nothing of forty below zero. After they had gone, the loneliness of the situation made itself unpleasantly felt. There were no other islands within six or seven miles, and though the mainland forests lay a couple of miles behind me, they stretched for a very great distance unbroken by any signs of human habitation. But, though the island was completely deserted and silent, the rocks and trees that had echoed human laughter and voices almost every hour of the day for two months could not fail to retain some memories of it all; and I was not surprised to fancy I heard a shout or a cry as I passed from rock to rock, and more than once to imagine that I heard my own name called aloud.

In the cottage there were six tiny little bedrooms divided from one another by plain unvarnished partitions of pine. A wooden bedstead, a mattress, and a chair, stood in each room, but I only found two mirrors, and one of these was broken.

The boards creaked a good deal as I moved about, and the signs of occupation were so recent that I could hardly believe I was alone. I half expected to find someone left behind, still trying to crowd into a box more than it would hold. The door of one room was stiff, and refused for a moment to open, and it required very little persuasion to imagine someone was holding the handle on the inside, and that when it opened I should meet a pair of human eyes.

A thorough search of the floor led me to select as my own sleeping quarters a little room with a diminutive balcony over the verandah roof. The room was very small, but the bed was large, and had the best mattress of them all. It was situated directly over the sitting-room where I should live and do my "reading," and the miniature window looked out to the rising sun. With the exception of a narrow path which led from the front door and verandah through the trees to the boat-landing, the island was densely covered with maples, hemlocks, and cedars. The trees gathered in round the cottage so closely that the slightest wind made the branches scrape the roof and tap the wooden walls. A few moments after sunset the darkness became impenetrable, and ten yards beyond the glare of the lamps that shone through the sitting-room windows—of which there were four—you could not see an inch before your nose, nor move a step without running up against a tree.

The rest of that day I spent moving my belongings from my tent to the sitting-room, taking stock of the contents of the larder, and chopping enough wood for the stove to last me for a week. After that, just before sunset, I went round the island a couple of times in my canoe for precaution's sake. I had never dreamed of doing this before, but when a man is alone he does things that never occur to him when he is one of a large party.

How lonely the island seemed when I landed again! The sun was down, and twilight is unknown in these northern regions. The darkness comes up at once. The canoe safely pulled up and turned over on her face, I groped my way up the little narrow pathway to the verandah. The six lamps were soon burning merrily in the front room; but in the kitchen, where I "dined," the shadows were so gloomy, and the lamplight was so inadequate, that the stars could be seen peeping through the cracks between the rafters.

I turned in early that night. Though it was calm and there was no wind, the creaking of my bedstead and the musical gurgle of the water over the rocks below were not the only sounds that reached my ears. As I lay awake, the appalling emptiness of the house grew upon me. The corridors and vacant rooms seemed to echo innumerable footsteps, shuf-flings, the rustle of skirts, and a constant undertone of whispering. When sleep at length overtook me, the breathings and noises, however, passed gently to mingle with the voices of my dreams.

A week passed by, and the "reading" progressed favourably. On the tenth day of my solitude, a strange thing happened. I awoke after a good night's sleep to find myself possessed with a marked repugnance for my room. The air seemed to stifle me. The more I tried to define the cause of this dislike, the more unreasonable it appeared. There was something about the room that made me afraid. Absurd as it seems, this feeling clung to me obstinately while dressing, and more than once I caught myself shivering, and conscious of an inclination to get out of the room as quickly as possible. The more I tried to laugh it away, the more real it became; and when at last I was dressed, and went out into the passage, and downstairs into the kitchen, it was with feelings of relief, such as I might imagine would accompany one's escape from the presence of a dangerous contagious disease.

While cooking my breakfast, I carefully recalled every night spent in the room, in the hope that I might in some way connect the dislike I now felt with some disagreeable incident that had occurred in it. But the only thing I could recall was one stormy night when I suddenly awoke and heard the boards creaking so loudly in the corridor that I was convinced there were people in the house. So certain was I of this, that I had descended the stairs, gun in hand, only to find the doors and windows securely fastened, and the mice and black-beetles in sole possession of the floor. This was certainly not sufficient to account for the strength of my feelings.

The morning hours I spent in steady reading; and when I broke off in the middle of the day for a swim and luncheon, I was very much surprised, if not a little alarmed, to find that my dislike for the room had, if anything, grown stronger. Going upstairs to get a book, I experienced the most marked aversion to entering the room, and while within I was conscious all the time of an uncomfortable feeling that was half uneasi-ness and half apprehension. The result of it was that, instead of reading, I spent the afternoon on the water paddling and fishing, and when I got home about sundown, brought with me half a dozen delicious black bass for the supper-table and the larder.

As sleep was an important matter to me at this time, I had decided that if my aversion to the room was so strongly marked on my return as it had been before, I would move my bed down into the sitting-room, and sleep there. This was, I argued, in no sense a concession to an absurd and fanciful fear, but simply a precaution to ensure a good night's sleep. A bad night involved the loss of the next day's reading—a loss I was not prepared to incur.

I accordingly moved my bed downstairs into a corner of the sitting-room facing the door, and was moreover uncommonly glad when the operation was completed, and the door of the bedroom closed finally upon the shadows, the silence, and the strange *fear* that shared the room with them.

The croaking stroke of the kitchen clock sounded the hour of eight as I finished washing up my few dishes, and closing the kitchen door behind me, passed into the front room. All the lamps were lit, and their reflectors, which I had polished up during the day, threw a blaze of light into the room.

Outside the night was still and warm. Not a breath of air was stirring; the waves were silent, the trees motionless, and heavy clouds hung like an oppressive curtain over the heavens. The darkness seemed to have rolled up with unusual swiftness, and not the faintest glow of colour remained to show where the sun had set. There was present in the atmosphere that ominous and overwhelming silence which so often precedes the most violent storms.

I sat down to my books with my brain unusually clear, and in my heart the pleasant satisfaction of knowing that five black bass were lying in the ice-house, and that to-morrow morning the old farmer would arrive with fresh bread and eggs. I was soon absorbed in my books.

As the night wore on the silence deepened. Even the chipmunks were still; and the boards of the floors and walls ceased creaking. I read on steadily till, from the gloomy shadows of the kitchen, came the hoarse sound of the clock striking nine. How loud the strokes sounded! They were like blows of a big hammer. I closed one book and opened another, feeling that I was just warming up to my work.

This, however, did not last long. I presently found that I was reading the same paragraphs over twice, simple paragraphs that did not require such effort. Then I noticed that my mind began to wander to other things, and the effort to recall my thoughts became harder with each digression. Concentration was growing momentarily more difficult. Presently I discovered that I had turned over two pages instead of one, and had not noticed my mistake until I was well down the page. This was becoming serious. What was the disturbing influence? It could not be physical fatigue. On the contrary, my mind was unusually alert, and in a more receptive condition than usual. I made a new and determined effort to read, and for a short time succeeded in giving my whole attention to my subject. But in a very few moments again I found myself leaning back in my chair, staring vacantly into space.

Something was evidently at work in my sub-consciousness. There was something I had neglected to do. Perhaps the kitchen door and windows were not fastened. I accordingly went to see, and found that they were! The fire perhaps needed attention. I went in to see, and found that it was all right! I looked at the lamps, went upstairs into every bedroom in turn, and then went round the house, and even into the ice-house. Nothing was wrong; everything was in its place. Yet something *was* wrong! The conviction grew stronger and stronger within me.

When I at length settled down to my books again and tried to read, I became aware, for the first time, that the room seemed growing cold. Yet the day had been oppressively warm, and evening had brought no relief. The six big lamps, moreover, gave out heat enough to warm the room pleasantly. But a chilliness, that perhaps crept up from the lake, made itself felt in the room, and caused me to get up to close the glass door opening on to the verandah.

For a brief moment I stood looking out at the shaft of light that fell from the windows and shone some little distance down the pathway, and out for a few feet into the lake.

As I looked, I saw a canoe glide into the pathway of light, and immediately crossing it, pass out of sight again into the darkness. It was perhaps a hundred feet from the shore, and it moved swiftly.

I was surprised that a canoe should pass the island at that time of night, for all the summer visitors from the other side of the lake had gone home weeks before, and the island was a long way out of any line of water traffic.

My reading from this moment did not make very good progress, for somehow the picture of that canoe, gliding so dimly and swiftly across the narrow track of light on the black waters, silhouetted itself against the background of my mind with singular vividness. It kept coming between my eyes and the printed page. The more I thought about it the more surprised I became. It was of larger build than any I had seen during the past summer months, and was more like the old Indian war canoes with the high curving bows and stern and wide beam. The more I tried to read, the less success attended my efforts; and finally I closed my books and went out on the verandah to walk up and down a bit, and shake the chilliness out of my bones.

The night was perfectly still, and as dark as imaginable. I stumbled down the path to the little landing wharf, where the water made the very faintest of gurgling under the timbers. The sound of a big tree falling in the mainland forest, far across the lake, stirred echoes in the heavy air, like the first guns of a distant night attack. No other sound disturbed the stillness that reigned supreme.

As I stood upon the wharf in the broad splash of light that followed me from the sitting-room windows, I saw another canoe cross the pathway of uncertain light upon the water, and disappear at once into the impenetrable gloom that lay beyond. This time I saw more distinctly than before. It was like the former canoe, a big birch-bark, with high-crested bows and stern and broad beam. It was paddled by two Indians, of whom the one in the stern—the steerer—appeared to be a very large man. I could see this very plainly; and though the second canoe was much nearer the island than the first, I judged that they were both on their way home to the Government Reservation, which was situated some fifteen miles away upon the mainland.

I was wondering in my mind what could possibly bring any Indians down to this part of the lake at such an hour of the night, when a third canoe, of precisely similar build, and also occupied by two Indians, passed silently round the end of the wharf. This time the canoe was very much nearer shore, and it suddenly flashed into my mind that the three canoes were in reality one and the same, and that only one canoe was circling the island!

This was by no means a pleasant reflection, because, if it were the correct solution of the unusual appearance of the three canoes in this lonely part of the lake at so late an hour, the purpose of the two men could only reasonably be considered to be in some way connected with myself. I had never known of the Indians attempting any violence upon the settlers who shared the wild, inhospitable country with them; at the same time, it was not beyond the region of possibility to suppose . . . But then I did not care even to think of such hideous possibilities, and my imagination immediately sought relief in all manner of other solutions to the problem, which indeed came readily enough to my mind, but did not succeed in recommending themselves to my reason.

Meanwhile, by a sort of instinct, I stepped back out of the bright light in which I had hitherto been standing, and waited in the deep shadow of a rock to see if the canoe would again make its appearance. Here I could see, without being seen, and the precaution seemed a wise one.

After less than five minutes the canoe, as I had anticipated, made its fourth appearance. This time it was not twenty yards from the wharf, and I saw that the Indians meant to land. I recognised the two men as those who had passed before, and the steerer was certainly an immense fellow. It was unquestionably the same canoe. There could be no longer any doubt that for some purpose of their own the men had been going round and round the island for some time, waiting for an opportunity to land. I strained my eyes to follow them in the darkness, but the night had completely swallowed them up, and not even the faintest swish of the paddles reached my ears as the Indians plied their long and powerful strokes. The canoe would be round again in a few moments, and this time it was possible that the men might land. It was well to be prepared. I knew nothing of their intentions, and two to one (when the two are big Indians!) late at night on a lonely island was not exactly my idea of pleasant intercourse.

In a corner of the sitting-room, leaning up against the back wall, stood my Marlin rifle, with ten cartridges in the magazine and one lying snugly in the greased breech. There was just time to get up to the house and take up a position of defence in that corner. Without an instant's hesitation I ran up to the verandah, carefully picking my way among the trees, so as to avoid being seen in the light. Entering the room, I shut the door leading to the verandah, and as quickly as possible turned out every one of the six lamps. To be in a room so brilliantly lighted, where my every movement could be observed from outside, while I could see nothing but impenetrable darkness at every window, was by all laws of warfare an unnecessary concession to the enemy. And this enemy, if enemy it was to be, was far too wily and dangerous to be granted any such advantages.

I stood in the corner of the room with my back against the wall, and my hand on the cold rifle-barrel. The table, covered with my books, lay between me and the door, but for the first few minutes after the lights were out the darkness was so intense that nothing could be discerned at all. Then, very gradually, the outline of the room became visible, and the framework of the windows began to shape itself dimly before my eyes.

After a few minutes the door (its upper half of glass), and the two windows that looked out upon the front verandah, became specially distinct; and I was glad that this was so, because if the Indians came up to the house I should be able to see their approach, and gather something of their plans. Nor was I mistaken, for there presently came to my ears the peculiar hollow sound of a canoe landing and being carefully dragged up over the rocks. The paddles I distinctly heard being placed underneath, and the silence that ensued thereupon I rightly interpreted to mean that the Indians were stealthily approaching the house . . .

While it would be absurd to claim that I was not alarmed—even frightened—at the gravity of the situation and its possible outcome, I speak the whole truth when I say that I was not overwhelmingly afraid for myself. I was conscious that even at this stage of the night I was passing into a psychical condition in which my sensations seemed no longer normal. Physical fear at no time entered into the nature of my feelings; and though I kept my hand upon my rifle the greater part of the night, I was all the time conscious that its assistance could be of little avail against the terrors that I had to face. More than once I seemed to feel most curiously that I was in no real sense a part of the proceedings, nor actually involved in them, but that I was playing the part of a spectator—a spectator, moreover, on a psychic rather than on a material plane. Many of my sensations that night were too vague for definite description and analysis, but the main feeling that will stay with me to the end of my days is the awful horror of it all, and the miserable sensation that if the strain had lasted a little longer than was actually the case my mind must inevitably have given way.

Meanwhile I stood still in my corner, and waited patiently for what was to come. The house was as still as the grave, but the inarticulate voices of the night sang in my ears, and I seemed to hear the blood running in my veins and dancing in my pulses.

If the Indians came to the back of the house, they would find the kitchen door and window securely fastened. They could not get in there without making considerable noise, which I was bound to hear. The only mode of getting in was by means of the door that faced me, and I kept my eyes glued on that door without taking them off for the smallest fraction of a second.

My sight adapted itself every minute better to the darkness. I saw the table that nearly filled the room, and left only a narrow passage on each side. I could also make out the straight backs of the wooden chairs pressed up against it, and could even distinguish my papers and inkstand lying on the white oilcloth covering. I thought of the gay faces that had gathered round that table during the summer, and I longed for the sunlight as I had never longed for it before.

Less than three feet to my left the passageway led to the kitchen, and the stairs leading to the bedrooms above commenced in this passageway, but almost in the sitting-room itself. Through the windows I could see the dim motionless outlines of the trees: not a leaf stirred, not a branch moved.

A few moments of this awful silence, and then I was aware of a soft tread on the boards of the verandah, so stealthy that it seemed an impression directly on my brain rather than upon the nerves of hearing. Immediately afterwards a black figure darkened the glass door, and I perceived that a face was pressed against the upper panes. A shiver ran down my back, and my hair was conscious of a tendency to rise and stand at right angles to my head.

It was the figure of an Indian, broad-shouldered and immense; indeed, the largest figure of a man I have ever seen outside of a circus hall. By some power of light that seemed to generate itself in the brain, I saw the strong dark face with the aquiline nose and high cheek-bones flattened against the glass. The direction of the gaze I could not determine; but faint gleams of light as the big eyes rolled round and showed their whites, told me plainly that no corner of the room escaped their searching.

For what seemed fully five minutes the dark figure stood there, with the huge shoulders bent forward so as to bring the head down to the level of the glass; while behind him, though not nearly so large, the shadowy form of the other Indian swayed to and fro like a bent tree. While I waited in an agony of suspense and agitation for their next movement little currents of icy sensation ran up and down my spine and my heart seemed alternately to stop beating and then start off again with terrifying rapidity. They must have heard its thumping and the singing of the blood in my head! Moreover, I was conscious, as I felt a cold stream of perspiration trickle down my face, of a desire to scream, to shout, to bang the walls like a child, to make a noise, or do anything that would relieve the suspense and bring things to a speedy climax.

It was probably this inclination that led me to another discovery, for when I tried to bring my rifle from behind my back to raise it and have it pointed at the door ready to fire, I found that I was powerless to move. The muscles, paralysed by this strange fear, refused to obey the will. Here indeed was a terrifying complication!

~§~

There was a faint sound of rattling at the brass knob, and the door was pushed open a couple of inches. A pause of a few seconds, and it was pushed open still further. Without a sound of footsteps that was appreciable to my ears, the two figures glided into the room, and the man behind gently closed the door after him.

They were alone with me between the four walls. Could they see me standing there, so still and straight in my corner? Had they, perhaps, already seen me? My blood surged and sang like the roll of drums in an orchestra; and though I did my best to suppress my breathing, it sounded like the rushing of wind through a pneumatic tube.

My suspense as to the next move was soon at an end—only, however, to give place to a new and keener alarm. The men had hitherto exchanged no words and no signs, but there were general indications of a movement across the room, and whichever way they went they would have to pass round the table. If they came my way they would have to pass within six inches of my person. While I was considering this very disagreeable possibility, I perceived that the smaller Indian (smaller by comparison) suddenly raised his arm and pointed to the ceiling. The other fellow raised his head and followed the direction of his companion's arm. I began to understand at last. They were going upstairs, and the room directly overhead to which they pointed had been until this night my bedroom. It was the room in which I had experienced that very morning so strange a sensation of fear, and but for which I should then have been lying asleep in the narrow bed against the window.

The Indians then began to move silently around the room; they were going upstairs, and they were coming round my side of the table. So stealthy were their movements that, but for the abnormally sensitive state of the nerves, I should never have heard them. As it was, their cat-like tread was distinctly audible. Like two monstrous black cats they came round the table toward me, and for the first time I perceived that the smaller of the two dragged something along the floor behind him. As it trailed along over the floor with a soft, sweeping sound, I somehow got the impression that it was a large dead thing with outstretched wings, or a large, spreading cedar branch. Whatever it was, I was unable to see it even in outline, and I was too terrified, even had I possessed the power over my muscles, to move my neck forward in the effort to determine its nature.

Nearer and nearer they came. The leader rested a giant hand upon the table as he moved. My lips were glued together, and the air seemed to burn in my nostrils. I tried to close my eyes, so that I might not see as they passed me; but my eyelids had stiffened, and refused to obey. Would they never get by me? Sensation seemed also to have left my legs, and it was as if I were standing on mere supports of wood or stone. Worse still, I was conscious that I was losing the power of balance, the power to stand upright, or even to lean backwards against the wall. Some force was drawing me forward, and a dizzy terror seized me that I should lose my balance, and topple forward against the Indians just as they were in the act of passing me.

Even moments drawn out into hours must come to an end some time, and almost before I knew it the figures had passed me and had their feet upon the lower step of the stairs leading to the upper bedrooms. There could not have been six inches between us, and yet I was conscious only of a current of cold air that followed them. They had not touched me, and I was convinced that they had not seen me. Even the trailing thing on the floor behind them had not touched my feet, as I had dreaded it would, and on such an occasion as this I was grateful even for the smallest mercies.

The absence of the Indians from my immediate neighbourhood brought little sense of relief. I stood shivering and shuddering in my corner, and, beyond being able to breathe more freely, I felt no whit less uncomfortable. Also, I was aware that a certain light, which, without apparent source or rays, had enabled me to follow their every gesture and movement, had gone out of the room with their departure. An unnatural darkness now filled the room, and pervaded its every corner so that I could barely make out the positions of the windows and the glass doors.

As I said before, my condition was evidently an abnormal one. The capacity for feeling surprise seemed, as in dreams, to be wholly absent. My senses recorded with unusual accuracy every smallest occurrence, but I was able to draw only the simplest deductions.

The Indians soon reached the top of the stairs, and there they halted for a moment. I had not the faintest clue as to their next movement. They appeared to hesitate. They were listening attentively. Then I heard one of them, who by the weight of his soft tread must have been the giant, cross the narrow corridor and enter the room directly overhead—my own little bedroom. But for the insistence of that unaccountable dread I had experienced there in the morning, I should at that very moment have been lying in the bed with the big Indian in the room standing beside me.

For the space of a hundred seconds there was silence, such as might have existed before the birth of sound. It was followed by a long quivering shriek of terror, which rang out into the night, and ended in a short gulp before it had run its full course. At the same moment the other Indian left his place at the head of the stairs, and joined his companion in the bedroom. I heard the "thing" trailing behind him along the floor. A thud followed, as of something heavy falling, and then all became as still and silent as before.

It was at this point that the atmosphere, surcharged all day with the electricity of a fierce storm, found relief in a dancing flash of brilliant lightning simultaneously with a crash of loudest thunder. For five seconds every article in the room was visible to me with amazing distinctness, and through the windows I saw the tree trunks standing in solemn rows. The thunder pealed and echoed across the lake and among the distant islands, and the flood-gates of heaven then opened and let out their rain in streaming torrents.

The drops fell with a swift rushing sound upon the still waters of the lake, which leaped up to meet them, and pattered with the rattle of shot on the leaves of the maples and the roof of the cottage. A moment later, and another flash, even more brilliant and of longer duration than the first, lit up the sky from zenith to horizon, and bathed the room momentarily in dazzling whiteness. I could see the rain glistening on the leaves and branches outside. The wind rose suddenly, and in less than a minute the storm that had been gathering all day burst forth in its full fury.

Above all the noisy voices of the elements, the slightest sounds in the room overhead made themselves heard, and in the few seconds of deep silence that followed the shriek of terror and pain I was aware that the movements had commenced again. The men were leaving the room and approaching the top of the stairs. A short pause, and they began to descend. Behind them, tumbling from step to step, I could hear that trailing "thing" being dragged along. It had become ponderous!

I awaited their approach with a degree of calmness, almost of apathy, which was only explicable on the ground that after a certain point Nature applies her own anæsthetic, and a merciful condition of numbness supervenes. On they came, step by step, nearer and nearer, with the shuffling sound of the burden behind growing louder as they approached.

They were already half-way down the stairs when I was galvanised afresh into a condition of terror by the consideration of a new and horrible possibility. It was the reflection that if another vivid flash of lightning were to come when the shadowy procession was in the room, perhaps when it was actually passing in front of me, I should see everything in detail, and worse, be seen myself! I could only hold my breath and wait—wait while the minutes lengthened into hours, and the procession made its slow progress round the room.

The Indians had reached the foot of the staircase. The form of the huge leader loomed in the doorway of the passage, and the burden with an ominous thud had dropped from the last step to the floor. There was a moment's pause while I saw the Indian turn and stoop to assist his companion. Then the procession moved forward again, entered the room close on my left, and began to move slowly round my side of the table. The leader was already beyond me, and his companion, dragging on the floor behind him the burden, whose confused outline I could dimly make out, was exactly in front of me, when the cavalcade came to a dead halt. At the same moment, with the strange suddenness of thunderstorms, the splash of the rain ceased altogether, and the wind died away into utter silence.

For the space of five seconds my heart seemed to stop beating, and then the worst came. A double flash of lightning lit up the room and its contents with merciless vividness.

The huge Indian leader stood a few feet past me on my right. One leg was stretched forward in the act of taking a step. His immense shoulders were turned toward his companion, and in all their magnificent fierceness I saw the outline of his features. His gaze was directed upon the burden his companion was dragging along the floor; but his profile, with the big aquiline nose, high cheek-bone, straight black hair and bold chin, burnt itself in that brief instant into my brain, never again to fade.

Dwarfish, compared with this gigantic figure, appeared the proportions of the other Indian, who, within twelve inches of my face, was stooping over the thing he was dragging in a position that lent to his person the additional horror of deformity. And the burden, lying upon a sweeping cedar branch which he held and dragged by a long stem, was the body of a white man. The scalp had been neatly lifted, and blood lay in a broad smear upon the cheeks and forehead.

Then, for the first time that night, the terror that had paralysed my muscles and my will lifted its unholy spell from my soul. With a loud cry I stretched out my arms to seize the big Indian by the throat, and, grasping only air, tumbled forward unconscious upon the ground.

I had recognised the body, and *the face was my own!* . . .

It was bright daylight when a man's voice recalled me to consciousness. I was lying where I had fallen, and the farmer was standing in the room with the loaves of bread in his hands. The horror of the night was still in my heart, and as the bluff settler helped me to my feet and picked up the rifle which had fallen with me, with many questions and expressions of condolence, I imagine my brief replies were neither self-explanatory nor even intelligible.

That day, after a thorough and fruitless search of the house, I left the island, and went over to spend my last ten days with the farmer; and when the time came for me to leave, the necessary reading had been accomplished, and my nerves had completely recovered their balance.

On the day of my departure the farmer started early in his big boat with my belongings to row to the point, twelve miles distant, where a little steamer ran twice a week for the accommodation of hunters. Late in the afternoon I went off in another direction in my canoe, wishing to see the island once again, where I had been the victim of so strange an experience.

In due course I arrived there, and made a tour of the island. I also made a search of the little house, and it was not without a curious sensation in my heart that I entered the little upstairs bedroom. There seemed nothing unusual.

Just after I re-embarked, I saw a canoe gliding ahead of me around the curve of the island. A canoe was an unusual sight at this time of the year, and this one seemed to have sprung from nowhere. Altering my course a little, I watched it disappear around the next projecting point of rock. It had high curving bows, and there were two Indians in it. I lingered with some excitement, to see if it would appear again round the other side of the island; and in less than five minutes it came into view. There were less than two hundred yards between us, and the Indians, sitting on their haunches, were paddling swiftly in my direction.

I never paddled faster in my life than I did in those next few minutes. When I turned to look again, the Indians had altered their course, and were again circling the island.

The sun was sinking behind the forests on the mainland, and the crimson-coloured clouds of sunset were reflected in the waters of the lake, when I looked round for the last time, and saw the big bark canoe and its two dusky occupants still going round the island. Then the shadows deepened rapidly; the lake grew black, and the night wind blew its first breath in my face as I turned a corner, and a projecting bluff of rock hid from my view both island and canoe.

Hand to Mouth

by Reggie Oliver

MY COUSIN JUSTIN is one of the undeserving rich. You won't want to know the details, but I'll just say he is something very high up in Grippmann-Savage, the international merchant bank and his bonuses alone amount to several million a year. That is how a couple of years back he could afford, on a whim, to buy a Château in the Dordogne. He told me all about it when we lunched together at his London club, Brummell's, that September. He was paying, of course. I am a frequently unemployed actor and the nearest I usually get to a meal out is my local Indian for a takeaway. Unlike my cousin I lead a hand to mouth existence.

I knew that this was not going to be a purely social lunch. Justin does not give away expensive food, even to his relations, for nothing. In a way, that is what I like about my cousin: you know exactly where you are with him. Everything he does is for his own convenience or financial benefit and he makes no secret of it. A hypocrite he is not.

I arrived at Brummell's punctually to find Cousin Justin waiting for me in the bar. He shook my hand and said: "We won't bother with a drink beforehand. Let's go straight into the dining room, shall we?"

Once we had sat down at our table Justin immediately began to choose what we were going to eat. For formality's sake I was handed a menu, but I was not even asked what I might like. From the waiter he ordered mulligatawny soup for both of us, followed by roast beef from the trolley, then he had a long consultation with the wine steward before finally settling on a decanter of the club claret. When this was done he gave a little sigh of satisfaction and smiled in my direction as if he had just done me an enormous favor.

"Now then, Cousin James, are you in any sort of gainful employment at the moment, or are you, as you say, 'resting'?"

People like my cousin Justin are under the illusion that we actors say we are "resting" when we are out of work. No actor in my experience

426

has ever used that expression. I told Justin that I had just finished a thirteen week tour of a successful farce; I went on to tell him about the company, and the theatres we had been to, but Justin did not even pretend to be interested. He actually waved at a passing high court judge as I was talking to him. Finally he interrupted me.

"Yes, yes . . . But what I mean is, are you likely to be working this winter?"

"Well, I don't know. I suppose I might get a pantomime at Christmas."

Justin looked shocked. "Pantomime! Pantomime? You mean being the back legs of a cow or something?"

"Usually, I do the villains. Like Abanazer in Aladdin, or—"

"No. Listen! I've got a proper job for you. Or the nearest thing to a proper job you'll ever do."

At that moment the waiter arrived with our soup and for a few brief seconds I was excited. Perhaps Cousin Justin had invested heavily in a movie and was going to use his influence to get me a part in it. Then he spoke again and the illusion was shattered.

"You know I've just bought this château in the Dordogne?"

I nodded. As it happens I did know—my sister had told me—but it was typical of his arrogance that he should assume I kept myself informed of his doings.

"It's called the Château de Bressac. Incredible place. On a bend of the Dordogne a few miles upstream of Beynac. Fantastic possibilities. Well, obviously, I can't get down there and do anything about it until next Spring, and the builders won't be in until then anyway, because it's pretty run down. Naturally I wanted someone to keep an eye on the place until then. You know: not just look in on it twice a day, but actually live there. See it doesn't get broken into. Well, I tried the locals but they wouldn't play ball. You know what locals are like." I nodded as if I too believed that "locals" belonged to a universal and predictable human category. "The long and the short of it is that no-one down there is actually prepared to live in the place and look after it over the winter months, so that was when I had my brain wave. I thought of you. I'll pay you, of course, but your tasks won't be exactly onerous. Just a bit of light dusting and general maintenance, I should imagine. There's an old *deux chevaux* down there that you can use, so you will be able to get about a bit. Not too much obviously, because your job is to be there and house sit. Château sit, I should say!" He laughed a good deal at his little joke and I politely joined in the mirth. "It could be a golden opportunity for you. You could—I don't know—read, write, study something useful like accounting, brush up your French. Well?"

By mid-October it was clear there was going to be no pantomime for me that year, so I agreed.

~§~

I got a cheap flight to Bergerac and splashed out on a taxi to Beynac. There I was picked up in the *deux chevaux* by a Monsieur Bobelet whom Justin had retained to keep an eye on the château grounds. Gaston Bobelet owned the farm that adjoined the château. He was one of those taciturn, permanently unshaven French rustics who seem to harbor a grudge against the world in general and foreigners in particular. His wife, whom I met later, was bright-eyed, almost completely spherical, and charming. She complimented me on my French and gave me a delicious *cassoulet* to eat on my first night at the château.

I had arrived in fine weather. It was the end of October and Southern France was enjoying an Indian Summer. As we drove towards the château along the banks of the Dordogne I couldn't help feeling exhilarated.

The grounds of the château are surrounded by a high brick wall, except for the Northern side where it is bounded by the river. There is only one entrance and that is through a gate of exquisite eighteenth century wrought iron work, now badly rusted. From there, there is a long straight drive through a park dotted with some fine old trees. To my right as Gaston took me down the drive in the deux chevaux I could just see through a belt of poplars and willows the broad stream of the Dordogne glittering in the afternoon sun.

The château itself was a tall irregular construction built mostly in the sixteenth century but with later additions. There were numerous turrets topped by conical slate roofs that gleamed dully like pewter in candlelight. It was not exactly a beautiful building, but it was imposing and picturesque, and, yes, I suppose its ancient grandeur gave it a sort of romantic beauty.

Madame Bobelet was waiting on the drive before the front door. She was far less taciturn than her husband, but she seemed nevertheless in a hurry to be done with her task. She showed me the main areas of the château and the bedroom on the first floor that she had made up for me to occupy. There was no electricity: lighting was by oil, candle or gas bottles, which also provided heat for the stove and a primitive boiler for hot water.

Madame Bobelet was extremely conscientious in providing me with practical information about my new home, but I noticed that when I asked her more general questions about the place and its former inhabitants she brushed them aside. Through the kitchen window, as she was showing me the stove, I caught sight of Gaston, pacing about on the drive puffing at the soggy end of a *Gauloise*. Suddenly Madame Bobelet finished her recitation, wished me a *bonne aprésmidi*, and a *bon appetit* (with regard to the cassoulet) and darted out of the kitchen door to join her husband.

I watched them as they walked down the straight drive to the château gates, leaving me with the *deux chevaux*, my evening meal and the vast unknown spaces of the Château de Bressac.

My first action when I was alone was to switch on my mobile phone. I could get no signal at all in the château so I walked out into the grounds. It took me some time before I found a spot that gave me a reasonable connection. It was quite a distance from the château and on the very banks of the Dordogne among the willows. I called Justin.

"Yes?"

I told him that I had arrived safely.

"Right. Well, you won't need to call me again. If you come across any problems, you and the Bobelets can sort it out between you. That's what you're there for, isn't it?"

Feeling that I needed to extract some sort of human response from him I said: "It's a beautiful place."

"Well of course it is! I know that!"

He was offended, I suppose, because he thought I was subtly accusing him of being a philistine. After that there seemed no point in pursuing the conversation so I rang off. Apart from the distant ripple of water there was no sound. High above in the cloudless blue air a pale bird of prey with long slow wingbeats circled. It was a short-toed eagle, quite common in those parts, though not usually so late in the year. I was proud of myself for having identified it and would have liked to share the moment with someone.

~§~

For the first ten days the weather continued fine and I settled into a routine of shopping, cooking and reading. I visited the Bobelets once in their farmhouse to return the *cassoulet* dish, and though Madame was very civil, it was made quite plain to me that they were both very busy people who had no time to spare talking to the indolent Englishman from the château.

I tried to be, as far as possible, a diligent caretaker and inspect every part of the building. It was an extraordinarily rambling structure with rooms of all different sizes organized in no particular order with numerous corridors and staircases. Nearly all the rooms were dusty, shuttered and void of furniture, apart from those great dark coffin-like *armoires* that the French go in for. I tried, for my own amusement really, to make a plan of the place for each of its three main floors, but it baffled me. Not even the tape measure I bought in Beynac for the purpose was any help. I couldn't make sense of it.

There seemed to be parts inside the château that were inaccessible. I remembered the story of Glamis Castle where there was said to be a secret room in which a monster was kept. One day the guests at a Glamis house party decided to hang a towel or cloth from every window they could find. If there was a window which was unmarked then that was the monster's window. I can't remember what was the result of the experiment, but I decided to do something similar with the château. I walked round it from the outside counting all the windows, then did the same from within. They more or less added up to the same total. Perhaps, I thought, the hidden parts of the building were internal and windowless.

One thing I did notice was that at the back of the château on the South West corner it looked as if there had once been a large octagonal tower of some kind which had either fallen down or had been destroyed. Against one outer wall I could see the remains of a fireplace and an overmantle clinging to it. Further up there was a series of stone steps which spiraled up into the château and were lost in darkness. I tried to look for that staircase from the inside, but without success.

Let me state categorically that I don't believe I have a psychic bone in my body, nevertheless there was something I didn't like about the Château de Bressac. It was not that there was some sort of atmosphere of evil or menace about it, at least as far as I could tell; in fact there seemed to be no atmosphere at all. That, I suppose, was what I didn't like. The place felt empty, not just physically but in some other way too. And it was silent, especially at night. With any normal old building you expect the odd creak or click, but this one was a tomb.

I discovered that there is a terrible thing about silence, especially the silence inside a building. Your ears become supersensitive. You find yourself tensed up, waiting for a noise to happen, but of course it doesn't, so you remain tense. I thought music might help. I had an MP3 player with earphones, but when I had it on in the château I caught myself not listening to the music at all, but somehow listening *through* it to see if there was any sound to be heard in the spaces beyond.

It was worse at night. For some reason the shutters of my bedroom window were jammed shut and no amount of shoving and banging could dislodge them. So, once I had extinguished my lamp or candle—no electricity, remember—I was left in complete darkness and silence. It was like being in a void. I wondered if death was like this. Only a tiny thread of pale light through a gap at the bottom of one of the shutters told me when it was morning.

In spite of this, the first ten days passed fairly easily; then the weather broke. I can remember it exactly. It was eleven fifteen at night according to my watch, and I was reading in bed by candlelight when suddenly there was a low roaring sound. I started violently. The rain had begun—a downpour in fact. I took my candle and went downstairs. Through the long windows in the hall I could see beyond the glass a vast, darkly glistening curtain of rain. There was a flash and the château's park was leprously illumined for a moment by a thunderbolt, like a great crack of light in a black wall. I counted slowly up to three before the thunder rumbled.

The innards of the building were still noiseless but we were now encased in sound, the rustle of rain, the groan of thunder. I began to walk upstairs to my bedroom. As I reached the first floor I did think I heard something else—something from inside but far off. It was such a tiny noise that I might have imagined it, but it was very distinct. It sounded like the cry of a baby, the senseless, angry yell of a newborn child pitched unwillingly into the world. It might have lasted a second, if that, then it was gone. I stood still for a long time waiting for the noise to repeat itself, but it didn't.

When I was in bed again I put my candle on the bedside table, but I did not blow it out. I let it burn down into its socket while I lay awake listening, but all I heard was rain and thunder.

For a few nights after that I kept a candle or a night-light on in my bedroom until at last I was ready to tell myself not to be a fool. The weather was getting colder. As well as the rain there was wind, which sometimes penetrated into the château, catching you unawares with cold blasts and occasionally slamming doors shut. There was a great fireplace in the main salon of the castle with a huge hooded overmantle in the French style on which was carved a heraldic escutcheon, presumably of the Bressac family. I lit a fire in this and ate my supper in front of it every night. It was the crackling of the fire as much as its heat and light that comforted me.

One night, about a week after the thunderstorm, I had sat long in front of the fire, finishing a bottle of the local wine. I was drinking a lot more wine these days because it was plentiful and cheap. I hoped vaguely I was not becoming an alcoholic, but, to be honest, I did not much care if I was. It was nearly midnight, the bottle was empty, and I had no more excuses for not going to bed, so I took my candle and stumbled upstairs. I managed to undress and put on a nightshirt, but when I accidentally knocked over my candle and it went out, I was drunk enough not to care. I got into bed and fell asleep almost immediately.

Some time later—how long I don't know—I was awake, or half-awake, or at least somehow aware of myself and my surroundings. I found that my cheek was rested against something rounded and firm and soft. It was not like my pillow: it yielded, but yielded less and it was very cold. Then the thing that touched me began to move restlessly as if alive. I pulled myself violently away from it and sat up in bed, letting out a stupid, involuntary, childish yelp.

I tried to find an explanation for my experience, but none came to me. I did not know what it was, but I knew exactly what it had felt like: a baby's belly, a baby's bottom perhaps, but a dead baby.

I felt around in the dark for the candle until I remembered that in my drunken carelessness I had left the matches downstairs.

On the nights following I once more kept a light on in the bedroom and barely slept. When I did, I sometimes felt again that touch of soft cold flesh against me, but more distantly and through the veil of dreams. I tried vainly to remember what the dreams were, because I thought they might be telling me something, but they never did. In the evenings before going upstairs I sometimes got through more than one bottle of wine.

One night I had gone to bed particularly drunk and, after a few hours of drugged sleep, I found myself suddenly, horribly awake. I had a headache from the wine, and the blood was thumping in my temples, but that was not what was making me sweat. It was the thing that was touching me again.

This time it felt like a hand, soft and cold. It was small—a baby's hand, it must have been. For a moment it played with my chin and then began to reach towards my mouth. Then tiny but perfectly formed little fingers were trying to force their way between my lips. The silky little digits were inexorable, insistent. I wanted to pull them away but my arms wouldn't move from my sides. I was both awake and somehow paralyzed. I might have prevented the thing from reaching further if I had bitten down on it, but that idea revolted me beyond words. The hand had reached inside my mouth, now numb with the cold, and was stretching out towards my throat. I could feel the fingers flickering inside me, tickling the roof of my mouth and the soft palate. They reached the back of my tongue. Then I began to choke. That convulsive movement jerked me up and into full consciousness. I was awake, alive, gasping for air in a cold black room.

I held my breath, waiting for something to break the silence, but nothing did. It was a windless night. I was entombed in silence and alone. Now, once more, I had to find something to explain what I had experienced. Of course it had been a dream, but what had caused such a vivid one? Had I unconsciously put my own hand into my mouth? Was that it? I tried it out, but I wasn't convinced. My fingers were far too big, and they were warm, comparatively speaking. Had it been some sort of animal? But what?

The following morning I decided I must do something about all this. It was time to see if there was any explanation to be found in the history of the château. Of course, if there wasn't, that would be something of a relief—or would it? I couldn't decide.

I drove into Beynac and represented myself at the municipal library in the Mairie as a scholar wishing to study the history of the district. I was shown to a rather dingy little room full of books that looked as if they had been haphazardly gathered together. There were large official-looking tomes full of maps and facsimile documents, huddled against town guides, biographies of local worthies, manuals on wine-making, boat building and other local trades.

Most of the guidebooks and local histories had little or nothing to say about the Château de Bressac. The most I could find out from a work in English was a passing mention in a book called *Rambles in the Dordogne:*

> *From the river you may see the Château de Bressac, home to the Counts of Bressac until the French Revolution. Since then, this imposing structure has passed through many hands and has never been occupied by one family for any great length of time. It is now believed to be more or less derelict. Permission to view the château and grounds is, to my certain knowledge, never granted.*

Finally, on a dusty shelf behind some bound volumes of old local newspapers, I discovered a work that looked as if it had what I was searching for. *Légendes et histoires de Beynac et ses environs* by Henri Fauvinard had been published in 1876 and did not appear to have been much consulted since that date. In it there was a chapter entitled "The noble house of Bressac" which gave the history of the Counts of Bressac who had inhabited the château since the sixteenth century. Until the mid-eighteenth century the family seems to have enjoyed a fairly uneventful run of aristocratic prosperity, then things began to get interesting. Here is a rough translation of the relevant passage:

> In the year 1763 Count Etienne de Bressac, then in his sixty-sixth year, married for a second time. He had been married as a young man, but his wife had died early and without issue. Since then, he had pursued a life of reckless and untrammeled libertinage, until it was borne in on him that unless he soon produced a legitimate heir, the great name of Bressac might perish with him. So the Count took a young bride of seventeen from the princely Italian house of Bartori. Why he chose this young woman from a foreign land is something of a mystery, but he had traveled much in Italy and had formed (it was said) strange ties with this ancient but ill-famed noble family.
>
> The Principessa Eleonora Bartori was a young girl of quite exceptional beauty: her skin was white, and her hair, which she did not powder as was then the fashion, was jet-black. Many remarked on the redness of her lips and the purity of her com-plexion. The old Count duly married her and she bore him a son, Armand, who was the delight of his old age. But as the Count grew older, increasingly his Countess seemed to rule over him, demanding that a great suite of rooms in the château be put at her exclusive disposal, and that none should be allowed to enter it, not even the Count, except by her permission.
>
> Her servants there were slaves, bought from the East, mostly blackamoors and all, save for one eunuch who was her personal steward, were dumb, their tongues having been cut out at the roots in the Eastern fashion.
>
> So the Count grew older but still would not die, and she, miraculously it seemed, remained the most beautiful woman for miles around. Her black hair showed not a thread of silver and her skin seemed, if anything, whiter and smoother, and her lips redder. Though many disliked the power she wielded and the strangeness of her personal retinue, no one could find anything against her. With the Count in his dotage and she still young and beautiful it might be

thought that she would take some young lover to herself, but she had no favorites, and this in itself was counted against her.

There were at that time many poor families in the village of Bressac and the surrounding district. When one of their children disappeared without trace, no great notice was taken of it at first, but this began to happen with more frequency. It was observed, more-over, that the children who disappeared were generally young girls who had received their first communion, and were about to reach puberty.

In 1784 the old Count died and Armand his son succeeded to the title, but his mother was still Countess and her influence was as great as when she had been the Count's consort. There were those in the neighborhood who tried to set Count Armand against the Dowager Countess in order to destroy her power, but in vain. They began to call her "The Old Countess" as a kind of insult, even though she seemed as young and as fresh as ever.

Finally a friend of the young Count, the Marquis d'Elboef, saw that the only way to depose this woman's influence was by means of another woman: Count Armand must marry, but he seemed in no hurry to do so. Suitable candidates were sought out and put forward, but each time the old Countess's machinations and the young Count's indifference dissipated the scheme. During this time it was noticed that Count Armand would spend many hours in the Countess's apartments.

A family named Duplessis moved into the district: a husband and wife and their eighteen-year-old daughter, Louise. The father was a Baron, and the family of Duplessis was a very wealthy one, having inherited estates from their great great uncle, Cardinal Richelieu.

Soon after their arrival, the Marquis d'Elboef held a great ball at his château in Montpeyroux and invited all the noble families for miles around, but his true purpose was to bring Louise Duplessis and Count Armand together, so breaking the hold that his mother had on the young man. It is said by some that the Marquis had conceived a great hatred for the Dowager Countess because of some wrong she had done him, but no one could say what it was.

Whatever the truth of this was, the Marquis' plan succeeded and a match was made between Louise Duplessis and the young Count Armand. The moment had come and the Countess saw no way of opposing the marriage without prejudice to her own position, so she bowed to the inevitable and even showed enthusiasm for it.

Nevertheless, she did not travel to Bergerac with Count Armand to see him united to Louise in the Cathedral there. She remained in the château saying that she was preparing it for the arrival of a new Countess. During that time two more children, both girls, went missing from the nearby village of Bressac.

And so Count Armand returned to the château from his wedding trip with his bride, pleasant enough to look at, with brown curls and blue eyes, but no match for the beauty of the Countess. She stood at the gate of the château to meet the young pair in a dress of scarlet satin, her ebon hair elaborately coifed and held in place by a tortoiseshell comb studded with diamonds and emeralds. She greeted her daughter-in-law effusively and for some months all seemed well, but during that time Louise began to show the strength of her character. She had none of the charm and skill of her mother-in-law, but she had a kind of resolute stubbornness, and her position as Count Armand's wife was inviolable. The Count, torn this way and that, seemed to have no will of his own. Meanwhile, Louise began to forge firm alliances with the servants and workers on the estate, as well as with her wealthier neighbors.

The Dowager Countess, isolated, made as much use as she could of her formidable allure. Whenever she emerged from her apart-ments all eyes, including those of her son, were upon her.

That winter a young servant girl at the château called Berthe disappeared. This might not have aroused much interest had it not been for the fact that Countess Louise had taken a great liking to the girl. Being dogged and stubborn by nature, Louise instituted a thorough search of the château, much to the disgust of the Countess, who regarded all this fuss over the disappearance of a mere servant as undignified and a waste of time.

It was when Louise ordered a search to be made in the Dowager Countess's apartments that the last battle was joined. The Dowager Countess seemed to prevail at first and Count Armand ordered that no one should enter her apartments without permission. But Louise was not to be rebuffed. She insisted that where the search was concerned nobody should be shown favor. Her persistence began to wear the Count down.

Then one day it was Louise who could not be found. Like Berthe she had vanished.

The scene in the Great Salon of the château that day was strange indeed. Count Armand sat alone by the fire, silent, gnawing his fingers, servants and retainers at a discreet distance. It was clear that he knew more than anyone there what had become of his wife. The silence intensified, and with it the Count's torment. At last he summoned his steward and four footmen to go with him to the Dowager Countess's apartments.

There was a fierce struggle at the entrance to the rooms. The dumb slaves of the Old Countess fought with their bare hands until the steward pointed his blunderbuss at them. Every room was searched, and then they came to a door behind which a low murmuring could be heard like a chant.

Here Count Armand hesitated for, although he had been in his mother's apartments many times, this was the one door that had always been barred to him. A kind of superstitious dread held him back. But the steward—who was my grandfather and I had it from him—turned the handle and opened the door.

The room was a bathhouse done up in the Turkish style. There was a great tessellated basin set into the floor and around it stood the Nubian eunuchs in attendance with precious vases of ointment to hand. The chief eunuch in ceremonial robes stood at one end of the bath muttering an incantation. In the bath itself stood the Countess, quite naked.

Never, said my grandfather, had she looked more lovely—at least for one brief moment. Her slender figure seemed rounder and fuller than usual; her pale skin was rosy from the heated water, and her lips were red. Then they noticed the little splashes of scarlet on her body, and that the gently steaming water around her feet was incarnadined. Above her was suspended, by an elaborate system of ropes and steel hoops, the white, drained corpse of Berthe the servant girl, her throat slashed, the wound no longer red but grey. At that moment the Countess was enjoying the last drops of her infernal shower bath. And in the corner, the poor naked body of the young Countess Louise—plump and pleasing, but no match for her mother-in-law—was being trussed up to provide a further supply of blood.

The learned reader may be aware that in some mystery religions of the East, particularly that of Cybele, the Mountain Mother, it was customary to be thus showered in the blood of bulls or goats as a rite of initiation, but it was only the blackest of sects which believed that the blood of virgins and young children would restore youth and preserve beauty. The Dowager Countess had been initiated into one of these hellish cults in her native Italy and, either through the release of dark power or from more natural causes, her looks had been preserved.

Countess Louise was at once set free. The Dowager Countess's unholy crew were taken away to be handed over to the jurisdiction of the local magistrate. As for The Dowager Countess herself, even as she was, naked and dabbled with her innocent victim's blood, she threw herself screaming at Count Armand's feet and begged for mercy. The speech she made was the most terrible that my grandfather can ever recall hearing, for in it she confessed to the slaughter of many of the district's missing children. Why she incriminated herself it is hard to say, unless she wanted, pitiless and inhuman as she was, to relieve her conscience. But one phrase, repeated over and over again, remained in the minds of everyone present: "Remember the child! Remember the child!"

Count Armand ordered that she be given a week's supply of food and drink and then, even as she was, shut up in that awful bathhouse with one candle, and all entrances to the place sealed. It was a fearful sentence, her agony being prolonged because Count Armand did not want to be immediately or directly responsible for her death.

Those who were appointed to lock the entrances to her tomb remembered that she never ceased to scream out for her son and to repeat that phrase: "Remember the child!"

Two weeks went by, at the end of which Count Armand could endure it no longer. He ordered that the bathhouse be broken into. This was done, and there the old Countess was found, dead—not from starvation, but from choking. The shock of her incarceration had brought on a pregnancy already sufficiently advanced, and she had given birth to a child—whether boy or girl I have been unable to ascertain. In the terrible pangs of her hunger, she had begun to devour the wretched infant. A tiny hand that had she tried to swallow whole had become lodged in her throat and she had choked herself to death. The baby's head remained intact, and those who saw its features swore that only her own son Armand could have been the father. Of the Countess's hair not a strand retained its natural blackness—it was all as white as the moon.

So the Countess's apartments were sealed up. The main en-trance was bricked over and, as I understand, only one secret entrance remained. Where this was situated only the Count knew.

As for Louise, she never spoke to Count Armand again, but she gave birth to a son and soon after, died. Count Armand lived on for a short while until the Revolution came. During this, he and his young son perished by the guillotine. No collateral heirs could be found to succeed to the title or estates, and so expired the noble house of Bressac.

It is said of course, that the Dowager's apartments in the Château are haunted, and the Countess's screams echo still in that empty bathhouse, but who has ever been in there to prove it?

~§~

I drove back to the château with reckless speed. Something like madness had taken hold of me, a madness that compelled me to see this through to the end. It was about 5:00 p.m. when I returned, and still light. The sun was setting in blood behind the trees. As I entered the hall, I picked up the big old electric torch that the Bobelets had left me. I switched it on and off a couple of times. The batteries appeared to be young.

As I was driving back a plan had formed in my mind. I had decided that I knew where the hidden entrance to the Countess's apartments might be. In my walks about the château I had come across a room on the first floor that was oddly shaped, like a right angled triangle. It might have been the corner of a much bigger room and it had running almost the length of its longest wall a huge fireplace with an elaborately carved overmantel, quite out of proportion to the size of the chamber. The carving in alabaster on the overmantel was badly damaged, but I noticed that it included a heraldic shield. The insignia carved on it were the arms of Bressac, as on the fireplace downstairs, but quartered with them on the shield was another armorial image: that of an eagle in full flight carrying a baby in its talons. I guessed that this could be the heraldic device of the Bartori family, and that the strangely situated fireplace might mark the entrance to the Old Countess's secret apartments.

It may have taken me an hour—perhaps longer—to find that three of the carved alabaster bosses on the overmantel, when turned anticlockwise, released some system of counterweights that allowed part of the wall of the fireplace's inglenook to slide back. A short dark passage with a flight of steps leading upwards at the end of it was revealed.

Putting a handy broken chair in the way of the stone door to prevent it from accidentally sliding shut, I switched on my torch and entered. At that moment I was too possessed with finishing and resolving what I had set out to find to think of the consequences.

I began to climb the steps. The masonry here was smooth and of the highest quality; its surface so polished that it dimly reflected the light of my torch. At the top of the steps I found a wooden door with a great ring handle of iron, richly wrought. I half-hoped the door would be locked and that my researches would end there. But I turned the ring and, after an initial protest, the latch rose easily on the other side. Rust had not corrupted: it was all too dry.

Beyond the door there was a series of small interconnecting chambers. The thing of which I was most immediately aware was an overpowering odor. The place reeked of decay and disintegration. As I looked around I saw the visible evidence of it. I was in a sort of lobby or anteroom, lavishly furnished. A Levantine Turkish rug was on the floor, its rich colors misted over with dust. Great hangings drooped in tatters from the walls. I was startled by a terrible scrabbling noise, only to find it was mice gouging a little city for themselves out of a divan.

I went into the second room, and there in the center was a great bed. It was roofed with a vast canopy of grey velvet dripping with golden thread. Moths and other creatures had gnawed great holes in its draperies, so it looked as if the bed was enmeshed in the web of a gigantic spider. Sheets and pillows were on the bed, the clothes slightly rumpled. If it wasn't for the dust you might have thought that someone had just got out of it.

The next room was a dining room, and even thicker with dust. The table was made of various marbles in the Italian pietra dura style; its surface, still visible under the grime, a dazzling patterned mosaic of color.

Silver plates and jugs, much tarnished, stood on the table. Cobwebs festooned the epergnes and candelabra. At one end of the room was a magnificent cupboard, made from all kinds of wood, with rustic scenes fashioned out of gilt and tortoiseshell on the doors. The doors opened up to reveal the miniature façade of a house in the Palladian style with pillars and pilasters, rusticated masonry on the lower range and a wonderfully carved pediment depicting Neptune in his chariot drawn by sea-horses and surrounded by conch-blowing Tritons. All this was in ivory, gilded here and there, with the windows made from the finest Venetian glass. The doors all opened to reveal spaces for keepsakes or old letters. Sections of the building could be pulled out as drawers by means of tiny golden knobs, and these drawers were filled with jewels of every kind, some loose, others made up into ornaments, and a hoard of gold and silver coins. I drew back from the sight, half afraid I might be tempted to steal them. I had a feeling that they were protected from theft by more than my own scruples.

Above the cupboard was a picture in a gilded wooden frame. It was the half-length of a woman in a powder-blue dress from about 1770. She was seated and leaning back idly on her left elbow, the hand caressing her cheek, one finger coquettishly playing over her lips as she stared out from the picture directly at the spectator. I was reminded of Boucher's famous portrait of Madame de Pompadour, except that this was the work of a competent journeyman and not a master. The face was white, the hair jet-black and shining like polished ebony, the lips red and perfectly formed, while in the green eyes the painter had captured an expression of malign suspicion. They seemed to glitter in the torchlight and fix me with a particular gaze, as if she were alive.

At the end of this suite of rooms was a door of wood, braced and ornamented with ironwork in the Arabic style. It had a great iron catch that lifted easily enough. On smooth, uncreaking hinges the door swung outwards towards me. I stepped into the next room, which was vast, with a coldness about it quite unlike the others.

I knew that I must be in the bathhouse of the Countess's apartments. I hardly had time to shine my torch over the Eastern sumptuousness of its marble and mosaic before a cold gust of wind from somewhere gave me such a shock that I dropped the torch. I saw it rolling away from me still alight. Then it disappeared, and I heard it smash against something and all light went out. It must have fallen into the bath. Then another blast of wind blew the door shut behind me.

The bang of the door was like a cannon shot, and the sound reverberated for what seemed like minutes. I knew terror then as I had never known it before—like a great marble fist thumping at my chest. Shaking and retching, I felt my way back to the door, murmuring little prayers like a child. I found the door, but it was shut fast and there was no way of opening it on my side. I tore my nails, scrabbling at the wood. I screamed and whimpered and banged until I was wet with blood and tears and perspiration. It was idiotic, I know. Nobody could possibly have heard me.

For a time—I have no idea how long—I was no better than a wild beast caught in a trap, and I only stopped shrieking finally out of exhaustion. If I had had the means to do so, I would have killed myself. I don't like to think about some of the things I screamed aloud. I was cursing a God I hardly believed in, then the next minute groveling and begging his forgiveness. The only excuse I can offer is that my terror drove me a little mad, and so perhaps did the almost palpable evil of this place. Oh yes, I felt it this time.

Once my emotions were spent, I felt a kind of calm coming to me. My senses were sharpened. I could see absolutely nothing as the place was pitch dark, but I could hear, feel and smell with great intensity. I felt again the cold blast of wind that had taken away my torch, then blown the door shut.

Well, I thought, if there is wind in the place, there must be some aperture through which it comes. I got up and began to walk around the bathhouse, keeping close to the walls. Many times I stopped, held my breath and listened. Had I heard something other than the sound I made? Was it a quiet, breathy, almost imperceptible snicker of laughter? The walls were damp, and once or twice I touched patches of slime. My feet slid gingerly over the floor in case I should meet with some obstacle. Once I tripped against something that rattled. I fell and, stretching out my right hand to protect my fall, I touched an object hard and round which rolled away. I stretched out again to grasp the thing. It had large holes in it. Some of its surface was smooth, some of it cracked and ragged. Then further down there were two rows of smaller objects like pebbles . . . or *teeth*. My hand first recoiled from the skull in horror, but then I picked it up and hurled it away from me. It gave me an odd satisfaction to hear the thing smash like a china vase against a wall.

Twice I went around those walls. The first time I seemed to come across a door, and I became elated. But no, it was the door that had closed on me. I confirmed my fears with a second tour. Then again I wanted to scream curses at God and die. I think I was closer to madness then than I have ever been, but something in me fought against it, silently in the dark. Slowly the urge to madness weakened, then it vanished as if it had never been. It was a victory of sorts, but I felt dull and lifeless after it. I was still going to die alone and never be found.

Slowly, my lethargy and despair lifted a little. I remembered that I had not yet located the source of the breeze and began to walk about feeling for it with my hands in front of me. The impression that I received was that it came up from somewhere. But it arrived in gusts, so that I had difficulty in following it to its source. Nevertheless, my attention was so fixed on feeling and hearing this one thing that I began to track it like a hound on a scent.

It was then that my enthusiasm almost betrayed me. As I began to feel this blast of air, I stepped forward confidently and my foot met emptiness. I threw myself backwards, and so just managed to prevent myself from falling into the sunken basin of the bathhouse. My caution returned. I crawled to the edge of the basin and let myself down into it.

The draught seemed to be coming from the floor of the bath, which was dry and had no trace of water in it, but though I was walking cautiously I nearly came to grief again. There was a hole in the floor. I knelt down and felt around it.

Part of the tiled base of the bath had given way and a hollow space underneath was exposed. I reached my hand inside. As far as I could tell the base of the pool was held up by brick pillars some two feet high. Evidently it had been heated in the ancient Roman manner by hot air from a furnace underneath. I climbed down into the spaces under the basin, where there was just room enough to crawl. If there had been a furnace under there, there would have been doors from which the fire was fed. It must have been from these that the breeze was coming. It was a small hope that I would be able to get through those doors, but it was the only hope I had.

I had to clear much debris before I began my journey under the bath and through the forest of brick pillars that supported it. In the pitch dark I was always bumping my head against them. Afraid that the floor above me might collapse, I moved gingerly. It was virtually impossible to tell where the breezes were coming from because the brick pillars were diverting their flow.

It might have been an hour, or more, or less—my situation had taken away from me all sense of time—before I ran up against a wall. I could have been going in circles for a long time before I met it. I worked my way along its brick surface, feeling carefully for any kind of door or aperture. I felt every crevice of the brick for a breath of wind. At last I could hear its whistling and moaning more distinctly. My hopes rose, but also my fears. I realized that I would soon know if there was a way of escape or not. Then my hands touched a pair of rusty metal plates under which the draught was blowing. These were the oven doors of the hypocaust. Would they open inwards or outwards?

I pushed, and they made no movement. There was no way of gripping them from the inside. With all the power that was available to me in that confined space, I heaved my shoulder against the metal. For that little effort I was deluged by an invisible but choking fall of dust and plaster. Even now the whole floor could collapse on top of me and I could die. Yet I fancied that the metal door had moved a little.

After a moment's thought I decided to brace myself against one of the brick pillars and thrust with my feet against the metal doors. They grated against the stone lintel at the first shove and opened a fraction. I saw a column of dazzling moonlight ahead of me and drank in a mouthful of cold air. One more thrust with my feet, and the doors were open just as a further deluge of tiles and plaster began to rain down on me.

I scrambled out feet-first onto the floor of a narrow, vaulted passageway. The moonlight was coming in from ragged holes in the roof. It was hideously cold, but the relief warmed me. To my left was a staircase going downwards, to my right a fall of rubble and masonry. My only way was down. I took a few steps before I realized that I was on the winding stair that I had seen on the outside of the château. I stopped before the steps did and hesitated again. I faced a drop of what? Thirty or forty feet? Death was still the likeliest option.

A small hand pushed me and I fell into dark open air.

~§~

Gaston Bobelet found me the following morning lying on the gravel path at the South West corner of the château. I was suffering from mild concussion and a sprained ankle, but no bones had been broken so he did not see fit to take me to hospital, and for that I was grateful to him. During the rest of my term as château caretaker I spent my nights in a room at the Bobelets' farmhouse, but Justin never knew that. When I returned to England I was not summoned to meet my cousin and make a report; I simply received a check through the post for the remainder of my house-sitter's salary. The following year I heard that Justin had sold the château: no reason was given.

Cousin Justin and I did not meet again until a family christening in the Spring of this year. My sister had produced a male child and, not being one to pass by such an opportunity, had decided to call him Justin and invite his wealthy namesake to be the godfather.

The ceremony at her little village church went well. Little Justin received the baptismal waters without complaint. Big Justin and the other godparents, of whom I was one, stood around the font as the vicar conducted the ceremony. When this was over my sister, perhaps for the benefit of photographers, handed the baby to his richest godfather to hold. I saw a troubled look pass across Cousin Justin's face, but he did his best to show willing. Like most childless men, he is not at ease with extreme infancy.

Justin junior emitted a gurgle of delight and stretched out a soft, plump little hand to caress his godfather's cheek. When the baby touched his mouth, my Cousin Justin started violently and nearly dropped him. I saw the look on his face, and it was one of sheer terror. When our eyes met across the font I smiled and lifted my fingers to my lips, flickering them a little as I did so. Justin's normally reddish complexion was now as grey as the surrounding stone. The baby began to cry, so my sister rapidly grabbed him back from his godfather's arms.

I felt at last that I had been paid in full for my time at the Château.

Part V

CANDLE SMOKE

gothic romances and delightfully malevolent folklore

GOTHIC FICTION is often imitated and there are attempts to rejigger it for each new generation, but why not read the real thing? There was once a time when authors had to scratch out their stories with quill and ink, when readers had to read by candlelight, and people had no choice but to wear squeaky shoes with funny brass buckles. Ah, the Napoleonic Era! Those were the good old days, when you didn't need a power outage to give you a good gothic feel. You merely crept around your house in the dark with a smoky candelabra sizzling the cobwebs overhead. Still, can you imagine reading Frankenstein by firelight after a heavy meal of mutton and taters, with a wicked storm shaking the trees and rattling the windows? That had to be the ultimate reading experience, comparable only to reading comic books at summer camp.

We don't have Frankenstein but we do have VIY, king of the gnomes. Also on tap are a headless horseman, a warlock with a voodoo doll, a noble knight lured to his doom, and a wailing ghost or two. I propose that we provide the gothic horrors and you provide the firelight. The raging storm must be left to the Great Almighty.

Most readers are familiar with Ichabod Crane and the Headless Horse-man, but few have read the original story by Washington Irving. "The Legend of Sleepy Hollow" delivers the first surprise in our box of delights. Told with a wink and a nod, the tale is blue-ribbon entertainment that effectively blends chortles and chills. Irving's writing is smooth, evocative, and amusing. Along the way one gains an insider's view of post-colonial America. When it first appeared it offered a new legend for a newborn country.

John Keats' "La Belle Sans Merci" was one of his last poems, written while he slowly succumbed to tuberculosis. When he died in 1821 he was only twenty-five and penniless, yet he left us with some of the best-loved poems ever written. Crafted as a romantic ballad, it is essentially a supernatural story in miniature. A knight is lured by love and yearning from his heroic purpose and later abandoned on the cold hillside, alone and withering. The poem grows darker *and more horrific with each stanza before fading to black with the final lines.*

Nikolai Gogol gave it his best shot at making a new monster with his creation of the VIY, an enormous bloodthirsty gnome whose eyelids hang down to his toes. A brief author's preamble to the story states that he drew upon traditional folklore in writing the tale, but that's a bit of playful misdirection. Gogol created the VIY out of whole cloth; it sprung entirely from his imagination. The novella is much better known and revered in Russia, where several movie and television versions have adapted it. The story is a neglected gem waiting for you to discovery its wicked charms.

With "The Leech of Folkstone" we get a tasty sample of the Ingoldsby Legends. The Legends (compiled and written by Richard Barham under the catchier penname, Thomas Ingoldsby) began to appear in 1837 in various British magazines. They proved so popular that they were compiled in book form a few years later. Subsequent editions (coming in all shapes and sizes, and featuring a variety of famous illustrators) sold steadily well into the next century. Neglected today, the Legends are begging for a relook, especially if they are as much fun to read as "The Leech of Folkstone".

Our final offering is "The Entail" by E. T. A. Hoffmann. Featuring flashbacks, foreshadowing and shifting points of view, the plotting of this novella has a cinematic quality that was well ahead of its time (1817). Alfred Hitchcock cited Hoffmann as an influence on his own work. Telling the tragic story of a multi-generational baronial castle, "The Entail" is packed with gothic characters, tropes, and trappings. Despite its dark subject matter the story is surprisingly endearing and emotionally satisfying. A new adaption of the work was created especially for Bruin's Midnight Reader. *We hope that it meets with your approval.*

The Legend of Sleepy Hollow

by Washington Irving

FOUND AMONG THE PAPERS OF THE
LATE DIEDRICH KNICKERBOCKER.

> *A pleasing land of drowsy head it was,*
> *Of dreams that wave before the half-shut eye;*
> *And of gay castles in the clouds that pass,*
> *Forever flushing round a summer sky.*
> CASTLE OF INDOLENCE.

IN THE BOSOM of one of those spacious coves which indent the eastern shore of the Hudson, at that broad expansion of the river denominated by the ancient Dutch navigators the Tappan Zee, and where they always prudently shortened sail and implored the protection of St. Nicholas when they crossed, there lies a small market town or rural port, which by some is called Greensburgh, but which is more generally and properly known by the name of Tarry Town. This name was given, we are told, in former days, by the good housewives of the adjacent country, from the inveterate propensity of their husbands to linger about the village tavern on market days. Be that as it may, I do not vouch for the fact, but merely advert to it, for the sake of being precise and authentic. Not far from this village, perhaps about two miles, there is a little valley or rather lap of land among high hills, which is one of the quietest places in the whole world. A small brook glides through it, with just murmur enough to lull one to repose; and the occasional whistle of a quail or tapping of a woodpecker is almost the only sound that ever breaks in upon the uniform tranquility.

I recollect that, when a stripling, my first exploit in squirrel-shooting was in a grove of tall walnut-trees that shades one side of the valley. I had wandered into it at noontime, when all nature is peculiarly quiet, and was startled by the roar of my own gun, as it broke the Sabbath stillness around and was prolonged and reverberated by the angry echoes. If ever I should wish for a retreat whither I might steal from the world and its distractions, and dream quietly away the remnant of a troubled life, I know of none more promising than this little valley.

From the listless repose of the place, and the peculiar character of its inhabitants, who are descendants from the original Dutch settlers, this sequestered glen has long been known by the name of Sleepy Hollow, and its rustic lads are called the Sleepy Hollow Boys throughout all the neighboring country. A drowsy, dreamy influence seems to hang over the land, and to pervade the very atmosphere. Some say that the place was bewitched by a High German doctor, during the early days of the settlement; others, that an old Indian chief, the prophet or wizard of his tribe, held his powwows there before the country was discovered by Master Hendrick Hudson. Certain it is, the place still continues under the sway of some witching power, that holds a spell over the minds of the good people, causing them to walk in a continual reverie. They are given to all kinds of marvellous beliefs, are subject to trances and visions, and frequently see strange sights, and hear music and voices in the air. The whole neighborhood abounds with local tales, haunted spots, and twilight superstitions; stars shoot and meteors glare oftener across the valley than in any other part of the country, and the nightmare, with her whole ninefold, seems to make it the favorite scene of her gambols.

The dominant spirit, however, that haunts this enchanted region, and seems to be commander-in-chief of all the powers of the air, is the apparition of a figure on horseback, without a head. It is said by some to be the ghost of a Hessian trooper, whose head had been carried away by a cannon-ball, in some nameless battle during the Revolutionary War, and who is ever and anon seen by the country folk hurrying along in the gloom of night, as if on the wings of the wind. His haunts are not confined to the valley, but extend at times to the adjacent roads, and especially to the vicinity of a church at no great distance. Indeed, certain of the most authentic historians of those parts, who have been careful in collecting and collating the floating facts concerning this spectre, allege that the body of the trooper having been buried in the churchyard, the ghost rides forth to the scene of battle in nightly quest of his head, and that the rushing speed with which he sometimes passes along the Hollow, like a midnight blast, is owing to his being belated, and in a hurry to get

back to the churchyard before daybreak.

Such is the general purport of this legendary superstition, which has furnished materials for many a wild story in that region of shadows; and the spectre is known at all the country firesides, by the name of the Headless Horseman of Sleepy Hollow.

It is remarkable that the visionary propensity I have mentioned is not confined to the native inhabitants of the valley, but is unconsciously imbibed by every one who resides there for a time. However wide awake they may have been before they entered that sleepy region, they are sure, in a little time, to inhale the witching influence of the air, and begin to grow imaginative, to dream dreams, and see apparitions.

I mention this peaceful spot with all possible laud, for it is in such little retired Dutch valleys, found here and there embosomed in the great State of New York, that population, manners, and customs remain fixed, while the great torrent of migration and improvement, which is making such incessant changes in other parts of this restless country, sweeps by them unobserved. They are like those little nooks of still water, which border a rapid stream, where we may see the straw and bubble riding quietly at anchor, or slowly revolving in their mimic harbor, undisturbed by the rush of the passing current. Though many years have elapsed since I trod the drowsy shades of Sleepy Hollow, yet I question whether I should not still find the same trees and the same families vegetating in its sheltered bosom.

In this by-place of nature there abode, in a remote period of American history, that is to say, some thirty years since, a worthy wight of the name of Ichabod Crane, who sojourned, or, as he expressed it, "tarried," in Sleepy Hollow, for the purpose of instructing the children of the vicinity. He was a native of Connecticut, a State which supplies the Union with pioneers for the mind as well as for the forest, and sends forth yearly its legions of frontier woodmen and country schoolmasters. The cognomen of Crane was not inapplicable to his person. He was tall, but exceedingly lank, with narrow shoulders, long arms and legs, hands that dangled a mile out of his sleeves, feet that might have served for shovels, and his whole frame most loosely hung together. His head was small, and flat at top, with huge ears, large green glassy eyes, and a long snipe nose, so that it looked like a weather-cock perched upon his spindle neck to tell which way the wind blew. To see him striding along the profile of a hill on a windy day, with his clothes bagging and fluttering about him, one might have mistaken him for the genius of famine descending upon the earth, or some scarecrow eloped from a cornfield.

His schoolhouse was a low building of one large room, rudely constructed of logs; the windows partly glazed, and partly patched with leaves of old copybooks. It was most ingeniously secured at vacant hours, by a withe twisted in the handle of the door, and stakes set against the window shutters; so that though a thief might get in with perfect ease, he would find some embarrassment in getting out—an idea most probably borrowed by the architect, Yost Van Houten, from the mystery of an eelpot. The schoolhouse stood in a rather lonely but pleasant situation, just at the foot of a woody hill, with a brook running close by, and a formidable birch-tree growing at one end of it. From hence the low murmur of his pupils' voices, conning over their lessons, might be heard in a drowsy summer's day, like the hum of a beehive; interrupted now and then by the authoritative voice of the master, in the tone of menace or command, or, peradventure, by the appalling sound of the birch, as he urged some tardy loiterer along the flowery path of knowledge. Truth to say, he was a conscientious man, and ever bore in mind the golden maxim, "Spare the rod and spoil the child." Ichabod Crane's scholars certainly were not spoiled.

I would not have it imagined, however, that he was one of those cruel potentates of the school who joy in the smart of their subjects; on the contrary, he administered justice with discrimination rather than severity; taking the burden off the backs of the weak, and laying it on those of the strong. Your mere puny stripling, that winced at the least flourish of the rod, was passed by with indulgence; but the claims of justice were satisfied by inflicting a double portion on some little tough wrong-headed, broad-skirted Dutch urchin, who sulked and swelled and grew dogged and sullen beneath the birch. All this he called "doing his duty by their parents;" and he never inflicted a chastisement without following it by the assurance, so consolatory to the smarting urchin, that "he would remember it and thank him for it the longest day he had to live."

When school hours were over, he was even the companion and playmate of the larger boys; and on holiday afternoons would convoy some of the smaller ones home, who happened to have pretty sisters, or good housewives for mothers, noted for the comforts of the cupboard. Indeed, it behooved him to keep on good terms with his pupils. The revenue arising from his school was small, and would have been scarcely sufficient to furnish him with daily bread, for he was a huge feeder, and, though lank, had the dilating powers of an anaconda; but to help out his maintenance, he was, according to country custom in those parts, boarded and lodged at the houses of the farmers whose children he instructed. With these he lived successively a week at a time, thus going the rounds of the neighborhood, with all his worldly effects tied up in a cotton handkerchief.

That all this might not be too onerous on the purses of his rustic patrons, who are apt to consider the costs of schooling a grievous burden, and schoolmasters as mere drones, he had various ways of rendering himself both useful and agreeable. He assisted the farmers occasionally in the lighter labors of their farms, helped to make hay, mended the fences, took the horses to water, drove the cows from pasture, and cut wood for the winter fire. He laid aside, too, all the dominant dignity and absolute sway with which he lorded it in his little empire, the school, and became wonderfully gentle and ingratiating. He found favor in the eyes of the mothers by petting the children, particularly the youngest; and like the lion bold, which whilom so magnanimously the lamb did hold, he would sit with a child on one knee, and rock a cradle with his foot for whole hours together.

In addition to his other vocations, he was the singing-master of the neighborhood, and picked up many bright shillings by instructing the young folks in psalmody. It was a matter of no little vanity to him on Sundays, to take his station in front of the church gallery, with a band of chosen singers; where, in his own mind, he completely carried away the palm from the parson. Certain it is, his voice resounded far above all the rest of the congregation; and there are peculiar quavers still to be heard in that church, and which may even be heard half a mile off, quite to the opposite side of the millpond, on a still Sunday morning, which are said to be legitimately descended from the nose of Ichabod Crane. Thus, by divers little makeshifts, in that ingenious way which is commonly denominated "by hook and by crook," the worthy pedagogue got on tolerably enough, and was thought, by all who understood nothing of the labor of headwork, to have a wonderfully easy life of it.

The schoolmaster is generally a man of some importance in the female circle of a rural neighborhood; being considered a kind of idle, gentlemanlike personage, of vastly superior taste and accomplishments to the rough country swains, and, indeed, inferior in learning only to the parson. His appearance, therefore, is apt to occasion some little stir at the tea-table of a farmhouse, and the addition of a supernumerary dish of cakes or sweetmeats, or, peradventure, the parade of a silver teapot. Our man of letters, therefore, was peculiarly happy in the smiles of all the country damsels. How he would figure among them in the churchyard, between services on Sundays; gathering grapes for them from the wild vines that overran the surrounding trees; reciting for their amusement all the epitaphs on the tombstones; or sauntering, with a whole bevy of them, along the banks of the adjacent millpond; while the more bashful country bumpkins hung sheepishly back, envying his superior elegance and address.

From his half-itinerant life, also, he was a kind of travelling gazette, carrying the whole budget of local gossip from house to house, so that his appearance was always greeted with satisfaction. He was, moreover, esteemed by the women as a man of great erudition, for he had read several several books quite through, and was a perfect master of Cotton Mather's "History of New England Witchcraft," in which, by the way, he most firmly and potently believed. He was, in fact, an odd mixture of small shrewdness and simple credulity. His appetite for the marvellous, and his powers of digesting it, were equally extraordinary; and both had been increased by his residence in this spell-bound region. No tale was too gross or monstrous for his capacious swallow. It was often his delight, after his school was dismissed in the afternoon, to stretch himself on the rich bed of clover bordering the little brook that whimpered by his schoolhouse, and there con over old Mather's direful tales, until the gathering dusk of evening made the printed page a mere mist before his eyes. Then, as he wended his way by swamp and stream and awful woodland, to the farmhouse where he happened to be quartered, every sound of nature, at that witching hour, fluttered his excited imagination—the moan of the whip-poor-will from the hillside, the boding cry of the tree toad, that harbinger of storm, the dreary hooting of the screech owl, or the sudden rustling in the thicket of birds frightened from their roost. The fireflies, too, which sparkled most vividly in the darkest places, now and then startled him, as one of uncommon brightness would stream across his path; and if, by chance, a huge blockhead of a beetle came winging his blundering flight against him, the poor varlet was ready to give up the ghost, with the idea that he was struck with a witch's token. His only resource on such occasions, either to drown thought or drive away evil spirits, was to sing psalm tunes and the good people of Sleepy Hollow, as they sat by their doors of an evening, were often filled with awe at hearing his nasal melody, "in linked sweetness long drawn out," floating from the distant hill, or along the dusky road.

Another of his sources of fearful pleasure was to pass long winter evenings with the old Dutch wives, as they sat spinning by the fire, with a row of apples roasting and spluttering along the hearth, and listen to their marvellous tales of ghosts and goblins, and haunted fields, and haunted brooks, and haunted bridges, and haunted houses, and particularly of the headless horseman, or Galloping Hessian of the Hollow, as they sometimes called him. He would delight them equally by his anecdotes of witchcraft, and of the direful omens and portentous sights and sounds in the air, which prevailed in the earlier times of Connecticut; and would frighten them woefully with speculations upon comets and shooting stars; and with the alarming fact that the world did absolutely turn round, and that they were half the time topsy-turvy!

But if there was a pleasure in all this, while snugly cuddling in the chimney corner of a chamber that was all of a ruddy glow from the crackling wood fire, and where, of course, no spectre dared to show its face, it was dearly purchased by the terrors of his subsequent walk homewards. What fearful shapes and shadows beset his path, amidst the dim and ghastly glare of a snowy night! With what wistful look did he eye every trembling ray of light streaming across the waste fields from some distant window! How often was he appalled by some shrub covered with snow, which, like a sheeted spectre, beset his very path! How often did he shrink with curdling awe at the sound of his own steps on the frosty crust beneath his feet; and dread to look over his shoulder, lest he should behold some uncouth being tramping close behind him! And how often was he thrown into complete dismay by some rushing blast, howling among the trees, in the idea that it was the Galloping Hessian on one of his nightly scourings!

All these, however, were mere terrors of the night, phantoms of the mind that walk in darkness; and though he had seen many spectres in his time, and been more than once beset by Satan in divers shapes, in his lonely perambulations, yet daylight put an end to all these evils; and he would have passed a pleasant life of it, in despite of the Devil and all his works, if his path had not been crossed by a being that causes more perplexity to mortal man than ghosts, goblins, and the whole race of witches put together, and that was—a woman.

Among the musical disciples who assembled, one evening in each week, to receive his instructions in psalmody, was Katrina Van Tassel, the daughter and only child of a substantial Dutch farmer. She was a blooming lass of fresh eighteen; plump as a partridge; ripe and melting and rosy-cheeked as one of her father's peaches, and universally famed, not merely for her beauty, but her vast expectations. She was withal a little of a coquette, as might be perceived even in her dress, which was a mixture of ancient and modern fashions, as most suited to set off her charms. She wore the ornaments of pure yellow gold, which her great-great-grandmother had brought over from Saardam; the tempting stomacher of the olden time, and withal a provokingly short petticoat, to display the prettiest foot and ankle in the country round.

Ichabod Crane had a soft and foolish heart towards the sex; and it is not to be wondered at that so tempting a morsel soon found favor in his eyes, more especially after he had visited her in her paternal mansion. Old Baltus Van Tassel was a perfect picture of a thriving, contented, liberal-hearted farmer. He seldom, it is true, sent either his eyes or his thoughts beyond the boundaries of his own farm; but within those everything was snug, happy and well-conditioned. He was satisfied with his wealth, but not proud of it; and piqued himself upon the hearty abundance, rather than the style in which he lived. His stronghold was situated on the banks of the Hudson, in one of those green, sheltered, fertile nooks in which the Dutch farmers are so fond of nestling. A great elm tree spread its broad branches over it, at the foot of which bubbled up a spring of the softest and sweetest water, in a little well-formed of a barrel; and then stole sparkling away through the grass, to a neighboring brook, that babbled along among alders and dwarf willows. Hard by the farmhouse was a vast barn, that might have served for a church; every window and crevice of which seemed bursting forth with the treasures of the farm; the flail was busily resounding within it from morning to night; swallows and martins skimmed twittering about the eaves; and rows of pigeons, some with one eye turned up, as if watching the weather, some with their heads under their wings or buried in their bosoms, and others swelling, and cooing, and bowing about their dames, were enjoying the sunshine on the roof. Sleek unwieldy porkers were grunting in the repose and abundance of their pens, from whence sallied forth, now and then, troops of sucking pigs, as if to snuff the air. A stately squadron of snowy geese were riding in an adjoining pond, convoying whole fleets of ducks; regiments of turkeys were gobbling through the farmyard, and Guinea fowls fretting about it, like ill-tempered housewives, with their peevish, discontented cry. Before the barn door strutted the gallant cock, that pattern of a husband, a warrior and a fine gentleman, clapping his burnished wings and crowing in the pride and gladness of his heart—sometimes tearing up the earth with his feet, and then generously calling his ever-hungry family of wives and children to enjoy the rich morsel which he had discovered.

The pedagogue's mouth watered as he looked upon this sumptuous promise of luxurious winter fare. In his devouring mind's eye, he pictured to himself every roasting-pig running about with a pudding in his belly, and an apple in his mouth; the pigeons were snugly put to bed in a comfortable pie, and tucked in with a coverlet of crust; the geese were swimming in their own gravy; and the ducks pairing cosily in dishes, like snug married couples, with a decent competency of onion sauce. In the porkers he saw carved out the future sleek side of bacon, and juicy relishing ham; not a turkey but he beheld daintily trussed up, with its gizzard under its wing, and, peradventure, a necklace of savory sausages; and even bright chanticleer himself lay sprawling on his back, in a side dish, with uplifted claws, as if craving that quarter which his chivalrous spirit disdained to ask while living.

As the enraptured Ichabod fancied all this, and as he rolled his great green eyes over the fat meadow lands, the rich fields of wheat, of rye, of buckwheat, and Indian corn, and the orchards burdened with ruddy fruit, which surrounded the warm tenement of Van Tassel, his heart yearned after the damsel who was to inherit these domains, and his imagination expanded with the idea, how they might be readily turned into cash, and the money invested in immense tracts of wild land, and shingle palaces in the wilderness. Nay, his busy fancy already realized his hopes, and presented to him the blooming Katrina, with a whole family of children, mounted on the top of a wagon loaded with household trumpery, with pots and kettles dangling beneath; and he beheld himself bestriding a pacing mare, with a colt at her heels, setting out for Kentucky, Tennessee —or the Lord knows where!

When he entered the house, the conquest of his heart was complete. It was one of those spacious farmhouses, with high-ridged but lowly sloping roofs, built in the style handed down from the first Dutch settlers; the low projecting eaves forming a piazza along the front, capable of being closed up in bad weather. Under this were hung flails, harness, various utensils of husbandry, and nets for fishing in the neighboring river. Benches were built along the sides for summer use; and a great spinning-wheel at one end, and a churn at the other, showed the various uses to which this important porch might be devoted. From this piazza the wondering Ichabod entered the hall, which formed the centre of the mansion, and the place of usual residence. Here rows of resplendent pewter, ranged on a long dresser, dazzled his eyes. In one corner stood a huge bag of wool, ready to be spun; in another, a quantity of linsey-woolsey just from the loom; ears of Indian corn, and strings of dried apples and peaches, hung in gay festoons along the walls, mingled with the gaud of red peppers; and a door left ajar gave him a peep into the best parlor, where the claw-footed chairs and dark mahogany tables shone like mirrors; andirons, with their accompanying shovel and tongs, glistened from their covert of asparagus tops; mock-oranges and conch-shells decorated the mantelpiece; strings of various-colored birds eggs were suspended above it; a great ostrich egg was hung from the centre of the room, and a corner cupboard, knowingly left open, displayed immense treasures of old silver and well-mended china.

From the moment Ichabod laid his eyes upon these regions of delight, the peace of his mind was at an end, and his only study was how to gain the affections of the peerless daughter of Van Tassel. In this enterprise, however, he had more real difficulties than generally fell to the lot of a knight-errant of yore, who seldom had anything but giants, enchanters, fiery dragons, and such like easily conquered adversaries, to contend with and had to make his way merely through gates of iron and brass, and walls of adamant to the castle keep, where the lady of his heart was confined; all which he achieved as easily as a man would carve his way to the centre of a Christmas pie; and then the lady gave him her hand as a matter of course. Ichabod, on the contrary, had to win his way to the heart of a country coquette, beset with a labyrinth of whims and caprices, which were forever presenting new difficulties and impediments; and he had to encounter a host of fearful adversaries of real flesh and blood, the numerous rustic admirers, who beset every portal to her heart, keeping a watchful and angry eye upon each other, but ready to fly out in the common cause against any new competitor.

Among these, the most formidable was a burly, roaring, roystering blade, of the name of Abraham, or, according to the Dutch abbreviation, Brom Van Brunt, the hero of the country round, which rang with his feats of strength and hardihood. He was broad-shouldered and double-jointed, with short curly black hair, and a bluff but not unpleasant countenance, having a mingled air of fun and arrogance. From his Herculean frame and great powers of limb he had received the nickname of *Brom Bones*, by which he was universally known. He was famed for great knowledge and skill in horsemanship, being as dexterous on horseback as a Tartar. He was foremost at all races and cock fights; and, with the ascendancy which bodily strength always acquires in rustic life, was the umpire in all disputes, setting his hat on one side, and giving his decisions with an air and tone that admitted of no gainsay or appeal. He was always ready for either a fight or a frolic; but had more mischief than ill-will in his composition; and with all his overbearing roughness, there was a strong dash of waggish good humor at bottom. He had three or four boon companions, who regarded him as their model, and at the head of whom he scoured the country, attending every scene of feud or merriment for miles round. In cold weather he was distinguished by a fur cap, surmounted with a flaunting fox's tail; and when the folks at a country gathering descried this well-known crest at a distance, whisking about among a squad of hard riders, they always stood by for a squall. Sometimes his crew would be heard dashing along past the farmhouses at midnight, with whoop and halloo, like a troop of Don Cossacks; and the old dames, startled out of their sleep, would listen for a moment till the hurry-scurry had clattered by, and then exclaim, "Ay, there goes Brom Bones and his gang!" The neighbors looked upon him with a mixture of awe, admiration, and good-will; and, when any madcap prank or rustic brawl occurred in the vicinity, always shook their heads, and warranted Brom Bones was at the bottom of it.

This rantipole hero had for some time singled out the blooming Katrina for the object of his uncouth gallantries, and though his amorous toyings were something like the gentle caresses and endearments of a bear, yet it was whispered that she did not altogether discourage his hopes. Certain it is, his advances were signals for rival candidates to retire, who felt no inclination to cross a lion in his amours; insomuch, that when his horse was seen tied to Van Tassel's paling, on a Sunday night, a sure sign that his master was courting, or, as it is termed, "sparking," within, all other suitors passed by in despair, and carried the war into other quarters.

Such was the formidable rival with whom Ichabod Crane had to contend, and, considering all things, a stouter man than he would have shrunk from the competition, and a wiser man would have despaired. He had, however, a happy mixture of pliability and perseverance in his nature; he was in form and spirit like a supple-jack—yielding, but tough; though he bent, he never broke; and though he bowed beneath the slightest pressure, yet, the moment it was away—jerk!—he was as erect, and carried his head as high as ever.

To have taken the field openly against his rival would have been madness; for he was not a man to be thwarted in his amours, any more than that stormy lover, Achilles. Ichabod, therefore, made his advances in a quiet and gently insinuating manner. Under cover of his character of singing-master, he made frequent visits at the farmhouse; not that he had anything to apprehend from the meddlesome interference of parents, which is so often a stumbling-block in the path of lovers. Balt Van Tassel was an easy indulgent soul; he loved his daughter better even than his pipe, and, like a reasonable man and an excellent father, let her have her way in everything. His notable little wife, too, had enough to do to attend to her housekeeping and manage her poultry; for, as she sagely observed, ducks and geese are foolish things, and must be looked after, but girls can take care of themselves. Thus, while the busy dame bustled about the house, or plied her spinning-wheel at one end of the piazza, honest Balt would sit smoking his evening pipe at the other, watching the achievements of a little wooden warrior, who, armed with a sword in each hand, was most valiantly fighting the wind on the pinnacle of the barn. In the meantime, Ichabod would carry on his suit with the daughter by the side of the spring under the great elm, or sauntering along in the twilight, that hour so favorable to the lover's eloquence.

I profess not to know how women's hearts are wooed and won. To me they have always been matters of riddle and admiration. Some seem to have but one vulnerable point, or door of access; while others have a thousand avenues, and may be captured in a thousand different ways. It is a great triumph of skill to gain the former, but a still greater proof of generalship to maintain possession of the latter, for man must battle for his fortress at every door and window. He who wins a thousand common hearts is therefore entitled to some renown; but he who keeps undisputed sway over the heart of a coquette is indeed a hero. Certain it is, this as not the case with the redoubtable Brom Bones; and from the moment Ichabod Crane made his advances, the interests of the former evidently declined: his horse was no longer seen tied to the palings on Sunday nights, and a deadly feud gradually arose between him and the preceptor of Sleepy Hollow.

Brom, who had a degree of rough chivalry in his nature, would fain have carried matters to open warfare and have settled their pretensions to the lady, according to the mode of those most concise and simple reasoners, the knights-errant of yore—by single combat; but Ichabod was too conscious of the superior might of his adversary to enter the lists against him; he had overheard a boast of Bones, that he would "double the schoolmaster up, and lay him on a shelf of his own schoolhouse;" and he was too wary to give him an opportunity. There was something extremely provoking in this obstinately pacific system; it left Brom no alternative but to draw upon the funds of rustic waggery in his disposition, and to play off boorish practical jokes upon his rival. Ichabod became the object of whimsical persecution to Bones and his gang of rough riders. They harried his hitherto peaceful domains; smoked out his singing school by stopping up the chimney; broke into the schoolhouse at night, in spite of its formidable fastenings of with and window stakes, and turned everything topsy-turvy, so that the poor schoolmaster began to think all the witches in the country held their meetings there. But what was still more annoying, Brom took all opportunities of turning him into ridicule in presence of his mistress, and had a scoundrel dog whom he taught to whine in the most ludicrous manner, and introduced as a rival of Ichabod's, to instruct her in psalmody.

In this way matters went on for some time, without producing any material effect on the relative situations of the contending powers. On a fine autumnal afternoon, Ichabod, in pensive mood, sat enthroned on the lofty stool from whence he usually watched all the concerns of his little literary realm. In his hand he swayed a ferule, that sceptre of despotic power; the birch of justice reposed on three nails behind the throne, a constant terror to evil doers, while on the desk before him might be seen sundry contraband articles and prohibited weapons, detected upon the persons of idle urchins, such as half-munched apples, popguns, whirligigs, fly-cages, and whole legions of rampant little paper gamecocks. Apparently there had been some appalling act of justice recently inflicted, for his scholars were all busily intent upon their books, or slyly whispering behind them with one eye kept upon the master; and a kind of buzzing stillness reigned throughout the schoolroom. It was suddenly interrupted by the appearance of a negro in tow-cloth jacket and trowsers, a round-crowned fragment of a hat, like the cap of Mercury, and mounted on the back of a ragged, wild, half-broken colt, which he managed with a rope by way of halter. He came clattering up to the school door with an invitation to Ichabod to attend a merry-making or "quilting frolic," to be held that evening at Mynheer Van Tassel's; and having delivered his message with that air of importance, and effort at fine language, which a negro is apt to display on petty embassies of the kind, he dashed over the brook, and was seen scampering away up the hollow, full of the importance and hurry of his mission.

All was now bustle and hubbub in the late quiet schoolroom. The scholars were hurried through their lessons without stopping at trifles; those who were nimble skipped over half with impunity, and those who were tardy had a smart application now and then in the rear, to quicken their speed or help them over a tall word. Books were flung aside without being put away on the shelves, inkstands were overturned, benches thrown down, and the whole school was turned loose an hour before the usual time, bursting forth like a legion of young imps, yelping and racketing about the green in joy at their early emancipation.

The gallant Ichabod now spent at least an extra half hour at his toilet, brushing and furbishing up his best, and indeed only suit of rusty black, and arranging his locks by a bit of broken looking-glass that hung up in the schoolhouse. That he might make his appearance before his mistress in the true style of a cavalier, he borrowed a horse from the farmer with whom he was domiciliated, a choleric old Dutchman of the name of Hans Van Ripper, and, thus gallantly mounted, issued forth like a knight-errant in quest of adventures. But it is meet I should, in the true spirit of romantic story, give some account of the looks and equipments of my hero and his steed. The animal he bestrode was a broken-down plow-horse, that had outlived almost everything but its viciousness. He was gaunt and shagged, with a ewe neck, and a head like a hammer; his rusty mane and tail were tangled and knotted with burs; one eye had lost its pupil, and was glaring and spectral, but the other had the gleam of a genuine devil in it. Still he must have had fire and mettle in his day, if we may judge from the name he bore of Gunpowder. He had, in fact, been a favorite steed of his master's, the choleric Van Ripper, who was a furious rider, and had infused, very probably, some of his own spirit into the animal; for, old and broken-down as he looked, there was more of the lurking devil in him than in any young filly in the country.

Ichabod was a suitable figure for such a steed. He rode with short stirrups, which brought his knees nearly up to the pommel of the saddle; his sharp elbows stuck out like grasshoppers'; he carried his whip perpendicularly in his hand, like a sceptre, and as his horse jogged on, the motion of his arms was not unlike the flapping of a pair of wings. A small wool hat rested on the top of his nose, for so his scanty strip of forehead might be called, and the skirts of his black coat fluttered out almost to the horses tail. Such was the appearance of Ichabod and his steed as they shambled out of the gate of Hans Van Ripper, and it was altogether such an apparition as is seldom to be met with in broad daylight.

It was, as I have said, a fine autumnal day; the sky was clear and serene, and nature wore that rich and golden livery which we always associate with the idea of abundance. The forests had put on their sober brown and yellow, while some trees of the tenderer kind had been nipped by the frosts into brilliant dyes of orange, purple, and scarlet. Streaming files of wild ducks began to make their appearance high in the air; the bark of the squirrel might be heard from the groves of beech and hickory-nuts, and the pensive whistle of the quail at intervals from the neighboring stubble field.

The small birds were taking their farewell banquets. In the fullness of their revelry, they fluttered, chirping and frolicking from bush to bush, and tree to tree, capricious from the very profusion and variety around them. There was the honest cock robin, the favorite game of stripling sportsmen, with its loud querulous note; and the twittering blackbirds flying in sable clouds; and the golden-winged woodpecker with his crimson crest, his broad black gorget, and splendid plumage; and the cedar bird, with its red-tipt wings and yellow-tipt tail and its little monteiro cap of feathers; and the blue jay, that noisy coxcomb, in his gay light blue coat and white underclothes, screaming and chattering, nodding and bobbing and bowing, and pretending to be on good terms with every songster of the grove.

As Ichabod jogged slowly on his way, his eye, ever open to every symptom of culinary abundance, ranged with delight over the treasures of jolly autumn. On all sides he beheld vast store of apples; some hanging in oppressive opulence on the trees; some gathered into baskets and barrels for the market; others heaped up in rich piles for the cider-press. Farther on he beheld great fields of Indian corn, with its golden ears peeping from their leafy coverts, and holding out the promise of cakes and hasty-pudding; and the yellow pumpkins lying beneath them, turning up their fair round bellies to the sun, and giving ample prospects of the most luxurious of pies; and anon he passed the fragrant buckwheat fields breathing the odor of the beehive, and as he beheld them, soft anticipations stole over his mind of dainty slapjacks, well buttered, and garnished with honey or treacle, by the delicate little dimpled hand of Katrina Van Tassel.

Thus feeding his mind with many sweet thoughts and "sugared suppositions," he journeyed along the sides of a range of hills which look out upon some of the goodliest scenes of the mighty Hudson. The sun gradually wheeled his broad disk down in the west. The wide bosom of the Tappan Zee lay motionless and glassy, excepting that here and there a gentle undulation waved and prolonged the blue shadow of the distant mountain. A few amber clouds floated in the sky, without a breath of air to move them. The horizon was of a fine golden tint, changing gradually into a pure apple green, and from that into the deep blue of the mid-heaven. A slanting ray lingered on the woody crests of the precipices that overhung some parts of the river, giving greater depth to the dark gray and purple of their rocky sides. A sloop was loitering in the distance, dropping slowly down with the tide, her sail hanging uselessly against the mast; and as the reflection of the sky gleamed along the still water, it seemed as if the vessel was suspended in the air.

It was toward evening that Ichabod arrived at the castle of the Heer Van Tassel, which he found thronged with the pride and flower of the adjacent country. Old farmers, a spare leathern-faced race, in homespun coats and breeches, blue stockings, huge shoes, and magnificent pewter buckles. Their brisk, withered little dames, in close-crimped caps, long-waisted short gowns, homespun petticoats, with scissors and pincushions, and gay calico pockets hanging on the outside. Buxom lasses, almost as antiquated as their mothers, excepting where a straw hat, a fine ribbon, or perhaps a white frock, gave symptoms of city innovation. The sons, in short square-skirted coats, with rows of stupendous brass buttons, and their hair generally queued in the fashion of the times, especially if they could procure an eel-skin for the purpose, it being esteemed throughout the country as a potent nourisher and strengthener of the hair.

Brom Bones, however, was the hero of the scene, having come to the gathering on his favorite steed Daredevil, a creature, like himself, full of mettle and mischief, and which no one but himself could manage. He was, in fact, noted for preferring vicious animals, given to all kinds of tricks which kept the rider in constant risk of his neck, for he held a tractable, well-broken horse as unworthy of a lad of spirit.

Fain would I pause to dwell upon the world of charms that burst upon the enraptured gaze of my hero, as he entered the state parlor of Van Tassel's mansion. Not those of the bevy of buxom lasses, with their luxurious display of red and white; but the ample charms of a genuine Dutch country tea-table, in the sumptuous time of autumn. Such heaped up platters of cakes of various and almost indescribable kinds, known only to experienced Dutch housewives! There was the doughty doughnut, the tender oly koek, and the crisp and crumbling cruller; sweet cakes and short cakes, ginger cakes and honey cakes, and the whole family of cakes. And then there were apple pies, and peach pies, and pumpkin pies; besides slices of ham and smoked beef; and moreover delectable dishes of preserved plums, and peaches, and pears, and quinces; not to mention broiled shad and roasted chickens; together with bowls of milk and cream, all mingled higgledy-piggledy, pretty much as I have enumerated them, with the motherly teapot sending up its clouds of vapor from the midst—Heaven bless the mark! I want breath and time to discuss this banquet as it deserves, and am too eager to get on with my story. Happily, Ichabod Crane was not in so great a hurry as his historian, but did ample justice to every dainty.

He was a kind and thankful creature, whose heart dilated in proportion as his skin was filled with good cheer, and whose spirits rose with eating, as some men's do with drink. He could not help, too, rolling his large eyes round him as he ate, and chuckling with the possibility that he might one day be lord of all this scene of almost unimaginable luxury and splendor. Then, he thought, how soon he'd turn his back upon the old schoolhouse; snap his fingers in the face of Hans Van Ripper, and every other niggardly patron, and kick any itinerant pedagogue out of doors that should dare to call him comrade!

Old Baltus Van Tassel moved about among his guests with a face dilated with content and good humor, round and jolly as the harvest moon. His hospitable attentions were brief, but expressive, being confined to a shake of the hand, a slap on the shoulder, a loud laugh, and a pressing invitation to "fall to, and help themselves."

And now the sound of the music from the common room, or hall, summoned to the dance. The musician was an old gray-headed negro, who had been the itinerant orchestra of the neighborhood for more than half a century. His instrument was as old and battered as himself. The greater part of the time he scraped on two or three strings, accompanying every movement of the bow with a motion of the head; bowing almost to the ground, and stamping with his foot whenever a fresh couple were to start.

Ichabod prided himself upon his dancing as much as upon his vocal powers. Not a limb, not a fiber about him was idle; and to have seen his loosely hung frame in full motion, and clattering about the room, you would have thought St. Vitus himself, that blessed patron of the dance, was figuring before you in person. He was the admiration of all the negroes; who, having gathered, of all ages and sizes, from the farm and the neighborhood, stood forming a pyramid of shining black faces at every door and window, gazing with delight at the scene, rolling their white eyeballs, and showing grinning rows of ivory from ear to ear. How could the flogger of urchins be otherwise than animated and joyous? The lady of his heart was his partner in the dance, and smiling graciously in reply to all his amorous oglings; while Brom Bones, sorely smitten with love and jealousy, sat brooding by himself in one corner.

When the dance was at an end, Ichabod was attracted to a knot of the sager folks, who, with Old Van Tassel, sat smoking at one end of the piazza, gossiping over former times, and drawing out long stories about the war.

This neighborhood, at the time of which I am speaking, was one of those highly favored places which abound with chronicle and great men.

The British and American line had run near it during the war; it had, therefore, been the scene of marauding and infested with refugees, cowboys, and all kinds of border chivalry. Just sufficient time had elapsed to enable each storyteller to dress up his tale with a little becoming fiction, and, in the indistinctness of his recollection, to make himself the hero of every exploit.

There was the story of Doffue Martling, a large blue-bearded Dutchman, who had nearly taken a British frigate with an old iron nine-pounder from a mud breastwork, only that his gun burst at the sixth discharge. And there was an old gentleman who shall be nameless, being too rich a mynheer to be lightly mentioned, who, in the battle of White Plains, being an excellent master of defence, parried a musket-ball with a small sword, insomuch that he absolutely felt it whiz round the blade, and glance off at the hilt; in proof of which he was ready at any time to show the sword, with the hilt a little bent. There were several more that had been equally great in the field, not one of whom but was persuaded that he had a considerable hand in bringing the war to a happy termination.

But all these were nothing to the tales of ghosts and apparitions that succeeded. The neighborhood is rich in legendary treasures of the kind. Local tales and superstitions thrive best in these sheltered, long-settled retreats; but are trampled under foot by the shifting throng that forms the population of most of our country places. Besides, there is no encouragement for ghosts in most of our villages, for they have scarcely had time to finish their first nap and turn themselves in their graves, before their surviving friends have travelled away from the neighborhood; so that when they turn out at night to walk their rounds, they have no acquaintance left to call upon. This is perhaps the reason why we so seldom hear of ghosts except in our long-established Dutch communities.

The immediate cause, however, of the prevalence of supernatural stories in these parts, was doubtless owing to the vicinity of Sleepy Hollow. There was a contagion in the very air that blew from that haunted region; it breathed forth an atmosphere of dreams and fancies infecting all the land. Several of the Sleepy Hollow people were present at Van Tassel's, and, as usual, were doling out their wild and wonderful legends. Many dismal tales were told about funeral trains, and mourning cries and wailings heard and seen about the great tree where the unfortunate Major André was taken, and which stood in the neighborhood. Some mention was made also of the woman in white, that haunted the dark glen at Raven Rock, and was often heard to shriek on winter nights before a storm, having perished there in the snow. The chief part of the stories, however, turned upon the favorite spectre of Sleepy Hollow, the Headless Horseman, who had been heard several times of late, patrolling the country; and, it was said, tethered his horse nightly among the graves in the churchyard.

The sequestered situation of this church seems always to have made it a favorite haunt of troubled spirits. It stands on a knoll, surrounded by locust-trees and lofty elms, from among which its decent, whitewashed walls shine modestly forth, like Christian purity beaming through the shades of retirement. A gentle slope descends from it to a silver sheet of water, bordered by high trees, between which, peeps may be caught at the blue hills of the Hudson. To look upon its grass-grown yard, where the sunbeams seem to sleep so quietly, one would think that there at least the dead might rest in peace. On one side of the church extends a wide woody dell, along which raves a large brook among broken rocks and trunks of fallen trees. Over a deep black part of the stream, not far from the church, was formerly thrown a wooden bridge; the road that led to it, and the bridge itself, were thickly shaded by overhanging trees, which cast a gloom about it, even in the daytime; but occasioned a fearful darkness at night. Such was one of the favorite haunts of the Headless Horseman, and the place where he was most frequently encountered. The tale was told of old Brouwer, a most heretical disbeliever in ghosts, how he met the Horseman returning from his foray into Sleepy Hollow, and was obliged to get up behind him; how they galloped over bush and brake, over hill and swamp, until they reached the bridge; when the Horseman suddenly turned into a skeleton, threw old Brouwer into the brook, and sprang away over the tree-tops with a clap of thunder.

This story was immediately matched by a thrice marvellous adventure of Brom Bones, who made light of the Galloping Hessian as an arrant jockey. He affirmed that on returning one night from the neighboring village of Sing Sing, he had been overtaken by this midnight trooper; that he had offered to race with him for a bowl of punch, and should have won it too, for Daredevil beat the goblin horse all hollow, but just as they came to the church bridge, the Hessian bolted, and vanished in a flash of fire.

All these tales, told in that drowsy undertone with which men talk in the dark, the countenances of the listeners only now and then receiving a casual gleam from the glare of a pipe, sank deep in the mind of Ichabod. He repaid them in kind with large extracts from his invaluable author, Cotton Mather, and added many marvellous events that had taken place in his native State of Connecticut, and fearful sights which he had seen in his nightly walks about Sleepy Hollow.

The revel now gradually broke up. The old farmers gathered together their families in their wagons, and were heard for some time rattling along the hollow roads, and over the distant hills. Some of the damsels mounted on pillions behind their favorite swains, and their light-hearted laughter, mingling with the clatter of hoofs, echoed along the silent woodlands, sounding fainter and fainter, until they gradually died away—and the late scene of noise and frolic was all silent and deserted. Ichabod only lingered behind, according to the custom of country lovers, to have a tête-à-tête with the heiress; fully convinced that he was now on the high road to success. What passed at this interview I will not pretend to say, for in fact I do not know. Something, however, I fear me, must have gone wrong, for he certainly sallied forth, after no very great interval, with an air quite desolate and chapfallen. Oh, these women! these women! Could that girl have been playing off any of her coquettish tricks? Was her encouragement of the poor pedagogue all a mere sham to secure her conquest of his rival? Heaven only knows, not I! Let it suffice to say, Ichabod stole forth with the air of one who had been sacking a henroost, rather than a fair lady's heart. Without looking to the right or left to notice the scene of rural wealth, on which he had so often gloated, he went straight to the stable, and with several hearty cuffs and kicks roused his steed most uncourteously from the comfortable quarters in which he was soundly sleeping, dreaming of mountains of corn and oats, and whole valleys of timothy and clover.

It was the very witching time of night that Ichabod, heavy-hearted and crestfallen, pursued his travels homewards, along the sides of the lofty hills which rise above Tarry Town, and which he had traversed so cheerily in the afternoon. The hour was as dismal as himself. Far below him the Tappan Zee spread its dusky and indistinct waste of waters, with here and there the tall mast of a sloop, riding quietly at anchor under the land. In the dead hush of midnight, he could even hear the barking of the watchdog from the opposite shore of the Hudson; but it was so vague and faint as only to give an idea of his distance from this faithful companion of man. Now and then, too, the long-drawn crowing of a cock, accidentally awakened, would sound far, far off, from some farmhouse away among the hills—but it was like a dreaming sound in his ear. No signs of life occurred near him, but occasionally the melancholy chirp of a cricket, or perhaps the guttural twang of a bullfrog from a neighboring marsh, as if sleeping uncomfortably and turning suddenly in his bed.

All the stories of ghosts and goblins that he had heard in the afternoon now came crowding upon his recollection. The night grew darker and darker; the stars seemed to sink deeper in the sky, and driving clouds occasionally hid them from his sight. He had never felt so lonely and dismal. He was, moreover, approaching the very place where many of the scenes of the ghost stories had been laid. In the centre of the road stood an enormous tulip-tree, which towered like a giant above all the other trees of the neighborhood, and formed a kind of landmark. Its limbs were gnarled and fantastic, large enough to form trunks for ordinary trees, twisting down almost to the earth, and rising again into the air. It was connected with the tragical story of the unfortunate André, who had been taken prisoner hard by; and was universally known by the name of Major André's tree. The common people regarded it with a mixture of respect and superstition, partly out of sympathy for the fate of its ill-starred namesake, and partly from the tales of strange sights, and doleful lamentations, told concerning it.

As Ichabod approached this fearful tree, he began to whistle; he thought his whistle was answered; it was but a blast sweeping sharply through the dry branches. As he approached a little nearer, he thought he saw something white, hanging in the midst of the tree: he paused and ceased whistling but, on looking more narrowly, perceived that it was a place where the tree had been scathed by lightning, and the white wood laid bare. Suddenly he heard a groan—his teeth chattered, and his knees smote against the saddle: it was but the rubbing of one huge bough upon another, as they were swayed about by the breeze. He passed the tree in safety, but new perils lay before him.

About two hundred yards from the tree, a small brook crossed the road, and ran into a marshy and thickly-wooded glen, known by the name of Wiley's Swamp. A few rough logs, laid side by side, served for a bridge over this stream. On that side of the road where the brook entered the wood, a group of oaks and chestnuts, matted thick with wild grape-vines, threw a cavernous gloom over it. To pass this bridge was the severest trial. It was at this identical spot that the unfortunate André was captured, and under the covert of those chestnuts and vines were the sturdy yeomen concealed who surprised him. This has ever since been considered a haunted stream, and fearful are the feelings of the schoolboy who has to pass it alone after dark.

As he approached the stream, his heart began to thump; he summoned up, however, all his resolution, gave his horse half a score of kicks in the ribs, and attempted to dash briskly across the bridge; but instead of starting forward, the perverse old animal made a lateral movement, and ran broadside against the fence. Ichabod, whose fears increased with the delay, jerked the reins on the other side, and kicked lustily with the contrary foot: it was all in vain; his steed started, it is true, but it was only to plunge to the opposite side of the road into a thicket of brambles and alder bushes. The schoolmaster now bestowed both whip and heel upon the starveling ribs of old Gunpowder, who dashed forward, snuffling and snorting, but came to a stand just by the bridge, with a suddenness that had nearly sent his rider sprawling over his head. Just at this moment a plashy tramp by the side of the bridge caught the sensitive ear of Ichabod. In the dark shadow of the grove, on the margin of the brook, he beheld something huge, misshapen and towering. It stirred not, but seemed gathered up in the gloom, like some gigantic monster ready to spring upon the traveller.

The hair of the affrighted pedagogue rose upon his head with terror. What was to be done? To turn and fly was now too late; and besides, what chance was there of escaping ghost or goblin, if such it was, which could ride upon the wings of the wind? Summoning up, therefore, a show of courage, he demanded in stammering accents, "Who are you?" He received no reply. He repeated his demand in a still more agitated voice. Still there was no answer. Once more he cudgelled the sides of the inflexible Gunpowder, and, shutting his eyes, broke forth with involuntary fervor into a psalm tune. Just then the shadowy object of alarm put itself in motion, and with a scramble and a bound stood at once in the middle of the road. Though the night was dark and dismal, yet the form of the unknown might now in some degree be ascertained. He appeared to be a horseman of large dimensions, and mounted on a black horse of powerful frame. He made no offer of molestation or sociability, but kept aloof on one side of the road, jogging along on the blind side of old Gunpowder, who had now got over his fright and waywardness.

Ichabod, who had no relish for this strange midnight companion, and bethought himself of the adventure of Brom Bones with the Galloping Hessian, now quickened his steed in hopes of leaving him behind. The stranger, however, quickened his horse to an equal pace. Ichabod pulled up, and fell into a walk, thinking to lag behind—the other did the same. His heart began to sink within him; he endeavored to resume his psalm tune, but his parched tongue clove to the roof of his mouth, and he could not utter a stave. There was something in the moody and dogged silence of this pertinacious companion that was mysterious

and appalling. It was soon fearfully accounted for. On mounting a rising ground, which brought the figure of his fellow-traveller in relief against the sky, gigantic in height, and muffled in a cloak, Ichabod was horror-struck on perceiving that he was headless!—but his horror was still more increased on observing that the head, which should have rested on his shoulders, was carried before him on the pommel of his saddle! His terror rose to desperation; he rained a shower of kicks and blows upon Gunpowder, hoping by a sudden movement to give his companion the slip; but the spectre started full jump with him. Away, then, they dashed through thick and thin; stones flying and sparks flashing at every bound. Ichabod's flimsy garments fluttered in the air, as he stretched his long lank body away over his horse's head, in the eagerness of his flight.

They had now reached the road which turns off to Sleepy Hollow; but Gunpowder, who seemed possessed with a demon, instead of keeping up it, made an opposite turn, and plunged headlong downhill to the left. This road leads through a sandy hollow shaded by trees for about a quarter of a mile, where it crosses the bridge famous in goblin story; and just beyond swells the green knoll on which stands the whitewashed church.

As yet the panic of the steed had given his unskillful rider an apparent advantage in the chase, but just as he had got half way through the hollow, the girths of the saddle gave way, and he felt it slipping from under him. He seized it by the pommel, and endeavored to hold it firm, but in vain; and had just time to save himself by clasping old Gunpowder round the neck, when the saddle fell to the earth, and he heard it trampled under foot by his pursuer. For a moment the terror of Hans Van Ripper's wrath passed across his mind—for it was his Sunday saddle; but this was no time for petty fears; the goblin was hard on his haunches; and (unskillful rider that he was!) he had much ado to maintain his seat; sometimes slipping on one side, sometimes on another, and sometimes jolted on the high ridge of his horse's backbone, with a violence that he verily feared would cleave him asunder.

An opening in the trees now cheered him with the hopes that the church bridge was at hand. The wavering reflection of a silver star in the bosom of the brook told him that he was not mistaken. He saw the walls of the church dimly glaring under the trees beyond. He recollected the place where Brom Bones's ghostly competitor had disappeared. "If I can but reach that bridge," thought Ichabod, "I am safe." Just then he heard the black steed panting and blowing close behind him; he even fancied that he felt his hot breath. Another convulsive kick in the ribs, and old Gunpowder sprang upon the bridge; he thundered over the resounding planks; he gained the opposite side; and now Ichabod cast a look behind to see if his pursuer should vanish, according to rule, in a flash of fire and brimstone. Just then he saw the goblin rising in his stirrups, and in the very act of hurling his head at him. Ichabod endeavored to dodge the horrible missile, but too late. It encountered his cranium with a tremendous crash—he was tumbled headlong into the dust, and Gunpowder, the black steed, and the goblin rider, passed by like a whirlwind.

~§~

The next morning the old horse was found without his saddle, and with the bridle under his feet, soberly cropping the grass at his master's gate. Ichabod did not make his appearance at breakfast; dinner-hour came, but no Ichabod. The boys assembled at the schoolhouse, and strolled idly about the banks of the brook; but no schoolmaster. Hans Van Ripper now began to feel some uneasiness about the fate of poor Ichabod, and his saddle. An inquiry was set on foot, and after diligent investigation they came upon his traces. In one part of the road leading to the church was found the saddle trampled in the dirt; the tracks of horses' hoofs deeply dented in the road, and evidently at furious speed, were traced to the bridge, beyond which, on the bank of a broad part of the brook, where the water ran deep and black, was found the hat of the unfortunate Ichabod, and close beside it a shattered pumpkin.

The brook was searched, but the body of the schoolmaster was not to be discovered. Hans Van Ripper as executor of his estate, examined the bundle which contained all his worldly effects. They consisted of two shirts and a half; two stocks for the neck; a pair or two of worsted stockings; an old pair of corduroy small-clothes; a rusty razor; a book of psalm tunes full of dog's-ears; and a broken pitch-pipe. As to the books and furniture of the schoolhouse, they belonged to the community, excepting Cotton Mather's "History of Witchcraft," a "New England Almanac," and a book of dreams and fortune-telling; in which last was a sheet of foolscap much scribbled and blotted in several fruitless attempts to make a copy of verses in honor of the heiress of Van Tassel. These magic books and the poetic scrawl were forthwith consigned to the flames by Hans Van Ripper; who, from that time forward, determined to send his children no more to school, observing that he never knew any good come of this same reading and writing. Whatever money the school-master possessed, and he had received his quarter's pay but a day or two before, he must have had about his person at the time of his disappearance.

The mysterious event caused much speculation at the church on the following Sunday. Knots of gazers and gossips were collected in the churchyard, at the bridge, and at the spot where the hat and pumpkin had been found. The stories of Brouwer, of Bones, and a whole budget of others were called to mind; and when they had diligently considered them all, and compared them with the symptoms of the present case, they shook their heads, and came to the conclusion that Ichabod had been carried off by the Galloping Hessian. As he was a bachelor, and in nobody's debt, nobody troubled his head any more about him; the school was removed to a different quarter of the hollow, and another pedagogue reigned in his stead.

It is true, an old farmer, who had been down to New York on a visit several years after, and from whom this account of the ghostly adventure was received, brought home the intelligence that Ichabod Crane was still alive; that he had left the neighborhood partly through fear of the goblin and Hans Van Ripper, and partly in mortification at having been suddenly dismissed by the heiress; that he had changed his quarters to a distant part of the country; had kept school and studied law at the same time; had been admitted to the bar; turned politician; electioneered; written for the newspapers; and finally had been made a justice of the Ten Pound Court. Brom Bones, too, who, shortly after his rival's disappearance conducted the blooming Katrina in triumph to the altar, was observed to look exceedingly knowing whenever the story of Ichabod was related, and always burst into a hearty laugh at the mention of the pumpkin; which led some to suspect that he knew more about the matter than he chose to tell.

The old country wives, however, who are the best judges of these matters, maintain to this day that Ichabod was spirited away by supernatural means; and it is a favorite story often told about the neighborhood round the winter evening fire. The bridge became more than ever an object of superstitious awe; and that may be the reason why the road has been altered of late years, so as to approach the church by the border of the millpond. The schoolhouse being deserted soon fell to decay, and was reported to be haunted by the ghost of the unfortunate pedagogue and the plowboy, loitering homeward of a still summer evening, has often fancied his voice at a distance, chanting a melancholy psalm tune among the tranquil solitudes of Sleepy Hollow.

POSTSCRIPT.

FOUND IN THE HANDWRITING OF MR. KNICKERBOCKER.

The preceding tale is given almost in the precise words in which I heard it related at a Corporation meeting at the ancient city of Manhattoes, at which were present many of its sagest and most illustrious burghers. The narrator was a pleasant, shabby, gentlemanly old fellow, in pepper-and-salt clothes, with a sadly humourous face, and one whom I strongly suspected of being poor—he made such efforts to be entertaining. When his story was concluded, there was much laughter and approbation, particularly from two or three deputy aldermen, who had been asleep the greater part of the time. There was, however, one tall, dry-looking old gentleman, with beetling eyebrows, who maintained a grave and rather severe face throughout, now and then folding his arms, inclining his head, and looking down upon the floor, as if turning a doubt over in his mind. He was one of your wary men, who never laugh but upon good grounds—when they have reason and law on their side. When the mirth of the rest of the company had subsided, and silence was restored, he leaned one arm on the elbow of his chair, and sticking the other akimbo, demanded, with a slight, but exceedingly sage motion of the head, and contraction of the brow, what was the moral of the story, and what it went to prove?

The story-teller, who was just putting a glass of wine to his lips, as a refreshment after his toils, paused for a moment, looked at his inquirer with an air of infinite deference, and, lowering the glass slowly to the table, observed that the story was intended most logically to prove—

"That there is no situation in life but has its advantages and pleasures—provided we will but take a joke as we find it:

"That, therefore, he that runs races with goblin troopers is likely to have rough riding of it.

"Ergo, for a country schoolmaster to be refused the hand of a Dutch heiress is a certain step to high preferment in the state."

The cautious old gentleman knit his brows tenfold closer after this explanation, being sorely puzzled by the ratiocination of the syllogism, while, methought, the one in pepper-and-salt eyed him with something of a triumphant leer. At length he observed that all this was very well, but still he thought the story a little on the extravagant—there were one or two points on which he had his doubts.

"Faith, sir," replied the story-teller, "as to that matter, I don't believe one-half of it myself."

— D. K.

La Belle Dame Sans Merci

by John Keats

Ah, what can ail thee, wretched wight,
  Alone and palely loitering;
The sedge is withered from the lake,
  And no birds sing.

Ah, what can ail thee, wretched wight,
  So haggard and so woe-begone?
The squirrel's granary is full,
  And the harvest's done.

I see a lilly on thy brow,
  With anguish moist and fever dew;
And on thy cheek a fading rose
  Fast withereth too.

I met a lady in the meads
  Full beautiful, a faery's child;
Her hair was long, her foot was light,
  And her eyes were wild.

I set her on my pacing steed,
  And nothing else saw all day long;
For sideways would she lean, and sing
  A faery's song.

I made a garland for her head,
  And bracelets too, and fragrant zone;
She looked at me as she did love,
  And made sweet moan.

She found me roots of relish sweet,
  And honey wild, and manna dew;
And sure in language strange she said,
  I love thee true.

She took me to her elfin grot,
  And there she gazed and sighed deep,
And there I shut her wild sad eyes—
  So kissed to sleep.

And there we slumbered on the moss,
  And there I dreamed, ah woe betide,
The latest dream I ever dreamed
  On the cold hill side.

I saw pale kings, and princes too,
  Pale warriors, death-pale were they all;
Who cried—"La belle Dame sans merci
  Hath thee in thrall!"

I saw their starved lips in the gloam
  With horrid warning gaped wide,
And I awoke, and found me here
  On the cold hill side.

And this is why I sojourn here
  Alone and palely loitering,
Though the sedge is withered from the lake,
  And no birds sing.

MRS. BOTHERBY'S STORY:
THE LEECH OF FOLKESTONE

by Thomas Ingoldsby of Tappington Manor
from the Ingoldsby Legends

READER, were you ever bewitched?—I do not mean by a "white wench's black eye," or by love-potions imbibed from a ruby lip;—but, were you ever really and bond fidê bewitched, in the true Matthew Hopkins sense of the word? Did you ever, for instance, find yourself from head to heel one vast complication of cramps?—or burst out into sudorific exudation like a cold thaw, with the thermometer at zero?—Were your eyes ever turned upside down, exhibiting nothing but their whites?—Did you ever vomit a paper of crooked pins? or expectorate Whitechapel needles?— These are genuine and undoubted marks of possession; and if you never experienced any of them—why, "happy man be his dole!"

Yet such things have been: yea, we are assured, and that on no mean authority, still are.

The World, according to the best geographers, is divided into Europe, Asia, Africa, America, and Romney Marsh. In this last-named, and fifth, quarter of the globe, a Witch may still be occasionally discovered in favourable, i. e., stormy, seasons, weathering Dungeness Point in an egg-shell, or careering on her broomstick over Dymchurch wall. A cow may yet be sometimes seen galloping like mad, with tail erect, and an old pair of breeches on her horns, an unerring guide to the door of the crone whose magic arts have drained her udder. —I do not, however, remember to have heard that any Conjuror has of late been detected in the district.

Not many miles removed from the verge of this recondite region, stands a collection of houses, which its maligners call a fishing-town, and its well-wishers a Watering-place. A limb of one of the Cinque Ports, it has, (or lately had,) a corporation of its own, and has been thought considerable enough to give a second title to a noble family. Rome stood on seven hills; Folkestone seems to have been built upon seventy. Its streets, lanes, and alleys—fanciful distinctions without much real difference—are agreeable enough to persons who do not mind running up and down stairs; and the only inconvenience, at all felt by such of its inhabitants as are not asthmatic, is when some heedless urchin tumbles down a chimney, or an impertinent pedestrian peeps into a garret window.

At the eastern extremity of the town, on the sea-beach, and scarcely above high-water mark, stood, in the good old times, a row of houses thendenominated "Frog-hole." Modern refinement subsequently euphonized the name into "East-street;" but "what's in a name?"—the encroachments of Ocean have long since levelled all in one common ruin.

Here, in the early part of the seventeenth century, flourished in somewhat doubtful reputation, but comparative opulence, a compounder of medicines, one Master Erasmus Buckthorne; the effluvia of whose drugs from within, mingling agreeably with the "ancient and fish-like smells" from without, wafted a delicious perfume throughout the neighbourhood.

At seven of the clock, on the morning when Mrs. Botherby's narrative commences, a stout Suffolk "punch," about thirteen hands and a half in height, was slowly led up and down before the door of the pharmacopolist by a lean and withered lad, whose appearance warranted an opinion, pretty generally expressed, that his master found him as useful in experimentalizing as in household drudgery; and that, for every pound avoirdupois of solid meat, he swallowed, at the least, two pounds troy-weight of chemicals and galenicals. As the town clock struck the quarter, Master Buckthorne emerged from his laboratory, and, putting the key carefully into his pocket, mounted the surefooted cob aforesaid, and proceeded up and down the acclivities and declivities of the town with the gravity due to his station and profession. When he reached the open country, his pace was increased to a sedate canter, which, in somewhat more than half an hour, brought "the horse and his rider" in front of a handsome and substantial mansion, the numerous gable-ends and bayed windows of which bespoke the owner a man of worship, and one well to do in the world.

"How now, Hodge Gardener?" quoth the Leech, scarcely drawing bit; for Punch seemed to be aware that he had reached his destination, and paused of his own accord; "How now, man? How fares thine employer, worthy Master Marsh? How hath he done? How hath he slept?—My potion hath done its office? Ha!"

"Alack! ill at ease, worthy sir—ill at ease," returned the hind; "his honour is up and stirring; but he hath rested none, and complaineth that the same gnawing pain devoureth, as it were, his very vitals: in sooth he is ill at ease."

"Morrow, doctor!" interrupted a voice from a casement opening on the lawn. "Good morrow! I have looked for, longed for, thy coming this hour and more; enter at once; the pasty and tankard are impatient for thine attack!"

"Marry, Heaven forbid that I should baulk their fancy!" quoth the Leech *sotto voce*, as, abandoning the bridle to honest Hodge, he dismounted, and followed a buxom-looking handmaiden into the breakfast parlour.

There, at the head of his well-furnished board, sat Master Thomas Marsh, of Marston-hall, a Yeoman well respected in his degree: one of that sturdy and sterling class which, taking rank immediately below the Esquire, (a title in its origin purely military,) occupied, in the wealthier counties, the position in society now filled by the Country Gentleman. He was one of those of whom the proverb ran:

> "A Knight of Cales,
> A Gentleman of Wales,
> And a Laird of the North Countree;
> A Yeoman of Kent,
> With his yearly rent,
> Will buy them out all three!"

A cold sirloin, big enough to frighten a Frenchman, filled the place of honour, counter-checked by a game-pie of no stinted dimensions; while a silver flagon of "humming-bub"—viz. ale strong enough to blow a man's beaver off—smiled opposite in treacherous amenity. The sideboard groaned beneath sundry massive cups and waiters of the purest silver; while the huge skull of a fallow deer, with its branching horns, frowned majestically above. All spoke of affluence, of comfort—all save the master, whose restless eye and feverish look hinted but too plainly the severest mental or bodily disorder. By the side of the proprietor of the mansion sat his consort, a lady now past the bloom of youth, yet still retaining many of its charms. The clear olive of her complexion, and "the darkness of her Andalusian eye," at once betrayed her foreign origin; in fact, her "lord and master," as husbands were even then, by a legal fiction, denominated, had taken her to his bosom in a foreign country. The cadet of his family, Master Thomas Marsh, had early in life been engaged in commerce. In the pursuit of his vocation he had visited Antwerp, Hamburg, and most of the Hanse Towns; and had already formed a tender connexion with the orphan offspring of one of old Alva's officers, when the unexpected deaths of one immediate, and two presumptive, heirs placed him next in succession to the family acres. He married, and brought home his bride: who, by the decease of the venerable possessor, heart-broken at the loss of his elder children, became eventually lady of Marston-Hall. It has been said that she was beautiful, yet was her beauty of a character that operates on the fancy more than the affections; she was one to be admired rather than loved. The proud curl of her lip, the firmness of her tread, her arched brow and stately carriage, showed the decision, not to say haughtiness, of her soul; while her glances, whether lightening with anger, or melting in extreme softness, betrayed the existence of passions as intense in kind as opposite in quality. She rose as Erasmus entered the parlour, and, bestowing on him a look fraught with meaning, quitted the room, leaving him in unrestrained communication with his patient.

"Fore George, Master Buckthorne!" exclaimed the latter, as the Leech drew near, "I will no more of your pharmacy—burn, burn—gnaw, gnaw—I had as lief the foul fiend were in my gizzard as one of your drugs. Tell me in the devil's name, what is the matter with me!"

Thus conjured, the practitioner paused, and even turned somewhat pale. There was a perceptible faltering in his voice, as, evading the question, he asked, "What say your other physicians?"

"Doctor Phiz says it is wind—Doctor Fuz says it is water—and Doctor Buz says it is something between wind and water."

"They are all of them wrong!" said Erasmus Buckthorne.

"Truly, I think so," returned the patient. "They are manifest asses; but you, good Leech, you are a horse of another colour. The world talks loudly of your learning, your skill, and cunning in arts the most abstruse; nay, sooth to say, some look coldly on you therefore, and stickle not to aver that you are cater-cousin with Beelzebub himself"

"It is ever the fate of science," murmured the professor, "to be maligned by the ignorant and superstitious. But a truce with such folly;— let me examine your palate."

Master Marsh thrust out a tongue long, clear, and red as beet-root. "There is nothing wrong there," said the Leech. "Your wrist:—no;—the pulse is firm and regular, the skin cool and temperate. Sir, there is nothing the matter with you!"

"Nothing the matter with me, Sir 'Potecary?— But I tell you there is the matter with me—much the matter with me. Why is it that something seems ever gnawing at my heart-strings?—Whence this pain in the region of the liver?—Why is it that I sleep not o' nights—rest not o' days? Why—"

"You are fidgety, Master Marsh," said the doctor.

Master Marsh's brow grew dark; he half rose from his seat, supported himself by both hands on the arms of his elbow-chair, and in accents of mingled anger and astonishment repeated the word "Fidgety!"

"Ay, fidgety," returned the doctor calmly. "Tut, man, there is nought ails thee save thine own over-weening fancies. Take less of food, more air, put aside thy flagon, call for thy horse; be boot and saddle the word! Why—hast thou not youth?"

"I have," said the patient.

"Wealth and a fair domain?"

"Granted," quoth Marsh cheerily.

"And a fair wife?"

"Yea," was the response, but in a tone something less satisfied.

"Then arouse thee, man, shake off this fantasy, betake thyself to thy lawful occasions—use thy good hap—follow thy pleasures, and think no more of these fancied ailments."

"But I tell you, master mine, these ailments are not fancied. I lose my rest, I loathe my food, my doublet sits loosely on me—these racking pains. My wife, too—when I meet her gaze, the cold sweat stands on my forehead, and I could almost think—" Marsh paused abruptly, mused awhile, then added, looking steadily at his visitor, "these things are not right; they pass the common, Master Erasmus Buckthorne."

A slight shade crossed the brow of the Leech, but its passage was momentary; his features softened to a smile, in which pity seemed slightly blended with contempt. "Have done with such follies, Master Marsh. You are well, and you would but think so. Ride, I say, hunt, shoot, do anything—disperse these melancholic humours, and become yourself again."

"Well, I will do your bidding," said Marsh, thoughtfully. "It may be so; and yet—but I will do your bidding. Master Cobbe of Brenzet writes me that he hath a score or two of fat ewes to be sold a pennyworth; I had thought to have sent Ralph Looker, but I will essay to go myself. Ho, there!—saddle me the brown mare, and bid Ralph be ready to attend me on the gelding."

An expression of pain contracted the features of Master Marsh as he rose and slowly quitted the apartment to prepare for his journey; while the Leech, having bidden him farewell, vanished through an opposite door, and betook himself to the private boudoir of the fair mistress of Marston, muttering as he went a quotation from a then newly-published play:

"Not poppy, nor mandragora,
Nor all the drowsy syrups of the world,
Shall ever medicine thee to that sweet sleep
Which thou own'dst yesterday."

~§~

Of what passed at this interview between the Folkestone doctor and the fair Spaniard, Mrs. Botherby declares she could never obtain any satisfactory elucidation. Not that tradition is silent on the subject—quite the contrary; it is the abundance, not paucity, of the materials she supplies, and the consequent embarrassment of selection, that makes the difficulty. Some have averred that the Leech, whose character, as has been before hinted, was more than threadbare, employed his time in teaching her the mode of administering certain noxious compounds, the unconscious partaker whereof would pine and die so slowly and gradually as to defy suspicion. Others there were who affirmed that Lucifer himself was then and there raised in propriâ personâ, with all his terrible attributes of horn and hoof. In support of this assertion, they adduce the testimony of the aforesaid buxom housemaid, who protested that the Hall smelt that evening like a manufactory of matches. All, however, seemed to agree that the confabulation, whether human or infernal, was con-ducted with profound secresy, and protracted to a considerable length; that its object, as far as could be divined, meant anything but good to the head of the family: that the lady, moreover, was heartily tired of her husband; and that, in the event of his removal by disease or casualty, Master Erasmus Buckthorne, albeit a great philosophist, would have no violent objection to "throw physic to the dogs," and exchange his labora-tory for the estate of Marston, its livestock included. Some, too, have inferred that to him did Madame Isabel seriously incline; while others have thought, induced perhaps by subsequent events, that she was merely using him for her purposes; that one José, a tall, bright-eyed, hook-nosed stripling from her native land, was a personage not unlikely to put a spoke in the doctor's wheel; and that, should such a chance arise, the Sage, wise as he was, would, after all, run no slight risk of being "bamboozled."

Master José, was a youth well-favoured, and comely to look upon. His office was that of page to the dame; an office which, after long remaining in abeyance, has been of late years revived, as may well be seen in the persons of sundry smart hobbledehoys, now constantly to be met with on staircases and in boudoirs, clad, for the most part, in garments fitted tightly to the shape, the lower moiety adorned with a broad stripe of crimson or silver lace, and the upper with what the first Wit of our times has described as "a favourable eruption of buttons." The precise duties of this employment have never, as far as we have heard, been accurately defined. The perfuming a handkerchief, the combing a lap-dog, and the occasional presentation of a sippet-shaped billet doux, are, and always have been, among them; but these a young gentleman standing five foot ten, and aged nineteen "last grass," might well be supposed to have outgrown. José, however kept his place, perhaps because he was not fit for any other. To the conference between his mistress and the physician he had not been admitted; his post was to keep watch and ward in the ante-room; and, when the interview was concluded, he attended the lady and her visiter as far as the courtyard, where he held, with all due respect, the stirrup for the latter, as he once more resumed his position on the back of Punch.

Who is it that says "little pitchers have large ears?" Some deep metaphysician of the potteries, who might have added that they have also quick eyes, and sometimes silent tongues. There was a little metaphorical piece of crockery of this class, who, screened by a huge elbow-chair, had sat a quiet and unobserved spectator of the whole proceedings between her mamma and Master Erasmus Buckthorne. This was Miss Marian Marsh, a rosy- cheeked laughter-loving imp of some six years old; but one who could be mute as a mouse when the fit was on her. A handsome and highly polished cabinet of the darkest ebony occupied a recess at one end of the apartment; this had long been a great subject of speculation to little Miss. Her curiosity, however, had always been repelled; nor had all her coaxing ever won her an inspection of the thousand and one pretty things which its recesses no doubt contained. On this occasion it was unlocked, and Marian was about to rush forward in eager anticipation of a peep at its interior, when, child as she was, the reflection struck her that she would stand a better chance of carrying her point by remaining *perdue*. Fortune for once favoured her: she crouched closer than before, and saw her mother take something from one of the drawers, which she handed over to the Leech. Strange mutterings followed, and words whose sound was foreign to her youthful ears. Had she been older, their import, perhaps, might have been equally unknown. —After a while there was a pause; and then the lady, as in answer to a requisition from the gentleman, placed in his hand a something which she took from her toilet. The transaction, whatever its nature, seemed now to be complete, and the article was carefully replaced in the drawer from which it had been taken. A long, and apparently interesting, conversation then took place between the parties, carried on in a low tone. At its termination, Mistress Marsh and Master Erasmus Buckthorne quitted the boudoir together. But the cabinet!-ay, that was left unfastened; the folding-doors still remained invitingly expanded, the bunch of keys dangling from the lock. In an instant the spoiled child was in a chair; the drawer so recently closed, yielded at once to her hand, and her hurried researches were rewarded by the prettiest little waxen doll imaginable. It was a first-rate prize, and Miss lost no time in appropriating it to herself. Long before Madame Marsh had returned to her *Sanctum*, Marian was seated under a laurestinus in the garden, nursing her new baby with the most affectionate solicitude.

~§~

"Susan, look here; see what a nasty scratch I have got upon my hand," said the young lady, when routed out at length from her hiding-place to her noontide meal.

"Yes, Miss, this is always the way with you! mend, mend, mend— nothing but mend! Scrambling about among the bushes, and tearing your clothes to rags. What with you, and with madam's farthingales and kirtles, a poor bower-maiden has a fine time of it!"

"But I have not torn my clothes, Susan, and it was not the bushes; it was the doll: only see what a great ugly pin I have pulled out of it! and look, here is another!" As she spoke, Marian drew forth one of those extended pieces of black pointed wire, with which, in the days of toupees and pompoons, our foremothers were wont to secure their fly-caps and head-gear from the impertinent assaults of "Zephyrus and the Little Breezes"

"And pray, Miss, where did you get this pretty doll, as you call it?" asked Susan, turning over the puppet, and viewing it with a scrutinizing eye.

"Mamma gave it me," said the child. —This was a fib!

"Indeed!" quoth the girl thoughtfully; and then, in half soliloquy, and a lower key, "Well! I wish I may die if it doesn't look like master!— But come to your dinner, Miss! Hark! the *bell is striking One!*"

Meanwhile Master Thomas Marsh, and his man Ralph, were threading the devious paths, then, as now, most pseudonymously dignified with the name of roads, that wound between Marston-Hall and the frontier of Romney Marsh. Their progress was comparatively slow; for though the brown mare was as good a roadster as man might back, and the gelding no mean nag of his hands, yet the tracts, rarely traversed save by the rude wains of the day, miry in the "bottoms," and covered with loose and rolling stones on the higher grounds, rendered barely passable the perpetual alternation of hill and valley.

The master rode on in pain, and the man in listlessness; although the intercourse between two individuals so situated was much less restrained in those days than might suit the refinement of a later age, little passed approximating to conversation beyond an occasional and half-stifled groan from the one, or a vacant whistle from the other. An hour's riding had brought them among the woods of Acryse; and they were about to descend one of those green and leafy lanes, rendered by matted and overarching branches alike impervious to shower or sunbeam, when a sudden and violent spasm seize'd on Master Marsh, and nearly caused him to fall from his horse. With some difficulty he succeeded in dismounting, and seating himself by the roadside. Here he remained for a full half-hour in great apparent agony; the cold sweat rolled in large round drops adown his clammy forehead, a universal shivering palsied every limb, his eye-balls appeared to be starting from their sockets, and to his attached, though dull and heavy serving-man, he seemed as one struggling in the pangs of impending dissolution. His groans rose thick and frequent; and the alarmed Ralph was hesitating between his disinclination to leave him, and his desire to procure such assistance as one of the few cottages, rarely sprinkled in that wild country, might afford, when, after a long-drawn sigh, his master's features as suddenly relaxed; he declared himself better, the pang had passed away, and, to use his own expression, he "felt as if a knife had been drawn from out his very heart." With Ralph's assistance, after a while, he again reached his saddle; and though still ill at ease, from a deep-seated and gnawing pain, which ceased not, as he averred, to torment him, the violence of the paroxysm was spent, and it returned no more.

Master and man pursued their way with increased speed, as, emerging from the wooded defiles, they at length neared the coast; then, leaving the romantic castle of Saltwood, with its neighbouring town of Hithe, a little on their left, they proceeded along the ancient paved causeway, and, crossing the old Roman road, or Watling, plunged again into the woods that stretched between Lympne and Ostenhanger.

The sun rode high in the heavens, and its meridian blaze was powerfully felt by man and horse, when, again quitting their leafy covert, the travellers debouched on the open plain of Aldington Frith, a wide tract of unenclosed country stretching down to the very borders of "the Marsh" itself.

Here it was, in the neighbouring chapelry, the site of which may yet be traced by the curious antiquary, that Elizabeth Barton, the "Holy Maid of Kent," had, something less than a hundred years previous to the period of our narrative, commenced that series of supernatural pranks which eventually procured for her head an unenvied elevation upon London Bridge; and though the parish had since enjoyed the benefit of the incumbency of Master Erasmus's illustrious and enlightened Namesake, still, truth to tell, some of the old leaven was even yet supposed to be at work. The place had, in fact, an ill name; and, though Popish miracles had ceased to electrify its denizens, spells and charms, operating by a no less wondrous agency, were said to have taken their place. Warlocks, and other unholy subjects of Satan, were reported to make its wild recesses their favourite rendezvous, and that to an extent which eventually attracted the notice of no less a personage than the sagacious Matthew Hopkins himself, Witchfinder-General to the British government.

A great portion of the Frith, or Fright, as the name was then, and is still, pronounced, had formerly been a Chase, with rights of Free-warren, &c., appertaining to the Archbishops of the Province. Since the Reformation, however, it had been disparked; and when Master Thomas Marsh, and his man Ralph, entered upon its confines, the open greensward exhibited a lively scene, sufficiently explanatory of certain sounds that had already reached their ears while yet within the sylvan screen which concealed their origin.

It was Fair-day: booths, stalls, and all the rude *paraphernalia* of an assembly that then met as much for the purposes of traffic as festivity, were scattered irregularly over the turf; pedlars, with their packs, horse-croupers, pig-merchants, itinerant venders of crockery and cutlery, wandered promiscuously among the mingled groups, exposing their several wares and commodities, and soliciting custom. On one side was the gaudy riband, making its mute appeal to rustic gallantry; on the other the delicious brandyball and alluring lollipop, compounded after the most approved receipt in the "True Gentlewoman's Garland," and "raising the waters" in the mouth of many an expectant urchin.

Nor were rural sports wanting to those whom pleasure, rather than business, had drawn from their humble homes. Here was the tall and slippery pole, glittering in its grease, and crowned with the ample cheese, that mocked the hopes of the discomfited climber. There the fugitive pippin, swimming in water not of the purest, and bobbing from the expanded lips of the juvenile Tantalus. In this quarter the ear was pierced by squeaks from some beleagured porker, whisking his well-soaped tail from the grasp of one already in fancy his captor. In that, the eye rested, with undisguised delight, upon the grimaces of grinning candidates for the honours of the horse-collar. All was fun, frolic, courtship, junketing, and jollity.

Maid Marian, indeed, with her lieges, Robin Hood, Scarlet, and Little John, was wanting; Friar Tuck was absent; even the Hobby-horse had disappeared: but the agile Maurice-dancers yet were there, and jingled their bells merrily among stalls well stored with gingerbread, tops, whips, whistles, and all those noisy instruments of domestic torture in which scenes like these are even now so fertile. —Had I a foe whom I held at deadliest feud, I would entice his favourite child to a Fair, and buy him a Whistle and a Penny-trumpet.

In one corner of the green, a little apart from the thickest of the throng, stood a small square stage, nearly level with the chins of the spectators, whose repeated bursts of laughter seemed to intimate the presence of something more than usually amusing. The platform was divided into two unequal portions; the smaller of which, surrounded by curtains of a coarse canvass, veiled from the eyes of the profane the *penetralia* of this moveable temple of Esculapius, for such it was. Within its interior, and secure from vulgar curiosity, the Quack-salver had hitherto kept himself ensconced; occupied, no doubt, in the preparation and arrangement of that wonderful *panacea* which was hereafter to shed the blessings of health among the admiring crowd. Meanwhile his attendant Jack-pudding was busily employed on the *proscenium*, doing his best to attract attention by a practical facetiousness which took wonderfully with the spectators, interspersing it with the melodious notes of a huge cow's horn. The fellow's costume varied but little in character from that in which the late (alas! that we should have to write the word—late!) Mr. Joseph Grimaldi was accustomed to present himself before "a generous and enlightened public:" the principal difference consisted in this, that the upper garment was a long white tunic of a coarse linen, surmounted by a caricature of the ruff then fast falling into disuse, and was secured from the throat downwards by a single row of broad white metal buttons; and his legs were cased in loose wide trousers of the same material; while his sleeves, prolonged to a most disproportionate extent, descended far below the fingers, and acted as flappers in the somersets and caracoles, with which he diversified and enlivened his antics. Con-summate impudence, not altogether unmixed with a certain sly humour, sparkled in his eye through the chalk and ochre with which his features were plentifully bedaubed; and especially displayed itself in a succession of jokes, the coarseness of which did not seem to detract from their merit in the eyes of his applauding audience.

He was in the midst of a long and animated harangue explanatory of his master's high pretensions; he had informed his gaping auditors that the latter was the seventh son of a seventh son, and of course, as they very well knew, an Unborn Doctor; that to this happy accident of birth he added the advantage of most extensive travel; that in his search after science he had not only perambulated the whole of this world, but had trespassed on the boundaries of the next: that the depths of the Ocean and the bowels of the Earth were alike familiar to him; that besides salves and cataplasms of sovereign virtue, by combining sundry mosses, gathered many thousand fathoms below the surface of the sea, with certain unknown drugs found in an undiscovered island, and boiling the whole in the lava of Vesuvius, he had succeeded in producing his cele-brated balsam of Crackapanoko, the never-failing remedy for all human disorders, and which, a proper trial allowed, would go near to reanimate the dead. "Draw near!" continued the worthy, "draw near, my masters! and you, my good mistresses, draw near, every one of you. Fear not high and haughty carriage: though greater than King or Kaiser, yet is the mighty Aldrovando milder than mother's milk; flint to the proud, to the humble he is as melting wax; he asks not your disorders, he sees them himself at a glance—nay, without a glance; he tells your ailments with his eyes shut!—Draw near! draw near! the more incurable the better! List to the illustrious Doctor Aldrovando, first physician to Prester John, Leech to the Grand Llama, and Hakim in Ordinary to Mustapha Muley Bey!"

"Hath your master ever a charm for the toothache, an't please you?" asked an elderly countryman, whose swollen cheek bespoke his interest in the question.

"A charm!—a thousand, and every one of them infallible. Tooth-ache, quotha! I had hoped you had come with every bone in your body fractured or out of joint. A toothache!—propound a tester, master o' mine—we ask not more for such trifles: do my bidding, and thy jaws, even with the word, shall cease to trouble thee!"

The clown, fumbling a while in a deep leathern purse, at length produced a sixpence, which he tendered to the jester. "Now to thy master, and bring me the charm forthwith."

"Nay, honest man; to disturb the mighty Aldrovando on such slight occasion were pity of my life: areed my counsel aright, and I will warrant thee for the nonce. Hie thee home, friend; infuse this powder in cold spring-water, fill thy mouth with the mixture, and sit upon thy fire till it boils!"

"Out on thee for a pestilent knave!" cried the cozened countryman; but the roar of merriment around bespoke the by-standers well-pleased with the jape put upon him. He retired, venting his spleen in audible murmurs; and the mountebank, finding the feelings of the mob enlisted on his side, waxed more impudent every instant, filling up the intervals between his fooleries with sundry capers and contortions, and discordant notes from the cow's horn.

"Draw near, draw near, my masters! Here have ye a remedy for every evil under the sun, moral, physical, natural, and supernatural! Hath any man a termagant wife?—here is that will tame her presently! Hath any one a smoky chimney?—here is an incontinent cure!"

To the first infliction no man ventured to plead guilty, though there were those standing by who thought their neighbours might have profited withal. For the last-named recipe started forth at least a dozen candidates. With the greatest gravity imaginable, Pierrot, having pocketed their groats, delivered to each a small packet curiously folded and closely sealed, containing, as he averred, directions which, if truly observed, would preclude any chimney from smoking for a whole year. They whose curiosity led them to dive into the mystery, found that a sprig of mountain ash culled by moonlight was the charm recommended, coupled, however, with the proviso that no fire should be lighted on the hearth during its exercise.

The frequent bursts of merriment proceeding from this quarter at length attracted the attention of Master Marsh, whose line of road necessarily brought him near this end of the fair; he drew bit in front of the stage just as its noisy occupant, having laid aside his formidable horn, was drawing still more largely on the amazement of "the public" by a feat of especial wonder—he was eating fire! Curiosity mingled with astonishment was at its height; and feelings not unallied to alarm were beginning to manifest themselves, among the softer sex especially, as they gazed on the flames that issued from the mouth of the living volcano. All eyes, indeed, were fixed upon the fire-eater with an intent-ness that left no room for observing another worthy who had now emerged upon the scene. This was, however, no less a personage than the *Deus ex machinâ*

—the illustrious Aldrovando himself.

Short in stature and spare in form, the sage had somewhat increased the former by a steeple-crowned hat adorned with a cock's feather; while the thick shoulder-padding of a quilted doublet, surmounted by a falling band, added a little to his personal importance in point of breadth. His habit was composed throughout of black serge, relieved with scarlet slashes in the sleeves and trunks; red was the feather in his hat, red were the roses in his shoes, which rejoiced moreover in a pair of red heels. The lining of a short cloak of faded velvet, that hung transversely over his left shoulder, was also red. Indeed, from all that we could ever see or hear, this agreeable alternation of red and black appears to be the mixture of colours most approved at the court of Beelzebub, and the one most generally adopted by his friends and favourites. His features were sharp and shrewd, and a fire sparkled in his keen grey eye, much at variance with the wrinkles that ran their irregular furrows above his prominent and bushy brows. He had advanced slowly from behind his screen while the attention of the multitude was absorbed by the pyrotechnics of Mr. Merryman, and, stationing himself at the extreme corner of the stage, stood quietly leaning on a crutch-handle walkingstaff of blackest ebony, his glance steadily fixed on the face of Marsh, from whose countenance the amusement he had insensibly begun to derive had not succeeded in removing all traces of bodily pain.

For a while the latter was unobservant of the inquisitorial survey with which he was regarded; the eyes of the parties, however, at length met. The brown mare had a fine shoulder; she stood pretty nearly sixteen hands. Marsh himself, though slightly bowed by ill health and the "coming autumn" of life, was full six feet in height. His elevation giving him an unobstructed view over the heads of the pedestrians, he had naturally fallen into the rear of the assembly, which brought him close to the diminutive Doctor, with whose face, despite the red heels, his own was about upon a level.

"And what makes Master Marsh here?—what sees he in the mummeries of a miserable buffoon to divert him when his life is in jeopardy?" said a shrill cracked voice that sounded as in his very ear. It was the Doctor who spoke.

"Knowest thou me, friend?" said Marsh, scanning with awakened interest the figure of his questioner: "I call thee not to mind; and yet—stay, where have we met?"

"It skills not to declare," was the answer; "suffice it we *have* met—in other climes perchance—and now meet happily again—happily at least

Geo. Cruikshank

The Leech of Folkstone

for thee."

"Why truly the trick of thy countenance reminds me of somewhat I have seen before; where or when I know not: but what wouldst thou with me?"

"Nay, rather what wouldst thou here, Thomas Marsh? What wouldst thou on the Frith of Aldington?—is it a score or two of paltry sheep? or is it something *nearer to thy heart?*"

Marsh started as the last words were pronounced with more than common significance: a pang shot through him at the moment, and the vinegar aspect of the charlatan seemed to relax into a smile half compass-sionate, half sardonic.

"Grammercy," quoth Marsh, after a long-drawn breath, "what knowest thou of me, fellow, or of my concerns? What knowest thou—"

"This know I, Master Thomas Marsh," said the stranger, gravely, "that thy life is even now perilled, evil practices are against thee; but no matter, thou art quit for the nonce—other hands than mine have saved thee! Thy pains are over. Hark! *the clock strikes One!*" As he spoke, a single toll from the bell-tower of Bilsington came, wafted by the western breeze, over the thick-set and lofty oaks which intervened between the Frith and what had been once a priory. Doctor Aldrovando turned as the sound came floating on the wind, and was moving, as if half in anger, towards the other side of the stage, where the mountebank, his fires extinct, was now disgorging to the admiring crowd yard after yard of gaudy-coloured riband.

"Stay Nay, prithee stay!" cried Marsh eagerly, "I was wrong; in faith I was. A change, and that a sudden and most marvellous, hath indeed come over me; I am free; I breathe again; I feel as though a load of years had been removed; and—is it possible?—hast thou done this?"

"Thomas Marsh!" said the doctor, pausing, and turning for the moment on his heel, "I have not: I repeat, that other and more innocent hands than mine have done this deed. Nevertheless, heed my counsel well! Thou art parlously encompassed; I, and I only, have the means of relieving thee. Follow thy courses; pursue thy journey; but as thou valuest life and more than life, be at the foot of yonder woody knoll what time the rising moon throws her first beam upon the bare and blighted summit that towers above its trees."

He crossed abruptly to the opposite quarter of the scaffolding, and was in an instant deeply engaged in listening to those whom the cow's horn had attracted, and in prescribing for their real or fancied ailments. Vain were all Marsh's efforts again to attract his notice; it was evident that he studiously avoided him; and when, after an hour or more spent in useless endeavour, he saw the object of his anxiety seclude himself once more within his canvass screen, he rode slowly and thoughtfully off the field.

What should he do? Was the man a mere quack? an impostor?—His name thus obtained?—that might be easily done. But then, his secret griefs: the doctor's knowledge of them; their cure; for he felt that his pains were gone, his healthful feelings restored!

True; Aldrovando, if that were his name, had disclaimed all co-operation in his recovery: but he knew, or he at least announced it. Nay, more; he had hinted that he was yet in jeopardy; that practices—and the chord sounded strangely in unison with one that had before vibrated within him—that practices were in operation against his life! It was enough! He would keep tryst with the Conjuror, if conjuror he were; and, at least, ascertain who and what he was, and how he had become acquainted with his own person and secret afflictions.

When the late Mr. Pitt was determined to keep out Bonaparte, and prevent his gaining a settle ment in the county of Kent, among other ingenious devices adopted for that purpose, he caused to be constructed what was then, and has ever since been, conventionally termed a "Military Canal" This is a not very practicable ditch, some thirty feet wide, and nearly nine feet deep—in the middle—extending from the town and port of Hithe to within a mile of the town and port of Rye, a distance of about twenty miles; and forming as it were, the cord of a bow, the arc of which constitutes that remote fifth quarter of the globe spoken of by travellers. Trivial objections to the plan were made at the time by cavillers; and an old gentleman of the neighbourhood, who proposed as a cheap substitute, to put down his own cocked-hat upon a pole, was deservedly pooh-pooh'd down; in fact, the job, though rather an expensive one, was found to answer remarkably well. The French managed, indeed, to scramble over the Rhine, and the Rhone, and other insignificant currents; but they never did, or could, pass Mr. Pitt's "Military Canal." At no great distance from the centre of this cord rises abruptly a sort of woody promontory, in shape almost conical; its sides covered with thick underwood, above which is seen a bare and brown summit rising like an Alp in miniature. The "defence of the nation" not being then in existence, Master Marsh met with no obstruction in reaching this place of appointment long before the time prescribed.

So much, indeed, was his mind occupied by his adventure and extraordinary cure, that his original design had been abandoned, and

Master Cobbe remained unvisited. A rude hostel in the neighbourhood furnished entertainment for man and horse; and here, a full hour before the rising of the moon, he left Ralph and the other beasts, proceeding to his rendezvous on foot and alone.

"You are punctual, Master Marsh," squeaked the shrill voice of the doctor, issuing from the thicket as the first silvery gleam trembled on the aspens above. "'Tis well: now follow me and in silence."

The first part of the command Marsh hesitated not to obey; the second was more difficult of observance.

"Who and what are you? Whither are you leading me?" burst not unnaturally from his lips; but all question was at once cut short by the peremptory tones of his guide.

"Hush! I say; your finger on your lip, there be hawks abroad: follow me, and that silently and quickly." The little man turned as he spoke, and led the way through a scarcely perceptible path, or track, which wound among the underwood. The lapse of a few minutes brought them to the door of a low building, so hidden by the surrounding trees that few would have suspected its existence. It was a cottage of rather extraordinary dimensions, but consisting of only one floor. No smoke rose from its solitary chimney; no cheering ray streamed from its single window, which was, however secured by a shutter of such thickness as to preclude the possibility of any stray beam issuing from within. The exact size of the building it was, in that uncertain light, difficult to distinguish, a portion of it seeming buried in the wood behind. The door gave way on the application of a key, and Marsh followed his conductor resolutely, but cautiously, along a narrow passage, feebly lighted by a small taper that winked and twinkled at its farther extremity. The Doctor, as he approached, raised it from the ground, and, opening an adjoining door, ushered his guest into the room beyond.

It was a large and oddly furnished apartment, insufficiently lighted by an iron lamp that hung from the roof, and scarcely illumined the walls and angles, which seemed to be composed of some dark-coloured wood. On one side, however, Master Marsh could discover an article bearing strong resemblance to a coffin; on the other was a large oval mirror in an ebony frame, and in the midst of the floor was described, in red chalk, a double circle, about six feet in diameter, its inner verge inscribed with sundry hieroglyphics, agreeably relieved at intervals with an alternation of skulls and cross bones. In the very centre was deposited one skull of such surpassing size and thickness as would have filled the soul of a Spurzheim or De Ville with wonderment. A large book, a naked sword, an hourglass, a chafing dish, and a black cat, completed the list of move-ables; with the exception of a couple of tapers which stood on each side of the mirror, and which the strange gentleman now proceeded to light from the one in his hand. As they flared up with what Marsh thought a most unnatural brilliancy, he perceived, reflected in the glass behind, a dial suspended over the coffin-like article already mentioned: the hand was fast verging towards the hour of nine. The eyes of the little Doctor seemed riveted on the horologe.

"Now strip thee, Master Marsh, and that quickly: untruss, I say! discard thy boots, doff doublet and hose, and place thyself incontinent in yonder bath."

The visitor cast his eyes again upon the formidable-looking article, and perceived that it was nearly filled with water. A cold bath, at such an hour and under such auspices, was anything but inviting: he hesitated, and turned his eyes alternately on the Doctor and the Black Cat.

"Trifle not the time, man, an you be wise," said the former: "Passion of my heart! let but yon minute-hand reach the hour, and thou not immersed, thy life were not worth a pin's fee!"

The Black Cat gave vent to a single Mew—a most unnatural sound for a mouser—it seemed as it were mewed through a cow's horn.

"Quick, Master Marsh! uncase, or you perish!" repeated his strange host, throwing as he spoke a handful of some dingy-looking powders into the brasier. "Behold the attack is begun!" A thick cloud rose from the embers; a cold shivering shook the astonished Yeoman; sharp pricking pains penetrated his ankles and the palms of his hands, and, as the smoke cleared away, he distinctly saw and recognised in the mirror the boudoir of Marston Hall.

The doors of the well-known ebony cabinet were closed; but fixed against them, and standing out in strong relief from the contrast afforded by the sable background, was a waxen image—of himself! It appeared to be secured, and sustained in an upright posture, by large black pins driven through the feet and palms, the latter of which were extended in a cruciform position. To the right and left stood his wife and José; in the middle, with his back towards him, was a figure which he had no difficulty in recognising as that of the Leech of Folkestone. The latter had just succeeded in fastening the dexter hand of the image, and was now in the act of drawing a broad and keen-edged sabre from its sheath. The Black Cat mewed again. "Haste or you die!" said the Doctor—Marsh looked at the dial; it wanted but four minutes of nine: he felt that the crisis of his fate was come. Off went his heavy boots; doublet to the right, galligaskins to the left; never was man more swiftly disrobed: in two minutes, to use an Indian expression, "he was all face!" in another he was on his back, and up to his chin, in a bath which smelt strongly as of brimstone and garlic.

"Heed well the clock!" cried the Conjuror: "with the first stroke of Nine plunge thy head beneath the water, suffer not a hair above the surface: plunge deeply, or thou art lost!"

The little man had seated himself in the centre of the circle upon the large skull, elevating his legs at an angle of forty-five degrees. In this position he spun round with a velocity to be equalled only by that of a tee-totum, the red roses on his insteps seeming to describe a circle of fire. The best buckskins that ever mounted at Melton had soon yielded to such rotatory friction—but he spun on—the Cat mewed, bats and obscene birds fluttered over-head; Erasmus was seen to raise his weapon, the clock struck!—and Marsh, who had "ducked" at the instant, popped up his head again, spitting and sputtering, half-choked with the infernal solution, which had insinuated itself into his mouth, and ears, and nose. All disgust at his nauseous dip, was, however, at once removed, when, casting his eyes on the glass, he saw the consternation of the party whose persons it exhibited. Erasmus had evidently made his blow and failed; the figure was unmutilated; the hilt remained in the hand of the striker, while the shivered blade lay in shining fragments on the floor.

The Conjuror ceased his spinning, and brought himself to an anchor; the Black Cat purred—its purring seemed strangely mixed with the self-satisfied chuckle of a human being. —Where had Marsh heard something like it before?

He was rising from his unsavoury couch; when a motion from the little man checked him. "Rest where you are, Thomas Marsh; so far all goes well, but the danger is not yet over!" He looked again, and perceived that the shadowy triumvirate were in deep and eager consultation; the fragments of the shattered weapon appeared to undergo a close scrutiny. The result was clearly unsatisfactory; the lips of the parties moved rapidly, and much gesticulation might be observed, but no sound fell upon the ear. The hand of the dial had nearly reached the quarter: at once the parties separated: and Buckthorne stood again before the figure, his hand armed with a long and sharp-pointed misericorde, a dagger little in use of late, but such as, a century before, often performed the part, of a modern oyster-knife, in tickling the osteology of a dismounted cavalier through the shelly defences of his plate armour. Again he raised his arm. "Duck!" roared the Doctor, spinning away upon his cephalic pivot:—the

Black Cat cocked his tail, and seemed to mew the word "Duck!" Down went Master Marsh's head—one of his hands had unluckily been resting on the edge of the bath: he drew it hastily in, but not altogether scatheless; the stump of a rusty nail, projecting from the margin of the hath, had caught and slightly grazed it. The pain was more acute than is usually produced by such trivial accidents; and Marsh, on once more raising his head, beheld the dagger of the Leech sticking in the little finger of the wax figure, which it had seemingly nailed to the cabinet door.

"By my truly, a scape o' the narrowest!" quoth the Conjuror: "the next course, dive you not the readier, there is no more life in you than in a pickled herring— What courage, Master Marsh; but be heedful; an they miss again, let them bide the issue!"

He drew his hand athwart his brow as he spoke, and dashed off the perspiration, which the violence of his exercise had drawn from every pore. Black Tom sprang upon the edge of the bath, and stared full in the face of the bather: his sea-green eyes were lambent with unholy fire, but their marvellous obliquity of vision was not to be mistaken—the very countenance, too!—Could it be?—the features were feline, but their expression was that of the Jack Pudding! Was the Mountebank a Cat?—or the Cat a Mountebank?—it was all a mystery;—and Heaven knows how long Marsh might have continued staring at Grimalkin, had not his attention been again called by Aldrovando to the magic mirror.

Great dissatisfaction, not to say dismay, seemed now to pervade the conspirators; Dame Isabel was closely inspecting the figure's wounded hand, while José, was aiding the pharmacopolist to charge a huge petronel with powder and bullets. The load was a heavy one; but Erasmus seemed determined this time to make sure of his object. Somewhat of trepidation might be observed in his manner as he rammed down the balls, and his withered cheek appeared to have acquired an increase of paleness; but amazement rather than fear was the prevailing symptom, and his countenance betrayed no jot of irresolution. As the clock was about to chime half-past nine, he planted himself with a firm foot in front of the image, waved his unoccupied hand with a cautionary gesture to his companions, and, as they hastily retired on either side, brought the muzzle of his weapon within half a foot of his mark. As the shadowy form was about to draw the trigger, Marsh again plunged his head beneath the surface; and the sound of an explosion, as of fire-arms, mingled with the rush of water that poured into his ears. His immersion was but momentary, yet did he feel as though half suffocated: he sprang from the bath, and, as his eye fell on the mirror, he saw—or thought he saw—the Leech of Folkestone lying dead on the floor of his wife's boudoir, his head shattered to pieces, and his hand still grasping the stock of a bursten petronel.

He saw no more; his head swam; his senses reeled, the whole room was turning round, and, as he fell to the ground, the last impressions to which he was conscious were the chucklings of a hoarse laughter, and the mewings of a Tom Cat!

Master Marsh was found the next morning by his bewildered serving-man, stretched before the door of the humble hostel at which he sojourned. His clothes were somewhat torn and much bemired! and deeply did honest Ralph marvel that one so staid and grave as Master Marsh of Marston should thus have played the roisterer, missing, perchance, a profitable bargain for the drunken orgies of midnight wassail, or the endearments of some rustic light-o'-love. Tenfold was his astonishment increased when, after retracing in silence their journey of the preceding day, the Hall, on their arrival about noon, was found in a state of uttermost confusion. —No wife stood there to greet with the smile of bland affection her returning spouse; no page to hold his stirrup, or receive his gloves, his hat, and riding-rod. —The doors were open, the rooms in most admired disorder; men and maidens peeping, hurrying hither and thither, and popping in and out, like rabbits in a warren. —The lady of the mansion was nowhere to be found.

José, too, had disappeared; the latter had been last seen riding furiously towards Folkestone early in the preceding afternoon; to a question from Hodge Gardener he had hastily answered, that he bore a missive of moment from his mistress. The lean apprentice of Erasmus Buckthorne declared that the page had summoned his master, in haste, about six of the clock, and that they had rode forth together, as he verily believed, on their way back to the Hall, where he had supposed Master Buckthorne's services to be suddenly required on some pressing emergency. Since that time he had seen nought of either of them: the grey cob, however, had returned late at night, masterless, with his girths loose, and the saddle turned upside down.

Nor was Master Erasmus Buckthorne ever seen again. Strict search was made through the neighbourhood, but without success; and it was at length presumed that he must, for reasons which nobody could divine, have absconded, together with Jos, and his faithless mistress. The latter had carried off with her the strong box, divers articles of valuable plate, and jewels of price. Her boudoir appeared to have been completely ransacked; the cabinet and drawers stood open and empty; the very carpet, a luxury then newly introduced into England, was gone. Marsh, however, could trace no vestige of the visionary scene which he affirmed to have been last night presented to his eyes.

Much did the neighbours marvel at his story: some thought him mad; others, that he was merely indulging in that privilege to which, as a traveller, he had a right indefeasible. Trusty Ralph said nothing, but shrugged his shoulders; and, falling into the rear, imitated the action of raising a wine-cup to his lips. An opinion, indeed, soon prevailed, that Master Thomas Marsh had gotten, in common parlance, exceedingly drunk on the preceding evening, and had dreamt all that he so circumstantially related. This belief acquired additional credit when they, whom curiosity induced to visit the woody knoll of Aldington Mount, declared that they could find no building such as that described, nor any cottage near; save one, indeed, a low-roofed hovel, once a house of public entertainment, but now half in ruins. The "Old Cat and Fiddle"—so was the tenement called—had been long uninhabited; yet still exhibited the remains of a broken sign, on which the keen observer might decipher something like a rude portrait of the animal from which it derived its name. It was also supposed still to afford an occasional asylum to the smugglers of the coast, but no trace of any visit from sage or mountebank could be detected; nor was the wise Aldrovando, whom many remembered to have seen at the fair, ever found again on all that country-side.

Of the runaways nothing was ever certainly known. A boat, the property of an old fisherman who plied his trade on the outskirts of the town, had been seen to quit the bay that night; and there were those who declared that she had more hands on board than Carden and his son, her usual complement; but, as the gale came on, and the frail bark was eventually found keel upwards on the Goodwin Sands, it was presumed that she had struck on that fatal quicksand in the dark, and that all on board had perished.

Little Marian, whom her profligate mother had abandoned, grew up to be a fine girl, and a handsome. She became, moreover, heiress to Marston Hall, and brought the estate into the Ingoldsby family by her marriage with one of its scions.

Thus far Mrs. Botherby.

It is a little singular that, on pulling down the old Hall in my grandfathers time, a human skeleton was discovered among the rubbish; under what particular part of the building I could never with any accuracy ascertain; but it was found enveloped in a tattered cloth, that seemed to have been once a carpet, and which fell to pieces almost immediately on being exposed to the air. The bones were perfect, but those of one hand were wanting; and the skull, perhaps from the labourer's pick-axe, had received considerable injury; the worm-eaten stock of an old-fashioned pistol lay near, together with a rusty piece of iron which a workman, more sagacious than his fellows, pronounced a portion of the lock, but nothing was found which the utmost stretch of human ingenuity could twist into a barrel.

The portrait of the fair Marian hangs yet in the Gallery of Tappington; and near it is another, of a young man in the prime of life, whom Mrs. Botherby affirms to be that of her father. It exhibits a mild and rather melancholy countenance, with a high forehead, and the peaked beard and moustaches of the seventeenth century. The signet-finger of the left hand is gone, and appears, on close inspection, to have been painted out by some later artist; possibly in compliment to the tradition, which, teste Botherby, records that of Mr. Marsh to have gangrened, and to have undergone amputation at the knuckle-joint. If really the resemblance of the gentleman alluded to, it must have been taken at some period antecedent to his marriage. There is neither date nor painter's name; but, a little above the bead, on the dexter side of the picture, is an escutcheon, bearing "Quarterly, Gules and Argent, in the first quarter a horse's head of the second;" beneath it are the words "Ætatis suæ; 26." Oh the opposite side is the following mark, which Mr. Simpkinson declares to be that of a Merchant of the Staple, and pretends to discover, in the monogram comprised in it, all the characters which compose the name of THOMAS MARSH, of MARSTON.

THE VIY

by Nicolai Gogol

(The "Viy" is a monstrous creation of popular fancy. It is the name which the inhabitants of Little Russia give to the king of the gnomes, whose eyelashes reach to the ground. The following story is a specimen of such folklore. I have made no alterations, but reproduce it in the same simple form in which I heard it. —AUTHOR'S NOTE.)

I

As soon as the clear seminary bell began sounding in Kieff in the morning, the pupils would come flocking from all parts of the town. The students of grammar, rhetoric, philosophy, and theology hastened with their books under their arms over the streets.

The "grammarians" were still mere boys. On the way they pushed against each other and quarreled with shrill voices. Nearly all of them wore torn or dirty clothes, and their pockets were always crammed with all kinds of things—push-bones, pipes made out of pens, remains of confectionery, and sometimes even young sparrows. The latter would sometimes begin to chirp in the midst of deep silence in the school, and bring down on their possessors severe canings and thrashings.

The "rhetoricians" walked in a more orderly way. Their clothes were generally untorn, but on the other hand their faces were often strangely decorated; one had a black eye, and the lips of another resembled a single blister, etc. These spoke to each other in tenor voices.

The "philosophers" talked in a tone an octave lower; in their pockets they only had fragments of tobacco, never whole cakes of it; for what they could get hold of, they used at once. They smelt so strongly of tobacco and brandy, that a workman passing by them would often remain standing and sniffing with his nose in the air, like a hound.

About this time of day the marketplace was generally full of bustle, and the market women, selling rolls, cakes, and honey-tarts, plucked the sleeves of those who wore coats of fine cloth or cotton.

"Young sir! Young sir! Here! Here!" they cried from all sides. "Rolls and cakes and tasty tarts, very delicious! I have baked them myself!"

Another drew something long and crooked out of her basket and cried, "Here is a sausage, young sir! Buy a sausage!"

"Don't buy anything from her!" cried a rival. "See how greasy she is, and what a dirty nose and hands she has!"

But the market women carefully avoided appealing to the philosophers and theologians, for these only took handfuls of eatables merely to taste them.

Arrived at the seminary, the whole crowd of students dispersed into the low, large classrooms with small windows, broad doors, and blackened benches. Suddenly they were filled with a many-toned murmur. The teachers heard the pupils' lessons repeated, some in shrill and others in deep voices which sounded like a distant booming. While the lessons were being said, the teachers kept a sharp eye open to see whether pieces of cake or other dainties were protruding from their pupils' pockets; if so, they were promptly confiscated.

When this learned crowd arrived somewhat earlier than usual, or when it was known that the teachers would come somewhat late, a battle would ensue, as though planned by general agreement. In this battle all had to take part, even the monitors who were appointed to look after the order and morality of the whole school. Two theologians generally arranged the conditions of the battle: whether each class should split into two sides, or whether all the pupils should divide themselves into two halves.

In each case the grammarians began the battle, and after the rhetoricians had joined in, the former retired and stood on the benches, in order to watch the fortunes of the fray. Then came the philosophers with long black moustaches, and finally the thick-necked theologians. The battle generally ended in a victory for the latter, and the philosophers retired to the different classrooms rubbing their aching limbs, and throwing themselves on the benches to take breath.

When the teacher, who in his own time had taken part in such contests, entered the classroom he saw by the heated faces of his pupils that the battle had been very severe, and while he caned the hands of the rhetoricians, in another room another teacher did the same for the philosophers.

On Sundays and Festival Days the seminarists took puppet-theatres to the citizens' houses. Sometimes they acted a comedy, and in that case it was always a theologian who took the part of the hero or heroine—Potiphar or Herodias, etc. As a reward for their exertions, they received a piece of linen, a sack of maize, half a roast goose, or something similar. All the students, lay and clerical, were very poorly provided with means for procuring themselves necessary subsistence, but at the same time very fond of eating; so that, however much food was given to them, they were never satisfied, and the gifts bestowed by rich landowners were never adequate for their needs.

Therefore the Commissariat Committee, consisting of philosophers and theologians, sometimes dispatched the grammarians and rhetoricians under the leadership of a philosopher—themselves sometimes joining in the expedition—with sacks on their shoulders, into the town, in order to levy a contribution on the fleshpots of the citizens, and then there was a feast in the seminary.

The most important event in the seminary year was the arrival of the holidays; these began in July, and then generally all the students went home. At that time all the roads were thronged with grammarians, rhetoricians, philosophers, and theologians. He who had no home of his own, would take up his quarters with some fellow-student's family; the philosophers and theologians looked out for tutors' posts, taught the children of rich farmers, and received for doing so a pair of new boots and sometimes also a new coat.

A whole troop of them would go off in close ranks like a regiment; they cooked their porridge in common, and encamped under the open sky. Each had a bag with him containing a shirt and a pair of socks. The theologians were especially economical; in order not to wear out their boots too quickly, they took them off and carried them on a stick over their shoulders, especially when the road was very muddy. Then they tucked up their breeches over their knees and waded bravely through the pools and puddles. Whenever they spied a village near the highway, they at once left it, approached the house which seemed the most considerable, and began with loud voices to sing a psalm. The master of the house, an old Cossack engaged in agriculture, would listen for a long time with his head propped in his hands, then with tears on his cheeks say to his wife, "What the students are singing sounds very devout; bring out some lard and anything else of the kind we have in the house."

After thus replenishing their stores, the students would continue their way. The farther they went, the smaller grew their numbers, as they dispersed to their various houses, and left those whose homes were still farther on.

On one occasion, during such a march, three students left the main-road in order to get provisions in some village, since their stock had long been exhausted. This party consisted of the theologian Khalava, the philosopher Thomas Brutus, and the rhetorician Tiberius Gorobetz.

The first was a tall youth with broad shoulders and of a peculiar character; everything which came within reach of his fingers he felt obliged to appropriate. Moreover, he was of a very melancholy disposetion, and when he had got intoxicated he hid himself in the most tangled thickets so that the seminary officials had the greatest trouble in finding him.

The philosopher Thomas Brutus was a more cheerful character. He liked to lie for a long time on the same spot and smoke his pipe; and when he was merry with wine, he hired a fiddler and danced the "tropak." Often he got a whole quantity of "beans," i.e. thrashings; but these he endured with complete philosophic calm, saying that a man cannot escape his destiny.

The rhetorician Tiberius Gorobetz had not yet the right to wear a moustache, to drink brandy, or to smoke tobacco. He only wore a small crop of hair, as though his character was at present too little developed. To judge by the great bumps on his forehead, with which he often appeared in the classroom, it might be expected that some day he would be a valiant fighter. Khalava and Thomas often pulled his hair as a mark of their special favor, and sent him on their errands.

Evening had already come when they left the high-road; the sun had just gone down, and the air was still heavy with the heat of the day. The theologian and the philosopher strolled along, smoking in silence, while the rhetorician struck off the heads of the thistles by the wayside with his stick. The way wound on through thick woods of oak and walnut; green hills alternated here and there with meadows. Twice already they had seen cornfields, from which they concluded that they were near some village; but an hour had already passed, and no human habitation appeared. The sky was already quite dark, and only a red gleam lingered on the western horizon.

"The deuce!" said the philosopher Thomas Brutus. "I was almost certain we would soon reach a village."

The theologian still remained silent, looked round him, then put his pipe again between his teeth, and all three continued their way.

"Good heavens!" exclaimed the philosopher, and stood still. "Now the road itself is disappearing."

"Perhaps we shall find a farm farther on," answered the theologian, without taking his pipe out of his mouth.

Meanwhile the night had descended; clouds increased the darkness, and according to all appearance there was no chance of moon or stars appearing. The seminarists found that they had lost the way altogether.

After the philosopher had vainly sought for a footpath, he exclaimed, "Where have we got to?"

The theologian thought for a while, and said, "Yes, it is really dark."

The rhetorician went on one side, lay on the ground, and groped for a path; but his hands encountered only fox-holes. All around lay a huge steppe over which no one seemed to have passed. The wanderers made several efforts to get forward, but the landscape grew wilder and more inhospitable.

The philosopher tried to shout, but his voice was lost in vacancy, no one answered; only, some moments later, they heard a faint groaning sound, like the whimpering of a wolf.

"Curse it all! What shall we do?" said the philosopher.

"Why, just stop here, and spend the night in the open air," answered the theologian. So saying, he felt in his pocket, brought out his timber and steel, and lit his pipe.

But the philosopher could not agree with this proposal; he was not accustomed to sleep till he had first eaten five pounds of bread and five of dripping, and so he now felt an intolerable emptiness in his stomach. Besides, in spite of his cheerful temperament, he was a little afraid of the wolves.

"No, Khalava," he said, "that won't do. To lie down like a dog and without any supper! Let us try once more; perhaps we shall find a house, and the consolation of having a glass of brandy to drink before going to sleep."

At the word "brandy," the theologian spat on one side and said, "Yes, of course, we cannot remain all night in the open air."

The students went on and on, and to their great joy they heard the barking of dogs in the distance. After listening a while to see from which direction the barking came, they went on their way with new courage, and soon espied a light.

"A village, by heavens, a village!" exclaimed the philosopher.

His supposition proved correct; they soon saw two or three houses built round a courtyard. Lights glimmered in the windows, and before the fence stood a number of trees. The students looked through the crevices of the gates and saw a courtyard in which stood a large number of roving tradesmen's carts. In the sky there were now fewer clouds, and here and there a star was visible.

"See, brother!" one of them said, "we must now cry 'halt!' Cost what it may, we must find entrance and a night's lodging."

The three students knocked together at the gate, and cried "Open!"

The door of one of the houses creaked on its hinges, and an old woman wrapped in a sheepskin appeared. "Who is there?" she exclaimed, coughing loudly.

"Let us spend the night here, mother; we have lost our way, our stomachs are empty, and we do not want to spend the night out of doors."

"But what sort of people are you?"

"Quite harmless people; the theologian Khalava, the philosopher Brutus, and the rhetorician Gorobetz."

"It is impossible," answered the old woman. "The whole house is full of people, and every corner occupied. Where can I put you up? You are big and heavy enough to break the house down. I know these philosophers and theologians; when once one takes them in, they eat one out of house and home. Go farther on! There is no room here for you!"

"Have pity on us, mother! How can you be so heartless? Don't let Christians perish. Put us up where you like, and if we eat up your provisions, or do any other damage, may our hands wither up, and all the punishment of heaven light on us!"

The old woman seemed a little touched. "Well," she said after a few moments' consideration, "I will let you in; but I must put you in different rooms, for I should have no quiet if you were all together at night."

"Do just as you like; we won't say any more about it," answered the students.

The gates moved heavily on their hinges, and they entered the courtyard.

"Well now, mother," said the philosopher, following the old woman, "if you had a little scrap of something! By heavens! my stomach is as empty as a drum. I have not had a bit of bread in my mouth since early this morning!"

"Didn't I say so?" replied the old woman. "There you go begging at once. But I have no food in the house, nor any fire."

"But we will pay for everything," continued the philosopher.

"We will pay early to-morrow in cash."

"Go on and be content with what you get. You are fine fellows whom the devil has brought here!"

Her reply greatly depressed the philosopher Thomas; but suddenly his nose caught the odour of dried fish; he looked at the breeches of the theologian, who walked by his side, and saw a huge fish's tail sticking out of his pocket. The latter had already seized the opportunity to steal a whole fish from one of the carts standing in the courtyard. He had not done this from hunger so much as from the force of habit. He had quite forgotten the fish, and was looking about to see whether he could not find something else to appropriate. Then the philosopher put his hand in the theologian's pocket as though it were his own, and laid hold of his prize.

The old woman found a special resting-place for each student; the rhetorician she put in a shed, the theologian in an empty storeroom, and the philosopher in a sheep's stall.

As soon as the philosopher was alone, he devoured the fish in a twinkling, examined the fence which enclosed the stall, kicked away a pig from a neighboring stall, which had inquiringly inserted its nose through a crevice, and lay down on his right side to sleep like a corpse.

Then the low door opened, and the old woman came crouching into the stall.

"Well, mother, what do you want here?" asked the philosopher.

She made no answer, but came with outstretched arms towards him.

The philosopher shrank back; but she still approached, as though she wished to lay hold of him. A terrible fright seized him, for he saw the old hag's eyes sparkle in an extraordinary way. "Away with you, old witch, away with you!" he shouted. But she still stretched her hands after him.

He jumped up in order to rush out, but she placed herself before the door, fixed her glowing eyes upon him, and again approached him. The philosopher tried to push her away with his hands, but to his astonishment he found that he could neither lift his hands nor move his legs, nor utter an audible word. He only heard his heart beating, and saw the old woman approach him, place his hands crosswise on his breast, and bend his head down. Then with the agility of a cat she sprang on his shoulders, struck him on the side with a broom, and he began to run like a race-horse, carrying her on his shoulders.

All this happened with such swiftness, that the philosopher could scarcely collect his thoughts. He laid hold of his knees with both hands in order to stop his legs from running; but to his great astonishment they kept moving forward against his will, making rapid springs like a Caucasian horse.

Not till the house had been left behind them and a wide plain stretched before them, bordered on one side by a black gloomy wood, did he say to himself, "Ah! it is a witch!"

The half-moon shone pale and high in the sky. Its mild light, still more subdued by intervening clouds, fell like a transparent veil on the earth. Woods, meadows, hills, and valleys—all seemed to be sleeping with open eyes; nowhere was a breath of air stirring. The atmosphere was moist and warm; the shadows of the trees and bushes fell sharply defined on the sloping plain. Such was the night through which the philosopher Thomas Brutus sped with his strange rider.

A strange, oppressive, and yet sweet sensation took possession of his heart. He looked down and saw how the grass beneath his feet seemed to be quite deep and far away; over it there flowed a flood of crystal-clear water, and the grassy plain looked like the bottom of a transparent sea. He saw his own image, and that of the old woman whom he carried on his back, clearly reflected in it. Then he beheld how, instead of the moon, a strange sun shone there; he heard the deep tones of bells, and saw them swinging. He saw a water-nixie rise from a bed of tall reeds; she turned to him, and her face was clearly visible, and she sang a song which penetrated his soul; then she approached him and nearly reached the surface of the water, on which she burst into laughter and again disappeared.

Did he see it or did he not see it? Was he dreaming or was he awake? But what was that below—wind or music? It sounded and drew nearer, and penetrated his soul like a song that rose and fell. "What is it?" he thought as he gazed into the depths, and still sped rapidly along.

The perspiration flowed from him in streams; he experienced simultaneously a strange feeling of oppression and delight in all his being. Often he felt as though he had no longer a heart, and pressed his hand on his breast with alarm.

Weary to death, he began to repeat all the prayers which he knew, and all the formulas of exorcism against evil spirits. Suddenly he experienced a certain relief. He felt that his pace was slackening; the witch weighed less heavily on his shoulders, and the thick herbage of the plain was again beneath his feet, with nothing especial to remark about it.

"Splendid!" thought the philosopher Thomas, and began to repeat his exorcisms in a still louder voice.

Then suddenly he wrenched himself away from under the witch, and sprang on her back in his turn. She began to run, with short, trembling steps indeed, but so rapidly that he could hardly breathe. So swiftly did she run that she hardly seemed to touch the ground. They were still on the plain, but owing to the rapidity of their flight everything seemed indistinct and confused before his eyes. He seized a stick that was lying on the ground, and began to belabor the hag with all his might. She uttered a wild cry, which at first sounded raging and threatening; then it became gradually weaker and more gentle, till at last it sounded quite low like the pleasant tones of a silver bell, so that it penetrated his innermost soul. Involuntarily the thought passed through his mind:

"Is she really an old woman?"

"Ah! I can go no farther," she said in a faint voice, and sank to the earth.

He knelt beside her, and looked in her eyes. The dawn was red in the sky, and in the distance glimmered the gilt domes of the churches of Kieff. Before him lay a beautiful maiden with thick, disheveled hair and long eyelashes. Unconsciously she had stretched out her white, bare arms, and her tear-filled eyes gazed at the sky.

Thomas trembled like an aspen-leaf. Sympathy, and a strange feeling of excitement, and a hitherto unknown fear overpowered him. He began to run with all his might. His heart beat violently, and he could not explain to himself what a strange, new feeling had seized him. He did not wish to return to the village, but hastened towards Kieff, thinking all the way as he went of his weird, unaccountable adventure.

There were hardly any students left in the town; they were all scattered about the country, and had either taken tutors' posts or simply lived without occupation; for at the farms in Little Russia one can live comfortably and at ease without paying a farthing. The great half-decayed building in which the seminary was established was completely empty; and however much the philosopher searched in all its corners for a piece of lard and bread, he could not find even one of the hard biscuits which the seminarists were in the habit of hiding.

But the philosopher found a means of extricating himself from his difficulties by making friends with a certain young widow in the market-place who sold ribbons, etc. The same evening he found himself being stuffed with cakes and fowl; in fact it is impossible to say how many things were placed before him on a little table in an arbor shaded by cherry-trees.

Later on the same evening the philosopher was to be seen in an ale-house. He lay on a bench, smoked his pipe in his usual way, and threw the Jewish publican a gold piece. He had a jug of ale standing before him, looked on all who went in and out in a cold-blooded, self-satisfied way, and thought no more of his strange adventure.

~§~

About this time a report spread about that the daughter of a rich colonel, whose estate lay about fifty versts distant from Kieff, had returned home one day from a walk in a quite broken-down condition. She had scarcely enough strength to reach her father's house; now she lay dying, and had expressed a wish that for three days after her death the prayers for the dead should be recited by a Kieff seminarist named Thomas Brutus.

This fact was communicated to the philosopher by the rector of the seminary himself, who sent for him to his room and told him that he must start at once, as a rich colonel had sent his servants and a kibitka for him. The philosopher trembled, and was seized by an uncomfortable feeling which he could not define. He had a gloomy foreboding that some evil was about to befall him. Without knowing why, he declared that he did not wish to go.

"Listen, Thomas," said the rector, who under certain circumstances spoke very politely to his pupils; "I have no idea of asking you whether you wish to go or not. I only tell you that if you think of disobeying, I will have you so soundly flogged on the back with young birch-rods, that you need not think of having a bath for a long time."

The philosopher scratched the back of his head, and went out silently, intending to make himself scarce at the first opportunity. Lost in thought, he descended the steep flight of steps which led to the courtyard, thickly planted with poplars; there he remained standing for a moment, and heard quite distinctly the rector giving orders in a loud voice to his steward, and to another person, probably one of the messengers sent by the colonel.

"Thank your master for the peeled barley and the eggs," said the rector; "and tell him that as soon as the books which he mentions in his note are ready, I will send them. I have already given them to a clerk to be copied. And don't forget to remind your master that he has some excellent fish, especially prime sturgeon, in his ponds; he might send me some when he has the opportunity, as here in the market the fish are bad and dear. And you, Jantukh, give the colonel's man a glass of brandy. And mind you tie up the philosopher, or he will show you a clean pair of heels."

"Listen to the scoundrel!" thought the philosopher. "He has smelt a rat, the long-legged stork!"

He descended into the courtyard and beheld there a kibitka, which he at first took for a barn on wheels. It was, in fact, as roomy as a kiln, so that bricks might have been made inside it. It was one of those remarkable Cracow vehicles in which Jews travelled from town to town in scores, wherever they thought they would find a market. Six stout, strong, though somewhat elderly Cossacks were standing by it. Their gold-braided coats of fine cloth showed that their master was rich and of some importance; and certain little scars testified to their valour on the battle-field.

"What can I do?" thought the philosopher. "There is no escaping one's destiny." So he stepped up to the Cossacks and said "Good day, comrades."

"Welcome, Mr. Philosopher!" some of them answered.

"Well, I am to travel with you! It is a magnificent vehicle," he continued as he got into it. "If there were only musicians present, one might dance in it."

"Yes, it is a roomy carriage," said one of the Cossacks, taking his seat by the coachman. The latter had tied a cloth round his head, as he had already found an opportunity of pawning his cap in the ale-house. The other five, with the philosopher, got into the capacious kibitka, and sat upon sacks which were filled with all sorts of articles purchased in the city.

"I should like to know," said the philosopher, "if this equipage were laden with salt or iron, how many horses would be required to draw it?"

"Yes," said the Cossack who sat by the coachman, after thinking a short time, "it would require a good many horses."

After giving this satisfactory answer, the Cossack considered himself entitled to remain silent for the whole of the rest of the journey.

The philosopher would gladly have found out who the colonel was, and what sort of a character he had. He was also curious to know about his daughter, who had returned home in such a strange way and now lay dying, and whose destiny seemed to be mingled with his own; and wanted to know the sort of life that was lived in the colonel's house. But the Cossacks were probably philosophers like himself, for in answer to his inquiries they only blew clouds of tobacco and settled themselves more comfortably on their sacks.

Meanwhile, one of them addressed to the coachman on the box a brief command: "Keep your eyes open, Overko, you old sleepyhead, and when you come to the ale-house on the road to Tchukrailoff, don't forget to pull up and wake me and the other fellows if we are asleep." Then he began to snore pretty loud. But in any case his admonition was quite superfluous; for scarcely had the enormous equipage begun to approach the aforesaid ale-house, than they all cried with one mouth "Halt! Halt!"

Besides this, Overko's horse was accustomed to stop outside every inn of its own accord.

In spite of the intense July heat, they all got out and entered a low, dirty room where a Jewish innkeeper received them in a friendly way as old acquaintances. He brought in the skirt of his long coat some sausages, and laid them on the table, where, though forbidden by the Talmud, they looked very seductive. All sat down at table, and it was not long before each of the guests had an earthenware jug standing in front of him. The philosopher Thomas had to take part in the feast, and as the Little Russians when they are intoxicated always begin to kiss each other or to weep, the whole room soon began to echo with demonstrations of affection.

"Come here, come here, Spirid, let me embrace thee!"

"Come here, Dorosch, let me press you to my heart!"

One Cossack, with a grey moustache, the eldest of them all, leant his head on his hand and began to weep bitterly because he was an orphan and alone in God's wide world. Another tall, loquacious man did his best to comfort him, saying, "Don't weep, for God's sake, don't weep! For over there—God knows best."

The Cossack who had been addressed as Dorosch was full of curiosity, and addressed many questions to the philosopher Thomas. "I should like to know," he said, "what you learn in your seminary; do you learn the same things as the deacon reads to us in church, or something else?"

"Don't ask," said the consoler; "let them learn what they like. God knows what is to happen; God knows everything."

"No, I will know," answered Dorosch, "I will know what is written in their books; perhaps it is something quite different from that in the deacon's book."

"O good heavens!" said the other, "why all this talk? It is God's will, and one cannot change God's arrangements."

"But I will know everything that is written; I will enter the seminary too, by heaven I will! Do you think perhaps I could not learn? I will learn everything, everything."

"Oh, heavens!" exclaimed the consoler, and let his head sink on the table, for he could no longer hold it upright.

The other Cossacks talked about the nobility, and why there was a moon in the sky.

When the philosopher Thomas saw the state they were in, he determined to profit by it, and to make his escape. In the first place he turned to the grey-headed Cossack, who was lamenting the loss of his parents. "But, little uncle," he said to him, "why do you weep so? I too am an orphan! Let me go, children; why do you want me?"

"Let him go!" said some of them, "he is an orphan, let him go where he likes."

They were about to take him outside themselves, when the one who had displayed a special thirst for knowledge, stopped them, saying, "No, I want to talk with him about the seminary; I am going to the seminary myself."

Moreover, it was not yet certain whether the philosopher could have executed his project of flight, for when he tried to rise from his chair, he felt as though his feet were made of wood, and he began to see such a number of doors leading out of the room that it would have been difficult for him to have found the right one.

It was not till evening that the company remembered that they must continue their journey. They crowded into the kibitka, whipped up the horses, and struck up a song, the words and sense of which were hard to understand. During a great part of the night, they wandered about, having lost the road which they ought to have been able to find blind-folded. At last they drove down a steep descent into a valley, and the philosopher noticed, by the sides of the road, hedges, behind which he caught glimpses of small trees and house-roofs. All these belonged to the colonel's estate.

It was already long past midnight. The sky was dark, though little stars glimmered here and there; no light was to be seen in any of the houses. They drove into a large courtyard, while the dogs barked. On all sides were barns and cottages with thatched roofs. Just opposite the gateway was a house, which was larger than the others, and seemed to be the colonel's dwelling. The kibitka stopped before a small barn, and the travelers hastened into it and laid themselves down to sleep. The philosopher however attempted to look at the exterior of the house, but, rub his eyes as he might, he could distinguish nothing; the house seemed to turn into a bear, and the chimney into the rector of the seminary. Then he gave it up and lay down to sleep.

When he woke up the next morning, the whole house was in commotion; the young lady had died during the night. The servants ran hither and thither in a distracted state; the old women wept and lamented; and a number of curious people gazed through the enclosure into the courtyard, as though there were something special to be seen. The philosopher began now to inspect the locality and the buildings, which he had not been able to do during the night.

The colonel's house was one of those low, small buildings, such as used formerly to be constructed in Russia. It was thatched with straw; a small, high-peaked gable, with a window shaped like an eye, was painted all over with blue and yellow flowers and red crescent-moons; it rested on little oaken pillars, which were round above the middle, hexagonal below, and whose capitals were adorned with quaint carvings. Under this gable was a small staircase with seats at the foot of it on either side.

The walls of the house were supported by similar pillars. Before the house stood a large pear-tree of pyramidal shape, whose leaves incessantly trembled. A double row of buildings formed a broad street leading up to the colonel's house. Behind the barns near the entrance-gate stood two three-cornered wine-houses, also thatched with straw; each of the stone walls had a door in it, and was covered with all kinds of paintings. On one was represented a Cossack sitting on a barrel and swinging a large pitcher over his head; it bore the inscription "I will drink all that!" Elsewhere were painted large and small bottles, a beautiful girl, a running horse, a pipe, and a drum bearing the words "Wine is the Cossack's joy."

In the loft of one of the barns one saw through a huge round window a drum and some trumpets. At the gate there stood two cannons. All this showed that the colonel loved a cheerful life, and the whole place often rang with sounds of merriment. Before the gate were two windmills, and behind the house gardens sloped away; through the tree-tops the dark chimneys of the peasants' houses were visible. The whole village lay on a broad, even plateau, in the middle of a mountain-slope which culminated in a steep summit on the north side. When seen from below, it looked still steeper. Here and there on the top the irregular stems of the thick steppe-brooms showed in dark relief against the blue sky. The bare clay soil made a melancholy impression, worn as it was into deep furrows by rain-water. On the same slope there stood two cottages, and over one of them a huge apple-tree spread its branches; the roots were supported by small props, whose interstices were filled with mold. The apples, which were blown off by the wind, rolled down to the courtyard below. A road wound round the mountain to the village.

When the philosopher looked at this steep slope, and remembered his journey of the night before, he came to the conclusion that either the colonel's horses were very sagacious, or that the Cossacks must have very strong heads, as they ventured, even when the worse for drink, on such a road with the huge kibitka.

When the philosopher turned and looked in the opposite direction, he saw quite another picture. The village reached down to the plain;

meadows stretched away to an immense distance, their bright green growing gradually dark; far away, about twenty versts off, many other villages were visible. To the right of these meadows were chains of hills, and in the remote distance one saw the Dnieper shimmer and sparkle like a mirror of steel.

"What a splendid country!" said the philosopher to himself. "It must be fine to live here! One could catch fish in the Dnieper, and in the ponds, and shoot and snare partridges and bustards; there must be quantities here. Much fruit might be dried here and sold in the town, or, better still, brandy might be distilled from it, for fruit-brandy is the best of all. But what prevents me thinking of my escape after all?"

Behind the hedge he saw a little path which was almost entirely concealed by the high grass of the steppe. The philosopher approached it mechanically, meaning at first to walk a little along it unobserved, and then quite quietly to gain the open country behind the peasants' houses. Suddenly he felt the pressure of a fairly heavy hand on his shoulder.

Behind him stood the same old Cossack who yesterday had so bitterly lamented the death of his father and mother, and his own loneliness. "You are giving yourself useless trouble, Mr Philosopher, if you think you can escape from us," he said. "One cannot run away here; and besides, the roads are too bad for walkers. Come to the colonel; he has been waiting for you for some time in his room."

"Yes, of course! What are you talking about? I will come with the greatest pleasure," said the philosopher, and followed the Cossack.

The colonel was an elderly man; his moustache was grey, and his face wore the signs of deep sadness. He sat in his room by a table, with his head propped on both hands. He seemed about five-and-fifty, but his attitude of utter despair, and the pallor on his face, showed that his heart had been suddenly broken, and that all his former cheerfulness had for ever disappeared.

When Thomas entered with the Cossack, he answered their deep bows with a slight inclination of the head.

"Who are you, whence do you come, and what is your profession, my good man?" asked the colonel in an even voice, neither friendly nor austere.

"I am a student of philosophy; my name is Thomas Brutus."

"And who was your father?"

"I don't know, sir."

"And your mother?"

"I don't know either; I know that I must have had a mother, but who she was, and where she lived, by heavens, I do not know."

The colonel was silent, and seemed for a moment lost in thought. "Where did you come to know my daughter?"

"I do not know her, gracious sir; I declare I do not know her."

"Why then has she chosen you, and no one else, to offer up prayers for her?"

The philosopher shrugged his shoulders. "God only knows. It is a well-known fact that grand people often demand things which the most learned man cannot comprehend; and does not the proverb say, 'Dance, devil, as the Lord commands!'"

"Aren't you talking nonsense, Mr. Philosopher?"

"May the lightning strike me on the spot if I lie."

"If she had only lived a moment longer," said the colonel sadly, "then I had certainly found out everything. She said, 'Let no one offer up prayers for me, but send, father, at once to the seminary in Kieff for the student Thomas Brutus; he shall pray three nights running for my sinful soul—he knows.' But what he really knows she never said. The poor dove could speak no more, and died. Good man, you are probably well known for your sanctity and devout life, and she has perhaps heard of you."

"What? Of me?" said the philosopher, and took a step backward in amazement. "I and sanctity!" he exclaimed, and stared at the colonel. "God help us, gracious sir! What are you saying? It was only last Holy Thursday that I paid a visit to the tart-shop."

"Well, she must at any rate have had some reason for making the arrangement, and you must begin your duties today."

"I should like to remark to your honor—naturally everyone who knows the Holy Scripture at all can in his measure—but I believe it would be better on this occasion to send for a deacon or subdeacon. They are learned people, and they know exactly what is to be done. I have not got a good voice, nor any official standing."

"You may say what you like, but I shall carry out all my dove's wishes. If you read the prayers for her three nights through in the proper way, I will reward you; and if not—I advise the devil himself not to oppose me!"

The colonel spoke the last words in such an emphatic way that the philosopher quite understood them.

"Follow me!" said the colonel.

They went into the hall. The colonel opened a door which was opposite his own. The philosopher remained for a few minutes in the hall in order to look about him; then he stepped over the threshold with a certain nervousness.

The whole floor of the room was covered with red cloth. In a corner under the icons of the saints, on a table covered with a gold-bordered, velvet cloth, lay the body of the girl. Tall candles, round which were wound branches of the "calina," stood at her head and feet, and burned dimly in the broad daylight. The face of the dead was not to be seen, as the inconsolable father sat before his daughter, with his back turned to the philosopher. The words which the latter overheard filled him with a certain fear:

"I do not mourn, my daughter, that in the flower of your age you have prematurely left the earth, to my grief; but I mourn, my dove, that I do not know my deadly enemy who caused your death. Had I only known that anyone could even conceive the idea of insulting you, or of speaking a disrespectful word to you, I swear by heaven he would never have seen his children again, if he had been as old as myself; nor his father and mother, if he had been young. And I would have thrown his corpse to the birds of the air, and the wild beasts of the steppe. But woe is me, my flower, my dove, my light! I will spend the remainder of my life without joy, and wipe the bitter tears which flow out of my old eyes, while my enemy will rejoice and laugh in secret over the helpless old man!"

He paused, overpowered by grief, and streams of tears flowed down his cheeks.

The philosopher was deeply affected by the sight of such inconsolable sorrow. He coughed gently in order to clear his throat. The colonel turned and signed to him to take his place at the head of the dead girl, before a little prayer-desk on which some books lay.

"I can manage to hold out for three nights," thought the philosopher; "and then the colonel will fill both my pockets with ducats."

He approached the dead girl, and after coughing once more, began to read, without paying attention to anything else, and firmly resolved not to look at her face.

Soon there was deep silence, and he saw that the colonel had left the room. Slowly he turned his head in order to look at the corpse. A violent shudder thrilled through him; before him lay a form of such beauty as is seldom seen upon earth. It seemed to him that never in a single face had so much intensity of expression and harmony of feature been united. Her brow, soft as snow and pure as silver, seemed to be thinking; the fine, regular eyebrows shadowed proudly the closed eyes, whose lashes gently rested on her cheeks, which seemed to glow with secret longing; her lips still appeared to smile. But at the same time he saw something in these features which appalled him; a terrible depression seized his heart, as when in the midst of dance and song someone begins to chant a dirge. He felt as though those ruby lips were colored with his own heart's blood. Moreover, her face seemed dreadfully familiar.

"The witch!" he cried out in a voice which sounded strange to himself; then he turned away and began to read the prayers with white cheeks. It was the witch whom he had killed.

II

When the sun had sunk below the horizon, the corpse was carried into the church. The philosopher supported one corner of the black-draped coffin upon his shoulder, and felt an ice-cold shiver run through his body. The colonel walked in front of him, with his right hand resting on the edge of the coffin.

The wooden church, black with age and overgrown with green lichen, stood quite at the end of the village in gloomy solitude; it was adorned with three round cupolas. One saw at the first glance that it had not been used for divine worship for a long time.

Lighted candles were standing before almost every icon. The coffin was set down before the altar. The old colonel kissed his dead daughter once more, and then left the church, together with the bearers of the bier, after he had ordered his servants to look after the philosopher and to take him back to the church after supper.

The coffin-bearers, when they returned to the house, all laid their hands on the stove. This custom is always observed in Little Russia by those who have seen a corpse.

The hunger which the philosopher now began to feel caused him for a while to forget the dead girl altogether. Gradually all the domestics of the house assembled in the kitchen; it was really a kind of club, where they were accustomed to gather. Even the dogs came to the door, wagging their tails in order to have bones and offal thrown to them.

If a servant was sent on an errand, he always found his way into the kitchen to rest there for a while, and to smoke a pipe. All the Cossacks of the establishment lay here during the whole day on and under the benches—in fact, wherever a place could be found to lie down in. More-over, everyone was always leaving something behind in the kitchen—his cap, or his whip, or something of the sort. But the numbers of the club were not complete till the evening, when the groom came in after tying up his horses in the stable, the cowherd had shut up his cows in their stalls, and others collected there who were not usually seen in the day-time. During supper-time even the tongues of the laziest were set in motion. They talked of all and everything—of the new pair of breeches which someone had ordered for himself, of what might be in the center of the earth, and of the wolf which someone had seen. There were a number of wits in the company—a class which is always represented in Little Russia.

The philosopher took his place with the rest in the great circle which sat round the kitchen door in the open-air. Soon an old woman with a red cap issued from it, bearing with both hands a large vessel full of hot "galuchkis," which she distributed among them. Each drew out of his pocket a wooden spoon, or a one-pronged wooden fork. As soon as their jaws began to move a little more slowly, and their wolfish hunger was somewhat appeased, they began to talk. The conversation, as might be expected, turned on the dead girl.

"Is it true," said a young shepherd, "is it true—though I cannot understand it—that our young mistress had traffic with evil spirits?"

"Who, the young lady?" answered Dorosch, whose acquaintance the philosopher had already made in the kibitka. "Yes, she was a regular witch! I can swear that she was a witch!"

"Hold your tongue, Dorosch!" exclaimed another—the one who, during the journey, had played the part of a consoler. "We have nothing to do with that. May God be merciful to her! One ought not to talk of such things."

But Dorosch was not at all inclined to be silent; he had just visited the wine-cellar with the steward on important business, and having stooped two or three times over one or two casks, he had returned in a very cheerful and loquacious mood.

"Why do you ask me to be silent?" he answered. "She has ridden on my own shoulders, I swear she has."

"Say, uncle," asked the young shepherd, "are there signs by which to recognise a sorceress?"

"No, there are not," answered Dorosch; "even if you knew the Psalter by heart, you could not recognize one."

"Yes, Dorosch, it is possible; don't talk such nonsense," retorted the former consoler. "It is not for nothing that God has given each some special peculiarity; the learned maintain that every witch has a little tail."

"Every old woman is a witch," said a grey-headed Cossack quite seriously.

"Yes, you are a fine lot," retorted the old woman who entered at that moment with a vessel full of fresh "galuchkis." "You are great fat pigs!"

A self-satisfied smile played round the lips of the old Cossack whose name was Javtuch, when he found that his remark had touched the old woman on a tender point. The shepherd burst into such a deep and loud explosion of laughter as if two oxen were lowing together.

This conversation excited in the philosopher a great curiosity, and a wish to obtain more exact information regarding the colonel's daughter. In order to lead the talk back to the subject, he turned to his next neighbor and said, "I should like to know why all the people here think that the young lady was a witch. Has she done harm to anyone, or killed them by witchcraft?"

"Yes, there are reports of that kind," answered a man, whose face was as flat as a shovel. "Who does not remember the huntsman Mikita, or the—"

"What has the huntsman Mikita got to do with it?" asked the philosopher.

"Stop; I will tell you the story of Mikita," interrupted Dorosch.

"No, I will tell it," said the groom, "for he was my godfather."

"I will tell the story of Mikita," said Spirid.

"Yes, yes, Spirid shall tell it," exclaimed the whole company; and Spirid began.

"You, Mr. Philosopher Thomas, did not know Mikita. Ah! he was an extraordinary man. He knew every dog as though he were his own father. The present huntsman, Mikola, who sits three places away from me, is not fit to hold a candle to him, though good enough in his way; but compared to Mikita, he is a mere milksop."

"You tell the tale splendidly," exclaimed Dorosch, and nodded as a sign of approval.

Spirid continued.

"He saw a hare in the field quicker than you can take a pinch of snuff. He only needed to whistle 'Come here, Rasboy! Come here, Bosdraja!' and flew away on his horse like the wind, so that you could not say whether he went quicker than the dog or the dog than he. He could empty a quart pot of brandy in the twinkling of an eye. Ah! he was a splendid huntsman, only for some time he always had his eyes fixed on the young lady. Either he had fallen in love with her or she had bewitched him—in short, he went to the dogs. He became a regular old woman; yes, he became the devil knows what—it is not fitting to relate it."

"Very good," remarked Dorosch.

"If the young lady only looked at him, he let the reins slip out of his hands, called Bravko instead of Rasboy, stumbled, and made all kinds of mistakes. One day when he was currycombing a horse, the young lady came to him in the stable. 'Listen, Mikita,' she said. 'I should like for once to set my foot on you.' And he, the booby, was quite delighted, and answered, 'Don't only set your foot there, but sit on me altogether.' The young lady lifted her white little foot, and as soon as he saw it, his delight robbed him of his senses. He bowed his neck, the idiot, took her feet in both hands, and began to trot about like a horse all over the place. Whither they went he could not say; he returned more dead than alive, and from that time he wasted away and became as dry as a chip of wood. At last someone coming into the stable one day found instead of him only a handful of ashes and an empty jug; he had burned completely out. But it must be said he was a huntsman such as the world cannot match."

When Spirid had ended his tale, they all began to vie with one another in praising the deceased huntsman.

"And have you heard the story of Cheptchicha?" asked Dorosch, turning to Thomas.

"No."

"Ha! Ha! One sees they don't teach you much in your seminary. Well, listen. We have here in our village a Cossack called Cheptoun, a fine fellow. Sometimes indeed he amuses himself by stealing and lying without any reason; but he is a fine fellow for all that. His house is not far away from here. One evening, just about this time, Cheptoun and his wife went to bed after they had finished their day's work. Since it was fine weather, Cheptchicha went to sleep in the courtyard, and Cheptoun in the house— no! I mean Cheptchicha went to sleep in the house on a bench and Cheptoun outside—"

"No, Cheptchicha didn't go to sleep on a bench, but on the ground," interrupted the old woman who stood at the door.

Dorosch looked at her, then at the ground, then again at her, and said after a pause, "If I tore your dress off your back before all these people, it wouldn't look pretty."

The rebuke was effectual. The old woman was silent, and did not interrupt again.

Dorosch continued.

"In the cradle which hung in the middle of the room lay a one-year-old child. I do not know whether it was a boy or a girl. Cheptchicha had lain down, and heard on the other side of the door a dog scratching and howling loud enough to frighten anyone. She was afraid, for women are such simple folk that if one puts out one's tongue at them behind the door in the dark, their hearts sink into their boots. 'But,' she thought to herself, 'I must give this cursed dog one on the snout to stop his howling!' So she seized the poker and opened the door. But hardly had she done so than the dog rushed between her legs straight to the cradle. Then Cheptchicha saw that it was not a dog but the young lady; and if it had only been the young lady as she knew her it wouldn't have mattered, but she looked quite blue, and her eyes sparkled like fiery coals. She seized the child, bit its throat, and began to suck its blood. Cheptchicha shrieked, 'Ah! my darling child!' and rushed out of the room. Then she saw that the house-door was shut and rushed up to the attic and sat there, the stupid woman, trembling all over. Then the young lady came after her and bit her too, poor fool! The next morning Cheptoun carried his wife, all bitten and wounded, down from the attic, and the next day she died. Such strange things happen in the world. One may wear fine clothes, but that does not matter; a witch is and remains a witch."

After telling his story, Dorosch looked around him with a complacent air, and cleaned out his pipe with his little finger in order to fill it again. The story of the witch had made a deep impression on all, and each of them had something to say about her. One had seen her come to the door of his house in the form of a hayrick; from others she had stolen their caps or their pipes; she had cut off the hair-plaits of many girls in the village, and drunk whole pints of the blood of others.

At last the whole company observed that they had gossiped over their time, for it was already night. All looked for a sleeping place—some in the kitchen and others in the barn or the courtyard.

"Now, Mr. Thomas, it is time that we go to the dead," said the grey-headed Cossack, turning to the philosopher. All four—Spirid, Dorosch, the old Cossack, and the philosopher—betook themselves to the church, keeping off with their whips the wild dogs who roamed about the roads in great numbers and bit the sticks of passers-by in sheer malice.

Although the philosopher had seized the opportunity of fortifying himself beforehand with a stiff glass of brandy, yet he felt a certain secret fear which increased as he approached the church, which was lit up within. The strange tales he had heard had made a deep impression on his imagination. They had passed the thick hedges and trees, and the country became more open. At last they reached the small enclosure round the church; behind it there were no more trees, but a huge, empty plain dimly visible in the darkness. The three Cossacks ascended the steep steps with Thomas, and entered the church. Here they left the philosopher, expressing their hope that he would successfully accomplish his duties, and locked him in as their master had ordered.

He was left alone. At first he yawned, then he stretched himself, blew on both hands, and finally looked round him. In the middle of the church stood the black bier; before the dark pictures of saints burned the candles, whose light only illuminated the icons, and cast a faint glimmer into the body of the church; all the corners were in complete darkness. The lofty icons seemed to be of considerable age; only a little of the original gilt remained on their broken traceries; the faces of the saints had become quite black and looked uncanny.

Once more the philosopher cast a glance around him. "Bother it!" said he to himself. "What is there to be afraid about? No living creature can get in, and as for the dead and those who come from the 'other side,' I can protect myself with such effectual prayers that they cannot touch me with the tips of their fingers. There is nothing to fear," he repeated, swinging his arms. "Let us begin the prayers!"

As he approached one of the side-aisles, he noticed two packets of candles which had been placed there.

"That is fine," he thought. "I must illuminate the whole church, till it is as bright as day. What a pity that one cannot smoke in it."

He began to light the candles on all the wall-brackets and all the candelabra, as well as those already burning before the holy pictures; soon the whole church was brilliantly lit up. Only the darkness in the roof above seemed still denser by contrast, and the faces of the saints peering out of the frames looked as unearthly as before. He approached the bier, looked nervously at the face of the dead girl, could not help shuddering slightly, and involuntarily closed his eyes. What terrible and extraordinary beauty!

He turned away and tried to go to one side, but the strange curiosity and peculiar fascination which men feel in moments of fear, compelled him to look again and again, though with a similar shudder. And in truth there was something terrible about the beauty of the dead girl. Perhaps she would not have inspired so much fear had she been less beautiful; but there was nothing ghastly or deathlike in the face, which wore rather an expression of life, and it seemed to the philosopher as though she were watching him from under her closed eyelids. He even thought he saw a tear roll from under the eyelash of her right eye, but when it was half-way down her cheek, he saw that it was a drop of blood.

He quickly went into one of the stalls, opened his book, and began to read the prayers in a very loud voice in order to keep up his courage. His deep voice sounded strange to himself in the grave-like silence; it aroused no echo in the silent and desolate wooden walls of the church.

"What is there to be afraid of?" he thought to himself. "She will not rise from her bier, since she fears God's word. She will remain quietly resting. Yes, and what sort of a Cossack should I be, if I were afraid? The fact is, I have drunk a little too much—that is why I feel so queer. Let me take a pinch of snuff. It is really excellent—first-rate!"

At the same time he cast a furtive glance over the pages of the prayer-book towards the bier, and involuntarily he said to himself, "There! See! She is getting up! Her head is already above the edge of the coffin!"

But a death-like silence prevailed; the coffin was motionless, and all the candles shone steadily. It was an awe-inspiring sight, this church lit up at midnight, with the corpse in the midst, and no living soul near but one. The philosopher began to sing in various keys in order to stifle his fears, but every moment he glanced across at the coffin, and involuntarily the question came to his lips, "Suppose she rose up after all?"

But the coffin did not move. Nowhere was there the slightest sound nor stir. Not even did a cricket chirp in any corner. There was nothing audible but the slight sputtering of some distant candle, or the faint fall of a drop of wax.

"Suppose she rose up after all?"

He raised his head. Then he looked round him wildly and rubbed his eyes. Yes, she was no longer lying in the coffin, but sitting upright. He turned away his eyes, but at once looked again, terrified, at the coffin. She stood up; then she walked with closed eyes through the church, stretching out her arms as though she wanted to seize someone.

She now came straight towards him. Full of alarm, he traced with his finger a circle round himself; then in a loud voice he began to recite the prayers and formulas of exorcism which he had learnt from a monk who had often seen witches and evil spirits.

She had almost reached the edge of the circle which he had traced; but it was evident that she had not the power to enter it. Her face wore a bluish tint like that of one who has been several days dead.

Thomas had not the courage to look at her, so terrible was her appearance; her teeth chattered and she opened her dead eyes, but as in her rage she saw nothing, she turned in another direction and felt with outstretched arms among the pillars and corners of the church in the hope of seizing him.

At last she stood still, made a threatening gesture, and then lay down again in the coffin.

The philosopher could not recover his self-possession, and kept on gazing anxiously at it. Suddenly it rose from its place and began hurtling about the church with a whizzing sound. At one time it was almost directly over his head; but the philosopher observed that it could not pass over the area of his charmed circle, so he kept on repeating his formulas of exorcism. The coffin now fell with a crash in the middle of the church, and remained lying there motionless. The corpse rose again; it had now a greenish-blue color, but at the same moment the distant crowing of a cock was audible, and it lay down again.

The philosopher's heart beat violently, and the perspiration poured in streams from his face; but heartened by the crowing of the cock, he rapidly repeated the prayers.

As the first light of dawn looked through the windows, there came a deacon and the grey-haired Javtuk, who acted as sacristan, in order to release him. When he had reached the house, he could not sleep for a long time; but at last weariness overpowered him, and he slept till noon. When he awoke, his experiences of the night appeared to him like a dream. He was given a quart of brandy to strengthen him.

At table he was again talkative and ate a fairly large sucking pig almost without assistance. But none the less he resolved to say nothing of what he had seen, and to all curious questions only returned the answer, "Yes, some wonderful things happened."

The philosopher was one of those men who, when they have had a good meal, are uncommonly amiable. He lay down on a bench, with his pipe in his mouth, looked blandly at all, and expectorated every minute.

But as the evening approached, he became more and more pensive. About supper-time nearly the whole company had assembled in order to play "krapli." This is a kind of game of skittles, in which, instead of bowls, long staves are used, and the winner has the right to ride on the back of his opponent. It provided the spectators with much amusement; sometimes the groom, a huge man, would clamber on the back of the swineherd, who was slim and short and shrunken; another time the groom would present his own back, while Dorosch sprang on it shouting, "What a regular ox!" Those of the company who were more staid sat by the threshold of the kitchen. They looked uncommonly serious, smoked their pipes, and did not even smile when the younger ones went into fits of laughter over some joke of the groom or Spirid.

Thomas vainly attempted to take part in the game; a gloomy thought was firmly fixed like a nail in his head. In spite of his desperate efforts to appear cheerful after supper, fear had overmastered his whole being, and it increased with the growing darkness.

"Now it is time for us to go, Mr. Student!" said the grey-haired Cossack, and stood up with Dorosch. "Let us betake ourselves to our work."

Thomas was conducted to the church in the same way as on the previous evening; again he was left alone, and the door was bolted behind him.

As soon as he found himself alone, he began to feel in the grip of his fears. He again saw the dark pictures of the saints in their gilt frames, and the black coffin, which stood menacing and silent in the middle of the church.

"Never mind!" he said to himself. "I am over the first shock. The first time I was frightened, but I am not so at all now—no, not at all!"

He quickly went into a stall, drew a circle round him with his finger, uttered some prayers and formulas for exorcism, and then began to read the prayers for the dead in a loud voice and with the fixed resolution not to look up from the book nor take notice of anything.

He did so for an hour, and began to grow a little tired; he cleared his throat and drew his snuff-box out of his pocket, but before he had taken a pinch he looked nervously towards the coffin.

A sudden chill shot through him. The witch was already standing before him on the edge of the circle, and had fastened her green eyes upon him. He shuddered, looked down at the book, and began to read his prayers and exorcisms aloud. Yet all the while he was aware how her teeth chattered, and how she stretched out her arms to seize him. But when he cast a hasty glance towards her, he saw that she was not looking in his direction, and it was clear that she could not see him.

Then she began to murmur in an undertone, and terrible words escaped her lips—words that sounded like the bubbling of boiling pitch. The philosopher did not know their meaning, but he knew that they signified something terrible, and were intended to counteract his exorcisms.

After she had spoken, a stormy wind arose in the church, and there was a noise like the rushing of many birds. He heard the noise of their wings and claws as they flapped against and scratched at the iron bars of the church windows. There were also violent blows on the church door, as if someone were trying to break it in pieces.

The philosopher's heart beat violently; he did not dare to look up, but continued to read the prayers without a pause. At last there was heard in the distance the shrill sound of a cock's crow. The exhausted philosopher stopped and gave a great sigh of relief.

Those who came to release him found him more dead than alive; he had leant his back against the wall, and stood motionless, regarding them without any expression in his eyes. They were obliged almost to carry him to the house; he then shook himself, asked for and drank a quart of brandy. He passed his hand through his hair and said, "There are all sorts of horrors in the world, and such dreadful things happen that—" Here he made a gesture as though to ward off something. All who heard him bent their heads forward in curiosity. Even a small boy, who ran on everyone's errands, stood by with his mouth wide open.

Just then a young woman in a close-fitting dress passed by. She was the old cook's assistant, and very coquettish; she always stuck something in her bodice by way of ornament, a ribbon or a flower, or even a piece of paper if she could find nothing else.

"Good day, Thomas," she said, as she saw the philosopher. "Dear me! what has happened to you?" she exclaimed, striking her hands together.

"Well, what is it, you silly creature?"

"Good heavens! You have grown quite grey!"

"Yes, so he has!" said Spirid, regarding him more closely. "You have grown as grey as our old Javtuk."

When the philosopher heard that, he hastened into the kitchen, where he had noticed on the wall a dirty, three-cornered piece of looking-glass. In front of it hung some forget-me-nots, evergreens, and a small garland—a proof that it was the toilette-glass of the young coquette. With alarm he saw that it actually was as they had said—his hair was quite grizzled.

He sank into a reverie; at last he said to himself, "I will go to the colonel, tell him all, and declare that I will read no more prayers. He must send me back at once to Kieff." With this intention he turned towards the door-steps of the colonel's house.

The colonel was sitting motionless in his room; his face displayed the same hopeless grief which Thomas had observed on it on his first arrival, only the hollows in his cheeks had deepened. It was obvious that he took very little or no food. A strange paleness made him look almost as though made of marble.

"Good day," he said as he observed Thomas standing, cap in hand, at the door. "Well, how are you getting on? All right?"

"Yes, sir, all right! Such hellish things are going on, that one would like to rush away as far as one's feet can carry one."

"How so?"

"Your daughter, sir . . . When one considers the matter, she is, of course, of noble descent—no one can dispute that; but don't be angry, and may God grant her eternal rest!"

"Very well! What about her?"

"She is in league with the devil. She inspires one with such dread that all prayers are useless."

"Pray! Pray! It was not for nothing that she sent for you. My dove was troubled about her salvation, and wished to expel all evil influences by means of prayer."

"I swear, gracious sir, it is beyond my power."

"Pray! Pray!" continued the colonel in the same persuasive tone. "There is only one night more; you are doing a Christian work, and I will reward you richly."

"However great your rewards may be, I will not read the prayers any more, sir," said Thomas in a tone of decision.

"Listen, philosopher!" said the colonel with a menacing air. "I will not allow any objections. In your seminary you may act as you like, but here it won't do. If I have you knouted, it will be somewhat different to the rector's canings. Do you know what a strong 'kantchuk' is?"

"Of course I do," said the philosopher in a low voice; "a number of them together are insupportable."

"Yes, I think so too. But you don't know yet how hot my fellows can make it," replied the colonel threateningly. He sprang up, and his face assumed a fierce, despotic expression, betraying the savagery of his nature, which had been only temporarily modified by grief. "After the first flogging they pour on brandy and then repeat it. Go away and finish your work. If you don't obey, you won't be able to stand again, and if you do, you will get a thousand ducats."

"That is a devil of a fellow," thought the philosopher to himself, and went out. "One can't trifle with him. But wait a little, my friend; I will escape you so cleverly, that even your hounds can't find me!"

He determined, under any circumstances, to run away, and only waited till the hour after dinner arrived, when all the servants were accustomed to take a nap on the hay in the barn, and to snore and puff so loudly that it sounded as if machinery had been set up there. At last the time came. Even Javtuch stretched himself out in the sun and closed his eyes. Tremblingly, and on tiptoe, the philosopher stole softly into the garden, whence he thought he could escape more easily into the open country. This garden was generally so choked up with weeds that it seemed admirably adapted for such an attempt. With the exception of a single path used by the people of the house, the whole of it was covered with cherry-trees, elder-bushes, and tall heath-thistles with fibrous red buds. All these trees and bushes had been thickly overgrown with ivy, which formed a kind of roof. Its tendrils reached to the hedge and fell down on the other side in snake-like curves among the small, wild field-flowers. Behind the hedge which bordered the garden was a dense mass of wild heather, in which it did not seem probable that anyone would care to venture himself, and the strong, stubborn stems of which seemed likely to baffle any attempt to cut them.

As the philosopher was about to climb over the hedge, his teeth chattered, and his heart beat so violently that he felt frightened at it. The skirts of his long cloak seemed to cling to the ground as though they had been fastened to it by pegs. When he had actually got over the hedge he seemed to hear a shrill voice crying behind him "Whither? Whither?"

He jumped into the heather and began to run, stumbling over old roots and treading on unfortunate moles. When he had emerged from the heather he saw that he still had a wide field to cross, behind which was a thick, thorny underwood. This, according to his calculation, must stretch as far as the road leading to Kieff, and if he reached it he would be safe. Accordingly he ran over the field and plunged into the thorny copse. Every sharp thorn he encountered tore a fragment from his coat. Then he reached a small open space; in the center of it stood a willow, whose branches hung down to the earth, and close by flowed a clear spring bright as silver. The first thing the philosopher did was to lie down and drink eagerly, for he was intolerably thirsty.

"Splendid water!" he said, wiping his mouth. "This is a good place to rest in."

"No, better run farther; perhaps we are being followed," said a voice immediately behind him.

Thomas started and turned; before him stood Javtuch.

"This devil of a Javtuch!" he thought. "I should like to seize him by the feet and smash his hang-dog face against the trunk of a tree."

"Why did you go round such a long way?" continued Javtuch. "You had much better have chosen the path by which I came; it leads directly by the stable. Besides, it is a pity about your coat. Such splendid cloth! How much did it cost an ell? Well, we have had a long enough walk; it is time to go home."

The philosopher followed Javtuch in a very depressed state.

"Now the accursed witch will attack me in earnest," he thought. "But what have I really to fear? Am I not a Cossack? I have read the prayers for two nights already; with God's help I will get through the third night also. It is plain that the witch must have a terrible load of guilt upon her, else the evil one would not help her so much."

Feeling somewhat encouraged by these reflections, he returned to the courtyard and asked Dorosch, who sometimes, by the steward's permission, had access to the wine-cellar, to fetch him a small bottle of brandy. The two friends sat down before a barn and drank a pretty large one. Suddenly the philosopher jumped up and said, "I want musicians! Bring some musicians!"

But without waiting for them he began to dance the "tropak" in the courtyard. He danced till tea-time, and the servants, who, as is usual in such cases, had formed a small circle round him, grew at last tired of watching him, and went away saying, "By heavens, the man can dance!"

Finally the philosopher lay down in the place where he had been dancing, and fell asleep. It was necessary to pour a bucket of cold water on his head to wake him up for supper. At the meal he enlarged on the topic of what a Cossack ought to be, and how he should not be afraid of anything in the world.

"It is time," said Javtuch; "let us go."

"I wish I could put a lighted match to your tongue," thought the philosopher; then he stood up and said, "Let us go."

On their way to the church, the philosopher kept looking round him on all sides, and tried to start a conversation with his companions; but both Javtuch and Dorosch remained silent. It was a weird night. In the distance wolves howled continually, and even the barking of the dogs had something unearthly about it.

"That doesn't sound like wolves howling, but something else," remarked Dorosch.

Javtuch still kept silence, and the philosopher did not know what answer to make.

They reached the church and walked over the old wooden planks, whose rotten condition showed how little the lord of the manor cared about God and his soul. Javtuch and Dorosch left the philosopher alone, as on the previous evenings.

There was still the same atmosphere of menacing silence in the church, in the center of which stood the coffin with the terrible witch inside it.

"I am not afraid, by heavens, I am not afraid!" he said; and after drawing a circle round himself as before, he began to read the prayers and exorcisms.

An oppressive silence prevailed; the flickering candles filled the church with their clear light. The philosopher turned one page after another, and noticed that he was not reading what was in the book. Full of alarm, he crossed himself and began to sing a hymn. This calmed him somewhat, and he resumed his reading, turning the pages rapidly as he did so.

Suddenly in the midst of the sepulchral silence the iron lid of the coffin sprang open with a jarring noise, and the dead witch stood up. She was this time still more terrible in aspect than at first. Her teeth chattered loudly and her lips, through which poured a stream of dreadful curses, moved convulsively. A whirlwind arose in the church; the icons of the saints fell on the ground, together with the broken window-panes. The door was wrenched from its hinges, and a huge mass of monstrous creatures rushed into the church, which became filled with the noise of beating wings and scratching claws. All these creatures flew and crept about, seeking for the philosopher, from whose brain the last fumes of intoxication had vanished. He crossed himself ceaselessly and uttered prayer after prayer, hearing all the time the whole unclean swarm rustling about him, and brushing him with the tips of their wings. He had not the courage to look at them; he only saw one uncouth monster standing by the wall, with long, shaggy hair and two flaming eyes. Over him something hung in the air which looked like a gigantic bladder covered with countless crabs' claws and scorpions' stings, and with black clods of earth hanging from it. All these monsters stared about seeking him, but they could not find him, since he was protected by his sacred circle.

"Bring the Viy! Bring the Viy!" cried the witch.

A sudden silence followed; the howling of wolves was heard in the distance, and soon heavy footsteps resounded through the church. Thomas looked up furtively and saw that an ungainly human figure with crooked legs was being led into the church. He was quite covered with black soil, and his hands and feet resembled knotted roots. He trod heavily and stumbled at every step. His eyelids were of enormous length. With terror, Thomas saw that his face was of iron. They led him in by the arms and placed him near Thomas's circle.

"Raise my eyelids! I can't see anything!" said the Viy in a dull, hollow voice, and they all hastened to help in doing so.

"Don't look!" an inner voice warned the philosopher; but he could not restrain from looking.

"There he is!" exclaimed the Viy, pointing an iron finger at him; and all the monsters rushed on him at once.

Struck dumb with terror, he sank to the ground and died.

At that moment there sounded a cock's crow for the second time; the earth-spirits had not heard the first one. In alarm they hurried to the windows and the door to get out as quickly as possible. But it was too late; they all remained hanging as though fastened to the door and the windows.

When the priest came he stood amazed at such a desecration of God's house, and did not venture to read prayers there. The church remained standing as it was, with the monsters hanging on the windows and the door. Gradually it became overgrown with creepers, bushes, and wild heather, and no one can discover it now.

~§~

When the report of this event reached Kieff, and the theologian Khalava heard what a fate had overtaken the philosopher Thomas, he sank for a whole hour into deep reflection. He had greatly altered of late; after finishing his studies he had become bell-ringer of one of the chief churches in the city, and he always appeared with a bruised nose, because the belfry staircase was in a ruinous condition.

"Have you heard what has happened to Thomas?" said Tiberius Gorobetz, who had become a philosopher and now wore a moustache.

"Yes; God had appointed it so," answered the bell-ringer. "Let us go to the ale-house; we will drink a glass to his memory."

The young philosopher, who, with the enthusiasm of a novice, had made such full use of his privileges as a student that his breeches and coat and even his cap reeked of brandy and tobacco, agreed readily to the proposal.

"He was a fine fellow, Thomas," said the bell-ringer as the limping innkeeper set the third jug of beer before him. "A splendid fellow! And lost his life for nothing!"

"I know why he perished," said Gorobetz; "because he was afraid. If he had not feared her, the witch could have done nothing to him. One ought to cross oneself incessantly and spit exactly on her tail, and then not the least harm can happen. I know all about it, for here, in Kieff, all the old women in the market-place are witches."

The bell-ringer nodded assent. But being aware that he could not say any more, he got up cautiously and went out, swaying to the right and left in order to find a hiding-place in the thick steppe grass outside the town. At the same time, in accordance with his old habits, he did not forget to steal an old boot-sole which lay on the ale-house bench.

THE ENTAIL

by E. T. A. Hoffman

specially adapted for this edition by Jonathan Eeds
based on the 1885 translation by J. T. Bealby
illustrations by Mario Laboccetta

I.

NOT FAR from the shore of the Baltic Sea can be found the ancestral home of the noble family Von R——. Known as R—sitten, the castle rises from a wild and desolate land. The surrounding grounds are barren except for patches of parched grass that ripple among the sand drifts. In contrast to the gardens, fountains and sweet-scented pathways that typically grace a baronial residence, unadorned gray walls mark the landward side and are braced by a thin forest of scraggly firs bent by wind and starved for rain. The forest's never-changing tapestry of gloom defied the bright spring sun. Instead of the joyous singing of little birds, nothing is heard but the ominous croak of the raven and the whirring scream of the storm-boding seagull.

Yet, merely a quarter of a mile away from the castle's shadow Nature suddenly changes. As if by magic the crumbling soil is transformed into thriving fields and verdant meadows. You see here, too, the large and prosperous village and the master of the borough's spacious house. A pleasant thicket of alders marks the foundation of a large manor, which one of the former owners had intended to erect, but that dream was never fulfilled. No one knows what happened exactly. The foundation lay abandoned, with thistle and clover now filling its imagined rooms. Not even Freiherr Roderick von R——, when he took up his residence on the ancestral estate, showed any interest in completing the manor. The lonely old castle and its brooding grounds was better suited to his dour temperament. He had its ruinous walls repaired as well as circumstances would permit, and then promptly shut himself up within them. Joining his isolation was a grim-faced servant who attended to his every need and a few domestics who kept things tidy.

He was seldom seen in the village, but he often walked and rode along the sea-beach; and people claimed to have heard him from a distance, talking to the waves and listening to the rolling and hissing of the surf, as though he could hear the answering voice of some sea spirit. Upon the topmost summit of the watchtower, the old Baron had a study fixed up and supplied with the latest telescopes and a complete set of astronomical apparatus. During daytime he frequently watched the ships sailing past on the distant horizon like white-winged seagulls. He spent the starlit hours engaged in astronomical, or, as some speculated, with astrological study, in which the old servant assisted him. The rumor was that he was devoted to the occult sciences or the so-called Black Arts, and that he had been driven out of Courland due to a failed experiment that endangered an august and princely house. The slightest allusion to his residence in Courland filled him with horror—he became unhinged, and through it all he blamed all the previous troubles on his predecessors because they had wickedly deserted the home of their ancestors. He believed the head of the family needed to be fettered to the ancestral castle, and so he converted all the baronial holdings into a "property of entail" to ensure that it could only pass into the hands of the eldest son in each successive generation. The ruling monarch was willing to ratify this special entail because it would forever secure for his country a family distinguished by chivalrous virtues—an eminent family which had already established roots in neighboring countries that could prove to be beneficial to the monarchy.

When old Baron Roderick died quiet suddenly—quite horribly, in fact—the provisions of the entail bequeathed the family fortunes entirely to the eldest son, Hubert.

~§~

Neither Roderick's son Hubert, nor the present Lord of the Entail, also named Roderick, would live in their ancestral castle; both preferred Courland. It is conceivable, too, that, being more cheerful and fond of life than the gloomy astrologer, they were repelled by the grim loneliness of the place. Life outside the walls of R—sitten had more to offer.

To maintain some sign of habitation in the castle, Freiherr Roderick granted shelter and subsistence on the property to two old maids—sisters of his father, who were living an impoverished but bearable life there. They, together with an aged serving-woman, occupied the small warm rooms of one of the wings. Other permanent residents included the cook, who had a large apartment on the ground floor adjoining the kitchen, and a worn-out cavalryman full of gruff stories, who tottered about through the lofty rooms and halls of the main building, and discharged the duties of castellan. The rest of the servants lived in the village with the land-steward.

The only time at which the desolated and deserted castle became the scene of life and activity was late in autumn, when the snow first began to fall and the season for wolf and boar hunting arrived. Then came Freiherr Roderick with his wife, attended by relatives and friends and a boisterous retinue from Courland. The neighboring nobility, and even amateur lovers of the chase who lived in the town nearby, came down in such numbers that the main building, together with the wings, barely sufficed to hold the crowd of guests. Well-stoked fires roared in all the stoves and fireplaces, while the spits were creaking from early dawn until late at night, and hundreds of light-hearted people, masters and servants, were running up and down stairs. Here was heard the jingling and rattling of drinking glasses and jovial hunting choruses, there the footsteps of those dancing to the sound of the shrill music—everywhere was loud mirth and jollity. So, as can be seen, the castle was for four or five weeks more like a first-rate hotel situated on a main highroad than the desolate abode of a country gentleman.

It was during this high-time that Freiherr Roderick withdrew from the revelry of the guests and devoted himself to the discharge of his duties as Lord of the Entail. It was his responsibility to do so. He not only had a complete statement of the revenues—the "books"—laid before him, but he listened to every proposal for improvement and listened to the complaints of his tenants. Although he allowed so little time for business affairs, he endeavored to establish order in everything, to check all wrongdoing and correct any injustice of the previous year.

In these matters of business he was honestly assisted by the old advocate V., who had been the law agent of the R—— family and Justitiarius of their estates in P——, a responsibility passed from father to son for many years. So to prepare, V. had to arrive at the estate at least a week before the arrival of the Freiherr. In the year 179— the time came round again when old V. was to start on his journey for R—sitten.

However strong and healthy the old man might feel—now that he was seventy—he was quite convinced that a helping hand would be a great benefit to his business. So he said to me one day as if in jest, "Cousin!" (I was his great-nephew, but he called me "cousin," owing to the fact that his own Christian name and mine were both the same)— "Cousin, I was thinking it would interesting if you went along with me to R—sitten and felt the sea-breezes blow about your ears. Besides giving me a hand, you may also experience the rollicking life of a hunter—to feel the excitement of a hunting lodge! . . . You see, it will be the perfect mix of business and pleasure: after drawing up a neatly-written document one morning, you will spend the afternoon glaring into the eyes of a sturdy brute—a snarling wolf or a wild boar with gnashing teeth, and you will have only an instant to take him down with a well-aimed shot. What do you say, young man? Doesn't that sound like fun?"

Naturally I could not resist such an offer from my dear old uncle. Since I was well-skilled in the sort of business he had to transact, I promised to work with tireless energy and relieve him of all care and trouble.

~§~

The next day we sat in the carriage on our way to R—sitten, well wrapped up in good fur coats, driving through a thick snowstorm, the first harbinger of the coming winter. On the journey the old gentleman told me many remarkable stories about the Freiherr Roderick, who had established the entail and appointed him (V.), in spite of his youth, to be

his Justitiarius and estate executor. He spoke of the harsh and violent character of the old nobleman, which seemed to be inherited by all the family, since even the present master of the estate, whom he had known as a mild-tempered and almost effeminate youth, acquired a wrathful brow as the years went by. He strongly advised me to behave with as much self-reliance and as little embarrassment as possible, if I desired to impress the Freiherr, who was sure to observe and judge me. He then went on to describe the apartments in the castle which he had selected to be his own: they were warm and cozy, and so conveniently positioned that we could withdraw from the raucous hilarity of the drunken festivities whenever we pleased. The two rooms, which were reserved for him on every visit, were small and hung with old tapestries on the walls. They were located close to the large hall of justice, in the wing opposite where the two old maids resided.

At last, after a rapid but wearying journey, we arrived at R—sitten. It was late at night as we drove through the village. The sounds of music, dancing, and merrymaking greeted us from the alehouse. The steward's house was lit up from basement to garret, and music and song were there too. Pipe-smoke and laughter drifted into our carriage. The happy sounds made it all the more striking as we left the village and drove into the desolate isolation of the castle. The sea-wind howled in sharp cutting currents all about us, whilst the somber firs, as if they had been roused by the wind from a deep-magic trance, groaned hoarsely in a responsive chorus. The bare black walls of the castle towered above the snow-covered ground. We drew up at the gates, which were locked tight. No amount of shouting or cracking of whips, nor knocking or hammering raised a single soul to our aid. The entire castle appeared dead: no light—not even a flickering candle—was visible at any of the windows.

The old gentleman shouted in his booming voice, "Francis, Francis, where the deuce are you? In the devil's name rouse yourself. We are all freezing here outside the gates. The snow is cutting our faces till they bleed. Why the devil don't you stir yourself?"

Then the watch-dog began to whine, and a wandering light was visible on the ground floor, passing from one window to another. There was a rattling of keys, and soon the ponderous wings of the gate creaked back on their hinges.

"Ha! a hearty welcome, a hearty welcome, Herr Justitiarius. Ugh! it's rough weather!" cried old Francis, holding the lantern above his head, so that the light fell full upon his withered face, which was drawn up into a curious grimace that was meant to pass for a friendly smile.

The carriage drove into the court, and we got out; then I obtained a full view of the old servant's extraordinary figure, almost hidden in his wide old-fashioned cavalryman's jacket, with its many extraordinary lace decorations. Whilst there were only a few grey locks on his broad white forehead, the lower part of his face wore the ruddy hue of health; and, notwithstanding that the strained muscles of his face gave it something of the appearance of a whimsical mask, yet the rather stupid good-nature which beamed from his eyes and played about his mouth compensated for all the rest.

"Now, old Francis," began my great-uncle, knocking the snow from his fur coat in the entrance hall, "now, old man, is everything prepared? Have you had the tapestries in my room well dusted, and the beds carried in? And have you had a big roaring fire going both yesterday and today?"

"No," replied Francis, quite calmly, "no, my worshipful Herr Justitiarius, we've got none of that done."

"Good Heavens!" burst out my great-uncle. "I wrote to you in proper time. You know that I always come at the time I say. Here's a fine piece of stupid carelessness! I shall have to sleep in rooms as cold as ice."

"But you see, worshipful Herr Justitiarius," continued Francis, most carefully clipping a burning thief from the wick of the candle with the snuffers and stamping it out with his foot, ". . . but, you see, sir, all that would not have been of much good, especially the fires—for the wind and the snow have taken up their quarters too much in the rooms, driving in through the broken windows, and then—"

"What!" cried my uncle, interrupting him as he spread out his fur coat and placing his arms akimbo. "Do you mean to tell me the windows are broken, and you, the castellan of the house, have done nothing to get them mended?"

"Err, worshipful Herr Justitiarius," resumed the old servant calmly, "we can't work on them owing to the great masses of stones, dust, and rubbish lying all over the room. Such a clutter . . ."

"Damn it all!" cried uncle. "And how can there be stones, dust, and rubbish in my room?"

I suddenly sneezed at the mere mention of dust.

"Your lasting health and good luck, young gentleman!" said the old man, bowing politely to me, but then he immediately turned back to my uncle. "They are the stones and plaster from the wall which collapsed from the great shock."

"You had an earthquake?" blazed up my uncle, now fairly in a rage.

"No, erm, not an earthquake, worshipful Herr Justitiarius," replied the old man, grinning all over his face, "but three days ago the heavy wainscot ceiling of the justice-hall caved-in with a tremendous crash. It shook the very foundation. I thought the world was ending."

"The devil you say—" My uncle was about to roar in his violent and passionate manner, but jerking up his right arm above his head and taking off his fox-skin cap with his left, he suddenly checked himself, nearly choking on his self-restraint. Turning to me at last, he said with a forced laugh, "By my word, cousin, we must hold our tongues; we mustn't ask any more questions, or else we shall hear of some still worse misfortune, or cause the whole castle to fall to pieces about our ears."

The old man nodded in complete agreement, smiling again.

"But," my uncle continued, wheeling round to the old servant, "bless me, Francis, could you not have had the common sense to get me another room cleaned and warmed? Could you not have quickly fitted up a room in the main building for the court-day?"

"All that has been already done," said the old man, pointing to the staircase with a gesture that invited us to follow him, and at once beginning to ascend them.

"Now there's a most curious noodle for you!" exclaimed my uncle as we followed old Francis.

The way led through long lofty vaulted corridors, in the dense darkness of which Francis's flickering light threw a strange reflection. The pillars, abutments, and multi-colored arches seemed as if they were floating before us in the air. Our own shadows stalked along beside us in gigantic shapes that slid along the wall and across the grotesque paintings hanging there. I could swear the portraits of the long-dead ancestors trembled as we passed. The stately subjects within their gilded frames seemed to whisper amid our echoing footsteps: "Wake us not, oh! wake us not—we whimsical spirits who sleep here in these old stones."

At last, after we had traversed a long suite of cold and gloomy apartments, Francis opened the door of a hall in which a fire blazed brightly in the grate. The fire offered us a home-like welcome with its pleasant crackling. I felt quite comfortable the moment I entered, but my uncle, standing still in the middle of the hall, looked round him and said in a tone which was so very grave as to be almost solemn, "And so this is to be the justice-hall!"

Francis held his candle above his head, so that my eye fell upon a light spot in the wide dark wall about the size of a door; then he said in a pained and muffled voice, "Justice has been already dealt out here."

"What's that? What possesses you, old man?" asked my uncle,

quickly throwing aside his fur coat and drawing near to the fire.

"It slipped out my lips. I couldn't help it," said Francis mysteriously, then he lit the great candles and opened the door of the adjoining room, which was very snugly fitted up for our reception.

In a short time a table was spread for us before the fire, and the old man served us with several well-dressed dishes, which were followed by a brimming bowl of punch, prepared in true Northern style—a very acceptable sight to two weary travelers.

My uncle then, tired with his journey, went to bed as soon as he had finished supper; but my spirits were too excited by the novelty and strangeness of the place, as well as by the intoxicating punch, for me to think of sleep. Meanwhile, Francis cleared the table, stirred up the fire, and bowing and scraping politely, left me alone.

Now I sat in the lofty spacious *Rittersaal* or Knight's Hall. The snowflakes had ceased to drift against the lattice, and the storm had ceased to whistle; the sky was clear, and the bright full moon shone in through the wide bay windows, illuminating with magical effect all the dark corners of the curious room into which the dim light of my candles and the fire could not penetrate. As one often finds in old castles, the walls and ceiling of the hall were decorated in a peculiar antique fashion. The cold stone walls were hung with fantastic paintings and carvings, gilded and colored in gorgeous tints. The ceiling was veneered with heavy wainscoting carved with a mixture of mythical forms and floral embellishments. Standing out conspicuously among the paintings, which represented for the most part wild bloody scenes of bear-baiting and wolf-hunts, were the heads of men and animals carved of dark burl. In the flickering light of the fire and the soft beams of the moon, the many ornaments made the room seem alive and charged with a terrible reality. Between these pictures were life-sized reliefs of knights walking along in hunting costume; undoubtedly they were the ancestors of the family who had delighted in the chase. Everything, both in the paintings and in the carved work, bore the dingy hue of extreme old age.

Contrary to this brooding antiquity was a bright bare patch on one of the walls, where two doors lead into adjoining apartments. I soon concluded that the bright patch must have also been a door at one time, now bricked up and shut-off. This new part of the wall, which had neither been painted like the rest, nor yet decorated with carvings, formed a striking contrast with the other wall surfaces.

Who would not be entranced by such a mysterious discovery? What mind would not be enthralled in the midst of such unusual and singularly strange circumstances? Even the dullest imagination is aroused when it comes into a valley girdled by fantastic rocks, or passes within the gloomy walls of a church or an abbey, or glimpses things it has never experienced before. When I add that I was but twenty years of age, and had drunk several glasses of strong punch, it will be easily understood that as I sat in the *Rittersaal* I was in an exceptional frame of mind.

Let the reader picture the stillness of the night within, and the rumbling roar of the sea without—the peculiar piping of the wind, which rang upon my ears like the tones of a mighty organ played upon by spectral hands—the passing of scudding clouds which, shining bright and white, often seemed to peep in through the rattling bay windows like giants sailings past. I felt, from the slight shudder which shook me, that possibly a new sphere of existences might now be revealed to me visibly and perceptibly. But this feeling was like the shivery sensations that one has upon hearing a well-told ghost story, such as we all like. At this moment it occurred to me that I should never be in a more seasonable mood for reading the book which I at that time carried about in my pocket. I mean of course Schiller's *Ghost-seer*, the sensational novel of necromancy. I read and read, and my imagination grew ever more and more excited. I came to the marvelously enthralling description of the wedding feast at Count Von V—'s.

Just as I was reading of the entrance of Jeronimo's bloody figure, the door leading from the gallery into the antechamber flew open with a tremendous bang. I jumped to my feet in terror; the book fell from my hands. In the very same moment, however, all was still again, and I began to be ashamed of my childish fears. The door must have been burst open by a strong gust of wind or in some other natural manner. *It is nothing*—I told myself; my over-strained fancy was converting every ordinary occurrence into something supernatural. Having thus calmed my fears, I picked up my book from the ground, and again threw myself in the arm-chair; but there came a sound of soft, slow, measured footsteps moving diagonally across the hall, whilst there was a sighing and moaning at intervals, and in this sighing and moaning was expressed the deepest trouble, the most hopeless grief, that a human being can know.

"Ha!" I assured myself. "It must be some sick animal locked up somewhere in the basement. Such acoustic deceptions at night, making distant sounds appear close at hand, are well known to everybody. Who in his right mind would allow himself to be terrified at such a thing as that?"

Thus I calmed my fears again. But now there was a scratching at the new portion of the wall—the pale patch, whilst louder and deeper sighs were audible, as if gasped out by someone in the last throes of mortal anguish.

"Yes, yes," I thought. "It is some poor animal locked up somewhere; I will shout as loudly as I can. I will stamp violently on the floor, then all will be still, or else the animal below will make itself known with its natural cries." But the blood ran cold in my veins. Beads of cold sweat formed on my forehead, and I remained sitting in my chair as if trans-fixed, quite unable to rise, still able less to cry out. At length the abomin-able scratching ceased, and I again heard the footsteps. Sensations ignited my brain. I leapt to my feet, and went two or three steps forward. But then there came an ice-cold draught of wind through the hall, whilst at the same moment the moon cast her bright light upon the statue of a grave and terrible-looking man.

And then, as though his warning voice rang through the louder thunders of the waves and the shriller piping of the wind, I heard distinctly, "No further, no further! or you will sink beneath the fearful horrors of the ghost-world." Then the door was slammed with the same violent bang as before, and I plainly heard the footsteps in the anteroom, then going down the stairs. The main door of the castle was opened with a creaking noise, and afterwards closed again. Then it seemed as if a horse were brought out of the stable, and after a while taken back again, and finally all was still.

At that same moment my attention was attracted to my old uncle in the adjoining room: he was groaning and moaning painfully. This brought me fully to consciousness again. I seized the candles and hurried into the room to him. He appeared to be struggling with an ugly, unpleasant dream.

"Wake up, wake up!" I cried loudly, taking him gently by the hand, and letting the full glare of the light fall upon his face.

He started up with a stifled shout, and then, looking kindly at me, said, "Ay, you have done quite right—that you have, cousin, to wake me. I have had a very ugly dream, and it's all solely owing to this room and that hall, for they made me think of past times and many mysterious things that have happened here. But now let us turn to and have a good sound sleep."

Therewith the old gentleman rolled himself in the bed-covering and appeared to fall asleep at once. But when I had extinguished the candles and likewise crept into bed, I heard him praying in a low tone to himself.

~§~

Next morning we began work in earnest. The land-steward brought his account-books, and various other people came forward, some to get a dispute settled, some to get arrangements made about other matters. At noon my uncle took me with him to the wing where the two old Baronesses lived. Uncle thought it fitting that we pay our respects to them.

Francis announced us. We had to wait some time before a little old dame, bent with the weight of her sixty years, and attired in gay-colored silks of noble ladies' lady-in-waiting, appeared and led us into the sanctuary. There we were received with comical ceremony by the old ladies, whose curious style of dress had gone out of fashion years and years before. I especially was an object of astonishment to them when my uncle, with considerable humor, introduced me as a young lawyer who had come to assist him in his business. Their expressions plainly indicated their belief that, owing to my youth, the welfare of the tenants of R—sitten was placed in jeopardy by my very presence. Although much of our conversation with the old ladies was humorously absurd, I was nevertheless still shivering from the terror of the preceding night. In my bones I felt as if I had encountered a churlish unseen power, or had brushed against that veil that separates this life from the next. One step across the thin barrier would be enough to plunge me irretrievably into destruction. Only by the exertion of willpower could I guard against that awful dread which never slackens and leads to incurable insanity.

And so it was that the old Baronesses, with their remarkable towering head-dresses, and their peculiar gowns decorated with gay flowers and ribbons, instead of striking me as merely ridiculous, had an appearance that was both ghostly and foreboding. They were very strange old girls, and this strange place made them stranger still. My fanciful thoughts were fueled by their withered yellow faces and blinking eyes. I imagined, by their queer ways, that they were on good footing with the ghosts who haunted the castle. The wretched French which they croaked, partly between their tightly-closed blue lips and partly through their long thin noses, led me to believe that they possessed the power and desire to stir mischief and disrupt our work. My uncle, who always had a keen eye for a bit of fun, entangled the old dames in his ironic way with such a mish-mash of nonsensical rubbish that, had I been in any other mood, would not have been able to swallow my laughter, but, as I have already explained, the foolish Baronesses and their unbearable twaddle were in my regard ghostly, unearthly. They merely served as an extension of my nightmare from the night before.

My old uncle, who had been attempting to amuse me with the old dames, gave me an astonished look. He could not decipher my innermost thoughts, but he could tell something bothered me.

~§~

After dinner, when we were alone together in our room, my uncle burst out, "In Heaven's name, cousin, tell me what is the matter with you? You don't laugh; you don't talk; you don't eat; and you don't drink. Are you ill, or is something else the matter with you?"

I now told him without hesitation all my terrible, awful experiences of the previous night. I concealed nothing, and above all I did not hide the fact that I had drunk a good deal of punch and had been reading Schiller's "Ghost-seer" beforehand. "This I must confess to," I added, "for only so can I credibly explain how it was that my over-strained and active imagination could create all those ghostly spirits, which only exist within the sphere of my own brain."

I fully expected that my uncle would now deservedly pepper me with the stinging pellets of his wit for my fanciful ghost-seeing; but, on the contrary, he grew very grave, and his eyes became riveted in a set stare upon the floor, until he jerked up his head and said, fixing me with his keen fiery eyes:

"Your book I am not acquainted with, dear cousin, but your ghostly visitors were due neither to it nor to the fumes of the punch. I must tell you that I dreamt exactly the same things that you saw and heard. Like you, I sat in the easy-chair beside the fire (at least I dreamt so); but what was only revealed to you as slight noises I saw and distinctly comprehended with my mind's eye. Yes, I beheld that foul fiend come in, stealthily and feebly step across to the bricked-up door, and scratch at the wall in hopeless despair until the blood gushed out from beneath his torn fingernails. Then he went downstairs, took a horse out of the stable, and finally put him back in the stall. Did you also hear the cock crowing in a distant farmyard up at the village? You came and awoke me, and I soon resisted the baneful ghost of that terrible man, who is still able to disturb in this fearful way the quiet lives of the living."

The old gentleman stopped, and I did not prompt him further questions, being well aware that he would explain everything to me at the proper time.

After sitting for a while, deeply absorbed in his own thoughts, he went on, "Cousin, do you think you have courage enough to encounter the ghost again now that you know all that happens—that is to say, along with me?"

Of course I declared that I now felt quite strong enough, and ready for what he wished.

"Then let us watch together during the coming night," the old gentleman went on to say. "There is a voice within me telling me that this evil spirit must fly, not so much before the power of my will as before my courage, which rests upon my firm conviction of what is good. I feel that it is not presumptive of me, but rather a just and pious deed that must be done. I am willing to risk life and limb to exorcise this foul fiend that is banishing the sons from the old castle of their ancestors."

My uncle paused thoughtfully, and I waited in silence for him to finish.

"The risks are great, of course," he continued. "If it should be God's will that this evil power be enabled to cause me harm, then you must bear witness, cousin, that I fell in honest Christian fight against a spirit from hell. As for yourself, keep at a safe distance so that you come to no harm."

~§~

Our attention was busily engaged with our assigned tasks until evening came. As on the day before, Francis had cleared away the remains of the supper, and brought us our punch. The full moon shone brightly through the gleaming clouds, the sea-waves roared, and the night-wind howled and shook the bay window till the panes rattled. Although inwardly excited, we forced ourselves to converse on indifferent topics.

The old gentleman had placed his pocket-watch on the table; finally, it chimed the midnight hour.

Then the door flew open with a terrific bang, and, just as on the preceding night, soft slow footsteps moved stealthily across the hall in a diagonal direction, whilst there were the same sounds of sighing and moaning. My uncle turned pale, but his eyes shone with an unusual brilliance. He rose from his armchair, stretching his tall figure up to its full height, so that as he stood there with his left arm propped against his side and with his right stretched out towards the middle of the hall. He had the appearance of a hero issuing his commands.

. . . But the sighing and moaning were growing every moment louder and more perceptible, and then the scratching at the wall began more

horribly even than on the previous night. My uncle strode forward straight toward the walled-up door with steps so firm that they echoed along the floor. He stopped immediately in front of the bright patch, where the scratching noise continued to grow worse and worse, and said in a strong solemn voice, such as I had never before heard from his lips:

"Daniel, Daniel! What are you doing here at this hour?"

Then there was a horrible unearthly scream, followed by a dull thud as if a heavy weight had fallen to the ground.

Uncle leaned over that terrible spot. He gripped his fist above the boards and said in a reverent tone, "Seek for pardon and mercy at the throne of the Almighty—*that* is your place. Away with you from the scenes of this life, in which you can nevermore play a part."

And as the old gentleman uttered these words in a tone still stronger than before, a feeble wail passed through the air and died in the blustering storm, which was just beginning to rage. Crossing over to the door, the old gentleman slammed it shut, so that the echo rang loudly through the empty room. There was something so supernatural almost in both his language and his gestures that I was deeply struck with awe.

On resuming his seat in his armchair his face appeared calm. He folded his hands and prayed inwardly. He passed the next several minutes in this way, and then asked me in that gentle tone which always went right to my heart, and which he always had so completely at his command, "Well, cousin?"

Agitated and shaken by awe, terror, fear, and pious respect and love, I threw myself upon my knees and rained down my warm tears upon the hand he offered me. He clasped me in his arms, and pressing me fervently to his heart said very tenderly, "Now we will go and have a good quiet sleep, good cousin."

And we did so. Shocked as I was, I did not think to ask my uncle how he knew the spirit's name. I thought only to put it all behind me. Since nothing of an unusual nature occurred on the following night, we soon recovered our former cheerfulness, much to the seething chagrin of the old Baronesses. Although there still seemed be something ghostly about them and their odd manners, their power to unnerve had dissipated with the departure of the midnight spirit.

~§~

Several days later the Baron finally made his appearance, along with his wife and a long train of servants devoted to the hunting party. The guests also arrived *en masse*, and the castle, now suddenly bustling with life, became a scene of the noisy revelry.

When the Baron came into our hall soon after his arrival, he seemed to be taken aback at the change in our quarters. Casting an ill-tempered glance towards the bricked-up door, he turned abruptly round and passed his hand across his forehead, as if attempting to banish some dark memory. My great-uncle mentioned the damage done to the justice-hall and the adjoining apartments, but the Baron dismissed the explanation and faulted Francis for not giving us better lodgings. He good-naturedly encouraged uncle to order anything he might want to make his new room comfortable, for the Baron recognized that he was given a poor substitute for the rooms he normally occupied.

On the whole, the Baron's bearing towards my old uncle was not merely cordial, but largely colored by reverence and respect, as if he viewed him more as a relative than a member of his staff. I must state, though, that this was the sole trait that could in any way soften me to his harsh, imperious character. The Baron exhibited a cold, hard demeanor that seemed to deepen more and more each day.

As for me, the Baron noticed me but little. If he did notice me at all, he saw me as nothing more than the usual secretary or clerk. On the occasion of the very first important memorandum that I drew up, he began to point out mistakes, as he conceived, in the wording. This made my blood boil, and I was about to make a caustic reply, when my uncle interposed, informing him briefly that I did my work exactly in the way he wished, and that in legal matters of this kind he alone was responsible. When we were left alone, I complained bitterly of the Baron, who would, I said, always inspire me with aggravation.

"I assure you, cousin," replied the old gentleman, "that the Baron, notwithstanding his unpleasant manner, is really one of the most excellent and kind-hearted men in the world. As I have already told you, he did not assume these manners until the time he became lord of the entail. Prior to that he was a modest, gentle youth. Besides, he is not, after all, so bad as you make him out to be. For my own understanding, though, I would like to know why you are so averse to him."

As my uncle said these words he smiled mockingly, and the blood rushed hotly and furiously into my face. I could not pretend to hide from myself. I saw it only too clearly, and felt it too firmly, that my peculiar antipathy to the Baron sprang from the fact that I loved, even to the point of madness, a being who appeared to me to be the loveliest and most fascinating of her sex who had ever trod the earth. This lady was none other than the Baroness von R— herself.

Her appearance placed a powerful and irresistible charm upon me at the very moment of her arrival, when I saw her traversing the apartments in her Russian sable cloak, which fitted close to the exquisite symmetry of her shape, and with a rich veil wrapped about her head. Moreover, the circumstance that the two old aunts, who were now adorned in yet more extraordinary fairytale gowns and be-ribboned head-dresses, were sweeping along one on each side of her and cackling their welcomes in French. So straddled by the old hags, the Baroness was looking about her in a way so gentle as to baffle all description, nodding graciously first to one and then to another, and then adding in her flute-like voice a few German words in the pure sonorous dialect of Courland. All this formed a truly remarkable and unusual picture and for some reason it triggered my imagination to recall the ghostly midnight visitor, but now that dreadful memory was brightened by the presence of the Baroness—my angel of light whose beauty vanquished the spectral powers of evil.

This wondrously lovely lady stood forth in startling reality before me. At that time she could hardly be nineteen years of age, and her face, as delicately beautiful as her form, bore the impression of the most angelic good-nature; but what I especially noticed was the indescribable fascination of her dark eyes, for a soft melancholy gleam of aspiration shone in them like dewy moonshine, whilst a perfect Elysium of rapture and delight was revealed in her sweet and beautiful smile. She often seemed completely lost in her own thoughts, and at such moments her lovely face was swept by dark and fleeting shadows. Many observers would have concluded that she was affected by some distressing pain; but it rather seemed to me that she was struggling with gloomy apprehend-sions of a future ripe with dark misfortunes. Strangely enough, I associa-ted the apparition of the castle with the brooding nature of the Baroness, though I could not give the least explanation of why I did so. I just knew intuitively that she and the ghost were connected somehow.

~§~

On the morning following the Baron's arrival, when the company assembled to breakfast, my old uncle introduced me to the Baroness. As usually happens with people in the frame of mind in which I then was, I behaved with indescribable absurdity. In answer to the beautiful lady's simple inquiries how I liked the castle, I entangled myself in the most extraordinary and nonsensical phrases. My gibbering alerted the old aunts, who ascribed my embarrassment simply and solely to my profound respect for the noble lady. My bumbling seemed to encourage the two fluffs to condescendingly to take up my part, which they did by praising me in French as a very nice and clever young man, and referring to me as a *garçon très joli* (handsome lad). This vexed me; so suddenly recovering my self-possession, I threw out a clever remark in better French than the old dames choke out; whereupon they opened their eyes wide in astonishment, and pampered their long thin noses with a liberal supply of snuff.

Judging by the Baroness's turning away from me with a more serious air to talk to some other lady, I perceived that my *bon mot* bordered on folly. This of course vexed me terribly, and I wished the two old ladies to the devil. Before this, my old uncle's ironic sense of timing had always rescued me from the languishing love-sick suitor stage— whenever it occurred—and the childish infatuation that comes with emphatic love-troubles. This time, however, I knew that the Baroness had made a deeper and more powerful impression upon my heart than any other woman had hitherto done. My uncle's humorous and endearing remarks had no effect on my beguiled state. I saw and heard nothing but her. Nevertheless I clearly understood that it would not only be absurd, but even utter madness to dream of an amorous adventure with this fair lady. Yet I could not help my gazing and adoring at a distance like a love-lorn boy.

Of such conduct I should have been perfectly ashamed. But what could I do? One does not ask for madness to come. What I resolved to do was to become more intimate with this beautiful girl without allowing her to get any glimpse of my real feelings, to drink the sweet poison of her lithe expressions and purring words, and then, when far away from her, to bear her image in my heart for many, many days—perhaps forever!

I was excited by this romantic and chivalric attachment to such a degree, that, as I restlessly pondered it during sleepless nights, I was childish enough to address myself in pathetic monologues, and even to sigh lugubriously, "Seraphina! *O Seraphina!*" till at last my old uncle woke up and cried, "Cousin, cousin! I believe you are dreaming aloud. Do it by daytime, if you can possibly contrive it, but at night have the goodness to let me sleep."

I was very much afraid that the old gentleman, who had not failed to notice my excitement with the Baroness's arrival, had heard the name and would overwhelm me with his sarcastic wit. But next morning all he said, as we went into the justice-hall, was, "God grant every man the strength to keep his head whenever his heart quivers. It's offsetting when a man transforms into an insufferable coxcomb without so much as a word of warning."

Then he took his seat at the great table and added amiably, "Time to work. Write neatly and distinctly, good cousin, that I may be able to read it without any trouble."

~§~

The respect, nay, the almost filial veneration which the Baron entertained towards my uncle, was apparent on all occasions. Thus, at the dinner table he had to occupy the seat—for which many envied him—beside the Baroness. As for me, chance threw me first in one place and then in another, but for the most part two officers from the neighboring capital unofficially adopted me. While in their company they rattled on about the latest news, spicing it all up with amusing anecdotes and observations, whilst they diligently passed the wine about.

Thus it happened that for several days in succession I sat at the end of the table at a great distance from the Baroness. Eventually chance brought me closer to her. Just as the doors of the dining-hall were thrown open for the assembled company, I happened to be engaged in a conversation with the Baroness's companion and confidante—a lady no longer in the bloom of youth, but by no means unattractive. I took her as intelligent as well because she seemed to take genuine interest in my rarified remarks. According to etiquette, it was my duty to offer her my arm, and I was very much pleased when she took her place quite close to the Baroness, who gave her a friendly nod.

It may be readily imagined that all I now said was intended not only for my fair neighbor, but also for the Baroness. My repressed feelings enlivened my words and my companion's attention became more riveted with every passing moment; in fact, she was at last utterly absorbed in the kaleidoscopic of my "brilliance." As remarked, she was an intelligent person, and it soon came to pass that our conversation, completely independent of the monotonous buzz of the other guests (which rambled about first to this subject and then to that), maintained its own free course and formed its own bubble of conversation.

During our discourse I observed that my companion occasionally directed meaningful glances to the Baroness, who took pains to listen to us. And this was particularly the case when the conversation turned to music and I began to speak with enthusiasm of this glorious and sacred art; nor did I conceal that, despite the fact of my having devoted myself to the dry tedious study of the law, I possessed tolerable skill on the harpsichord, could sing, and had even set several songs to music.

The majority of the company had drifted into another room to take coffee and liqueurs, but I found myself near the Baroness, who was still talking with her confidante. She turned to me, asking in a cordial manner how I liked living in the castle. I told her that for the first few days the ancient castle affected me strangely. Perhaps it was because of its wind-blown desolation, or due its proximity to the restless ocean, over which the towers hang in a kind of obstinate defiance of gravity. Even in this mood, I assured her, I possessed a deep interest in the ancestral home and was delighted to work on behalf of the family with my uncle. I ended by confiding in a hushed tone that my only wish was to be excused from the hunt planned for the next day, for I was not accustomed to such things.

The Baroness smiled and said, "I can easily believe that this wild life of ours in the fir forests cannot be very congenial to you. You are a musician, and,unless I am utterly mistaken, a poet as well. I am passionately fond of both arts. I can also play the harp a little, but I have to do without it here in R—sitten, for my husband does not like me to bring it with me. Its soft strains would not harmonize with the wild shouts of the hunters and the ringing blare of their bugles, which are the only sounds that ought to be heard here. And O heaven! How I should like to hear a little music!"

I protested that I would exert all the skill I had at my command to fulfil her wish, for there must surely be an instrument of some kind in the castle, even it were only an old harpsichord.

Then the Lady Adelheid (the Baroness's confidante) burst out into a silvery laugh.

"Didn't you know," she chided playfully, "that no other instrument had ever been heard in the castle except blaring trumpets and hunting-horns, twanging fiddles, untuned violoncellos, and the braying oboes of the village musicians?"

The Baroness reiterated her wish that she would like to have some real music, and especially wanted to hear me play. Both she and Adelheid racked their brains to devise some way they could get a decent pianoforte brought to the Castle.

At this moment old Francis crossed the room.

"Here's the man who always can give the best advice, and can procure everything, even things previously unheard of and unseen." With these words the Lady Adelheid called him to her, and as she endeavored to make him understand what was wanted.

The Baroness listened with her hands clasped and her head bent forward, looking upon the old man's face with a gentle smile. She made for a most attractive picture, like some lovely, winsome child that is all eagerness to have a wished-for toy in her hands.

Francis, in his typically roundabout way, pointed out why it would be downright impossible to procure such a wonderful instrument in a big hurry. Finally, stroking his beard with an air of self-flattery, he said, "But the land-steward's lady up at the village performs on the manichord—or whatever is the outlandish name they now call it—with uncommon skill, and sings to it so fine and mournful-like that it makes your eyes red, just like onions do, and makes you feel as if you would like to dance with both legs at once."

"And you say she has a pianoforte?" interposed Lady Adelheid.

"Aye, to be sure," continued the old man; "it came straight from Dresden; a—"

"Oh, that's fine!" interrupted the Baroness.

"—a beautiful instrument," went on the old man, "but a little fragile; for not long ago, when the organist began to play on it the hymn 'In all Thy works,' he broke it all to pieces, so that—"

"Good gracious!" chimed the Baroness and Lady Adelheid.

"—so that," went on the old man again, his patience holding steady through the interruptions, "it had to be taken to R—— to be mended, and cost a lot of money."

"But has it come back again?" asked Lady Adelheid impatiently.

"Aye, to be sure, my lady, and the steward's lady will reckon it a high honor—"

At this moment the Baron chanced to pass. He looked across at our group rather astonished, and whispered with a sarcastic smile to the Baroness, "So you have to take counsel from Francis again, I see?"

The Baroness cast down her eyes blushing, whilst old Francis breaking off terrified, suddenly threw himself into military posture, his head erect, and his arms close and straight down his side.

The old aunts came sailing down upon us in their stuffed gowns and carried off the Baroness. Lady Adelheid followed her, and I was left alone as if spellbound.

A struggle began to rage within me between my rapturous anticipations of now being able to be near her whom I adored, who completely swayed all my thoughts and feelings . . . and my sulky ill-humor and annoyance at the Baron, whom I regarded as a barbarous tyrant. If he were not so barbarous, would the grey-haired old servant have assumed such a slavish attitude?

~§~

"Do you hear me? Can't you see the obvious, I say?" cried my great-uncle, tapping me on the shoulder. He had pulled me away and we were trudging upstairs to our own apartments.

"Don't force yourself so on the Baroness's attention," he said when we reached the room. "What good can come of it? Leave that to the young fops who like to pay court to ladies; there are plenty of them to do it."

I explained how it had all come about and challenged his reproof of my actions. His only reply to this was, "Humph! humph!" as he struggled into his dressing-gown. Then, having lit his pipe, he took his seat in his easy-chair and began to talk about the adventures of the hunt on the preceding day, pestering me mercilessly over my bad shots. I fumed in silence and watched the sun die down.

~§~

All was quiet in the castle; the visitors, both gentlemen and ladies, were busy in their own rooms dressing for the evening. The musicians with their twanging fiddles, untuned violoncellos, and braying oboes (of whom Lady Adelheid had spoken) were expected soon, and a merry-making of a grand sort was anticipated. My old uncle, preferring a quiet sleep to such foolish pastimes, stayed in his chamber. I, however, had just finished dressing when there came a light tap at our door and Francis entered. Smiling in his self-satisfied way, he announced to me that the manichord had just arrived in a sledge from the land-steward's lady, and had been carried into the Baroness's apartments. Lady Adelheid sent her compliments and asked if I could come at once.

How my heart pounded! With a delicious tremor I opened the door of the room in which I was to find her. Lady Adelheid came to meet me with a joyful smile. The Baroness, already in full dress for the ball, was sitting in a meditative attitude beside the mysterious crate, in which slumbered the music that I was called upon to awaken. When she rose, her beauty shone upon me with such glorious splendor that I stood staring at her unable to utter a word.

"Come, Theodore," she addressed me in the more formal northern fashion. "Come, Theodore," she coaxed pleasantly, "the instrument has arrived."

"Heaven grant it's not unworthy of your skill!" Lady Adeheud added.

I paused, then stiffly stepped forward. As I opened the lid I was greeted by the rattling of a score of broken strings, and when I attempted to strike a chord, the effect was hideous and abominable, for all the strings which were not broken were completely out of tune.

"It seems our friend the organist has been putting his delicate little hands upon it again," said Lady Adelheid, laughing at the calamity.

But the Baroness was very much annoyed and said, "Oh, it really is a slice of bad luck! I am doomed, I see, never to have any pleasure here."

I searched in the case of the instrument, and fortunately found some coils of strings, but no tuning-key anywhere. Hence fresh laments.

"Any key will do if the ward fits on the pegs," I explained; then both Lady Adelheid and the Baroness ran backwards and forwards in gay spirits, and before long a whole magazine of bright keys lay before me on the sounding-board.

Then I set to work diligently, and both the ladies assisted me all they could, trying first one peg and then another. At length one of the tiresome keys fitted, and they exclaimed joyfully, "This will do! it will do!" But when I had drawn the first creaking string up to just proper pitch, it suddenly snapped, and the ladies recoiled in alarm. The Baroness, handling the brittle wires with her delicate little fingers, gave me the numbers as I wanted them, and carefully held the coil whilst I unrolled it. Suddenly one of them coiled itself up again with a whipping *whirr*, making the Baroness utter an impatient "Oh!"

Lady Adelheid enjoyed a hearty laugh, whilst I pursued the tangled coil to the corner of the room. After we had all united our efforts to extract a perfectly straight string from it, and had tried it again, to our mortification it again broke; but at last—at last we found some good coils; the strings began to hold, and gradually the discordant jangling gave place to pure melodious chords.

"Ha! it will go! it will go! The instrument is getting in tune!" exclaimed the Baroness, looking at me with her lovely smile.

How quickly did this common interest banish all the strangeness and shyness which the artificial manners of social decorum imposes. A kind of confidential familiarity arose between us, which, burning through me like an electric current, consumed the timorous nervousness and constraint which had lain like ice upon my heart. That peculiar mood of diffused melting sadness which is engendered of such love as mine had quite left me. When the pianoforte was brought into something like tune, instead of interpreting my deeper feelings in dreamy improvisations, as I had intended, I began with those sweet and charming *canzonets* which have reached us from the South. During this or the other *Senza di te* (Without thee), or *Sentimi idol mio* (Hear me, my darling), or *Almen se nonpos'io* (At least if I cannot), with numberless *Morir mi sentos* (I feel I am dying), and *Addios* (Farewell), and *O dios!* (O Heaven!), a brighter and brighter brilliancy shone in Seraphina's eyes. She had seated herself close beside me at the instrument. I felt her breath fanning my cheek, and as she placed her arm behind me on the chair-back, a white ribbon fluttered loose from her beautiful ball-dress and fell across my shoulder. My singing and Seraphina's soft sighs gave life to the ribbon and it continually caressed my cheek, like a true love-messenger. It is a wonder how I kept from losing my head.

As I was running my fingers aimlessly over the keys, thinking of a new song, Lady Adelheid, who had been sitting in one of the corners of the room, ran across to us, and, kneeling down before the Baroness, begged her, as she took both her hands and clasped them to her bosom, "Oh, dear Baroness! darling Seraphina! now you must sing too."

To this she replied, "Whatever are you thinking about, Adelheid? How could I dream of letting our virtuoso friend hear such poor singing as mine?" And she looked so lovely. Like a shy-hearted child, she cast down her eyes and blushed, timidly contending with the desire to sing.

I then added my entreaties for her to sing. I rose to make way for her at the piano, but she would not permit me to do so, asserting that she could not play a single chord, and for that reason, since she would have to sing without accompaniment, her performance would be poor and uncertain.

Nonetheless, sing she did. She began in a sweet voice, pure as a bell, that came straight from her heart, and sang a song whose simple melody bore all the characteristics of those *Volkslieder* which possess such a lustrous brightness that we bask in the glad-light that surrounds us in our own higher poetic nature. On her beginning the second verse of the song I played an *arpeggio* accompaniment. The inspiration which now took possession of me, stolen from the Baroness's own lips, doubtless made me to appear a great maestro, for they overwhelmed me with enthusiastic praise.

The lights and illuminations from the ballroom, situated in one of the wings of the castle, now shone across into the Baroness's chamber, whilst a discordant bleating of trumpets and French horns announced that it was time to gather for the ball.

"Oh, now I must go," said the Baroness, causing me to rise from the pianoforte. "You have afforded me a delightful hour; these have been the pleasantest moments I have ever spent in R—sitten."

She then offered me her hand. Enwrapped within the extreme intoxication of delight I pressed it to my lips. I felt her fingers close upon my hand with a sudden convulsive tremor.

I do not know how I managed to reach my uncle's chamber, and still less how I got into the ballroom. There was a certain Gascon who was afraid to go into battle since he was all heart, and every wound would be fatal to him. I might be compared to him; and so might everybody else who is in the same mood that I was in; every touch was then fatal. The Baroness's hand—her tremulous fingers—had affected me like a poisoned arrow; my blood was burning in my veins.

~§~

On the following morning my old uncle, without asking any direct questions, had soon drawn from me a full account of the hour I had spent in the Baroness's society, and I was abashed when the smile vanished from his lip—along with the jocular note from his voice—and he grew serious all at once, saying, "Cousin, I beg you will resist this folly that is taking such a powerful hold on you. Let me tell you that your present conduct, as harmless as it now appears, may lead to the most terrible consequences. In your blind infatuation you are standing on thin ice, which will break before you are aware of its cracking, and you will plunge into the frigid depths. No love, no fulfillment—only drowning in sorrow. I shall take good care not to hold you fast by the coattails, for I know you will scramble out again on your own, and then, when you are lying sick, feeling a forgery of death, you will say, 'I caught this fever in a dream.' But I warn you that a malignant sickness will gnaw at your vitals, and years will pass before you recover yourself and are a man again. Unafraid—a real man. The devil take your music if you can put it to no better use than to seduce sentimental young women out of their quiet peace of mind."

"But—" I began, interrupting the old gentleman, "but have I ever thought of insinuating myself as the Baroness's lover?"

"You puppy!" cried the old gentleman, "if I thought so I would pitch you out of this window."

At this juncture the Baron entered and put an end to the painful conversation. The business at hand rescued me from my love-sick reveries, in which I saw and thought of nothing but Seraphina.

~§~

In general society the Baroness only exchanged a few friendly words with me, but hardly an evening passed without a secret message coming to me through Lady Adelheid—a whispered summons to my Seraphina. It soon came to pass that our music alternated with conversations on diverse topics. Whenever I and Seraphina began to get too absorbed in sentimental dreams and vague aspirations, the Lady Adelheid, though now hardly young enough to be so naïve and droll as she once was, intervened with all sorts of merry and somewhat chaotic nonsense. From several hints she let fall, I soon discovered that the Baroness really had something preying upon her mind—the same sensation I read in her eyes the very first moment I saw her. Hidden behind that somber veil of hers, I clearly discerned the hostile influence of the castle's ghostly apparition. Something terrible had happened or was yet to happen. I felt compelled to tell Seraphina how I had come in contact with the invisible enemy—the clawing spirit at the bricked-up wall. I wanted to assure her that my old uncle had banished the spectre, undoubtedly forever. And yet I felt my tongue constrained by a hesitation which was inexplicable even to myself.

One day the Baroness failed to appear at the dinner table. It was said that she was a little unwell and could not leave her room. Sympathetic inquiries were addressed to the Baron as to whether her illness was of a grave nature. He smiled in a very disagreeable way—it was almost like bitter irony—and said, "Nothing more than a slight congestion, which she often catches from our blustering sea-breezes. The salt-winds torture any sweet voices; the only sounds they will endure are the vibrant calls of the hunt."

At these words the Baron hurled a keen searching look at me across the table, for I sat obliquely opposite to him. He had not spoken to his neighbor, but directly to me.

Lady Adelheid, who sat beside me, blushed a scarlet red. Fixing her eyes upon the plate in front of her, and scribbling about on it with her fork, she whispered, "And yet you must see Seraphina today; your sweet songs shall today also bring soothing and comfort to her poor heart."

Adelheid innocently addressed these words to me, but at this moment it struck me that I was entangled in a base and forbidden intrigue with the Baroness, which could only end in some terrible crime. My old uncle's warning fell heavily upon my heart. What should I do? Not see her again? That was impossible so long as I remained in the castle; and even if I might leave the castle and return to K——, I had not the will to do it. Oh! I was not strong enough to shake myself out of this dream, which was mocking me with delusive hopes of happiness.

I came to regard Adelheid as a common go-between, but I also sensed that she was a sly troublemaker, manipulating me in order to salve the exhausted aspirations of her own youth. I knew I would come to despise her, and yet, upon second thoughts, I could not help being ashamed of my actions—my part, my folly. Had anything ever happened during those blissful evening hours to bring me closer to Seraphina other than was permissible by propriety and morality? How dare I nurture the thought that the Baroness would ever entertain any warm feeling for me? And yet I was convinced that my situation was dangerous, impending . . . and that made it even more alluring.

~§~

We broke up from dinner earlier than usual to chase after some wolves which had been seen in the fir-wood close by the castle. A little hunting was just the thing for me in my excited frame of mind. I expressed to my uncle my resolve to accompany the party; he gave me an approving smile and said, "Very good! I am glad you are going out with them for once. I shall stay at home, so you can take my rifle with you, and buckle my hunting-knife round your waist. It is a good and trusty weapon, if you only keep your presence of mind."

That part of the wood in which the wolves were supposed to prowl was surrounded by the huntsmen. It was bitterly cold; the wind howled through the firs, and drove the light snow-flakes right in my face and filled my eyelashes with ice-crystals. By dusk I could scarcely see six paces before me. Quite benumbed by the cold, I left the place that had been assigned to me and sought shelter deeper in the wood. There, leaning against a tree, with my rifle under my arm, I forgot the wolf-hunt entirely. My thoughts traveled back to Seraphina's cozy room.

After a time shots were heard in the distance; but at the same moment there was a rustling in the reed-bank, and I saw not ten paces from me a huge wolf emerge from cover and prepare to pounce. I took aim and fired, but shot high and wide. The brute sprang towards me with glaring eyes. I would have been lost had I not thought to draw my hunting-knife. Just as the brute was flying at me, I drove it deep into his throat, so that the blood spurted out over my hand and arm.

One of the Baron's keepers, who had stood not far from me, came running up with a loud shout, and at his repeated "Halloo!" all the rest soon gathered round us.

The Baron hastened up to me, saying, "For God's sake, you are bleeding—you are bleeding. Are you wounded?"

I assured him that I was not. Then he turned to the keeper, who had stood nearest to me, and harangued him for not having shot after me when I missed. And notwithstanding that the man maintained this to have been perfectly impossible, since in the very same moment the wolf had rushed upon me, and any shot would have been at the risk of hitting me, the Baron persisted in saying that he ought to have taken special care of me as a less experienced hunter. Meanwhile the keepers had lifted the dead animal up for all to admire. It was one of the largest that had been seen for a long time, and everybody admired my courage and resolve, although I felt what I had done to be quite natural. Had I thought for a moment of the danger I would have run like a rabbit. The Baron especially took great interest in the matter. He worried that although I was not physically wounded by the brute, I would suffer emotional after-effects from such a brutal attack.

As we went back to the castle, the Baron took me by the arm like a friend, and I had to give my rifle to a keeper to carry. He continued to talk about my heroic deed, so that eventually I came to believe in my own heroism, and lost all my constraint and embarrassment, and felt that I had established myself in the Baron's eyes as a man of courage and uncommon resolution. The schoolboy had passed his examination successfully, was now no longer a schoolboy, and all the submissive nervousness of the schoolboy had left him.

I was convinced that I had earned a right to woo Seraphina's favor. Everybody knows of course what ridiculous thoughts and fancies a love-sick youth is capable of. In the castle, over the misty punchbowl, by the fireside, I was the hero of the hour. Other than me, the Baron was the only one of the party who had killed a wolf—also a formidable one. The rest of the hunting party had to be content with ascribing their bad shots to the weather and the darkness, and with relating thrilling stories of their former exploits in hunting and the dangers they had escaped. I thought, too, that I might reap a special share of praise and admiration from my old uncle as well; and so, with a view to this end, I related to him my adventure at considerable length, nor did I forget to paint the savage brute's wild and bloodthirsty appearance in very startling colors.

The old gentleman, however, only laughed in my face and said, "God pities the weak."

~§~

Tired of drinking and bored of conversation, I was going quietly along the corridor towards the justice-hall when I saw a figure with a light slip in before me. On entering the hall I saw it was Lady Adelheid.

"This is the way we have to wander about like ghosts or sleep-walkers in order to catch you, my brave slayer of wolves," she whispered, taking my arm. The words "ghosts" and "sleep-walkers," fell like lead upon my heart; they immediately brought to my recollection the ghostly apparitions of those two awful nights. As then, the wind came howling in from the sea in deep organ-like cadences, rattling the bay windows again and again and whistling fearfully through them, whilst the moon cast her pale gleams exactly upon the mysterious part of the wall where the scratching had been heard. I fancied I discerned stains of blood upon it. Doubtless Lady Adelheid, who still had hold of my hand, must have felt the cold icy shiver which ran through me.

"What's the matter with you?" she whispered softly. "What's the matter with you? You are as cold as marble. Come, I will call you back into life. Do you know how very impatient the Baroness is to see you? And until she does see you she will not believe that the ugly wolf has not really bitten you. She is in a terrible state of anxiety about you. Why, my friend—oh! how have you awakened this interest in the little Seraphina? I have never seen her like this. Ah!—so now the pulse is beginning to prickle; see how quickly the dead man comes to life! Well, come along— but softly, still! Come, we must go to the little Baroness."

I allowed myself to be led away in silence. The way in which Adelheid spoke of the Baroness seemed to me undignified, and the innuendo of an understanding between us positively shameful. When I entered the room along with Adelheid, Seraphina, uttering a breathy "*Oh!*", advanced three or four paces quickly to meet me; but then, as if restraining herself, she stood still in the middle of the room. I ventured to take her hand and press it to my lips. Allowing it to rest in mine, she asked, "But, for Heaven's sake!—is it your business to meddle with wolves? Don't you know that the fabulous days of Orpheus and Amphion are long past, and that wild beasts have quite lost all respect for even the most admirable of singers?"

But this gleeful turn, by which the Baroness at once effectually guarded against all misinterpretation of her warm interest in me, I was put immediately into the proper key and the proper mood. Why I did not take my usual place at the pianoforte I cannot explain, even to myself, nor why I sat down beside the Baroness on the sofa. Her question, "And what were you doing then to get into danger?" was an indication of our tacit agreement that conversation, not music, was to engage our attention for that evening.

After I had narrated my adventure in the wood, and mentioned the warm interest which the Baron had taken in it, delicately hinting that I had not thought him capable of so much feeling.

The Baroness responded in a tender and almost melancholy tone: "Oh! how violent and rude you must think the Baron; but I assure you it is only whilst we are living within these gloomy, ghostly walls, and during the time there is hunting going on in the dismal fir-forests, that his character completely changes—at least his outward behavior does.

"What principally disquiets him—constantly haunts him—is that something terrible will happen here. And that undoubtedly accounts for the fact of his being so greatly upset by your adventure, which fortunately had a happy outcome. He would not endanger even the meanest of his servants, if he knows it—still less a new-won friend whom he has come to like. I am certain that Gottlieb, whom he blames for leaving you in the lurch, will be punished. Even if he escapes being locked up in a dungeon, he will suffer a punishment more mortifying to a hunter: to join the next hunt with only a club in his hand.

"The hunts here are rife with danger. Even though the Baron continually fears some tragic accident, he is so fond of hunting that he cannot resist provoking the demon of mischief. That demon is tied to the entail. Sometimes I think the hunts, taken on the harshest nights in the darkest woods, are a debt—nay, I say more a *penance* paid to the entail. Many queer stories are told about his ancestor who established the entail. There is some dark family secret locked within these walls like a horrible ghost which drives away the owners, and makes it impossible for them to bear it any longer than a few weeks at a time—and only when surrounded by a tumult of jovial guests.

"But, oh! how lonely I am in the midst of this noisy, merry company! And how the ghostly influences that breathe upon me from the walls stir and excite my heart! You, my dear friend, have given me, through your musical skill, the first cheerful moments I have spent here. How can I thank you sufficiently for your kindness!"

I kissed the hand she offered to me. Melting inside, I told all. I confessed that on the very first day—or rather the very first night, I experienced firsthand the ghostliness of the place. The Baroness fixed her staring eyes upon my face, as I went on to describe the ghostly character of the justice-hall. I gave her the barest of details but it was enough to greatly disturb her.

She cried vehemently, "Something dreadful has happened to you in that hall, which I never enter without shuddering. I beg you—pray, pray, tell me all you know."

Seraphina's face had grown deadly pale, and I saw plainly that it would be better to give her a faithful account of all that I had experienced than allow her excited imagination to run free and conjure up some apparition far more horrible than what I had actually encountered. As she listened to me her fear and anxiety mounted moment by moment. When I mentioned the scratching on the wall she screamed, "It's horrible! Yes, yes, it's in that wall that the awful secret is concealed!"

But as I went on to describe how my old uncle had banished the spirit, she sighed deeply, as though she had shaken off a heavy burden. She leaned back in the sofa and held her hands before her face. It was then that I first noticed that Adelheid had left us. A considerable pause ensued, and as Seraphina remained silent, I softly rose, strode to the pianoforte and endeavored in swelling chords to invoke the bright spirits of consolation. I wanted to deliver Seraphina from the dark influence that my narration had placed her. I began to sing softly. The melancholy strains of *Ochi, perchè piangete* (O eyes, why weep you?) roused Seraphina out of her dreams, and she listened to me with a gentle smile upon her face, and bright pearl-like tears in her eyes.

How am I to rationalize that I knelt down before her, that she bent towards me, that I threw my arms about her, that a long ardent kiss was placed on my lips? How can I say this without losing my senses? I tore myself from her arms, and, quickly rising to my feet, hurried back to the pianoforte. Turning from me, the Baroness took a few steps towards the window, then she turned round again and approached me with an air of proud dignity, which was not at all usual with her. Looking me straight in the face, she said, "Your uncle is the worthiest old man I know. He is the guardian-angel of our family. May he include me in his pious prayers!"

I was unable to utter a word. The subtle poison that I had imbibed with her kiss burned and boiled in my every pulse and nerve. Lady Adelheid then came into the room but her entry was not enough to suppress my roiling emotions. The violence of my inward conflict burst out in a passionate flood of tears, which I was embarrassingly unable to contain. Adelheid looked at me with wonder and then smiled ironically—I could have murdered her.

The Baroness gave me her hand, and said with inexpressible gentleness, "Farewell, my dear friend. Fare you right well; and remember that nobody perhaps has ever understood your music better than I have. Oh! these notes! they will echo long, long in my heart."

I forced myself to utter a few stupid, disconnected words, and hurried to my uncle's room. The old gentleman had already gone to bed and was snoring. I stayed in the hall, and falling upon my knees, I wept aloud. I called upon my beloved by name, I gave myself up completely and regardless to all the absurd folly of a love-sick lunatic, until at last the extravagant noise awoke my uncle.

His loud call disrupted my misery: "Cousin, I believe you have gone batty, or else you're having another tussle with a wolf. Be off to bed with you if you will be so very kind."

His words—so common, so innocent and affectionate—compelled me to enter his room, where I got into bed with the fixed resolve to dream only of Seraphina.

~§~

It would be somewhere past midnight when I thought I heard distant voices, a running backwards and forwards, and an opening and banging of doors—for I had not yet fallen asleep. I listened attentively; I heard footsteps approaching the corridor. The hall door was opened, and soon there came a knock at our door.

"Who is there?" I cried.

A voice from without answered, "Herr Justitiarius, Herr Justitiarius, wake up, wake up!"

I recognized Francis's voice and asked, "Is the castle on fire?"

The old gentleman, awake now, shouted, "Where—*where* is there a fire? Is it that cursed apparition again? Where is it?"

"Oh! please get up, Herr Justitiarius," said Francis, "Please get up. The Baron wants you."

"What does the Baron want me for?" inquired my uncle. "What does he want me for at this time of night? Does he not know that all law business goes to bed along with the lawyer, and sleeps as soundly as he does?"

"Oh!" cried Francis, now anxiously. "Please, Herr Justitiarius, good sir, please get up. My lady the Baroness is dying."

I started up with a cry of dismay.

"Open the door for Francis," said the old gentleman to me. I stumbled about the room almost distracted, and could find neither door nor lock; my uncle had to come and help me.

Francis came in, his face pale and troubled, and lit the candles. We had scarcely thrown on our clothes when we heard the Baron calling in the hall, "Can I speak to you, good V.?"

"But what have you dressed for, cousin?" asked the old gentleman on the point of going out. "The Baron only wanted me."

"I must go down—I must see her and then die," I replied tragically, and as if my heart were torn by hopeless grief.

"Ay, just so; right you are, cousin," he said and banged the door shut in my face. Then I heard him lock it from the outside. At first, deeply incensed by this restraint, I thought of bursting the door open with my shoulder, but I quickly reflected that this would appear to be an outrageous piece of insanity. I resolved to await the old gentleman's return; then however, let the cost be what it may, I would escape his watchfulness and investigate for myself. I heard him talking vehemently with the Baron, who several times distinctly said my name, but I could not discern anything further. Every moment my position grew more intolerable. I was outraged, panicked. At length I heard someone bring a message to the Baron, who immediately hurried off.

My old uncle entered the room again.

"She is dead!" I cried, running towards him.

"And you are a stupid fool," he interrupted coolly; then he laid hold upon me and forced me into a chair.

"I must go down," I cried, "I must go down and see her, even though it cost me my life."

"Do so, good cousin," said he, locking the door, taking out the key, and putting it in his pocket.

I now flew into a perfectly frantic rage. Stretching out my hand towards the rifle, I screamed, "If you don't instantly open the door I will send this bullet through my brains."

Then the old gentleman planted himself immediately in front of me, and fixing his keen piercing eyes upon me said, "Boy, do you think you can frighten me with your idle threats? Do you think I should set much value on your life if you can go and throw it away in childish folly like a broken plaything? What have you to do with the Baron's wife? Who has given you the right to insinuate yourself, like a tiresome puppy, where you have no claim to be, and where you are not wanted? Do you wish to go and act the love-sick suitor of a married woman above your station—at the solemn hour of her death? Can you tell me how that possibly makes any sense at all?"

I sank back in my chair utterly confounded. After a while the old gentleman went on more gently, "And now that we've cleared the air, let me tell you that this pretended illness of the Baroness is in all probability *nothing*. Lady Adelheid always loses her head at the least little thing. If a raindrop falls upon her nose, she screams, 'What fearful weather it is!' Unfortunately the noise stirred the old aunts, and they, in the midst of an unseasonable flood of tears already unleashed by Adelheid, put in an appearance armed with an entire arsenal of worsening wails, elixirs of life, and the deuce knows what else . . . A fainting-fit. That's all—"

The old gentleman checked himself. Doubtless he observed the struggle that was going on within me. He took a few turns through the room, then again planting himself in front of me, he had a good hearty laugh and said, "Cousin, cousin, what nonsensical folly have you now got in your head? Ah well! I suppose it can't be helped. The devil must play his pretty games in many ways. You have tumbled very nicely into his clutches, and now he's making you dance to a sweet tune."

He took a few turns up and down the carpet and went on: "It's no use thinking of sleep now, and it occurs to me that we might have a pipe and await the dawn."

With these words he took a clay pipe from the cupboard, and proceeded to fill it slowly and carefully, humming a song to himself; then he rummaged through a heap of papers, until he found a blank sheet, which he plucked out, rolled into a thin cone and lighted.

I know not how it was, but the calm, quiet behavior of the old gentleman operated strangely upon me. I seemed to be no longer in R—sitten, and the Baroness was so far, far distant from me that I could only reach her on the wings of thought. My tranquility was fleeting, however, for the old gentleman blasted the mood with one of his sardonic quips.

Blowing the tobacco-smoke from him in thick clouds, he said, speaking between his teeth, "Well, cousin, what was that story about the wolf?"

The question annoyed me.

"Do you find my hunting exploit so amusing?" I blurted. "You think it a joke?"

"By no means," he rejoined, his eyebrows raised like arching wings. "By no means, cousin mine. I only advise you to not get carried away by all the fuss you are receiving over that beast. Don't let it go to your head. It might give you the wrong idea about things. You were certainly out of your depth out there in the woods. You are a law clerk, not a hunter. Let me better make my point . . . I once had a college friend who was a quiet, sober fellow, and always on good terms with himself. By accident he became entangled in an affair of honor—I say by accident, because he himself was never in any way aggressive; and although most of the fellows looked upon him as a poor thing, as a coward, he yet showed so much firm and resolute courage in this affair as greatly to excite everybody's admiration. But from that time onwards he was completely changed. The sober and industrious youth became a bragging, insufferable bully. He was always drinking and rioting, and fighting about all sorts of childish trifles, until he was run through in a duel by the senior officer of an exclusive corps. I merely tell you the story, cousin; you are at liberty to think what you please about it . . . But to return to the Baroness and her illness—"

At this moment light footsteps were heard in the hall. I fancied, too, there was an unearthly moaning in the air. "She is dead!" the thought shot through me like a fatal flash of lightning.

The old gentleman quickly rose to his feet and called out, "Francis,

Francis!"

"Yes, my good Herr Justitiarius," he replied from without.

"Francis," went on my uncle, "rake the fire together a bit in the grate, and if you can manage it, you had better make us a good cup or two of tea. It is devilish cold," and then turning to me, "and I think we had better go and sit round the fire and talk a little."

He opened the door, and I followed him mechanically. "How are things going on below?" I asked.

"Oh!" replied Francis; "there was not much the matter. The Lady Baroness is all right again, and ascribes her bit of a fainting-fit to a bad dream."

I was going to break out into an extravagant manifestation of joy and gladness, but a stern glance from my uncle kept me quiet.

"On second thought," he said, "I think it would be better if we lay down for an hour or two. You need not mind about the tea, Francis."

"As you think well, Herr Justitiarius," replied Francis, and he left the room with the wish that we might have a good night's rest, albeit the cocks were already crowing.

"See here, cousin," said the old gentleman, knocking the ashes out of his pipe on the grate. "I think, cousin, that it's a very good thing no harm has come to you either from wolves or loaded rifles. I expect you to someday inherit all my beautiful papers, quills, wax seals, notary stamps, books of law, and best of all, my list of ever-needy clients who sometimes forget to pay. Until then, sleep well."

I acquiesced with a nod. I now saw things in the right light, and was ashamed of myself for giving the old gentleman good grounds for treating me like a spoiled child.

~§~

Next morning my uncle said to me, "Be so good as to step down, good cousin, and inquire how the Baroness is. You need only ask for Lady Adelheid; she will supply you with a full account, I have no doubt."

You may imagine how eagerly I hastened downstairs. But just as I was about to give a gentle knock at the door of the Baroness's anteroom, the Baron hurriedly came out of the same. He stood still in astonishment, and scrutinized me with a gloomy searching look.

"What do you want here?" burst from his lips.

Notwithstanding that my pounding heart, I controlled myself and replied in a firm tone, "To inquire on my uncle's behalf how my lady, the

Baroness, is?"

"Oh! it was nothing—one of her usual nervous attacks. She is now having a quiet sleep, and will, I am sure, make her appearance at the dinner-table quite well and cheerful. Tell him that—tell him that." This the Baron said with a certain degree of passionate vehemence, which seemed to me to imply that he was more concerned about the Baroness than he was willing to show.

I turned to go back to my uncle, when the Baron suddenly seized my arm and said, whilst his eyes flashed fire, "I have a word or two to say to you, young man."

Here I saw the deeply injured husband before me, and feared there would be a scene which would perhaps end ignominiously for me. I was unarmed; but at that moment I remembered I had in my pocket the ingeniously-made hunting-knife which my uncle had presented to me after we got to R—sitten. I now followed the Baron, who rapidly led the way. The situation agitated me beyond sensibility and restraint. I determined not to spare his life if I ran any risk of being treated dishonorably.

We entered the Baron's own room, the door of which he locked behind him. Now he began to pace restlessly back and forth, with his arms folded one over the other; then he stopped in front of me and repeated, "I have a word or two to say to you, young man."

I had wound myself up to a pitch of most daring courage, and I replied, raising my voice, "I hope they will be words I hear without resentment."

He stared hard at me in astonishment, as though he had failed to understand me. Then, fixing his eyes gloomily upon the floor, he threw his arms behind his back, and again began to stride up and down the room. He took down a rifle and put the ramrod down the barrel to see whether it were loaded or not. My blood boiled in my veins as I observed this obvious attempt at intimidation. Grasping my knife, I stepped close up to him, so as to make it impossible for him to take aim at me.

"That's a handsome weapon," he said, replacing the rifle in the corner. ". . . Sorry. I got distracted by it."

I withdrew a few paces, the Baron following me. Slapping me on the shoulder, perhaps a little more violently than was necessary, he said, "I daresay I seem to you, Theodore, to be excited and irritable; and I really am so, owing to the anxieties of a sleepless night. My wife's nervous attack was not in the least dangerous; that I now see plainly. But here— here in this castle, which is haunted by an evil spirit, I always dread something terrible happening . . . and then it's the first time she has been ill here. And you—you alone were to blame for it."

"How that can possibly be?" I replied calmly. "I don't understand."

"I wish," continued the Baron, "I wish that damned piece of mischief —the pianoforte, were chopped into a thousand pieces, and that you—but no, no; it was to be so, it was inevitably to be so, and I alone am to blame for all. I ought to have told you—the moment you began to play music in my wife's room—of my wife's unstable mind."

I was about to speak, but the Baron silenced me with a raised hand. "Let me go on," he said. "I must prevent your forming any rash judgment. You probably regard me as an uncultivated fellow, averse to the arts; but I am not so by any means. I *do* have a deep conviction that some music can powerfully affect a person's mind. My wife suffers from a morbid excitability, which will finally destroy all the happiness of her life."

He strolled in a semi-circle around me, his arm crooked like the blade of a windmill.

"Within these strange walls she is never free of that strained over-excited condition, which at times is fleeting, and at others is the forerunner of a serious illness. You will ask me, and quite reasonably too, why I do not spare my delicate wife the necessity of coming to live in this weird castle, and mix amongst the confusion of a hunting-party. Well, call it a selfish weakness. I cannot bear to leave her behind. I would worry too much. Additionally, I thought that this bracing environment would make her stronger. But by my soul the sea-breezes, the wild woods, the baying hounds, and hunting-horns cannot drown out the sickly sentiments of your damned *piano*. No man should play in that way. It's enough to make a blind angel cry. I shudder to recall it . . ."

He spun around to face me.

"I tell you, you are deliberately torturing my wife to death!"

He uttered these words with great emphasis, whilst his eyes flashed with a restless fire. The blood mounted to my head. I raised my fist at the Baron. I was about to speak—to shout, but he cut me short— "I know what you are going to say," he began. "I full well know what you are going to say, but I must repeat that you are going down the right road to kill my wife. But I cannot of course for a moment maintain that you intend this outcome. Yet you will understand that I must put a stop to it. Your playing and singing overexcites her, and then, just when she drifts about without anchor and rudder on the boundless sea of dreams which your music places her, like some vile charm, you plunge her down into the depths of horror with a tale about a fearful apparition which you say came and played pranks upon you in the justice-hall . . . Your great-uncle has told me everything. Everything!"

I was speechless. The Baron paused to catch his breath, and I could see for the first time that his emotions were boggled by some strong liqueur. "But, pray," he finally continued in a more subdued manner, "I must know for myself. Repeat to me all you saw, or did not see. Tell me what you heard, felt, or divined by instinct on that frightful night."

I braced myself up and narrated calmly how everything had happened from beginning to end, the Baron merely interposing at intervals a few words expressive of his astonishment. When I came to the part where my old uncle had met the ghost with trustful courage and had exorcised him with a few powerful words, the Baron clasped his hands, raised them folded towards Heaven, and said with deep emotion, "Yes, he is the guardian-angel of the family. His mortal remains shall rest in the vault of my ancestors."

When I finished my narration, the Baron murmured to himself, "Daniel, Daniel, what are you doing here at this hour?" as he folded his arms and strode up and down the room.

"And was that all you wanted me for, Herr Baron?" I asked, making a movement as though I would retire to my room. The past few minutes had been too much for me, and I needed a bracer of brandy.

Starting up as if out of a dream, the Baron took me kindly by the hand and said, "Yes, my good friend, but linger one moment more. My wife, whose soul you have beguiled without meaning to—you must play for her again. I see now that your music can also be a *cure*—a tincture that poisons the evil embodiments. You alone can cure her."

I felt myself blushing, and had I stood opposite a mirror should undoubtedly have seen in it a very drawn and absurd face. The Baron seemed to exult in my embarrassment; he kept his eyes fixed intently upon my face, smiling with perfectly galling irony.

"How in the world can I cure her?" I managed to stammer out at length with an effort.

"Well," he said, pouncing on my shaken confidence, "you have no dangerous patient to deal with at any rate. There is no gentler soul than Seraphina. I now make an express claim upon your skill to save her. Since the Baroness has been drawn into the enchanted circle of your music, it would be both foolish and cruel to drag her out of it all of a sudden. *Go on* with your music, therefore. You will always be welcome during the evening hours in my wife's apartments. But here is the plan for recovery: gradually select a more energetic kind of music, and effect a clever alternation of the cheerful sort with the serious; and above all things, repeat your story of the fearful ghost very, very often. Make light of it if you will. The Baroness will grow familiar with it; she will forget that a ghost haunts this castle, and the story will have no stronger effect upon her than any other tale of enchantment which is put before her in a romance or a ghost-story book. Pray, do this, my good friend."

With these words the Baron left me. I went away as well. I felt annihilated—to be thus humiliated like a foolish and insignificant child. Fool that I thought jealousy stirred his heart! He himself sends me to Seraphina; he sees me only as a blind instrument to be used and then tossed aside. A few minutes previously I had really feared the Baron. Deep within my heart lurked the pang of guilt and I expected retaliation, but that guilt—unwanted yet deserved—mingled with a yearning for a higher life and a grander station that was decidedly not deserved yet passionately wanted. Now all had disappeared in the blackness of night, and I saw only the stupid boy who in childish obstinacy had persisted in taking the paper crown, mistaking it for a golden one.

~§~

I hurried away to my uncle, who was waiting for me.

"Well, cousin, why have you been so long? Where have you been staying?" he cried as soon as he saw me.

"I have been having some words with the Baron!" I quickly replied, carelessly and in a low voice, without being able to look at the old gentleman.

"God damn it all," said he, feigning astonishment. "Good gracious, boy! That's just what I thought. I suppose the Baron has challenged your honor, cousin?"

The ringing peal of laughter which the old gentleman immediately afterwards broke out into taught me that this time too, as always, he had seen me through and through. I bit my lip, and dare not speak a word, for I knew it would only encourage the old gentleman to barrage me with a torrent of teasing.

~§~

Sometime later the Baroness appeared at the dinner-table in an elegant morning-robe, the dazzling whiteness of which exceeded that of fresh-fallen snow. She looked worn and low-spirited, but she began to speak in her soft and melodious accents. On raising her dark eyes there shone a sweet yearning in their voluptuous glow, and a fugitive blush flitted across her porcelain cheeks. She was more beautiful than ever . . . But who can fathom the follies of a young man who has got a cauldron of hot blood in his head and heart? I felt bitterness and loss; my nerves grated one atop another. The entire business seemed a foul mystification so misunderstood that it could never be unraveled. I had to bring order, to act rational. I was now determined to show that I possessed acute common-sense and extraordinary sagacity. I was having difficulty lidding the boiling pot, however, so I sought a cagy self-banishment. Like a petu-

lant child, I shunned the Baroness and escaped Adelheid when she pursued me. I found a place where I could hide, at the very end of the table between the two officers, with whom I began to carouse with merrily. We kept our glasses going gaily during dessert, and I was, as is so frequently the case in moods like mine, extremely noisy and loud in my joviality.

A servant brought me a plate with some bonbons on it and announced that they were from Lady Adelheid. I certainly wasn't in in the mood for sweets, but when I looked closer at the plate I was astounded to spy the words *"and Seraphina"* scratched into one of the chocolates. It must have been done with a brooch pin. I popped this one in my mouth to hide the evidence.

My blood coursed tumultuously in my veins. I sent a glance in Adelheid's direction, which she met with a most sly and archly cunning look; and taking her glass in her hand, she gave me a slight nod. Almost mechanically I murmured to myself, "Seraphina!" then taking up my glass in my turn, I drained it at a single draught. My glance fell in her direction. I perceived that she also had drunk at the very same moment and was setting down her glass. Our eyes met, and a malignant demon whispered in my ear, "Unhappy wretch, she does love you!"

One of the guests now rose, and, in conformity with the custom of the North, proposed the health of the lady of the house. Our glasses rang in the midst of tumultuous joy. My heart was torn with rapture and despair. The wine burned like fire within me. Everything spun round in circles. I felt as if I must hasten to her, throw myself at her feet, and there sigh out my life.

"What's the matter with you, my friend?" asked my neighbor, rousing me from my self-absorption. When I looked about, Seraphina had left the hall. We rose from the table. As I was making for the door Adelheid held me fast, and she began to ramble on about many different matters. I neither heard nor understood a single word. She grasped both my hands and, laughing, shouted something in my ear. I remained dumb and motionless, as though affected by catalepsy. All I remember is that I finally took a glass of liqueur out of Adelheid's hand in a mechanical way and drank it off, and then I recollect being alone, slumping in a window bench, and after that I rushed out of the hall, down the stairs, and ran out into the woods like some kind of steaming beast.

The snow was falling in thick flakes. The fir-trees were moaning as they waved to and fro in the wind. Like a maniac I ran round and round in wide circles, laughing and screaming loudly, "Look, look and see. Aha! Aha! The devil is having a fine dance with the boy who thought he would taste the forbidden fruit!"

Who can tell what would have been the end of my mad prank if I had not heard my name called loudly from the outside of the wood? The storm had abated; the moon shone out brightly through the broken clouds; I heard dogs barking, and perceived a dark figure approaching me. It was the old man Francis. I have no idea how he found me.

"Why, why, my good Herr Theodore," he began, "you have quite lost your way in the rough snow-storm. The Herr Justitiarius is awaiting you with much impatience."

I followed the old man in silence. I found my great-uncle working in the justice-hall. "You have done well," he cried, on seeing me, "you have done a very wise thing to go out in the open air a little and chill that hot head of yours. Don't drink quite so much wine next time. You are far too young, and it's not good for you."

I did not utter a word in reply. I merely took my place at the table in silence.

"But now tell me, good cousin, what it was the Baron really wanted you for?" I told him all, and concluded by stating that I would not lend myself for the doubtful cure which the Baron had proposed. "And it would not be practicable," the old gentleman interrupted, "for tomorrow morning early we set off for home, cousin."

And so it was that I never saw Seraphina again.

~§~

As soon as we arrived in K—— my old uncle complained that he felt the effects of the wearying journey this time more than ever. His moody silence, broken only by violent outbreaks of the worst possible ill-humor, announced the return of his crippling gout.

One day I was suddenly called in. I found the old gentleman confined to his bed and unable to speak, suffering from a paralytic stroke. He held a letter in his hand, which he had crumpled up tightly in a spasmodic fit. I recognized the handwriting of the land-steward of R— sitten. Upset by my uncle's condition, I did not venture to take the letter out of the old gentleman's hand. I did not doubt that his end was near. But his pulse began to beat again, even before the physician arrived; the old gentleman's remarkably tough constitution resisted the mortal attack, although he was in his seventieth year. That self-same day the doctor pronounced him out of danger.

We had a more severe winter than usual. This was followed by a rough and stormy spring, which caused uncle's gout to intensify—a consequence of the inclement season. The pain kept him confined to his bed. During this period he made up his mind to retire from business. He transferred his responsibilities of Justitiarius to others, and so I was cut off from all hope of ever again going to R—sitten. The old gentleman would allow no one to attend him but me, and it was to me alone that he looked to for all amusement and every cheerful diversion. In the hours when he was free from pain, his good spirits returned and he had no lack of jests. He even made mention of past hunting exploits, and so I fully expected him to come round to me and make a butt of my heroic deed when I had killed the wolf with my knife, yet never once did he allude to our visit to R—sitten. As may well be imagined, I was very careful, from natural shyness, not to lead him directly to the subject. My persistent anxiety and continual attendance of the old gentleman had thrust Seraphina's image into the background. But as soon as his sickness abated somewhat, my thoughts returned with more liveliness to that moment in the Baroness's room, which I now looked upon as a star—a bright star—that had set, for me at least, forever.

There came an occurrence that revived all the pain I had formerly felt. One evening, as I was opening the pocket-book which I had carried whilst at R—sitten, there fell out of the papers I was unfolding a dark curl, wrapped about with a white ribbon. I immediately recognized it as Seraphina's hair. But, on examining the ribbon more closely, I distinctly perceived the mark of a spot of blood on it! Perhaps, in the final days of our visit to R—sitten, during one of my moments of passionate insanity, Adelheid had skillfully contrived to hide it among my things. But why was the spot of blood there? It engendered something terrible in my mind, transforming this pastoral love-token into an awful warning—a warning pointing to a passion which might lead to a loss of precious blood. It was the same white ribbon that had fluttered in my face the first time I sat near Seraphina, when the Mysterious Night had forever stamped upon my soul the emblem of mortal injury.

An inner voice sounding very much like my uncle whispered: *boys must not play with powers they do not understand.*

~§~

At last the storms of spring had ceased to bluster, and summer asserted her rights; and if the cold had formerly been unbearable, so now too was the heat when July came in. The old gentleman visibly gathered strength, and following his usual custom, went out to a garden in the suburbs. One still, warm evening, as we sat in the sweet-smelling jasmine arbor, he was in unusually good spirits, and not, as was generally the case, overflowing with sarcasm and irony, but in a gentle and almost soft and melting mood.

"Cousin," he began, "I don't know why it is, but I feel so nice and warm and comfortable all over today. I have not felt like it for many years. I believe it is a sign that I shall die soon."

I exerted myself to drive these gloomy thoughts from his mind.

"Never mind, cousin," he said. "I won't let you spoil my good mood with your worrying. In any case I'm not long for this world, and so I will now discharge a debt I owe you. Do you still remember our autumn in R—sitten?"

This question thrilled through me like a lightning-flash, so before I was able to make any reply he continued . . .

"It was Heaven's will that your time in that castle should be crystalized by memorable circumstances, and that you should become involved against your own will in the deepest secrets of the house. The time has now come when you must learn all. We have often talked about things which you, cousin, rather dimly guessed at than really understood. The time has come to hear an old man's wisdom.

"In the changing of the seasons nature represents, symbolically, the cycle of human life. That is a trite remark, but I interpret it differently from everybody else. The dews of spring dissipate, summer's mists fade away, and it is the pure atmosphere of autumn which clearly reveals the distant landscape, and then finally earthly existence is swallowed in the long night of winter. The governance of the Inscrutable Power is more plainly revealed in the clear-sightedness of old age. We are granted glimpses of the promised land, but the final pilgrimage must begin with a death on earth. At this moment I clearly see the dark destiny of that house—an ancient place I am knitted to by firmer ties than any blood relationship can weave! Everything lies revealed to the eyes of my spirit. And yet I cannot tell you in words the things which I now see, for no man's mind could interpret such a place. R—sitten exists beyond the normal sphere of man.

"But listen, my son, I do not mean to be so cryptic. I will tell you as well as I am able. Now that the danger has passed for you I can tell you. Be assured that the powers that created an irresistible cascade in your heart have passed. The mysterious relations into which you ventured to enter, not perhaps without being summoned, might have ended in your destruction—but—that's all over now. Hear me . . ."

~§~

The history of the entail, which my old uncle told me on that summer's day, is so faithfully retained in my memory that I can even now repeat it in his own words. For the next hour he spoke of himself in the third person, as if he was talking about somebody else. It was a strange way to describe his experiences at R—sitten, but perhaps he wanted to distant himself from all that had happened. Perhaps he wanted to ensure that all powers behind the memories remained in the past.

II.

ONE stormy night in the autumn of 1760 the servants of R—sitten were startled out of the midst of their sleep by a terrific crash, as if the whole of the spacious castle had tumbled into a thousand pieces. In a moment everybody was out of bed and lights were lit. The house-steward, his face deadly pale with fright and terror, came up panting with his keys. They proceeded through the passages, halls and rooms—suite after suite—and found all safe. All that was heard in the appalling silence was the creaking rattle of the locks, which were difficult to open, and the ghost-like echo of their own footsteps. They looked at one another, utterly astounded. Nowhere was there the least trace of damage.

The old house-steward was overwhelmed by an ominous feeling of apprehension. He climbed the stairs into the great Knight's Hall, which had a small adjoining room where Freiherr Roderick von R— used to sleep while engaged in making his astronomical observations. Between the door of this room and that of a second was a side entrance—a postern —leading through a narrow passage immediately into the astronomical tower. As Daniel (that was the house-steward's name) opened this postern the storm, blustering and howling terrifically, drove a heap of rubbish and broken pieces of stones all over him. He recoiled in terror and dropped the candles, which went out with a hiss on the floor.

"O God! O God!" he screamed. "The Baron! He must be miserably dashed to pieces!"

At the same moment Daniel heard sounds of lamentation wailing from the Freiherr's sleeping-chamber, and on entering it he saw the servants gathered around their master's corpse. They had brought him up from the rubble and made him as presentable as possible. His dusty hair and lacerated face contrasted sharply with the finery he wore. The Baron was dressed in his best ceremonial custom—something normally reserved for only the most esteemed occasions. It was as if he had expected to greet and bow before a king. His unflinching, determined expression appeared calm and earnest. He sat upright in his spacious, richly decorated arm-chair as though resting after a session of exhaustive study.

But his rest was the rest of the dead.

~§~

When day dawned it was seen that the crowning turret of the tower had collapsed. The huge square stones had broken through the ceiling and floor of the observatory-room, and then, carrying down in front of them a powerful beam that ran across the tower. The tumbling stones dragged down a portion of the castle walls and crushed a portion of the narrow connecting-passage. Not a single step could be taken beyond the postern threshold without risk of falling at least eighty feet into a deep chasm.

The old Freiherr, capable astrologer that he was, had foreseen the very hour of his death and had sent word of it to his sons days before his fatal accident. And so it happened that the very next day saw the arrival of Wolfgang, Freiherr von R——, eldest son of the deceased, and now suddenly lord of the entail. Relying confidently upon the probable truth of the old man's foreboding, he had left Vienna immediately after he received the ominous letter, and hastened to R—sitten as fast as he could travel. The house-steward had draped the great hall in black, and laid the old Freiherr on a magnificent state-bed in the clothes in which he had been found. He surrounded the temporary resting place with tall silver candlesticks with burning wax-candles. Quiet shadows sadly flickered on the walls.

Wolfgang ascended the stairs, entered the hall, and approached his father's corpse without speaking a word. There he stood with his arms folded on his chest, gazing gloomily into his father's pale face. He was like a statue; not a tear came to his eyes. At length, with an almost convulsive movement of the right arm towards the corpse, he murmured hoarsely, "Did the stars compel you to make the son whom you loved miserable?"

Throwing his hands behind his back and stepping a short pace backwards, the Baron raised his eyes upwards and said in a low and broken voice, "Poor, infatuated old man! Your carnival farce with its shallow delusions is now over. Now you no doubt see that the possessions which are so stingily dealt out to us here on earth have nothing in common with the Hereafter beyond the stars. What will—what *power*—

can reach from beyond the grave?" The Baron was silent again for some seconds, then he cried passionately, "No, your perversity shall not rob me of a single grain of my earthly happiness, which you strove so hard to destroy!"

He took a folded paper out of his pocket and held it up to one of the burning candles that stood close beside the corpse. The paper was caught by the flame. As the reflection flickered and played upon the corpse's face, it looked as if its muscles moved—as though the old man uttered toneless words. The illusion was so realistic that the servants who stood some distance off were filled with great horror. Ignoring the sudden restless rustling behind him, the Baron calmly finished what he was doing by carefully stamping out the last fragment of paper that fell still ablaze on the floor. Then, casting yet another moody glance upon his father's corpse, he hurriedly left the hall.

~§~

On the following day Daniel reported to the Freiherr the damage that had been done to the tower, and described at great length all that had taken place on the night when their dear dead master died. He concluded by saying that it would be wise to have the tower repaired at once, for, if a further fall were to take place, there would be some danger of the entire castle collapsing.

"Repair the tower?" the Freiherr interrupted the old servant curtly, whilst his eyes flashed with anger, "Repair the tower? Never, never! Don't you see, old man," he went on more calmly, "don't you see that the tower could not fall in this way without some special cause? What if it was my father's own wish that the place where he carried out his unholy astrological experiments should be destroyed? What if he personally made certain preparations that enabled him to bring down the turret whenever he pleased—to destroy the tower at will? Gunpowder charges prepositioned at the supporting beams? Oh, don't look at me like that—"

The Baron paused to gather his thoughts.

". . . Regarding your proposal to make repairs, let me say this: I shan't care if the whole castle tumbles down. I shan't care! I shall be glad, in fact. Do you imagine that I am going to dwell in this weird owls' nest? No! My wise ancestor, who had the foundations of a new castle laid in the beautiful valley yonder, had begun a work which I intend to finish."

Daniel, now crestfallen, said, "Then will all your faithful old servants have to take up their bundles and go?"

"That I am not going to be waited upon by helpless, weak-kneed old fellows like you is quite certain; but for all that I shall turn none away. You may all enjoy the bread of charity without working for it."

"And am I," cried the old man, greatly hurt, "am I, the house-steward, to be forced to lead such a worthless life?"

Then the Freiherr, who had turned his back upon the old man and was about to leave the room, wheeled suddenly round, his face perfectly ablaze with passion, strode up to the old man as he stretched out his doubled fist towards him, and shouted in a thundering voice, "You, you hypocritical old villain! It's you who helped my old father in his unearthly practices up in his—his—*star chamber*. You lay upon his heart like a vampire; and perhaps it was *you* who basely took advantage of the old man's mad folly—to plant in his mind those diabolical ideas which brought me to the brink of ruin. I ought, I tell you, to kick you out like a mangy cur."

The old man was so terrified at these harsh words that he threw himself upon his knees beside the Freiherr; but the Baron, as he spoke these last words, threw forward his right foot, perhaps quite unintention-ally (as is frequently the case in anger, when the body mechanically obeys the mind,) and hit the old man so hard on the chest that he rolled over with a stifled scream. Rising painfully to his feet and uttering the cry of a mortally wounded animal, Daniel glared at the Freiherr with a fierce expression that mingled rage and despair. The Freiherr threw down a purse of money as he went out of the room, but the old man left it on the floor untouched.

~§~

Meanwhile all the nearest relatives of the family who lived in the neighborhood had arrived, and the old Freiherr was interred with much pomp within the family vault in the R—sitten chapel.

After the invited guests had departed, the new lord of the entail appeared to shake off his gloomy mood, and to be fully prepared to enjoy his inherited property. Along with V., the old Freiherr's Justitiarius who had already earned his full confidence, the Baron made an exact calculation of his sources of income. Working together they determined how much could be devoted to making improvements, and how much could be devoted to building of the new manor near the village.

V. was of opinion that the old Freiherr could not possibly have spent all his income every year. There must certainly be money concealed somewhere, since he had found nothing amongst his papers except one or two banknotes for insignificant sums, and the cash in the iron safe was but very little more than a thousand thalers. Who other than Daniel could explain the discrepancy? An obstinate self-willed old man, Daniel was probably only waiting to be asked about it. The Baron was greatly troubled by the thought that Daniel, whom he had so grossly insulted, might let large sums molder somewhere rather than reveal any secrets. His reticence could not possibly be motivated by self-interest, for of what use could even the largest sum of money be to him—a childless old man, whose only wish was to end his days in the castle of R—sitten?

Before they carried the discussion any further, the Baron thought it best to explain his troubled relationship with Daniel. He feared Daniel may be nurturing a desire to take vengeance and had a reason to not cooperate. He gave V. a circumstantial account of the entire scene with Daniel, and concluded by saying that that he had strong evidence that it was Daniel *alone* who had infected the old Freiherr's mind with the inexplicable aversion to seeing his sons living in R—sitten.

The Justitiarius declared that this information was perfectly false, since there was not a human creature on the face of the earth who would have been able to twist the Freiherr's thoughts in any way, let alone determine them for him. The Justitiarius then assured the Baron that he would deal with Daniel.

Good to his word, he undertook finally to draw the secret of the hidden treasure from Daniel. His task proved far easier than he had anticipated. He pulled the old steward aside and said, "How is it, Daniel, that your old master has left so little funds in the coffers?"

Daniel replied, with a repulsive smile, "Do you mean the few trifling thalers, Herr Justitiarius, which you found in the little strong box? Oh! Yes. The rest is lying in the vault beside our gracious master's sleeping-chamber. But the best," he went on to say, whilst his smile passed over into an abominable grin, and his eyes flashed with malicious fire, "but the best of all—several thousand gold pieces—lies buried at the bottom of the chasm beneath the ruins."

The Justitiarius at once summoned the Freiherr. All three proceeded to the observatory and entered the sleeping-chamber, where Daniel pushed aside the wainscot in one of the corners. A small lock was revealed. Whilst the Freiherr was regarding the polished lock with covetous eyes, and making preparations to try and unlock it with the great bunch keys he dragged with some difficulty out of his pocket, Daniel drew himself up to his full height, and looked down with almost malignant pride upon his master, who had now stooped down in order to see the lock better.

Daniel's face was deadly pale, and he said, his voice trembling, "If I am a dog, my lord Freiherr, I have also at least a dog's fidelity." Therewith he held out a bright steel key to his master, who greedily snatched it out of his hand. He easily succeeded in opening the door. They stepped into a small and low-vaulted apartment, in which stood a large iron coffer with the lid open, containing many money-bags, upon which lay a strip of parchment, written in the old Freiherr's familiar handwriting, large and old-fashioned.

> Here find one hundred and fifty thousand Imperial thalers in old Frederichsdor, saved from the revenues of the estate and intended for upkeep of the castle. Further, the lord of the entail who succeeds me in the possession of this money shall, upon the highest hill situated eastward from the old tower of the castle (which he will find in ruins), erect a lighthouse for the benefit of mariners. It is my wish that a fire be kindled within it every night.

> R—sitten, on Michaelmas Eve of the year 1760.

> Roderick, Freiherr von R.

The Freiherr lifted up the bags one after the other and let them fall again into the coffer, delighted at the ringing clink of so much gold coin. Then he turned round abruptly to the old house-steward, thanked him for the loyalty he had shown, and assured him that it was vile and slanderous rumors which had induced him to treat him so harshly. He should not only remain in the castle, but should also continue to discharge his duties without hindrance as house-steward, and at double the wages he was currently earning.

"I owe you a large compensation. If you will take the money, help yourself to one of these bags." As he concluded with these words, the Baron stood before the old man, with his eyes bent upon the ground, and pointed to the coffer; then, approaching it again, he once more ran his eyes over the bags. A burning flush suddenly mounted into the old house-steward's cheeks, and he uttered that awful howling whimper again—a noise as of an animal wounded to death, just as had been described to the Justitiarius by the Baron. The Justitiarius shuddered, for the words which the old man murmured between his teeth sounded like, "*Blood for gold.*" Absorbed in the contemplation of the treasure before him, the Freiherr had not heard the bitter words.

Daniel tottered in every limb, as if shaken by an malarial fit. Approaching the Freiherr with bowed head in a humble attitude, he kissed his hand, and drawing his handkerchief across his eyes under the pretense of wiping away his tears, said in a whining voice, "Alas! my good

and gracious master, what am I, a poor childless old man, to do with money? But the doubled wages I accept with gladness, and will continue to do my duty faithfully and zealously."

The Freiherr, who had paid no particular heed to the old man's words, now let the heavy lid of the coffer fall to with a bang, so that the whole room shook, and then, locking the coffer and carefully withdrawing the key, he said carelessly, "Very well, very well, old man." But after they entered the hall he went on talking to Daniel, "But you said something about a quantity of gold pieces buried underneath the ruins of the tower?"

Silently the old man stepped towards the postern, and after some difficulty unlocked it. But so soon as he threw it open the storm drove a thick mass of snowflakes into the hall. A raven was disturbed and flew in croaking and screaming and dashed with its black wings against the window, but regaining the open postern it disappeared downwards into the chasm. The Freiherr stepped out into the corridor, but one single glance downwards, and he started back trembling.

"A fearful sight!—I'm giddy!" he stammered as he sank almost fainting into the Justitiarius' arms. But quickly recovering himself with some effort, he fixed a sharp look upon the old man and asked, "Down there, you say?"

Meanwhile the old man had been locking the postern, and was now leaning against it with all his bodily strength, and was gasping and grunting to get the great key out of the rusty lock. This at last accomplished, he turned round to the Baron, and, changing the huge key about backwards and forwards in his hands, replied with a peculiar smile, "Yes, there are thousands and thousands down there—all my dear dead master's beautiful instruments—telescopes, quadrants, globes, dark mirrors, they all lie smashed to atoms underneath the ruins, between the stones and the big beams."

"But money—the coined money," interrupted the Baron, "you spoke of gold pieces, old man?"

"I only meant things which had cost several thousand gold pieces," he replied; and not another word could be squeezed from him.

The Baron appeared highly delighted to have all at once come into possession of all the means needed to carry out his favorite plan—namely, that of building a new and magnificent manor. The Justitiarius asserted his views at this point. He stated that in his opinion, according to the will of the deceased, the money could only be applied to the repair and finishing of the interior of the old castle. And furthermore, any new construction would hardly equal the commanding size and simple character of the old ancestral castle. The Freiherr, however, persisted in his intention and maintained that the deceased cannot overrule the living. At the same time he assured V. that he understood it to be his sacred duty to improve R—sitten . . . that is, as far as the climate, soil, and environs would permit, for it was his intention to soon bring home his dearly loved wife—a lady who was in every respect worthy of the greatest sacrifices.

This gave the Justitiarius pause for thought. It was the first time that he had heard about the Baron's wife. The air of mystery with which the Freiherr spoke of his marriage, which possibly had been already consummated in secret, cut short all further questions from the Justitiarius. Nevertheless he found in it to some extent a redeeming feature, for the Freiherr's eager grasping after riches now appeared to be due not so much to avarice strictly speaking as to the desire to make one dear to him forget the more beautiful country she was relinquishing for his sake.

Otherwise he could not acquit the Baron of being avaricious, or at any rate insufferably close-fisted. He was witness to some evidence of greed.

Even though rolling in money, the Baron could not help bursting out with the peevish grumble, "I know the old rascal has concealed from us the greatest part of his wealth, but next spring I will have the ruins of the tower turned over under my own eyes."

~§~

The Freiherr had architects come, and discussed with them at great length what would be the most expeditious way to proceed with his castle-building. He rejected one drawing after another; in none of them was the style of architecture sufficiently rich and grandiose. He now began to draw plans himself, and, spirited by this employment, which constantly placed before his eyes a sunny picture of the happiest future, brought himself into such a genial humor that it often bordered on wild exuberance—an exuberance heartily felt by all those about him. His generosity and profuse hospitality belied all imputations of avarice at any rate.

Daniel also seemed to have now forgotten the insult that had been put upon him. To the Freiherr, whose mistrustful eyes often followed him about on account of the treasure buried in the chasm, he presented a bearing that was both quiet and humble. But what struck everybody as extraordinary was that the old man appeared to grow younger from day to day. Possibly this might be because he had begun to forget his grief for his old master, which had stricken him severely, and possibly also because he had not now, as he once had, been forced to spend the cold nights in the tower mapping the stars without sleep. He also got better food and good wine such as he liked. But whatever the cause might be, the old greybeard seemed to be growing into a vigorous man with red cheeks and well-nourished body, who could walk firmly and laugh loudly whenever he heard a jest to laugh at.

~§~

The pleasant tenor of life at R—sitten was disturbed by the arrival of a man who seemed quite at home there. This was Wolfgang's younger brother Hubert.

When Wolfgang laid eyes on Hubert he screamed out—his face as pale as a corpse's: "Unhappy wretch, what do you want here?"

Hubert threw himself happily into his brother's arms, but Wolfgang, fuming, led him away up to a disused room in a quiet wing, where he locked himself in with him. They remained closeted several hours, at the end of which time Hubert came down, greatly agitated, and called for his horses.

The Justitiarius intercepted him on the way out. Hubert tried to pass him, but V., intent to snip in the bud what appeared to be the start of a bitter life-long quarrel between the brothers, beseeched him to stay—at least a few hours.

At the same moment the Freiherr came down the sweeping staircase calling, "Stay here, Hubert! you will think better of it."

Hubert's expression brightened. He assumed an air of composure, and quickly pulling off his costly fur coat, and throwing it to a servant behind him, he grasped V.'s hand and went with him into the room, saying with a scornful smile, "So the lord of the entail will tolerate my presence here after all, it seems."

V. thought that the unfortunate misunderstanding would assuredly be smoothed away now. Hubert took up the steel tongs which stood near the fire-grate. As he proceeded to rake the fire and break up a knotty piece of wood that would only smolder, he said to V., "You see what a good-natured fellow I am, Herr Justitiarius, and that I am skillful in all domestic matters. But Wolfgang is full of the most extraordinary prejudices, and also . . . a bit of a miser."

V. did not deem it advisable to attempt to explore further the relations between the brothers, especially since Wolfgang's face, conduct and voice plainly showed that he was shaken to the very depths of his nature by a wild mix of violent passions.

Late in the evening V. took the opportunity to visit Freiherr's room to hear his decision about a routine matter connected with the terms of the inheritance—the estate-tail. He found the Baron pacing up and down the room with long strides, his arms crossed on his back, and his demeanor seeped in anger.

On seeing the Justitiarius he stood still, and then, taking him by both hands and looking him gloomily in the face, he said in a broken voice, "My brother has come. I know what you are going to say," he proceeded almost before V. had opened his mouth to pose a question. "Unfortunately you know nothing about him. You don't know that my unfortunate brother—yes, I will not call him anything worse than *unfortunate*—that, like a spirit of evil, he crosses my path everywhere, destroying my peace of mind, disrupting my life. It is not his fault that I have not been made permanently miserable, for he has done his best to make me so . . . but Heaven willed it otherwise. I have avoided his craft of misery. Ever since he has known of the conversion of the property into an entail, fixing the properties to me alone, he has persecuted me with deadly hatred. He envies me this property, which in his hands would only be scattered like chaff. He is the wildest spendthrift I ever heard of. His load of debt exceeds by a long way the half of the *un*entailed property in Courland that fell to him, and now, relentlessly pursued by his creditors, he hurries here to me to beg for money. That is who he is. That is why he is here."

"And you, his brother, refuse to give him any share of the fortune?" V. said.

The Freiherr, letting V.'s hands fall, and taking a long step backwards, went on in a loud and vehement tone.

"Of course I refused! I neither can nor *will* give away a single thaler of the revenues of the entail. Listen, and I will explain the proposal that I made the insane fellow a few hours ago—a proposal made in vain. Hear my terms and then pass judgment upon my intentions . . .

"Our unentailed possessions in Courland are, as you are aware, considerable. I am willing to renounce the half that falls to me. I yield that much because Hubert has married a beautiful but impoverished lady in Courland. She and the children she has borne him are starving. The estates should be put under trust. Sufficient sums should be set aside out of the revenues to support him and his new family. His creditors can be convinced to be repaid by arrangement of a regular schedule. But what does he care for a quiet life—a life free of anxiety? What does he care for his wife and child? Money, ready-money, and large quantities, is what he will have, that he may squander it in infamous folly. Some demon has made him aware of the secret of the hundred and fifty thousand thalers, half of which he in his mad way demands, maintaining that this money is transferable property and quite apart from the entailed portion. This, however, I must and will refuse him, but the feeling haunts me that he is plotting my destruction in his heart."

No matter how much V. tried to persuade the Freiherr not to question his brother's motives, he could not break down that wall of suspicion. Since the Justitiarius was not acquainted with the more circumstantial details of the disagreement, he could only appeal to the Baron on broad and somewhat superficial moral principles. His efforts to keep the family peace could not compete against a lifetime of bad blood. In fact, the Freiherr, who was quite certain of the situation, ordered V. to stop his pleas for peace and deal directly with his hostile and avaricious brother. V. would negotiate terms since the Baron had failed to achieve the results he sought.

V. proceeded to do so with all the circumspection he could muster. He was surprised and was gratified when Hubert later declared, "Be it so then! I will accept my brother's proposals, but upon condition that he will now, since I am on the point of losing both my honor and my good name due to my severe creditors, make me an advance of a thousand Fredericks d'or in hard cash, and further grant that I may, from time to time, take up my residence in our beautiful R—sitten. Hunting season is the preferred time, of course."

~§~

"Never, never!" exclaimed the Freiherr violently, when V. laid his brother's amended counter-proposals before him. "I will never consent that Hubert stay in my house even a single minute after I have brought my wife home. Go, my good friend, tell this bad-egg of a brother that he shall have two thousand Fredericks d'or, not as an advance, but as a gift— only, bid him go, bid him go now!"

The Baron's words swirled in V.'s brain and he had the sudden revelation that everything centered on the Baron's wife. Had he married without his departed father's knowledge or consent? Was he afraid that Hubert would attempt to leverage this sensitive fact to his own advantage? As go-between for two warring brothers, he was on tenuous ground—especially since he did not have all the facts.

V. returned to Hubert's room and continued negotiations without mentioning Wolfgang's wife. Hubert listened to the Justitiarius proudly and calmly, and when he finished speaking replied in a hoarse and hollow tone, "I will think it over; but for the present I shall stay a few days in the castle."

V. made another attempt to convince the discontented Hubert that the Freiherr, by turning over his share of their unentailed property, was really doing all he possibly could do to be fair—that on the whole he had no room for complaint against his brother. At the same time he admitted that the restrictive nature of an ancestral *primogeniture*, which gave sole advantages in the eldest-born and left the remaining children with the mere dribs of fortune, was in many respects a hateful and unfair tradition. He could sympathize with Hubert's position.

Hubert tore his waistcoat open from top to bottom like a man whose breast was cramped and he wanted to relieve it with fresh air. Thrusting one hand into his open shirt-frill and planting the other in his side, he spun round on one foot in a quick pirouette and cried in a sharp voice, "*Fie!* What is hateful is born of hatred." Then erupting into a shrill fit of laughter, he said, "What graciousness my Lord of the Entail shows by throwing his gold pieces to the poor beggar!"

V. saw plainly now that any hope of reconciliation between the brothers was quite out of the question.

To the Freiherr's annoyance, Hubert rooted himself in the rooms in one of the side wings of the castle. It appeared that he was planning a very long stay. He was observed to hold frequent and long conversations with the house-steward. Old Daniel was sometimes even seen to accompany him when he went out wolf-hunting. Otherwise he was very little seen, and studiously avoided meeting his brother alone, for which the latter was very glad.

V. felt how strained and unpleasant this state of things was, and was obliged to confess to himself what Hubert said and did was meant to destroy the pleasure of the place. He now perfectly understood why the Freiherr had shown such alarm upon seeing his brother. He was a poison pill.

One day, as V. was sitting by himself in the justice-room amongst his law-papers, Hubert came in with a grave and more composed manner than usual, and said in a voice that bordered upon melancholy, "I will accept my brother's last proposals. If you will arrange that I receive the two thousand Fredericks d'or today, I will leave the castle this very night—on horseback—alone."

"With the money?" V. asked.

"Yes," replied Hubert. "I know what you are thinking: *oh*, the weight! How can you carry so much gold on horseback? Give it me in bills on Isaac Lazarus of K——. For I am going to K—— this very night. Something is driving me away from this place. The old fellow has bewitched it with evil spirits."

"Do you mean your father, Herr Baron?" asked V. sternly. Hubert's lips trembled. He had to cling to the chair to keep from falling, but then suddenly recovering himself, he cried, "Today then, please, Herr Justitiarius," and staggered to the door with some effort.

~§~

"He now sees that no deceptions can help him," said the Freiherr whilst drawing up the bills on Isaac Lazarus in K——. "He realizes that he is helpless against my firm will."

The Baron gladly gathered the satchel of money. A burden was lifted from his heart by the departure of his inimical brother. He was in high spirits at supper. The Baron and his Justitiarius sat alone at the table. Hubert had sent his excuses, and there was not one who regretted his absence.

~§~

The room which V. occupied was somewhat sequestered, and its windows had a hidden view upon the castle-yard below. Later that night he was suddenly startled from his sleep. As he sat up and rubbed his eyes he had impression that he had been awakened by a distant and pitiable moan. He listened for another cry but all remained quiet as the grave, and so he concluded that the sound was only the delusion of a dream. Still he could not go back to sleep. He was seized with such a peculiar feeling of breathless anxiety and terror that he could not stay in bed.

He rose and approached the window. It was not long, however, before the castle door was flung open and a figure with a blazing torch came out and strode across the courtyard. V. recognized the figure as that of old Daniel and watched as he opened the stable-door and went in. Soon afterwards he brought out a saddled horse. Now a second figure came into view out of the darkness, well wrapped in furs, and with a fox-skin cap on his head. V. perceived that it was Hubert; but after he had spoken excitedly with Daniel for some minutes, he returned inside the castle. Daniel led back the horse into the stable and locked the door, then locked the castle door, and returned across the courtyard. It was evident Hubert had intended to go away on horseback, but had suddenly changed his mind. It was evident to V. that there was a dangerous understanding of some sort between Hubert and the old house-steward.

V. looked forward to the morning with burning impatience; he would acquaint the Freiherr with the occurrences of the night. It was imperative now to take precautionary measures against the attacks of Hubert's malice. V. was now convinced of Hubert's dark designs, although he did not understand their exact nature.

~§~

Next morning, at the hour when the Freiherr was in the habit of rising, V. heard people running all about—doors opened and slammed shut, and there sounded a tumultuous confusion of agitated voices. Upon leaving his room he met servants everywhere, who, without heeding him, ran past him with ghastly pale faces, upstairs, downstairs, in and out rooms. At length he ascertained that the Freiherr was missing, and that they had been looking for him for him in vain.

Late the previous evening, the Freiherr had gone to bed in the presence of his personal attendant, which was the last time anyone saw him. Afterwards he must have gotten up and gone away somewhere in his dressing-gown and slippers, taking the large candlestick with him, for these articles were also missing.

V.—his mind agitated with dark forebodings—leapt up the stairs and entered the adjoining cabinet that Wolfgang—like his father—had chosen for his own bedroom. The postern leading to the tower stood wide open. A brush of ice-cold air stung his face as he stepped toward the threshold.

With a cry of horror V. shouted, "There—he lies dashed to pieces at the bottom of the ravine!"

And so it was. There had been a fall of snow, so that all they could distinctly make out from above was the rigid arm of the unfortunate man protruding from between the stones. Many hours passed before the workmen succeeded, at great risk of life, in descending by means of ladders bound together, and drawing up the corpse by the aid of ropes. In the last agonies of death the Baron had kept a tight hold upon the silver candlestick—the hand in which it was clenched was the only uninjured part of his body, which had been shattered in the most hideous way by smashing against the sharp stones.

Just as the corpse was drawn up and carried into the hall—laid upon the very same spot on the large table where a few weeks before old Roderick had lain dead—Hubert burst in, his face distorted by the frenzy of despair.

Quite overpowered by the fearful sight he wailed, "Brother! O my poor brother! No! I never wanted this. I never prayed for it from the demons that curl my heart."

This suspicious exclamation of innocence made V. tremble. He immediately assumed Hubert to be the murderer of his brother. Hubert, however, had fallen on the floor senseless. The servants carried him to bed, but after taking strong restoratives he soon recovered.

A short time later, Hubert appeared in V.'s room, pale and sorrow-stricken, and with his eyes half clouded with grief. Too weak to stand, he slowly sank down into an easy-chair, saying, "I have wished for my brother's death—only because my father had left him the best part of the property through that foolish entail. But he has found a fearful death—a horrifying, undeserving end. I am now lord of the estate-tail, but my heart is rent with pain. I shall never be happy."

Now looking at V. directly, Hubert's voice dropped into a low business-like tone: "I grant a continuance of your legal authority. You shall be invested with all the powers you require to independently manage the estate. I can no longer bear to live here."

Hubert then left the room, and after two or three hours of preparation was on his way to K——.

~§~

All the circumstance surrounding the Baron's freak death were examined, and the likeliest scenario indicated that the unfortunate Wolfgang had arisen in the night, probably with the intention of going into the other cabinet where there was a library. In the stupor of sleep he had mistaken the door and had opened the postern, blindly taken a step out, and plunged headlong into the rubble.

But after all had been said, there was nevertheless a good deal that was strained and unlikely in this explanation. If the Baron was unable to sleep and wanted to get a book out of the library, this of itself excluded all idea of sleep-stupor. If he was awake enough to read, he was awake enough to walk. Additionally, the postern door was always kept locked, and required a good deal of exertion to unlock it. V. remembered how Daniel had struggled with the lock when they examined the crumbled tower.

V. questioned the domestics about these improbabilities. At first his inquiry was met with dumbfounded silence, then Francis, who had served as Freiherr's personal groomer, said, "Nay, nay, my good Herr Justitiarius; it couldn't have happened in that way."

"Well, how then?" asked V. abruptly and sharply.

But Francis, a faithful, honest fellow, who would have followed his master into his grave, was unwilling to speak out in front of the others. He would only make his comments to the Justitiarius in private. That was arranged and V. learned that the Freiherr would often to talk to Francis about the vast treasure which he believed lay buried beneath the ruins of the tower. Frequently at night, as if goaded by some malicious fiend, the Baron would open the postern with the key that Daniel had been obliged to give him, and he would gaze with longing eyes down into the chasm where the supposed riches lay.

V. thanked Francis for this information and quietly turned the situation over in his mind. There was now no doubt about it: on that ill-omened night the Freiherr, after his servant had left him, must have taken one of his usual walks to the postern, where he had been most likely suddenly seized with dizziness, and had fallen into the jagged pit.

Daniel, who also appeared to be very upset by the Freiherr's terrible end, thought it would be a good thing to have the dangerous postern walled up; and this was done at once.

~§~

Freiherr Hubert von R——, who was now claimant of the entail, went back to Courland without once showing himself at R—sitten for a very long time. V. was invested with full powers for the absolute management of the property. The building of the new castle was not started; but on the other hand the old structure was put in as good a state of repair as possible.

Several years passed before Hubert came again to R—sitten, late in the autumn, but after he had remained shut up in his room with V. for several days, he went back to Courland. Passing on his way through K—— he deposited his will with the government authorities there.

During his short stay at R—sitten, Hubert, whose character appeared to have undergone a complete transition into a humble and haunted man, spoke obsessively of what he sensed was his impending death. The inevitability of his doom was seen in his sallow face and slumping shoulders. V. attempted to calm him—encourage him even. But these apprehensions proved prophetic, for he died in the very next year.

~§~

Soon after the Baron's untimely but not entirely unexpected passing, the Baron's son, who was also named Hubert, arrived from Courland to take possession of his rich inheritance. He was followed by his mother and sister. The youth seemed to unite in his personality all the bad qualities of his ancestors. He proved himself to be proud, arrogant, impetuous, avaricious—all of which was brazenly demonstrated within the very first moments of his arrival at R—sitten. He had notions of how things should run and he wanted all the "irregularities" corrected then and there, regardless of how nonsensical or difficult his ideas were. To begin with, he kicked the cook out of the kitchen because of the unappetizing smell, and then attempted to thrash the coachman with his own whip because his horse snorted mucus onto his lapel. He did not succeed in whipping him, however, for the big brawny fellow had the impudence not to submit to it. So, young Hubert was quickly on the road to assuming the role of a harsh and severe lord of the entail, which he seemed to be born for.

Thankfully, before things got out of hand, V. intervened in his firm and earnest manner. The Justitiarius declared most explicitly that not a single chair should be moved, a rug be beaten, or even a cat be booted from the house if she wishes to stay. Nothing—absolutely nothing—was to be changed until after the will had been opened.

"You have the presumption to tell *me*," began the fledgling Baron, "the *lord* of the entail—"

V., however, cut short the young man, who was foaming with rage, and said, whilst he measured him with a keen searching glance: "Don't be in too great a hurry, Herr Baron. At all events, you have no right to exercise authority here until after the opening of your father's will. It is I—I alone—who am now master here; and I shall know how to meet violence with violent measures. Please to recollect that by virtue of my powers as executor of your father's will, as well as by virtue of the arrangements which have been made by the court, I am empowered to forbid your remaining in R—sitten if I think fit to do so. And so! if you wish to spare me this disagreeable step, I would advise you to go away quietly to K—— and wait for me to summon you."

The lawyer's earnestness, and the resolute tone in which he spoke, lent the proper emphasis to his words. Hence the young Baron, who seemed to be wearing two sharply-pointed horns, felt the weakness of his weapons against the firm bulwark, and found it better to cover the shame of his retreat with a burst of scornful laughter.

"We'll see who holds the power after the will is read," he said menacingly and left with his entourage.

~§~

Three months passed and the day was come on which, in accordance with the expressed wish of the deceased, Hubert's will was to be opened at K——, where it had been deposited.

In the chambers, besides the officers of the court, the Baron, and V., there was present a previously unknown young man of noble appearance. He was accompanying V., and so it was assumed that he was V.'s law clerk, especially since the lad had a parchment deed sticking out from the breast of his buttoned-up coat.

The Baron treated the clerk as he did with nearly everyone—with scornful contempt. His impetuous squawking cut through the solemn air of the room. He demanded that they should forego with all their tiresome ceremonies and proceed as quickly as possible without excessive words

and scribblings. He couldn't for the life of him make out why a will was needed in any case, especially in the case of entailed property. No matter what provisions were made in the will, it would depend entirely upon his decision as to whether they should be observed or not. After all, he was the Lord of the Entail.

So, despite his demand for brevity he managed to extend the proceedings with his snooty demands. As soon as he ran out of words, the proceedings began in earnest.

After casting a hasty and surly glance at the handwriting and the seal, Hubert-the-younger acknowledged them to be those of his dead father. Then he slumped into silence. Throwing his right arm carelessly over the back of his chair and leaning his left on the table, he drummed his fingers on its green cover whilst he sat and stared indifferently out of the window.

Once the Baron looked comfortably set, the will was read and its contents came as a shock to all.

After a brief preamble, the deceased Freiherr Hubert von R—— declared that he had never possessed the estate-tail as its lawful owner, but that he had only managed it in the name of the deceased Freiherr Wolfgang von R——'s only son, called Roderick after his grandfather; and it was he to whom, according to the rights of family priority, the estate had fallen upon his father's death.

Amongst Hubert's papers would be found an exact account of all revenues and expenditure, as well as of existing movable property. The will went on to relate that Wolfgang von R—— had, during his travels, made the acquaintance of Mdlle. Julia de St. Val in Geneva, and had fallen so deeply in love with her that he resolved never to leave her side again. She was very poor; and her family, although noble and of good repute, did not, however, rank amongst the most illustrious, for which reason Wolfgang dared not expect to receive the consent of old Roderick to a union with her, for the old Freiherr's aim and ambition was to promote by all possible means the establishment of a powerful family.

Nevertheless he ventured to write from Paris to his father, acquainting him with the fact that his affections were engaged. But what he had foreseen was actually realized. The old Baron declared categorically that he had himself chosen the future mistress of the entail, and therefore there could never be any mention made of any other. Wolfgang, instead of crossing the Channel into England, as he was to have done, returned into Geneva under the assumed name of Born, and married Julia, who after the lapse of a year bore him a son, and this son became on Wolfgang's death the real lord of the entail.

In explanation of the facts why Hubert, though acquainted with all this, had kept silent so long and had represented himself as lord of the entail, various reasons were assigned, based upon agreements formerly made with Wolfgang, but they seemed for the most part insufficient and devoid of any real foundation.

The young Baron sat staring at the clerk of the court as if thunderstruck, whilst the latter went on proclaiming all this bad news in a provokingly monotonous and jarring tone.

When he finished, V. rose, and taking the young man whom he had brought with him by the hand, said, as he bowed to the assembled company, "Here I have the honor to present to you, gentlemen, Freiherr Roderick von R——, lord of the entail of R—sitten."

Baron Hubert looked at the youth, who had, as it were, fallen from the clouds to deprive him of the rich inheritance together with half the unentailed Courland estates. With suppressed fury in his gleaming eyes, and threatening him with his doubled fist, he ran out of the court without uttering a word.

Baron Roderick, on being challenged by the court-officers, produced the documents by which he was to establish his identity as the person whom he represented himself to be. He handed in an attested extract from the register of the church where his father was married, which certified that on such and such a day Wolfgang Born, merchant, born in K——, had been united in marriage with the blessing of the Church to Mdlle. Julia de St. Val, in the presence of certain witnesses, who were named. Further, he produced his own baptismal certificate (he had been baptized in Geneva as the son of the merchant Born and his wife Julia, née De St. Val, begotten in lawful wedlock), and various letters from his father to his mother, who was long since dead, but they none of them had any other signature than "W".

V. looked through all these papers with a cloud upon his face; and as he put them together again, he said, somewhat troubled, "Ah well! God will help us in all His wisdom!"

~§~

The very next morning Freiherr Hubert von R——, accompanied by a newly acquired advocate, appeared before the government authorities in K—— and presented a statement of protest. The petition called upon them to immediately surrender of the entail of R—sitten to him.

Hubert's lawyer maintained that the deceased Freiherr Hubert Von R—— did not possess the power to dispose of the entailed property in any way he pleased. It broke the tenets of the original entail . . .

. . . The testament in question, therefore, is nothing more than an statement of facts, written down and deposited with the court, to the effect that Freiherr Wolfgang von R—— had bequeathed the estate-tail to a son who was at that time still living. Accordingly, this evidence had no greater weight than that of any other witness, and so could not by any possibility legitimately establish the claims of the person who claimed to be Freiherr Roderick von R——.

Hence it was the duty of this new claimant to prove his alleged rights of inheritance. This he did not do. Since there was no evidence to back his claim, his rude pretense as the rightful heir is expressly disputed and denied. Therefore, according to the laws of succession, the entail falls to Baron Hubert von R——. Upon the father's death the property immediately came into the hands of the son. There was no need for any formal declaration to be made of his entering into possession of the inheritance, since the succession could not be alienated. At any rate, the present owner of the estate will not be disturbed by claims which are perfectly groundless. Whatever reasons the deceased may have had for calling forth another heir of entail are quite irrelevant. And it should be remembered that he had himself had an intrigue in Switzerland, as could be proved if necessary from the papers he had left behind him. It is quite possible that the person whom he alleged to be his brother's son was in fact his own son, the fruit of an unlawful love, for whom—out of a momentary fit of remorse—he had wished to secure the entail. A dead man's guilty conscience does not upend the iron-clad provisions of the entail.

Regardless of the will's revelations, the opposing views had to be considered. However revolted the judges were by this new appeal—particularly by the last clauses of the protest in which the son accused his dead father of a crime—they had to take them seriously. Hubert clearly represented the family namesake. On the other hand, young Roderick now appeared to be something of an upstart, although a seemingly pleasant one.

The judges were on the verge of ruling in favor of Hubert when V. vaulted this utter disaster by temporarily swaying them with the promise of new evidence. He begged for a little time with explicit and solemn assurance that he would acquire proof that would establish Freiherr Roderick von R—— as the legitimate heir. Due to V.'s passion, fortitude, and flawless reputation, the surrender of the estate to the young Baron was delayed pending further discovery.

~§~

V. knew too well how difficult it would be for him to keep his promise. He had turned over all old Roderick's papers without finding the slightest trace of a letter or any kind of a statement bearing upon Wolfgang's relation to Mdlle. de St. Val. He was sitting rapt in thought in old Roderick's sleeping-chamber—every hole and corner of which he had searched—and was working on a statement of the case that he intended dispatching to a certain notary in Geneva, who had been recommended to him as a shrewd and energetic man. He asked the notary to procure and forward certain documents which would put the young Freiherr's cause on firm ground.

It was midnight. The full moon shone in through the windows of the adjoining hall, the door of which stood open. V. heard someone coming slowly and heavily up the stairs. Each ponderous step jingled a set of keys. His attention was arrested. He rose to his feet and went into the hall, where he plainly made out that there was someone crossing the ante-room and approaching the door of the hall where he was. Soon afterwards the door was opened and a man slowly shuffled in. He was dressed in night-clothes, his face ghastly pale and distorted. He bore a candle-stick with the candles burning in one hand, and a huge bunch of keys in the other.

V. at once recognized the old house-steward, Daniel, and was on the point of addressing him and inquiring what he wanted so late at night, when he was arrested by an icy shiver. There was something so unearthly and ghost-like in the old man's manner and bearing as well as in his set, pallid face. He perceived that he was in presence of a somnambulist.

Crossing the hall obliquely with measured strides, the old man went straight to the walled-up postern that had formerly led to the tower. Halting in front of it, he uttered a wailing sound that seemed to come from the bottom of his heart. The cry was so awful, so loud, that the whole apartment rang with it and caused V. to tremble with dread. Then, setting the candlestick down on the floor and hanging the keys on his belt, Daniel began to scratch at the wall with both hands. He scratched so fervently that blood soon dripped from his fingernails. All the while he was moaning and groaning as if tortured by a nameless agony.

After placing his ear against the wall in a listening attitude he waved his hand as if hushing someone, then he stooped down and picked up the candlestick. Finally he stole back to the door with soft measured footsteps.

V. took his own candle in his hand and cautiously followed him. They both went downstairs, one after the other. The old man unlocked the great main door of the castle, and V. cleverly slipped through before it shut. Then they went to the stable, where old Daniel—to V.'s perfect astonishment—placed his candlestick so skillfully that the entire interior of the building was fully lit. Having fetched a saddle and bridle, he put them on one of the horses which he had coaxed from the manger. While the horse stood in quiet dismay, he carefully tightened the girth and drew up the stirrup-straps. Pulling the tuft of hair on the horse's forehead outside the front strap, he took him by the bridle and led him out of the stable, clicking with his tongue and patting his neck with one hand. On getting outside in the courtyard he stood several seconds in the attitude of one receiving commands, which he promised by sundry nods to carry out. Then he led the horse back into the stable, unsaddled him, and tied him to the manger. This done, he took his candlestick, locked the stable, and returned to the castle, finally disappearing in his own room, the door of which he carefully bolted.

V. was deeply agitated by this scene. He had years before witnessed just such a scene played out in the dead of night by Daniel and Hubert. Was this a dream-time reenactment of that event? Was Daniel haunted by Hubert's spirit?

Sleep was slain for the night.

~§~

The next day, just as dusk was starting, Daniel came into the Justitiarius' room to receive some instructions relating to his department of the household. V. took him by the arms, and forcing him into a chair, began in a confidential way:

"See here, my old friend Daniel, I have long been wishing to ask you what you think of all this confused mess into which Hubert's peculiar will has tumbled us. Do you really think that Roderick is Wolfgang's son, begotten in lawful marriage?"

The old man, leaning over the arm of his chair, and avoiding V.'s eyes, for V. was watching him most intently, replied doggedly, "Bah! Maybe he is; maybe he is not. What does it matter to me? It's all the same to me who's master here now."

"But I believe," V. went on, moving nearer to the old man and placing his hand on his shoulder, "but I believed you possessed the old Freiherr's full confidence, and in that case he assuredly would not have concealed from you the real state of affairs regarding his sons. He told you, I dare say, about the marriage which Wolfgang had made against his will, did he not?"

"I don't remember to have ever heard him say anything of that sort," replied the old man, yawning with the most ill-mannered loudness.

"You are sleepy, old man," said V. "Perhaps you have had a restless night?"

"Not that I am aware," he rejoined coldly, "but I must go and order supper." Whereupon he rose heavily from his chair and rubbed his bent back, yawning again, and that still more loudly than before.

"Stay a little while, old man," cried V., taking hold of his hand and endeavoring to force him to resume his seat, but Daniel preferred to stand in front of the study-table.

Propping himself upon the desk with both hands, and leaning across towards V., he asked sullenly, "Well, what do you want? What have I to do with the will? What do I care about the quarrel over the estate?"

"Well, well," interposed V., "we'll say no more about that now. Let us turn to some other topic, Daniel. You are out of humor and yawning, and all that is a sign of great weariness. I am almost inclined to believe that it really was you last night, who—"

"Well, what did I do last night?" asked the old man without changing his position.

V. went on: "Last night, when I was sitting upstairs in your old master's sleeping-chamber next the great hall, you came in at the door, your face pale and rigid—and you went across to the bricked-up postern and scratched at the wall with both your hands, groaning as if in very great pain. You scratched until your fingers bled. You can see your injured fingertips now. Do you walk in your sleep, Daniel?"

The old man dropped back into the chair which V. quickly managed to place for him . . . but not a sound escaped his lips. His face could not be seen, owing to the gathering dusk of the evening. V. only noticed that he took his breath in short gasps and that his teeth were rattling together.

". . . Yes," continued V. after a short pause, "there is one thing that is very strange about sleep-walkers. On the day after they have been in this peculiar state in which they have acted as if they were perfectly wide awake, they don't remember the least thing that they did."

Daniel did not move.

"I have come across something like your condition once before in the course of my experience," V. proceeded. "I had a friend who regularly began to wander about at night as you do whenever it was full moon; he often sat down and wrote letters . . . sometimes addressing them to the dead. But what was most extraordinary was that if I began to whisper softly in his ear I could soon manage to make him speak, and he would answer correctly all the questions I put to him—even things that he would most jealously have concealed when awake now fell from his lips unbidden, as though he were unable to offer any resistance to the power that was exerting its influence over him.

"Deuce take it! I really believe that—if a man who's given to walking in his sleep had ever committed any crime, and hoarded it up as a secret ever so long—it could be extracted from him by questioning when he was in this peculiar state. Happy are they who have a clean conscience like you and me, eh, Daniel! We may walk as much as we like in our sleep. There's no fear of anybody extorting the confession of a crime from us.

"But come now, Daniel! when you scratch so hideously at the bricked-up postern, you want, I dare say, to go up the astronomical tower, don't you? I suppose you want to go and experiment like in the old days with Baron Roderick—eh? Engage in some sorcery of the stars? . . . Well, next time you come sleep-walking I shall ask you what you are up to."

Whilst V. was speaking, the old man was shaken with continually increasing agitation. With V.'s last words his whole frame seemed to heave and rock convulsively past all hope of cure, and in a shrill voice he began to utter a string of unintelligible gibberish.

Seeing Daniel's quick descent, V. rang for the servants. They brought lights; but as the old man's fit did not abate, they lifted him up as though he had been a mere automaton, not possessed of the power of voluntary movement, and carried him to bed. After continuing in this frightful state for about an hour, he fell into a profound sleep resembling a dead faint. When he awoke he asked for wine. After he had got what he wanted, he sent everyone away and locked himself in his room as usual.

~§~

While thinking back on his conversation with the old steward, V. could not forget two facts. In the first place, Daniel, having now been made aware of his propensity to walk in his sleep, would probably adopt every measure of precaution to avoid him; and on the other hand, confessions made whilst in this condition would not be enough to support legal proceedings. In spite of this, however, he returned to the hall on the approach of midnight, hoping that Daniel, as frequently happens to those afflicted in this way, would sleepwalk again.

About midnight there arose a great noise in the courtyard. V. plainly heard a window broken in; then he went downstairs, and as he traversed the passages he was met by rolling clouds of suffocating smoke, which, he soon perceived were pouring out of the open door of the house-steward's room. The steward himself was just then being carried out, to all appearance dead.

The servants related that about midnight one of the under-grooms had been awakened by a strange hollow knocking. He thought something had befallen the old man, and so was preparing to get up and go and see if he could help him, when the night watchman in the court shouted, "Fire! Fire! The Herr House-Steward's room is burning!" At this outcry several servants at once appeared on the scene, but all their efforts to burst open the room door were unavailing. Whereupon they hurried out into the court. By now the resolute watchman had already broken in the window—for the room was low and on the basement story—and had torn down the burning curtains and extinguished them by pouring a few buckets of water on the fire.

They found Daniel lying on the floor in the middle of the room, all in a swoon. His hand still held the candlestick tightly clenched, and it was the burning candles that had started the fire. Some of the blazing rags had fallen upon the old man, burning his eyebrows and a large portion of the hair off his head. If the watchman had not seen the fire the old man would have been helplessly burned to death. Moreover, the servants, to their great astonishment, found the room door secured from the inside by two heavy bolts—two new bolts, which had been fastened to the door jamb since the previous evening, for they had not been there before.

V. perceived that the old man had wished to make it impossible for him to get out of his room, for he knew that he could not resist the blind impulse to wander in his sleep.

Due to the fire, the old man became seriously ill. He did not speak. He took but little nourishment. He lay staring before him with the reflection of death set in his eyes, just as if he were clasped in the vice-like grip of some hideous thought. V. believed he would never rise from his bed again.

~§~

Meanwhile, V. had done all that could be done for his client. Now he could only await the outcome, and so he decided to return to K——. His departure was fixed for the following morning. As he was packing his papers together late at night, he happened to lay his hand upon a little sealed packet which Freiherr Hubert von R—— had given him, bearing the inscription, "To be read after my will has been opened," and which for some unaccountable reason had hitherto escaped his notice. He was on the point of breaking the seal when the door opened and Daniel came in with still, ghostlike step. Placing upon the table a black portfolio which he carried under his arm, he sank upon his knees with a deep groan, and grasping V.'s hands with a convulsive clutch he said, in a voice so hollow and hoarse that it seemed to come from the bottom of a grave, "I should not like to die on the scaffold! There is One above who judges!"

Then, rising with some trouble and with many painful gasps, he left the room as he had come.

V. spent the whole of the night in reading what the black portfolio and Hubert's packet contained. Both agreed in all circumstantial evidence, and naturally suggested what further steps were to be taken.

~§~

On arriving at K——, V. immediately presented himself to Freiherr Hubert von R——, who received him with ill-mannered pride. . . . But the remarkable result of the interview, which began at noon and lasted on without interruption until late at night, was that the next day the Freiherr made a declaration before the court that he acknowledged the claimant to be, in accordance to his father's will, the son of Wolfgang von R——, eldest son of Freiherr Roderick von R——, and begotten in lawful wedlock with Mdlle. Julia de St. Val, and furthermore acknowledged him as rightful and legitimate heir to the entail.

On leaving the court he found his carriage harnessed with post-horses and waiting at the door. He stepped in and was driven off at a rapid rate, leaving his mother and his sister behind him. They would perhaps never see him again, he wrote in a quickly scribbled letter to them, adding a few perplexing statements that baffled them. His sudden departure left them empty and confused.

Roderick was astonished at this unexpected turn in the case. He pressed V. to explain how this wonder had come about—what mysterious power was at work in the matter? V., however, evaded his questions but promised to explain all at some future time, after he came into full possession of the estate. For the surrender of the entail to him could not be effected immediately, since the court, not content with Hubert's declaration, required that Roderick should also first prove his own identity to their satisfaction.

V. proposed to the Baron that he should go and live at R—sitten, adding that Hubert's mother and sister, momentarily embarrassed by his sudden departure, would prefer to go and live quietly on the ancestral property rather than stay in the gossipy town. The prospect of dwelling under the same roof with the Baroness and her daughter enlivened Roderick's face with a delighted smile, betraying the deep impression which the lovely and graceful Seraphina had made upon him. In fact, the Freiherr made such good use of his time in R—sitten that, at the end of a few weeks, he had won Seraphina's love as well as her mother's cordial approval of her marriage with him.

All this was for V. rather too quick work, since Roderick's claims to be lord of the entail continued to be rather doubtful. The life of idyllic happiness at the castle was interrupted by letters from Courland. Hubert had not shown himself at all at the Courland estates, but had traveled directly to St Petersburg, where he had accepted military service and was now in the field against the Persians, with whom Russia happened to be just then waging war. This obliged the Baroness and her daughter to set off immediately for their Courland estates, where everything was in confusion and disorder. Roderick, who had already regarded himself a member of the family, insisted upon accompanying his beloved. And so, since V. had likewise returned to K——, the castle was left in its previous state of utter loneliness.

Left alone with his tortured memories, Daniel's malignant guilt grew worse and he fell into a deep, listless melancholy. Lacking the resolve to manage even the most mundane tasks, he conferred his duties to an old chasseur named Francis—Wolfgang's faithful servant.

~§~

After a very long wait, V. finally received some favorable news from Switzerland. The priest who had married Roderick was long since dead, but there was found in the church register a memorandum in his handwriting which stated that the man by the name of Born, whom he had joined in the bonds of wedlock with Mdlle. Julia de St. Val, had established completely to his satisfaction his identity as Freiherr Wolfgang von R——, eldest son of Freiherr Roderick von R—— of R—sitten. Besides this, two witnesses of the marriage had been discovered—a merchant of Geneva and an old French captain, who had since moved to Lyons. Wolfgang had also confided in them his real name. Furthermore, their sworn affidavits confirmed the priest's notice in the church register.

With these memoranda in his hands, drawn up with proper legal formalities, V. now succeeded in securing his client the complete possession of his rights. The full power of the entail was to be put into his hands in the coming autumn.

Meanwhile the sad report arrived that Hubert had fallen in his very first skirmish, thus sharing the fate of his younger brother, who had likewise been slain in battle a year before his father's death. Thus the entire Courland estates fell to Baroness Seraphina von R——, and this made a handsome dowry for her marriage to Roderick.

Nowhere in the world was there a happier man than Roderick, Master of R—sitten.

~§~

The Baroness, along with Roderick and his betrothed, arrived at R—sitten on a chilly November afternoon. The formal surrender of the estate-tail to the young Baron took place, and then his marriage with Seraphina was solemnized. Many weeks passed amid a continual whirl of pleasure. Eventually the wearied guests began to depart from the castle—much to V.'s great satisfaction, for he made up his mind to remain at R—sitten until he had fully initiated the young lord in all the relations and duties connected with the entail. Roderick's uncle had kept an account of all revenues and disbursements with the most detailed accuracy. Since Hubert had only retained a small sum annually for his own support, the surplus revenues increased the capital left by the old Freiherr. The total now amounted to a considerable sum. Hubert had only employed the income of the entail for his own purposes during the first three years, but to cover this he had given a mortgage of his share of the Courland property as security.

Now that the family was settled, V. turned his mind more and more to the old steward. From the time when old Daniel had revealed himself as a somnambulist, V. had chosen old Roderick's bedroom for his own sitting-room, in order that he might keep a watchful eye on him. Hence it was in this room and in the adjoining great hall that V. conducted business with the Freiherr.

Once they were both sitting at the great table by the bright blazing fire. V. had his pen in his hand, and was noting down various totals and calculating the riches of the lord of the entail, whilst the latter, leaning his head on his hand, was blinking at the open account-books and formidable-looking documents. Neither of them heard the hollow roar of the sea, nor the anxious cries of the sea-gulls as they dashed against the windowpanes, flapping their wings and flying backwards and forwards, announcing the oncoming storm. Neither of them heeded the storm, which arose about midnight, and was now roaring and raging with wild fury round the castle walls. The sounds of ill-omen awoke in the fire-grates and narrow passages, and began to whistle and shriek in a weird, unearthly way. At length, after a terrific blast of wind, which made the whole castle shake, the hall was suddenly illuminated by the murky glare of the full moon.

"Awful weather!" V. exclaimed, shuddering where he sat.

The Freiherr, quite absorbed in the consideration of the wealth which had fallen to him, replied indifferently, as he turned over a page of the receipt-book with a satisfied smile, "It is indeed; very stormy!"

But, as if clutched by the icy hand of dread, he started to his feet as the door of the hall flew open and a pale spectral figure became visible, striding in with the stamp of death upon its face. It was Daniel, who, lying helpless under the power of disease, was deemed by everybody incapable of moving a single limb . . . but here he was again sleepwalking under the embrace of the full moon. He had, it appeared, been unable to resist it.

The Freiherr stared at the old man without uttering a sound; and when Daniel began to scratch at the wall, and moan as though in the painful agonies of death, Roderick's heart was filled with horrible dread. With his face ashy pale and his hair standing straight on end, he leapt to his feet and strode towards the old man in a threatening attitude and cried in a loud firm voice, so that the hall rang again:

"Daniel, *Daniel*, what are you doing here at this hour?"

Then the old man uttered that same unearthly howling whimper, like the death-cry of a wounded animal, which he had uttered when Wolfgang had offered to reward his fidelity with gold so . . . so . . . long ago.

As the animal cry died in his lungs he fell flat on the floor.

V. summoned the servants and they raised the old man up, but all attempts to resuscitate him proved fruitless.

Then the Freiherr cried, almost beside himself, "Good God! Good God! Now I remember to have heard that a sleepwalker may die on the spot if anybody calls him by his name. Oh! oh! unfortunate wretch that I am! I have killed the poor old man! I shall never more have a peaceful moment so long as I live."

The servants carried the corpse away and the hall was empty again.

V. took the Freiherr, who was still quivering from guilt and shame, by the hand and led him in silence to the walled-up postern. There he said, "The man who fell down dead at your feet, Freiherr Roderick, was the atrocious murderer of your father."

The Freiherr fixed his staring eyes upon V. as though he saw the foul fiends of hell. But V. went on, "The time has come now for me to reveal to you the hideous secret which, weighing upon the conscience of this monster and burdening him with curses, compelled him to roam abroad in his sleep. The Eternal Power has seen fit to make the son take vengeance upon the murderer of your father. The words which you thundered in the ears of that fearful night-walker were the last words that your unhappy father spoke. The exact words!"

V. sat down in front of the fire, and the Freiherr, trembling and unable to utter a word, took his seat beside him. V. began to tell him the contents of the document which Hubert had left behind him, and the seal of which he (V.) was not to break until after the opening of the will. Hubert testified, to the deepest remorse, the implacable hatred of his older brother—a hatred that took root in him from the moment that old Roderick, the elder-baron, had established the entail and named Roderick its benefactor. He was deprived of all weapons, for the entail could not be broken. It was only when Wolfgang formed his secret bond with Julia de St. Val in Geneva that Hubert saw his way to effecting his brother's ruin. And that was the time when he came to an understanding with Daniel, who had his own reasons for revenge. Together they secretly worked to circumvent the entail. It was in fact Daniel who devised a plan, engineered by villainous devices, to provoke the old Baron into disowning Roderick.

Daniel was aware that old Roderick believed the only way to ensure an illustrious future for the family for all time was through an alliance with one of the oldest families in the country. The old man foresaw this alliance in the stars, and any disobedience of the constellations would only entail destruction upon the family he had founded. He saw Wolfgang's union with Julia as a sinful crime—a betrayal of the family fates, committed against the ordinances of the Power which had stood by him through all his worldly undertakings. He would have regarded any measures leading to Julia's ruination as justified, for Julia had, he conceived, arranged herself against him like some demoniacal principle. She shook the very foundation of the universe and was certain to cause the castle to crumble. The astral forces demanded her removal.

Hubert knew that his brother loved Julia passionately, almost to madness in fact, and that the loss of her would infallibly make him miserable beyond measure, perhaps even kill him. And Hubert was ever ready to assist the old man in his diabolical plans as he had himself conceived an unlawful affection for Julia, and he hoped to win her for himself.

It was, however, determined by Providence that all attacks, even the most virulent, were to spare Wolfgang's ambition for a happy life. Unknown to either his father or brother, he hastened to marry Julia in a quiet civil ceremony, and soon after a son was born to them. He kept both his wife and son a secret.

The celestial messages were murky at times, but Old Roderick could sense that his aspirations were unravelling. He was also certain that he was nearing the end of his days. The storm clouds of an impending death fogged his eyes, but the approaching precipice gave him a prescient clarity. He somehow knew that Wolfgang had already married the pretty Julia who was so hostile to his plans. Reacting to this belief, he sent a letter to his son which commanded him to appear at R—sitten on a given day to take possession of the entail. He concluded his summons with a threat: he cursed Wolfgang if he did not sever his connection with Julia.

This was the letter that Wolfgang burnt beside his father's corpse.

~§~

Before his death in the tower collapse, the old man had also written to Hubert, saying that Wolfgang had already married Julia, but that he ordered him to dissolve the union and part from her. Hubert took this to be another of father's fancy visions. Assuming that, he was greatly dismayed when upon reaching R—sitten, Wolfgang—with perfect frankness—not only confirmed the old man's supposition, but also went on to add that Julia had borne him a son. He hoped in a short time to surprise her with the pleasant revelation of his high rank and great wealth, for she had hitherto taken him for Born, a merchant from M——. He intended going to Geneva himself to fetch his beloved wife.

But before he could carry out this plan he was overtaken by death. He had joined the rubble pile that had claimed his father.

~§~

Hubert considered every strategy available to him. He carefully concealed what he knew about the existence of a son born to Wolfgang in lawful wedlock with Julia. By doing so he handily usurped the property that really belonged to his nephew.

But only a few years passed before he became a prey to bitter remorse. He was reminded of his guilt by destiny—as if in some dark mirror there reflected the hatred that grew between his own two sons.

"You are a poor starving beggar!" said the elder, a boy of twelve, to the younger, "but I shall be lord of R—sitten when father dies, and then you will have to be humble and kiss my hand when you want me to give you money to buy a new coat."

The younger, goaded to ungovernable fury by his brother's proud and scornful words, threw the knife at him which he happened to have in his hand, and almost killed him.

Hubert, for fear of some dire misfortune, sent the younger away to St. Petersburg. He had a military bent and later served as officer under Suwaroff. Sadly he fell fighting against the French. It was another dark mark on Hubert's heart.

Hubert could not bring himself to reveal to the world the dishonest and deceitful way in which he had acquired possession of the estate-tail. He could not bear the shame and disgrace which would have come upon him, but he would not rob the rightful owner of a single penny more. He sent an investigator to Geneva and learned from this that Madame Born had died of grief at the incomprehensible disappearance of her husband, but that young Roderick Born was being brought up by a worthy man who had adopted him.

When the adoptive father perished at sea, Hubert arranged to be introduced to the local solicitor under an assumed name as a relative of Born the merchant. He accomplished this without formally meeting young Roderick, but he was able to glimpse his fine form from the shadows of a church steeple. Fully coming to terms with his obligations, Hubert thereon secretly sent sufficient sums to give the young heir of the entail a good and respectable education. In the meanwhile, he carefully grew the surplus revenues from the estate . . . and how he drew up the terms of his will, we already know.

The string of baffling statements within the will were now coming to clarity, like a sloop slipping out of the fog and showing the tack of its sails. In the body of the will, while paying respects to his departed brother, Hubert spoke in strangely obscure terms, but his words allowed this much to be inferred: that there must be some mystery about Wolfgang's death, and that he had taken part—indirectly, at least—in some heinous crime.

~§~

The contents of the black portfolio made everything clear. Along with Hubert's traitorous correspondence with Daniel was a sheet of paper written and signed by Daniel. V. read the confession and was appalled. His hands were trembling by the time he had reached Daniel's thorny signature. And so V. learned that it was at Daniel's encouragement that Hubert had come to R—sitten, and it was Daniel again who had written and told him about the one hundred and fifty thousand thalers that had been found.

It has been already described how Hubert was received by his brother, and how—deceived in all his hopes and wishes—was about to depart for good when he was innocently convinced by V. to stay. Concurrent to this, unsuspected by anyone, Daniel's heart was tortured by an insatiable thirst for vengeance—a writhing wounded rage which he was determined to unleash on the young man who threatened to kick him out like a mangy cur. It was he who was relentlessly and incessantly fanned the flame of passion by which Hubert's desperate heart was consumed. It was he who poured vile poison into the family veins.

There came a time when Daniel and Hubert mingled their hatred. Whilst in the fir forests hunting wolves, out in the midst of a blinding snowstorm, Daniel and Hubert had agreed to assure his destruction. Roderick had fallen back from the main hunting party and they trailed him, unknown.

"Make away with him!" murmured Hubert, looking askance and taking aim with his rifle. Through the snow-ladened boughs Hubert held Roderick in his muzzle-sights. His jaw was tight, his frosty breath billowing out.

"Yes, do away with him," snarled Daniel, touching Hubert's elbow and gently drawing it down, "but not in that way, not in that way! I have a better way."

And he made the most solemn declaration that he would murder the Freiherr and not a soul in the world would be the wiser. Hubert went all-in with Daniel, but he would soon change his mind. Once Roderick offered his brother money, Hubert repented of the murder-plot and decided to depart the castle in peace. He determined to go away in order to shun all further temptation of enacting some foul deed.

Daniel himself saddled his horse and brought it out of the stable.

As the Baron was about to mount his horse, Daniel said to him in a sharp, strained voice, "I thought you would stay on the entail, Freiherr Hubert, now that it has just fallen to you, for the proud lord of the entail lies dashed to pieces at the bottom of the ravine, below the tower."

The steward had observed that Wolfgang, tormented by his thirst for gold, would often to rise in the night, go to the postern which formerly led to the tower, and stand gazing with longing eyes down into the chasm, where, according to his (Daniel's) testimony, vast treasures lay buried. Relying upon this habit, Daniel waited near the hall-door on that ill-omened night; and as soon as he heard the Freiherr open the postern leading to the tower, he entered the hall and proceeded to where the Freiherr was standing, close to the edge of the chasm.

On becoming aware of the presence of his villainous servant, in whose eyes the gleam of murder shone, the Freiherr turned round and said with a cry of terror, "Daniel, Daniel, what are you doing here at this hour?"

But then Daniel shrieked wildly, "Down with you, you mangy cur!" and with a powerful push of his foot he hurled the unhappy man over into the deep chasm. He heard the crash of his body and lingered as the dust rose from the shaft and choked his eyes.

Learning of his father's terrible murder, the young Baron could find no peace in the castle. He went to his Courland estates, and only visited R—sitten once a year, in autumn.

Francis—old loyal Francis—who had strong suspicions as to Daniel's guilt, maintained that he often haunted the place at full moon—the time when he walked in his sleep and reenacted his treacherous betrayal. Francis described the nature of the apparition's habits so accurately that V., who later experienced the haunting for himself, was able to exorcise the spirit with a few well-chosen words.

It was also the disclosure of these circumstances which stamped Hubert's memory with dishonor—a dishonor that shook the entire family like a terrible storm. When his son, the young Freiherr Hubert, learned the truth he went into self-exile, where he attempted to regain his family's honor with a suicidal charge against the enemy's battlements. Instead he was buried with little ceremony in a pit piled with the mangled dead of his military brothers.

~§~

This was my old uncle's story.

Now he took my hand, and whilst his eyes filled with tears, he said, in a broken voice, "Cousin, cousin! And she too—the beautiful lady—has fallen a victim to the dark destiny, the grim, mysterious power which has established itself in that old ancestral castle. Two days after we left R—sitten the Freiherr arranged an excursion on sledges as the concluding event of the visit. He drove his wife himself; but as they were going down the valley the horses, for some unexplained reason, suddenly taking fright, began to snort and kick and plunge most savagely. 'The old man! The old man is after us!' screamed the Baroness in a shrill, terrified voice. At this same moment the sledge was overturned with a violent jerk, and the Baroness was hurled a considerable distance. They picked her up lifeless—she was quite dead. The Freiherr is now profoundly inconsolable, and has settled down into a state of passivity that will kill him. We shall never go to R—sitten again, cousin!"

Here my uncle paused. There were no more words in the old man. As I left him my heart was torn by emotion. Nothing but the all-soothing hand of time could assuage the deep pain which I feared would cost me my life. I had come so, so close to immersing myself in the curse that haunts each generation of the Roderick family. My dear uncle saved me from the fate I recklessly and blindly sought. My dear uncle . . .

~§~

Years passed. V. was resting in his grave, and I had left my native country. Then I was driven northwards, as far as St. Petersburg, by the devastating war which was sweeping over all Germany. On my return journey, not far from K——, I was driving one dark summer night along the shore of the Baltic, when I perceived in the sky before me a remarkably large bright star. Approaching nearer I realized that the red flickering flame I had taken for a star must be a large fire, but I could not understand how it could be so high in the sky.

"Postilion, what fire is that before us yonder?" I asked the man who was driving me.

"Oh! why, that's not a fire. It's the beacon tower of R—sitten."

"R—sitten!" I cried and stared at it intently.

The postilion's casual response had reawakened all the experiences of those eventful autumn days which I had spent there. The memories flooded my mind with lifelike reality. I saw the Baron—Seraphina—and also the remarkably eccentric old aunts—myself as well, with my bare milk-white face, my hair elegantly curled and powdered, and wearing a delicate sky-blue coat—nay, I saw myself in my love-sick folly, sighing like a furnace, and making lugubrious odes on my mistress's eyebrows.

The somber, melancholy mood into which these memories plunged me was relieved by the bright recollection of V.'s genial jokes, shooting up like flashes of colored light, and I found them now even more entertaining than they had been so long ago.

Thus agitated by pain mingled with a most peculiar pleasure, I reached R—sitten early in the morning and got out of the coach in front of the post-house, where it had stopped. I recognized the house as that of the land-steward; I inquired after him.

"Begging your pardon," said the clerk of the post-house, taking his pipe from his mouth and giving his night-cap a tilt, "begging your pardon—there is no land-steward here. This is a Royal Government office, and the Herr Administrator is still asleep."

On making further inquiries I learnt that Freiherr Roderick von R——, the last lord of the entail, had died sixteen years before without descendants, and that the entail in accordance with the terms of the original deeds had now reverted to the state.

I went up to the castle. It was a mere heap of ruins. I was informed by an old peasant, who came out of the fir-forest, that a large portion of the stones had been employed in the construction of the beacon-tower. He also could tell the story of the ghost which was said to have haunted the castle, and he affirmed that people often heard unearthly cries and lamentations amongst the stones, especially at full moon.

Poor short-sighted old Roderick! What a malignant destiny did you conjure up to destroy with the breath of poison, in the first moments of its growth, that race which you intended to plant with firm roots to last on till eternity!

I turned my back to the memory of those cold towers and wound my way down the path, away from R——sitten.

PART VI

A Midnight Novel

something old that's something new

Our Midnight novel, "The Thing in the Woods", has an intriguing publishing history. It is the only horror novel written by Margery Williams, who is much better known for her children's book "The Velveteen Rabbit". That lovable tale about a child's stuffed toy is a perennial favorite—one of the most famous books in children's literature in fact, and it's guaranteed to be on the shelf of your local bookstore today, one hundred years after it was first published in 1922.

Nine years before Williams achieved fame for "The Velveteen Rabbit", her novel of beastly murder was quietly released in England. "The Thing in the Woods" (1913) is set in rural Pennsylvania, where Williams spent her formative years after immigrating from the UK with her mother. When the novel was finally published in the US in 1924, the title remained the same but the author assumed the pseudonym Harper Williams for this new publication. Presumably, this was done to protect the on-going success of "The Velveteen Rabbit". A beloved children writer suddenly releasing a hair-raising horror novel would have caused a confusing situation for fans of the cuddly bunny. In any case, that's the theory and it was probably a wise marketing move.

There was long thought to be little difference between the 1913 and 1924 versions, but the rarity of both books made it difficult to sort out. Recent scholarship by Russ Bernard and Douglas A. Anderson discovered significant changes to the final chapters of the novel. In addition to the Americanization of British spelling, final scenes were added or expanded, leaving less doubt about what the "Thing" is. The American edition adds more tension to the narrative and better fleshes out the beast's origin story, and so that is the version we are presenting here.

More than a novel of the supernatural, "The Thing is the Woods" is also a superb murder mystery. In many ways the narrative follows the tried and true form of golden age mysteries. An outsider arrives in a small, isolated community and is introduced to an quirky mix of locales—some likable, some loathsome, and none of them above suspicion. An improbable murder occurs that points to something supernatural or super-human. Some red-herrings are introduced to further mystify the reader. The novel may also be the first fictional reference to The Jersey Devil—a bit of regional interest thrown into the mash. There was a rash of Jersey Devils sightings in the South Jersey pine barrens in 1909, about the time Lawrence was writing the first version of her novel. There were so many sightings that monster possies were formed to comb the woods with shotguns, and of course the obligatory monster posse pitchforks and torches.

So now we present "The Thing in the Woods". Pitchforks and torches are not required, but you may want to pack a bookmark.

Editor's note: In preparing "The Thing in the Woods" for this anthology a few minor corrections were made, but the text otherwise closely follows the 1924 American edition. Reflective of the time and place it appeared, the novel may contain outdated and offensive cultural references and depictions.

THE THING IN THE WOODS

by Margery Williams

1

LENNOX SAYS GOOD-BYE

I HAD just made my rounds of the wards for the last time, that June evening, fifteen years ago, when Murchison, my chief, came to me with the open letter in his hand.

"Here's the very chance to suit you, Haverill," he said. "Read that! A chap named Lennox, in Pennsylvania, wants a substitute for three months. Small country practice—no work of any account, I imagine—and a good holiday thrown in. Just reached me tonight, by chance."

I had finished my term as *interne,* and was leaving the hospital the next day. The whole summer was before me, for after three years of heavy work I owed myself one good vacation before settling to the task of building up a private practice, and I was glad enough of the chance to turn it to advantage. Every dollar I had saved I had put aside for the future struggle, and Murchison knew it. How to take a three months' vacation on next to nothing was no easy problem, and only such an opportunity as this, for which I had been searching vainly for weeks past, could solve it.

I glanced at the signature below the letter. "George Lennox . . . I used to know a George Lennox at college."

"Probably the same man. He asks me to recommend someone reliable. Funny idea. He can't have much opinion of his country colleagues, or he'd simply hand the patients over. There can't be so many of them, in a place like that. Rather fussy, I gather! Well, it might suit you. I thought I'd ask you before I spoke to anyone else."

621

It suited me so well, in prospect, that I sat down at Murchison's desk and wrote off my application then and there. Lennox's answer came promptly, dated from the small town in Pennsylvania where he had been settled for the past five years. Beyond a few details about the place, his letter told me very little. He was leaving for his health, to take a three months' holiday abroad, and he wanted a substitute as early as possible. The practice was that of the average country doctor in a not over-populous neighborhood. It was a bracing district, not far from the moun-tains; there was good fishing, and some shooting in the fall, and with the arrangements he offered it fell in perfectly with my own plans. He was urgent that I should take over the work as soon as I could, and after a brief correspondence I settled up my affairs in the city—they were not many—packed my few belongings, and went down.

It was a small and primitive station at which I was deposited, after a somewhat uninteresting train journey. The place struck me, even in those days, as a survivor of an earlier age; one of those little backwaters left behind in the flow of progress. As I stood looking about me at the stretch of dusty road, the hotel, and the few clustered shops that marked the beginning of the village street, the station-master came up.

"You're for Doctor Lennox, ain't you?" he began. "His buggy's there waitin'. I reckon Pete's over at the saloon, puttin' in time! I'll step over an' tell him."

I put my valise in the solitary vehicle he indicated, with a smart roan mare in the shafts, and a moment later "Pete" appeared, drawing a furtive black hand over his mouth. I addressed him curtly; if he was to be my factotum during the next three months there would have to be less of these rather free-and-easy ways. He eyed me civilly, with some curiosity, muttering a darkie's invariable ready excuses; climbed to the buggy seat, tilting his straw hat over his eyes, and we set off.

The village was not large. It seemed that Lennox's place was some mile and a half out, and our road led for the most part through woods. It was pretty country. The trees were tall and close-growing, hickory and oak, with young saplings pushing a sturdy growth between. There were boulders everywhere, the sullen granite that in this district crops out through the earth's scant surface, making the small farmer's life a per-petual harvest of stone picking. To me, fresh from the city pavements, it was picturesque enough. Once a hare loped across our path, and I saw Pete shift the reins to scrabble in his coat pocket. He cast a half-sheepish glance at me as he did so.

"Have you lost something?" I asked.

"No, sah! I jest recollected suthin'. Raikon dat hyar remin' me!"

"Meeting a rabbit is supposed to be lucky, isn't it?" I remarked, lighting a cigarette. "It seems to me I've heard so."

He looked at me suspiciously, and I knew that I had divined correctly the reason of that sudden dive. "Dat so, sah?" he said guilelessly. "I 'spect all dem things jes' depend!"

A few yards farther the road took a bend. Along the narrow footpath at the side a girl was walking. She was dressed in a short golf-skirt and cotton blouse, with a man's Panama on her head, and from her look I took her for a chance summer visitor rather than a resident. I noticed her only casually, but as the buggy drew abreast she lifted her head, and instantly I felt Pete swerve against me on the seat. His clumsy action made the horse start. The girl laughed, a little mocking ripple—I heard her with a glow of annoyance—and we shot off at increased pace up the road.

I turned to the man angrily; he had drunk even more than I supposed. His face was actually pale, as pale as a darkie's can be. His hand was in his pocket again, and he turned my blame promptly on the horse.

"Yoh clumsy trash, ain' yoh look whar yoh goin' a-skeerin' folks that way! I'se lam yoh suthin' some day!"

"What's the matter with you?" I said. "Can't you drive steadily?"

He fell to muttering, apologetic, conciliatory.

"'Deed, sah, dat hoss ain' got no sainse! I done druv dat boss two years, an' I *know* her, sah! Dere ain' no hoss round got less sainse. Sho as we met dat hyar I knew there was suthin' boun' ter happen! I ain' got no use fur meetin' hyars in de mawnin'—no, sah! I ain' doin' no *business* wiv 'em!"

We reached Lennox's house without further incident. It was a grey stone house, standing back in a pleasant garden, with barn and small orchard adjoining. Lennox was out on the porch to welcome me. Pete led the mare swiftly round to the side and began to unharness; I think he was anxious to escape any possible comment I might make to the doctor on his condition.

"Well, so you've got here!" Lennox said as we shook hands. "I'm very glad. Did you have a tiresome journey? Come inside. I'm very glad to see you!"

His tone was cordiality itself. To my ears it had even a note of relief. It struck me instantly, as I looked at him, that he had been through some recent stress of worry, if not ill-health. He had aged considerably. He was older than I, and his hair already a little grey at the temples. His face was lined and troubled, and he had an uneasy way with his hands I did not like. I had known him always as a rather steady-going, plodding sort of fellow, not given to excess of nervous energy in any form, and his present appearance gave me something of a shock.

He led the way into the house. Dinner was already served. Lennox followed the country custom in dining early. I don't know how the staid elderly woman, who was both cook and housekeeper, and who was to fulfil the same offices for me, would take to such an innovation as dinner at seven. I ate well after my journey, Lennox but sparingly. He offered me a highball with the meal, but drank only water himself.

"I've got into country ways," he said. "I'm afraid you'll find the place a bit dull, Haverill, but you'll manage all right. You can get most things you want, down here; the tradespeople aren't bad."

Over our meal we talked chiefly of the University days when we had been more or less friends—though Lennox was already a senior when I entered—of the men we had mutually known and of their careers, and lightly only, of our own. Lennox was not over-talkative, but he seemed more at ease as the day wore on. I could see he was glad to have me definitely there, was anxious to start, but I was not quite prepared for his answer when I asked him what day he thought of leaving.

"Oh, tomorrow! I shall get the twelve-thirty to the city. Everything is ready."

I suppose I looked rather blank, for I had counted on a couple of days at least in his company before I was left alone.

"You'll find everything easy to hand. I'll go over things with you this evening. It isn't a specially busy place here, you know!"

"And you'll be away three months?" I asked.

"More or less. . . . My dear fellow, I want a change! I want it frightfully!" I agreed with him. His eyes were wandering round the room as he spoke. "The work's nothing here—worse luck! You'll have practically a holiday. But I'm quite run down. There've been some . . . some family worries. What's the matter, Pete?"

The coloured man had come into the room.

"De mare's done got anudder shoe loose. I 'specs I'll hev to take her into town."

"Again? You should have had it seen to this morning early." He spoke irritably. "Take her in, and don't be late back!"

"Yessah!"

Pete went out lingeringly, and I more than suspected from his entry that he had been listening, or attempting to listen, to our talk.

"That man," I said when he had gone. "Do you find him all right?"

"Pete?" Lennox lit a cigar. "He's invaluable! You'll find him a spleen-did servant. He's been with me three years, and I wouldn't part with him for a good deal. He has his faults, as all darkies have, but he's thoroughly trustworthy!"

I thought of the furtive groping in his pocket when we passed the hare.

"A bit superstitious, eh?"

"What do you mean," Lennox fairly wheeled on me. "Has he been talking?"

"I imagine he carries an assortment of amulets about with him."

"Oh, that!" He looked vaguely relieved. "All of 'em do. He's a walking catalogue of superstitions. It's the only thing we have rows about. I detest all that nonsense!"

"I'll have a talk with him, some day," I said.

"I wouldn't advise you to. In fact, I wouldn't advise you to encourage him on the subject in any way. I think it's better to leave those things alone. Darkies are darkies, and no power on earth would persuade Pete against his rabbit's foot. No! Steer clear of that, my dear fellow, and you'll find him all right."

We spent the afternoon in the surgery. Lennox showed me a detailed account of his cases—they were very few—in a notebook. He had evidently been at pains that I should find no trouble in taking over the work.

"I've left some things in rather a mess," he said. "I told you I'd been upset lately . . . but I think you'll find it all right."

Supper was at six. Pete, true to his word, brought the mare back well before dusk. I could hear him whistling in the coach-house as he hung the harness away.

"I suppose you'd find use for a motorcycle here?" I asked Lennox as we sat in the dining-room after supper. It was barely dark outside, but the housekeeper had already drawn the curtains and lighted the lamp. I would have infinitely preferred my pipe on the porch, but if Lennox chose to stew indoors in this weather it was no business of mine, and it would only be forced on me for one evening.

"I used to have one," he said, "but I gave it up. The roads aren't very good here, and I found a horse better. Did you bring one?"

"It's coming on tomorrow."

"Oh? Well, you'll suit yourself. The roads aren't very good at night, but the mare is used to them. Not that I have many night calls."

It was a few minutes after that he looked at me suddenly as we sat opposite one another across the unlighted hearth.

"I suppose you're fit—in good health and all that? I didn't ask."

"Perfectly."

"That's good. Never had any nerve trouble, for instance?"

"Not an atom!"

"I'm glad. It's as well to be sure, you know." He laughed, rather apologetically. "I was quite lucky to get you."

It seemed that Lennox kept early hours. It was barely half-past ten when he proposed turning in. The heavy country air had made me sleepy, and I was ready enough to follow his lead. Lennox's room was directly over the surgery, with which it communicated by a little staircase, convenient for night calls. Both the surgery and the room above it had been built as a later addition to the house. The bedroom would be mine later; for the present I was put into a small extra bedroom across the landing from his own.

I slept heavily, but a little after midnight, as I judged, I was roused by hearing movements below stairs. People were talking; I fancied I heard a woman's voice, low and querulous. Evidently it was not a call too urgent to wait for daylight, for a few moments later I heard the floor of Lennox's room creak as he returned to bed. I fell asleep again easily, and when I woke the second time it was broad daylight.

I asked Lennox at breakfast if there was any fresh call for the day. He looked at me narrowly.

"Only the scarlatina case in the village and the woman at the Bend," he said, referring to the two cases he had mentioned the day before. "The woman is doing all right, but you might look in during the afternoon. The buggy will be back by one o'clock."

I smoked a pipe out in the orchard while he finished his packing. No one came up the road the whole morning except the baker and a travelling tinsmith; Lennox was right when he said I could take my work easily. The house stood in a pretty enough position. There were woods behind and about, skirting the orchard, and in front, on the other side of the road, a strip of pasture sloped to a little brook. The nearest dwelling was some two hundred yards away, down the road to the village. It belonged to a small farmer, I learned, a Pennsylvania Dutchman, as were most of the people about.

At twelve the mare was hitched and waiting, and Lennox came to bid me goodbye, after a few final instructions. We shook hands, and as he climbed into the buggy and took up the reins I don't think I ever saw a man's face express more utter and absolute relief.

2

THE LIGHT IN THE WOODS

MY first week passed uneventfully. I was called out twice only, on trivial cases, and I put in my spare time exploring the neighborhood generally. I was jaded with city life, and hospital work in particular, and it was a perfect tonic to do nothing. I was too lazy even to fish, though an excellent trout stream ran not far from the house, through the woods at the back. Neighbors were not likely to trouble me, nor I them. So far I had had but little intercourse with the people about, except for professional visits and the usual country exchange of greetings when I drove into the town for my mail. In Lennox's time this task had fallen to Peter, but it was some years since I had enjoyed the use of a horse, and I took pleasure in these short trips.

The housekeeper was subdued but efficient; she looked after my wants methodically enough and rarely offered conversation, which suited me. With Peter I got on all right. As Lennox had said, he was docile, willing and capable, and did his work reliably. He seemed devoted to the mare, and would converse with her at great length over the morning grooming.

Lennox had a fairly good library. In ways the house was comfortable enough, and I fancy he must have had some small private income in addition to the proceeds of his practice.

I had my first tiff with Pete when I had been there nearly a fortnight. Kerosene had given out; the oilman had omitted to call as usual, and Mrs. Searle, the housekeeper, only made me aware of the deficiency at suppertime. After the meal I ordered Peter to hitch up and drive down to the village to get it.

To my utter amazement he refused almost point-blank to go. He had a lot of work to do; the buggy wasn't washed down yet; the mare hadn't finished her feed. He'd go first thing in the morning.

"Nonsense, Pete," I said. "The oil's wanted now. The mare hasn't done five miles today, and it'll do her good! You washed the buggy this afternoon, because I saw you."

"Dat so, sah?" He rubbed his head. "Yes, I specs dat's so, now I

627

think. I disremembered it."

"Then hurry up. You can be back by eight."

His eyes rolled on me.

"But it done get *dark* by eight, sah!"

"Well, you can take the carriage lamps!"

"I ain't gwine take no kerridge lamps—no, sah! All de time I wuk fur Doc' Lennox he ain' ask me to do no thing like that—no, sah; an' ef he ask me *now* I ain' gwine do it."

"But you've driven the doctor at night, you fool, time and again!" I cried, losing patience with him. "Don't stand there and tell me lies!"

He kept his ground, obstinate, deferential.

"Yessir, I done druv Doc' Lennox. I ain' sayin' nothin' 'bout that. I'se gwine drive you, doctah, ef yoh ask me, but I ain' gwine no village affer dark tonight ter git no ker'sine. I ain' gwine monkeyin' wi' no ha'ants, an' I d'want no ha'ants monkeyin' wid *me!*"

That potent darkie word "ha'ants" gave me a clue. I strode out into the kitchen to Mrs. Searle.

"What's this nonsense with Peter? What is he afraid of?" I asked her.

Mrs. Searle's grey faded eyes rested on me a moment inquisitively. Then she went on with her dish-washing.

"I reckon Peter's scared of the dark, sir," she answered civilly. "Them niggers is jest like that! The oil can wait, as well as not. There's more'n I thought, or I wouldn't have mentioned it to you."

"It isn't going to wait," I said. "I'm not going to have this absurdity in any house I live in!"

I went back to Pete in the dining-room. I had left the doors purposely open, and I swear he fairly squirmed when he saw me come in.

"Now, Pete," I said. "You put the mare in at once. You're going after that oil and I'm going with you, if you're such a holy coward that you're afraid to drive a mile of road after dark alone!"

If I had hoped to shame him, it was without result.

"All right, sah!" he answered grandly, though I saw the relief in his eyes. "Ef you'se gwine I'se gwine. Dey ain' no one gwine call *me* no cowa'd, doctah!"

He went off to put the mare in, and in ten minutes I heard the grate of wheels before the house. It was already dark outside, but a moon was rising, and before we had driven far the carriage lamps were scarcely needed. Pete was subdued; I think he was trying to preserve his dignity in silence. I was tempted to a lecture, but remembered what Lennox had said of the futility of trying to combat darkie superstition. I was sure that

Pete still carried his beloved rabbit foot, and I hope it gave him comfort on the drive.

We reached the village, took in our can of oil, which Pete stowed under the buggy seat, and started to drive back. The moon was full overhead now, but obscured more or less by fleeting clouds. I saw Pete glancing several times at the buggy lamps. Presently he slackened the reins a little.

"I reckon we mought put dem out now, sah! Dey ain' no need er dem lamps to see by."

"As you like, Pete. Get down and put them out. I'll hold the reins."

"I ain't got no need er gittin' out, sah! I kin raich 'em from here."

He leaned over the splashboard at some inconvenience and extinguished the lamps, it seemed to me with unnecessary alacrity. I could not put his anxiety down altogether to the price of kerosene.

"What's your worry about those lamps, Pete?" I asked.

He turned guileless yet uneasy eyes upon me.

"Dey jest ain' no *sainse* burnin' 'em! Dey worry a pusson drivin' dem lamps do."

I let it go as one of his unplumbed darkie mysteries, and we drove on. We were just entering upon the densest stretch of wood between the house and the village when a curious sound caught my ears. It was like the scrambling rush of some big bird through the trees to the left of us; a night-hawk, probably, though the confused wing-flaps were more like a turkey-buzzard. Coming unexpectedly in the silence it startled me, but before I could turn to Pete he had dropped the reins and flung himself upon me, a frenzied babbling lump. He clung and muttered, while I strove to hold him off, and the mare, taking fright at the moment, sent the light buggy rocking from side to side on the road. I gave the man a push that nearly threw him out. Once free of his clutch it was only a moment's work to secure the reins, but we shaved a bad accident by the skin of our teeth. Luckily we were not far from the house. My grip startled Pete into sanity—it was at least flesh and blood that had him there—and by the time I had pulled the mare to a standstill before the gate he was able to get out, shaking still miserably from head to foot, and seize the bridle.

Between us we got the mare unharnessed and into the stable. She was in a lather over head and shoulders, and I stood over the cringing Pete while he rubbed her down. I think he never ceased praying the whole time.

Whatever the noise was that had frightened him—and I put it down to no worse than an owl at the most—it had frightened him thoroughly. There was no use attempting reason or rebuke with the abject tooth-chattering being that followed me to the house, and I sent him to bed with a grim reminder that I would talk to him on the morrow. He did not go up immediately, however. For a long while I heard his voice in confabulation with Mrs. Searle in the kitchen, where I did not doubt he had made haste to secure every door and window against the outside air.

I lit a pipe and threw myself down in an armchair in the surgery, where I had been in the habit of spending the last few evenings, putting things to rights after my own fashion. If Pete's superstition was going to obsess him to this extent my summer was likely to be a lively one! No bird that ever flew was sufficient to justify the extraordinary state into which he had thrown himself. Whiskey might be at the root of it, despite Lennox's faith; I had kept him under my eye in the village, but I knew that no human vigilance is sharp enough to keep a darkie from drink if he has the tendency. The sideboard was usually unlocked, but tomorrow I determined to take the key into my own possession.

Wanting something to read, and too lazy to go back into the sitting-room, I fell to examining the contents of the surgery bookshelves. There were the usual array of medical books, some new, some old; apparently Lennox had kept himself more or less up to date. At one end, on the upper shelf, were several volumes on mental diseases, "Lunacy and its Causes," Hoffman's "Congenital Insanity," and one or two recent patho-logical treatises that I knew only by title. There was a well-known medical work on criminology among them also, and from their number and disposition, and the several paper bookmarks that caught my eye here and there, I judged that this particular study must have had some attraction for Lennox. There was nothing, however, that interested me for the moment, or that promised cheerful reading. I had not come down here to dive into works on mental disorders or the bound reports of Lunacy Commissions as preliminary to passing a healthful holiday, and I fell back on a month-old magazine that was lying on the surgery table.

When I had finished it I turned the lamp slightly down and went out on the porch, with the idea of trying to locate again the noise that had caused such catastrophe that evening.

The woods about were very still; not a leaf moved. The silence had an intensity that was almost oppressive. Clouds had gathered, obscuring the moon, and it was quite dark.

Presently, above the line of the farther treetops, a gleam of light shot up. It moved and swept, like a white arm outstretched against a black curtain. So near as I could judge, it came from the direction of Sliefer's dam, a point some two miles away, and at first glimpse I thought it might be a fire, but the whiteness of it put that out of the question. It had the appearance of a crude searchlight, but it was less definite in ray and moved less steadily. More than anything else, it reminded me of those "jackies" that children love to make with a bit of prism refracted on a wall.

For several minutes I watched it, then, as suddenly, it was extinguished, twitching back into darkness, and I turned and went.

3

A MYSTERIOUS CALL

I HAD prepared a stern lecture for Pete while I was shaving next morning, but I was destined not to give it. While I was yet in my room Mrs. Searle called me from below stairs. "You're wanted over to the Bend, doctor, for Mr. Lessing."

I finished my dressing quickly and went downstairs. Coffee was on the table. Mrs. Searle sniffed as she set a cup before me.

"You'd best take something to eat before you start, doctor. It's a two'n-a-half-mile drive.

"Who is this Mr. Lessing? Did they say what it was for?"

I fancied she looked at me rather curiously.

"He has the new bungalow in the woods there. It's just before the turnin' to Sliefer's dam."

She spoke as though with a reluctance to name either the house or its owner, and there flashed across my mind instantly a remembrance of the first day Peter had driven me to the Bend, a few clustered cottages, hardly enough to be called a village, situated some few miles up the road. We had passed near the house then, just visible through the trees, and I had asked him who lived there. He had answered with the same reluctance I traced in Mrs. Searle's reply. Evidently this Mr. Lessing had for some reason managed to make himself unpopular in the district.

Peter had the buggy ready, and I started off. The mare was fresher than usual this morning, and covered the two and a half miles at a brisk pace.

The road ran level for some distance, then dipped to the little hollow known as Dutchman's Hollow, where it crossed a shallow stream, nearly dry in the summer. At the top of the hill, when you had crossed the stream, was the turning to the new bungalow.

The woods were emerald with early sunlight, and the dew hung heavily on brambles and undergrowth. Birds were everywhere, and I saw a Baltimore oriole, a rare flash of black and orange, fly across my path as we neared the stream. Above the marshy space at the foot of the hollow many dragonflies were glancing, jeweled and wonderful, and a small spotted turtle flopped from his stone in midstream at the near crunch of wheels.

I let the mare take her own pace climbing the hill. The morning was too fine for hurry, even on an unknown errand. When we reached the top, a glint of unpainted timber through the trees led me to the left, and a few yards up the crossroad I came out on a little clearing in which the house stood.

It was an ordinary one-story cottage, newly built, and as yet with no attempt at garden or enclosure. What struck my eye immediately was a curious sort of annex standing near it. It was a rather high, square building, windowless, but with one big skylight like an artist's studio. Yet it had not the look of a studio, and the skylight was so raised on four glass sides as to suggest a rude attempt at an observatory.

I tied the mare to a sapling in the shade, and went up to the house. The front door stood open, and the interior showed the usual living room of a summer cottage. It was furnished scantily but artistically. There were a few good rugs on the floor, a divan heaped with cushions, a piano, and a set of low bookshelves supporting a great bronze jar filled with wild-flowers. There were few ornaments about, but those few were chiefly of Eastern origin and good of their kind. It looked a room belonging to people of taste rather than wealth.

The divan was so placed in one corner, near a window screened by drawn curtains, that it was a full moment before I realized that it was occupied. A man lay there face downward among the tumbled cushions, in what seemed the apathy of complete exhaustion. He was clothed only in a suit of thin woolen pajamas, that showed the meagerness of his frame. He was so thin and slight that he seemed to fill scarcely any space on the wide couch. He was evidently not asleep, but he had not turned his head at my entrance—I could see only a patch of rumpled dark hair against the pillows—and I crossed the room and paused beside him.

"Mr. Lessing. . . ."

He moved, looking at me with petulant, questioning eyes from a face that showed every sign of physical and nervous exhaustion.

"Who are you? I sent for Doctor Lennox."

"My name is Haverill. I am taking Doctor Lennox's place for a few months."

"The devil you are!" He lifted his head, regarding me again intently with those queer dark eyes, the eyes of a boy set in a prematurely worn face. "Then Lennox has bolted!"

"He has gone to Europe for the summer," I said, looking him full in the face. "He told me he needed a change, and I gathered from his looks he was pretty overworked. So I'm afraid you'll have to put up with me for a while."

"That's like old Lennox! I thought he'd do it some day." He slipped back again among the cushions. "Where are you from?"

I told him. He repeated the name of the hospital after me mechanically. "I didn't know Lennox had gone when I sent over."

The tone was ungracious, but it was more the ungraciousness of a child than a rational being. I could see that the man's nerves were fairly on the raw. Judging roughly, I should say that he had not slept for several nights. I ignored the hint.

"As I'm here," I said pleasantly, "I might as well look you over, don't you think? What's the trouble?"

For a full minute he did not answer. I fancied he was turning me over very closely in his mind.

"The usual thing," he said then. "Overwork—like Lennox's!" A grim smile flashed momentarily on me. "I've been scratched up. That's what I want you to see to."

"An accident?"

"You may call it a dog!"

He turned, with a visible effort. Until now he had been lying almost upon his face. The light came obscured from the window, but as I bent forward I realized with a thrill of what extraordinary physical endurance that slight body was capable. The right sleeve of his pajamas had been torn down—it seemed that one single rip-and the edges of the flannel were caked and sodden with blood. As he threw open the jacket with the other hand I saw two long parallel scratches of the same depth running transversely across his chest.

My first act was to draw the curtain aside. He lay there blinking at me in the full light, watchful to see what change my face betrayed.

"What you think, eh?"

"I think," I said quietly, "that the sooner that dog is shot the better."

I made a movement to draw the jacket down, but at the touch of my hand on his shoulder he winced for the first time.

"I must have warm water," I said. "I suppose you are not alone here?"

Almost as I spoke a woman came into the room by a second door; evidently his wife. She was young, and her face would have been noticeably beautiful but for its expressionlessness. She had deep eyes, well-molded features, and a very clear pallid complexion, but her whole appearance suggested a slatternliness, evinced in the tumbled silk wrapper, the carelessly combed-back hair. I think I have never seen a woman, least of all in any crisis, look so utterly stupid and bewildered. Her eyes were pink about the edges, where powder had been hastily dabbed to hide recent tear-marks. I imagined that her first impulse in any emergency would be to weep.

"Have you warm water in the house?"

"I'll get it."

She disappeared toward the kitchen, and I followed her in. I wanted for the moment to be out of range of the man on the couch, and I thought it would give her a chance to say something to me herself of what had happened. She took up a bowl haphazard from the dresser, put it down again and took another, always with the scurrying half-frightened movement with which she had entered the room; went finally through a doorway into what appeared to be an outer kitchen to fetch the water. There I heard another woman's voice, clear-cut, decisive, with what seemed an undertone of forced cheerfulness to it. Scraps of a conversation reached me while I waited.

"They won't send it up. I'll have to go down later. And Scholl will let us have bread if I fetch it. I thought I'd better bring three now."

"Mary, it's awful!"

"Did that new man get here?"

Mrs. Lessing's voice was discreetly dropped, drowned by the accompanying splash of water from a kettle. But I heard the other say: "Is he any good?"

"Mary, *sh-h*!"

She fluttered back, and I took the bowl of water from her hands. Lessing was stretched on the divan just as I had left him, waiting my return. There was no chair near, and I looked about me impatiently for something on which to set the bowl, while the woman stood by in a sort of helpless indecision. Just as I was about to put it on the floor someone pushed Mrs. Lessing gently but promptly aside and came forward. It was the girl whose voice I had heard in the kitchen, and I saw in the second's glance I gave her that it was she whom I had seen on the road the first morning I came down.

"Give me the bowl," she said. "You can manage better if I hold it."

I stripped Lessing's jacket off as gently as I could, sponging the sleeve where it adhered to the torn flesh. He must have been lying untended there for some considerable time before my arrival. When I had laid bare his chest and shoulder to the light I set my lips to an involuntary whistle. The man looked as if he had been fighting with some wild animal. No dog had made those wounds. They were not bites; they were long raking cuts, as if the flesh had been torn by heavy blunt-pointed claws. A bear might have done it, but there was no sign of bruising or tooth-prints. The scratch on the shoulder was a good half-inch deep in one place—it nearly laid bare the bone.

He had bled freely; the jacket sleeve was soaked and stiff. I set to work to cleanse the blood from his chest, and as I did so I saw other wounds of the same order, some old cicatrices, others newly healed scars of perhaps a month old, but none so deep as the present ones. I glanced sharply at the man's hands. They were well kept, the fingers stained a little with acids as though in photography, the nails smooth and closely trimmed.

The scratches were ugly. I had slipped an emergency case of tabloids into my pocket on starting, and asking for fresh water, I dissolved two in it. The girl watched me steadily, holding the bowl of solution while I cleansed the cuts carefully, bit by bit, and I fancied that in her presence Lessing was at particular pains not to flinch. The man's endurance was extraordinary. I had noticed something else on his arm, but of that I did not immediately speak.

"You want iodoform?" said the girl. "There is some in the house."

She fetched it, with diachylon and a roll of sterilized gauze such as is used in hospitals, from the drawer of a Japanese cabinet. I dressed the cuts—it took some little time—and helped him into the clean shirt she brought me. When I straightened my back at last we were alone.

"Do you mind," said Lessing, "going to the cabinet there and getting me a bottle that's in the top left-hand cupboard? There's a glass with it."

I found both. I drew the glass stopper from the bottle and smelled it. It contained a familiar cardiac stimulant.

"It's all right. It's the stuff Lennox gave me."

I poured him a dose and he drank it. Then he dropped back on the cushions again, watching me. I drew a chair up, but on second thought remained standing.

"Well, Mr. Lessing," I said, "I don't know that I'm able to do anything more for you under the present circumstances. If you feel like wanting me, you know where to send."

"What are you in a hurry for?"

"I am in no hurry."

"Then sit down."

"If you think there is anything to be gained."

I sat down. I had dealt with his type before, and I waited.

"Well?" he said.

"You must know, my good fellow, that there's no use calling a medical man in to tell this kind of nonsense! I'm not a fool."

"Then there," he answered, "you differ most charmingly from old Lennox!"

I could no more be angry with him than with a sick child.

"No dog made these scratches!"

"I said you might call it a dog," he reminded me.

"I might call it an orangutan and be nearer the mark! Am I to conclude that you keep a menagerie in your house, Mr. Lessing?"

"Suppose I told you I did it myself?"

"I should call you a liar," I said. "I have seen your hands."

"Old Lennox swore I did. I told you he was a fool."

"We'll drop the scratches," I said, walking to the window. "I don't know that it really matters if you choose to tell me they were done by a tame mud-turtle in the back yard. But one or two things you'll have to stop if I'm looking after you."

"Such as?"

"You want sleep, man! You look as if you hadn't seen bed for a week."

"I sleep in the daytime. I have to work at night."

"What—photography?"

"Chemistry . . . of sorts."

"Chemistry doesn't have to be done at night, of necessity," I answered. "You're overworked and you're using yourself up. You know you've hardly a whole nerve left in your body at this moment."

"I've plenty in my shoulder," he returned drily, and I smiled involuntarily as our eyes met. There was a fascination in the man, despite his eccentricity, his absurd persistence in what seemed to be a tissue of childish and reasonless lies, to which I held no clue.

"That won't hurt you long. I'll look in again tomorrow." I wheeled on him abruptly, of purpose. "How long have you been taking morphia?"

I expected denial. Instead his eyes merely narrowed, appreciatively.

"A year, more or less. I take it when I can't sleep."

"Lately?"

"Not for several weeks."

"Yes, you have," I thought. Aloud I said: "I'll make you up something else, for a change. Can you sleep now?"

"I'll have a try."

"Better get to bed."

"I sleep better here," he said, and without more ado turned over with his face to the wall. I waited a moment, but he took no further notice of my presence, and I went out.

The girl who had helped me with the dressing was outside, feeding sugar to the mare. The two seemed old friends. I saw, as I drew near, that she bore a strong resemblance to Lessing himself, sufficient to proclaim her his sister. She had the same deep hazel eyes, but her hair was lighter; it showed a bronze glint as she stood bare-headed in the sunshine. It would have been an attractive face but for a look of cynicism, almost a hardness, in the lines of her mouth. I was glad that it was she I encountered instead of Mrs. Lessing. Here was at least one practical person in this puzzling household. She turned as I came near, but without moving.

"Your brother will do all right," I said without preamble. "Keep him quiet today, and if possible make him sleep. He wants rest badly."

She nodded, brushing the crumbs of sugar from her hands.

"How long has this been going on?"

"The not sleeping?" She looked at me sharply. "About four or five nights."

"I thought so. Can't you make him?"

She looked at me almost contemptuously, as though wondering that my interview with Lessing had taught me so little. "Does he look as if I could?"

"You can do it if anyone can," I said. "I shall be back tomorrow. If by any chance I am wanted . . ."

"I'll come and fetch you," she said.

"Good." I turned to unfasten the mare, then paused. "You have a dog here, I think. May I see it?"

For a moment she seemed about to hesitate. "If you like," she said then.

I followed her round to the side of the house. A small sort of toolshed stood not far from the odd building I had noticed, and which I saw now was not an annex, but separate from the house. The door of the shed was closed, and from within a whining and scratching greeted our approach. Without a word she turned the key and threw open the door.

A magnificent orange setter rushed out nearly knocking her down. There was nothing savage in his demeanor; he licked her hands and face and even tried to include me in the demonstration, but what caught my attention was his inexplicable behavior the next moment. He bounded straight toward the big outbuilding, but within a few paces of it he stopped, whining and sniffing, his ears laid back, his body trailed near to the ground, as though in some abject fear. Whining still, he dragged himself back to our feet and crouched there, trembling. Miss Lessing's voice broke the silence.

"Do you advise," she said, "that he should be destroyed as dangerous?"

"I think," I replied, "that is hardly necessary, at present. What's the matter with him?"

Her lip curled a little as she looked at me. She shrugged her shoulders.

"He is frightened. Do you believe in the instinct of dogs, Doctor Haverill?"

"What is that building used for?" I asked curtly.

"It is my brother's laboratory."

"Then what in heaven's name—?" I checked the exclamation on my lips. She was looking at me as her brother had done, but she seemed, at all events, to make up her mind more quickly. "Come with me," she said quietly.

We walked to the building. There was a door at the side fitted with a Yale lock, but it stood slightly ajar. She pushed it open. The interior consisted of one single room, that seemed from its fittings half laboratory, half workshop. There were shelves around, containing bottles, chemical apparatus, a few books stacked together. A long table, littered with tubes and glasses, stood almost directly under the skylight.

One corner of the room, to the right of the table, was screened off to form a darkroom, with the ordinary square of red glazed fabric let into the door.

I looked around the place with curiosity. There was nothing here to account for the dog's behavior. The contents of the table at one end were confused and overthrown, and a strip of cocoa matting, which had evidently lain under or near the table, had been rolled and flung in one corner. The boards were noticeably cleaner where it had been lying, and near the edge of this clean space there was a stain, smudged as though purposely by someone's foot, but to my eyes an obvious bloodstain.

Directly under the skylight, which was some four feet square, was the apparatus that for the moment puzzled me. It was mounted on a high stand that brought it near to the glass, and it looked like an acetylene lamp with very powerful concave reflectors; the kind of reflector, on a smaller scale, that is used in some lighthouses. The size of the lamp was quite outside the requirements of the room for ordinary lighting purposes, and the reflector seemed planned to throw the light outside the building, and in any desired direction. As I looked at it there flashed across my mind the recollection of the curious sort of searchlight I had seen the night before from my porch. Here was the solution of it, but I was puzzled to imagine what Lessing could be doing with an apparatus of this kind in such a place.

I turned to Miss Lessing.

"Was it here that your brother spent last evening?"

"Yes. He came out here about nine o'clock, after dinner. He often works late, and we never sit up for him. My sister-in-law went to bed soon after; she had one of her bad headaches that she has been subject to for the last eighteen months. I sleep in the room next to hers, and I went to bed about eleven. I am an early riser, as a rule, and when I came out of my room this morning I met my brother just coming into the house." She paused, and I could see that she was struggling with the recollection. "He wouldn't let me touch him, and he only said something about wanting to sleep, and that I should send Doctor Lennox up to him. I left him in the sitting-room and went straight off."

"Cycled?"

"No, walked. I have no cycle here. My brother doesn't like me using one. If I had, it would have saved time. I came through the woods."

"You were quick, anyway," I said approvingly. "Now listen, Miss Lessing. Your brother has had a severe shock; of what sort I know no more than you. He will probably tell us in his own time. For the present, I don't want him worried in any way. I shall come again tomorrow. If I may advise you, I would lock this place and keep the key until he asks you for it. Have you touched anything in the room since this morning?"

"No. It is as he left it."

Then Lessing himself had removed the telltale carpet. I thought a moment.

"Was your brother wearing pajamas when he went out last evening?"

"He changed into them after dinner, I remember. It is hot in here of an evening, and he nearly always wears them to work in."

"Did you hear any noise last night?"

"No." She hesitated a moment. "My sister-in-law was very restless last night, and she was talking in her sleep. She seemed to be in pain, so I went in to her, but she was sound asleep and I went back to bed. I heard nothing outside."

"Where was the dog?"

"Shut up. We used to have him loose, but he's sometimes noisy at night, and lately my brother has taken a fancy to have him shut up."

"It doesn't seem likely that he would trouble him here," I said.

She bit her lip.

"Doctor Haverill, what is it?"

"My dear young lady," I said, "I can know nothing until your brother is able to give us some account." I had almost said "chooses," but I changed the word on a look at her face.

"After all," I said lightly, "you must remember I am here only as a doctor, and a stranger at that!"

I turned back to where the mare was waiting, and she followed me, locking the door behind her.

"I shall be at the house all day if I'm wanted, but I don't think I shall be. Meantime, you'll remember what I've told you. Your brother will have to make up sleep before he can tell us anything at all."

She seemed to take it quite as a matter of course that I should be giving my directions to her instead of Mrs. Lessing. It was as if she took the responsible place instinctively in the household. I climbed into the buggy, turning the mare around, and she nodded a good-bye to me. My last glimpse, as I left the house, was of her slim bare-headed figure, wistful in its very air of self-reliance, standing there in the sunshine with the setter by her side.

4

DUTCHMAN'S HILL

TO say the thing puzzled me would be to put it lightly enough. For the rest of the day my thoughts kept turning to that enigmatic household at the Bend. The most puzzling point of all, to my mind, was why Lennox, in speaking of the people about, had not so much as mentioned Lessing's name. Here was a patient to whom he had, as I surmised, been called once before at least on the same mysterious errand as my own that morning, with whom he was more or less on terms of intimacy, and who must have provided almost his sole educated companionship in the village, and yet he had not seen fit so much as to touch upon Lessing's existence in my talk with him. Considering the words with which my own advent had been that morning greeted, I would have given much to be able to corner Lennox just then for ten minutes' conversation.

I had heard nothing from him so far, and the following morning, on the chance of there being a letter, I drove down to the village after breakfast. As I entered the post office Miss Lessing was just coming out. She had a brown paper parcel—an obvious butcher's parcel—in her hand, together with a couple of mail packets, and as I stood aside to let her pass she stopped to exchange a few words with me. Her brother was better, she said; he looked forward to seeing me that afternoon. We chatted a moment, and when she turned to go I said naturally:

"You might let me give you a lift up the road. I'm going straight back."

She smiled. "I'm used to walking, thanks all the same! Besides, there's a short cut through the woods I've found. It takes off nearly half the distance."

"You don't mind the woods alone?"

"I've got the dog with me."

I watched her straight slim little figure up the street, the dog following at her heels, and turned into the post office. The clerk had grown familiar during our daily intercourse. He handed me two letters with a ready grin—Lennox's handwriting was not among them—then leaned his elbows on the shabby counter and spat reflectively into the space below.

"Mr. Lessing had another attack, ain't he?"

"What do you mean," I said curtly.

"I heer'd you was called over thar, yesterday. Reckon you'll have enough to do if you take on with all the crazy folks round here."

I looked at him hard.

"Oh, I ain't got nothing special against Mr. Lessing. He's a pleasant-spoken chap, all I've seen of him. On'y when a man gits to meddlin' with things it ain't no person's business to meddle with he's liable to git called crazy—ef not worse. I ain't holdin' with what people say when they get to talkin'—no sir! I got enough to do tendin' my own business. But there's plenty won't go near Mr. Lessing's place after dark nor no other time, an' if you was to listen to them I reckon they got their reasons. They say his wife's as crazy as he is. Seems when he ain't traipsin' round the woods all hours o' the night he's shut up there in that stoodio place doin' his vivisectin'—"

"What?"

I laughed in spite of myself. Mr. Johnson looked sulky.

"Ain't that what they call it? I ain't no doctor."

"Mr. Lessing happens to be a student of chemistry, not a medical student, so if anyone's been trying to get round you with bogy tales they're talking nonsense. I'm surprised at a man of your education, Mr. Johnson, listening to such absurdities!"

"Then what does he shut himself up for, with a lamp you can see two miles off, unless he's up to suthin' he don't want folks to know?"

"Probably because he doesn't want a pack of ignoramuses meddling with his affairs."

"Well, that's what they say, and there's folks as believes it," he said sullenly. "An' as fur his walkin' in the woods, I ain't tellin' you anything but what's so. He was seen the same night as Jake Menning got killed goin' down Dutchman's Hill. It was Jakey's half-brother as seen him, an' Aaron ain't one to be tellin' lies. No, sir! An' if Doctor Lennox was here now he would tell you the same, for he was called out to see a sick child at the Bend that same night and it was him as found Jake Menning there the next mornin'."

"Do you know you're saying things you might get into trouble over?" I asked sternly.

"Oh, I ain't sayin' he had no hand in it," he returned promptly. "Everyone knows Jakey got killed through bein' too drunk to look whar he was goin'!"

I pushed a quarter over to him.

"Well, give me some stamps, Mr. Johnson. If you take my advice you won't pay quite so much attention to idle gossip."

I drove home, thinking. Lennox, or someone, had been chattering; that was clear. How far I had no means at present of knowing, for I was not going to pursue any further conversation with Johnson, ready as he was. A doctor who gives himself to gossip is no better than an old hen. I felt a sharp contempt for Lennox that overrode whatever interest I might once have had for him. If he had got himself into any tangle down here he deserved it thoroughly.

A light covered wagon, such as hucksters use, was outside the gate when I got back, and a man, who had evidently been bargaining with Mrs. Searle at the back door, came round and climbed into it. I had to pull the mare up to one side to give him room to drive off, and as I waited I happened to notice him rather closely, the more so as he gave me a civil but obvious scrutiny himself as he climbed over the wagon-wheel. He was a man of about forty, in a tightly buttoned coat of greasy black oilskin and a peaked cap, which might have belonged earlier in its career to a sea-faring man, pulled down over his forehead. His face, with unpleasantly close-set eyes, was scarred by smallpox, and apart from the repugnance which this disfigurement always inspires more or less, I think I have seldom seen a countenance which impressed me more disagree-ably. He was a man whom I would have ordered off my own premises anywhere at first sight, and I replied with a curt nod to his over-subservient greeting.

I left the mare in the yard and went into the parlor. Mrs. Searle had evidently been interrupted in her morning tidying, and she came back, duster in hand, as I stood there. I had enough experience to know her for a woman who did not give herself to gossip, though she probably knew all that was afoot, by the curious intuitive sense so highly developed in all women of her class. With her I would be perfectly safe in any inquiries I chose to make.

She apologized for her intrusion and set about completing her tour of the furniture, with noiseless briskness.

"I see you've been down to the village, sir," she said after a moment. "I was going to ask whether you'd order some more coal up for tomorrow, from Harkness's. It's most finished."

"I'll send Pete this afternoon. He can walk in. By the way, Mrs. Searle, what was this story about Jake Menning? I just heard something of it in the village today."

"Jake Menning . . ." She paused in her dusting, setting back a vase carefully on the mantelshelf. "I suppose you'd have heard of it, sir. He was killed last March, goin' down Dutchman's Hill. There isn't much water now, but it's generally deep there, long after the spring rains. Some did say it was done a-purpose, but the most of 'em thinks he jest had a fit an' fell in. Doctor Lennox found him, about six o'clock in the mornin', driving back from a night call. He was lyin' jest at the foot of the hollow, where them planks begin, with his face in the water. It wasn't deep enough to drown anyone ordinarily, an' that's why they thought it was a seizure.

"There was two half-brothers, Jake an' Aaron, both livin' over near the Bend. Aaron's took the whole business over now. Jake was always kind o' queer; they called him crazy sometimes, round the village. They was as like as two peas, which was queer, seein' they was on'y half related, so to speak. Down to the smallpox scars an' all. They'd both took the smallpox, but Jake took it worse, and they said that was what affected his brain some. You couldn't tell 'em apart, on'y for Aaron's stutterin'.

"Aaron was the best of the two. He's a good chapel member, and he's done a lot better in the business since Jakey's out of it. I heard they used to quarrel a lot in Jake's lifetime. Aaron's savin', and a bit close with his money too, and I recon he kep' Jake under some. He was an awful ill-lookin' man, Jake Menning—not that I like to say wrong of the dead, but I know a bad-lookin' man when I see one, an' Jake was that, for all his craziness. There weren't anyone liked him much, so they said he was harmless as a child, and right smart in business, an' now they ain't content with his being dead but they must get to startin' nonsense about his walking—excuse me mentionin' any such silly talk to you, sir!"

"Walking?" I stared.

"What they call it, sir," she explained apologetically. "You see," she went on, taking up her duster again, "Dutchman's Hill always did have a bad name, account of a pedlar bein' drowned there years ago, and now with this other business they try to make out the place is haunted again. They don't seem to know rightly whether it's Crazy Jake or the pedlar I told you of, but there's quite a lot of folks now won't go nigh the place after dark, no more'n if it had the plague."

"So that's what all this nonsense has been about!" I said, a light beginning to dawn on me. "I suppose Pete is right in it all?"

"Pete is like all the niggers, sir. They ain't happy unless they've got some sort of a ha'nt to tell about. Not that the other folks here is any better, an' I will say that of 'em. I never met such a gossipin' set in my life till I come here!"

Mrs. Searle herself was originally from New England, and eight years' residence here had not altered her original opinion of the people. For this reason, if for none other, I knew that she kept herself very sternly aloof from the minor scandal-making of the place.

"I suppose there was an inquest on this man?"

"Oh, yes, sir. They brought it in accidental causes, an' Doctor Lennox seemed to think the man died of heart-failure, an' he must have been dead before he fell in. Anyway it wasn't drownin', simple. I don't know. It was Aaron had heart-weakness in the family, as I heard, so it was queer Jake bein' the one took off that way!"

I rose.

"Well, I suppose the people here have precious little to gossip about, and they like to make a mystery of whatever does happen!"

"That's about as I take it, sir." She moved toward the door. "An' now I think, it was funny your asking me about Jake Menning, just this moment. That was Aaron as came round to the back door a while ago, as you drove up. He wanted to know if we'd like any chickens, so I took one for Sunday, seen' he only gets round once a fortnight now he has the whole business to attend to. I don't know whether it's thinkin' over it, but it seems to me he's getting to look more like Jakey every day. If it wer'n't for his stutterin' I could take him for a ghost myself!"

So that was Aaron Menning. Well, he might be a good chapel member, but he had a face that would hang him if my impressions went for anything. All the same, this put me no nearer to clearing up the mystery at the Bend, which was what interested me at the moment. Jake Menning and the alleged ghost of Dutchman's Hill were ordinary enough features in a village drama, but they could have no direct bearing on the problem that occupied my mind.

After lunch I told Peter to put the mare in. He lingered about the buggy when I came out, making unnecessary adjustments to the harness. I could see he was anxious to learn the outcome of yesterday's visit, and where I was going now.

"Is yoh gwine by de village, doctah?" he asked finally, with the air of one with a commission to request.

"No, I'm going to the Bend. There is no need for you to drive me," I added as I took the reins up.

I could have sworn the old sinner looked relieved as he went back to the coach-house. When I reached the bungalow I found Lessing himself on the porch. As he rose to greet me I saw that he was taller than I had thought; there was a certain wiry strength about him when he stood upright. What amazed me was the man's extraordinary endurance and resiliency; his face showed scarcely a sign of the exhaustion of yesterday. He was dressed in corduroy trousers and a soft silk shirt, under which the outline of the bandaging was visible as he moved.

"Well, how are you?" I asked as we shook hands.

"All right. Come into the house—or shall we stay here?"

"I'll have a look at you first." I followed him into the room. "A bit stiff?"

"Nothing much."

"Sleep?"

"Like a log."

I need hardly have asked him. He stripped up his shirt and I made a brief readjustment of the dressings. The wounds were going on all right. He must have had a magnificent constitution despite his slightness of build. We sat down on the divan, and Lessing produced a box of cigarettes.

There was a small wooden table near the window, littered with testtubes and odds and ends, and I nodded toward it.

"Been busy?"

"I was just working out something. I have a sort of laboratory fitted outside, though. I had it built."

"That sort of studio place?"

"It's just like a workshop—where I muddle occasionally! I'll show you sometime, if you like."

"I should be delighted."

"My experiments have, unfortunately, given rather a bad name to the place. They had a bad effect on old Lennox, too. I believe I was too progressive for him. You wouldn't expect that from a medical man, would you? Did you know Lennox very well?"

He knocked the ash off his cigarette, waiting for my reply. If he was guarded, so was I.

"I knew him at the University, a good while ago. Since then I had not seen him till the other day."

"He's a queer old bird! I used to tell him he made the ideal country practitioner. It made him mad because it was so exactly true. We used to disagree frightfully, you know. It's the only relaxation in a place like this. I shall miss Lennox . . ."

It struck me he was trying, in a casual way, to find out how far Lennox had spoken of him to me, and whether we had been at any time since his departure in correspondence.

"Lennox has quaint theories," he went on, leaning back against the cushions. "One of them is that nothing exists outside the pharmacopoeia and Burton's 'North American Fauna.' We used to argue it at great length.

I don't believe he's convinced yet."

"He was never an easy man to convince."

"So? It's habit that survives. How do you like it down here, by the way?"

"Oh, I'm putting in a good time," I smiled. "I fish a little, tramp a little. There ought to be good shooting in these woods by and by."

"They are interesting," said Lessing drily.

"Have you been here long?" I asked.

"Over a year." He rose and went into the kitchen, whence he returned a moment later, saying: "I thought I heard my wife there. We might as well have some tea."

It was Miss Lessing who brought the tea in, a few minutes later. She greeted me pleasantly, setting the tray down on the little table I pulled forward for her.

"Kate is lying down for a while," she said to her brother. "She has a headache. Do you take sugar, Doctor Haverill?"

I sat chatting there for nearly an hour. Lessing seemed at all events disposed to be friendly. All the while I was trying to reconcile this man who sat talking boyishly on trivial subjects with the outstretched figure I had seen twenty-four hours ago. If I had felt any resentment for his treatment of me yesterday it would have vanished utterly, and his complete absence of restraint now showed me, if I had needed it, how all memory of that mood had changed with his physical condition.

When I rose to go it was under promise to dine with them the following week. I fancied that Miss Lessing glanced hesitatingly at her brother before she seconded his invitation. It might have been only fancy; she was certainly cordial enough as we shook hands. "Next Thursday, then," Lessing called after me from the doorway. I drove home no less mystified than before.

5

THE DEAD CYCLIST

LENNOX sent me a note from Queenstown. I wondered, reading the brief cheerful account of his crossing, if he guessed how much I would give to have him cornered for a half-hour's interview. That he could throw considerable light on the puzzle I did not doubt, any more than that he had promptly put the ocean between us with a view to avoiding the very question I wanted to put to him. Anyway he was securely out of reach, and there was no use in wasting speculation.

My motorcycle had arrived some time ago, but up to now I had not made use of it. It was housed in the carriage-shed, to Peter's great curiosity. Once I had caught him meddling with it surreptitiously, and my lecture, garnished with many lies as to what would happen to him if he pursued investigations, wrought the desired effect on his superstitious mind. Devils offered to Peter the most natural explanation for anything he failed to understand. Having a free morning, it occurred to me to put the engine in order, and Peter, cleaning harness nearby, watched my proceedings with distrustful curiosity.

"Is yoh kwine *ride* dat 'ar thing, doctah?" he asked me.

"Sure!" I stood up, wiping my grimed hands on a piece of cotton waste. "Don't you think it's a likely thing to scare the ha'nts with, Pete?"

"Yoh talk er de ha'nts, doctah, 'cause yoh ain' done *seen* 'em. When yoh's done *seen* 'em, doctah, I raikon yose gwine talk er suthin' else."

"If I meet one on this, Pete, it'll give him such fits he won't do any han'ting for a week. Give me that monkey-wrench."

He eyed me gloomily.

"Dat ar thing's got a debbil in 'um sure, an' yoh ain' git no better er one debbil by mixin' 'um up wid anuffer—no, *sah!*"

"Peter," I said, "you are too conservative."

"I d'know dat. I d'know dat! De debbil's de dibbil, an' dar ain' no good yet come er mixin' up wid him. 'Tain' in de Bible nor 'tain' in nature, an' I ain' holdin' wid no such dealin's."

"Well, Pete, I'm going to back my devil against your rabbit's foot, anyhow."

Pete looked suspicious.

"Who's been talkin' 'bout rabbit's foots, doctah?"

"No one. Turn your pockets out, Pete!"

His hand clapped involuntarily to the side of his trousers.

"I got ter put dat harness away, an' I ain' got the time t' be hindered in! Sholy to Gawd, doctah, yob ain' s'pose *I* carry no trash like that!"

He straightened himself with dignity, hanging the harness up on its pegs. I finished my job and went into the surgery. I had written to the city for the drug I wanted for Lessing. It arrived yesterday, and I had made up the powders. They were lying on the desk with a rubber band about them, and the packet caught my eye as I came in. I called to Pete.

"I want you to take a prescription over to Mr. Lessing," I said. "You can take the buckboard and bring back that sack of feed from Sliefer's at the same time."

I held the packet out to him. He eyed first it, then me.

"Well?" I said impatiently.

"I'se gwine, I'se gwine. I was thinkin' on'y dis mawnin' how dat feed done oughter be fotched. Yessir, I was sayin' dat out in de car'ge-house. It done oughter be fotched *today.*"

"It'll be right on your road after you leave Mr. Lessing's."

"Yessir, dat so! On'y dat packet, doctah . . . I was jest considerin' dat packet. Ef I was to put dat packet in de buckboard longer de feed sack I'd be right scared 'er losing it. It don't seem to me, doctah, dat 'ar packet gwine t' be very safe dat way."

"But you've got a pocket, you old idiot!"

"Yessir, I done got pockets. I was on'y jest a-studyin,' doctah. I don' recommend pockets, not when a pusson's got a commission to 'tend to. When a pusson puts suthin' in his pocket, it happens sometime dat a pusson's gwine *forget* it."

"If it happens to you," I assured him, "I'll find a way of operating on your memory, so you'd better be careful!"

He took the packet without more ado and went off to get the buckboard ready. It was too fine a day to waste about the house, and I had it in mind to take the cycle out for a spin. Telling Mrs. Searle I would probably be away for lunch, I got into my cycling suit and set off.

I followed the road for some distance past the Bend, and then branched off to the right, joining the Pike. The machine was in good running order, and I did some twenty miles before I slowed up finally at a little village with the hope of getting something to eat.

There was the usual hotel and saloon combined, with its array of spruce bushes in tubs before the entrance. I leaned my cycle against the porch and went in to interview the landlord about a meal.

Dinner was by luck just ready. I cleaned off some of the grime of my ride and wandered into the commercial room, which was garnished with horsehair furniture, a mildewed engraving of Washington, and two plates of sticky fly-paper, buzzing and noxious, set out on the soiled tablecloth. There was one other midday guest, a young man in a gray suit who sat watching the struggles of the latest addition to the fly-paper colony while he waited for dinner. I placed him immediately as a newspaper man, and the first dozen words we exchanged, as I took my place opposite to him at the table, proved me right. He had been sent down on the trial of one of those dull and elusive scandals which serve to lighten the papers during the dead season, and had to put in two hours' waiting for his train back to the city.

He had a considerable fund of anecdotes which needed only the barest encouragement to set going, and he transferred his interest from the fly-paper to myself with complimentary promptitude. He had a trick of raising his voice a full three tones at the beginning of each sentence, and as his dissertations were lengthy I found myself speculating as to what new and rasping height his voice might next reach.

There was a week-old copy of a local paper lying on the table, and in a pause of the meal he pushed it over to me.

"There's a thing that might interest you, being a cyclist," he said. "What do you make of that kind of an accident?"

I read the paragraph he pointed out. It was the account of an inquest held on the body of a young man identified as one George Powell, salesman in a Philadelphia dry-goods store. He had been found on a stretch of road a few miles beyond Coopersville by a farmer taking an early load of milk to the Coopersville creamery. The handlebars and front part of his wheel, nearby, were damaged, and the broken lamp was picked up a few yards further on. The man was dead, but the curious part, which had evidently struck my acquaintance also, was that there were no injuries found on the body except a single diagonal scratch across the face, which was of sufficient depth to have destroyed one eye and to lay the entire cheek open. This in itself had not produced death, and the coroner's autopsy had revealed no symptom of concussion. The medical officer's verdict had been death from heart failure.

The injuries suggested attack, but there had been no robbery, and though the man's clothing was torn his pockets were apparently untouched. They contained thirty-five dollars in notes, in a pocket-book, some small change, and the papers that had led to his identification.

"Well?" said my acquaintance.

"It looks queer."

He laid a finger on the paragraph.

"You see the body was picked up fifteen yards from the edge of the wood. If anyone had laid for him, they'd have laid right in the woods, where there was cover. But whatever hit him, it hit him before he reached there."

"He might have run into something."

"As what?"

"I don't know." And there struck me instantly the thought that my companion put into words. "If you run into anything on a bicycle, at full speed, it doesn't generally happen that the handle-bars get the worst injury. You see that the front wheel was not much broken. And he was riding toward the woods, and it's going to take a pretty phenomenal shock to throw a man and his bicycle fifteen yards backwards. I'll tell you another thing. I happen to know that stretch of road, because I spent part of last summer near there with some people. It's a level stretch, cleared both sides, and there isn't anything larger than a stone to run into."

I waited, wondering what he was driving at. He chose a toothpick from the holder and began to employ it, leisurely.

"You'd reckon those things would strike the jury, wouldn't you? But they're so dam' simple down here that they're content to come up against facts like that, and they say: 'Well, here's a man got killed and we don't know what hit him. Guess we'll let it go at misadventure and go get a drink!' That's their mental attitude, and there isn't anything going to shake them out of it."

"What's your theory?" I asked.

He revolved the toothpick meditatively.

"If I knew, I guess I'd be up against a story that would make every newspaper in the country sit up. There's something queer there, and I'll tell you why, and you'll see just how enterprising these country juries are. Last April"—he raised his voice again, giving the toothpick an extra twirl in emphasis—"precisely the same thing happened to another man, not twelve miles from where this was. He was killed under much about the same circumstances, and the jury then returned the same old verdict, with a caution about the dangers of scorching. I happen to know, because I was down there on some story the time the thing occurred. I saw the man." He paused, and without knowing why I felt my pulses quicken suddenly in anticipation. "He had marks on his body that a wild-cat couldn't have made! He was picked up at the side of the path, among some stiff underbrush, so of course they said the fall did it. I tell you he was ripped, like I've seen a dog's face ripped by a badger. I've seen murder cases and I've seen accidents, but I've never seen the precise accident that would leave that kind of marks."

"You think it was murder?"

"The man wasn't murdered. He hit his head against a stone and died of concussion that time, right enough. But it was near enough to murder, if you assume an assailant who'd strap two-inch steel claws on to his hands." He laughed. "It's an original outfit! But that's what I'm asking *you?* What's the animal that goes round in these woods that's strong enough to wreck the steel tubing of a bicycle, that attacks with its claws and not with its teeth, and that's quick enough to knock a man down without the chance of a struggle?"

"There were no traces?"

"None. Not a single footprint."

All the while he spoke there had been before my mind the picture of Lessing—Lessing with those inexplicable scratches on his chest. Whatever had attacked these two had attacked Lessing also; that I would swear to. I was conscious that the young man was watching me rather closely.

"Heard something of this before, have you?"

"No. It interests me. But I think you're on a wrong tack."

"How?"

"Man alive, you don't suppose there could conceivably be any animal of that kind loose in the country without people *knowing* it! Someone would have seen it."

"I guess two people did see it," he suggested.

"If anything escaped from a menagerie there'd be a hue and cry raised. The woods around here couldn't give cover to any animal of that size and ferocity for three months without some track of it being found."

He said: "How about the murders in the Rue Morgue?"

"Those scratches weren't made by a monkey!"

I was unguarded. He looked up sharply.

"You didn't see them."

"You have described them," I reminded him. "Besides, an ape's instinct is to strangle."

"Not necessarily."

"Put the first down as a murder. The second might not have had any connection. There is nearly three months between. The medical officer suggested himself that the injuries might have been caused by falling on the broken bicycle framework."

"Medical officers aren't infallible. They've got to say something."

I laughed. "Well, stick to your escaped simian theory! If a third case turns up we'll see who's right."

I rose, paid my bill and went out, leaving him, I have no doubt, with the impression that I was a particularly hidebound idiot. But I had my own reasons for making no further contribution to his data. I would see this thing through without any assistance from a too enterprising press.

6

A BOYCOTTED HOUSEHOLD

THURSDAY evening found me at the Lessing's bungalow. Mrs. Lessing was in evidence this time, in a soft black gown that accentuated the pallor of her face. The evening did not correct my first impressions of her. She shook hands limply, contributed a few remarks about the weather, and then subsided on the couch in silence. Dinner was laid on a small round table near the window, and Mary Lessing came in from the kitchen with rolled-up sleeves and a big apron tied about her.

"We do our own chores here, Doctor Haverill," she said. "Do you want to make yourself useful?"

I rose promptly. Lessing had not yet appeared and my *tete-a-tete* with his wife was not exhilarating. I followed her out into the kitchen, where she gave me a can-opener and a box of sardines.

"Turn those out for me, please. And if you have any hygienic aversion to canned goods, smother it. We live on them here."

"You find it far from the village?"

She smiled, quizzically. "A good way. Besides, the tradespeople here aren't exactly genial. So we subsist on boxes from the city. It gives you all the real pleasure of a desert island without the risks. Put them on that plate, will you? You see, by the time the box arrives and gets hauled up from the station we've generally forgotten what we ordered, so there's all the excitement of discovery as well. This time it was olives. Do you realize the joy of unexpected olives in the wilderness?"

"I'm going to."

"That's the right spirit! Living in the country teaches one a becoming humility. There are more things to open. Perhaps it was a mistake to ask you out here, but in any case I could hardly have palmed off these peaches as grown in our own garden, because we haven't got one."

She was standing at the table, drying crisp salad on a white cloth. The position showed me only her profile, with a little wave of bronze hair escaping near one ear. "Do you think gardening is worth the trouble?"

"When things like this grow in every department store? Perhaps not. Good heavens, Doctor Haverhill, but you must *wash* that can-opener! Give it to me!"

I gazed at the jagged gash already achieved in the peach-can.

"Don't tell anyone and they won't taste it!"

"I thought bachelors knew how to do everything."

"Sardines and peaches go excellently together," I maintained. "They call it *salade de fruits poissonnés.*"

Lessing lounged in.

"I admire the way Mary sets you to work," he said. "She has a talent for being industrious by proxy. Here—" He pulled a parcel out of his pocket. "I've brought your cheese, but I won't answer for the state of it."

Miss Lessing cast a quick glance at me. "Where—?"

"Not at Johnson's. I don't know if my sister has explained to you, Doctor Haverhill, that we are a boycotted household? We find it quite amusing. It leads to a practice of expedience which is excellent training for the young. Mary has learned to make quite creditable bread already."

"Out of the sawdust they pack the canned goods in," put in his sister promptly. "Carry that dish in without spilling it, Dick, and don't talk nonsense!"

We sat down to one of the most cheerful meals four young people have ever enjoyed. I would except Mrs. Lessing, but that even her limp and monosyllabic presence failed to dampen our spirits. Afterwards Lessing made Turkish coffee over a spirit lamp while the two girls cleared the table, refusing my assistance highhandedly.

I moved about the room in the familiarity which our informal meal had fostered, looking at the knick-knacks, the row of books on the shelves. They were a pretty varied collection, poetry, some modern French scientific books and novels, and one of the most complete collections of detective literature I have ever encountered, side by side with a few textbooks on chemistry and some volumes on occultism and black magic, some familiar to me by title, others unknown. There was a monthly magazine lying near which I recognized as occupying itself largely with the subject of psychic phenomena, and turning it over I noticed Lessing's name in the index.

"You write?" I asked.

"Once in a blue moon!" He looked up from a critical stage in his coffee-making. "Does that sort of thing interest you?"

"Indifferently—if it happens to be genuine."

"There's so little genuine." He withdrew the coffee deftly, blowing out the lamp, and stood the little copper pot aside. "That's the worst of it. One endures hours of boredom for no result."

"You belong to the P.R.S.?"

"A most respectable and unexciting body." He smiled. "I would give in my demission, only they afford me a patient hearing from time to time. Besides, it gives me the opportunity of wrangling with someone, and contention is the spice of life, as I was saying. It was with that truism that I strove to console Lennox, when I bored him to extinction."

Involuntarily my ears pricked.

"Was that often?"

"No, I can't say the boredom predominated, in the long run." He surveyed his coffee with the air of an artist, his boyish head on one side.

"Where are those cups, Mary?"

"Your system of boredom seemed to have a remarkable effect on Lennox, anyway," slipped from me involuntarily.

Lessing laughed. "Oh, that was when the boredom ended! He stood it nobly to a point." He turned toward me. "Would you like to see what frightened Lennox, sometime?"

Before I could answer Mary Lessing came in with the coffee-cups, and the subject was dropped.

It was ten o'clock when I rose to leave, my departure hastened by a suspicion that Mrs. Lessing had glanced several times of purpose at the clock. They all came out on the porch to say good night, and at the last moment Lessing added: "I'll walk down the hill with you."

"I've got my motorbike," I said quickly, as Miss Lessing looked up. "There's no need to bring you out."

"Oh, it'll do me good!"

It was a still, sultry night, with a humidity in the air that had arisen since nightfall. We walked leisurely, smoking, as far as the crossroad at the top of Dutchman's Hill. The hollow below was alive with fireflies, gleaming and vanishing alternately in the soft dusk. There should be a moon, but within the past hour premonitory rainclouds had gathered, blotting it out. Lessing glanced at the sky .

"How long will it take you to get back?"

"Ten minutes, more or less. It won't rain till I get there."

I scratched a match, stooping toward my cycle lantern.

"Is it necessary to light that?" he asked.

"Why not? There's a bad bit of road at the bottom there."

"I find the glare of a lamp like that always makes it worse. What is it, acetylene?"

He bent over the lantern to examine it, and in the pause the match burned down and went out. I felt for the box again in my pocket, and as I did so Lessing let go his hold on the bicycle. The machine slipped by its weight, and reaching quickly to catch it I heard the unmistakable sound of escaping air.

"Now you've done it!" cried Lessing boyishly.

"Damn!" I groped for the rear tire. It was flat. "Here's a cheerful business. How the dickens—"

Lessing laughed. "We'll have to walk it now! Never mind. I know the road."

"I'm not going to bring you all that way," I said. "I shall be all right."

"Nonsense! I like a walk before I turn in."

He took hold of the cycle on one side, I on the other, and together we set off to walk down the hill. There is an exhilaration in walking through woods at night, even tempered by the necessity of pushing a heavy motorcycle before you, and my brief annoyance at the accident rapidly vanished. Lessing was boyishly high-spirited; between us we made a fairly rowdy trip of it. We had just finished the ascent of the other side of the hollow when he laid a sudden hand on my arm.

"Did you hear anything?"

"No. Why?"

I thought he was still joking, but his cloak of nonsense had dropped from him abruptly. He pulled me to the side of the road.

"Listen!"

There seemed nothing to listen for. I waited, rather impatiently. Lessing threw back his head, scanning the line of the trees that shut us in. "There!"

It was still in my mind that he was trying to play some game on me.

"It's nothing but a bird," I said.

"Bird? You heard nothing else?"

"No."

"Come on," Lessing said. He seemed abruptly sobered, and I fancied he was at pains to quicken our pace over the remaining stretch
of road. When we sighted the glimmer of the orchard palings I pulled up.

"Come on into the house and have a drink," I said.

"No, thanks, I must get back. By the way, do you carry a revolver?"

"What on earth for?"

"I only wondered. I should advise you to, around here." His hand slipped down to his pocket, and I heard a soft click.

"What are you going to do?"

"Have a pot at the birds, going back." He smiled. "Good night. Look in sometime during the week."

And he went off without further delay, whistling softly.

7

WHAT HAPPENED IN THE LABORATORY

INSTEAD, it was Lessing who came a day or two later to see me. He lounged in one evening when I was sitting smoking on the porch, after supper, and my first advice of his presence was the clatter of a zinc pail which Pete let fall promptly in the side yard. When Lessing rounded the corner of the porch he was grinning.

"Your nigger must have a bad conscience," he said. "I never saw anyone so afraid of the devil in all my life!"

I made a sound of annoyance. Evidently I had not finished with Pete yet. "He's a born idiot!" I said.

"I'm not so sure," Lessing returned. "He has a very practical regard for his own skin. I appreciate that."

"You ought to."

He gave me one of those habitual quick looks, his head on one side.

"Thanks! Do you find the mosquitoes bad around here? I got all bitten up coming past Dutchman's Hollow."

I took the hint.

"We'll sit indoors," I said. "It's pretty cool in the surgery."

He followed me into the room, glancing curiously about him.

"So this is where old Lennox hung out . . . the place has a look of him. What's that, butterflies? He always had a weakness for things he could stick a pin into and label nicely!"

"Have you never been here before?"

"Never. He used to come to my place. I have an idea you know, that Lennox still thinks I'm not right in the head."

I lit the student lamp on the table and set out whisky and a couple of glasses. Lessing settled himself in the shabby armchair opposite me, and for a little while we smoked in silence. In the half-shadow beyond the ring of lamplight I could see his face, fine and clear cut against the shabby morocco of the chair back, the dark hair tumbled over his forehead. He was staring up at the smoke wreaths in a curious intensity of abstraction.

"I suppose," he began at last, "that I owe you some sort of an explanation, as things go."

657

I made a little gesture of indifference. I was beginning to know my man. If it pleased him to work upon my curiosity I was prepared to give him the least possible satisfaction.

"You offered me one," I corrected him. "I believe we decided to let it go at that."

He turned his gaze upon me, with a rather charming impertinence.

"That was when I took you for a fool. As I admit the error you ought to forgive my expression of it. The truth is . . ." He paused so long that I reached for a fresh cigarette to break the interval. "I'll be damned if I know what the truth is myself!" He finished almost violently. "I can give you facts—all you want. When it comes to putting things together. . . . Do you know how maddening it is to have your hand on a thing—actually on it—and feel it all the while slipping through your fingers?"

He threw his cigarette away. "Let's drop all this nonsense, anyway. I came over here tonight to have a talk with you. I tell you frankly, because you're about the only sane man I'm likely to cross down here. I tried Lennox once, and Lennox thought I was batty, and there the matter ended. But I've got to a point now where it's absolutely necessary, for the sake of my own mental balance, that I should have someone else's opinion about things. I'm going to put certain facts before you, and you'll say what you think about them."

I nodded.

"About eighteen months ago," Lessing began, "my wife was in rather bad health. It was some sort of nervous trouble, which I need not enter into here, but the doctor said she needed complete change, and that she must positively live in the country for some time, a year or two at least. We came down here. I bought the piece of ground up the hill there and built the little bungalow we are living in, with the idea of using it later on, when her health is restored, simply as a summer cottage. I have a fondness for dabbling in chemistry, as I think I told you, and shortly after we moved down here I built that sort of outdoor study you have seen, so that I could have a place, perfectly quiet, that I could work in without being disturbed, and without messing the house up with my things. I am not a good sleeper. I sit up pretty late at night as a rule, and it worries me to know I'm disturbing other people in the house or that the women are liable to drop in in their dressing-gowns at half past one or so, to ask whether I'm going to bed or not.

"My laboratory has a top light for day use, and I have rigged up an acetylene lamp just over my table, with a pretty strong light. One night last fall I happened to be working rather late. As a rule I have no difficulty whatever about keeping awake—it's the other way about, in fact—but along about one o'clock I began to get rather drowsy. It might have been the fumes of the chemicals I was using, but I'm used to that, and anyway I don't think they could have affected me. My interest in what I was doing was still awake, but the other side of my mind seemed to get drowsy at the same time. I fought against it a long while, and then gradually I seemed to get the consciousness of something—some presence—in or near the room. I don't know if you have ever attended a seance, Haverill?"

"Never—of any account."

My cigarette had burned down to my fingers, and I threw it away. I was beginning to get keenly interested in his story.

"Well, if you had, you would know that one sometimes gets the sense of a materialization some minutes before it actually takes place. I suppose the subconscious part of one's mind acts more quickly than the senses in receiving an impression. Anyway that was what seemed to happen with me. I waited. I was awake; I want you to understand that clearly. I was as awake as I am now. I saw everything about me, but I seemed to see it in a quite impersonal sort of way.

"The top light is arranged to open in sections, the top as well as the four sides. The side glasses were my idea for bad weather, so that I could always have ventilation on one side or the other without rain driving in, as it will with an ordinary skylight. I had the middle section raised, and one side open as well. Presently I was conscious that something was trying to enter at the glass. There were no sound on the roof itself, which is galvanized, but I could hear plainly a sort of scraping at the window. The inside light was so strong that I could see nothing, but something was gradually obscuring the opening. I had a conviction that the thing, whatever it was, was attracted by my light, and I made an effort, with the strange drowsiness gaining on me, to reach the lamp and turn it out.

"I was on my feet, reaching across the table, with the glare of the lamp full in my eyes, when something—I don't know what—struck me and threw me to the ground. My hand was already on the lamp, and I must have managed to turn it out actually in the moment of falling. I have a recollection of struggling for a moment there in the darkness, of trying, with some sort of hazy instinct, to drag myself under cover of the table, and then I suppose I became unconscious.

"When I came to it was broad daylight. I was lying on the floor, near the table. There was broken glass near me, and I seemed to remember the crash of it before I lost consciousness. My clothes were torn, my arms and chest were badly scratched—I must have somehow defended my face without knowing it—and I was stiff all over when I moved. When I got into the open I was seized with an intense nausea, which lasted for several minutes. My wife and sister are used to my being up till all hours, so that my absence had caused no uneasiness. I went into the house, washed myself as well as I could, and went to sleep. It was then five o'clock, so that I must have been nearly four hours unconscious."

"Did you notice any other symptoms besides the nausea?" I interrupted.

"Yes; an intense fatigue. It was not sleepiness. I was tired out, as if I had been through some great exertion."

"Well?" I said, for I knew he had not finished.

"That was last October, the twenty-fourth, to be exact. Since then the thing has happened twice again. On each occasion I have had the same premonitory drowsiness. I have struggled against it, and it has mastered me at just the critical moment. The second time when I came to I was more badly hurt than before. My sister happened to be up early that morning, and there was no disguising my condition from her. She went off for Lennox. When he came he fixed me up and gave me a sleeping draught—which I didn't need—and I slept nearly the whole day. He held the opinion, which I wrested from him later, that I had had some sort of seizure, the result of overwork, and that I had inflicted the injuries on myself during unconsciousness. The rest he put down to hallucination. He was a fool, and I told him so. Whatever the thing was, it was no hallucination."

"How wide was the skylight open?"

"About eighteen inches."

"Did you find any traces in the morning?"

"Not a mark. The building is high, as you know, and the sides are of perfectly plain boarding. There is nothing that could give foothold, except to a monkey, and the nearest tree is eight feet off. Oh, I went over the whole ground carefully! Whatever it was that came, it did not reach me from the ground."

I moved impatiently. "But what other way could it have reached you?"

"That's what I ask myself," said Lessing grimly. "Do I look like a man subject to brain trouble?"

"No," I said. "I gave that theory up almost immediately."

"Then what do you make of it?" be asked quietly.

"Make of it!" I cried. "Good heavens, man, do you realize that you're asking me to believe a thing that's outside the range of all human possibility!"

"Human possibility! What is human possibility? I tell you the thing as it happened, simply." He rose and began to pace to and fro in the room. "I'm a sane man. I'm not given to imaginary things. And besides-you saw yourself—"

"Wait a moment," I said. "About this light. Have you used the same lamp right along?"

Lessing gave a quick look. I wondered if he had divined my visit to the laboratory that first morning.

"No. I altered it after the second time. There was an interval of over four months when nothing happened at all. I tried to reason it all out, and I concluded that in some way the lamp had had to do with it. From the position of the building, and the woods about it, the light I was at first using could be visible only from one certain direction. I wanted to investigate the whole thing systematically, and with that idea I raised the lamp and fitted a strong reflector that would throw the light outside the building at will, and in any direction."

His description corresponded with the light I had seen above the tree-tops, the night of Pete's adventure with the turkey-buzzard.

"You were using this the last time?"

"Yes. I had been experimenting with it, off and on, for several weeks."

"Have you any idea of the shape of the thing?" I asked him.

"So far as I could make out anything, outside the glass, I might describe it as some kind of dog. It seemed to be greyish. . . . But that as a theory is sheer nonsense. You know that no dog could have made the scratches you saw."

One thing still puzzled me.

"You say that you put the light out yourself the first time?"

"Yes."

"And the second?"

"There was scarcely time to get any definite impression," he answered evasively. "I was struck down almost at once."

"But you had the impression of a dog?"

"What does it matter?" he cried, with a sudden change of voice. "I tell you, Haverill, it was like nothing that I can describe!"

We sat there for some minutes in silence. I can see now the turn of Lessing's head, the restless movement of his fingers on the chair-arm. It seemed incongruous that we should be sitting here in this common place room, amid surroundings which spoke so emphatically of the practical routine of life, discussing that which should have branded us both as madmen.

It was Lessing who broke the silence first.

"What the good?" he said, with a short laugh. "I've told you the whole business, and it's up to you to make what you choose of it. The only conclusion seems to be that we are up against something which is, as you put it, outside the range of experience. Good. But suppose I told you that it wasn't outside the range of experience—that what I saw has been seen by other people, upon independent testimony, ten, twenty, thirty years ago?"

I thought of the reporter's story. But there would be time to contribute my data presently, after Lessing had told me all that he knew.

"Did you ever hear of an apparition called the Jersey Devil?" he asked.

"I don't remember it."

"You probably wouldn't," Lessing replied. He took a fresh cigarette from the box and lit it. "The tale afforded some stray paragraphs in the papers, at different times, much as the periodical accounts of 'authentic' ghosts do, but I don't believe anyone gave the slightest credence to it. The Jersey Devil, to sum up all that I have been able to glean on the subject, was a legendary monster, reputed to have been seen, on the evidence of several persons, at different periods during the past fifty or sixty years. The legend goes back, I believe, to just before the Civil War. According to the story, its appearance gives warning to some national trouble or calamity. It was said to have been seen before Lincoln's assassination, before the Spanish-American War, and before the assassination of President McKinley. It is described as a creature having the body of a bat and the head of a horse—sometimes as a quasi-human head on a winged animal body—and it haunts certain counties of New Jersey, chiefly Monmouth and Ocean counties, and has also been seen as far north as Pennsylvania. The legend goes that it is a changeling, that is to say, a devil which took possession of a child's body at birth and flew off in the shape of a monster. Why it should have developed the sort of national solicitude they claim for it is unexplained. Of course the evidence is almost entirely that of superstitious country people who saw it, or thought they saw it, but the fact remains that the evidence in every case tallies, even after intervals of ten or twenty years.

"We may take it that very legend has somewhere some natural origin, however much it may be subsequently exaggerated or distorted. Why, if this particular legend is purely imaginary, should it be confined to certain districts and not to others? We are not dealing with an apparition reputed to haunt one particular place. It has a pretty wide range of country, on the contrary, and its appearance has been vouched for, almost simultaneously, in places a great many miles apart. Why should it be seen in one certain county and not in the adjoining ones, where the inhabitants are probably equally superstitious? Also it is not seen actually at the time of trouble, when people's minds might be most naturally influenced by superstition, but days and sometimes weeks before the event. That fact in itself I attach no importance to. There is a coincidence, and people naturally connect the two ideas. But I mention it to prove that in no instance was the thing seen because it was expected to be seen; its appearance in each case was entirely without warning or predisposition."

I moved in my chair.

"We've got enough to deal with as the thing stands. If you're going to back it up with any old wives' tales of a bat-winged horse—"

"I'm not backing it up," Lessing retorted.

"I'm only asking myself whether the experiences that give rise to the tale of the Jersey Devil have any connection with my own. The details don't matter. I want to get at the origin of the thing."

"The two don't even tally!" I spoke sharply, for I had still uncomfortably before my eyes the vision of the dead cyclist on the stretch of empty road.

"They don't, on this point," Lessing continued coolly. "The Jersey Devil has never, to my knowledge, been credited with any malevolent intent. At the worst, assuming the tales to have some basis of truth, it has merely scared one or two respectable farmers driving home at night. Now the thing that attacked me, attacked me deliberately, and with an almost extraordinary ferocity of onslaught. I don't think there can be any question about that. That fact alone puts the apparition theory out of the game. We are not dealing with any mere visual phenomena. We are dealing with some actual existing menace. There is just one point that can lead up to the connection, if there is one, between the two."

"The attraction of the lamp?"

"Exactly. Those other people may have been carrying a lamp or they may not. In any case, it was probably a lantern of so slight a power as to escape notice. I said that the thing attacked me. But the real object of its attack might very well have been the lamp, and not me at all. I merely happened in each instance to be near it."

"But even admitting," I objected, "for the sake of argument, that the thing was a bat, I am not certain about bats being actually attracted by light. They blunder into it."

"Nor am I. As I say, I give you my only theory. And if you assume a bat, you must assume a bat of sufficient size to strike a man down at one blow. The whole thing's grotesque."

He pulled out his watch, and rose abruptly. "I must get back, or Mary will be worrying about me. We'll talk over this another time. If you go into the thing with me, we'll go into it thoroughly. Only you know now why I warned you against cycling with a strong lantern."

"Even to the extent of slitting my bicycle tire?"

"Even to that extent," returned Lessing gravely. "You see, I wasn't taking any risks."

We shook hands, and I followed him out to the porch. There was a clear moon, and the road glimmered white between the black line of the woods. As I watched the swing of his shoulders down the path I was left, I admit, with a definite sense of comfort at the proximity of my own four walls. And before sleep overtook me that night the words of the reporter came back again and again to my mind:

"What's the animal that goes round in these woods that's strong enough to wreck the steel tubing of a bicycle, that attacks with its claws instead of its teeth, and that's quick enough to knock a man down without the chance of a struggle?"

8

I GO FISHING

THE next morning was one of the most glorious that I remember in that whole summer. I rose early, throwing the windows wide open while I dressed to let in the full blaze of sunshine, and set myself, while the morning common-sense mood was still upon me, to go over carefully in my mind every detail of Lessing's story. Somewhere there must be a natural explanation; it was only the question of finding it. Among other things it occurred to me that someone, for reasons unknown, might be playing a series of practical jokes upon him, but it was difficult to credit a hoax of such malignant and serious intent, and even assuming for a moment that Lessing was the victim of any such plot, it did not explain those mysterious deaths which, I felt more and more convinced, were in some way connected with his own experiences.

It was at least certain that I was in for a fairly interesting vacation. I remembered with grim humor Lennox's assurance that I would find the practice a quiet one; opinions might well differ on that point. Even if Lennox came back at the time agreed upon, I had still another six weeks before me, and in six weeks a good deal might happen. It would be my own fault if I did not get some part of the mystery cleared up before then.

Everyone has his own private specific for clearing the mind. Mine was fishing. After breakfast I hunted out my tackle, asked Mrs. Searle to pack me a lunch, and set out resolutely, with the determination to remain in the open air until nightfall.

Part of the creek that lay behind the house I had already explored, and this morning I decided to work upstream, in the direction of the dam. The air was clear and fresh and the woods were alive with birds. Here and there the sumac and poison ivy were already beginning to turn color, showing patches of tawny scarlet against the green of the undergrowth. Great painted butterflies flitted across my path, and once, as I sat quietly on a boulder in midstream, a kingfisher flashed near me in the broken sunlight.

The creek ran with a pleasant sound in its bed, now swirling between great boulders, now trickling over shallows of waving bronze-tinted weed, here and there forming deep pools, outside the stress of the current, where one might catch a glimpse of shadowy forms moving through the gold-brown sun-shot water.

I made desultory casts, taking more interest in the morning and in my surroundings than in the actual pursuit upon which I was engaged. Out here under the trees, with the music of the stream in one's ear, it was impossible to feel anything but sane and healthy.

The silence of these woods was intense. In pine woods there is always some stir of movement, however faint, but these trees, giant hickories and dense-foliaged oaks, grew so tall that sound seemed lost amid their branches. One had the impression of miles of far-reaching solitude. To break the spell I began to whistle as I moved upstream, pausing now and then to try some likely pool, picking my way over the big rocks that dotted the bed of the stream. The creek was fairly deep in places; a child, losing its footing, could be easily drowned in the strong current. It was an ideal stream for sport, but either the fish were wary this morning or I was giving but scant attention to my task, for by midday I had only one small half-pounder and a missing hook to my score. Mrs. Searle's luncheon packet bulged in my pocket, reminding me presently of hunger. I was reeling in, preparatory to settling down by some comfortable tree trunk, when something rushed at me with a splash and a scurry. I was standing at the moment on a rounded boulder near midstream, and the impact threw me off my balance knee-deep into the water. I turned to see the Lessings' orange setter.

"Oh, you *bad* dog!" a voice exclaimed from the bushes. "Whatever— Oh, Doctor Haverill, I am so sorry!"

Mary Lessing stood on the bank, bareheaded, in a short golf-skirt and up-rolled sleeves. The dog bounded back to her, and she dealt him a summary and ineffectual cuff on the ear.

"Don't do that!" I cried. "I was just thinking how cool it looked in here, anyway!"

I waded to the shore and joined her. "I can't shake hands, because I'm wet," I added. "How are you? I've been trying to fish, but the trout here are entirely too sophisticated!"

"You've frightened them for good now!" she laughed. "What a shame! Did you catch anything?"

"One wretched half-pounder. I put him back for luck."

"A poor luck!"

"I'm not so sure," I rejoined, smiling, and she stooped hastily down to address the setter, who sat regarding us with lolling tongue.

"When are you going to learn manners, you wretched animal? You haven't even the grace to apologize!" The setter put up a muddied paw and scraped appealingly at her skirt. "You deserve to go without biscuits for a month," she continued. "Go away from me; don't shake yourself here!"

The command came too late, and we both dodged to avoid the jubilant shower of water drops. Mary Lessing shook her skirt and sat down.

"Do you often explore up this way?" she asked.

"No. It's the first time. I've no idea now how far I've come."

"You're about ten minutes from the dam," she said. "Our cottage is not very far off. I was just going back to lunch."

"And I was just going to have mine here." I clapped a sudden hand to my pocket; the paper parcel was still luckily intact. "Suppose we were to consider it a picnic? I don't know what Mrs. Searle has put up for me, but I have a recollection that she baked apple cake yesterday. It's too entirely gorgeous a day to eat indoors."

"Oh, as for that—" she began.

"As for that, you must admit that lunch indoors doesn't tempt you in the very least."

"It doesn't," she said. "I came out here this morning because—"

She stopped rather abruptly. I was looking about me for a likely spot in the shade, and when I had found it, at the base of two towering hickories, I pulled Mrs. Searle's parcel out from my pocket. The setter watched my proceedings with a keen interest, intent on the chance of the moment.

"I'm convinced," she objected, "that you ought to go home and change your boots."

"It's impertinent," I reminded her, untying the pink grocery string from the parcel, "to give medical advice to a doctor. Do you like Uneeda biscuits? Because they seem to have occupied an important place in my housekeeper's mind this morning."

We sat down on the moss beneath the hickories, and I divided the single gigantic sandwich with my pocket-knife. Luckily Mrs. Searle had over-estimated my hunger. We ate healthily, with open-air appetites, and what was left over the setter finished at one watchful snap.

"When does Doctor Lennox come home?" Mary asked presently.

"He's due in another six weeks, unless he finds Europe too fascinating. Then I shall have to go back and grind, I suppose. It won't be an attractive prospect, after this holiday."

"You have a practice in New York?"

"Not yet. I've been *interne* up to now. I expect it'll end in the East Side. A friend of mine has a settlement there, and I'd like to join him if I can. There's always plenty to do."

"I know," she nodded. "I've seen something of it. Do you know a man named Herrick, there?"

"Herrick!" I sat upright. "If you mean Jack Herrick, that's the friend I was speaking of. Then you—"

"Then *you*," she corrected, "are the college chum he was always talking about. Why, I've known Jack Herrick ever since I used to play dolls!"

"Three and a half years . . ." I said pensively. "The world's a small place."

"You are rude, Doctor Haverill. It's a long enough time, anyway."

She was looking at the branches overhead, and in her upturned face I caught fleetingly a likeness that had puzzled me more than once before. I knew now. On Herrick's mantelshelf, in his shabby comfortable room at the settlement, there had stood always a photograph in a silver frame. It was the portrait of a child of perhaps thirteen, in a gingham overall, and with her hair braided in two short tails down her back. Herrick had said once: "That's an old sweetheart of mine."

Singularly enough, the recollection did not at this moment greatly please me. But I merely said: "You wore your hair in two pig-tails."

She brought her eyes to earth swiftly. "Who told you?"

"All proper little girls do at that age," I reminded her shamelessly.

"I see. But we were talking of John Herrick."

"Go on."

"Don't you think he's splendid?" she continued, turning to me. "He's done no end of good. And he works . . . I don't believe he ever takes a real holiday. Doctor Haverill, you ought to get him—"

"To come down here for a while? I will if it would please you."

She looked at me so frankly that I was at once ashamed.

"Why, of course it would! But I don't know why I said that. I don't suppose he'd take the time."

I watched a dragonfly that was wheeling over the stream. She sat near me, her hands locked about her knees.

"My brother was at your house last night," she said after a moment.

"Yes."

I could feel her eyes fixed on me, and I knew what was in her mind.

"He told you something?"

"We were talking about chemistry," I said. "It's a subject your brother is very interested in."

"Chemistry!" She put out her hand with a little gesture. "Doctor Haverill, do you take me for a child? What is the matter? You can tell me; he has spoken to you. I want to know."

"What do you want to know?" I said, lamely enough.

"The whole thing—what is happening here. I know something threatens him, that he is in danger, and neither he nor you will tell me what it is."

"How can I tell you," I fenced, "what I don't even know myself?"

She was quick. "Then there *is* something?"

I ignored the unfinished sentence.

"Miss Lessing, why can't you get your brother to go away from here, for a time?"

"I can't. I've tried. He wouldn't leave, now. You don't know him. He's the last person in the world to give a thing up until he's proved it down to the ground, one way or another. Whatever's at the bottom of this, he won't rest till he's found it out. It's just a scientific problem to him, and nothing else."

"And you?" I said.

"I?" She moved her shoulders. "What can I think? I had hoped just now—But I only know what he has told me, what I have seen. If one began to think—"

"Listen to me," I said. "You must not think! You and I are two sane people. Look at these woods around! I ask you, is it possible to feel anything but sane and incredulous in a place like this? I want you to get into your head, right now, that there is nothing—nothing at all in this world—that a man has any reason to be afraid of. And there are very few things in the world, to my belief, that cannot be explained. Has it ever occurred to you that this whole conviction of your brother's may be nothing more than hallucination?"

"But the injuries—"

"I have known hysteric patients, before now, inflict as severe injuries upon themselves without consciousness or recollection. I don't say it is your brother's case; I'm only trying to form a possible rational explanation such as any doctor would put forward. I have had one or two such cases within my own experience. What I propose to do is this, but I shall do it only with your consent. I will write to Herrick and ask him down here for a fortnight. It will be a new brain to bear on the problem, and I shall ask your brother to let us join these investigations with him."

"You'll do that." She put out her hand to me impulsively.

"I'll do it tonight. Only . . . I shall have to give Herrick a detailed account of everything that has happened, so far as we know it, and I can't do that without your brother's approval."

"Yes . . . I see."

"You will excuse one question. Are they on good terms?"

It struck me that I had never heard Lessing mention his name.

"Yes." She paused doubtfully. "It's funny you should ask that. They had a disagreement about two years ago. It was when my brother first took up this . . . this kind of study. Having seances and that. Doctor Herrick wanted him to give it up."

I moved involuntarily. Here was a new light on Lessing's attitude of mind, which he himself had been at pains, it seemed to me, to touch on very lightly. I remembered stray references of his, the signed article I had noticed on my first evening at the house.

"Your brother used to attend seances often?"

"Didn't he tell you? I don't know that I would have mentioned it, but I don't see that it matters. It was before I came to live with them. He and some friends of his were very interested, and Doctor Herrick used to join them too sometimes. They met at a friend's studio. Doctor Herrick was rather against it from the first, but I know he used to be there. Of course I understand very little about it, but . . . things did happen. I don't mean that they banged on tambourines or rapped out the alphabet or anything like that. It wasn't spiritualism. And then Doctor Herrick stopped. I think he knew more than any of them, but he said it was dangerous and it didn't lead to anything, and he wanted my brother to give it up altogether. Kate—that's my sister-in-law, you know—was their medium, and I think it was on her account. Doctor Herrick thought it was bad for her. And then one night something happened, I don't know just what, but Kate got some sort of a shock. She's very highly strung at any time, and I always supposed something frightened her, but anyway she was quite ill for a long time after that. She used to get queer sort of nervous spells, and she couldn't be left alone, and that was why I first came to live with them, on her account. Of course my brother gave the whole business up then. The physician who attended her said simply that she was in poor health, and had had a nervous breakdown, and he told her she must live in the country awhile till she got stronger, but I know Doctor Herrick thought at the time that the seances had been the cause of it. He told my brother so."

I listened attentively. It was news to me that Herrick, the essential level-headed, should have lent himself at any time to experiments of this order. He had never mentioned the subject to me in our many talks, and I had even gathered, as one gathers an impression without any very definite grounds, that he was a confirmed sceptic on all matters of occultism.

"You say they had a disagreement?"

"It was exactly that," she made haste to say. "They didn't quarrel, but I know Herrick was very much opposed to Dick's views, and they used to have arguments. But it didn't amount to more than that."

"Good!"

She had risen to her feet, and at her movement the setter himself lazily rose and came towards us.

"Then we're going to see this thing out?" I said.

"We'll see it out."

We shook hands, and I fancied that her fingers rested in mine a moment voluntarily before she drew them away.

"Are you coming up to see my brother today?" she asked.

"Presently . . . I'd like to." I looked at my watch. "I thought of taking a stroll up to the dam, as I'm so close; I've never been there. You say it's only a few minutes?"

"Not more than ten, through the woods."

"Let's walk up together," I suggested, "if you aren't too tired."

She assented readily, and we struck off up a little footpath, barely traceable, that followed the course of the stream. It was, as she had said, a scant ten minutes before the sound of the sluice broke on our ears, and through a sudden clearing of the woods the dam lay before us, a black sinister sheet of water, covered with masses of floating weed and pond-lilies, and darkened by the trees and underbrush that grew closely down to its edge. An old scow, long past use and sunken low in the water, lay padlocked to a slimy stump near the shore.

Following an old cart-track, we skirted the edge of the dam in the direction of the sawmill, a dilapidated building with broken roof, that seemed to have stood for many years of disuse. To reach it we had to cross the sluice itself, and Mary Lessing, who was a few paces ahead of me, paused to look down over the single rough handrail that protected one from a misstep.

There is something forbidding about a mill-sluice at any time, especially when dissociated, as this was, from the companionable sound of human labor. The sheer depth, the knowledge of the vast imprisoned force behind one, the sound of water gushing here and there between the slimy weed-grown timbers, give always, to me at least, an indefinable sense of the sinister.

I leaned my rod against the railing, and we looked side by side down at the black oozing wall below.

"I like this place," Mary Lessing said. "There's something queer and creepy about it. I often come here. I suppose they haven't worked the sluice for years."

"I doubt if the machinery would move now," I said. "Of course this is never opened. There should be a smaller sluice for the millstream further on."

I glanced as I spoke at the clumsy wooden levers near me that controlled the sluice. They looked to be rotting in their place, but as I pushed one, idly, a sudden change in the sound of escaping water below warned me that the machinery was not in such ill repair as it would seem. I exerted my strength to pull the lever back, and my attention was momentarily distracted from the girl beside me. She was leaning out over the hand-rail, and when I turned it was with a sudden cry of warning.

"Look out!" I said. "That may not be safe!"

I caught her arm instinctively as I spoke, and on the instant the rail bent outward with a slight sound of cracking. In another moment she would have been over the edge. We looked at one another, and Mary laughed, a little nervously on the stillness. Her face had flushed.

"I thought that rail was all right," she said rather awkwardly.

"Dick walked over here with me not a week ago, and we tested it then to see."

"It isn't all right now," I returned sharply.

I put my two hands on the rail, giving it a slight wrench outward. It gave easily to my touch, and looking closer, I saw that the surface towards the water had been half cut through. Someone had tampered with it deliberately and within the last few days.

"What is it?" Mary Lessing asked.

"Merely rotten, as I thought!"

I turned away, and walked thoughtfully on towards the sawmill. The thing puzzled me, but it had an ugly look. It was no idle mischief that had prompted the act. Whoever had done it, had done it maliciously, and the purpose was not very far to seek. Hitherto I had not attached much importance to the Lessings' occasional laughing references to their un-popularity in the village. Now it assumed suddenly a significance.

I turned to Mary Lessing, walking beside me.

"I want you to promise me something," I said, "whether it seems to you irrelevant or not. I want you not to come here again by yourself, at any time. It's a lonely place and it isn't particularly safe. If you come at all, bring your brother with you."

The smile that was on her lips at first faded abruptly, leaving her face serious.

"The rail was cut," she said quietly. "Is that what you mean? It must have been, because it was perfectly solid a few days ago."

"Someone has been up to mischief. If there are characters of that kind in the neighborhood, it's best to run no risks, that's all."

We walked on a few paces, silently. The mill was on our right, a desolate-looking building enough, with its surrounding litter of sodden chips and piles of cut logs lying here and there In the open. A heavy smell of decaying wood was in the air; added to the stagnant odor of the dam itself.

The setter was in front of us, sniffing to and fro on the trail of the rats that infested the wood piles. Suddenly he stood still, his ears laid back, growling ominously. A short, thick-set figure slipped from the angle of the mill wall and vanished in the woods on the farther side of the cart-track.

"Aaron Menning," Miss Lessing said. She put her hand and called the dog back. I was staring up the track where the chicken-huckster had so adroitly disappeared.

"Does he live near here?"

"Not very far off. I suppose he comes here to fish. There are a good many in the dam."

"Very probable," I said.

"I dislike that man," Mary said after a moment. "I guess it's mutual, too. The other one, Jake, you know, had a quarrel with my brother one time. He was always loitering round the house, and Dick turned him away. Aaron's always very civil when we meet, but I don't believe he likes us any more than Jakey did."

We took a turning past the mill that led us, without further event, to the Lessings' bungalow. Within sight of the house I parted from her. I wanted to see Lessing again, but there were a few points that needed readjustment in my own mind first. As I walked slowly home down the familiar slope of Dutchman's Hill I was thinking that the industrious and chapel-going Aaron might very well bear a little watching.

9

PROBLEMS

I WROTE to Herrick that same evening and his answer came a couple of days later, saying that he hoped to get away towards the end of the month. I had said nothing in my letter about the events of the summer, but merely mentioned that the Lessings were my neighbors for the time being.

Herrick wrote: 'I shall be glad to meet Lessing again. He seems to have buried himself in obscurity for the last twelve months. Is he still as enthusiastic a theorist as ever, or has the country sobered his ideas? In any case you are to be congratulated on having for neighbors three of the most charming people it has ever been my luck to meet."

I smiled at the "three." In my own mind I could have substituted another numeral which would explain much of Herrick's promptitude in accepting my invitation. He was very much mistaken if he thought that any such artless device would put me off the track. In imagination I already saw myself playing the role of a reluctant gooseberry during his visit.

Lessing, when I mentioned my expected guest, made a comment almost identical with Herrick's own.

"Herrick?" he said. "Good! We shall have some arguments, Haverill, that will eclipse even your own. If Herrick gets to the bottom of this by any of his cut-and-dried theories and deductions I'll give him best once and for all!"

One thing at least pleased me. I gathered from both their remarks that whatever difference had occurred between them had been, purely a battle of opinion, and had no influence on their fundamental regard for one another. Meantime my meeting with Mary Lessing, and the subsequent incident of the broken handrail, had settled my mind on one point at least. There was some malicious influence at work in the neighborhood which was distinctly and obviously human, whether it bore any relation to the laboratory experiences or not, and at any cost, even if necessary in the face of Lessing's opposition, she must be kept clear of it.

Three-fourths of the neighboring population were Pennsylvania Dutch, and I had learned enough, in my own infrequent dealings with them, to recognize their sullen aloofness, amounting almost to a hostility, towards any stranger settled in their midst. The Lessings were for some reason disliked in the village, and I fancied that much of the distrust towards them was due to their having chosen for their dwelling a spot which already had a sufficiently bad reputation in the eyes of the country people about. Lessing was by no means the sort of man to make himself popular here, or even friendly. He was more or less of a recluse; he had erected a mysterious building in which, engaged upon equally mysterious pursuits, he chose to isolate himself until all hours of the night, and he displayed an open indifference towards all the current gossip and superstition of the neighborhood. Following the primitive psychology of these people, narrow-minded to a degree and distrustful of anything unfamiliar, his habits alone were sufficient to brand him as an ungodly character. According to his sister, he had already fallen foul of Jake Menning soon after his arrival, and I had no doubt whatever that Aaron, out of reyenge, had since done his best to foster the already antagonistic feeling towards him. The huckster's trade lends itself to all the backdoor gossip of the countryside, and it seemed to me that I could trace easily enough the fruit of Aaron's house-to-house visits. Aaron himself was civil-spoken, industrious, religious to all accounts, and a highly respected member of the community, but all this did not weigh very far against the man's face. Whatever ill blood ran in the Menning family, it was certainly not confined to the deceased Jakey.

I mentioned my suspicions to Lessing a day or two later, when I was at the bungalow.

"Oh, the man's right enough," he returned. "I don't like his kind, that's all. I had a row with Jakey because I didn't want him hanging round the place and I told him so. Aaron has never annoyed us in any way; on the contrary, he takes pains to be particularly civil. I think he's like all the rest around, glad enough to keep clear of Dutchman's Hill and all its inhabitants, dead or living!"

Mary Lessing had asked me, on our homeward walk, not to mention the cut railing to her brother, and I had not done so. It was sufficient for the moment that she had agreed to keep away from the mill-dam and its immediate neighborhood. She was a sensible girl and I had no fear that she would break her promise out of any spirit of bravado or curiosity.

We were in the sitting-room. Mary had gone down to the village on an errand, and Mrs. Lessing was as usual invisible. For the time being we were free from interruption, and it struck me as a good moment to tell Lessing what I had heard from the reporter concerning the two mysterious cycling fatalities.

He took it even more seriously than I had expected. It was even with scant patience that he heard me out.

"But good heavens, man," he cried, "why didn't you tell me all this sooner? Don't you see that it's what I've been expecting, what I've been watching the papers for month after month? It puts my experience clear of all doubt. I have felt certain—as certain as I am standing here—that sooner or later some accident of this sort would turn up."

"It was a good fifteen miles from here," I said. "Besides—"

"What's fifteen miles? I don't care if it was fifty! Have you got the cutting with you?"

I had. I had torn off the corner with the paragraph, unobserved of my reporter friend, and I took the fragment now from my pocketbook and gave it to Lessing. He read it through eagerly.

"The facts correspond. The man was killed in the open; he had no chance of shelter. The thing hit him as he was riding."

"It's not proved."

"There's the damage to the bicycle."

"There's exactly that," I said, "which to my mind puts a different light on the whole thing. If the impact of the blow was sufficient to damage the bicycle to that extent, how was it that the rider escaped all injury except a single scratch on the face? It's out of all reason. There were no marks on the body. That is testified to. If a man is knocked off his bicycle while riding at even an average speed, he'll have some marks to show for it. He died from heart failure, probably resultant upon fright and the shock of the wound. Very good. But that doesn't account for the bicycle. It seems to me that whatever attacked him wreaked its spite on the machine afterwards."

"He had time to dismount?"

"Possibly. It doesn't say how near to the bicycle he was lying. If he fell at all he must have fallen clear of it. The lamp was picked up several yards away."

"The lamp . . ." said Lessing.

The same thought was in both our minds.

"What date did this happen?" he asked.

"It was a week-old paper. I was there . . . wait a moment." I made a rough calculation in my mind. "This happened, apparently, on the Thursday previous. That should bring it to about the third of the month."

"The third was a Thursday," said Lessing. He pulled out an almanac from the bookshelves and ran the pages over. I saw him frown.

"There was a full moon on that evening. It is just possible he was riding without a light at all. If so, that throws my whole theory out."

"The whole thing," said I, "looks to me like the work of a maniac. Take the lamp. It was picked up some yards away. Now a bicycle lantern isn't merely hung on; it's screwed on, and you can't imagine any sort of blow struck from above that would dislodge it and throw it that distance. It must have been either unscrewed or torn off deliberately, and that in itself suggests human agency."

Lessing barely heard me. He was staring at the scrap of paper spread out on his knee.

"The first man, according to your reporter was killed actually in the woods. The second was picked up some twenty feet from the edge of the woods, on the open road. That's important. It was a clear night. Why should he be attacked in the open when there were woods within half a dozen yards that would have given ample ambush?" Unconsciously he was repeating the reporter's argument. "That doesn't look like the work of a human being. Besides, the man wasn't robbed. I tell you, Haverill, there's something that doesn't satisfy me in all this. Either they made some extraordinary mistake, or . . . but he was riding *towards* the woods!"

"Apparently."

"On what evidence?"

"I suppose the position of the bicycle," I said lamely.

"There had been no rain for some days. The roads are hard about here, and a bicycle wouldn't be likely to leave tracks, especially on the edge of the path. You're a doctor, Haverill. Suppose a man died from heart failure, would he necessarily die at the instant of the shock?"

"Only in romances. Actually, there would be several seconds' interval at least."

"He might run, say, twenty feet and then drop?"

"Quite possibly. But I don't see how that helps."

"It means just this," said Lessing, "that according to my idea the man was not riding towards the woods at all. He was attacked actually in the woods or at the edge of them, and he ran the twenty feet to where his body was found. Listen. The moon did not rise that evening until 10:30. Anyone riding through the woods the earlier part of the evening would have used a lamp. He was a stranger in the district and was identified only by papers. No one in Coopersville knew him or had apparently ever seen him before. Coopersville is not a large place, and a case like this makes sufficient talk. If he had passed through there during the evening someone would have seen him, and it would have been mentioned at the inquest. The chances are that he had come from a distance, and that he was riding *towards* Coopersville with the idea of putting up there for the night. Assuming that, and that he was carrying a lamp at the time, we have our facts fairly clear. He was attacked just within cover of the woods, that is to say, where the light would be more clearly noticeable than on an open stretch of moonlit road. The overhanging trees would break the attack more or less, which accounts for the comparative slightness of his own injury. The primary object of attack being the lamp, the rider would have the chance of escape, whereas if he had been struck actually in the open, at full force, he would have been probably killed on the spot."

The whole theory was fairly ingenious, but it didn't account for the wrecking of the bicycle, for its being found where it was, some distance clear of the woods and near the man's own body. I told Lessing so. He looked at me queerly.

"Have you ever seen a dog worry a stick?" he asked.

"We aren't dealing with dogs."

"Whatever wrecked the bicycle could have dragged it that distance."

"If your theory has anything in it the bicycle was carried. If it had been dragged they would have found traces. Don't tell me that any animal capable of such insensate fury as you suggest would have had the intelligence to conceal its tracks!"

We were both getting rather heated over the argument. It seemed to me that Lessing was bent obstinately on maintaining his own views, to the point of extravagance. For my part, I was equally positive that the affair was due to some human agency. Neither of us, therefore, was aware of a shadow in the doorway until Mary Lessing's pleasant mocking voice broke in upon our discussion.

"What on earth," she said, "are you two people scrapping about so vehemently?"

"We weren't scrapping," I smiled. "We were discussing a problem— you might call it a scientific riddle. It concerns the law which governs the movement of bodies through space."

Mary turned on me her invariable reproachful glance when she suspected that anyone was making fun of her. She sat down, pulling the pins from her hat, and let the sunlight strike on her roughened bronze-colored hair.

"Is it anything," she inquired, "with which my inferior feminine mind might be capable of grappling?"

"Certainly," I returned promptly. "We will illustrate it with the simple objects now before us. How would it be possible, for instance, for that extremely solid bookcase to be moved, say, to the other end of the room, without being dragged or carried?"

Mary affected to consider, her head on one side.

"Simple enough," she said, laughing. "It would have to fly through the air, that's all."

There was a moment's silence in the room, while I looked at Lessing and he looked at me.

"Suppose we have some tea?" he said then.

10

THE CHICKEN-HUCKSTER'S HOUSE

IT was the last weekend in August that Herrick arrived. For nearly two days before it had rained steadily, and I had spent the time indoors, discounting old scores in the shape of letters, and enlivened only by a visit from Lessing, who walked over in oilskins on the Thursday after-noon to spend a couple of hours smoking on a sheltered corner of the front porch. The weather lifted on Friday night, and by Saturday morning the roads were passable. As I did not expect Herrick before the 5:40 train I took my bicycle out after lunch and went for a spin to stretch my limbs.

I set out by way of the village, posting my letters on the way, and intending to make a circuit that would bring me home from the opposite direction. I managed, however, to lose my bearings, and after some fruitless bungling stopped at a farmhouse to ask my way. The farmer seemed rather less taciturn than most of the folk about, and readily pointed me out a short cut which, according to him, would bring me out at the crossroads just above the dam.

The road, which lay for the first few miles through cultivated land, entered eventually upon a stretch of sparsely wooded country, desolate and inhospitable enough. Stunted spruce trees, powdered with blue berries, clung tenaciously to the barren ground, and everywhere the grey monotonous boulders cropped out, scattered as though in the idle finish to some giant's play. Their uncouth rounded outlines suggested from a distance a field dotted with grey misshapen sheep, forever movelessly browsing. The road was bad; a horse would have had difficulty in picking his way, and I cursed the well-meaning farmer roundly as I dismounted to push my heavy machine.

A little distance on, however, things became better. I reached the beginning of a wood, gaunt ragged hickories interspersed with tangles of wild grapevine, and matted creepers, and a few hundred yards beyond a broken snake-fence suggested the whereabouts of a house.

I came upon it at the turn of the road, a square, red-painted frame house and barn, surrounded by a medley of small sheds and outhouses in every degree of dilapidation. There was no gate, merely a couple of bars let down in the fencing, and I left the bicycle a moment and went inside.

The yard upon which I entered was a litter of old junk of every description, ancient packing cases, broken barrels, scrap-iron, and bones flung into piles. The wagon-ruts leading up to the house were sunken deep in filth, and an indescribable odor filled the air, in which the smell of badly kept fowls predominated. They ran everywhere, a ragged nondescript crew, scratching, cackling, gazing at me from evil yellow-rimmed eyes. Many more were confined in the coops, mere oblong boxes of lath from which protruded gaunt heads and outstretched necks, whose mournful protest mingled with the clamor of their untrammeled brethren. So far as I could see, every shed held its prisoners, all in the same state of filth and neglect, a sore to the eyes and offence to the nostrils. There was that in the look and smell of the place that stuck in my throat, used as I was to poverty in both town and country. There seemed no one about, and after a moment's hesitation I retraced my steps across the black mire of the yard and regained the roadway.

On the opposite side of the way a little ragged girl of about thirteen watched my retreat with keen eyes. She had been in the woods gathering the small uneatable nuts that children call pig-hickories; her apron was filled with the green unripe hulls. She grinned, backing a little at my approach.

"Hello, sis," I said. "Who lives in that house there?"

" 'S Mister Menning's."

"Ah!" I took another backward glance at the ill-kept yard, with its indescribable litter. As I did so a low moan, almost human in its misery, came from the barn behind the jumbled sheds. It was repeated, long-drawn and mournful, the protest of a dumb thing exhausted by suffering. I turned to the child sharply.

"What's the matter there?"

"It's the cow." She shuffled her bare toes in the dust, looking with a fascinated curiosity towards the place whence the sound came. "She hollers awful sometimes."

"Is it ill?"

"Mennin beats her." She said with the curious indifference of the country-bred child towards animal suffering. "He's allus beatin' her. Gran'pap's spoke to him, onct. He says she don't make no profit an' Gran'pa says she can't make no profit if he's allus beatin' her."

I remembered her face suddenly.

"Aren't you Mrs. Nevill's little girl, from the Bend?"

"Yep. Gran'pa's house is jest back there." She jerked her head up the road.

"How's your mother? I'll step in and see her, as I'm here."

"Mother's up. She's been washin'."

She began to retreat up the road, with the sudden movement of a half-wild thing, and I followed her, glad enough to turn my back on the chicken-huckster's dwelling. The moaning of the cow was in my ears again as I walked on.

I knew the Nevills' cottage, and my road from there lay straight enough. I had never approached the Bend before from this side, and so the lie of the land was unfamiliar to me. The Nevills were one of the few Irish families about.

The household consisted of a rheumatic old grandfather, his daughter, whom I had attended a short while ago, and her husband, a steady young fellow who worked at a harness factory in the village.

Paddy was an old sinner if there ever lived one, but now, along in the green seventies, he confined himself to the cultivation of religion and the smoking of a particularly vile corncob pipe. He had been employed most of his life on the railway, and his rheumatism was the result of six weeks' work in a flooded cutting. Providence had released him some two years ago from a vituperative wife, whose latter years had been soured by the burden of an invalid husband; I gathered from the old man's talk that she had to her last day regarded his rheumatism as a form of criminal idleness, and since her death Paddy had taken a fresh lease of life.

I found him on his usual corner of the cottage porch, his square old head with its bristly jaws—Paddy still shaved once a week—framed by the window-ledge and its row of flowering plants in tin cans. His daughter was inside, getting supper, and the new baby lay in a ramshackle baby-coach near Paddy's elbow. He was rocking the coach with one toe on the wheel while he smoked, the smell of his unspeakable tobacco mingling with that of the frying onions in the kitchen, through the open door.

I always felt like holding my breath when I approached the Nevill cottage. The stuffiness was of that permanent, impenetrable sort which seems to encompass the house solidly for a radius of five yards at least.

I sat down on the porch step and asked after Paddy's rheumatism. He looked down at his feet, shapeless in list slippers, like fearsome parcels.

"I ain't long fur this world, doctor, and that's truth I'm tellin' yer. Don't I know it? We ain't a long-lived fam'ly. Me father died at seventy-eight an' me brother at eighty, an' I'm thinkin' I won't be long after thim." He raised his voice suddenly to a shout, without turning. "Mary, git a cheer out fur th' doctor!"

I refused the chair hastily; the porch step at least bordered on fresh air.

"I've just come round by Aaron Menning's place," I said. "I met the little girl there."

Paddy's face darkened.

"Ain't I allus tellin' the young limb I won't hev her hangin' round the likes of thim dirty Dutchmen! It's her mother'll be after takin' the strap to her fur that. The place ain't fit fur a dog these days. Did ye take heed to the cow there?"

I nodded.

"The poor baste do be after cryin' day an' night, like a Christian. I've told him again an' again, but he's a bad man is Aaron. He's took after his brother, an' that's sayin' ill enough of anyone. Ye wouldn't mind Jake Mennin', doctor?"

"No. It was before I came here."

"Sure I've lived neighbors to thim fifteen years, an' I've seen things to turn your stomach on yer. He had a bad streak in him, Jake, an' it was the devil took him in the end. They had a little girl there workin', the year before Jake died. . . . That's why I tell Lizzie I'll break her neck before I see her hangin' round there. The ould mother's a decent woman, or used to be. God knows the poor soul's had enough to turn her crazy."

"There is a mother, then?"

"Sure, but ye don't see her nowadays. 'Tis Aaron keeps her to the house, most like. I used to be civil spoke to Aaron a while back, but sence Jake died there ain't no good to him at all. Would any Christian man treat a dumb baste the way he does? An' he treats his ould mother the same, if all's known."

He pulled on his pipe.

"Two weeks ago, it would be, as we saw her last. Yes, I mind now it was the day I was thinkin' of puttin' the new winder-pane in. She come over to borry a half-cup o' sugar, an' I says to Mary to let her have it, the poor soul. She had her hand all wrapped up to here"—he measured a space on his gaunt grimy wrist—"an' she says to Mary as she'd scalded it in the kitchen. Aaron was away with the wagon, or she wouldn't 'a' come then."

"I suppose Aaron does a good business," I said casually.

"By the talk he does. I do be thinkin' he does most of it in the next county, fur I don't see him drivin' the village way more'n onct in a week or so. He'll be gone three days on a stretch wid the wagon, an' Lizzie's seen him come home momin's wid the poor baste in a lather. Lizzie says he has hundreds o' chickens there, an' he can't be after sellin' thim all. They die on him all the time, fur she's seen him pull 'em out o' the coops and throw 'em to the pigs."

I asked after his son and rose to go, after turning the half of my tobacco pouch into Paddy's old tin box. It was getting on toward five o'clock, and I would have just time to clean up, get the mare put in, and drive to the depot for the afternoon train.

11

JAKEY WALKS

IT did me good to see Herrick's cheery face on the platform, and to feel the hand-grip he gave me. Our friendship dated back to college days, and unlike so many of those early intimacies, it had strengthened instead of decreased with the passage of time. Then, as now, Herrick had been the same curious mixture of enthusiast and practical hard-headed worker, and in spite of the inevitable schooling of experience and years of exacting and often discouraging labor, he had carried into the early forties a certain boyish confidence, a freshness of outlook, which gave to one instinctively, on meeting him, the impression of indomitable health and vitality.

When we had tucked his valise into the back of the buggy and turned the mare about, he looked at me with a laugh.

"Well, Haverill, you look quite the country practitioner already! Seven weeks' change—ye gods! But you haven't grown a beard yet!"

"I'm keeping the beard for my leisure moments," I told him. "So far they haven't been many."

"Don't tell me this place is in the throes of an epidemic! It looks like one of those ideal Sleepy Hollows where you get about one call for whooping-cough every six months. I came here for repose, you know."

"Oh, you'll get it," I assured him. "You'll get the kind of repose that keeps you awake nights wondering where it's going to hit you next. They don't want a doctor down here; they want a new lunacy commission officer, and the first suspect will be me. Oh, I'm going to make you work, Jack! Have no idle dreams on the subject."

"Work! You look as if you'd forgotten the meaning of the word! If ever a man had the luck to stumble on a good excuse for a holiday it's you. This air, this sky, these woods to fish and loaf in—Hello, what's up? The whooping-cough I spoke of, or have you arranged a little semblance of business for my benefit! That good lady seems about to welcome us with open arms."

A woman was hurrying down the road toward us, from the direction of my house. She had a gingham sunbonnet on which flapped at each step as she walked, and on catching sight of the buggy with the familiar roan mare in the shafts she waved her hand in unmistakable signal. I pulled Bess up, and by the time the woman came pantingly abreast of us I recognized her for Mrs. Sliefer, who lived in the first farm-house beyond the Bend, past the crossroads.

"I been to your house, doctor," she began, "an' Mis' Searle told me you weren't to hum, so I come right on. My niece is took bad an' she's been queer sence the mornin', and I'd like you to come straight back with me an' see her."

She spoke with an air somewhat of indignation, born of her toilsome walk. Mrs. Sliefer was a stout lady, to put it at the mildest, and the heat and exercise had obviously tried her. I leaned from the buggy.

"Get right up, Mrs. Sliefer! There's plenty of room, and you can tell me as we drive."

She hoisted herself laboriously into the buggy, with our combined help, and collapsed, rather than sat down, between us. Luckily the seat was a broad one. As it was, her generous proportions all but crushed us.

I kept the mare at a walk while Mrs. Sliefer told her errand. Briefly, as I gathered from her rather spasmodic utterance, the facts were these. Her niece, Rebecca Dum, who lived with Mr. and Mrs. Sliefer at the farm, was keeping company with the young man from Haskell's grocery store. The young couple were in the habit of meeting of an evening, after Rebecca had washed her supper dishes, in the woods near the sawmill, some fifteen minutes from the farm-house and in the line of the short cut which the young man used to walk up from the village. They usually took a short stroll about the dam before returning to the farm, to finish the evening in the older folks' company on the home porch. Yesterday, as I have said, was rainy, and Rebecca had expected her sweetheart at the house.

As he did not arrive, however, and the weather had lifted since five o'clock, Rebecca, thinking he might possibly have gone to the usual trysting-place, put on a shawl and her rubber shoes and went out to find him. He was not to be seen, and she loitered a few moments in the neighborhood of the dam before returning home. It was then just getting dusk. According to her account, she was strolling near the sawmill when the ghost of Jakey Menning, surrounded by light and with flames coming from his mouth, sprang out from the bushes and yelled at her. Rebecca, struck of a heap, as she expressed it, had still the sense to turn and run, and being a sturdy young woman she speedily outdistanced the alleged ghost and gained the shelter of her own home. Once on the porch, however, she collapsed in hysterics, and it was not until she came to, a good half-hour after, that her aunt and uncle could learn what had happened. Rebecca's sweetheart had meantime arrived, and being a strong-minded young man had at once induced Mr. Sliefer to set out with him, armed with a stout cudgel and the farmer's shotgun, to investigate. They patrolled the neighborhood of the sawmill thoroughly, but needless to say nothing was found.

Rebecca recovered, but this morning, on the matter being mentioned at breakfast, had promptly gone off again into hysterics, a state which had lasted all day, off and on, and which her aunt had been unable to check. The hysteria had brought on sickness, and the girl, so Mrs. Sliefer told me, was now in bed in a state of utter collapse.

I told Herrick I would drop him at the house.

"On the contrary," he returned, "I'll come along, with Mrs. Sliefer's permission."

We drove on accordingly, the three of us, covering the distance past Dutchman's Hill and the Lessing's bungalow at a smart trot. A few minutes beyond the sawmill, along the road Mary Lessing and I had taken some mornings ago, the Sliefer's farmhouse came in sight, a comfortable low-built dwelling standing back in a good-sized orchard with the barn and outbuildings clustered near it.

We found Rebecca in an upper bedroom, watched over by a mute and scared-looking neighbor, who had been fetched in to sit with her while her aunt was away. The girl lay in bed, her eyes rolling, her hands twitching nervously on the covers. There was nothing alarming in her condition, which had been brought about as much by Mrs. Sliefer's well-meant home physicking as by the original fright.

I went to the bedside and put my hand on her wrist.

"Now then," I said, "what's all this nonsense about bogies? A big strong girl like you ought to have better sense than to imagine such things."

She began to whimper.

"I seen it—I seen it! It was all spoutin' fire! It was Jakey Menning as sure as there's a livin' God! Oh-h-I don't want to look at it . . . I don't want to!"

She went off into another hysterical spasm, and it took all my force to hold her still while her aunt went for water. When it was over, and she lay back on the pillows, still sobbing exhaustedly, I took Mrs. Sliefer aside.

"Give me pen and ink," I said, "and have someone drive down to the drug store with this prescription at once. I'll wait here till it's brought back. Your niece will probably be all right tomorrow, after a night's sleep, but keep her in bed a day in any case."

She took the prescription and gave it to her husband. We heard his heavy boots creaking out to the back door. I turned to Mrs. Sliefer.

"And now," I said, "you're a clever, sensible woman. What's your idea of all this nonsense?"

Mrs. Sliefer was obviously flattered by my description. She mopped her flat round face, still shining from the walk.

"Rebecca ain't no liar," she said. "She's a good up-standin' girl, an' she ain't never showed no foolishness before this. We was talking about Dutchman's Hill on'y a few nights ago, and Rebecca was the first to laugh about it. 'I'd like to see the ghost'd scare me!' she said, right there. No. Rebecca seen suthin, or she wouldn't ha' come home the state she did. An' as for it's bein' Jakey, she'd oughter know Jakey Mennin' well enough, seein' he's brought the wagon round here time an' ag'n when Aaron was busy."

"You don't tell me *you* believe in the foolish talk there's been, Mrs. Sliefer!"

She stiffened.

"No, an' I ain't sayin' I do, but sperrits or no sperrits, Mr. Sliefer's goin' to get to the bottom of this. Seems to me there' a law had ought to deal with respectable girls bein' frightened out of their wits ten yards from their own doorstep!"

"Listen," I said. "It seems that your niece has been the victim of a very cruel and foolish practical joke, but there's no good going into the matter here and now. Only look after her. If anyone is playing tricks around the sawmill, keep her away from there. She's in no state to risk any more shocks. Don't let her go wandering about alone."

"I wouldn't ha' let her last night, on'y she was so sure of findin' George Freeman there. Rebecca was born an' brought up here, and she knows the woods as well as our own front yard. But there'll be an end of these doin's, an' I told her so."

"That's right." I paused a moment. "Who was here, the evening that your niece spoke of not being frightened?"

"Only us an' Mis' Scholl there, an' George Freeman. There wasn't one of 'em would play a trick on her. An' George Freeman was in at the house a'ready when Rebecca come runnin' back."

I did not leave until the farmer returned, and I had seen Rebecca already quiet and subdued under the influence of the sleeping draught I had prescribed for her. Then Herrick and I drove home through the dusk to the ruined supper which Mrs. Searle had prepared so painstakingly for six o'clock.

"Well," I said to him, "what do you make of it?"

Herrick smiled.

"Ghosts don't usually 'holler,'" he said, "and Rebecca seems to have been very clear on the hollering, if on nothing else. I think we may dismiss the theory of the defunct Jakey. And by the way, who *was* Jakey Menning, and what is this extraordinary tangle about a place called Dutchman's Hill?"

I gave the mare a light touch with the whip.

"We are passing Dutchman's Hill at this moment," I said, "and I'll give you the history over our supper."

12

MR. CROWFOOT

I OUTSLEPT Herrick by a good hour the next morning; in fact, he was already up and out by the time I came down to a belated breakfast. I had one call to make in the village, and after that, Herrick being still absent, I sat down on the porch with my pipe and a newspaper to await his return.

There was no mail for me at the office, only a couple of letters for Herrick, forwarded from New York, and as I slipped these in my pocket I wondered again at the curious silence of Lennox. Since that short note from Queenstown I had heard nothing from him, and he had neglected even to provide me with the promised address by which I could communicate with him in case of need, an oversight by which he had certainly secured to himself a free and uninterrupted holiday, and which left me no choice meantime but to await his return or such news as he might ultimately choose to send. I must admit that Lessing's phrase "bolted" stuck unpleasantly in my mind, little as it accorded with my estimate of Lennox's character. His haste to be off, the lack of any communication from him since, had more than a look of flight, but why, or from what he had bolted I was still at a loss to understand.

I was still turning this over in my mind when Herrick sauntered into view down the road, accompanied by a stranger. Visitors were sufficiently rare in the neighborhood, and as the two approached the house leisurely I studied the newcomer with some curiosity. He was a small man, of apparently some fifty years, sparsely bearded, and dressed in a very shabby knickerbocker suit of greenish tweeds. A soft felt hat covered his head and at least half his forehead; he wore dark glasses and carried a botanical collecting-box slung over his shoulder. There was something quaintly rabbit-like in his appearance, enhanced by the air of timidity with which he hung back while Herrick strode forward to the porch to greet me.

"I want to introduce Mr. Crowfoot," Herrick said, with a gesture which had an effect of herding the mild little man up to the porch step as he might have herded some curious and inoffensive zoological specimen. "He is down here hunting orchids, and I came across him in the woods and brought him along to have a chat with you. You might be able to give him some hints about the country."

I shook hands with the little man and gave him a chair on the porch, where he settled himself shyly, his collecting-box across his knee.

"I'm afraid I don't know much about the flora round here," I said, "but I imagine Mr. Crowfoot will find a good deal to interest him."

"Oh, I am only an amateur," said the little man. "I s—I s— I s-s—"

He undoubtedly did, and the reason for his shyness stood forthwith revealed. He stammered, and had more than the usual sensitiveness of his infirmity.

"S-simply indulge a hobby," he finished heroically. "It gives me an object for my leisure time. I s-s—*presume* you have lived here some time, Mr.—?"

"H a v e r i l l –Doctor Haverill," Herrick prompted.

"Haverill." He repeated it in a certain childlike way, as though to place the name definitely in his memory, and immediately I was conscious of a liking for him. He was at once so diffident and so meticulously polite.

"On the contrary, I've been here only a month or so, taking a friend's place for the time. The country about is delightful, so far as I know it."

"Delightful!" he echoed, and lapsed into a pleased silence, which lasted so long that Herrick rose.

"I want to change my shoes," he said. "I've been up to the neck in bog. I don't know our resources, Austin, but I guess we can offer Mr. Crowfoot a drink?"

"Water—I should l-like very much a plain glass of water," said the little botanist.

"And a cigar at all events," I supplemented. "I should have some pretty decent cigars somewhere around that my predecessor left here. Look in the drawer in the surgery, Jack, will you?"

Herrick reappeared a moment later with the box.

"Excellent," said our new friend as he helped himself. "Excellent! Apparently you d-d-don't care for these cigars then, Doctor Haverill?"

I laughed. "Oh, I only smoke a pipe, as a rule!"

"You make, if I may-s-say so, a great error," he said gravely.

He smoked for a few moments tranquilly, his gaze, behind the dark glasses, seeming to rest dreamily on the stretch of road before the house.

"I suppose you are staying in the village?" I asked.

"Over there." He made a vague gesture which included half the visible landscape. "With some excellent people of the name of S-S-Sliefer."

"Oh, Sliefer's," I said, interested. "I know them slightly. The big farmhouse past the sawmill."

"Precisely," he agreed, and gave me a look before relapsing again into silence.

Our conversation, if it could be called so, languished. It was evident to me that his shyness was battling with the desire to be off—I judged that Herrick had fairly dragged him here out of a mistaken cordiality—and after the exchange of a few more spasmodic sentences I accepted his courteous and timid explanation that the Sliefers dined at midday and would be expecting him back, and rose to shake hands.

"A queer chicken!" said Herrick as we watched his jerky little figure disappear down the road. "I picked him up back in the woods there, grubbing around the sawmill, and brought him along for your benefit—a quaint example of the Pennsylvanian fauna! *Timidicus professus*, or ground-dwelling goo-goo bird. Difficult of approach and does not thrive in captivity. Guess he's more than a bit batty, by his looks."

"Mrs. Sliefer never mentioned a boarder," I remarked. "He must be a new arrival. It's to be hoped he won't come to any grief in his grubbing around, as you call it."

"Oh, the gods protect the innocent," laughed Herrick. "Even the alleged ghost of Jakey Menning would have pity. By the way, the fair Rebecca's tale is still firmly believed in, by the Sliefers at any rate. The latest village version is that she was chased clear to the garden fence and that her skirt still shows five scorched prints where the ghostly fingers clutched. The neighborhood must have been quite worked up. It was bad enough when Jakey had the decency to keep to one place at least, but now he has taken, like the wind, to blowing where he listeth, folks are getting scary. I got that much from our guileless little friend, though he professes himself to be quite indifferent on the subject. Of course you, as the village doctor, are above such gossip, so I thought I'd go gleaning for you."

"Someone's doing it," I said.

"Of course someone did, in the case of Rebecca at least. Real ghosts don't holler, as I said before, and the blue-fire details smell strongly of the common or garden matchbox. But as our little professor-bird spends most of his time in the woods about there, I thought his observations might come in useful."

"Private detective, eh?"

Herrick smiled.

"Oh, I'm sufficiently interested in the Lessing problem to be anxious to clear out the undergrowth, if you follow me. That done, one can judge a bit more clearly. If there's any foolery going on we'll run it to the ground, and Crowfoot may come in useful there."

"I've a good notion," I said, knocking my pipe out, "to try some watching round that locality myself one of these nights."

"It wouldn't be any good," he returned, "for the simple reason that Jakey wouldn't demonstrate to you or me any more than he's demonstrated to Lessing. He chooses those he wants to favor. As a matter of fact, by the aid of my bedroom window, the convenience of which you have probably underestimated, Austin, I spent last night prowling myself. No, I didn't let you into it because I wanted to be alone. Needless to say, there was nothing doing. But I've found out one thing. There's someone else interested in the game besides us. I don't know who. But we narrowly escaped collision, and gave each other mutually a wide berth."

"It couldn't have been the ghost himself, whoever he is?"

"I think not. It was too obvious we were both out on the same errand. Like the Irishman, we each thought we were someone else and when we met it was neither of us!" He smiled at the recollection. "Well, I suppose we'll get at the root of the thing some day!"

13

AN AFTERNOON DRIVE

IT was towards the end of that week that we drove over to the bungalow, one afternoon, for tea. The teacups were set out on the porch, and Mary Lessing, in a white frock, sprang up from one of the big basket-chairs to greet us with a comical dismay.

"I've dragged you over here," she began promptly, "and now I'll tell you the worst at once. There is not—one—lump—of sugar in the entire house. I've looked. So either you will drink your tea sugarless, smile sweetly, and say it doesn't matter, or else one of you has got to come right down to the village with me and get some. You can take your full choice about it. I'm glad to see you had the thoughtfulness to drive, anyway."

Herrick sat down with alacrity.

"I am a tired man," he announced, "supposed to be on a holiday, and I'm not going to the village to get anything till I've had tea, and I'm not going to drink tea without sugar, not even if you promise to smile in the teacup, Mary Lessing. So I guess it's up to you and Haverill. And I think that after all my excellent instructions of the past fourteen years you ought to be a better housekeeper. It's scandalous and disgusting of you. Where's Dick?"

"In the laboratory."

"A day like this! I'll rout him out of that in just two seconds. Ho, Dick!"

There was no response, and he rose grumbling, and trailed round to the laboratory door. Mary looked at me.

"Do you mind?" she said meekly.

I slipped off the mare's hitching-strap, and Mary climbed into the buggy beside me. We took the road past Sliefer's, and it is to be admitted that I made no effort to hurry. Our errand might reasonably be supposed to take an hour, and since chance had so obligingly given me that hour I was going to make the most of it.

As a matter of fact, I got precious little good out of it.

Romance probably demands, here, that I should describe how Mary and I drove side by side through the mellow autumn-tinted woods, how we spoke of the beauty of nature around us, and how gradually a sweet sense of companionship grew up in our young and sympathetic souls.

Instead Mary spoilt the whole thing by her hurry to get that sugar. If the life of the whole household, including Herrick, had depended upon it, she couldn't have been more sternly anxious to get to the village, to buy that sugar and to convey that sugar swiftly and relentlessly home. Looking back, I can see now that her attitude in the matter was only part of a constraint that had been growing between us subtly ever since Herrick's arrival. A certain frank comradeship, as I had been pleased to think it, that had sprung into being on the morning of our impromptu picnic, had wavered and dropped, leaving nothing in its place. I could not decide that she actually avoided me, though she certainly devoted a good deal of attention to Herrick when we were all together. Be that as it may, her professed anxiety on the sugar question that afternoon justly irritated me. We began with constraint, and ended in something very like open warfare.

It was probably not the first time that a perverse imp of circumstance, or call it what you will, has induced two young people, who started out on apparently good terms, to waste the precious moments of each other's uninterrupted company in being pointedly and deliberately disagreeable, and that for no reason that either of them could frame. The imbecility of that drive stands out in my memory now. We should both of us have known better. The whole thing had begun in such a meaningless way as to have no possible excuse. We had started, as I say, on good terms, with every equipment for a pleasant hour, and instead we each, in our own way, chose to behave abominably.

After one unique and disastrous attempt at conversation, I remember, we said no more, but drove on side by side in a ridiculous and stony silence, each thinking how disagreeable the other was, and wondering mutually what we had ever liked in one another.

There was the usual group of loafers gathered on the porch of Haskell's grocery store when we reached the village. I left Mary seated in the buggy outside while I went in to buy the sugar. A brisk-mannered young man, with fair hair, served me, and it was my fancy that he dawdled a little over making up the parcel. The proprietor was busy nearby at the time, and from the side-glance the assistant gave him I gathered that the latter was purposely stretching out his task to gain time. I was not wrong. Upon the proprietor crossing to the back of the store, where the cash register stood, the young man leaned forward across the counter.

"Doctor," he began, "I would like a few words with you sometime when you aren't busy."

"Why, certainly," I answered. "Any time you like. You want advice about something?"

It was almost the first time I had had occasion to go into the store, and the assistant was quite a stranger to me. I was probably known to him by sight, but I wondered at his choosing such a confidential way to approach me if he merely wanted medical advice! I kept the same office hours as Lennox had done, and everyone in the village knew where and when to find me.

"I'm George Freeman," he said. "It wasn't advice exactly. I just . . . wanted to see you."

George Freeman . . . suddenly I remembered. It was the name of

Rebecca Dum's sweetheart, the young man who had shown such decision on the evening of the ghost scare at Sliefer's farm. I looked at him with new interest.

"I shall be in this evening after nine o'clock," I said. "Come round to the house. You know where it is?"

"Yes. I'll be round."

"All right." I put down a quarter on the counter, taking up the parcel he held out to me. As I did so a step creaked behind me and I turned quickly.

Aaron Menning stood near us. For a second his eyes moved shiftily from one to the other; then he put up a hand to the greasy peaked cap he wore.

"Artemoon, doctor," he drawled; "artemoon, F-Freeman. Gimme some p-plug terbaccer."

His face was impassive and stupid, but when he pushed his cap back I noticed the veins on his temples stand out. He approached the counter with something of a swagger, his hands in the pockets of his black oilskin coat, and spat on the floor. There was something in the movements of the man which I disliked, at that moment, more intensely than ever. He had a curious shambling way when he walked, which, added to his thick-set figure, gave me the feeling of something half animal, almost simian. It amounted to an actual repugnance. I gave him a curt nod while I waited for my change, and lost no time in hastening out to the buggy.

I put the parcel under the seat and took the reins from Mary's hands. Curiously, my mood of a few moments ago was all but forgotten as I climbed in beside her.

"Did the fellow say anything to you?" I asked her as we drove off. A sudden suspicion had struck me when I came out and found her waiting there.

"Who?"

"Aaron Menning."

"No. I just saw him go into the store."

She spoke with a studied indifference that put me on the alert. Instantly I was sure that he had spoken.

"Why do you ask?"

I set my teeth.

"Because if he had," I answered rashly, "I'd take the occasion to break his neck next time we meet."

Mary gave a soft little laugh.

"Really, Doctor Haverill, I didn't know you were so violent."

"I'm not," I retorted, "at least, not as a rule. But the sight of that man always rouses in me a peculiar and earnest desire to kick him."

"I dare say he's really quite a simple and kind-hearted man," said Mary, with no other purpose, I felt sure, than to irritate me.

"The rugged exterior that hides a beautiful soul," I suggested, remembering that sinister farmyard beyond the Bend. "That's as it may be. The exterior is good enough for me, or bad enough, as you choose to put it. If I get the report of a S.P.C.A. inspector on that farm of his, as I intend to do one of these days, we'll see how Aaron's simple kind-heartedness stands out."

The words slipped out almost without my knowledge. Mary looked at me quickly.

"What's wrong at the place?"

"Merely that the condition of it isn't particularly pretty. I shouldn't have mentioned it. Only a man that keeps animals in the filth and neglect that he does ought to be made an example of in any civilized community. I don't know that there's anything to be gained by interfering at the present moment, but I've seen enough to make me keep an eye on him."

For a little time we drove in silence. Mary's face was grave and troubled. I was angry with myself. I was a fool to mention Menning or his place at all. Presently I turned to her.

"Look here, you're not upset by what I said just now? Because you've no need to think twice about it. I said it because . . . well, because I hated to hear you speak about him that way, even for a minute."

"No. I wasn't thinking about Aaron just then." She gave me a queer little smile. "Doctor Haverill, I guess I've behaved pretty abominably this afternoon."

I flicked the mare with the whip.

"Shall we say we both did, and call it quits? I suppose it was in the air, somehow."

"In the air," she repeated, smiling again, then shivered suddenly. "Things are in the air . . . that's just it. I had a dream last night. I suppose you'll call it silly nonsense, but it's made me queer and restless all day. Doctor Haverill, has Herrick said anything to you about my brother yet?"

"We talked one evening."

"Well?"

"We . . . didn't get to any conclusions, that's all. He has some theory. He hasn't told me yet what it is."

She looked at me steadily.

"If he said that, it is because he knows something. I am absolutely certain of that. And if he knows . . . Doctor Haverill, you are keeping something back from me, you and Herrick together!"

"I am not. I wouldn't do it." I looked at the girl beside me. "If you want me to swear."

"No." She put out a hand. "Yes, one thing. Can you swear to me that to your knowledge there is no suspicion in his mind of any . . . brain trouble with Dick?"

"Yes, I can swear to that, absolutely!"

"I am glad." She was looking straight ahead, down the road before us. "I don't think even Herrick would have kept that from me, if he thought it. Well . . . I suppose I've got to wait."

We spoke of other things during the rest of the drive, and she did not once mention Herrick's name, or her brother's, again. We were passing Sliefer's place when I caught sight once of our queer little acquaintance of the morning. He was just turning in at the gateway, his hat pulled well forward, his little tin box under his arm, and I nodded to him as we drove by. He jerked his head in response, peering short-sightedly up at the buggy through his round dark glasses.

"What a funny little man!" said Mary, after we had passed by. "Is he staying down here?"

"At the Sliefers'. Herrick found him in the woods this morning. He appears to spend his time orchid-hunting in the neighborhood."

"Orchid-hunting . . ." said Mary. She turned her head and looked back at Mr. Crowfoot rather deliberately. Following her gaze, I was surprised to see that he too had turned, and was standing looking after us from the Sliefers' gateway. Seeing himself observed, he moved hurriedly, and disappeared in the direction of the house like a disturbed rabbit going abruptly to earth.

14

THE CRY IN THE NIGHT

A FEW minutes after we reached the bungalow Mrs. Searle appeared. She brought a letter for Herrick which had come by the afternoon mail.

"It had a special-delivery stamp on, so I thought it might be important," she said. "Pete was busy, so I took the liberty of bringin' it over myself. I was glad of the walk, anyway."

I had my own opinion of Pete's busyness, when it came to an errand up the hill, and I tried to catch Mrs. Searle's eye, but her gaze was discreetly lowered.

"It's awfully good of you," said Herrick. He slipped the envelope in his pocket, with a glance at the writing. "Won't you rest a minute, Mrs. Searle? I'm sure Miss Lessing would like you to."

Mary was getting tea at the moment, but Lessing seconded him promptly. Mrs. Searle shook her head.

"I'll be gettin' back, sir, thanks just the same. There's things to see to. It's done me good to get the walk."

"You needn't walk back, anyway," I put in. "I'd be glad for the mare to be home, and Mr. Herrick and I can walk over, later. You can drive yourself, Mrs. Searle, can't you?"

"Certainly, sir, if you'd rather."

She untied the mare and turned the buggy carefully around before getting in. "Ask Pete to give her a good rub down," I called. "Mr. Herrick and I will be back by supper-time."

As it happened, we stayed fairly late. The tea resolved itself into a semi-supper, with the addition of chocolate cake, canned pineapple, and sardines prepared by some special and deadly recipe of Lessing's in a chafing-dish. It was a combination that induced a certain languor afterwards in soul and body. Later, Lessing having re-engaged Herrick in the game of chess that our return had interrupted, Mary and I found ourselves once more left to each other's company at the far end of the porch. She had attempted some quite ridiculous excuse about dishwashing, but either the sense of Herrick's near presence or the meal just finished lent me moral courage to vanquish her objections on the spot.

"Either you invite people to your house," I said, "or you don't invite them. If you do, it's your business to entertain them. I'm not an exacting person, but if it comes to contesting my rights against those of mere crockery, I warn you that I'm going to be exceedingly disagreeable."

Our talk on the homeward drive had broken the aloofness of the past week, and I was minded not to let her slip back into it at will. She sat down on the wicker armchair opposite me, her hands folded on her lap.

"Would you like to see the family photograph album?" she suggested. "We none of us collect picture-postcards, so I'm afraid that's the only interesting object I can offer you. Or I might take you round the garden and show you the site for next year's rose bushes."

"I should be delighted!" I said ruthlessly.

She made a mouth at me.

"I don't think you are in a mood to appreciate the exquisite sentiment of next year's rose bushes," she returned. "It calls for a totally different range of sympathies from yours."

I lit a cigarette.

"You don't know anything about my range of sympathies," I remarked. "For all you know, they may extend to objects even more ethereal than unborn roses."

"Impossible!" She pulled a spray off the woodbine that grew round the porch pillar, and began to pull it to pieces, leaf by leaf. "By the way," she said after a moment, "did you tell me that that queer little friend of yours was a botanist?"

"Of Herrick's," I corrected. "I entirely disclaim him. He described himself as an amateur, whatever he may mean by that. I gather that it's his way of amusing himself on a holiday. There are a good many people who seem to feel lost unless they have some definite hobby for their vacations. I suppose really it gives him mild exercise and an excuse for grubbing about in the open."

"He takes other mild exercise," said Mary, her mouth curving in sudden recollection. "He was engaged in some the other morning, and that's what made me so interested. I'm afraid I interrupted him."

"You'd seen him before, then?"

She laughed.

"I was taking Leo for a run before breakfast, down the hill, the other morning, and I came upon him just in the hollow there near where the stream is, and I'd give you a hundred dollars to guess his occupation. I don't know if you've ever noticed a cedar there, Doctor Haverill, growing quite near the road, on the right-hand side? It branches off some little way from the ground. Well, there he was engaged, of all things in the world, in solemnly climbing up into this tree and jumping out again. I was walking along the footpath where the ground is soft, so he never heard me coming, and the performance struck me as so interesting that I stood still for a minute and watched him. He did it four or five times, and it looked as if he was trying to see how far he could jump. The last time he landed quite near to the edge of the stream, and that seemed to satisfy him, for he didn't try any more after that. Then he looked about on the ground and began to smooth over all the footprints he'd made. He'd just finished when he caught sight of me. He had taken his glasses off for jumping, I suppose in case he smashed them, and as soon as he saw me he grabbed them out of his pocket and walked off. It was for all the world as if he was ashamed at having been caught doing it. I suppose it did look ridiculous for a man of his age to go doing stunts like a schoolboy. I guess it was some sort of an exercise, and he does it pretty often, for he was certainly active at it. I thought maybe he was a physical-culture crank."

"A mild lunatic, more like!" I smiled. "Perhaps the giddiness of youth returns to him at times and he has to work it off. Maybe it's a religious exercise—some obscure sect of jumping Baptists. I'll ask him when we meet."

Mary laughed, but her brows were drawn in a puzzled frown.

"Do you know," she said, "I have a conviction that I have seen that man before. I don't know in the least why. Generally I remember people quite well. I feel that I have not only seen him, but spoken to him. A thing like that bothers me, because I ought to remember it. I will sometime."

"You'd remember if you had spoken to him," I said. "He stammers quite badly."

"Then that settles it," returned Mary gaily. "I have only known two people who stammered in my whole life, with the exception of Aaron Menning, and one was a chemistry professor at school and the other a spinster aunt!"

My appointment with George Freeman was at nine, and it was nearly that hour when we left the bungalow. Herrick and I walked briskly down the hill, and as we passed Dutchman's Hollow I cast a curious glance at the tree which had been the scene of Mr. Crowfoot's acrobatic performances. It stood, as Mary had said, almost overhanging the foot-path, a strong twisted-limbed cedar, noticeable as being the only tree of its kind along the road. The fork was a good six feet from the ground, and I reflected that Crowfoot must possess more agility than his appearance warranted.

Herrick followed my glance.

"A queer tree, that," he said. "Looks as if it had been stuck there for some purpose. Do you ever notice, Haverill, how some inanimate things-if I may call a tree inanimate—strike one unpleasantly? Now that tree, to me, suggests a suicide every time I look at it. A man might hang himself among the upper branches, and you'd merely take his body for a part of the tree."

"Another horror to the mystery of Dutchman's Hill!" I said lightly. "Heaven's sake, Jack, but you're in a cheerful mood tonight! You seem to have creepy things on the brain. If you stood and looked at any tree long enough you could hypnotize yourself into seeing things."

"I merely called it unpleasant," returned Herrick argumentatively.

"To me it is. You think that because I have taken a fancy to dislike a tree I'm ready to imagine unpleasant things about it. I believe that if it impresses me that way, for no apparent reason, it is because the unpleasant things have in all probability already happened."

"Oh, argue that stuff with Lessing," I protested good-humoredly. "It's more in his line. I heard you at it tonight. I'm a normal man, and I object to having my free imagination harrowed over things that don't count. That tree is a tree, and that's all about it."

Our fooling had brought us to a pause at the beginning of the little plank bridge, and Herrick, leaning against the rail, had employed the interval in making a cigarette. He smiled, slipping his tobacco pouch back, and began to feel through his pockets for the little automatic tinderbox he always carried. He was methodical over trifling things to a degree that occasionally irritated me.

"Then go up and touch it," he said. "I would like to test that sensitiveness which you boast that you don't possess."

"All right."

I walked up to the tree, impatient at my own encouragement of such nonsense, and laid my hand on the trunk. Almost as my fingers touched the bark I heard distinctly a low cry, cut suddenly and horribly short. The woods, especially at night, are deceptive both as to direction and distance, and, already half-expectant of some trick, I could have sworn that Herrick himself had done it. I wheeled on him angrily. He was standing in the roadway, the cigarette at his lips, the tiny flame of the tinderbox flickering in his lifted hand, and by its light I saw his face white and startled.

"Did you do that?"

"Do you think I'm a fool?" He caught my arm and swung me round, facing the woods, of a sudden ominously silent. For a moment we listened acutely. Then Herrick flung his unlighted cigarette away. "Come on. It was over there."

He started forward, in the direction where the dam lay, breaking through the underbrush. I followed at his heels. Along the road there had been still a glimmer of light, but once under cover of the trees we stumbled through dense blackness, with nothing to guide us save Herrick's vague sense of direction. Once he stood still to shout. There was no answer.

"Follow the stream," I said.

We had struck the edge of it again; I felt my boots sink in marshy ground, and thereafter we made quicker pace. The brook was narrow at this time of year, running a mere trickle in its bed. It branched off from the creek just below the mill sluice, and in spring carried off some of the excess of water when the creek itself was swollen. Just now, as I knew, there was a scant foot of water at its deepest. I was taking no particular heed therefore to my steps when Herrick, a few paces to my left, called out.

"Take care!" he said. "We're nearly in the creek!"

As he spoke I heard, somewhere near us in the darkness, the unmistakable sound of rushing water. I stopped abruptly, bewildered, with the sense of having somehow lost my bearings. As we were going, the creek should have been a good hundred yards on our left.

And the sound was not the sound of the creek. I had paused at the moment near the edge of the brook; I could feel soft, saturated moss underfoot, and I fancied that it grew even softer and damper as I stood. Something swirled at my ankles, and taking a step forward I was knee-deep in sudden icy flood.

Incredible as it seemed, the stream was rising. I had barely grasped the meaning of it when Herrick shouted again. This time he was answered. A strong shout caught up the echo of his voice.

"Hello, there! Where are you?" It was Herrick.

And the answer came promptly, near at hand now in the darkness:

"Hello! By the dam. Keep clear of the stream; the sluice-gate is giving!"

15

SUSPICIONS

THE warning came just in time. Herrick sang out and sprang, and I could hear the splash as he landed close beside me. Together we forced a way through the bushes and tall weeds and began to scramble up the sloping bank. It was a thicket of alders and brambles; the briars caught and tore at our clothes as we pushed through. We came out not far from the sluice, with the rush of escaping water still in our ears, and above the turmoil of it I called again.

"Where are you? Is there something wrong?"

"I want help here!"

The voice answered almost from under our feet, midway down the bank up which we had just scrambled. In a cleared space of the little thicket a man was standing; my eyes, used by now to the darkness, could make out his figure outlined against the surrounding bushes. It was Mr. Crowfoot, and he was bending over something that lay stretched and ominous among the trampled weeds at his feet. I had not recognized his voice in the darkness, though it sounded vaguely familiar. Herrick reached him first, and was on his knees beside the prostrate figure when I came up.

"An accident, Haverill. I thought so. No, he's alive. How did it happen?"

"He must have fallen off the gate," said Crowfoot. In the excitement he forgot to stammer. "I heard him call out and went down after him. I had only just time to drag him out."

Herrick wiped his hand on the grass.

"Cut his head open," he said briefly. "I think there's an arm broken. Give me a hand, Austin. We must get him up to the top."

"Compound fracture and a broken collarbone," said Crowfoot in his precise tones, oddly precise even in this moment. "I'm glad you gentlemen came along. The head wound isn't much, but there's probably a slight concussion. If you will help me—"

It struck me that he took the man's injuries with a remarkable coolness, utterly at variance with the impression of nervousness he had given me that morning. It was as if he were the medical man and we mere lay beings who had happened along. Herrick growled. He had found his tinder-box, and it flashed a tiny glimmer on the man's face.

"George Freeman!" I exclaimed.

"You know him?" said Herrick quickly.

"The sweetheart of that girl at Sliefer's. He had an appointment with me this evening. He must have been on his way—"

I stopped short. I thought Crowfoot gave a faint exclamation, but he said nothing. Together we got the limp figure to the roadway at the top of the bank, and laid him down. Herrick turned to Crowfoot.

"Was he with you?"

"No. I was walking along the side of the dam. I often take a stroll of an evening; I sleep rather badly without. He was lying at the bottom of the sluice-gate when I found him, half in the water, and I dragged him out. I supposed he had missed his footing in the dark and cried out as he fell."

Herrick and I exchanged glances. So far the story might be true; we had both heard the cry.

"Isn't there a railing?" Herrick asked.

"It was broken," said Crowfoot, "and has never been properly repaired. I have spoken about it several times at the farm, but Mr. Sliefer has neglected to mend it."

"That's so," I confirmed. "It's been broken a good three weeks. Hardly anyone passes this way, now the mill isn't working, so I suppose they haven't bothered."

"Well . . ." said Herrick. He rose from his knees. "As he's known at the farm he'd better be taken there. He must be properly moved. We can't handle him like this."

"I'll go and get help," said Crowfoot.

Herrick looked at him squarely.

"I prefer that we should go together," he said drily. "Austin, do you mind staying here for ten minutes? I suppose you haven't your revolver?"

I hadn't. I carried one usually in accordance with Lessing's suggestion, but at this moment it was locked in one of the surgery drawers.

"Never mind," I said. "I don't need it."

Mr. Crowfoot hesitated. Then his hand slipped to his pocket. Herrick had been cleverer than I gave him credit for.

"If you allow me, Doctor Haverill," he said gravely, "I will leave you my own. I should much prefer it. We are two, and it would be better that you should not remain here unarmed."

Again Herrick and I glanced at one another.

"Do you usually carry a revolver when you take your evening strolls, Mr. Crowfoot?" he asked.

"It is a precaution," replied the little botanist, "which I consider to be quite harmless. As you put a similar question to your friend just now I presume the habit is not confined to myself."

"Take it," said Herrick curtly. "We'll be back in a quarter of an hour." And he disappeared with Crowfoot along the path toward Sliefer's farm.

Left alone, my first and perhaps pardonable impulse was to examine the chambers of the revolver Mr. Crowfoot had just given me. One of the cartridges had been discharged. I slipped it back into my jacket pocket, where it would be ready to hand, and took out my cigarette case. There was nothing to be done for the man beside me until further help arrived. I reassured myself as to his condition. It was as Crowfoot had said. The head wound had bled freely, but we had already partially stanched it with Herrick's handkerchief. The right arm and shoulder were fractured, and I suspected a rib as well. He could not have fallen directly from the sluice-gate, but from one side, with the bushes and the water to break his fall. If he had struck one of the heavy timbers immediately below he would have had his back broken on the spot. As it was he was in no immediate danger, unless from a concussion the extent of which we could not as yet ascertain.

I sat down on the beam which marked the beginning of the sluice-wall, and fell to thinking. The thing had not, to me, entirely the look of an accident. Crowfoot, on a moment's consideration, and in spite of the empty cartridge, I exonerated. Freeman had not been shot, and Crowfoot could have had no object in pushing him over only to rescue him afterwards, and undoubtedly he had saved his life. Possibly they had quarreled, and Freeman had lost his footing, which would account for Crowfoot's prompt action. Crowfoot was staying at the Sliefers', in the same house with Freeman's sweetheart, and where a young woman like Rebecca is concerned there is always a possibility of misunderstandings; but the idea of little Crowfoot playing the rustic Don Juan seemed rather absurd. And that question of the sluice-gate worried me. It had been a dry season, the water in the dam was even lower than usual; there was no earthly reason why the gate should give way just then with no extra pressure to account for it.

Sitting on the wall, swinging my feet, with the sound of the water in my ears, I found myself listening mechanically to its rush. Suddenly a thought occurred to me. There had been no increase in the volume of sound since I had been sitting there. If the sluice-gate had given way only in part, the force of the escaping water would by this time have widened the fissure.

I rose, and walked the few paces to the top of the gate.

It was as I thought. The lever that controlled the sluice had been pulled half over. Bracing my feet firmly, I threw all my strength against it. I had the force of the water to contend with; as I pushed, the whole neglected structure of the gate seemed to vibrate and tremble, but little by little I could hear the gush gradually decreasing, the seething and bubbling below me quieted.

I pushed the lever back as far as I could; it refused to go the whole way, and I feared to do further damage unwittingly by forcing it. But the greater part of the escape was checked. I went back to the wall again and waited.

The minutes dragged. It was a relief to see presently the glimmer of a light through the trees and to hear Mr. Sliefer's anxious deepthroated hail. They had taken one of the stable doors off its hinges, and Herrick and the farmer carried it between them while Crowfoot walked ahead with the lantern.

I saw Crowfoot glance toward the sluice, but he said nothing. With as little jarring as might be we lifted Freeman's unconscious weight on to the door, and I took Herrick's place in the slow procession back to the farmhouse.

Mrs. Sliefer, with Rebecca, white-faced and stricken, met us in the yard. They had prepared a room upstairs, and there we got Freeman to bed and did all that was possible for him. Unconsciousness spared him the pain of our handling; the fracture was as ugly a one as I have seen. The concussion was graver even than we had supposed; it would be days certainly, possibly weeks, before he would be in a state to answer any questions.

I decided to stay the night, and Herrick, with the Sliefers' hired man, drove over in the buggy to take a message to Mrs. Searle and bring back what was needful from the surgery.

In his absence I set myself to gather what information I could from the Sliefers themselves. George Freeman had been there that evening. He had arrived earlier than usual, it being his weekly evening off, and stayed only a short time, saying that he had an appointment in the village. On Rebecca teasing him, he had said that it was a business appointment and that she should hear all about it in good time.

He had left the house at a quarter-past eight. His appointment was for nine, and it would have taken him nearly that time to walk over, even by the short cut. It was already close upon nine when we left the Lessing's cottage to walk home, and at least twenty minutes must have elapsed before we heard Freeman's cry. How had he employed that interval, and with what object had he lingered nearly three-quarters of an hour near the dam? Instinctively I thought of Crowfoot. He was not in the room, and in the light of what had happened I felt no hesitation in questioning the Sliefers about their guest.

He had come to them a fortnight ago, engaging his room by letter. They often took a boarder in the summer, and someone who once stayed there had recommended them to him. He was quiet and pleasant-mannered, and anxious to give no trouble, an ideal boarder from Mrs. Sliefer's point of view, though Rebecca inclined to consider him "queer." He had stipulated for a ground-floor room, explaining that for some heart affection he was forbidden to mount stairs. (I smiled, thinking of the acrobatic exercises Mary Lessing had witnessed.) They had accordingly arranged the back parlor for him, which had a door opening directly on the side porch. His meals were served to him there. Beyond the necessary service they had very little to do with him. He was not at all talkative on account of his infirmity, but always pleasant in manner. To their knowledge, George Freeman had never so much as spoken to him, though it was his unfailing joke to tease Rebecca about the "handsome young city gentleman."

So much for Mr. and Mrs. Sliefer's account. Rebecca differed. Rebecca didn't hold with "queerness," nor with mucking one's room up with rubbishy weeds, nor with going out at night to hunt toadstools.

"Toadstools?" I said.

"Fungy, he calls 'em. It's the same thing. He says there's some that shines in the dark, like rotten wood. I've never seen 'em, nor I wouldn't go touchin' 'em if I did. Anything would need to shine good and hard for him to see it with those blue goggles on!"

"Rebecca's jest set against him because he wears glasses," said Mrs. Sliefer.

"I like to see a folk's eyes," Rebecca insisted. "I hate to have 'em lookin' at you when you think they ain't."

For some reason she seemed to distrust Crowfoot, but there was certainly no suspicion, even in her mind, of any possible quarrel between the two men. Rebecca herself admitted his courage in having pulled Freeman out. No mention was made of the sluice, and I concluded that neither Herrick nor Crowfoot had spoken of it at the house.

Mrs. Sliefer volunteered to sit up with Freeman the first part of the night, and having seen her settled in a capacious armchair near his bed, I returned to Herrick in the parlor below. There was a couch in the room, but we were neither inclined to make use of it. It was my first chance of speaking privately to Herrick since his return to the house, and having closed the staircase door leading upstairs, I told him briefly all that I had learned that evening.

"Crowfoot couldn't have opened the sluice," he said when I had finished. "How does the thing work? Do you suppose Freeman could have caught at the lever as he fell and pulled it over on him? It doesn't sound likely."

"Impossible. The lever works in the opposite direction."

Herrick pondered.

"He might have been fooling with the thing and opened it, and then lost his balance trying to get it back."

I shook my head.

"He knows the dam well enough, and he doesn't strike me as the sort of man to go fooling with a thing like that out of mischief. Besides, he didn't fall from where the lever is. If he had, and the sluice was already open, he'd have been soaked through and probably drowned to boot. Remember the rush of that water! Crowfoot got him out, and Crowfoot was only wet to the knees. He must have fallen partially clear of the pool, across one of the timbers. The thing looks much more to me as though someone had deliberately opened the sluice on them while they were both down there. Either the machinery stuck, or they were interrupted before they could do the worst. In any case Crowfoot knows more than he has chosen to tell us. He may be shielding someone; the whole business looks ugly."

"I'm going to handle Crowfoot in the morning," said Herrick grimly. "It's a case where he'll find it best to tell all he knows. A man who goes hunting toadstools at night with a revolver lays himself open to miscon-struction." He stared a moment at the purple crocheted mat on which the Sleifers' parlor lamp sat enthroned. "Why on earth was he so keen on your keeping that revolver, I wonder?"

"Possibly for the same reason that had caused him to fire one of the cartridges himself, this evening," I said drily.

"He had?" Herrick looked up. "Why didn't we hear the shot?"

"It happens to be one of those special revolvers which are built to make as slight a report as possible. I know the pattern. The sound carries practically no distance. If Crowfoot carries that revolver habitually it is because he has good reason to be afraid of someone, and he wouldn't have used it without serious cause."

"Have you any idea," asked Herrick, "what Freeman wanted to see you about tonight?"

"Yes," I said slowly, "I have. You know the night you came down here, Jack? It was Freeman who was the most determined to sift that ghost story to the bottom, if you remember. From all accounts, he is not the young man to take half-way measures in a thing that concerns his sweetheart. I think that he has been working on his own initiative, that he found out something, and it was about that that he wanted to see me. He made the appointment for after dark, at an hour when he was not likely to be seen coming or going from my house, and he even took the precaution of coming by way of the woods. Someone had an interest in preventing him from keeping the appointment. They watched him to the Sliefers' house, and laid up for him by the sluice, which he would have to cross on his way to me."

"You mean Crowfoot himself?"

"Crowfoot wasn't here at the time of the ghost scare, and he didn't know of Freeman's appointment tonight. Moreover, I don't think he had even an idea who the man was till you flashed your lamp on him. Remember it was pretty dark there. But two people might have known of it. They were both in the store at the time. One was Mr. Haskell, whom I think we may dismiss immediately. The other was Aaron Menning."

"Aaron Menning . . ." There was that in Herrick's tone that confirmed instantly my own conclusions. "Then if that's so, Aaron Menning is at the bottom of the ghost business, and of the whole Dutchman's Hill story. Aaron; the pious chapel member! But why in heaven's name—?"

"There's a streak of insanity in the whole family," I said. "Don't forget that Jakey was said to be half crazy. Aaron has the look of a criminal degenerate. How on earth he has maintained his reputation in the village so long I can't think. He is cunning and malicious, if no worse."

"I'd like to know just what hold that type of man could have over Crowfoot," Herrick said. "Crowfoot comes in somewhere. If it was Aaron pushed Freeman over, what reason could Crowfoot have for shielding him deliberately? There's more behind it yet than we can lay hand on."

There was, but our plans for finding out were destined to receive a rude shock in the morning.

About two o'clock I left Herrick on the couch and went to take Mrs. Sliefer's place upstairs. Against my will I half dozed in the chintz-covered armchair, and through my brain there chased puzzling dreams in which Herrick and I were trying feverishly to conceal George Freeman's body in the mill-dam, while Crowfoot, continually changing and rechanging into the likeness of Aaron, leapt up and down from the dizzy heights of a butternut tree and chattered at us angrily as he sprang.

Herrick was already drinking coffee when I came downstairs. Rebecca had brought it in, and with it a note addressed to me.

I broke it open. There was a second bulkier envelope inside with the note. Both note and address were printed in small, neat capitals, such as a child might use.

"MY DEAR HAVERHILL,
    "I REGRET THAT I HAVE BEEN OBLIGED TO
LEAVE FOR THE CITY BY AN EARLY TRAIN, AND
SO MUST POSTPONE THE PLEASURE OF MEETING
YOU AND YOUR FRIEND AGAIN TILL A LATER
DATE.
               "ALEXANDER CROWFOOT."

On the second envelope was printed:

> "To BE OPENED ONLY IF NOT RECLAIMED
> WITHIN THREE DAYS."

"Stung!" said Herrick.

16

I CATCH A BURGLAR

I FOUND Rebecca in the kitchen, weeping. It was easy to see that she had spent half the night crying, and I hastened to reassure her so far as I could as to her sweetheart's condition.

"And now about Mr. Crowfoot," I said. "What time did he leave here?"

"It must have been early," Rebecca answered. "I was down an' about by five."

"He gave you the note?"

"He left it in his room. I went to put his coffee like I always do, outside, an' the door was open. He left another envelope for mother with his week's board in. His bed hadn't been slept in. He was writin' in his room all last evenin', after he came in."

"And his things?"

"He didn't have more'n a suitcase, and he must have took that with him."

I went back to Herrick in the parlor. Crowfoot's enclosure still lay on the table, and as I took it up to put it in my pocket I felt sorely tempted to break the seal there and then.

"So he's lit out, temporarily," said Herrick. "Well . . . it doesn't look particularly wise under the circumstances, but I suppose he knows his own business."

"Should we open the letter?"

"No," Herrick said decidedly. "That point is quite clear. The instructions are definite. He gives us a certain date, and if he does not reclaim his letter personally by then we are free to act on our discretion, but not before. Meantime we can only put two and two together. Crowfoot was down here on some job in which he anticipated personal danger, or he wouldn't have gone armed. The cartridge he used was not fired on Freeman, and unless I am much mistaken the affair of last night upset, or at all events abruptly altered, his own schemes. He's learned something that we haven't, and I'd give a good deal to know just what, but we can't force his hand. Unless I underestimate him, he'll turn up to claim that letter all right."

"Unless—" I recalled the provisional clause on the envelope.

Herrick smiled.

"He doesn't strike me as the sort of person to step off a plank bridge in the dark! That's a pure bit of dramatic effect, in my opinion."

When we had finished breakfast I drove down to the drug store and telephoned for a trained nurse. She arrived by the midday train, and Freeman's condition being satisfactory, I was able to leave him in her charge and go home with Herrick.

We refused the farmer's buggy and walked over, following the short cut that had so nearly proved fatal to one man at least the night before. The water below the sluice-gate was at its normal level, but looking over we could see the line of uptorn weeds and flattened grasses that showed where the brief flood had swept. An alder bush on the left side, overhanging the timbered edge of the pool, was partly broken, indicating the point of Freeman's fall.

We examined the upper part of the sluice-gate carefully. On the wood near the lever I found a few dried spots of blood. Herrick nodded appreciatively when he saw them.

"Looks as if Crowfoot's cartridge wasn't wasted! Someone got hit, though not badly; there's none tracked along the road. My respect for our friend increases. Austin, why was he so careful we didn't see his handwriting?"

"Give it up. He's a queer bird anyway."

I told him of what Mary Lessing had seen that morning, by Dutchman's Hill. Hitherto it had presented itself to me merely as a whim on Crowfoot's part. Now I began to think he might have had some object in the performance. Herrick smiled when it came to the jumping, but his face grew serious again immediately.

"Austin," he said, "I give you a problem. What is it about that particular tree that attracts me and attracts Crowfoot? There's something more than coincidence in it. Crowfoot wasn't amusing himself. To my

mind, he was testing a theory, and if we knew what that theory was. . . ."
He broke off, thoughtfully, and I turned to him.

"Well?"

"Nothing much. Austin, whereabouts was Jake's body found, last spring?"

"Face downwards in the water, just near the plank bridge. Why?"

"Taken with Crowfoot's action, does that suggest anything to you?"

"Nothing to do with suicide. Jake had a fit and fell in the water."

"Exactly." He walked a few paces in silence. "Has it ever occurred to you what a really admirable country coroner you would make?"

"I don't see what that's got to do with it."

"Listen." He swung round. "Jake's death was not accident, though he may have died actually in a fit. He was frightened by someone or something that sprang out at him from that tree as he passed, and Crowfoot, depend upon it, was merely trying to find out whether that jump was within the limits of an ordinarily active man."

We were both tired that evening and we turned in early after supper. I had left instructions to call me if there was any change in Freeman's condition, but I anticipated none before the morning. The nurse seemed a competent woman, and I felt easy in leaving him to her care. I slept like a log, my rest untroubled by any dreams.

Towards morning, as it seemed to me, I woke up with that curious sense of something happening which arouses one at times by appeal through some subconscious perception. Five minutes before a thunderstorm would have failed to rouse me; now instinct dragged me up sitting in my bed, of a sudden keenly and alertly awake.

I listened. Someone was moving in the surgery below. Mrs. Searle went to bed always at ten, and I had the impression of having slept already for several hours. I struck a match softly and looked at my watch. It was a quarter to twelve, earlier than I had thought. I felt on the bureau for my revolver, which I had taken to my room that evening, and opened the door noiselessly.

It was not Herrick, for I could hear his regular breathing through the keyhole opposite. At the foot of the little flight of stairs a faint light glimmered. The stairs opened directly from the surgery, and it was my custom to leave the door at the bottom open during the night. Now it was closed, and the light that I saw filtered through the crack. I crept quietly down and pushed it open, revolver in hand.

A pocket electric lamp lay on the desk, and by its light a man was searching through one of the desk drawers. It was a small drawer which had been always locked; I fancied that it contained some private papers and affairs of Lennox's which he had put together there before leaving. The man's back was towards me, but I recognized instantly the shabby tweed coat, the soft felt hat pulled low down over his head.

It was Crowfoot.

I don't know what I had expected; certainly not him. I lowered the revolver and stepped forward.

"Were you looking for anything, Mr. Crowfoot?"

At the sound of my voice he turned; his hand shot out towards the electric lamp, and instantly the room was in darkness.

For a second we stood there, neither moving, and we could hear each other's breathing across the room.

"Light that lamp," I said quietly. "If you have any explanation I am ready to hear it.   I have a revolver in my hand, and if you attempt to move I shall be compelled to treat you like any other common housebreaker."

"Listen here," he began, "and don't for heaven's sake play the fool!" His voice sounded excited, impatient, but with an assurance in it that was somehow vaguely familiar to me, and, as on the night before, there was no trace of his usual stammering. It was the voice of a man interrupted in important business rather than caught red-handed in an attempt at common theft. "Put that revolver down, Haverill. I tell you, you don't know what you're meddling with! I'm in a hurry. Let me go out of the house now, without any questions, and I swear to heaven I'll come back tomorrow and tell you everything you want to know. I'll tell you *everything!* But don't stop me now!"

"You will, eh?"

I laid the revolver down on a chair that stood behind me, but only to have both hands free. He made a movement, chancing the darkness, but the room was too small. I collided with him somewhere near the arm-chair—the solid mahogany caught my knee an ugly whack through my thin pajamas—and for a moment we grappled together fruitlessly.

"Haverill, you idiot—let me go!"

He gasped and struggled, but I held my grip.

"Not so easy. I want the lamp."

He swore, wrenching an arm free, and the little white bulb glowed out. He must have slipped it in his pocket when he turned. The light shone on our two blinking faces. Crowfoot's hat had fallen off in the struggle, and for the first time I saw him without his black glasses.

It was Lennox! Stupefied, I let go my hold. "Now will you let me go?"

he snarled.

"I thought you were in Europe! What's it all about? Are you crazy?"

"Oh, you idiot!" There was a savage patience in his voice. "Get on your trousers, then, and come along. You were always an obstinate devil, Haverill! Bring that revolver with you and don't wake the house, and don't for God's sake stand wasting any more time! I'll wait for you."

I ran upstairs. A hundred wild ideas passed through my mind as I groped my way hurriedly into sweater and trousers in the dark, not even staying to light a candle. I hardly knew, in my bewilderment, whether Lennox had been impersonating Crowfoot or Crowfoot Lennox; the whole thing seemed inextricably and extravagantly mixed. Curiously, Herrick had not even been roused by our scuffle. I carried my boots down to avoid waking him now, and pulled them on in the surgery.

"Take your revolver," said Lennox.

We passed out through the door; he had used his own latchkey to come in with.

"Will you tell me—?" I began, when we were clear of the house.

"All in good time."

A few paces up the road an automobile was standing. Two men were already seated in it, besides the chauffeur. One leaned out, watching, and he gave an exclamation as the two of us stepped into the light of the lamps.

"It's all right," said Lennox. He almost pushed me into the tonneau, where I tumbled into a big broad-shouldered Irishman, and swung up himself to the front seat. "This is Doctor Haverill; he's coming along. Haverill, this is Mr. Keary, the county sheriff, and Inspector McWade."

The chauffeur let in the clutch and the big car swung forward in the direction of Dutchman's Hill.

"And now, Haverill," Lennox said, turning to me, "you wanted to be in it, and you're in it. These gentlemen are accompanying me to the Bend with a warrant for the arrest of the man known as Aaron Menning."

"Ah!" I looked at the burly Irish inspector beside me, and the conviction of yesterday grew clear in my mind. "For assault on George Freeman!"

"No," said the sheriff, speaking for the first time. "For the manslaughter of his brother on the seventeenth of last March."

17

A MIDNIGHT CHASE

WE swept on at a steady pace, through a silence broken only by the throbbing of the engine and the hissing whir of tires over the dust. On either side of the road the woods stretched black and inscrutable. Just before we came to Dutchman's Hill Lennox said a word to the chauffeur, and he paused to extinguish the two headlights. Thereafter we drove more slowly.

A few paces beyond the bridge, at the beginning of the hill, the car stopped suddenly. Something had gone wrong with the engine, and while the chauffeur got out to attend to it Lennox and the sheriff took the opportunity to walk back to the bridge we had just crossed.

"Have to get a light on it," the chauffeur said, unhooking one of the side lamps. "The blame thing might have held out a bit longer! We ain't far from Dutchman's Hill, by all accounts."

"This is Dutchman's Hill," I said.

"It is, eh?" He glanced at the inspector; who was holding the lamp for him. "Well, they say one cuss leads to another, and be damned if I don't give this place a worse name than it's had yet!"

Alone in the car, I leaned back against the cushions, speculating as to the chance that had drawn me into this midnight adventure and what its outcome would be—the climax, for aught I knew, of all the summer's mysteries. Of Lennox's part in it I could but guess, but the experience of the last forty-eight hours gave me a confidence in him that overrode all earlier impressions. Mentally I contrasted the vision of Crowfoot, alert, cool-headed, decisive, with the Lennox of my first evening's arrival, and marveled at the grip he had brought to bear on himself in the two months' interval.

The air was still and oppressive in the hollow; the stench of gasoline rose in a warm reek mingled with the stagnant smell of the swamp close by. The mosquitoes were thick; they descended in swarms upon us with the stopping of the car, and a host of moths and midges fluttered round the lamp, attracted by its glare. The two men, bent over the engine, joked and grumbled in undertones, as cheerfully as though we were out on no

713

more serious errand than a mere pleasure ride. The sheriff rejoined us.

"How long will you be, Jackson?"

The chauffeur straightened his back.

"Twenty minutes, sir, more or less. I can't fix it under."

There was a brief consultation, and the sheriff turned to Lennox.

"How far are we from the Bend?"

"Three-quarters of a mile, by road. We can strike a short cut at the top of the hill."

"We'd better walk it. There's no good wasting time. Get your job through, Jackson, bring the car on to the top of the hill and wait for us there, along the road. I suppose . . ."

Lennox caught my eye.

"I can rely on Doctor Haverill," he said promptly. "As we are one man short already I don't think it advisable that we should divide."

"Very good. Have either of you gentlemen an extra revolver?"

I pulled mine out and gave it to the chauffeur. He grinned cheerfully as he slipped it in his pocket.

"Right, sir! If any spook puts a game on me I won't start tellin' my beads! Give me twenty minutes, Mr. Keary, and I'll have the car right there!"

We left him at his task and set off up the hill, following the little footpath at the side of the road, Lennox and the sheriff in front, the inspector and myself at the rear. When we were nearly at the top the inspector paused.

"There's fire somewhere," he said. "I can smell it."

"Someone been burning bush, most likely," said Lennox. "We can tell further on."

At the top of the hill it was unmistakable, a sickly charred odor that hung heavily on the air. Lennox gave an exclamation and quickened his pace involuntarily. A moment later the Lessing bungalow came in sight; there were lights in the windows, and I caught sight of a slim shawl-wrapped figure on the porch. Lennox and the sheriff were well ahead, and as they reached the bungalow someone stepped out and joined them in the roadway. I heard Lessing's voice raised in amazement. "Lennox, by all that's holy!"

"It's Menning's place," said Lennox as we came up. "I thought as much! The game's up."

"Burned to tinder an hour ago," said Lessing cheerfully. "Hello, Haverill! Have you all joined the local fire-brigade?" He caught sight of the inspector's square shoulders behind me, and whistled. "So that's it! Well, if you're wanting an interview with Menning, I guess his present address is somewhere in the woods between here and Coopersville!"

We ran on hastily to the Bend, taking a short cut across the fields behind the bungalow. It was as Lessing had said. The fire had broken out some three hours ago, and his first intimation had been the sudden lurid glare across the treetops as he sat on the porch smoking a final cigarette before turning in. The house, a dilapidated structure at best, had caught from the basement upward, and by the time he arrived on the scene it was already beyond hope of saving. He had given what help he could to the neighbors, hastily collected, but with the limited appliances at hand the task was hopeless from the first.

The huckster's yard with its strewn debris, desolate enough by daylight, was made doubly sinister by the red wavering light that still played and flickered among the broken boxes and tumble-down sheds, lit up the loathsome scrapheaps and the trampled mire underfoot. The prisoned chickens, startled from sleep, kept up a mournful squawking, pushing and struggling in their coops. The efforts of the men had been directed to the barn and cowshed. They stood now, an awed, strangely silent little group, gathered near a broken bureau and a pile of household goods that had been dragged somewhere from the burning and huddled forlornly in the open yard. I remember that a wooden clock, still ticking, and a filthy and ancient foot-tub were among the collection. I spoke to one of the men; it was old Paddy's son-in-law.

"We done all we could; the old place was no better'n tinder. Pop was fur lettin' it burn an' not lift a hand. We got Miss Mennin' out. Hiram Scholl he bust the door in an' got her. She's over to the house now. Aaron ain't here. It's funny about him. He ain't took the horse anyway. They was sayin' . . ."

He stopped short and looked at me, the glare of the fire on his sweat-streaked face.

"They was sayin' he started it. I dunno. It broke out downstairs. They ain't no one seen Aaron."

And after a moment he added: "He'd oughter be insured. There's no savin' anything."

I went back to Lennox and the sheriff, standing a little apart.

"Aaron's gone," I said.

"I know. There's nothing to be done here. We'll go and see the old woman."

I stayed behind with the inspector and Lessing while the other two went over to the Nevills' cottage, and together we made a thorough search of the barn and outhouses. There was nothing to be learned. Filth and disorder reigned everywhere. To describe the condition of the place, as we found it, would only be to recall the actual physical sickness that overtook me during the task.

The neighbors had gradually dispersed during our search. By the time the others rejoined us the place was deserted. The fire had completely burned itself out; only a tiny smoldering flame pulsed up here and there, to die down again immediately into blackness.

McWade and the sheriff exchanged a few words, and the latter turned. "Well, gentlemen, I think there's nothing more to be done," he said. "I expect Jackson has the car ready by now. We'll walk back to the house, and if Mr. Lessing has no objection I should like a few words with him before we go."

We did not meet the car, nor was it in sight when we reached the bungalow. Mary Lessing was on the porch, and while the others went indoors I stayed outside to smoke a cigarette in the open air and watch the road in case Jackson turned up.

"I'm glad it was Menning's house, if it had to be somebody's," said Mary, with really feminine lucidity. "I wanted to go, but Dick wouldn't let me. I guess I wouldn't have been much use. Doctor Haverill, is it . . . Aaron they're after?"

"They think he had something to do with that business last spring. It's Lennox's story. I haven't had a chance to talk to him yet. Anyway I'll take back all I said against him last night."

She had heard nothing of the accident at the dam, and I told her as briefly as I could all that had happened since we left the bungalow last evening. She listened breathlessly.

"So it was Doctor Lennox all the time! Now I know why he didn't want to meet me that morning. I was sure I knew him, somehow."

"You were smarter than we were," I admitted. "He took us in. Only I don't see why, now."

"Sliefer's is near to Aaron's place," said Mary, "and if he was watching Aaron he wouldn't want anyone to know who he was. You think it was Aaron who attacked Freeman last night?"

"I am nearly sure of it."

Mary shivered. "It's horrible," she said.

"It's horrible! I wish now—"

"What?"

"I wish I'd known," she said quickly. "That poor girl! I shall go over and see her first thing tomorrow. I know Rebecca quite well. We get our milk from there."

"Do," I said. "You'll cheer her up a bit." I rose as I spoke and peered down the road. "It's time that car put in an appearance."

"Your car? Where did you leave it?"

"Just down the hill there. It had a breakdown," I explained. "The man was going to catch us up."

"I thought I heard a car," she said, "a little while ago. It was while you were over at the fire. It didn't come past here. Do you suppose Menning knew what you came for?"

"Lennox thinks he must have suspected it. Anyhow he's far enough away by this time."

She looked at me, as I thought, a little uneasily.

"You aren't afraid of Menning?" I exclaimed. "Far or near, he'll take good enough care to keep out of anyone's way just now. Well, I'll go and see if I can find the car. He may have misunderstood the directions. You might tell the others if they're looking for me."

As it happened, I had barely gone a dozen paces up the road before I heard the cheerful approaching throb of a motor, and a moment later the car, with Jackson in it, swung into sight.

"I was just coming along to look for you," I said as he drew up. "I thought you'd missed us."

"Thought the spooks had got me!" He grinned appreciatively. "No, sir! I just pulled up the road a bit—didn't know which way you'd gone. I guess they weren't huntin' company tonight." He laughed. "Mighty thick these woods are. I don't know this part of the country much. Do you get any big animals, round about?"

"Nothing bigger than a badger," I said. "Why?"

"There was something crossed my path, coming up the hill there. It might have been a dog, now I think of it, but it didn't look like no dog I've ever seen. Rather high in the hindquarters, and grayish . . . I on'y saw the back of it. It slunk off in the bushes as I come up."

"There aren't any very big dogs that I know," I said, "except Mr. Lessing's setter, and that's generally chained up at night."

"It weren't no setter," said Jackson. "Weren't the build of a setter. And it weren't no badger, for I've seen 'em. Low-running, brownish beasts they are . . . Is this the house, sir?"

We drew up outside the bungalow, and I jumped down to join the others, waiting on the porch.

"It wasn't anything *like* a dog, now I think of it," said Jackson.

18

LENNOX'S STORY

LENNOX'S FACE, when the car had deposited us once more at our door, expressed utter chagrin and annoyance. He flung himself down in the surgery armchair and lit a cigar.

"That's what comes of not acting on the minute," he said. "I had my hand on the man last night. I tell you, Haverill, you can't drive plain facts into people's heads. There's formality and formality, and the end is your man gets a clear twelve hours to lay his plans and the game's up."

"Bad luck," I rejoined.

He sat staring moodily down at the carpet. "While I think of it," I remembered, "I've got some property of yours. You might as well have it back."

I pulled out the envelope he had left for me that morning. Lennox took it without a glance and thrust it into his pocket.

"Considering that I didn't have the opportunity to open it," I remarked, "I think you might let me into the story now."

He pulled out his watch. "Well, I don't know but what sleep's out of the question anyway, tonight. Get the whisky out, Haverill, there's a good chap, and we'll go into it."

"One moment," I said as I unlocked the cupboard. "Have you any objection if I fetch Herrick down?"

"Not in the least."

I roused Herrick accordingly, and he bundled sleepily into a dressing-gown and joined us below, where his sleepiness rapidly vanished in the few moments that it took to grasp the new turn of events, and the part that Lennox himself had played in last night's happenings.

Put briefly, this was the story as Lennox put it to us, gathered round the surgery table in the chilly half-hour that precedes dawn.

The Menning household, when Lennox first came here, had consisted of the two half-brothers, Jake and Aaron, and the old mother, who kept house for them and helped more or less in the business. They were of Westphalian origin, but had settled in this country for two generations. The mother, according to Lennox, was a curious survival of the original peasant stock. Stolid, hard-working, and uncommunicative, she preserved always a certain aloofness from her neighbors, a taciturnity that marked her out even among the Dutch families about. She had preserved a great deal of her native superstition and traditions, and was reputed to have a great knowledge of herbs and some skill in home doctoring and decoctions, when she could be induced to use it, by reason of which the neighbors, ready enough in such gossip, believed her to have actual powers of witchcraft. Superstition dies hard, even in a new country, and there was at all events a marked unwillingness among them to annoy or "cross" her in any way. About thirty years ago she had married a young Pennsylvania Dutchman, Menning by name, who had deserted her shortly after. Aaron, their son, had his mother's characteristics in a modified degree. He was inclined to be friendly, if not sociable, a good businessman, thrifty but honest-dealing, and very religious. Jake, the half-brother, was some years older than Aaron, and, in Lennox's phrase, a "throw-back." There was considerable mystery and gossip about his birth. Some said that he was born before the mother's marriage, some after. He was certainly only half related to Aaron, and the wide difference between them was in curious contrast to their strong physical resemblance, a result in both cases of the virile persistence of the mother's peasant type. Jakey was mentally deficient, but not enough to debar him from ordinary tasks. He occupied himself in the huckstering business, and took the wagon round in turn with Aaron, week and week about. In many ways he could be trusted, but he was malicious and cunning, and the bad streak seemed to predominate with age. Lennox never considered him safe. There was always the possibility, in his opinion, of a serious outbreak, and he had even gone so far as to suggest to Aaron the advisability of having him put under definite restraint. At first Aaron had been disposed to consider the idea favorably, then later, for no given reason, he changed his mind. His manner, at about this time, in regard to any discussion about Jakey, changed also so noticeably that Lennox supposed there must have been words between Aaron and the mother about his (Lennox's) interference in the matter, and that Aaron had perhaps been naturally induced to range himself upon the mother's side. Lennox urged him at least to have his brother medically examined, but he always met with a dogged refusal.

"Jakey's all right in the daytime," Aaron persisted. "He ain't doin' harm to nobody. Nights we lock him in."

Once only he went so far as to say that if it became necessary he would take his own steps in the matter, rather implying a resentment at outside interference, and Lennox, to avoid making further bad blood, was forced to let the matter drop. So things went on till last March, and the events which led to the finding of Jakey's body by the creek at Dutchman's Hill.

Lennox saw the body, and there was no doubt in his mind at the time that death was due to an epileptic seizure. There were no marks of any sort on the body. The ground was fairly soft at the time—a thaw had set in that same afternoon—but there were no footprints to be found other than those of the man himself, leading down to the creek, and the tracks of some large dog which had evidently passed that way in the night, sniffed at the body and gone on.

At the word "large dog" I saw Herrick shift in his chair.

"Do the Mennings keep a dog?" he asked.

"A watchdog, I believe. Most people do."

"Nothing else was found near the place?"

"Nothing but this, which I myself happened on a few days later. Either of the brothers might have dropped it, or it might have been dropped by another person altogether. It was lying some little distance from the creek, beyond the bridge there. The inspector attached no particular importance to it. There is a certain amount of traffic along this road, and there is no indication that this wasn't dropped by some passing person a day or two after the body was found."

He drew from his waistcoat pocket a small round silver object, slightly larger than a pea.

"Looks like some boy's treasure," I said.

"A button, isn't it?"

"It has been a button," Herrick said. "The shank has been broken off and it's been hammered. Well, Lennox, go on."

"Of course there was an inquest," Lennox said. "They found that the man died during an epileptic seizure, which carried out my own conclusions. And now I am coming to the queer part of my tale. It was Aaron who formally identified the body. I saw him and spoke with him at the inquest, and I saw him again the day after Jakey's funeral."

He paused.

"Six weeks after the inquest, Haverill, I was walking down the short cut from the Bend, and I met Jake Menning face to face. I am as certain of it as that I am sitting here. He made off without giving me a chance to speak to him. But that it was Jake, in solid flesh and blood, I had no shadow of a doubt.

"The next day I went to the house. I asked for Aaron. The old woman met me. She said that Aaron was away with the wagon. I asked when I could see him, and she became evasive. It seemed that he was very busy, that he was away a good deal of the time; she could not say at all when he was likely to be found.

"Her answers, and more particularly her manner, set me to thinking. I had not seen Aaron since the day after Jakey's funeral. No one, so far as I could learn without pushing inquiries unduly, had seen much of Aaron since the inquest. His trade had always lain further afield than the immediate neighborhood, where most people raised their own chickens for use, and few in sufficient quantity to sell. Mrs. Searle had seen him, certainly, and Mrs. Searle had remarked a change in him. She said that he was queer and silent; she thought that the shock of his brother's death had preyed on his mind. In her own words, he was 'getting just like Jakey in his ways.'

"It was about this time that the talk first began about the haunting of Dutchman's Hill. I am not a credulous man where ghosts are concerned, and I scoffed any idea of the supernatural. One stranger, a peddler, said that a 'something' had jumped out and chased him to the bridge, where it stopped. Others declared that it was the ghost of Jakey that haunted the place. On top of all this came the—er—the very singular attacks upon Mr. Lessing. I don't want to go into Lessing's case now. His own story was of course untenable, and I strongly believe that he knew a great deal more than he chose to tell me at the time—in other words, that he found amusement in trying, deliberately, to see how much I would believe. We were always strongly opposed on certain questions, though in general I found him a most courteous and charming man, and I am afraid he was not above trying, in this matter, to take a rise out of me, as they say. If he had taken me into his confidence then, instead of inventing the ridiculous sort of bogy-tale he did, we should have been at the truth of this matter much earlier."

Herrick and I exchanged glances. I fancied he was about to speak, but on second thoughts changed his mind. Lennox continued.

"The problem resolved itself into this. If Jakey was still alive, and I could swear to it that he was, whose was the body that had been identified and buried in March, and how was it that no one, save myself, guessed at his continued existence? *Who was Aaron Menning?*

"I tell you, Haverill, the thing became a nightmare. I had no proof to go upon, nothing but my own instinct. The more I thought over it, the more clear it grew to me. The man whose body had been found at Dutchman's Hill was not Jakey at all, it was Aaron."

"But—"

"Listen here, Haverill," Lennox said. "I know what I am saying sounds incredible to you. But consider for a moment, on what superficial observations we base our recognition of people, every day. Remember the very strong likeness which existed between the two brothers, even to the scarring and thickening of the skin by smallpox, which in itself blunts the individuality of a face. The face of the dead man was swollen both by the manner of death and the partial immersion in mud. Remember that there were no intimate relatives to impose upon, for the mother undoubtedly knew the truth. The farmer who found the body identified it as that of a huckster named Menning who had called upon him the week before. Aaron was away from home that night, and he did not return with the wagon till the afternoon. It was the mother who first identified the body as that of Jakey, and the news was already spread when I arrived on the scene. Aaron appeared at the inquest, but with the exception of myself there were not three men there who knew him at all intimately, or who could have sworn to his actual identity *unless* they saw the two brothers side by side. Both Aaron and the mother opposed the inquest strongly, and the neighbors told me that she would let no one help her in preparing the body for burial. She had always kept herself rather aloof, as I said, and at the time her refusal did not strike me as peculiar.

"Given the clue, the thing was easy enough to construct. I believe myself it was fear of his brother's placing him under restraint that first suggested the attack. He must have concealed himself in the tree near the footbridge, knowing that Aaron had an errand in the village and would pass that way, and so sprung out upon him. The impact of his body bore them both down to the edge of the stream. There was no struggle. The shock brought on the seizure in which Aaron died, and Jakey, leaving him there, had sufficient cunning either to follow the stream or swing himself up by the bridge, and so avoid leaving any traces. He returned to the house, and with his mother concocted the story of Aaron's absence with the wagon, harnessed the horse and made off ready to return the following afternoon, when the dead man's identity would have been safely established. People might have suspected Jakey of killing Aaron, but no one would suspect Aaron of killing Jakey.

"I think now that he was on his guard against me at the inquest, and that his suspicion must have deepened as time went on. I was morally convinced that the man was a dangerous homicidal lunatic, but I had no evidence to convict him. He would have been cunning enough to defeat me, since no one would have credited my story. Aaron was known and respected. It would have been folly to bring any hasty charge against him. Convinced that he already mistrusted me, and that my only safety was in disarming his suspicion, I took the only course possible. I determined to go away for a time, and I took the precaution of letting it be supposed that I went for my health. I wanted Menning to think that he had driven me away, and I believe I succeeded. Up to last night he had no suspicion of my identity with Crowfoot. I counted on his relaxing his caution once I was out of the way, and I was right.

"Freeman must have suspected something of the truth, since that Rebecca swore she had seen Jakey's ghost near the mill-dam, and if it had not been for Freeman's well-meant imprudence we should have had Jakey under lock and key at this moment. He got suspicious of Freeman, laid up for him last night, and pushed him over the sluice. I heard Freeman's cry and the splash, and guessed instinctively what had happened. It was then that Jakey's mania came out. He disappeared when Freeman fell, but in a paroxysm of rage and fear came back and tried to pull the gate open on us while we were both down there. I had to fire on him in defense, and he made off. He had taken the alarm, how-ever, and instead of waiting the one more day I had intended, I judged it best to post straight off and lay my facts as I knew them before the sheriff then and there. The rest of course you know."

"Then you had no intention of going to Europe?" I asked.

"Not in the least. A friend posted my note from Queenstown, a wise precaution, since Menning would undoubtedly hear of it through the postmaster's gossip. I went to the Sliefers' because they were near enough to the Bend to enable me to carry out a few investigations without arous-ing too much interest, and also because they happened to be about the only people in the village whom I never attended professionally, and they would therefore be less likely to recognize me. You were the only person I was afraid of, Haverill, and you I had to chance. We spent only a few hours together before I left, and before that we hadn't met for years; it was only my voice that troubled me, and there I took a leaf out of Jakey's book. Mr. Herrick would make a better detective than you. He played me a neat trick over that revolver last night!"

Herrick smiled. "You must admit that things looked ugly for you! Now I see why you were so reluctant to be dragged up to the house that morning."

"My old training in college theatricals came in useful anyway!" He looked at his watch.

"Give me another of those cigars of which you are so lavish, Haverill, and I'll turn in. I'm dog-tired, and there's plenty before me tomorrow, yet."

He betook himself with a blanket to the dining-room sofa, to get a few hours' sleep. The first violet light of dawn was already filtering between the curtains, and Herrick stood up abruptly and extinguished the lamp.

"Lord," he said, "it's stuffy in here! Well, Austin, what do you make of it all?"

"It may be true," I said. "It throws sufficient doubt anyway for the arrest of this man. They might prove manslaughter. Lennox's idea evidently is that if he can be once arrested on this charge they can have him medically examined, and the whole truth will come out."

"Exactly." He walked to the window, pulling aside the curtains, and threw up the sash. The clean fresh air of the dawn, faintly cold, swept past him into the room. "Austin, what points struck you particularly in this story?"

"If he really saw Jakey that disposes of the ghost tales. Only one doesn't know . . ."

"His doubts about his own judgment, in the earlier case, weakens this," Herrick supplemented. "I agree. He seems certain at one moment and uncertain at another. But he is more positive, I take it, on that point, than on any other. It was *apparently* Jakey's body, it was *apparently* Aaron at the inquest, but it was definitely Jakey himself whom he saw and recognized later."

"Jakey is alive. Whether Aaron was actually killed, or whether Jakey in some extraordinary way came to life again . . . There have been cases."

"There have been cases," Herrick said. "The inquest was held the next day, and no one apparently saw the body after the inquest. People have been buried alive before now. And we must remember that Lennox, for all the skill and ingenuity he has brought to bear in this matter afterwards, has only the experience of the average country practitioner. You know what that's worth."

"It seems to me," I said, grappling with an idea which had somehow forced itself upon me all through Lennox's narrative, "that—I don't want to criticize unduly—but I do feel that Lennox's tale has been more evolved to fit existing facts than suggested by them. He seems to me to be trying to convince himself just as much as us. And—"

"Yes?" said Herrick.

I hesitated.

"I—well, hang it all, Herrick, I *saw* the man before he left, and whatever the cause, or however temporary the effect, I am pretty sure that the story he told us tonight is not sufficient to account for the state of nerves he was in then. You saw how touchy he was about Lessing?"

Herrick nodded.

"Lessing said once that Lennox only cared for things he could stick a pin into and label."

"And unless I am much mistaken," said Herrick quietly, "it will take a bolder man than Lennox to label the real truth of this business. However, Austin, we'll drop that part of it for the moment. There are one or two points I want to recall to you particularly."

"Well?"

"They are these." He spoke deliberately.

"The character of Menning's mother. She is important. The rather curious isolation in which the family seem always to have kept themselves. Aaron's sudden change of mind about having Jakey put under restraint. And . . . the two other details to which Lennox himself seems to attach the least importance. One is that of the footprints, presumably of a dog—a large dog—noticed near the spot where Menning's body was found."

"And the other?"

"The other," said Herrick, "I have here in my hand, and to me it provides the most significant clue in the whole case."

He opened his hand, and I saw lying on the palm the battered silver button that had been picked up on Dutchman's Hill.

19

THE MILL DAM

I COULD get nothing further from Herrick just then. He went back to his room, but not to sleep, for I could hear him pacing up and down overhead. For myself, I dozed fitfully in the surgery armchair, and when I finally opened my eyes with a start it was to find the room filled with sunlight and Herrick standing over me, fully dressed, a cup of steaming coffee in his hand.

"Wake up, Austin," he said. "I've stolen a march on Mrs. Searle. It's hot, if it isn't otherwise drinkable."

I rubbed my eyes.

"Where's Lennox?"

"Sleeping the sleep of the just. By the look of him he won't wake up till midday. That's the reward of an easy conscience for you— 'Something accomplished, something done.' Which reminds me. Are you using your motorcycle today?"

"I don't think so." I drank the coffee—it was strong and scalding hot, and it pulled me together. "Why, do you want it?"

"I'd like it for today, yes."

"Sure." I looked at him curiously. "Have you got something in mind?"

"Only a little tour of investigation. You needn't look injured, Austin! Just something I want to check up on. Are you going over to Sliefer's today?"

"Later on. I've got two calls in the village."

"Well, if you see the Lessings tell them I'll be over tomorrow—or tonight if I get back in time."

We got the cycle out without rousing Pete, and I watched Herrick off down the road. When he had gone I lit my pipe and set out for a little stroll until such time as the household should be awake.

There had been a heavy fall of dew, and the weeds by the roadside were drenched and silvered. Spider webs like jewel-work upon the brambles. I was reminded of the first time I had driven over to the bungalow, early in the summer, on just such a morning as this, and of how little thought had been in my mind then of what I should find at my journey's end. To me, then, these far stretching woods, dense and close-grown, the hollow with its rank growth of teeming insect life, the little creek that followed threadlike among the emerald mosses and tufts of sedge, suggested nothing more than the idle peace and pleasure of a summer's holiday. I had envied whoever lived here all the year round. These cool depths of shadow, with the freckled at nothing more dreadful than the tragedy of play of sunlight through the branches, hinted weasel and rabbit, of hawk and thrush. Now their aspect was to me indefinably changed. I felt them sinister, secretive, their peace a mere deceptive veil for the evil that lurked beneath.

What was the secret that overshadowed the place? What had Herrick meant by his insistence upon the silver button and those queer footprints by the cedar where Aaron had met his death? Did Lennox's story after all explain anything? I felt that it did not and yet I felt, in a strange, unexplained way, that somehow, in connection with the Mennings, and the Menning homestead, loathsome and sinister, was to be found the answer to our whole problem. But how?

Retracing my steps, I reached the house to find smoke curling cheerfully from the chimney and Lennox, contrary to Herrick's prophecy, dressed and on the porch. Mrs. Searle had breakfast ready, bacon, buckwheat cakes and coffee which obliterated the lingering taste of the decoction Herrick had pressed upon me before starting out.

Lennox was not very communicative. I think he was still inwardly chagrined by the failure of last night's expedition.

After breakfast Pete hitched the mare and I set out on my rounds. The news of the fire had already spread. Everyone was talking about it, and from what I could gather no one had any sympathy over it, unless it was for the old woman now rendered houseless. The current belief was that Menning, heavily insured, had fired the place himself. There was even a suggestion that he had intended the old woman to perish with the house. Disaster works strangely in loosening people's tongues, and I gathered that though the supposed Aaron had outwardly enjoyed the respect of the community there was inwardly very little liking lost between him and his neighbors. At all events they were ready enough now to speak of his queerness, his surliness, the way the farm was kept—in itself a sufficient ground of condemnation in a hardworking neighbor-hood— and above all of the way he had, of late months, neglected and illtreated his old mother. Odds and ends of scandal, restrained up to now I imagined, through a lurking fear of Menning himself, found free tongue. But in all this talk there was no clear idea as yet of the real reason for the sheriff's visit. Menning was "wanted" for something, but no one quite knew what, and gossip confined itself so far to dark hints and speculations which fell very wide of the real mark.

I reached the Sliefers' house about midday. Freeman was progressing favorably, though not yet out of danger. Mrs. Sliefer pressed me to eat dinner with them, and over the meal the talk turned naturally on the excitement of the night before. Mrs. Sliefer was very definite in her opinion of the Menning household, almost as vehement as old Paddy had been that day I talked to him of his neighbors.

"If there was ever call for a place to be burned," she declared, "it was that one, though I ain't one for wishing ill to my neighbors without cause. But there's a bad streak in that family an' always has been. The old woman's grown feeble of late and I'm sorry enough for her, poor soul, by all I hear, but there was a day when I'd 'a crossed the road sooner than pass the time of day with her, and so would many another. I never believed all these ignorant tales of old Ma Menning bein' a witch, for there ain't no witches and we well know it, but there was something about her that wasn't like other folks, and though we was neighbors in a way, she never took to me nor I to her. Things did get better in the two years Jakey was away, an' then it did seem like Aaron had a chance to take hold an' run things decent, till he come back again. And after his death one would have thought there'd been a turn for the better, but it didn't last. I guess the bad streak was in the whole family, an' after Jakey died I suppose it preyed on Aaron's mind, in a way, an' he got to goin' the same road as his brother."

It was on my tongue to mention the truth, but I checked myself in time. Evidently the police hoped to gain something by keeping the real facts dark, at least until after Jakey's arrest.

After dinner I drove round, by way of the Bend, to the Lessings' bungalow. The Menning place was a mere charred ruin, except for the outhouses which stood empty and deserted. The few remaining chickens —Menning had sold out the greater part of his stock a few days before the fire, which was another reason why his neighbors thought it premeditated—had been taken elsewhere; the cow, filthy and gaunt from weeks of neglect, poor brute, was grazing hungrily in a small stony pasture adjoining, thankful to be at liberty.

Old Paddy, with a greasy, old velvet cap on and his feet in slashed shoes, was leaning over his fence-railing, smoking his black pipe. I asked about Menning's mother.

"The old woman, she's took an' cleared out. Scared er Aaron, I guess. She got a wheelbarrer an' loaded her bits o' truck on it, an' carted it up to that little empty shack back off the road yonder, what belongs to Scholl. Reckon the Scholls don't mind her usin' it. She wouldn't have no help neither—carted the lot herself, in two journeys, an' I'll say she's still pretty spry on her feet fur an old lady, though she does look so feeble. My darter, she was sorry fur the old soul, an' she gives her some potatoes an' a bag o' flour, but she didn't git so much as a thank you for it. Jest chucked 'em on the barrer an' went off. Kinder dazed that night, she was, but she come round pretty quick once the excitement was over."

He paused to spit, with precision, at a white stone by the fence rail.

"No one ain't seen nothin' of Aaron."

"No," I said.

"Guess they won't, neither. He's cleared out for good, by the looks of it."

"Maybe it's well."

"No one round here ain't grumblin'. It's a case o' good riddance. I don't trust Aaron. My darter, she ain't lettin' her young 'un run through the woods, neither. He'd orter be jailed an' done with it."

I found Mary and Lessing on the porch. They hailed me cheerfully, and I hitched the mare in the shade and joined them.

"Poor old Crowfoot," said Lessing. "I don't think the arm of the law was best pleased at being fetched out on a wild goose chase last night. It's my private opinion that Lennox has solaced his loneliness by reading up on detective novels. I always thought he had some bats in his belfry. Did he tell you anything more last night?"

"Quite a lot."

I told them the story as briefly as I could.

"Lennox is crazy," Dick said when I had finished. "The thing doesn't hang together. And when he gets to a point where he can't trust his judgment as to the identity of a man in one case, how can he trust it in another? What did Herrick think?"

"He didn't say definitely."

"So like Herrick! What?"

"He seemed to lay more stress on the dogs' footprints and the button Lennox picked up than on anything else. Oddly enough, someone else spoke of dogs, now I think of it." And I told him what the chauffeur had said last night.

"Queer," said Lessing. "You'd think he'd know a dog when he saw one. I'd like to have a look at that button."

"Herrick has it."

"He has . . ." Lessing was silent a moment. "Even if Jakey did kill Aaron, and Aaron is really his brother—hang it all, the thing's so mixed—I don't see that that gets us any further on. Does Lennox think he's at the back of everything? What's he playing at?"

"He was at the back of Rebecca's scare, and that business of Freeman. If Freeman were only well enough to speak . . . I don't know that he could tell us much then, that we haven't found out for ourselves."

"Grant that Jakey did kill his brother, and has succeeded in putting it over. He was at the bottom of all these Dutchman's Hill scares, and that business with Rebecca. Freeman found out something, and he laid for Freeman . . . and got him. That doesn't explain the cyclist affair, nor what happened to me."

"And it doesn't explain another thing, either," said Mary, breaking in for the first time. "It doesn't explain what the one point was that Lennox himself was unwilling to face, what it was he tried to avoid by ridiculous explanations that wouldn't satisfy a child. I don't mean recently, I mean further back, almost in the beginning, the second time he was here to attend Dick." She turned to her brother. "Perhaps I haven't told you this before. But it did strike me at the time, and afterwards I've been thinking of it more and more.

"I was standing out here on the porch, wondering whether I could leave you with Kate and slip over to Lennox's house, or whether I could get hold of anyone to send, when Lennox himself came by, driving. I ran out to stop him and tell him what had happened. He pulled up as soon as he saw me, before I had time to call out, and I tell you if I ever saw a man frightened it was then. He was afraid, and he was afraid before he saw me, or even knew what I had to say. Something had happened, something that gave him a shock, before he came up the road there. He tried to pass it off, but I'm not a fool; I know when a person is just puzzled, and I know when he is afraid, and I tell you that Lennox was afraid. And I'd like to know just what it *was* that frightened him."

"Where was he coming from?" Lessing asked.

"Down the road here, the way Austin came just now. He came from the Bend."

"From Menning's place."

"It might have been. I don't know. He didn't say and I didn't ask him. But something, that morning, had happened to upset him before he got here. And it was as if he knew or at least expected, what he was going to find."

"Did you ask him?"

"I said something about it. He told me he'd been up all night on a case some miles away, that he'd only left at daybreak to drive back, and that he felt all in. But it was something more than that, I feel certain, to have thrown him into the state he was in."

"I shall ask him tonight," I said. "If he's keeping anything back—"

"Ask him!" said Mary. "Ask him, and get the truth! You can tell him just what I said."

I had promised to look in at the Sliefers' again, later in the evening, and instead of doing so on my way back, Mary proposed that I should walk across with her, after tea, while Lessing got some letters written.

"I want some cream for supper," she said, "and I want to see Rebecca too. I meant to go this morning. If you don't mind the walk we'll take Leo along. He hasn't had a run today yet."

She called the setter and he came bounding up, glad enough of the prospect of a walk.

"Poor old Leo!" Mary said. "He doesn't get half enough exercise.

We'll take the leash, Austin, if you don't mind. There's a collie at the farm and the two are sworn enemies. I always have to fasten him if I go there."

I put the leash in my pocket and we set off through the woods by a short cut that brought us out eventually upon the cart-track near the old sawmill. On the other side of this road the Sliefers' land began, and only a couple of pasture fields, with low snake-fences, separated us from the farm. Leo had dropped behind after we passed the mill, and as we stopped by the fence to wait for him we saw a woman coming along the path. She wore a faded check cotton dress and a sunbonnet that almost hid her face, and she was carrying a basket filled with chips, evidently gathered near the mill. As she drew near I caught a flash of very keen eyes, set in a dark wrinkled face, directed upon us in a glance that was by no means friendly.

Mary stepped forward and spoke to her, and I saw her slip something into the old woman's hand. The gnarled fingers closed on it unwillingly; she muttered something and passed on.

"Do you know her?" I asked.

"It's old Mrs. Menning," Mary said. "Poor old soul! She's crotchety, but I can't help feeling sorry for her. Is it true they are sending her to the poorhouse?"

"I've no idea. Old Paddy Nevill told me she'd moved her things up to some little empty shack near her old place. I suppose they'll let her stay there till something can be arranged."

I watched the bent, dragging figure out of sight. As Paddy had said, she covered the ground fairly spryly, for all her feebleness of gait. It was my first acquaintance with this woman to whose personality Herrick had particularly drawn my attention the night before. If Lennox were right, she had played an almost incredibly cunning part throughout, even if her brain had not itself evolved the whole plot.

"You'd think she could find chips nearer than the sawmill," Mary said. "It's a good walk from the Nevills' place, if she's near there. I wouldn't wonder if the old body were unhinged by the fire altogether. She's never friendly at her best, but she looked quite queer just now. Did you notice how she was muttering to herself?"

I let down the bars and we passed through into the field.

"Austin," Mary said, as we picked our way over the boulder-strewn pasture, "do you know that I've got a confession to make, and it's worrying me."

I smiled.

"Anything very dreadful?"

"I just don't know," she said. "It's about last night. You know I stayed out on the porch while you were all over at the fire. Well, it was while I was sitting there, about a quarter of an hour after you went, I saw Menning come up by the road. I don't think he even saw me. He was going at a sort of shambling trot, and he never looked up when he passed the house. I am sure it was he, though."

"And you never told us!" I exclaimed.

"I knew you'd be angry, but I couldn't help it. I didn't know about this whole story then, and—and I hate the idea of any man being hunted that way, no matter what he's done. I thought he might have some sort of chance to get away, and that's why I didn't say anything last night, even to Dick!"

"Which way was he going?"

"Toward the hill. Your chauffeur must surely have met him. That's what I couldn't make out."

"He saw no one at all. The man may have turned off into the woods when he saw the car. I suppose you know what the sheriff would say to this?"

"Compounding a felony!" Mary laughed. "Anyway he never asked me, so I didn't have to tell any lies about it. Only after what you said last night it worried me, and I thought I'd better own up. Now if he is caught it won't be on my conscience that I had a direct hand in it."

"Oh, woman!" I exclaimed.

"You'd have done the same in my case," she retorted. "Besides, I wasn't supposed to know. You never told me anything."

"You are *sure* it was Menning?"

"Quite sure. I had left the house door open, and he passed right into the light. I wondered why he was going away from the fire instead of toward it, and I thought at first he might be going to get more help. I didn't know then. He hadn't been there all along."

We reached the farm, and I left her below while I saw my patient. Either I was longer than I thought, or we must have loitered unconsciously on our way over, for when I joined her again on the porch the light was already fading. Then there was a delay about the cream. Rebecca had to fetch it, and while she was gone Mary turned to me.

"This farm is still bewitched," she said. "It's the cream-pans now. Rebecca swears that the milk has gone, these last few nights. Last night she set out three pans in the spring-house and this morning one of them was two-thirds empty. I suspect cats, but anyway the problem takes Rebecca's mind off her other trouble, poor girl. Here she is. Can you spare this, Rebecca?"

"It's a bit scant, Miss Lessing, but it's the best I can do. We'll be short for churning this week, as it is. Whatever ails the milk I don't know! I've never had it go before."

"Well, it isn't witches' work;" Mary smiled. "They turn the milk, you know, Rebecca, they don't steal it! I'd keep an eye on the cat. If you'll take Leo a moment, Austin, till we're out of the grounds, I'll carry the pail—no, it isn't heavy, and I don't trust men anyway. They spill everything. Good night, Rebecca!"

"Carry your old cream yourself," I retorted. "I won't help you—not after that. And the way I've condoned your offences, too! Come on, Leo! Can I let him loose here, do you think?"

"Wait till we're quite clear of the house. He had a dreadful fight here once. It'll be all right now. We'd better take the path along the dam; it's a little shorter."

We followed the footpath along which they had carried Freeman that night to the house. Given any other time and place, I should have been tempted to do my best in prolonging this stroll, but I had none too pleasant associations with the place and its surroundings, and with twilight closing rapidly upon us I was in no mind to loiter. A stagnant weedy smell rose from the dam, a gloomy stretch of water with enclosing frees that darkened it still more effectually. Frogs croaked in monotonous chorus from the weeds at the edge and the midges were thick. In the end Mary had to give in ignominiously, and I carried the pail while she fought their attacks off with a handkerchief.

It was here that Rebecca and her sweetheart used to walk of an evening, and I wondered at their choice of a trysting-place.

"It's romantic," said Mary, "in a way. Can't you imagine this the deserted moat, with the ruined castle of Lord Thingummy in the background? I am sure that Rebecca reads Laura Jean Libbey on the sly. What spot more suggestive of lovers' vows and maidens palely loitering! Rebecca's too healthy not to be romantic at her age."

"Romance?" I said. "Fiddlesticks! The Sliefers ought to have this place drained if they aren't going to work the mill anymore. As a plain medical man I have no use for picturesque sheets of water that smell bad after sunset."

"So you'd sacrifice all this—" she waved the hand that was not occupied in keeping midges at bay— "and plant cabbages on it!"

"Why cabbages?"

"Aren't they the symbol of all that is practical?"

"Including myself!" I snapped. I was getting badly bitten, and with no opportunity for redress.

"Oh, I didn't say that!" She stopped short. "Did you see that big fish jump just then? Right beyond the pond-lilies there. This place must be full of them."

"Carp, most likely. It's pretty deep up at this end."

She stopped to watch the circle widen and disappear, leaving the water black. "Austin . . . do you suppose I ought to have spoken about Menning before?"

"I don't know that it matters. They'll get him anyhow."

There was no good in mere speculation, and I didn't want to enlarge on the subject of Menning. She had come into contact with sufficient ugliness this summer already. "It's more than probable that he has cleared out altogether by this time. In any case, until we know, I think it would be better that you kept near the house unless one of us is with you. There's no good running any risks."

We had passed the mill and were just turning into the little path that would bring us to the road near the bungalow, when Lessing met us.

"I thought you two would never turn up," he said. "I'm dying of hunger. How's the patient, Austin?"

"Getting on. You can carry the pail if you want to work. Where's that dog got to?"

I had released the setter some little way back, and he had kept within sight nearly all the way. Missing him now, I turned to whistle, and saw Leo, a pale shadow in the dusk, nosing eagerly about the scattered logs that lay in the clearing near the mill. Lessing called him several times by name, sharply, but he paid no attention.

"Got a rabbit, most likely. Wait a minute. I'll soon fetch him out of that."

He walked back the few paces to the clearing, and Mary sat down at the edge of the path with a little sigh of resignation. I offered her a cigarette, and for some minutes we smoked in silence, listening for her brother's step. Presently Mary stood up.

"I'm not going to wait here all evening! We'll go on to the house and let him catch up to us."

We had nearly reached the bungalow before Lessing overtook us. He was holding Leo by a handkerchief knotted through his collar. The dog came unwillingly, cringing against his master's legs, the hair along his spine bristling and his ears laid back.

"Why, look at that!" Mary exclaimed. "I've never seen him act that way before. You haven't been beating him, Dick?"

"I'd like to!" Lessing stooped to take a fresh grip on the dog's collar. "Be quiet, you brute! You aren't going back there now."

Mary patted the setter's head. "Poor old boy! Did he get a rat, and wouldn't they let him have it! Was it a good rat, Leo?"

But the dog only twisted impatiently from her touch, his head turned backwards and his nose working.

"It was a dam good rat," said Lessing, "but he won't have it now. Go open the shed door, Mary, till I get him in."

She threw open the door of the toolshed, and Lessing thrust the dog inside, pushing him in with his foot, and fastened the latch.

"That's that! Aren't you staying for supper, Austin?"

"Wish I could! I must get the mare back, and I want to be there when Herrick gets in."

I untied the mare and backed her around. Mary was standing on the porch.

"Do you notice you can smell that stagnant water at the dam? We seem to get it in whiffs, every once in a while. I noticed it very strongly last night, sitting out here. I wonder the Sliefers can stand it, living as close as they do."

There was a slight taint on the air. As Mary said, it seemed to come in whiffs. It might have been the dam, but it carried my mind back, as a smell will do, to some vague recollection I could not quite place.

"There's a lot of rotting vegetation there. Maybe it isn't so bad at their end. Sometimes you smell things much more at a distance."

"It just comes and goes. I don't notice it now. You'll be over this evening?"

"I'll bring Herrick along if he's back."

I paused, held by a vague trouble in her eyes.

"You aren't worried, Mary?"

"Worried? No. I just feel . . . restless. It's the sort of feeling you get before a storm. As if we were all waiting for something, and you don't know what."

"You've been upset about this Menning affair."

"It isn't that. I don't know what it is. The place, maybe . . . I always liked woods before, and now I feel as if I should never like them again." Her grave clear eyes held mine "Austin, I wish I *knew*. If only . . . sometimes I almost wish we'd never come to this place at all."

"Mary, you don't really wish that?"

"No, I don't. I ought to, but I can't. But . . . I do wish we were all away—out of here—somewhere else."

"We shall be, soon enough." I was thinking of the end of my holiday, the breaking-up of a summer that, if it had brought danger and ugliness and all but tragedy, had brought also something infinitely precious into my life—something I was far from ready to lose.

"The summer has done Kate good, anyway. We had a letter from her this morning."

"Where is she?" I knew that Mrs. Lessing had left a few days before, to stay with some friends.

"On Long Island. A place on the Sound. We'll probably join her there in a couple of weeks. I wish you could come—you and Jack both. I think the sea air would blow sense into all of us!" She laughed. "I'm talking like an old woman, and I've got Dick's supper to get and nothing ready! Well, we'll see you tonight."

"Would you rather I stayed?"

"Nonsense! You'll begin to think I'm developing nerves, next!"

She waved her hand as I climbed into the buggy. Gathering up the reins, I turned the mare's head homeward. It was already nearly dark, but I could still see the road before me. Was it presage, or only the desire for Mary's company that made me wish, even before I had turned the corner by Dutchman's Hill, that I had after all accepted Lessing's invitation and stayed on?

As I reached the point where the road dipped to the hollow it seemed to me that I could smell once more that queer unplaceable odor of which Mary had spoken.

20

WHAT WE FOUND IN THE SAWMILL

HERRICK had not yet returned when I reached the house. Lennox was just sitting down to supper, in which I joined him. While we were lingering over our coffee I remembered what Mary had said that morning, and asked him point-blank about it.

He gave me a curious look before replying:

"So Mary Lessing told you that, did she? Well, I give her credit for observation. I remember that morning perfectly. She was quite right;

something *had* happened."

He paused to light a cigar over the lamp-chimney before saying: "Shall we go into the surgery, Haverill?"

I followed him in, leaving the dining-room to Mrs. Searle, and closed the door between us, while Lennox threw himself back into the armchair and smoked for a few moments in silence.

"I've told you, Haverill, that between one thing and another my nerves were in a pretty unreliable state early this summer. I mention that now, because I still think it had a certain bearing on what happened. When Mary Lessing stopped me that morning in the road it was just a case of one shock on top of another."

"Then—"

"Wait a minute," Lennox said. "If I tell this thing I've got to tell it my own way. I'll tell you just what happened and I haven't got any explanation of it at all. You can take it or leave it. And you'll understand that I don't even claim to be telling you facts. The whole thing might have been just an impression in my own mind. That's what I want to make clear, regardless of any effect it may have had on me at the time.

"I had been out on an all-night case. I was physically tired, and through a particular anxiety in this instance, just about all in. I had a seven-mile drive home, and I could almost have fallen asleep there in the buggy. I had left my patient out of danger, and coming back I remembered that Mrs. Searle wanted a couple of chickens from Aaron and that I'd told her the day before I would stop in some time and get them. It was very little after daybreak, but I chanced the Mennings being early risers and turned out of my way to go by the Bend. There was smoke coming from the chimney, so I got out and knocked at the door, and the old woman opened it. I guess she was just dressing; she looked half asleep, and she told me Aaron wasn't up yet, but that the chickens were ready, and she'd get them for me if I didn't mind waiting a minute.

"I stood about outside. It was a chilly morning, and a bit foggy. I guess I had my mind more on a cup of hot coffee than anything else, and I wondered if the old woman would give me some if I asked for it when she came back, though I'd be needing coffee pretty badly before I'd drink it in that house. You knew the Menning place, before it was burned?"

I nodded.

"There are a lot of tumble-down outbuildings there where they used to keep the chickens he bought, and one in particular—I don't know if you noticed it—a sort of lean-to near the open wagon shed, painted green. I don't know what it was built for, but it had a door and a square window-hole, high up, about the height of a man's head. I don't suppose the whole floor space inside would be more than about eight foot square, about the size of a calf-pen, and I shouldn't wonder if that was what it was. I'd walked over to it because I wanted to get my pipe started, out of the breeze. The door was shut, and I'm certain there wasn't anything moving in there, or I'd have heard it. "I'd struck a match, and was just bending over to draw on my pipe when something shot past me. It seemed to come out of the uncleared patch of woods back of the sheds. I didn't get more than a half glimpse of it, and I can't even tell you what it looked like, except that it was biggish, and it seemed to shamble on all fours, and it panted, the way an animal does that's been running, and it *smelt* like an animal too. I seemed to get a whiff of it as it went past. It came by me so close I could almost have touched it, and flung itself straight at that window-hole and slithered through, and I could hear the thud of its body on the inside.

"I'm a short man. That window-hole was well above the level of my head. My first thought was to pull myself up and look through, and then—well, you can put it down to what you like, but the thing had given me such a queer turn when it shot past, like cold water down my spine, and I believe if I could have touched that window I wouldn't have had the physical strength to pull myself up and look through. Instead I backed away and just stood there, staring. The door was tight shut. It had all happened in such a flash that I began to wonder, then, if I'd imagined the whole thing. I might have stood there for a couple of minutes, though it seemed to me longer, and then suddenly the door was flung wide open and Aaron himself or as I know now, Jakey-walked out.

"The door opened outward, and I could see straight past into the shed. There was a heap of broken harness and some rags lying in one corner, and except for that the place was as bare as my hand.

"I daresay I must have looked queer—I know I felt it—for Menning gave me a pretty surly look. He asked me what I wanted, and I told him I'd stopped for the chickens. He said they weren't ready, that he'd bring them over, but just at that minute his mother came out from the house with them in her hand, and I tell you I was glad enough to grab those chickens and drive off. I didn't want to ask questions or to stop near the place."

"This thing—what did you think it looked like?"

"I can't even tell you. It—it didn't look like anything."

"But it ran?"

"Yes, it ran. It's no good trying to tell you what my impression was, any more than I have done."

"Do you suppose Menning kept something shut up there?"

"If he did, where was it when he opened the door? I tell you the shed was empty."

"There was no trapdoor?"

"I went back to see. I didn't just give it up, either. I went back a few days later, one time when Menning had passed our house and I knew he'd be away on his rounds some time. I saw the old woman. She was surly in a way, but friendly to me. You see, I'd tended her before when Menning had been beating her up—oh yes, he'd done that more than once to my knowledge. The Nevills knew it, but there was no good interfering; she'd deny it, and no one dared tackle Menning. But she had to come to me, once, and though she put up some story, I could tell what had happened. Well, I chatted with her there, and just to see what she'd say I asked her if they didn't keep some sort of a dog on the place. She said no, that they'd had a dog and her son shot it because it howled at night. After a while I left her settled there in the kitchen and before I left I took my chance to go over every hole and corner out of doors. Except for the cow and a couple of pigs there wasn't the sign of any animal round the place bigger than a cat. And there was no opening in that shed except the window and the door Menning came out by.

"So now you know the whole thing—all Mary Lessing claimed I was keeping back from you—and I imagine you're about as wise as I am, and that isn't much."

"Why didn't you tell us sooner?" I asked.

"What could I do? If I went telling that around anyone would have a right to say I was crazy and that I'd imagined the whole thing. You might say—and I've tried to think myself—that what I heard was just something running in the bushes and what I saw was an old hen fluttering in at the window. And maybe it was. And I've known men who've been just as startled, and have told circumstantial tales, over nothing more."

"You could have told it at its face value."

"No," said Lennox, "I couldn't. My mind doesn't work that way. I've got to weigh things. And I've got to exhaust every possible reasonable explanation, including my own physical state at the time, before I'll admit that a thing is so when I know it can't be so. If I've kept this to myself it's because I wanted to find some sort of explanation in my own mind first."

He faced me, stolid and obstinate. Even in that moment I admired his self-possession, his dogged, common-sense determination not to be drawn into admission of the existence of anything that, as Lessing said, he couldn't stick a pin into and label. And I knew, too, that it had cost him something to tell me that story.

"Well," I said, "that's only one more to the list of things we don't seem able to clear up. There's one point; that whatever the explanation may be, it all seems to center, in the end, round Menning himself."

Lennox rose and went to his desk. "It's what I've always said," he threw back over his shoulder. "Get Menning, and you get the root of all this mystery."

I sat pondering his story. It was not long before my ears caught the sound of a motorcycle along the road, and a few minutes after Herrick appeared. He looked as if he had ridden far and fast; his clothes were covered with dust and there were grimy circles round his eyes.

"No, I don't want to eat," he said. "I got a sandwich coming along. Just let me get this dirt off, that's all."

He went through to the kitchen, and we could hear him splashing at the sink. When he came back, still vigorously toweling his face, Lennox had already mixed him a drink at the sideboard.

"Well," Herrick said, settling himself in the chair Lennox had vacated, "let's begin at the beginning. When I left this morning, Austin, I couldn't tell you where I was going, because I didn't know myself. I had to pick up my information on the way. I was on the track of something which, it seems to me, none of us has so far taken into account, and that is, Jakey Menning's early life."

"He was born right in this county," said Lennox.

"He was not. That's where you make your mistake. He was between eight and nine years old when he first came here. His mother, when we first hear of her, was employed with a travelling show, owned by a German Jew called Goldstein, a sort of fourth rate circus that used to do one-night stands in the small towns and villages. She cooked for the men and looked after the wardrobe. While she was working with them Jakey was born. No one seems to have known just who his father was. The mother passed as a kind of half-wit. She was cunning under an appearance of heavy stupidity, spoke a poor English, was easily teased and enraged, and seems to have been treated as the butt of the company. They wintered usually in Pottsville, where the proprietor's brother kept a saloon. The proprietor's wife took rather a fancy to Jakey, and later on, when Jakey's mother, during the slack season, took a job as cook in a cheap eating-joint there, she simply abandoned the baby to the circus people. While she was employed there she met Menning, married him, and doesn't seem to have troubled about Jakey for several years. Probably she never told Menning of his existence.

"They settled in the country, where Aaron was born, and a few years after, for reasons unknown, Menning deserted her. Then, for the first time, she seems to have remembered Jakey, now growing to an age when he might begin to make himself useful about the farm. She set about claiming him. The circus people, from what I could hear, made some opposition. Jakey was being trained as an acrobat and showed some promise, though he was a difficult child to manage. Moreover, they had kept him all this time and expected some return. Times, however, were slack, they probably foresaw trouble with the school inspectors also, and in the end they let the boy go.

"He worked about the farm, off and on, for some eight or ten years, and got himself thoroughly disliked, as you know, by all the Mennings' neighbors. The criminal streak in him was already apparent, though in those days it only took the form of spitefulness and mental deficiency. He was idle and vagrant and finally, at about seventeen years old, took himself off one fine day and went back to the travelling show, which he managed to trace up through the Pottsville saloon-keeper. They took him back as an extra hand, to help with the wagons. He was not good enough for a performer, his training being interrupted, but the proprietor about that time had the idea of running one or two freak side-shows, and they tried Jakey out as the hoary old fake of 'wild man.'"

Herrick paused a moment to light a fresh cigarette, and in that instant I saw Lennox's eye turn to me with something very like relief.

"It seems," Herrick went on, "that he was quite a successful attracttion and I can certainly believe it. There was naturally something apish and uncouth about him, and very little make-up would have turned the trick most naturalistically. He stayed with the show nearly two years, doing odd jobs by day and playing his wild-man stunt at the performances. And then some sort of queer thing must have happened.

"I couldn't get the whole truth of it from the Pottsville brother, who told me most of the story. Either he didn't know or he was unwilling to tell, but the gist of it is that there was some row and Jakey got suddenly fired. From what the Pottsville brother 'guessed,' Jakey played his role too realistically, and the proprietor refused then and there to keep him another day. He had a little money in his pockets, he turned up in Pottsville, where he hung about for two or three days, and then made his way back to the farm.

"I would give a great deal to have ten minutes with Goldstein himself, and know exactly what did happen and why Jakey was fired. I gathered that it was something pretty unpleasant. But Goldstein is somewhere out in Ohio, and try as I would, I could get nothing more from the brother than what I have told you. I think myself there was something hushed up at the time, and that he is afraid even now of its coming out. But I got enough, I think, to throw some interesting light on what has happened since."

"Did you get any idea," Lennox asked, "of Jakey's make-up when he was with these people?"

"No. Why?"

"Tell him your story, Lennox," I said. He repeated briefly what he had already told me. Herrick listened, his face intent.

"So that was—" He pulled himself up short. "Well, it isn't difficult to put two and two together. The obvious explanation is that Jakey has fallen back on his old circus stunt as a means of terrorizing the neighborhood. It wouldn't be difficult. No one here, from what I can make out—possibly not even his own family—knew how he spent those two years while he was away. There is a form of mania which takes just that expression, and it is possible that in Jakey's case it began out of sheer maliciousness, and developed later into something a great deal worse—a fixed mania which, with the rousing of the homicidal instinct, turned him actually, at moments, into the wild beast he pretended to be."

"You think it was Menning—it was—well, what I saw—that attacked Lessing?"

"I am certain of it. Go over the thing carefully, Lennox. There was no stunt outside the possibility of a man with unusual physical strength and ability, who had had acrobatic training in boyhood. And remember that a maniac can perform feats that in his sane moments might be outside his powers. We are not dealing with a normal person. That's the one thing in this whole business we've got to remember." He rose. "Austin, will you come over to the bungalow with me? I'd like to see Lessing tonight."

I looked at my watch. "Ten o'clock. I told them I'd be over. We'll take the cycle. It'll carry two of us."

He had left the motorcycle outside the porch. As we wheeled it out to the roadway I said: "You think that is the explanation of the whole thing?"

Herrick gave me a quick look.

"I said it was the obvious explanation. It is. But there's more mixed up with it than that. And it's the other side of it that we shall never get to the truth of until we get hold of Menning himself."

I thought of Lennox's description of what he had seen, in that fleeting glimpse, and in spite of myself a shudder went over me.

"Do you mean that mania can actually transform a human being to that degree?"

"Haven't you seen enough, Austin, in your own experience, to answer that question?"

I was silent. Every doctor, I imagine, has had experiences which he is glad enough to put out of his mind, and though my own were limited so far, I had heard enough tales of abnormality, at second hand, to know that there was truth in Herrick's words.

I took my seat on the back of the motorcycle, and in a few minutes we had reached the rise of hill. Turning the corner, we could see the bungalow through the trees. There was still a light burning. As we approached, the deep melancholy howl of the dog broke on our ears. Evidently Lessing had not yet let him out.

We left the cycle against a tree and went up to the porch. The door stood wide open, the light streaming through it from the lamp on the table inside. Of Lessing or his sister there was no sign. Except for the steady howling of the dog in the shed, the place was absolutely silent.

We went through the empty rooms, came out again on the porch. A chair was drawn up near the doorway, with a book dropped in it face-downward, as though someone had risen in haste. That, and the lamp left flaring on the table, gave me for the first time a definite thrill of uneasiness.

Herrick went back and lowered the flame. "They can't have gone far," he said. "They wouldn't have left the light that way. Let's try the studio."

We crossed the little space of ground beside the house. The studio was dark; the door was locked and the key on the outside. As we passed the tool-shed there was a tumult within. The dog, hearing our footsteps, flung himself against the door in a frenzy of eagerness, whining, scratching, tearing at the wood with his nails. There was something in the deep, agonized, almost human anxiety in his voice, raised, not in yelps, but in steady entreaty, that sent a queer thrill down by spine. Herrick felt it too. He stopped short.

"What's got that dog?"

"Lessing shut him in this evening. It was after—"

I paused. All at once there came back to my mind the dog's behavior that afternoon, when Lessing dragged him back from the sawmill, bristling and rebellious—Lessing's own face when he joked about the rat. It was near the identical spot where we had missed the dog before, when he broke away from us on our way down, just before we saw Menning's mother. Menning's mother . . . and Menning himself had been seen in the neighborhood the night before. In a flash I saw the whole thing clearly—Freeman's action, the ghost that haunted the mill-dam, Rebecca's rifted cream-pans and the old woman with her basket of chips. What a fool I had been!

In a moment I had drawn the bolt and the setter was free. He barely stopped to notice us; with a flash of his white chest and a wide-flung yelp of relief he was off across the road and into the woods.

I caught Herrick's arm. "Lessing is at the sawmill. Come on—I'll tell you later!"

"The sawmill?"

I saw his hand slip down to his pocket as we ran. The same thought was in both our minds. We broke through the underbrush on the far side of the road, stumbled by chance on the footpath and were racing along it, shoulder to shoulder, while the setter's barking still echoed in our ears.

For a while his voice guided us. Then, abruptly, he was silent. We paused on the edge of the clearing to take breath. All was still—that closed-in stillness of the woods at night, when all daytime life hushed. Before us loomed the old mill, its broken roof and ruined timbers black against the sky. For a moment there was no sound but the pounding of the blood in our ears, the dry rustle of a dead bush as Herrick leaned forward, listening.

Then suddenly, from somewhere in the recesses of the old building itself, there broke on that tense stillness another sound—more horrible to me than anything else—the hoarse choking breaths and muffled worrying of a dog at grips with his enemy. It came, not from the main floor of the mill, but from the basement where the water-wheel hung. There was a doorway on the near side of the mill, formerly used for carting away the sawdust, but it had been nailed up, and remembering this I called to Herrick as I ran directly for the steep slope on the side by the sluice. Here there was open space to squeeze through, and with Herrick close on my heels I trampled a way through the breast-high weeds and bushes round the corner of the building and gained an entrance.

Within all was pitch black. The water was shut off, but a little trickle still flowed through, dripping from the slimy motionless bulk of the great wheel above us. The air was warm, heavy with the smell of rotting saw-dust and of something else, fetid and nauseous. The worrying had ceased; we could hear the broken rapid breathing of two bodies, there, unseen, somewhere within a few feet of us in the darkness. I made a step forward, but Herrick clutched my arm, and as he did so the fight broke out again with renewed fury, somewhere it seemed up in the far corner, among the drifted sawdust. I could recognize the setter's deep-throated snarls, the snap of teeth seeking a grip, and with it was another voice, deeper and more guttural—something wholly strange and horrible—something that snarled and panted and coughed in choking gasps. The darkness moved; there came the breath of a warm animal body, the straining of a heavy weight flung against resisting wood, and then the nailed planks gave way, the sudden square of the doorway was obscured by a tumbling, heaving mass and the next instant we were alone—alone in the darkness with silence round us and that fetid unforgettable smell on the air.

It was the same smell that Mary had complained of that evening, wafted to us as we sat on the porch—the smell, I knew now, that I had first noticed on the day I passed the Mennings' place in the early summer.

"Phew!" said Herrick.

He struck a match, shielding the flame with his hands. The little flicker threw out shadows high on the piled sawdust and gray ruined walls. We could make out the huge mass of the wheel, the shafts that ran to the story above, the great beams supporting the broken flooring over our heads. The match spluttered and went out, but in that instant it had shown us what we sought, a dark motionless figure lying huddled in the far corner, where the sawdust sloped up in a shadowy drift under the rafters.

Herrick reached it first, his feet sinking deep at every step as he scrambled up. I heard him draw his breath in sharply as I struck another match, and by its gleam saw Lessing, one arm doubled under him and the clothes nearly torn from his body, lying unconscious in a saturated pool of blood.

Of Mary there was no sign.

21

THE THING IN THE WOODS

TOGETHER we managed to get Lessing back to the house and laid him on the couch, and while Herrick held the lamp I did the best I could for his injuries with the means at my disposal. It was an ugly job. One arm and shoulder were badly mangled and the collar bone broken; he had lost a great deal of blood and there was a nasty contused wound above the temple. A flicker of consciousness came back while I was working over him, but the loss of blood told, and he lapsed back again almost immediately. There were stitches to be taken; nothing much could be done except to check the bleeding with temporary bandages and as soon as I could manage single-handed Herrick rode off to Lennox for help.

In reality it was not long, though it seemed to me an eternity that I kept that nightmare vigil, my ears strained for any sound from without, bending all my will-power on my task to keep me from the one thought that I dared not face, Mary. Where had she gone—what had happened to her? I went over a thousand possibilities, trying to find some reasonable explanation to which I might cling, though as each moment went by the stillness became more and more a torture. If she had merely missed her brother and gone down the road to call for him we should have met her, or she would be back by now. If she had been with him at the mill, or had followed there . . . I thought of the deep blackness of the water at the end of the dam, where we had passed that evening, the sheer drop blow the sluice-gates, and shuddered.

It was with infinite relief I caught the approaching noise of the motorcycle and saw Herrick reappear, followed only a few moments later by Lennox with the light spring-wagon. It was decided to take Lessing straightway to the doctor's house, where he could be better looked after than in the bungalow. We laid a mattress in the bottom of the wagon and lifted him onto this, and Herrick and I on the motorcycle accompanied Lennox beyond the hollow at the foot of the hill. Before we started Herrick, his face grim and set in the lamplight, pulled out the revolver I had lent him that morning and handed it to me.

"Keep that, Austin. I bought another today. Lennox has his own."

"There was an extra box of cartridges," I said, "in the table-drawer."

"Lennox gave them to me."

When we had seen the wagon well along the road we turned, and rode back to the bungalow.

"Now," said Herrick, when we stood once more in the lighted room, "the first thing is to find Mary. And then . . . there has got to be an end to this. Are you ready to face it?"

He did not need to ask me. I looked round on the little room, gay and friendly with its rugs and books and the great bowls of wildflowers that Mary loved—the countless little signs of her occupation, a sweater flung across a chair, her work-basket of Indian grass on the table—the room in which I had spent so many happy hours, now suddenly sinister in its desertion. And then my eye fell on the couch where we had laid Lessing, and the hideous litter I had left in my haste—stained wads of cotton and the torn strips from his shirt with which we had striven to check the blood before we carried him up from the mill.

"For God's sake," I exclaimed impulsively, "let's get that cleared away before she gets back!"

Before Mary got back . . . the words died in my throat. But I gathered up the telltale evidence all the same—every last scrap and fragment—and thrust them out of sight behind the kitchen wood-box, before I turned to Herrick.

"We'll try Sliefers' first," he said. "There's just the possibility she is there."

It was a slight chance, and as it proved, fruitless. The farmer was still up, and opened the door to us in stockinged feet. No one there had seen Mary since the afternoon. Sliefer heard our errand with a grave face.

"There's no house she'd have come to but this," he said. "There's only Scholl's and Nevill's at the Bend, and they were both asleep as you passed? They're a-bed by ten. Besides, if there was anything out of the way they'd either one of them have sent over here straight. No. Unless the young lady's missed her way, or met with some accident . . ."

He looked at us doubtfully. It was no time to mince matters. We told him, as briefly as we could, what had happened that evening and how we had found Lessing at the mill.

He heard us out, his jaw set grimly. When we had finished he rose without a word, a tall, still stalwart figure in his stockinged feet, and crossing the kitchen took down his gun that hung on a rack above the door.

"I guess I'm coming with you," he said.

I glanced at Herrick. He nodded.

"Three are better than two, Austin. We may be glad of an extra hand before the night's out." He turned to Sliefer, who had laid his gun on the table, and was pulling on a pair of heavy boots. "Have you got a good dog? I don't mean the collie."

"Aye. There's old Spot, back in the barn. He'd pick up a trail anywheres. Nor he ain't none too friendly to Menning, either, that's one reason we've kep' him tied up, most of the time. Now I guess I'll step up an' leave word with Mother."

He opened the stairway door and tip-toed up, curiously noiseless on his heavy feet. We heard whispering, a smothered exclamation; then he came down, gently closing the door behind him.

"I ain't told her nothing, only that you'd missed Miss Lessing and we was going out to hunt her up. There's no need she should know about the rest of it. This ain't no woman's job, nor it ain't no sheriff's job either. If they'd come to me first off I know every track in these woods back an' forth, and it won't be easy for anyone to get away from me, not once we pick his trail up. Menning can run these woods like a fox, but he won't run far, not when I got a gun in my hand. Not that I'd be scared to meet him anywheres, gun or no gun, and I bet he knows it."

A strange expression flitted across Herrick's face as he measured the farmer's sturdy figure with his eye. But he only said gravely: "You're a good neighbor, Mr. Sliefer. As you say, this is no sheriff's job now; it's up to us. And we're going to see it through."

We closed the door behind us.

"I told Mother to bolt that, once we're gone," Sliefer said. "Reckon we don't need no lantern."

"Better not," Herrick said.

The old man crossed to the barn and came back a few minutes later with the dog on a chain, a cross-bred hound by the look of him, heavily built and brindled white and brown.

"That's what they used to call a bear-dog," the farmer said, "when I was a boy. The breed's pretty well died out now. I've had old Spot here eleven years, and I had his mother an' grandmother before him. You don't see 'em nowadays, anymore. They raise these light-built hounds now, but they ain't the fighters these dogs were."

The farmer was a brisk walker. He picked his way through the woods, turning here, pausing there, at what seemed to us invisible signs and landmarks, making his way unerringly through the trees and undergrowth, the hound close to his heels, till presently we stood once more on the open road a little below the bungalow. I looked eagerly towards the house, only to see the turned down light burning just as we had left it.

"We'll try here first," Sliefer said.

He took two or three turns about the road and clearing, but the dog took no interest. We recrossed the road to the farther side, and here, among the underbrush near the path Herrick and I had taken, he showed the first signs of keenness, sniffing to and fro, his nose laid close to the ground. In a few moments he was off at a leisurely trot along the path.

"Picked up the other dog's scent, most like," said Sliefer, watching him. "Come on. We'll find him at the mill."

He took us by a short cut through the bushes, across a cleared space of stumps and blackberry vines, and turning into the woods at the left again, brought us in a few minutes on the sawmill road. The hound was there before us, moving shadow-like about the clearing. When we came up to him he was clearly puzzled and uneasy. He moved warily, his fore-feet stiffly braced, his ears laid back, the hair along his spine bristling as he snuffed to and fro.

I touched Herrick's shoulder. "Do you see that? It's the same way Leo was acting this afternoon."

"Give him time," said Sliefer. "I know Spot. He ain't made his mind up yet."

Shifting the gun under his arm, he pulled out a can of tobacco and began to roll a cigarette. Somehow that natural matter-of-fact action did much to relax my tense nerves. With Herrick I watched the hound closely. He approached the broken doorway, sniffed, peered, circled off a couple of times and then, as though suddenly making up his mind to it, plunged inside, only to reappear an instant after and set off, head down, with a queer muffled whine, through the underbrush. I made a move to follow but Sliefer checked me.

"Wait a bit. He ain't sure yet. He'll give us the holler when he's sure started."

He was right. After a little while Spot came back, breaking cover near the back of the mill, and returned to us, uneasiness and perplexity in every line of his taut body. With his eyes fixed on his master's face he waited, eager and yet strangely reluctant, and again with a thrill I noticed that involuntary bristling of his spine, the trembling of his lower jaw, as though at some unfamiliar and disturbing proximity. Twice the farmer spoke to him encouragingly, and twice the dog circled off, checked abruptly and came back. Sliefer grew impatient.

"I don't know what's got into the dog. He ain't never acted that way before. Hey there, Spot! Get to it! Fetch em' boy!"

For a moment the hound eyed him. Then, with the same abruptness with which he had entered the mill he raised his head, gave a low whine, and was off in a straight line through the underbrush. Almost immediately we heard his first call, the warning bell-like note of a hound on the found trail.

"He's picked it up all right," the farmer said. "Come on. I back Spot to keep a scent once he's got it."

We started after him, keeping as steady a pace as we could in the darkness. It was well that Sliefer was with us. He made his way with the unerring ease of a man used to the woods from boyhood, to whom night is almost the same as day, and all we needed to do was to follow in his tracks. The hound seemed to be keeping an even course, some couple of hundred yards ahead of us; his deep warning cry, pitched always on the same two notes, rang out at intervals and Sliefer had no difficulty in guiding his way by the sound.

Once, in the neighborhood of the Menning house, the dog was at fault; he hesitated and all but turned aside towards the out-buildings, but in the end picked up the scent again and struck out in a northerly direction through the woods.

For nearly an hour we followed him, through tracts of dense second growth and across spaces of stony pasture, out again on a back road, with an occasional darkened house tranquil in its grassy yard, looping and turning here and there, but on the whole keeping a fairly straight course. We crossed two sloping pastures, plunged into a thicket of young trees, and presently found ourselves on a space of rising ground, strewn with huge boulders and set with stunted juniper and spruce.

Ahead of us the hound's voice rang out clear and mournful, as it seemed to me with a deepening note. Sliefer paused and looked about him. The moon was rising. It showed the sharp line of hills, densely wooded on either side, with the dark cleft of a gorge between. Through the gap in a ruined stone fence we could see a cart track, all but obliterated, that wound into obscurity.

"I know this place," the farmer said. "It's near what they call Rocky Hollow. I haven't been here in years, but I used to know it well when I was a boy. I sort of suspicioned he was heading for here, right along. Once in them big rocks in there you won't trap a man easy, not if he knows his way. If we'd had time to head him off, now."

I glanced at Herrick. He was staring straight at that narrow closed-in gorge, his eyes keen and fixed.

"Is there any other outlet there?"

"Not easy. It's straight-up rock at the far end and the woods are pretty thick. A man would have to make slow going, either way he took it. If he's in there—"

We followed the cart track till it ended in a little grassy clearing from which a few steps brought us to the spot Sliefer had called "Rocky Hollow." It was a small, narrow valley, filled with masses of piled boulders, some enormous, some small, the remains evidently of some ancient moraine. They looked as if giant hands had flung them there in sport, one upon another. Seen by daylight, with the black wooded hillside shutting it in, the place would be desolate enough; by the faint growing moonlight it had a look indescribably grim and sinister. Here, one felt, among those barren stones and piled boulders, that took fantastic shapes in the play of light and shadow, would be a fit hiding-place for anything evil.

Higher up the ravine, near us but hidden from sight, the hound was baying furiously, no longer the bell-like note that had guided us through the woods, but a hoarse deep voice of warning and anger. We made our way towards the sound, scrambling over the stones, and found him standing before an opening between two boulders, where an overhanging rock formed a sort of rough cavern. There was a glimpse of something white within, and for a moment my heart turned sick with fear. But it was only a sheet of crumpled greasy newspaper that had evidently contained food. There were the charred remains of a small campfire and an old tin can lay in one corner.

Sliefer caught the dog by his collar as we peered inside. He picked up the crumpled sheet.

"A week old," he said. "Here's where he hung out, all right. No tramp ever comes here; it's too far off the main road."

Stooping forward, I had rested my hand on the rock at one side. It was warm to the touch, and I turned quickly to the blackened embers near.

"He's not far off, either. That fire—"

"Is cold," returned Herrick quickly, touching the ashes.

The stone was warm, I could have sworn it. Somebody, only a moment ago, had lain there. There was a sudden oath from Sliefer, and I turned to see, a hundred feet down the gorge, something that twisted and moved, a stealthy misshapen shadow, between the gray boulders. It was a bare glimpse, seen in a flash and blotted out immediately against the grayish rocky background, but in that second I thought of Lennox and I too felt cold down my spine.

The farmer's face had gone a curious sickly white. He stood holding his gun stupidly, with fingers that shook.

"That . . . that weren't no man . . . that . . ."

"Did you see?" cried Herrick.

There was a sharp note of excitement in his voice. I nodded. "I . . . went off down there."

Sliefer had pulled himself together. He swung round, his face suddenly savage.

"Man or beast, by God, we'll get him now! *That* shan't run the woods another night, not if I drop in my tracks!"

He shouted to the dog, but the hound, with the rare stupidity of his race, was still snuffing round the cave. Dragged away, he tried one scent and another in and out the boulders, but the tracks had been crossed and confused a dozen times and we lost precious minutes before he picked up his right trail at last, halfway down the gorge, and was off again on his slow loping gait.

He ran silently this time, and in deadly earnest. Only occasionally his voice came back to us, low-pitched and warning. Downhill, over the shoulder of that same sloping pasture we had crossed before, then a wide detour to the right, skirting a swamp where our feet sunk deep between the tussocks—more open fields and then again back to the woods. On we kept doggedly, through hours it seemed to me—more slowly now, for the steady pace was beginning to tell on us—in silence only broken by Sliefer's heavy breathing as he forged ahead, his ear bent always for the sound of the dog's voice. By his old hunter's instinct he knew which way the hound was running, and was able to save many a turn by short cuts which we followed unquestionably, relying on that seventh sense of his which never seemed to fail us.

It was getting on towards dawn when Sliefer paused finally at a cross-road which seemed to me familiar.

"See that?" he said. "There's the right-hand fork that turns back to the Bend, past the old Sullivan house. He's circling back on his old tracks. A while back I thought he was trying to make that tract of woods the other side of the State road, but the dog's headed him out of that. It's getting on for daylight now, and the way I figure it he'll try and make for some place he knows. He daren't show up round the village and I reckon he'll keep clear of the old house, for he knows that's been watched. By the way he's headed now, it's either the sawmill or some other place near it. He knows he can't give Spot the slip again in the woods and he's hard pushed—ain't got much chance now to pick an' choose. I say we won't waste time but jest chance it and cut in right here towards the mill. There's an old wood-road just a little ways further up that'll be easier going than if we took the long way round."

"Right," said Herrick. He loosened the revolver in his belt. "Are we agreed? Whatever we see, close in on it, but don't fire unless you have to."

Sliefer gave him a quick, grim look.

"I reckon nothin'll get by me again. That don't happen' twice. We ain't any bunch of girls that he can fool with his damn play-acting."

Again that queer look flitted across Herrick's face, but he said nothing, only fell in silently beside me as we followed Sliefer into the path.

It was darker here. The trees shut in close about us. Sliefer was a few paces ahead. Presently I felt Herrick's hand on my arm.

"Less than half an hour to daybreak! God, Austin, if we can only beat him to it!"

He quickened pace as he spoke.

"What do you mean? We'll get him anyhow."

"We'll get Menning, yes . . . but we mayn't get the thing that attacked Dick. Yes, they're the same, but—Austin, I can't explain to you now, but I tell you we've got to make every effort in these last few minutes. If Sliefer's right, and he's doubled back, we're all right. Otherwise . . ."

"But he must know—"

"He *knows*. He isn't playing for safety; he knows that's over. He wasn't playing for safety when he made that big detour, he's playing for time. It's time that matters, and it's there we've got to beat him. Austin, Sliefer talks of play-acting, but is it play-acting that can keep a man ahead of a dog for the best part of the night? Was it play-acting that half-killed Lessing? No, if we're ever to know the truth we've got to know it now, within these next twenty minutes. Ah!"

It was the hound again, sudden, sharp, and near at hand. Sliefer had been right after all. We were within a few steps of the sawmill clearing, but the dog was there before us. He was circling the ground, barking furiously as he had done in the gorge, his attention divided between the mill itself and the group of trees, with an old dead chestnut among them, that stood within a dozen feet of the building and a little nearer the sluice gate. But he left the trees when we came up and flung himself savagely against the boarded doorway.

"That was open when we left it, Herrick—do you remember?"

He took out his revolver.

"Go round to the back, Sliefer, and take the dog with you. Austin, watch this end from outside. I'll go through; I've got the flashlight."

"I'm coming with you," Sliefer said.

"All right. One must stay outside, in case . . . Austin, it'll be you, then. If anything—*anything*, you understand—tries to get past you, shoot to cripple it. Fire low. Remember what I told you!"

He flung the door open; I heard the quick rush of the dog's feet. With every nerve tense to straining-point I listened, but the seconds slowly passed and there was no further sound. I moved a few paces back, to get a clearer view of the building and waited.

From within I fancied once I could hear Sliefer's voice. The flashlight moved to and fro, its gleam visible through the cracks of the old walls. Now they were going through the upper floor.

There was a stillness in the air, that chill hush which comes just before dawn. Already the light was changing, becoming faintly clear and shadowless. Somehow, with this drawing-near of daylight, of the return to common day shapes and things, the nightmare feeling of those dark hours dropped from me; I seemed to see it as something fantastic, monstrous, a bad dream. All the events of the last few hours crowded in upon me—the finding of Lessing, Mary's disappearance, our grim chase through the night woods. How far were these things connected—what was Herrick's idea? What were we after—a criminal, hunted and desperate, endowed with animal strength and cunning, but yet a man like ourselves—or a figment of Herrick's brain?

From within the building I heard an exclamation, the dog's sharp whine. Nerves suddenly taut, I waited, my eyes fixed on the broken doorway. And then some instinct—I don't know what—made me turn and look up.

I was standing almost directly under the old dead chestnut, near which the dog had been nosing when we arrived. It's bare greyish limbs, gnarled and twisted, stretched above me, bare in the growing light. Bare —but as I looked one of those twisted boughs seemed to stir and change, heave slowly, detach itself in some monstrous way from the rest and take living shape. I tried to cry out, dragged helplessly at my revolver, but before I could get it free something fell on me, clutching, I was borne to the ground beneath a hairy living weight, bestial, loathsome, an unnamable horror.

For an eternity, it seemed to me, we struggled there. The thing was stronger than I, and strive as I would I could get no clear view of it. Coarse long fur, indescribably filthy, was against my mouth and nose, and my clutching hands met in it helplessly. I made a supreme effort and twisted my head to one side till my face pressed the earth, in a blind instinct of preservation. Long curved nails caught at my throat, and once I fancied a hand that was partly human. Strangely, through it all, I kept my mind somehow clear; the fear of losing consciousness was stronger in me than any other. This, I remember thinking, was the Thing that had attacked Lessing, that had killed the two cyclists, falling on them as it had fallen on me. Herrick was right . . . I would tell Herrick . . . and I wondered what they would say when they found me. Darkness shut down; I was lying under a heavy mountain, and then the mountain lifted, I heard the hoarse snarl of the dog and an oath and Herrick's voice crying sharply: "Don't shoot!"

There was a blinding report close to me. Somehow I staggered to my feet. Herrick was supporting me. The smoke cleared away, and through it I could see Sliefer, the gun in his hands, and on the ground something that writhed and twisted in beastlike shape and yet cried out with a human voice and dragged itself, still dreadfully crying, up the slope to the water's edge, swayed there for a sickening instant and fell with a splash into the black depths below.

22

THE SILVER BULLET

PALE CLEAR SUNLIGHT; early twittering of birds; the clean freshness of dawn . . .

The lamp was still burning on the table when we reached the bungalow. Herrick put it out. Then he laid a hand on my shoulder.

"Austin—"

There was a clatter of wheels on the road outside. Someone had pulled up outside the house. It was a boy—Hiram Scholl's boy—taking his load of milk-cans over to the creamery.

"I don't know as you've missed that yeller dog that belongs here," he called out, "but if the folks were looking for him I thought I'd tell you. He's over to the little house back on our wood-lot up the road. I called to him, an' I dunno but he's hurt or something, for he's just layin' there an' he wouldn't come. So if you want to go after him I guess he's still there."

"Leo!" I exclaimed.

Herrick turned to me quickly as the boy drove off. "What house is that?"

"Hiram Scholl's. It was empty, but someone said that Menning's mother—Herrick, there's just a chance!"

I sprang for the motorcycle, leaning where we had left it the night before, by the side of the house. In a moment I had it out on the road and Herrick swung to the seat behind me as I started the engine up.

Five minutes brought us to the spot where the house stood, a tiny frame shack set on a space of half-cleared woodland back from the road. To reach it we had to climb the slope of stony pasture that divided Scholl's land from the woods, and as we came in sight of the house, half-hidden among the stunted spruce and juniper trees my eyes caught a yellowish spot stretched on the doorstone.

It was the setter. He whined as I called to him, but without turning, his gaze fixed on the closed door. His fine coat was draggled and matted with blood about the throat; he sprang to his feet as we came near and began to paw at the doorway.

I knocked. No one moved within. The one window was close shuttered, but I fancied, listening, I could hear a faint crooning sound from inside.

Together we set our shoulders to the door. It gave way, and we found ourselves in the one tiny living-room of the house. It was dark and close there was a disorder of household things piled here and there. On a small broken rocker in the middle of the floor, Mrs. Menning sat huddled, swaying to and fro, with the low crooning mutter we had heard from outside. She had an old colored handkerchief tied over her head and a small silver cross was hung on a thin chain round her wrinkled neck. Her aged face was impassive; her eyes, uncannily keen and bright, seemed to look straight through us into distance.

"Where is Miss Lessing?" I asked.

She made no sign of having heard me, only kept up that faint unintelligible muttering. Herrick went over and shook her gently by the shoulder.

"Where is Miss Lessing? You got to tell us." She twisted her shoulder from his grasp and sunk lower into the chair, her eyes averted. My ears had caught a sound overhead. There was no stairway in the room, but behind a pile of furniture a wooden button betrayed a door that I had taken for an ordinary closet. Hastily, I began to drag the things aside. The old woman saw my purpose and slipped with sudden agility to her feet, her eyes blazing with anger, but Herrick thrust her aside and in an instant we had the door open and were upstairs, the dog at our heels.

"Mary!"

I caught her in my arms—unhurt, thank God—and carried her down, through the shuttered room, past the old muttering woman—out into the open and the clean air.

"Oh, Austin, that old woman! She met me on the road—I had gone to call for Dick, and she said she was looking for me; that Dick had had an accident and they'd brought him to this house and sent for me. She told me to go upstairs, that he was there, and she shut the door and wouldn't let me out. There was no window; no one could have heard me from outside. And then Leo found me, I heard him barking and she tried to drive him away, but he wouldn't go. Good old Leo!" She put her arm round the setter, who was trying hard to reach her face with his tongue. "I knew he'd help you to find me. Austin, where is Dick?"

I had to tell her, breaking it as gently as I could.

"Will you take me to him at once, please—now! Austin, I knew something was going to happen—I felt it. That's why I was worried, last night—I couldn't explain. And then shut up alone there, not knowing what it was . . . That old woman—she was dreadful, but she wasn't unkind to me. Do you suppose she knew—that she just wanted to get me somewhere safe?"

Who knew? Was there perhaps a spark of human feeling in that strange warped soul, half unhinged by her own troubles, something that Mary's chance kindness, that afternoon by the sawmill, had reached and touched? It might have been.

We walked down the hill, and I took Mary on the motorcycle behind me as far as Lennox's, leaving Herrick to follow on foot. Dick was better. He had passed a feverish night, Lennox said, but the fever had left him with dawn and he was in an exhausted but normal sleep when we arrived.

I left Mary with him, and walked back along the road to meet Herrick.

"And now," I said, "tell me—tell me the whole thing. Jack, what was it?"

We were near the old twisted cedar by the hollow, the tree by which Aaron had met his death that spring. Herrick sat down on a boulder by the roadside and began to scrape slowly at his pipe.

"I told you about Menning and his wild-man stunt—all that I found out the other day. Menning had a criminal twist and he knew how to turn that trick to his own ends. It is far easier to simulate the grotesque—the superhuman, if you like—than most people suppose. Isn't that, after all, the basis of the witch-doctors' power? Even an ordinary man becomes horrible if you put a mask on him. And remember that Menning had a streak of abnormality to start with, and the thing may very easily, as I said, have become an obsession with him. Anyway that's the best explanation one can put on it, and the one that Lennox and our friend Sliefer, and Lessing himself, will agree upon. After all, it pretty well covers the facts."

I remembered his words the night before.

"Then what did you mean about the dawn?"

Herrick was silent a moment.

"We're all well out of a bad business, Austin," he said then. "Don't you think we'd better let it go at that?"

"But you had another theory. You had it that morning, after the fire. You wouldn't tell me what it was. But I don't imagine you've changed your mind altogether."

"No, I didn't change my mind," Herrick said. He put his hand into his pocket. When he withdrew it there lay, on his palm, the little battered silver button that Lennox had first shown us.

"You remember, Austin," he said, "that I recalled one or two facts to your mind that evening. This was one of them. I want you to look at it again."

"It is a button," I said. "A button such as you find on some European peasants' costumes."

"Westphalian peasants, such as Menning's mother came from. Lennox overlooked that fact, though as the button is badly defaced we can excuse him. I'll help you out, Austin. It is of pure silver, very soft, and it has been hammered to form a rough bullet that could be fired from an old-fashioned muzzle-loading gun."

"I don't see how that helps you."

"I want you to think," he said, "what particular associations there are with a silver bullet."

I stared at the little pellet in my hand, striving with some vague recollection at the back of my mind.

"They were used against . . . against . . . some sort of witchcraft," I said at last. "I don't see—"

"They were used against lycanthropy," said Herrick.

I stared at him. I suppose I looked stupid. I felt it. It was as though some spectre, strange, ghastly, altogether of another world, had risen up suddenly there before us in these quiet Pennsylvania woods.

"A mania—subject imagines himself some beast, resulting in actual physical transformations—exhibits depraved appetites—frequently homicidal," I recalled haltingly the words of an old treatise.

"They did more than believe they were animals," said Herrick dryly. "They seem to have succeeded in impressing their belief pretty strongly upon their neighbors and relatives. Did you ever dig into old records of that sort, Austin? The were-wolf stories of the Middle Ages? They're rather grim reading."

I was silent.

"Remember our facts," he went on. "Menning's mother came from Westphalia, one of the parts of Europe where the belief in lycanthropy is most widely spread and where its existence is still credited among the peasants of today. Lycanthropy was believed to be a hereditary taint, as transmissible as insanity, which may lie dormant through one or more generations, so much so that at one time the relatives of an accused man or woman were all held suspect. There seems to have been more or less of a mystery about the Mennings altogether, chiefly on account of the mother's character, and most particularly in regard to Jakey. Remember also what Lennox said about the strong persistence of type in both sons, although of different paternity. We have Lennox's assertion that there was something peculiar, 'animal', about Jakey, which certainly impressed him, but which he seemed rather at a loss to describe. Then there is that unexplained incident when Jakey was with the circus. Whatever it was, it was something that gave such a shock to the proprietor—who, remember, had originally conceived the idea of the wild-man stunt himself, so wasn't likely to have been taken in by acting—that he sacrificed his best drawing card then and there sooner than have Jakey remain another night with the show. All the brother would say was that he 'guessed Jakey acted too well,' which in itself is fairly significant.

"That Aaron knew, or suspected, certain facts about his brother, there is no doubt. Why else should he so obstinately oppose any medical examination, and particularly the idea of Jakey being removed even temporarily from their control? Why did he make the very singular statement that Jakey was 'all right in the daytime,' and that *at night they shut him up*?"

"And the bullet?" I asked.

"Do you remember that Aaron promised if it became necessary he would take steps? What those steps were he did not say, but I believe myself that this silver bullet answers the question. Remember the horror in which lycanthropy was held, the revulsion it excited, and think whether he would not have resorted to the gravest measures sooner than have the whole concealed story come to light.

"I think that Aaron had already determined that night, unknown to their mother, to put an end to the whole thing; that he went out to seek his half-brother at the time, and under that form, when alone it would be possible to bring himself to do that which he felt had to be done. Jakey must have suspected. There was a struggle between the two, and it was Aaron who was killed, before he had time to use the silver bullet which he dropped, there, in the moment of unexpected attack. The old mother must have known the truth; through all her horror and superstition her love for her first son survived, and together they concocted the story of Aaron's absence with the wagon. That she paid bitterly, many times over, for her impulse, there is no doubt. She was now completely under Jakey's dominion—the dominion of a being little better than a monster, whom she dared not now denounce, for who would have believed her story?

"It is certain that what we saw last night is what attacked Lessing, and had attacked him previously. It reached him through the sky- light, but not altogether as he thought. It climbed. You will remember that in every instance the attack was from overhead."

"But the thing that . . . that I touched . . ." I cried. "It was *furry!* It—"

I stopped short, taken with a sudden shudder.

"I know," said Herrick.

"I had hoped," he went on, "that you didn't retain any very definite impression. That's why—"

"You saw it."

"We all saw something. We thought we did."

"And Sliefer . . ." I paused. "Herrick, there was something else. I remember now. You were holding me. And you told Sliefer not to fire. I wondered . . ."

"They say there is a change, one way or another, at the moment of death," Herrick said. "I knew it. I tried to stop him." He paused a moment. "I was too late. That's all."

We sat there for a moment, not speaking. Then Herrick knocked his pipe out against the boulder and rose to his feet.

"Come on back to the house. Mrs. Searle will have breakfast for us, and we both look rather a wreck!" He laid a hand on my shoulder. "Take my advice, Austin, and put this whole thing out of your mind. I told you in the beginning—there's the other explanation; why not stand by it? As I say, it covers all the facts. The rest is between us three. Look at it how you will, whatever happened last night happened for the best."

I remembered the thing that had cried and twisted on the ground, and was silent. Herrick was right.

~§~

As soon as Lessing was able to travel we went down, the three of us, to the little cottage on the Sound which they had rented for the remainder of the fall. Herrick came down for an occasional long weekend, and it was during one of these, when we were lounging out on the beach before supper, that he handed me without comment a little cutting from a Pennsylvania local paper.

It was headed "Man's Body found in Millpond" and stated briefly how some boys, fishing in Sliefer's dam, had discovered the body of a man, believed to be that of a certain Aaron Menning, chicken peddler, who had disappeared from the neighborhood mysteriously some weeks before. The body, which had lain for a considerable time in the water, showed the trace of two bullet wounds, but owing to the difficulties of medical evidence after so long a time had elapsed, it was not possible to prove that either of these had been sufficient to cause death, which was brought in, on the finding of the coroner's jury, as accidental. "It will be remembered," the article concluded, "that equally mysterious circumstances attended, less than a year ago, the death of Menning's stepbrother, whose body was found at a spot not half a mile from the scene of this later tragedy. Though there was no suggestion of foul play at the time, rumor later connected Aaron's name, in no uncertain terms, with his stepbrother's death, a rumor which his disappearance served to strengthen in many persons' minds. Whatever the circumstances which led to this second tragedy, and how far the two may be connected, will remain forever a mystery, since Aaron's death closes definitely the last chapter in the story of this singularly ill-fated family."

"What's that?" asked Lessing.

I slipped the cutting into my pocket. My compact with Herrick still held good.

"Only some more nonsense of Jack's."

Lessing grinned up at me from where he lounged, one bandaged arm stretched above his head, in the deck-chair.

"I should think, as an engaged man, you ought to be getting impervious by this time."

"I am. Don't you worry!"

Over the lawn, through the warm-scented dusk, came Mary's voice from the porch.

"Austin!" she called. "Dick! Are you three going to sit there all night?"

Herrick moved away.

"Come on," he said over his shoulder. "Supper is ready, and I won't risk being told again that I monopolize you all the day!"

A special thanks to:

Joe Bandel, who contributed the new translation of "Typhoid Mary". Joe lives in Brainerd, Minnesota and has translated several books by Hanns Heinz Ewers. This includes the first uncensored versions of The *Sorcerer's Apprentice*; *Alraune*; and *Vampire*. His translation of *Alraune* was published by Side Real Press in a limited edition. Side Real Press also published his translation of *The Hanns Heinz Ewers Brevier* and plans to publish his translation of *Vampire*. Other books by Hanns Heinz Ewers include *Hanns Heinz Ewers Volume* I; *Hanns Heinz Ewers Volume II* and *Hanns Heinz Ewers Illustrated Stories*.

Culpeo S. Fox, who translated "In the Penal Colony" and created many of the illustrations for *Bruin's Midnight Reader*. Culpeo is a long-time contributing artist for Bruin Books, illustrating *Quest for Fire* and *Tom's A-cold,* among others. Culpeo has a B.A. in Graphic Design and is based in Germany.

Douglas A. Anderson and Russ Bernard, who recommended *The Thing in the Woods* to us.

Douglas A. Anderson is an American writer and editor on the subjects of fantasy and medieval literature, specializing in textual analysis of the works of J. R. R. Tolkien. He is a winner of the Mythopoeic Award for scholarship. He started Nodens Books to revive the work of forgotten authors. Together with Mark Valentine he founded the *Wormwoodiana* blogspot, which is devoted to fantasy, supernatural and decadent literature. A discussion of *The Thing in the Woods* can be found there.

Russ Bernard has collected books for over 40 years, with primary focus older Fantasy, Speculative Literature and Children's books. He started collecting Margery Williams originally because he was curious about the early editions of *The Velveteen Rabbit* but later discovered *The Thing in the Woods*. His exhaustive side-by-side comparison of the two versions of the novel was essential to the selection made for this anthology.

Additional stories and poems not listed on the copyrights page:

The Most Dangerous Game by Richard Connell first appeared in the January 19, 1924 issue of *Collier's*.

The Doll's Ghost by F. Marion Crawford was posthumously published in *Wandering Ghosts* in 1911.

The Boy Who Sought the Shudders by the Brothers Grimm was first collected in manuscript form around 1810.

Lost Hearts by M. R. James was first published in 1895 and later collected in his story collection *Ghost Stories of an Antiquary* (1904).

Seaton's Aunt by Walter de la Mare was originally published in *The Riddle and Other Stories* (1923).

The Dead Valley by Ralph Adams Cram was first published in 1895 in *Black Spirits and White*, Stone & Kimball (Chicago).

The Willows by Algernon Blackwood was originally published in his 1907 collection *The Listener and Other Stories*.

That Damned Thing by Ambrose Bierce was first published in *Town Topics: The Journal of Society* (NYC) on December 7, 1893.

The Raven (poem) by Edgar Allan Poe first appeared in *The American Review* February 1845 issue under the pseudonym "Quarles".

The Love Song of J. Alfred Prufrock (poem) by T. S. Eliot was first published in the June 1915 issue of *Poetry: A Magazine of Verse*.

The Monkey's Paw by W. W. Jacobs originally appeared in the 1902 story collection *The Lady of the Barge*.

A Haunted Island by Algernon Blackwood was first published in *The Empty House* in 1906.

The Legend of Sleepy Hollow by Washington Irving was originally published in 1819 in a collection of essays and stories entitled *The Sketch Book of Geoffrey Crayon, Gent.*

La Belle Dame Sans Merci (poem) by John Keats was originally written in 1819 then revised in 1820—the version appearing in *BMR*.

The VIY by Nicolae Gogol was first published in Volume 1 of his collection of tales entitled *Mirgorod* (1835).

The Leech of Folkstone by Thomas Ingoldsby of Tappington Manor (Richard Harris Barham) was first collected as part of the Ingldsby Legends in 1840.

The Entail by E.T.A. Hoffmann was first published in *Tales of Hoffmann* in 1819; the *BMR* version was adapted by Jonathan Eeds in 2021.

The Thing in the Woods by Margery Williams; first published in 1913 by London publisher Duckworth and CO.; text expanded and published in 1924 by New York publisher Robert McBride & Company. American version published under the pseudonym Harper Williams.

Printed in Great Britain
by Amazon

15785024R00445